'Zelazny's stories are fabul[...]
has not read them and is a[...]

'His stories are sunk to their knees in maturity and wisdom, in bravura writing that breaks rules most writers only suspect exist. His concepts are fresh, his attacks bold, his resolutions generally trenchant'   Harlan Ellison

'Roger Zelazny can be as realistic as Hemmingway, as fanciful as Kenneth Graham; he is by turns a hard-nosed naturalist and a poet of exquisite sensibility'   Thomas Burnett Swann

'Zelazny, telling of gods and wizards, uses magical words as if he himself were a wizard'   Philip Jose Farmer

The ULTIMATE FANTASIES sequence

Conan

Elric

Lankhmar

Lud-in-the-Mist

Lyonesse

The Broken Sword

The Chronicles of Amber

The Dragon Waiting

CHRONICLES OF AMBER

ROGER ZELAZNY

For my mother

The right of Roger Zelazny to be identified as the author of this work has
been asserted by him in accordance with the
Copyright, Designs and Patents Act 1988.

This edition published in Great Britain in 2008 by
Gollancz
An imprint of the Orion Publishing Group
Orion House, 5 Upper St Martin's Lane, London WC2H 9EA
An Hachette Livre UK Company

1 3 5 7 9 10 8 6 4 2

A CIP catalogue record for this book
is available from the British Library

ISBN 978 0 57508 2 694

Typeset at The Spartan Press Ltd,
Lymington, Hants

Printed and bound in the UK by
CPI Mackays, Chatham ME5 8TD

The Orion Publishing Group's policy is to use papers that
are natural, renewable and recyclable products and made
from wood grown in sustainable forests. The logging and
manufacturing processes are expected to conform to the
environmental regulations of the country of origin.

www.orionbooks.co.uk

NINE PRINCES IN AMBER

1

It was starting to end, after what seemed most of eternity to me.

I attempted to wriggle my toes, succeeded. I was sprawled there in a hospital bed and my legs were done up in plaster casts, but they were still mine.

I squeezed my eyes shut, and opened them, three times.

The room grew steady.

Where the hell was I?

Then the fogs were slowly broken, and some of that which is called memory returned to me. I recalled nights and nurses and needles. Every time things would begin to clear a bit, someone would come in and jab me with something. That's how it had been. Yes. Now, though, I was feeling halfway decent. They'd have to stop.

Wouldn't they?

The thought came to assail me: *Maybe not.*

Some natural skepticism as to the purity of all human motives came and sat upon my chest. I'd been over-narcotized, I suddenly knew. No real reason for it, from the way I felt, and no reason for them to stop now, if they'd been paid to keep it up. So play it cool and stay dopey, said a voice which was my worst, if wiser, self.

So I did.

A nurse poked her head in the door about ten minutes later, and I was, of course, still stacking Z's. She went away.

By then, I reconstructed a bit of what had occurred.

I had been in some sort of accident, I remembered vaguely. What had happened after that was still a blur; and as to what had happened before, I had no inkling whatsoever. But I had first been in a hospital and then brought to this place, I remembered. Why? I didn't know.

However, my legs felt pretty good. Good enough to hold me up, though I didn't know how much time had lapsed since their breaking – and I knew they'd been broken.

So I sat up. It took me a real effort as my muscles were very tired. It was dark outside and a handful of stars were standing naked beyond the window. I winked back at them and threw my legs over the edge of the bed.

I was dizzy, but after a white it subsided and I got up, gripping the rail at the head of the bed, and I took my first step.

Okay. My legs held me.

So, theoretically, I was in good enough shape to walk out.

I made it back to bed, stretched out and thought I was sweating and shaking. Visions of sugar plums, etc.

In the State of Denmark there was the odor of decay . . .

It had been an accident involving an auto, I recalled. One helluva one . . .

Then the door opened, letting in light, and through slits beneath my eyelashes I saw a nurse with a hypo in her hand.

She approached my bedside, a hippy broad with dark hair and big arms.

Just as she neared, I sat up.

'Good evening,' I said.

'Why – good evening,' she replied.

'When do I check out?' asked.

'I'll have to ask Doctor.'

'Do so,' I said.

'Please roll up your sleeve.'

'No thanks.'

'I have to give you an injection.'

'No you don't. I don't need it.'

'I'm afraid that's for Doctor to say.'

'Then send him around and let him say it. But in the meantime, I will not permit it.'

'I'm afraid I have my orders.'

'So did Eichmann, and look what happened to him,' and I shook my head slowly.

'Very well,' she said. 'I'll have to report this . . .'

'Please do,' I said, 'and while you're at it, tell him I've decided to check out in the morning.'

'That's impossible. You can't even walk – and there were internal injuries . . .'

4

'We'll see,' said I. 'Good night.'

She swished out of sight without answering.

So I lay there and mulled. It seemed I was in some sort of private place – so somebody was footing the bill. Who did I know? No visions of relatives appeared behind my eyes. Friends either. What did that leave? Enemies?

I thought a while.

Nothing.

Nobody to benefact me thus.

I'd gone over a cliff in my car, and into a lake, I suddenly remembered. And that was all I remembered.

I was . . .

I strained and began to sweat again.

I didn't know *who* I was.

But to occupy myself, I sat up and stripped away all my bandages. I seemed all right underneath them, and it seemed the right thing to do. I broke the cast on my right leg, using a metal strut I'd removed from the head of the bed. I had a sudden feeling that I had to get out in a hurry, that there was something I had to do.

I tested my right leg. It was okay.

I shattered the cast on my left leg, got up, went to the closet.

No clothes there.

Then I heard the footsteps. I returned to my bed and covered over the broken casts and the discarded bandages.

The door swung inward once again.

Then there was light all around me, and there was a beefy guy in a white jacket standing with his hand on the wall switch.

'What's this I hear about you giving the nurse a hard time?' he asked, and there was no more feigning sleep.

'I don't know,' I said. 'What is it?'

That troubled him for a second or two, said the frown, then, 'It's time for your shot.'

'Are you an M.D.?' I asked.

'No, but I'm authorized to give you a shot.'

'And I refuse it,' I said, 'as I've a legal right to do. What's it to you?'

'You'll have your shot,' he said, and he moved around to the left side of the bed. He had a hypo in one hand, which had been out of sight till then.

It was a very foul blow, about four inches below the belt buckle, I'd say, and it left him on his knees.

'— —!' he said, after a time.

'Come within spitting distance again,' I said, 'and see what happens.'

'We've got ways to deal with patients like you,' he gasped.

So I knew the time had come to act.

'Where are my clothes?' I said.

'— —!' he repeated.

'Then I guess I'll have to take yours. Give them to me.'

It became boring with the third repetition, so I threw the bed-clothes over his head and clobbered him with the metal strut.

Within two minutes, I'd say, I was garbed all in white, the color of Moby Dick and vanilla ice cream. Ugly.

I shoved him into the closet and looked out the latticed window. I saw the Old Moon with the New Moon in her arms, hovering above a row of poplars. The grass was silvery and sparkled. The night was bargaining weakly with the sun. Nothing to show, for me, where this place was located. I seemed to be on the third floor of the building though, and there was a cast square of light off to my left and low, seeming to indicate a first floor window with someone awake behind it.

So I left the room and considered the hallway. Off to the left, it ended against a wall with a latticed window, and there were four more doors, two on either side. Probably they let upon more rooms like my own. I went and looked out the window and saw more grounds, more trees, more night, nothing new. Turning, I headed in the other direction.

Doors, doors, doors, no lights from under any of them, the only sounds my footsteps from the too big borrowed shoes.

Laughing Boy's wristwatch told me it was five forty-four. The metal strut was inside my belt, under the white orderly jacket, and it rubbed against my hip bone as I walked. There was a ceiling fixture about every twenty feet, casting about forty watts of light.

I came to a stairway, off to the right, leading down. I took it. It was carpeted and quiet.

The second floor looked like my own, rows of rooms, so I continued on.

When I reached the first floor I turned right, looking for the door with light leaking out from beneath it.

I found it, way up near the end of the corridor, and I didn't bother to knock.

The guy was sitting there in a garish bathrobe, at a big shiny desk, going over some sort of ledger. This was no ward room. He looked up at me with burning eyes all wide and lips swelling toward a yell they didn't reach, perhaps because of my determined expression. He stood, quickly.

I shut the door behind me, advanced, and said:

'Good morning. You're in trouble.'

People must always be curious as to trouble, because after the three seconds it took me to cross the room, his words were:

'What do you mean?'

'I mean,' I said, 'that you're about to suffer a lawsuit for holding me incommunicado, and another one for malpractice, for your indiscriminate use of narcotics. I'm already suffering withdrawal symptoms and might do something violent . . .'

He stood up.

'Get out of here,' he said.

I saw a pack of cigarettes on his desk. I helped myself and said, 'Sit down and shut up. We've got things to talk about.'

He sat down, but he didn't shut up:

'You're breaking several regulations,' he said.

'So we'll let a court decide who's liable,' I replied. 'I want my clothes and my personal effects. I'm checking out.'

'You're in no condition—'

'Nobody asked you. Pony up this minute, or answer to the law.'

He reached toward a button on his desk, but I slapped his hand away.

'Now!' I repeated. 'You should have pressed that when I came in. It's too late now.'

'Mr Corey, you're being most difficult . . .'

Corey?

'I didn't check in here,' I said, 'but I damn well have a right to check me out. And now's the time. So let's get about it.'

'Obviously, you're in no condition to leave this institution,' he replied. 'I cannot permit it. I am going to call for someone to escort you back to your room and put you to bed.'

'Don't try it,' I said, 'or you'll find out what condition I'm in. Now, I've several questions. The first one's: Who checked me in, and who's footing my bill at this place?'

'Very well,' he sighed, and his tiny, sandy mustaches sagged as low as they could.

He opened a drawer, put his hand inside, and I was wary.

I knocked it down before he had the safety catch off: a .32 automatic, very neat; Colt. I snapped the catch myself when I retrieved it from the desk top; and I pointed it and said: 'You will answer my questions. Obviously you consider me dangerous. You may be right.'

He smiled weakly, lit a cigarette himself, which was a mistake, if he intended to indicate aplomb. His hands shook.

'All right, Corey – if it will make you happy,' he said, 'your sister checked you in.'

'?' thought I.

'Which sister?' I asked.

'Evelyn,' he said.

No bells. So, 'That's ridiculous. I haven't seen Evelyn in years,' I said. 'She didn't even know I was in this part of the country.'

He shrugged.

'Nevertheless . . .'

'Where's she staying now? I want to call her,' I said.

'I don't have her address handy.'

'Get it.'

He rose, crossed to a filing cabinet, opened it, riffled, withdrew a card.

I studied it. *Mrs Evelyn Flaumel* . . . The New York address was not familiar either, but I committed it to memory. As the card said, my first name was Carl. Good. More data.

I stuck the gun in my belt beside the strut then, safety back on, of course.

'Okay,' I told him.' 'Where are my clothes, and what're you going to pay me?'

'Your clothes were destroyed in the accident,' he said, 'and I must tell you that your legs were definitely broken – the left one in two places. Frankly, I can't see how you're managing to stay on your feet. It's only been two weeks—'

'I always heal fast,' I said. 'Now, about the money . . .'

'What money?'

'The out-of-court settlement for my malpractice complaint, and the other one.'

'Don't be ridiculous!'

'Who's being ridiculous? I'll settle for a thousand, cash, right now.'

'I won't even discuss such a thing.'

'Well, you'd better consider it – and win or lose, think about the name it will give this place if I manage enough pretrial publicity. I'll certainly get in touch with the AMA, the newspapers, the—'

'Blackmail,' he said, 'and I'll have nothing to do with it.'

'Pay now, or pay later, after a court order,' I said. 'I don't care. But it'll be cheaper this way.'

If he came across, I'd know my guesses were right and there was something crooked involved.

He glared at me, I don't know how long.

Finally, 'I haven't got a thousand here,' he said.

'Name a compromise figure,' I said.

After another pause, 'It's larceny.'

'Not if it's cash-and-carry, Charlie. So, call it.'

'I might have five hundred in my safe.'

'Get it.'

He told me, after inspecting the contents of a small wall safe, there was four-thirty, and I didn't want to leave fingerprints on the safe, just to check him out. So I accepted and stuffed the bills into my side pocket.

'Now what's the nearest cab company that serves this place?'

He named it, and I checked in the phone book, which told me I was upstate.

I made him dial it and call me a cab, because I didn't know the name of the place and didn't want him to know the condition of my memory. One of the bandages I had removed *had* been around my head.

While he was making the arrangement I heard him name the place: it was called Greenwood Private Hospital.

I stubbed out my cigarette, picked up another, and removed

perhaps two hundred pounds from my feet by resting in a brown upholstered chair beside his bookcase.

'We wait here and you'll see me to the door,' I said.

I never heard another word out of him.

2

It was about eight o'clock when the cab deposited me on a random corner in the nearest town. I paid off the driver and walked for around twenty minutes. Then I stopped in a diner, found a booth and had juice, a couple of eggs, toast, bacon, and three cups of coffee. The bacon was too greasy.

After giving breakfast a good hour I started walking, found a clothing store, and waited till its nine-thirty opening.

I bought a pair of slacks, three sport shirts, a belt, some underwear, and a pair of shoes that fit. I also picked up a handkerchief, a wallet, and pocket comb.

Then I found a Greyhound station and boarded a bus for New York. No one tried to stop me. No one seemed to be looking for me.

Sitting there, watching the countryside all autumn-colored and tickled by brisk winds beneath a bright, cold sky, I reviewed everything I knew about myself and my circumstances.

I had been registered at Greenwood as Carl Corey by my sister Evelyn Flaumel. This had been subsequent to an auto accident some fifteen or so days past, in which I had suffered broken bones which no longer troubled me. I didn't remember Sister Evelyn. The Greenwood people had been instructed to keep me passive, were afraid of the law when I got loose and threatened them with it. Okay. Someone was afraid of me, for some reason. I'd play it for all it was worth.

I forced my mind back to the accident, dwelled upon it till my head hurt. It was no accident. I had that impression, though I didn't know why. I would find out, and someone would pay. Very, very much would they pay. An anger, a terrible one, flared within the middle of my body. Anyone who tried to hurt me, to use me, did so at his own peril and now he would receive his due, whoever he was, this one. I felt a strong desire to kill, to destroy whoever had been responsible, and I knew that it was not the first time in my life that I had felt this thing, and I knew, too, that I followed through on it in the past. More than once.

I stared out the window, watching the dead leaves fall.

When I hit the Big City, the first thing I did was to get a shave and haircut in the nearest clip joint, and the second was to change my shirt and undershirt in the men's room, because I can't stand hair down my back. The .32 automatic, belonging to the nameless individual at Greenwood, was in my right-hand jacket pocket. I suppose that if Greenwood or my sister wanted me picked up in a hurry, a Sullivan violation would come in handy. But I decided to hang onto it. They'd have to find me first, and I wanted a reason. I ate a quick lunch, rode subways and buses for an hour, then got a cab to take me out to the Westchester address of Evelyn, my nominal sister and hopeful jogger of memories.

Before I arrived, I'd already decided on the tack I'd take.

So, when the door to the huge old place opened in response to my knock, after about a thirty-second wait, I knew what I was going to say. I had thought about it as I'd walked up the long, winding, white gravel driveway, between the dark oaks and the bright maples, leaves crunching beneath my feet, and the wind cold on my fresh-scraped neck within the raised collar of my jacket. The smell of my hair tonic mingled with a musty odor from the ropes of ivy that crowded all over the walls of that old, brick place. There was no sense of familiarity. I didn't think I had ever been here before.

I had knocked, and there had come an echo.

Then I'd jammed my hands into my pockets and waited.

When the door opened, I had smiled and nodded toward the mole-flecked maid with a swarthy complexion and a Puerto Rican accent.

'Yes,' she said.

'I'd like to see Mrs Evelyn Flaumel, please.'

'Who shall I say is calling?'

'Her brother Carl.'

'Oh come in please,' she told me.

I entered a hallway, the floor a mosaic of tiny salmon and turquoise tiles, the walls mahogany, a trough of big-leafed green things occupying a room divider to my left. From overhead, a cube of glass and enamel threw down a yellow light.

The gal departed, and I sought around me for something familiar.

Nothing.

So I waited.

Presently, the maid returned, smiled, nodded, and said, 'Please follow me. She will see you in the library.'

I followed, up three stairs and down a corridor past two closed doors. The third one to my left was open, and the maid indicated I should enter it. I did so, then paused on the threshold.

Like all libraries, it was full of books. It also held three paintings, two indicating quiet landscapes and one a peaceful seascape. The floor was heavily carpeted in green. There was a big globe beside the big desk with Africa facing me and a wall-to-wall window behind it, eight stepladders of glass. But none of these was the reason I'd paused.

The woman behind the desk wore a wide-collared, V-necked dress of blue-green, had long hair and low bangs, all of a cross between sunset clouds and the outer edge of a candle flame in an otherwise dark room, and natural I somehow knew, and her eyes behind glasses I didn't think she needed were as blue as Lake Erie at three o'clock on a cloudless summer afternoon; and the color of her compressed smile matched her hair. But none of these was the reason I'd paused.

I knew her, from somewhere, though I couldn't say where.

I advanced, holding my own smile.

'Hello,' I said.

'Sit down,' said she, 'please,' indicating a high-backed, big-armed chair that bulged and was orange, of the kind just tilted at the angle in which I loved to loaf.

I did so, and she studied me.

'Glad to see you're up and around again.'

'Me, too. How've you been?'

'Fine, thank you. I must say I didn't expect to see you here.'

'I know,' I fibbed, 'but here I am, to thank you for your sisterly kindness and care.' I let a slight note of irony sound within that sentence just to observe her response.

At that point an enormous dog entered the room – an Irish wolfhound – and it curled up in front of the desk. Another followed and circled the globe twice before lying down.

'Well,' said she, returning the irony, 'it was the least I could do for you. You should drive more carefully.'

'In the future,' I said, 'I'll take greater precautions, I promise.' I didn't know what sort of game I was playing, but since she didn't know that I didn't know, I'd decided to take her for all the information I could. 'I figured you would be curious as to the shape I was in, so I came to let you see.'

'I was, am,' she replied. 'Have you eaten?'

'A light lunch, several hours ago,' I said.

So she rang up the maid and ordered food. Then, 'I thought you might take it upon yourself to leave Greenwood,' she said, 'when you were able. I didn't think it would be so soon, though, and I didn't think you'd come here.'

'I know,' I said, 'that's why I did.'

She offered me a cigarette and I took it, lit hers, lit mine. 'You always were unpredictable,' she finally told me. 'While this has helped you often in the past, however, I wouldn't count on it now.'

'What do you mean?' I asked.

'The stakes are far too high for a bluff, and I think that's what you're trying, walking in here like this. I've always admired your courage, Corwin, but don't be a foot. You know the score.'

Corwin? File it away, under 'Corey'.

'Maybe I don't,' I said. 'I've been asleep for a while, remember?'

'You mean you haven't been in touch?'

'Haven't had a chance, since I woke up.'

She leaned her head to one side and narrowed her wonderful eyes.

'Rash,' she said, 'but possible. Just possible. You might mean it. *You* might. I'll pretend that you do, for now. In that case, you may have done a smart, safe thing. Let me think about it.'

I drew on my cigarette, hoping she'd say something more. But she didn't, so I decided to seize what seemed the advantage I'd obtained in this game I didn't understand with players I didn't know for stakes I had no inkling of.

'The fact that I'm here indicates something,' I said.

'Yes,' she replied, 'I know. But you're smart, so it could indicate more than one thing. We'll wait and see.'

Wait for what? See what? Thing?

Steaks then arrived and a pitcher of beer, so I was temporarily freed from the necessity of making cryptic and general statements for her to ponder as subtle or cagey. Mine was a good steak, pink inside and full of juice, and I tore at the fresh tough-crusted bread with my teeth and gulped the beer with a great hunger and a thirst. She laughed as she watched me, while cutting off tiny pieces of her own.

'I love the gusto with which you assail life, Corwin. It's one of the reasons I'd hate to see you part company with it.'

'Me, too,' I muttered.

And while I ate, I pondered her. I saw her in a low-cut gown, green as the green of the sea, with full skirts. There was music, dancing, voices behind us. I wore black and silver and . . . The vision faded. But it was a true piece of my memory, I knew; and inwardly I cursed that I lacked it in its entirety. What had she been saying, in her green, to me in my black and silver, that night, behind the music, the dancing and the voices?

I poured us more beer from the pitcher and decided to test the vision.

'I remember one night,' I said, 'when you were all in green and I in my colors. How lovely things seemed – and the music . . .'

Her face grew slightly wistful, the cheeks smoothing.

'Yes,' she said. 'Were not those the days? . . . You really have not been in touch?'

'Word of honor,' I said, for whatever that was worth.

'Things have grown far worse,' she said, 'and the Shadows contain more horrors than any had thought . . .'

'And . . . ?' I inquired.

'He still has his troubles,' she finished.

'Oh.'

'Yes,' she went on, 'and he'll want to know where you stand.'

'Right here,' I said.

'You mean . . . ?'

'For now,' I told her, perhaps too quickly, for her eyes had widened too much, 'since I still don't know the full state of affairs,' whatever that meant.

'Oh.'

And we finished our steaks and the beer, giving the two bones to the dogs.

We sipped some coffee afterward, and I came to feel a bit brotherly but suppressed it. I asked, 'What of the others?' which could mean anything, but sounded safe.

I was afraid for a moment that she was going to ask me what I meant. Instead, though, she leaned back in her chair, stared at the ceiling, and said, 'As always, no one new has been heard from. Perhaps yours was the wisest way. I'm enjoying it myself. But how can one forget – the glory?' I lowered my eyes, because I wasn't sure what they should contain, 'One can't,' I said. 'One never can.'

There followed a long, uncomfortable silence, after which she said: 'Do you hate me?'

'Of course not,' I replied. 'How could I – all things considered?'

This seemed to please her, and she showed her teeth, which were very white.

'Good, and thank you,' she said. 'Whatever else, you're a gentleman.'

I bowed and smirked.

'You'll turn my head.'

'Hardly,' she said, 'all things considered.'

And I felt uncomfortable.

My anger was there, and I wondered whether she knew who it was that I needed to stay it. I felt that she did. I fought with the desire to ask it outright, suppressed it.

'Well, what do you propose doing?' she finally asked, and being on the spot I replied, 'Of course, you don't trust me . . .'

'How could we?'

I determined to remember that *we*.

'Well, then. For the time being, I'm willing to place myself under your surveillance. I'll be glad to stay right here, where you can keep an eye on me.'

'And afterward?'

'Afterward? We'll see.'

'Clever,' she said, 'very clever. And you place me in an awkward position.' (I had said it because I didn't have any place else to go, and my blackmail money wouldn't last me too long. 'Yes, of course you may stay. But let me warn you' – and here she fingered what I had thought to be some sort of pendant on a chain about her neck – 'this is an ultrasonic dog whistle. Donner and Blitzen here have four brothers, and they're all trained to take care of nasty people and they all respond to my whistle. So don't start to walk toward any place where you won't be desired. A toot or two and even you will go down before them. Their kind is the reason there are no wolves left in Ireland, you know.'

'I know,' I said, realizing that I did.

'Yes,' she continued, 'Eric will like it that you are my guest. It should cause him to leave you alone, which is what you want, *n'est ce pas?*'

'*Oui*,' I said.

Eric! It meant something! I *had* known an Eric, and it had been very important, somehow, that I did. Not recently. But the Eric I had known was still around, and that was important.

Why?

I hated him, that was one reason. Hated him enough to have contemplated killing him. Perhaps I'd even tried.

Also, there was some bond between us, I knew.

Kinship?

Yes, that was it Neither of us liked it being – brothers . . . I remembered, I remembered . . .

Big, powerful Eric, with his wet curly beard, and his eyes – just like Evelyn's!

I was racked with a new surge of memory, as my temples began to throb and the back of my neck was suddenly warm.

I didn't let any of it show on my face, but forced myself to take another drag on my cigarette, another sip of beer, as I realized that Evelyn was indeed my sister! Only Evelyn wasn't her name. I couldn't think of what it was, but it wasn't Evelyn. I'd be careful, I resolved. I'd not use any name at all when addressing her, until I remembered.

And what of me? And what was it that was going on around me?

Eric, I suddenly felt, had had some connection with my accident. It should have been a fatal one, only I'd pulled through. *He* was the one, wasn't he? Yes, my feelings replied. It had to be Eric. And Evelyn was working with him, paying Greenwood to keep me in a coma. Better than being dead, but . . .

I realized that I had just somehow delivered myself into Eric's hands by coming to Evelyn, and I would be his prisoner, would be open to new attack, if I stayed.

But she had suggested that my being her guest would cause him to leave me alone. I wondered. I couldn't take anything at face value. I'd have to be constantly on my guard. Perhaps it would be better if I just went away, let my memories return gradually.

But there was his terrible sense of urgency. I had to find out the full story as soon as possible and act as soon as I knew it. It lay like a compulsion upon me. If danger was the price of memory and risk the cost of opportunity, then so be it. I'd stay.

'And I remember,' Evelyn said, and I realized that she had been talking for a while and I hadn't even been listening. Perhaps it was because of the reflective quality of her words, not really requiring any sort of responses – and because of the urgency of my thoughts.

'And I remember the day you beat Julian at his favorite game and he threw a glass of wine at you and cursed you. But you took the prize. And he was suddenly afraid he had gone too far. But you laughed then, though, and drank a glass with him. I think he felt badly over that show of temper, normally being so cool, and I think he was envious of you that day. Do you recall? I think he has, to a certain extent, imitated many of your ways since then. But I still hate him and hope that he goes down shortly. I feel he will . . .'

Julian, Julian, Julian. Yes and no. Something about a game and my baiting a man and shattering an almost legendary self-control. Yes, there was a feeling of familiarity; and no, I couldn't really say for certain what all had been involved.

'And Caine, how you gulled *him*! He hates you yet, you know . . .'

I gathered I wasn't very well liked. Somehow, the feeling pleased me.

And Caine, too, sounded familiar. Very.

Eric, Julian, Caine, Corwin. The names swam around in my head, and in a way, it was too much to hold within me.

'It's been so long . . .' I said almost involuntarily, and it seemed to be true.

'Corwin,' she said, 'let's not fence. You want more than security, I know that. And you're still strong enough to get something out of this, if you play your hand just right I can't guess what you have in mind, but maybe we can make a deal with Eric.' The *we* had obviously shifted. She had come to some sort of conclusion as to my worth in whatever was going on. She saw a chance to gain something for herself, I could tell. I smiled, just a little. 'Is that why you came here?' she continued. 'Do you have a proposal for Eric, something which might require a go-between?'

'I may,' I replied, 'after I've thought about it some more. I've still so recently recovered that I have much pondering to do. I wanted to be in the best place, though, where I could act quickly, if I decided my best interests lay with Eric.'

'Take care,' she said. 'You know I'll report every word.'

'Of course,' I said, not knowing that at all and groping for a quick hedge, 'unless your best interests were conjoined with my own.'

Her eyebrows moved closer together, and tiny wrinkles appeared between them.

'I'm not sure what you're proposing.'

'I'm not proposing anything, yet,' I said. 'I'm just being completely open and honest with you and telling you I don't know. I'm not positive I want to make a deal with Eric. After an . . .' I let the words trail off on purpose, for I had nothing to follow them with, though I felt I should.

'You've been offered an alternative?' She stood up suddenly, seizing her whistle. 'Bleys! Of course!'

'Sit down,' I said, 'and don't be ridiculous. Would I place myself in your hands this calmly, this readily, just to be dog meat because you happen to think of Bleys?'

She relaxed, maybe even sagged a little, then reseated herself.

'Possibly not,' she finally said, 'but I know you're a gambler, and I know you're treacherous. If you came here to dispose of a partisan, don't even bother trying. I'm not that important. You should know that by now. Besides, I always thought you rather liked me.'

'I did, and I do,' I said, 'and you have nothing to worry about, so don't. It's interesting, though, that you should mention Bleys.'

Bait, bait, bait! There was so much I wanted to know!

'Why? *Has* he approached you?'

'I'd rather not say,' I replied, hoping it would give me an edge of some kind, and now that I knew Bleys' gender: 'If he had, I'd have answered him the same as I would Eric – "I'll think about it." '

'Bleys,' she repeated, and *Bleys*, I said to myself inside my head, *Bleys. I like you. I forget why, and I know there are reasons why I shouldn't – but I like you. I know it.*

We sat awhile, and I felt fatigue but didn't want to show it. I should be strong. I knew I had to be strong.

I sat there and smiled and said, 'Nice library you've got here,' and she said, 'Thank you.'

'Bleys,' she repeated after a time. 'Do you really think he has a chance?'

I shrugged.

'Who knows? Not I, for certain. Maybe he does. Maybe not, too.'

Then she stared at me, her eyes slightly wide, and her mouth opening.

'Not you?' she said. 'You're not going to try yourself, are you?'

I laughed then, solely for purposes of countering her emotion.

'Don't be silly,' I said when I'd finished. 'Me?'

But as she said it, I knew she'd struck some chord, some deep-buried thing which replied with a powerful 'Why not?'

I was suddenly afraid.

She seemed relieved, though, at my disavowal of whatever it was I was disavowing. She smiled then, and indicated a built-in bar off to my left.

'I'd like a little Irish Mist,' she said.

'So would I, for that matter,' I replied, and I rose and fetched two.

'You know,' I said, after I'd reseated myself, 'it's pleasant to be together with you this way, even if it is only for a short time. It brings back memories.'

And she smiled and was lovely.

'You're right,' she said, sipping her drink. 'I almost feel in Amber with you around,' and I almost dropped my drink.

Amber! The word had sent a bolt of lightning down my spine!

Then she began to cry, and I rose and put my arm around her shoulders to comfort her.

'Don't cry, little girl. Please don't. It makes me unhappy, too.' *Amber! There was something there, something electrical and potent!* 'There will be good days once again,' I said, softly.

'Do you really believe that?' she asked.

'Yes,' I said loudly. 'Yes, I do!'

'You're crazy,' she said. 'Maybe that's why you were always my favorite brother too. I can almost believe anything you say, even though I know you're crazy.'

Then she cried a little more and stopped.

'Corwin,' she said, 'if you do make it – if by some wild and freakish chance out of Shadow you should make it – will you remember your little sister Florimel?'

'Yes,' I said, knowing it to be her name. 'Yes, I will remember you.'

'Thank you. I will tell Eric only the essentials, and mention Bleys not at all, nor my latest suspicions.'

'Thank you, Flora.'

'But I don't trust you worth a damn,' she added. 'Remember that, too.'

'That goes without saying.'

Then she summoned her maid to show me to a room, and I managed to undress, collapsed into the bed, and slept for eleven hours.

3

In the morning she was gone, and there was no message. Her maid served me breakfast in the kitchen and went away to do maid-things. I'd disregarded the notion of trying to pump information of the woman, as she either wouldn't know or wouldn't tell me the things I wanted to know and would no doubt also report my attempt to Flora. So, since it seemed I had the run of the house, I decided I'd return to the library and see what I could learn there. Besides, I like libraries. It makes me feel comfortable and secure to have walls of words, beautiful and wise, all around me. I always feel better when I can see that there is something to hold back the shadows.

Donner or Blitzen, or one of their relatives, appeared from somewhere and followed me up the hallway, walking stiff-legged and sniffing after my spoor. I tried to make friends with him, but it was like exchanging pleasantries with the state trooper who signaled you to pull off the road. I looked into some of the other rooms as I went along, and they were just places, innocuous-looking ones.

So I entered the library, and Africa still faced me. I closed the door behind me to keep the dogs out, and I strolled around the room, reading the titles on the shelves.

There were lots of history books. In fact, they seemed to dominate her collection. There were also many art books, of the big and expensive variety, and I leafed through a few of these. I usually do my best real thinking when I'm thinking about something else.

I wondered at the sources of Flora's obvious wealth. If we were related, did that mean that perhaps I enjoyed somewhat of opulence, also? I thought about my economic and social status, my profession, my origins. I had the feeling that I'd never worried much about money, and that there'd always been enough, or ways of getting it, to keep me satisfied. Did I own a big house like this? I couldn't remember.

What did I do?

I sat behind her desk and examined my mind for any special caches of knowledge I might possess. It is difficult to examine yourself this way, as a stranger. Maybe that's why I couldn't come up with anything. What's yours is yours and a part of you and it just seems to belong there, inside. That's all.

A doctor? That came to mind as I was viewing some of Da Vinci's anatomical drawings. Almost by reflex, in my mind, I had begun going through the steps of various surgical operations. I realized then that I had operated on people in the past.

But that wasn't it. While I realized that I had a medical background, I knew that it was a part of something else. I knew, somehow, that I was not a practicing surgeon. What then? What else was involved?

Something caught my eye.

Seated there at the desk, I commanded a view of the far wall, on which, among other things, hung an antique cavalry saber, which I had overlooked the first time around the room. I rose and crossed over to it, took it down from its pegs.

In my mind, I *tsked* at the shape it was in. I wanted an oily rag and a whetstone, to make it the way it should be once again. I knew something about antique arms, edged weapons in particular.

The saber felt light and useful in my hand, and I felt capable with it. I struck an *en garde*. I parried and cut a few times. Yes, I could use the thing.

So what sort of background was that? I looked around for new memory joggers.

Nothing else occurred to me, so I replaced the blade and returned to the desk. Sitting there, I decided to go through the thing.

I started with the middle one and worked my way up the left side and down the right, drawer by drawer.

Stationery, envelopes, postage stamps, paper clips, pencil stubs, rubber bands – all the usual items.

I had pulled each drawer all the way out though, and held it in my lap as I'd inspected its contents. It wasn't just an idea. It was part of some sort of training I'd once received, which told me I should inspect the sides and bottoms as well.

One thing almost slipped by me, but caught my attention at the last instant: the back of the lower right-hand drawer did not rise as high as the backs of the other drawers.

This indicated something, and when I knelt and looked inside the drawer space I saw a little box-like affair affixed to the upper side.

It was a small drawer itself, way in the back, and it was locked.

It took me about a minute of fooling around with paper clips, safety puts, and finally a metal shoehorn I'd seen in another drawer. The shoehorn did the trick.

The drawer contained a packet of playing cards.

And the packet bore a device which caused me to stiffen where I knelt, perspiration suddenly wetting my brow and my breath coming rapidly.

It bore a white unicorn on a green field, rampant, facing to the dexter.

And I knew that device and it hurt me that I could not name it.

I opened the packet and extracted the cards. They were on the order of tarots, with their wands, pentacles, cups, and swords, but the Greater Trumps were quite different.

I replaced both drawers, being careful not to lock the smaller one, before I continued my inspection.

They were almost lifelike in appearance, the Greater Trumps ready to step right out through those glistening surfaces. The cards seemed quite cold to my touch, and it gave me a distinct pleasure to handle them. I had once had a packet like his myself, I suddenly knew.

I began spreading them on the blotter before me.

The one bore a wily-looking little man, with a sharp nose and a laughing mouth and a shock of straw-colored hair. He was dressed in something like a Renaissance costume of orange, red, and brown. He wore long hose and a tight-fitting embroidered doublet. And I knew him. His name was Random.

Next, there was the passive countenance of Julian, dark hair hanging long, blue eyes containing neither passion nor compassion. He was dressed completely in scaled white armor, not silver or metallic-colored, but looking as if it had been enameled. I knew, though, that it was terribly tough and shock-resistant, despite its decorative and festive appearance. He was the man I had beaten at his favorite game, for which he had thrown a glass of wine at me. I knew him and I hated him.

Then came the swarthly, dark-eyed countenance of Caine, dressed all in satin that was black and green, wearing a dark three-cornered hat set at a rakish angle, a green plume of feathers trailing down the back. He was standing in profile, one arm akimbo, and the toes of his boots curled upwards, and he wore an emerald-studded dagger at his belt. There was ambivalence in my heart.

Then there was Eric. Handsome by anyone's standards, his hair was so dark as to be almost blue. His beard curled around the mouth that always smiled, and he was dressed simply in a leather jacket and leggings, a plain cloak, high black boots, and he wore a red sword belt bearing a long silvery saber and clasped with a ruby, and his high cloak collar round his head was lined with red and the trimmings of his sleeves matched it. His hands, thumbs hooked behind his belt, were terribly strong and prominent. A pair of black gloves jutted from the belt near his right hip. He it was, I was certain, that had tried to kill me on that day I had almost died. I studied him and I feared him somewhat.

Then there was Benedict, tall and dour, thin; thin of body, thin of face, wide of mind. He wore orange and yellow and brown and reminded me of haystacks and pumpkins and scarecrows and the *Legend of Sleepy Hollow*. He had a long, strong jaw and hazel eyes and brown hair that never curled. He stood beside a tan horse and leaned upon a lance about which was twined a rope of flowers. He seldom laughed. I liked him.

I paused when I uncovered the next card, and my heart leaped forward and banged against my sternum and asked to be let out.

It was me.

I knew the me I shaved and this was the guy behind the mirror. Green eyes, black hair, dressed in black and silver, yes. I had on a cloak and it was slightly furled as by a wind. I had on black boots, like Eric's, and I too wore a blade, only mine was heavier, though not quite as long as his. I had my gloves on and they were silver and scaled. The clasp at my neck was cast in the form of a silver rose.

Me, Corwin.

And a big, powerful man regarded me from the next card. He resembled me quite strongly, save that his jaw was heavier, and I knew he was bigger than I, though slower. His strength was a thing out of legend. He wore a dressing gown of blue and gray clasped about the middle with a wide, black belt, and he stood laughing. About his neck, on a heavy cord, there hung a silver hunting horn. He wore a fringe beard and a light mustache. In his right hand he held a goblet of wine. I felt a sudden affection for him. His name then occurred to me. He was Gérard.

Then came a fiery bearded, flame-crowned man, dressed all in red and orange, mainly of silk stuff, and he held a sword in his right hand and a glass of wine in his left, and the devil himself danced behind his eyes, as blue as Flora's, or Eric's. His chin was slight, but the beard covered it. His sword was inlaid with an elaborate filigree of a golden color. He wore two huge rings on his right hand and one on his left: an emerald, a ruby, and a sapphire, respectively. This, I knew, was Bleys.

Then there was a figure both like Bleys and myself. My features, though smaller, my eyes, Bleys' hair, beardless. He wore a riding suit of green and sat atop a white horse, heading toward the dexter side of the card. There was a quality of born strength and weakness, questing and abandonment about him. I both approved and disapproved, liked and was repelled by, this one. His name was Brand, I knew. As soon as I laid eyes upon him, I knew.

In fact, I realized that I knew them all well, remembered them all, with their strengths, their weaknesses, their victories, their defeats.

For they were my brothers.

I lit a cigarette I'd filched from Flora's desk box, and I leaned back and considered the things I had recalled.

They were my brothers, those eight strange men garbed in their strange costumes. And I knew that it was right and fitting that they should dress in whatever manner they chose, just as it was right for me to wear the black and the silver. Then I chuckled, as I realized what I was wearing, what I had purchased in the little clothing store of that little town I had stopped in after my departure from Greenwood.

I had on black slacks, and all three of the shirts I had purchased had been of a grayish, silvery color. And my jacket, too, was black.

I returned to the cards, and there was Flora in a gown green as the sea, just as I'd remembered her the previous evening; and then there was a black-haired girl with the same blue eyes, and her hair hung long and she was dressed all in black, with a girdle of silver about her waist. My eyes filled with tears, why I don't know. Her name was Deirdre. Then there was Fiona, with hair like Bleys or Brand, my eyes, and a complexion like mother of pearl. I hated her the second I turned over the card. Next was Llewella, whose hair matched her jade-colored eyes, dressed in shimmering gray and green with a lavender belt, and looking moist and sad. For some reason, I knew she was not like the rest of us. But she, too, was my sister.

I felt a terrible sense of distance and removal from all these people. Yet somehow they seemed physically close.

The cards were so very cold on my fingertips that I put them down again, though with a certain sense of reluctance at having to relinquish their touch.

There were no more, though. All the rest were minor cards. And I knew, somehow, that *somehow*, again – ah, somehow! – that several were missing.

For the life of me, however, I did not know what the missing Trumps represented.

I was strangely saddened by this, and I picked up my cigarette and mused.

Why did all these things rush back so easily when I viewed the cards – rush back without dragging their contexts along with them? I knew more now than I'd known before, in the way of names and faces. But that was about all.

I couldn't figure the significance of the fact that we were all done up on cards this way. I had a terribly strong desire to own a pack of them, however. If I picked up Flora's, though, I knew she'd spot in a hurry that they were missing, and I'd be in trouble. Therefore, I put them back in the little drawer behind the big drawer and locked them in again. Then, God, how I racked my brains! But to little avail.

Until I recalled a magical word.

Amber.

I had been greatly upset by the word on the previous evening. I had been sufficiently upset so that I had avoided thinking of it since then. But now I courted it. Now I rolled it around my mind and examined all the associations that sprang up when it struck.

The word was charged with a mighty longing and a massive nostalgia. It had, wrapped up inside it, a sense of forsaken beauty, grand achievement, and a feeling of power that was terrible and almost ultimate. Somehow, the word belonged in my vocabulary. Somehow, I was part of it and it was a part of me. It was a place name, I knew then. It was the name of a place I once had known. There came no pictures, though, only emotions.

How long I sat so, I do not know. Time had somehow divorced itself from my reveries.

I realized then, from the center of my thoughts, that there had come a gentle rapping upon the door. Then the handle slowly turned and the maid, whose name was Carmella, entered and asked me if I was interested in lunch.

It seemed like a good idea, so I followed her back to the kitchen and ate half a chicken and drank a quart of milk.

I took a pot of coffee back to the library with me, avoiding the dogs as I went. I was into the second cup when the telephone rang.

I longed to pick it up, but I figured there must be extensions all over the house and Carmella would probably get it from somewhere.

I was wrong. It kept ringing.

Finally, I couldn't resist it any longer.

'Hello,' I said, 'this is the Flaumel residence.'

'May I speak with Mrs Flaumel please?'

It was a man's voice, rapid and slightly nervous. He sounded out of breath and his words were masked and surrounded by the faint ringing and the ghost voices that indicate long distance.

'I'm sorry,' I told him. 'She's not here right now. May I take a message or have her call you back?'

'Who am I talking to?' he demanded.

I hesitated, then, 'Corwin's the name,' I told him.

'My God!' he said, and a long silence followed.

I was beginning to think he'd hung up. I said, 'Hello?' again, just as he started talking.

'Is she still alive?' he asked.

'Of course she's still alive! Who the hell am I talking to?'

'Don't you recognize the voice, Corwin? This is Random. Listen, I'm in California and I'm in trouble. I was calling to ask Flora for sanctuary. Are you in with her?'

'Temporarily,' I said.

'I see. Will you give me your protection, Corwin?' Pause, then, 'Please?'

28

'As much as I can,' I said, 'but I can't commit Flora to anything without consulting her.'

'Will you protect me against her?'

'Yes.'

'Then you're good enough for me, man. I'm going to try to make it to New York now. I'll be coming by a rather circuitous route, so I don't know how long it will take me. If I can avoid the wrong shadows, I'll be seeing you whenever. Wish me luck.'

'Luck,' I said.

Then there was a click and I was listening to a distant ringing and the voices of the ghosts.

So cocky little Random was in trouble! I had a feeling it shouldn't have bothered me especially. But now, he was one of the keys to my past, and quite possibly my future also. So I would try to help him, in any way I could, until I'd learned all I wanted from him. I knew that there wasn't much brotherly love lost between the two of us. But I knew that on the one hand he was nobody's fool; he was resourceful, shrewd, strangely sentimental over the damnedest things; and on the other hand, his word wasn't worth the spit behind it, and he'd probably sell my corpse to the medical school of his choice if he could get much for it. I remembered the little fink all right, with only a touch of affection, perhaps for a few pleasant times it seemed we had spent together. But trust him? Never. I decided I wouldn't tell Flora he was coming until the last possible moment. He might be made to serve as an ace, or at least a knave, in the hole.

So I added some hot coffee to what remained in my cup and sipped it slowly.

Who was he running from?

Not Eric, certainly, or he wouldn't have been calling here. I wondered then concerning his question as to whether Flora was dead, just because I happened to be present here. Was she really that strongly allied with the brother I knew I hated that it was common knowledge in the family that I'd do her in, too, given the chance? It seemed strange, but then he'd asked the question.

And what was it in which they were allied? What was the source of this tension, this opposition? Why was it that Random was running?

Amber.

That was the answer.

Amber. Somehow, the key to everything lay in Amber, I knew. The secret of the entire mess was in Amber, in some event that had transpired in that place, and fairly recently, I'd judge. I'd have to be on my toes. I'd have to pretend to the knowledge I didn't possess, while piece by piece I mined it from those who had it. I felt confident that I could do it. There was enough distrust circulating for everyone to be cagey. I'd play on that I'd get what I needed and take what I wanted, and I'd remember those who helped me and step on the rest. For this, I knew, was the law by which our family lived, and I was a true son of my father . . .

My headache came on again suddenly, throbbing to crack my skull. Something about my father I thought, guessed, felt was what had served to set it off. But I wasn't sure why or how.

After a time, it subsided and I slept, there in the chair. After a much longer time, the door opened and Flora entered. It was night outside, once more.

She was dressed in a green silk blouse and a long woolen skirt that was gray. She had on walking shoes and heavy stockings. Her hair was pulled back behind her head and she looked slightly pale. She still wore her hound whistle.

'Good evening,' I said, rising.

But she did not reply. Instead, she walked across the room to the bar, poured herself a shot of Jack Daniels, and tossed it off like a man. Then she poured another and took it with her to the big chair.

I lit a cigarette and handed it to her.

She nodded, then said, 'The Road to Amber – is difficult.'

'Why?'

She gave me a very puzzled look.

'When is the last time you tried it?'

I shrugged.

'I don't remember.'

'Be that way then,' she said. 'I just wondered how much of it was your doing.'

I didn't reply because I didn't know what she was talking about. But then I recalled that there was an easier way than the Road to get to the place called Amber. Obviously, she lacked it.

'You're missing some Trumps,' I said then suddenly, in a voice which was almost mine.

She sprang to her feet, half her drink spilling over the back of her hand.

'Give them back!' she cried, reaching for the whistle. I moved forward and seized her shoulders.

'I don't have them,' I said. 'I was just making an observation.'

She relaxed a bit, then began to cry, and I pushed her back down, gently, into the chair.

'I thought you meant you'd taken the ones I had left,' she said. 'Rather than just making a nasty and obvious comment.'

I didn't apologize. It didn't seem right that I should have to.

'How far did you get?'

'Not far at all.' Then she laughed and regarded me with a new light in her eyes.

'I see what you've done now, Corwin,' she said, and I lit a cigarette in order to cover any sort of need for a reply.

'Some of those things were yours, weren't they? You blocked my way to Amber before you came here, didn't you? You knew I'd go to Eric. But I can't now. I'll have to wait till he comes to me. Clever. You want to draw him here, don't you? He'll send a messenger, though. He won't come himself.'

There was a strange tone of admiration in the voice of this woman who was admitting she'd just tried to sell me out to my enemy, and still would – given half a chance – as she talked about something she thought I'd done which had thrown a monkey wrench into her plans. How could anyone be so admittedly Machiavellian in the presence of a proposed victim? The answer rang back immediately from the depths of my mind: it is the way of our kind. We don't have to be subtle with each other. Though I thought she lacked somewhat the finesse of a true professional.

'Do you think I'm stupid, Flora?' I asked. 'Do you think I came here just for purposes of waiting around for you to hand me over to Eric? Whatever you ran into, it served you right.'

'All right, I don't play in your league! But you're in exile, too! That shows you weren't so smart!'

Somehow her words burned and I knew they were wrong.

'Like hell I am!' I said.

She laughed again.

'I knew that would get a rise out of you,' she said. 'All right, you walk in the Shadows on purpose then. You're crazy.'

I shrugged.

She said, 'What do you want? Why did you really come here?'

'I was curious what you were up to,' I said. 'That's all. You can't keep me here if I don't want to stay. Even Eric couldn't do that. Maybe I really did just want to visit with you. Maybe I'm getting sentimental in my old age. Whatever, I'm going to stay a little longer now, and then probably go away for good. If you hadn't been so quick to see what you could get for me, you might have profited a lot more, lady. You asked me to remember you one day, if a certain thing occurred . . .'

It took several seconds for what I thought I was implying to sink in.

Then she said, 'You're going to try! You're really going to try!'

'You're goddamn right I'm going to try,' I said, knowing that I would, whatever it was, 'and you can tell that to Eric if you want, but remember that I might make it. Bear in mind that if I do, it might be nice to be my friend.'

I sure wished I knew what the hell I was talking about, but I'd picked up enough terms and felt the importance attached to them, so that I could use them properly without knowing what they meant. But they *felt* right, so very right . . .

Suddenly, she was kissing me.

'I won't tell him. Really, I won't, Corwin! I think you can do it. Bleys will be difficult, but Gérard would probably help you, and maybe Benedict. Then Caine would swing over, when he saw what was happening—'

'I can do my own planning,' I said.

Then she drew away. She poured two glasses of wine and handed one to me.

'To the future,' she said.

'I'll always drink to that.'

And we did.

Then she refilled mine and studied me.

'It had to be Eric, Bleys, or you,' she said. 'You're the only ones with any guts or brains. But you'd removed yourself from the picture for so long that I'd counted you out of the running.'

'It just goes to show: you never can tell.'

I sipped my drink and hoped she'd shut up for just a minute. It seemed to me she was being a bit too obvious in trying to play on every side available. There was something bothering me, and I wanted to think about it.

How old was I?

That question, I knew, was a part of the answer to the terrible sense of distance and removal that I felt from all the persons depicted on the playing cards. I was older than I appeared to be. (Thirtyish, I'd seemed when I looked at me in the mirror – but now I knew that it was because the Shadows would lie for me.) I was far, far older, and it had been a very long time since I had seen my brothers and my sisters, all together and friendly, existing side by side as they did on the cards, with no tension, no friction among them.

We heard the sound of the bell, and Carmella moving to answer the door.

'That would be brother Random,' I said, knowing I was right. 'He's under my protection.'

Her eyes widened, then she smiled, as though she appreciated some clever thing I had done.

I hadn't, of course, but I was glad to let her think so.

It made me feel safer.

4

I felt safe for perhaps all of three minutes.

I beat Carmella to the door and flung it open.

He staggered in and immediately pushed the door shut behind himself and shot the bolt. There were lines under those light eyes and he wasn't wearing a bright doublet and long hose. He needed a shave and he had on a brown wool suit. He carried a gabardine overcoat over one arm and wore dark suede shoes. But he was Random, all right – the Random I had seen on the card – only the laughing mouth looked tired and there was dirt beneath his fingernails.

'Corwin!' he said, and embraced me.

I squeezed his shoulder. 'You look as if you could use a drink,' I said.

'Yes. Yes. Yes . . .' he agreed, and I steered him toward the library.

About three minutes later, after he had seated himself, with a drink in one hand and a cigarette in the other, he said to me, 'They're after me. They'll be here soon.'

Flora let out a little shriek, which we both ignored.

'Who?' I asked.

'People out of the Shadows,' he said. 'I don't know who they are, or who sent them. There are four or five though, maybe even six. They were on the plane with me. I took a jet. They occurred around Denver. I moved the plane several times to subtract them, but it didn't work – and I didn't want to get too far off the track. I shook them in Manhattan, but it's only a matter of time. I think they'll be here soon.'

'And you've no idea at all who sent them?'

He smiled for an instant.

'Well, I guess we'd be safe in limiting it to the family. Maybe Bleys, maybe Julian, maybe Caine. Maybe even you, to get me here. Hope not, though. You didn't, did you?'

' 'Fraid not,' I said. 'How tough do they look?'

He shrugged. 'If it were only two or three, I'd have tried to pull an ambush. But not with that whole crowd.'

He was a little guy, maybe five-six in height, weighing perhaps one thirty-five. But he sounded as if he were talking dead serious talk. I felt reasonably sure that he meant it when he said he'd take on two or three bruisers, singlehanded. I wondered suddenly about my own physical strength, being his brother. I felt comfortably strong. I knew I'd be willing to take on any one man in a fair fight without any special fears. How strong was I?

Suddenly, I knew I would have a chance to find out.

There came a knocking at the front door.

'What shall we do?' asked Flora.

Random laughed, undid his necktie, tossed it atop his coat on the desk. He stripped off his suit jacket then and looked about the room. His eyes fell upon the saber and he was across the room in an instant and had it in his hand. I felt the weight of the .32 within my jacket pocket and thumbed off the safety catch.

'Do?' Random asked. 'There exists a probability that they will gain entrance,' he said. 'Therefore, they will enter. When is the last time you stood to battle, sister?'

'It has been too long,' she replied.

'Then you had better start remembering fast,' he told her, 'because it is only a matter of small time. They are guided, I can tell you. But there are three of us and at most only twice as many of them. Why worry?'

'We don't know what they are,' she said.

The knocking came again.

'What does it matter?'

'Nothing,' I said. 'Shall I go and let them in?'

They both blanched slightly.

'We might as well wait . . .'

'I might call the cops,' I said.

They both laughed, almost hysterically.

'Or Eric,' I said, suddenly looking at her.

But she shook her head.

'We just don't have the time. We have the Trump, but by the time he could respond – if he chose – it would be too late.'

'And this might even be his doing, eh?' said Random.

'I doubt it,' she replied, 'very much. It's not his style.'

'True,' I replied, just for the hell of it, and to let them know I was with things.

The sound of knocking came once again, and much more loudly.

'What about Carmella?' I asked, upon a sudden thought.

Flora shook her head.

'I have decided that it is improbable that she will answer the door.'

'But you don't know what you're up against,' Random cried, and he was suddenly gone from the room.

I followed him, along the hallway and into the foyer, in time to stop Carmella from opening the door.

We sent her back to her own quarters with instructions to lock herself in, and Random observed, 'That shows the strength of the opposition. Where are we, Corwin?'

I shrugged.

'If I knew, I'd tell you. For the moment at least, we're in this together. Step back!'

And I opened the door.

The first man tried to push me aside, and I stiff-armed him back.

There were six, I could see that.

'What do you want?' I asked them.

But never a word was spoken, and I saw guns.

I kicked out and slammed the door again and shot the bolt.

'Okay, they're really there,' I said. 'But how do I know you're not pulling something?'

'You don't,' he said, 'but I really wish I were. They look wild.'

I had to agree. The guys on the porch were heavily built and had hats palled down to cover their eyes. Their faces had all been covered with shadows.

'I wish I knew where we are,' said Random.

I felt a hackle-raising vibration, in the vicinity of my eardrums. I knew, in that moment, that Flora had blown her whistle.

When I heard a window break, somewhere off to my right, I was not surprised to hear a growled rumbling and some baying, somewhere off to my left.

'She's called her dogs,' I said, 'six mean and vicious brutes, which could under other circumstances be after us.'

Random nodded, and we both headed off in the direction of the shattering.

When we reached the living room, two men were already inside and both had guns.

I dropped the first and hit the floor, firing at the second. Random leaped above me, brandishing his blade, and I saw the second man's head depart his shoulders.

By then, two more were through the window. I emptied the automatic at them, and I heard the snarling of Flora's hounds mixed with gunfire that was not my own.

I saw three of the men upon the floor and the same number of Flora's dogs. It made me feel good to think we had gotten half them, and as the rest came through the window I killed another in a manner which surprised me.

Suddenly, and without thinking, I picked up a huge overstuffed chair and hurled it perhaps thirty feet across the room. It broke the back of the man it struck.

I leaped toward the remaining two, but before I crossed the room, Random had pierced one of them with the saber, leaving him for the dogs to finish off, and was turning toward the other.

The other was pulled down before he could act, however. He killed another of the dogs before we could stop him, but he never killed anything again after that. Random strangled him.

It turned out that two of the dogs were dead and one was badly hurt. Random killed the injured one with a quick thrust, and we turned our attention to the men.

There was something unusual about their appearance.

Flora entered and helped us to decide what.

For one thing, all six had uniformly bloodshot eyes. Very, very bloodshot eyes. With them, though, the condition seemed normal.

For another, all had an extra joint to each finger and thumb, and sharp, forward-curving spurs on the backs of their hands.

All of them had prominent jaws, and when I forced one open, I counted forty-five teeth, most of them longer than human teeth, and several looking to be much sharper. Their flesh was grayish and hard and shiny.

There were undoubtedly other differences also, but those were sufficient to prove a point of some sort.

We took their weapons, and I hung onto three small, flat pistols.

'They crawled out of the Shadows, all right,' said Random, and I nodded. 'And I was lucky, too. It doesn't seem they suspected I'd turn up with the reinforcements I did – a militant brother and around half a ton of dogs.' He went and peered out the broken window, and I decided to let him do it himself. 'Nothing,' he said, after a time. 'I'm sure we got them all,' and he drew the heavy orange drapes closed and pushed a lot of high-backed furniture in front of them. While he was doing that, I went through all their pockets.

I wasn't really surprised that I turned up nothing in the way of identification.

'Let's go back to the library,' he said, 'so I can finish my drink.'

He cleaned off the blade, carefully, before he seated himself, however, and he replaced it on the pegs. I fetched Flora a drink while he did this.

'So it would seem I'm temporarily safe,' he said, 'now that there are three of us sharing the picture.'

'So it would seem,' Flora agreed.

'God, I haven't eaten since yesterday!' he announced.

So Flora went to tell Carmella it was safe to come out now, so long as she stayed clear of the living room, and to bring a lot of food to the library.

As soon as she left the room, Random turned to me and asked, 'Like, what's it between you?'

'Don't turn your back on her.'

'She's still Eric's?'

'So far as I can tell.'

'Then what are you doing here?'

'I was trying to sucker Eric into coming around after me himself. He knows it's the only way he'll really get me, and I wanted to see how badly he wanted to.'

Random shook his head.

'I don't think he'll do it. No percentage. So long as you're here and he's there, why bother sticking his neck out? He's still got the stronger position. If you want him, you'll have to go after him.'

'I've just about come to the same conclusion.'

His eyes gleamed then, and his old smile appeared. He ran one hand through his straw-colored hair and wouldn't let go of my eyes.

'Are you going to do it?' he asked.

'Maybe,' I said.

'Don't "maybe" me, baby. It's written all over you. I'd almost be willing to go along, you know. Of all my relations, I like sex the best and Eric the least.'

I lit a cigarette, while I considered.

'You're thinking,' he said while I thought, ' "How far can I trust Random this time? He is sneaky and mean and just like his name, and he will doubtless sell me out if someone offers him a better deal." True?'

I nodded.

'However, brother Corwin, remember that while I've never done you much good, I've never done you any especial harm either. Oh, a few pranks, I'll admit. But, all in all, you might say we've gotten along best of all in the family – that is, we've stayed out of each other's ways. Think it over. I believe I hear Flora or her woman coming now, so let's change the subject . . . But quick! I don't suppose you have a deck of the family's favorite playing cards around, do you?'

I shook my head.

Flora entered the room and said, 'Carmella will bring some food shortly.'

We drank to that, and he winked at me behind her back.

The following morning, the bodies were gone from the living room, there were no stains upon the carpet, the window appeared to have been repaired, and Random explained that he had 'taken care of things'. I did not see fit to question him farther.

We borrowed Flora's Mercedes and went for a drive. The countryside seemed strangely altered. I couldn't quite put my finger on what it was that was missing or new, but somehow things felt different. This, too, gave me a headache when I attempted to consider it, so I decided to suspend such thinking for the nonce.

I was at the wheel, Random at my side. I observed that I would like to be back in Amber again – just to see what sort of response would obtain.

'I have been wondering,' he replied, 'whether you were out for vengeance, pure and simple, or something more,' thereby shifting the ball back to me, to answer or not to answer, as I saw fit.

I saw fit. I used the stock phrase:

'I've been thinking about that, too,' I said, 'trying to figure my chances. You know, I just might "try".'

He turned toward me then (he had been staring out of the side window) and said:

'I suppose we've all had that ambition, or at least that thought – I know I have, though I dismissed me early in the game – and the way I feel about it, it's worth the attempt. You're asking me, I know, whether I'll help you. The answer is "yes". I'll do it just to screw up the others.' Then, 'What do you think of Flora? Would she be of any help?'

'I doubt it very much,' I said. 'She'd throw in if things were certain. But then, what's certain at this point?'

'Or any,' he added.

'Or any,' I repeated, so he'd think I knew what sort of response I would obtain.

I was afraid to confide in him as to the condition of my memory. I was also afraid to trust him, so I didn't. There were so very many things I wanted to know, but I had no one to turn to. I thought about it a bit as we drove along.

'Well, when do you want to start?' I asked.

'Whenever you're ready.'

And there it was, right in my lap, and I didn't know what to do with it.

'What about now?' I said.

He was silent. He lit a cigarette, I think to buy time. I did the same.

'Okay,' he finally said. 'When's the last time you've been back?'

'It's been so damn long,' I told him, 'that I'm not even sure I remember the way.'

'All right,' he said, 'then we're going to have to go away before we can come back. How much gas have you got?'

'Three-quarters of a tank.'

'Then turn left at the next corner, and we'll see what happens.'

I did this thing, and as we drove along all the sidewalks began to sparkle.

'Damn!' he said. 'It's been around twenty years since I've taken the walk. I'm remembering the right things too soon.'

We kept driving, and I kept wondering what the hell was happening. The sky had grown a bit greenish, then shaded over into pink.

I bit my lip against the asking of questions.

We passed beneath a bridge and when we emerged on the other side the sky was a normal color again, but there were windmills all over the place, big yellow ones.

'Don't worry,' he said quickly, 'it could be worse.'

I noticed that the people we passed were dressed rather strangely, and the roadway was of brick.

'Turn right.'

I did.

Purple clouds covered over the sun, and it began to rain. Lightning stalked the heavens and the skies grumbled above us. I had the windshield wipers going full speed, but they weren't doing a whole big lot of good. I turned on the headlights and slowed even more.

I would have sworn I'd passed a horseman, racing in the other direction, dressed all in gray, collar turned high and head lowered against the rain.

Then the clouds broke themselves apart and we were riding along a seashore. The waves splashed high and enormous gulls swept low above them. The rain had stopped and I killed the lights and the wipers. Now the road was of macadam, but I didn't recognize the place at all. In the rear-view mirror there was no sign of the town we had just departed. My grip tightened upon the wheel as we passed by a sudden gallows where a skeleton was suspended by the neck, pushed from side to side by the wind.

Random just kept smoking and staring out of the window as our road turned away from the shore and curved around a hill. A grassy treeless plain swept away to our right and a row of hills climbed higher on our left. The sky by now was a dark but brilliant blue, like a deep, clear pool, sheltered and shaded. I did not recall having ever seen a sky like that before.

Random opened his window to throw away the butt, and an icy breeze came in and swirled around inside the car until he closed the window again. The breeze had a sea scent to it, salty and sharp.

'All roads lead to Amber,' he said, as though it were an axiom.

Then I recalled what Flora had said the day before. I didn't want to sound like a dunce or a withholder of crucial information, but I had to tell him, for my sake as well as his own, when I realized what her statements implied.

'You know,' I began, 'when you called the other day and I answered the phone because Flora was out, I've a strong feeling she was trying to make it to Amber, and that she found the way blocked.'

At this, he laughed.

'The woman has very little imagination,' he replied. 'Of course it would be blocked at a time like this. Ultimately, we'll be reduced to walking, I'm sure, and it will doubtless take all of our strength and ingenuity to make it, if we make it at all. Did she think she could walk back like a princess in state, treading on flowers the whole way? She's a dumb bitch. She doesn't really deserve to live, but that's not for me to say, yet.

'Turn right at the crossroads,' he decided.

What was happening? I knew he was in some way responsible for the exotic changes going on about us, but I couldn't determine how be was doing it, where he was getting us to. I knew I had to learn his secret, but I couldn't just ask him or he'd know I didn't know. Then I'd be at his mercy. He seemed to do nothing but smoke and stare, but coming up out of a dip in the road we entered a blue desert and the sun was now pink above our heads within the shimmering sky. In the rear-view mirror, miles and miles of desert stretched out behind us, far as I could see. Neat trick, that.

Then the engine coughed, sputtered, steadied itself, repeated the performance.

The steering wheel changed shape beneath my hands.

It became a crescent; and the seat seemed further back, the car seemed closer to the road, and the windshield had more of a slant to it.

I said nothing, though, not even when the lavender sandstorm struck us.

But when it cleared away, I gasped.

There was a godawful line of cars all jammed up, about half a mile before us. They were all standing still and I could hear their horns.

'Slow down,' he said. 'It's the first obstacle.'

I did, and another gust of sand swept over us.

Before I could switch on the lights, it was gone, and I blinked my eyes several times.

All the cars were gone and their horns silent. But the roadway sparkled now as the sidewalks had for a time, and I heard Random damning someone or something under his breath.

'I'm sure I shifted just the way he wanted us to, whoever set up that block,' he said, 'and it pisses me off that I did what he expected – the obvious.'

'Eric?' I asked.

'Probably. What do you think we should do? Stop and try it the hard way for a while, or go on and see if there are more blocks?'

'Let's go on a bit. After all, that was the only the first.'

'Okay,' he said, but added, 'who knows what the second will be?'

The second was a thing – I don't know how else to describe it.

It was a thing that looked like a smelter with arms, squatting in the middle of the road, reaching down and picking up cars, eating them.

I hit the brakes.

'What's the matter?' Random asked. 'Keep going. How else can we get past them?'

'It shook me a bit,' I said, and he gave me a strange, sidelong look as another dust storm came up.

It had been the wrong thing to say, I knew.

When the dust cleared away, we were racing along an empty road once more. And there were towers in the distance.

'I think I've screwed him up,' said Random. 'I combined several into one, and I think it may be one he hasn't anticipated. After all, no one can cover all roads to Amber.'

'True,' I said, hoping to redeem myself from whatever faux pas had drawn that strange look.

I considered Random. A little, weak-looking guy who could have died as easily as I on the previous evening. What was his power? And what was all this talk of Shadows? Something told me that whatever Shadows were, we moved among them even now. How? It was something Random was doing, and since he seemed at rest physically, his hands in plain sight, I decided it was something he did with his mind. Again, how?

Well, I'd heard him speak of 'adding' and 'subtracting' as though the universe in which he moved were a big equation.

I decided – with a sudden certainty – that he was somehow adding and subtracting items to and from the world that was visible about us to bring us into closer and closer alignment with that strange place Amber, for which he was solving.

It was something I'd once known how to do. And the key to it, I knew in a flash, was remembering Amber.

But I couldn't.

The road curved abruptly, the desert ended, to give way to fields of tall, blue, sharp-looking grass. After a while, the terrain became a bit hilly, and at the foot of the third hill the pavement ended and we entered upon a narrow dirt road. It was hard-packed, and it wound its way among greater bills upon which small shrubs and bayonet-like thistle bushes now began to appear.

After about half an hour of this, the hills went away, and we entered a forest of squat, big-boled trees with diamond-shaped leaves of autumn orange and purple.

A light rain began to fall, and there were many shadows. Pale mists arose from mats of soggy leaves. Off to right somewhere, I heard a howl.

The steering wheel changed shape three more times, its latest version being an octagonal wooden affair. The car was quite tall now, and we had somewhere acquired a hood ornament in the shape of a flamingo. I refrained from commenting on these things, but accommodated myself to whatever positions the seat assumed and new operating requirements the vehicle obtained. Random, however, glanced at the steering wheel just as another howl occurred, shook his head, and suddenly the trees were much higher, though festooned with hanging vines and something like a blue veiling of Spanish Moss, and the car was almost normal again. I glanced at the fuel gauge and saw that we had half a tank.

'We're making headway,' my brother remarked, and I nodded.

The road widened abruptly and acquired a concrete surface. There were canals on both sides, full of muddy water. Leaves, small branches, and colored feathers glided along their surfaces.

I suddenly became lightheaded and a bit dizzy, but 'Breathe slowly and deeply,' said Random, before I could remark on it. 'We're taking a short cut, and the atmosphere and the gravitation will be a bit different for a time. I think we've been pretty lucky so far, and I want to push it for all it's worth – get as close as we can, as quickly as we can.'

'Good idea,' I said.

'Maybe, maybe not,' he replied, 'but I think it's worth the gam— Look out!'

We were climbing a hill and a truck topped it and came barreling down toward us. It was on the wrong side of the road. I swerved to avoid it, but it swerved, too. At the very last instant, I had to go off the road, onto the soft shoulder to my left, and head close to the edge of the canal in order to avoid a collision.

To my right, the truck screeched to a halt. I tried to pull off the shoulder and back onto the road, but we were stuck in the soft soil.

Then I heard a door slam, and saw that the driver had climbed down from the right side of the cab – which meant that he probably was driving on the proper side of the road after all, and we were in the wrong. I was sure that nowhere in the States did traffic flow in a British manner, but I was certain by this time that we had long ago left the Earth that I knew.

The truck was a tanker. It said ZUNOCO on the side in big, blood-red letters, and beneath this was the motto 'Wee covir the werld'. The driver covered me with abuse, as I stepped out, rounded the car, and began apologizing. He was as big as I was, and built like a beer barrel, and he carried a jack handle in one hand.

'Look, I said I'm sorry,' I told him. 'What do you want me to do? Nobody got hurt and there was no damage.'

'They shouldn't turn goddamn drivers like you loose on the road!' he yelled. 'You're a friggin' menace!'

Random got out of the car then and said, 'Mister, you'd better move along!' and he had a gun in his hand.

'Put that away,' I told him, but he flipped the safety catch off and pointed.

The guy turned around and started to run, a look of fear widening his eyes and loosening his jaw.

Random raised his pistol and took careful aim at the man's back, and I managed to knock his arm to the side just as he pulled the trigger.

It scored the pavement and ricocheted away.

Random turned toward me and his face was almost white.

'You bloody fool!' he said. 'That shot could have hit the tank!'

'It could also have hit the guy you were aiming at.'

'So who the hell cares? We'll never pass this way again, in this generation. That bastard dared to insult a Prince of Amber! It was *your* honor I was thinking about.'

'I can take care of my own honor,' I told him, and something cold and powerful suddenly gripped me and answered, 'for he was mine to kill, not yours, had I chosen,' and a sense of outrage filled me.

He bowed his head then, as the cab door slammed and the truck took off down the road.

'I'm sorry, brother,' he said. 'I did not mean to presume. But it offended me to hear one of them speak to you in such a manner. I know I should have waited to let you dispose of him as you saw fit, or at least have consulted with you.'

'Well, whatever,' I told him, 'Let's get back onto the road and get moving, if we can.'

The rear wheels were sunken up to their hubcaps, and as I stared at them, trying to decide the best way to go about things, Random called out, 'Okay, I've got the front bumper. You take the rear and we'll carry it back to the road – and we'd better deposit it in the left lane.'

He wasn't kidding.

He'd said something about lesser gravitation, but *I* didn't feel that light. I knew I was strong, but I had my doubts about being able to raise the rear end of a Mercedes.

But on the other hand, I had to try, since he seemed to expect it of me, and I couldn't tip him off as to any gaps in my memory.

So I stooped, squatted, grasped, and started to straighten my legs. With a sucking sound, the rear wheels freed themselves from the moist earth. I was holding my end of the car about two feet above the ground! It was heavy – damn! it was heavy! – but I could do it!

With each step that I took, I sank about six inches into the ground. But I was carrying it! And Random was doing the same with his end.

We set it down on the roadway, with a slight jouncing of springs. Then I took off my shoes and emptied them, cleaned them with swatches of grass, wrung out my socks, brushed off the cuffs of my trousers, threw my footgear into the rear seat and climbed back into the front, barefooted.

Random jumped in, on the passenger's side, and said, 'Look, I want to apologize again—'

'Forget it,' I said. 'It's over and done with.'

'Yes, but I don't want you to hold it against me.'

'I won't,' I told him. 'Just curb your impetuosity in the future, when it involves life-taking in my presence.'

'I will,' he promised.

'Then let's get rolling,' and we did.

We moved through a canyon of rocks, then passed through a city which seemed to be made entirely of glass, or glass-like substance, of tall buildings, thin and fragile-appearing, and of people through whom the pink sun shone, revealing their internal organs and the remains of their last meals. They stared at us as we drove by. They mobbed the corners of their streets, but no one attempted to halt us or pass in front of us.

'The Charles Forts of this place will doubtless quote this happening for many years,' said my brother.

I nodded.

Then there was no roadway whatsoever, and we were driving across what seemed an eternal sheet of silicon. After a while it narrowed and became our road, and after another while there were marshes to our left and our right, low, brown, and stinking. And I saw what I'd swear to be a Diplodocus raise its head and stare down upon us. Then, overhead, an enormous bat-winged shape passed by. The sky was now a royal blue, and the sun was of fallow gold.

'We've now got less than a quarter tank of gas,' I commented.

'Okay,' said Random, 'stop the car.'

I did this and waited.

For a long time – like maybe six minutes – he was silent, then, 'Drive on,' he said.

After about three miles we came to a barricade of logs and I began driving around it. A gate occurred on one side, and Random told me, 'Stop and blow your horn.'

I did so, and after a time the wooden gate creaked upon its huge iron hinges and swung inward.

'Go on in,' he said. 'It's safe.'

I drove in, and off to my left were three bubble-headed Esso pumps, the small building behind them being one of the kind I had seen countless times before, under more ordinary circumstances. I pulled up before one of the pumps and waited.

The guy who emerged from the building was about five feet tall, of enormous girth, with a strawberry-like nose, and his shoulders maybe a yard across.

'What'll it be?' he asked, 'Fill 'er up?'

I nodded. 'With regular,' I said.

'Pull it up a bit,' he directed.

I did, and asked Random, 'Is my money any good here?'

'Look at it,' he told me, and I did.

My wallet was stuffed with orange and yellow bills, Roman numerals in their corners, followed by the letters 'D.R.'

He grinned at me as I examined the sheaf.

'See, I've taken care of everything,' he said.

'Great. By the way, I'm getting hungry.'

We looked around us, and we saw a picture of a gent who sells Kentucky Fried Chicken in another place, staring down at us from a big sign.

Strawberry Nose sloshed a little on the ground to make it come out even, hung up the hose, approached, and said, 'Eight Drachae Regums.'

I found an orange note with a 'V D.R.' on it and three more with 'I D.R,' and passed them to him.

'Thanks,' he said, and stuffed them in his pocket. 'Check your oil and water.'

'Yeah.'

He added a little water, told me the oil level was okay, and smeared the windshield a bit with a dirty rag. Then he waved and walked back, into the shack.

We drove over to Kenni Roi's and got us a bucket full of Kentucki Fried Lizzard Partes and another bucket of weak, salty-tasting beer.

Then we washed up in the outbuilding, beeped the horn at the gate, and waited till a man with a halberd hanging over his right shoulder came and opened it for us.

Then we hit the road again.

A tyrannosaurus leaped before us, hesitated for a moment, then went on his way, off to the left. Three more pterodactyls passed overhead.

'I am loath to relinquish Amber's sky,' said Random, whatever that meant, and I grunted back at him.

'I'm afraid to try it all at once, though,' he continued. 'We might be torn to bits.'

'Agreed,' I agreed.

'But on the other hand, I don't like this place.'

I nodded, so we drove on, till the silicon plain ended and bare rock lay all about us.

'What are you doing now?' I ventured.

'Now that I've got the sky, I'm going to try for the terrain,' he said.

And the rock sheet became rocks, as we drove along. There was bare, black earth between. After a while, there was more earth and fewer rocks. Finally, I saw splotches of green. First a bit of grass here and there. But it was a very, very bright green, of a kind like yet unlike that common on Earth as I knew it.

Soon there was much of it.

After a time there were trees, spotted occasionally along our way.

Then there was a forest.

And what a forest!

I had never seen trees such as this – mighty and majestic, of a deep, rich green, slightly tinged with gold. They towered, they soared. They were enormous pines, oaks, maples, and many others which I could not distinguish. Through them crept a breeze of fantastic and lovely fragrance, when I cracked the window a bit. I decided to open it all the way and leave it like that after I'd had a few whiffs.

'The Forest of Arden,' said the man who was my brother, and I knew he was right, and somehow I both loved and envied him for his wisdom, his knowledge.

'Brother,' said I, 'you're doing all right. Better than I'd expected. Thank you.'

This seemed to take him somewhat aback. It was as if he'd never received a good word from a relative before.

'I'm doing my best,' he said, 'and I'll do it all the way, I promise. Look at it! We've got the sky, and we've got the forest! It's almost too good to be true! We've passed the halfway point, and nothing's bugged us especially. I think we're very fortunate. Will you give me a Regency?'

'Yes,' I said, not knowing what it meant, but willing to grant it, if lay within my powers.

He nodded then and said, 'You're okay.'

He was a homicidal little fink, who I recalled had always been sort of a rebel. Our parents had tried to discipline him in the past, I knew, never very successfully. And I realized, with that, that we had shared common parents, which I suddenly knew was not the case with me and Eric, me and Flora, me and Caine and Bleys and Fiona. And probably others, but these I'd recalled, I knew for sure.

We were driving on a hard, dirt roadway through a cathedral of enormous trees. It seemed to go on forever and ever. I felt safe in the place. Occasionally, startled a deer, surprised a fox crossing or standing near the road. In places, the way was marked with hoofprints. The sunlight was sometimes filtered through leaves, angling like tight golden strings on some Hindu musical instrument. The breeze was moist and spoke of living things. It came to me that I knew this place, that I had ridden this road often in the past. I had ridden through the Forest of Arden on horseback, walked through it, hunted in it, lay on my back beneath some of those great boughs, my arms beneath my head, staring upward. I had climbed among the branches of some of those giants and looked down upon a green world, constantly shifting.

'I love this place,' I said, only half realizing I had said it aloud, and Random replied, 'You always did,' and there might have been a trace of amusement in his voice. I couldn't be sure.

Then off in the distance I heard a note which I knew to be the voice of a hunting horn.

'Drive faster,' said Random suddenly. 'That sounds to be Julian's horn.'

I obeyed.

The horn sounded again, nearer.

'Those damn-hounds of his will tear this car to pieces, and his birds will feed on our eyes!' he said. 'I'd hate to meet him when he's this well prepared. Whatever he hunts, I know he'd willingly relinquish it for quarry such as two of his brothers.'

' "Live and let live" is my philosophy these days,' I remarked.

Random chuckled.

'What a quaint notion. I'll bet it will last all of five minutes.'

Then the horn sounded again, even nearer, and he remarked, 'Damn!'

The speedometer said seventy-five, in quaint, runic numerals, and I was afraid to go any faster on that road.

And the horn sounded again, much nearer now, three long notes, and I could hear the baying of hounds, off to the left.

'We are now very near to the real Earth, though still far from Amber,' said my brother. 'It will be futile to run through adjacent Shadows, for if it is truly us that be follows, he will pursue us. Or his shadow will.'

'What shall we do!'

'Speed, and hope it is not us that he follows.'

And the horn sounded once again, almost next to as this time.

'What the hell is he riding, a locomotive?' I asked.

'I'd say he is riding the mighty Morgenstern, the fastest horse he has ever created.'

I let that last word roll around in my head for a while, wondering at it and wondering at it. Yes, it was true, some inner voice told me. He did create Morgenstern, out of Shadows, fusing into the beast the strength and speed of a hurricane and a pile driver.

I remembered that I had call to fear that animal, and then I saw him.

Morgenstern was six hands higher than any other horse I'd ever seen, and his eyes were the dead color of Weimaraner dog's and his coat was all gray and his hooves looked like polished steel. He raced along like the wind, pacing the car, and Julian was crouched in his saddle – the Julian of the playing card, long black hair and bright blue eyes, and he had on his scaled white armor.

Julian smiled at us and waved, and Morgenstern tossed his head and his magnificent mane rippled in the wind, like a flag. His legs were a blur.

I recalled that Julian had once had a man wear my castoff garments and torment the beast. This was why it had tried to trample me on the day of a hunt, when I'd dismounted to skin a buck before it.

I'd rolled the window shut once more, so I didn't think it could tell by scent that I was inside the car. But Julian had spotted me, and I thought I knew what that meant. All about him ran the Storm Hounds, with their tough, tough bodies and their teeth like steel. They too had come out of Shadow, for no normal dog could run like that. But I knew, for a certainty, that the word 'normal' did not really apply to anything in this place.

Julian signaled us to stop then, and I glanced at Random and he nodded. 'If we don't, he'll just run us down,' he said. So I hit the brakes, slowed, stopped.

Morgenstern reared, pawed the air, struck the earth with all four hooves and cantered over. The dogs milled about, their tongues hanging out, their sides heaving. The horse was covered with a glistening sheen that I knew to be perspiration.

I rolled down the window.

'What a surprise!' said Julian, in his slow, almost impeded way of speaking; and a great hawk that was black and green circled and settled upon his left shoulder.

'Yes, isn't it,' I replied. 'How have you been?'

'Oh, capital,' he decided, 'as always. What of yourself and brother Random?'

'I'm in good shape,' I said, and Random nodded and remarked, 'I thought you'd be indulging in other sports at a time like this.'

Julian tipped his head and regarded him crookedly, through the windshield.

'I enjoy slaughtering beasts,' he said, 'and I think of my relatives constantly.'

A slight coldness worked its way down my back.

'I was distracted from my hunt by the sound of your motor vehicle,' he said. 'At the time, I did not expect it to contain two such as you. I'd assume you are not simply riding for pleasure, but have a destination in mind, such as Amber. True?'

'True,' I agreed. 'May I inquire why you are here, rather than there?'

'Eric set me to watching this road,' he replied, and my hand came to rest upon one of the pistols in my belt as he spoke. I had a feeling a bullet couldn't breach that armor, though. I considered shooting Morgenstern.

'Well, brothers,' he said, smiling, 'I welcome you back and I wish you a good journey. I'll doubtless see you shortly in Amber. Good afternoon,' and with that he turned and rode towards the woods.

'Let's get the hell out of here,' said Random. 'He's probably planning an ambush or a chase,' and with this he drew a pistol from his belt and held it in his lap.

I drove on at a decent speed.

After about five minutes, when I was just beginning to breathe a bit easily, I heard the horn. I pushed down on the gas pedal, knowing that he'd catch us anyhow, but trying to buy as much time and gain as much distance as I could. We skidded around corners and roared up hills and through dales. I almost hit a deer at one point, but we made it around the beast without cracking up or slowing.

The horn sounded nearer now, and Random was muttering obscenities.

I had the feeling that we still had quite a distance to go within the forest, and this didn't hearten me a bit.

We hit one long straight stretch, where I was able to floor it for almost a minute. Julian's horn notes grew more distant at that time. But we then entered a section where the road wound and twisted and I had to slow down. He began to gain on us once again.

After about six minutes, he appeared in the rear-view mirror, thundering along the road, his pack all around him, baying and slavering.

Random rolled down his window, and after a minute he leaned out and began to fire.

'Damn that armor!' he said. 'I'm sure I hit him twice and nothing's happened.'

'I hate the thought of killing that beast,' I said, 'but try for the horse.'

'I already have, several times,' he said, tossing his empty pistol to the floor and drawing the other, 'and either I'm a lousier shot than I thought, or it's true what they say: that it will take a silver bullet to kill Morgenstern.'

He picked off six of the dogs with his remaining rounds, but there were still about two dozen left.

I had passed him one of my pistols, and he accounted for five more of the beasts.

'I'll save the last round,' he said, 'for Julian's head, if he gets close enough!'

They were perhaps fifty feet behind me at that point, and gaining, so I slammed on the brakes. Some of the dogs couldn't halt in time, but Julian was suddenly gone and a dark shadow passed overhead.

Morgenstern had leaped over the car! He wheeled then, and as horse and rider turned to face us I gunned the engine and the car sped forward.

With a magnificent leap, Morgenstern got them out of the way. In the rear-view mirror, I saw two dogs drop a fender they'd torn loose and renew the pursuit. Some were lying in the road, and there were about fifteen or sixteen giving chase.

'Good show,' said Random, 'but you're lucky they didn't go for the tires. They've probably never hunted a car before.'

I passed him my remaining pistol, and 'Get more dogs,' I said.

He fired deliberately and with perfect accuracy, accounting for six.

And Julian was beside the car now, a sword in his right hand.

I blew the horn, hoping to spook Morgenstern, but it didn't work. I swerved toward them, but the horse danced away. Random crouched low in his seat and aimed past me, his right hand holding the pistol and resting upon his left forearm.

'Don't fire yet,' I said. 'I'm going to try to take him.'

'You're crazy,' he told me, as I hit the brakes again.

He lowered his weapon, though.

As soon as we came to a halt, I flung open my door and leaped out – barefooted yet! Damn it!

I ducked beneath his blade, seized his arm, and hurled him from the saddle. He struck me once on the head with his mailed left fist, and there were Roman candles going off all around me and a terrible pain.

He lay where he had fallen, being groggy, and there were dogs all round me, biting me, and Random kicking them. I snatched up Julian's blade from where it lay and touched his throat with its point.

'Call them off!' I cried. 'Or I'll nail you to the ground!'

He screamed orders at the dogs and they drew back. Random was holding Morgenstern's bridle and struggling with the horse.

'Now, dear brother, what do you have to say for yourself?' I asked.

There was a cold blue fire within his eyes, and his face was without expression.

'If you're going to kill me, be about it,' he said.

'In my own good time,' I told him, somehow enjoying the sight of dirt on his impeccable armor. 'In the meantime, what is your life worth to you?'

'Anything I've got, of course.'

I stepped back.

'Get up and get into the back seat of the car,' I told him.

He did this thing, and I took away his dagger before he got in.

Random resumed his own seat, and kept his pistol with the single remaining round aimed at Julian's head.

'Why not just kill him?' he asked.

'I think he'll be useful,' I said. 'There is much that I wish to know. And there is still a long way to travel.'

I began to drive. I could see the dogs milling around. Morgenstern began cantering along after the car.

'I'm afraid I won't be worth much to you as a prisoner,' Julian observed. 'Although you will torture me, I can only tell you what I know, and that isn't much.'

'Start with that then,' I said.

'Eric looks to have the strongest position,' he told us, 'having been right there in Amber when the whole thing broke loose. At least this is the way I saw it, so I offered him my support. Had it been one of you, I'd probably have done the same thing. Eric charged me with keeping guard in Arden, since it's the one of the main routes. Gérard controls the southern seaways, and Caine is off in the northern waters.'

'What of Benedict?' Random asked.

'I don't know. I haven't heard anything. He might be with Bleys. He might be off somewhere else in Shadow and not even have heard of this thing yet. He might even be dead. It's been years since we've heard from him.'

'How many men have you got in Arden,' asked Random.

'Over a thousand,' he said. 'Some are probably watching you right now.'

'And if they want you to go on living, that's all they'll do,' said Random.

'You are doubtless correct,' he replied. 'I have to admit, Corwin did a shrewd thing in taking me prisoner rather than killing me. You just might make it through the forest this way.'

'You're just saying that because you want to live,' said Random.

'Of course I want to live. May I?'

'Why?'

'In payment for the information I've given you.'

Random laughed.

'You've given us very little, and I'm sure more can be torn from you. We'll see, as soon as we get a chance to stop. Eh, Corwin?'

'We'll see,' I said 'Where's Fiona?'

'Somewhere to the south, I think,' Julian replied.

'How about Deirdre?'

'I don't know.'

'Llewella?'

'In Rebma.'

'Okay,' I said, 'I think you've told me everything you know.'

'I have.'

We drove on in silence, and finally the forest began to thin. I'd lost sight of Morgenstern long ago, though I sometimes saw Julian's falcon pacing us. The road took a turn upward, and we were heading toward a pass between two purple mountains. The gas tank was a little better than a quarter full. Within an hour, we were passing between high shoulders of stone.

'This would be a good place to set up a road block,' said Random.

'That sounds likely,' I said. 'What about it, Julian?'

He sighed.

'Yes,' he agreed, 'you should be coming upon one very soon. You know how to get by it.'

We did. When we came to the gate, and the guard in green and brown leather, sword unsheathed, advanced upon us, I jerked my thumb toward the back seat and said, 'Get the picture?'

He did, and he recognized us, also.

He hastened to raise the gate, and he saluted as we passed by.

There were two more gates before we made it through the pass – and somewhere along the way it appeared we had lost the hawk. We had gained several thousand feet in elevation now, and I braked the car on a road that crawled along the face of a cliff. To our right hand, there was nothing other than a long way down.

'Get out,' I said. 'You're going to take a walk.'

Julian paled.

'I won't grovel,' he said. 'I won't beg you for my life.' And he got out.

'Hell,' I said, 'I haven't had a good grovel in weeks! Well . . . go stand by the edge there. A little closer, please.' And Random kept his pistol aimed at his head. 'A while back,' I told him, 'you said that you would probably have supported anyone who occupied Eric's position.'

'That's right.'

'Look down.'

He did. It was a long way.

'Okay,' I said, 'remember that, should things undergo a sudden change. And remember who it was who gave you your life where another would have taken it.

'Come on, Random. Let's get moving.'

We left him standing there, breathing heavily, his brows woven together.

We reached the top and were almost out of gas. I put it in neutral, killed the engine, and began the long roll down.

'I've been thinking,' said Random; 'you've lost none of your old guile. I'd probably have killed him, myself, for what he tried. But I think you did the right thing. I think he will throw us his support, if we can get an edge on Eric. In the meantime, of course, he'll report what happened *to* Eric.'

'Of course,' I said.

'And you have more reason to want him dead than any of us.'

I smiled.

'Personal feelings don't make for good politics, legal decisions, or business deals.'

Random lit two cigarettes and handed me one.

Staring downward through the smoke, I caught my first glimpse of that sea. Beneath the deep blue, almost night-time sky, with that golden sun hanging up there in it, the sea was so rich – thick as paint, textured like a piece of cloth, of royal blue, almost purple – that it troubled me to look upon it. I found myself speaking in a language that I hadn't realized I knew. I was reciting 'The Ballad of the Water-Crossers,' and Random listened until I had finished and asked me, 'It has often been said that you composed that. Is it true?'

'It's been so long,' I told him, 'that I don't really remember any more.'

And as the cliff curved further and further to the left, and as we swung downward across its face, heading toward a wooded valley, more and more of the sea came within our range of vision.

'The Lighthouse of Carba,' said Random, gesturing toward an enormous gray tower that rose from the waters, miles out to sea. 'I had all but forgotten it.'

'And I,' I replied. 'It is a very strange feeling – coming back,' and I realized then that we were no longer speaking English, but the language called Thari.

After almost half an hour, we reached the bottom. I kept coasting for as far as I could, then turned on the engine. At its sound, a flock of dark birds beat its way into the air from the shrubbery off to the left. Something gray and wolfish-looking broke from cover and dashed toward a nearby thicket; the deer it had been stalking, invisible till then, bounded away. We were in a lush valley, though not so thickly or massively wooded as the Forest of Arden, which sloped gently but steadily toward the distant sea.

High, and climbing higher on the left, the mountains reared. The further we advanced into the valley, the better came our view of the nature and full extent of that massive height of rock down one of whose lesser slopes we had coasted. The mountains continued their march to the sea, growing larger as they did so, and taking upon their shoulders a shifting mantle tinged with green, mauve, purple, gold and indigo. The face they turned to the sea was invisible to us from the valley, but about the back of that final, highest peak swirled the faintest veil of ghost clouds, and occasionally the golden sun touched it with fire. I judged we were about thirty-five miles from the place of light, and the fuel gauge read near empty. I knew that the final peak was our destination, and an eagerness began to grow up within me. Random was staring in the same direction.

'It's still there,' I remarked.

'I'd almost forgotten . . .' he said.

And as I shifted gears, I noticed that my trousers had taken on a certain sheen which they had not possessed before. Also, they were tapered considerably as they reached toward my ankles, and I noted that my cuffs had vanished. Then I noticed my shirt.

It was more like a jacket, and it was black and trimmed with silver; and my belt had widened considerably.

On closer inspection, I saw that there was a silver line down the outer seams of my pants legs.

'I find myself garbed effectively,' I observed, to see what that wrought.

Random chuckled, and I saw then that he had somewhere acquired brown trousers streaked with red and a shirt of orange and brown. A brown cap with a yellow border rested on the seat beside him.

'I was wondering when you'd notice,' he said. 'How do you feel?'

'Quite good,' I told him, 'and by the way, we're almost out of gas.'

'Too late to do much about that,' he said. 'We are now in the real world, and it would be a horrible effort to play with Shadows. Also, it would not go unnoticed. I'm afraid we'll have to hoof it when this gives out.'

It gave out two and a half miles later. I coasted off to the side of the road and stopped. The sun by now was westering farewell, and the shadows had grown long indeed.

I reached into the back seat, where my shoes had become black boots, and something rattled as my hand groped after them.

I drew forth a moderately heavy silver sword and scabbard. The scabbard fit my belt perfectly. There was also a black cloak, with a clasp like a silver rose.

'Had you thought them lost forever?' asked Random.

'Damn near,' said I.

We climbed out of the car and began walking. The evening was cool and briskly fragrant. There were stars in the east already, and the sun was diving toward its bed.

We trudged along the road, and Random said:

'I don't feel right about this.'

'What do you mean?'

'Things have gone too easily, thus far,' he told me. 'I don't like it. We made it all the way through to the Forest of Arden with barely a hitch. True, Julian tried to take care of us there – but I don't know . . . We've made it so very far so readily that I'd almost suspect we were permitted to do it.'

'This thought has also crossed my mind,' I lied. 'What do you think it portends?'

'I fear,' said he, 'that we are walking into a trap.'

We walked on for several minutes in silence.

Then, 'Ambush?' said I. 'These woods seem strangely still.'

'I don't know.'

We made maybe two miles, and then the sun was gone. The night was black and studded with brilliant stars.

'This is no way for two such as we to move,' Random said.

'True.'

'Yet I fear to fetch us steeds.'

'And I, also.'

'What is your assessment of the situation?' Random asked.

'Death and *dreck*,' said I. 'I feel they may be upon us soon.'

'Do you think we should abandon the roadway?'

'I've been thinking about it,' I lied again, 'and I don't see that it would hurt any for us to walk off to the side a bit.'

So we did.

We passed among trees, we moved past the dark shapes of rocks and bushes. And the moon slowly rose, big, of silver, and lighting up the night.

'I am taken by this feeling that we cannot do it,' Random told me.

'And what reliance can we give this feeling?' I asked.

'Much.'

'Why?'

'Too far and too fast,' he responded. 'I don't like it at all. Now we're in the real world, it is too late to turn back. We cannot play with Shadows, but must rely on our blades.' (He wore a short, burnished one himself.) 'I feel, therefore, that it is perhaps Eric's will that we have advanced to this point. There is nothing much to do about it now, but now we're here, I wish we'd had to battle for every inch of the way.'

We continued for another mile and paused for cigarettes, which we held cupped in our hands.

'It's a lovely night,' I said, to Random and the cool breeze.

'I suppose . . . What was that?'

There was a soft rustling of shrubbery a bit of a way behind us.

'Some animal, maybe.'

His blade was in his hand.

We waited, several minutes, but nothing more was heard.

So he sheathed it and we started walking again.

There were no more sounds from behind us, but after a time I heard something from up ahead.

He nodded when I glanced at him, and we began to move more cautiously.

There was a soft glow, as from a campfire, away, far, in the distance.

We heard no more sounds, but his shrug showed acquiescence to my gesture as I headed toward it, into the woods, to the right.

It was the better part of an hour before we struck the camp. There were four men seated about the fire and two sleeping off in the shadows. The girl who was bound to a stake had her head turned away from us, but I felt my heart quicken as I looked upon her form.

'Could that be . . . ?' I whispered.

'Yes,' he replied, 'I think it may.'

Then she turned her head and I knew it was.

'Deirdre!'

'I wonder what the bitch has been up to?' Random said. 'From those guys' colors, I'd venture they're taking her back to Amber.'

I saw that they wore black, red, and silver, which I remembered from the Trumps and from somewhere else to be the colors of Eric.

'Since Eric wants her, he can't have her,' I said.

'I never much cared for Deirdre,' Random said, 'but I know you do, so . . .' and he unsheathed his blade.

I did the same.

'Get ready,' I told him, rising into a crouch.

And we rushed them.

Maybe two minutes, that's about what it took.

She was watching us by then, the firelight making her face into a twisted mask. She cried and laughed and said our names, in a loud and frightened voice, and I slashed her bonds and helped her to her feet.

'Greetings, sister. Will you join us on the Road to Amber?'

'No,' she said. 'Thanks for my life, but I want to keep it. Why do you walk to Amber, as if I didn't know.'

'There is a throne to be won,' said Random, which was news to me, 'and we are interested parties.'

'If you're smart, you'll stay away and live longer,' she said, and God! She was lovely, though a bit tired-looking and dirty.

I took her into my arms because I wanted to, and squeezed her. Random found a skin of wine and we all had a drink.

'Eric is the only prince in Amber,' she said, 'and the troops are loyal to him.'

'I'm not afraid of Eric,' I replied, and I knew I wasn't certain about that statement.

'He'll never let you into Amber,' she said. 'I was prisoner myself, till I made it out one of the secret ways two days ago. I thought I could walk in Shadows till all things were done, but it is not easy to begin this close to the real place. So his troops found me this morning. They were taking me back. I think he might have killed me, had I been returned – though I'm not sure. At any rate, I'd have remained a puppet in the city. I think Eric may be mad – but again, I'm not sure.'

'What of Bleys?' Random inquired.

'He sends things out of the Shadows, and Eric is greatly disturbed. But he has never attacked with his real force, and so Eric is troubled, and the disposition of the Crown and Scepter remains uncertain, though Eric holds the one in his right hand.'

'I see. Has he ever spoken of us?'

'Not of you, Random. But of Corwin, yes. He still fears the return of Corwin to Amber. There is relative safety for perhaps five more miles – but beyond that, every step of the way is studded with peril. Every tree and rock is a booby trap and an ambush. Because of Bleys and because of Corwin. He wanted you to get at least this far, so that you could not work with Shadows nor easily escape his power. It is absolutely impossible for either of you to enter into Amber without falling into one of his traps.'

'Yet you escaped . . .'

'That was different. I was trying to get out, not in. Perhaps he did not guard me so carefully as he would one of you, because of my sex and my lack of ambition. And nevertheless, as you can see, I did not succeed.'

'You have now, sister,' I said, 'so long as my blade is free to swing on your behalf,' and she kissed my brow and squeezed my hand. I was always a sucker for that.

'I'm sure we're being followed,' said Random, and with a gesture the three of us faded into the darkness.

We lay still beneath a bush, keeping watch on our trail.

After a time, our whispers indicated that there was a decision for me to make. The question was really quite simple: What next?

The question was too basic, and I couldn't stall any more. I knew I couldn't trust them, even dear Deirdre, but if I had to level with anybody, Random was at least in this thing with me, up to his neck, and Deirdre was my favorite.

'Beloved relatives,' I told them, 'I've a confession to make,' and Random's hand was already on the hilt of his blade. That's how far we could trust one another. I could already hear his mind clicking: *Corwin brought me here to betray me*, he was saying to himself.

'If you brought me here to betray me,' he said, 'you won't take me back alive.'

'Are you kidding?' I asked. 'I want your help, not your head. What I have to say is just this: I don't know what the hell's going on. I've made some guesses, but I don't really know where the devil we are, what Amber is, what Eric is doing, who Eric is, or why we're crouched here in the bushes hiding from his troopers,' I told him, 'or for that matter, who I am, really.'

There was an awfully long silence, and then Random whispered, 'What do you mean?'

'Yes,' said Deirdre.

'I mean,' I said, 'that I managed to fool you, Random. Didn't you think it strange that all I did on this trip was drive the car?'

'You were the boss,' he told me, 'and I figured you were planning. You did some pretty shrewd things along the way. I know that you're Corwin.'

'Which is a thing I only found out a couple of days ago, myself,' I said. 'I know that I am the one you call Corwin, but I was in an accident a while back. I had head injuries – I'll show you the scars when we've got more light – and I am suffering from amnesia. I don't dig all this talk about Shadows. I don't even remember much about Amber. All I remember is my relatives, and the fact that I can't trust them much. That's my story. What's to be done about it?'

'Christ!' said Random. 'Yes, I can see it now! I understand all the little things that puzzled me along the way . . . How did you take Flora in so completely?'

'Luck,' I said, 'and subconscious sneakiness, I guess. No! That's not it! She was stupid. Now I really need you, though.'

'Do you think we can make it into the Shadows,' said Deirdre, and she was not speaking to me.

'Yes,' said Random, 'but I'm not for it. I'd like to see Corwin in Amber, and I'd like to see Eric's head on a pole. I'm willing to take a few chances to see these things, so I'm not turning back to the Shadows. You can if you want. You all think I'm a weakling and a bluff. Now you're going to find out. I'm going to see this through.'

'Thanks, brother,' I said.

'Ill-met by moonlight,' said Deirdre.

'You could still be tied to a stake,' said Random, and she did not reply.

We lay there a while longer and three men entered the campsite and looked about. Then two of them bent down and sniffed at the ground.

Then they looked in our direction.

'*Weir*,' whispered Random, as they moved in our direction.

I saw it happen, though only in shadow. They dropped to all fours and the moonlight played tricks with their gray garments. Then there were the six blazing eyes of our stalkers.

I impaled the first wolf on my silver blade and there was a human howl. Random beheaded one with a single blow, and to my amazement, I saw Deirdre raise one in the air and break its back across her knee with a brittle, snapping sound.

'Quick, your blade!' said Random, and I ran his victim through, and hers, and there were more cries.

'We'd better move fast,' said Random. 'This way!' and we followed.

'Where are we going?' asked Deirdre, after perhaps an hour of furtive movement through the undergrowth.

'To the sea,' he replied.

'Why?'

'It holds Corwin's memory.'

'Where? How?'

'Rebma, of course.'

'They'd kill you there and feed your brains to the fishes.'

'I'm not going the full distance. You'll have to take over at the shore and talk with your sister's sister.'

'You mean for him to take the Pattern again?'

'Yes.'

'It's risky.'

'I know . . . Listen, Corwin,' he said, 'you've been decent enough with me recently. If by some chance you're not really Corwin, you're dead. You've got to be, though. You can't be someone else. Not from the way you've operated, without memory even. No, I'll bet your life on it. Take a chance and try the thing called the Pattern. Odds are, it'll restore your memory. Are you game?'

'Probably,' I said, 'but what is the Pattern?'

'Rebma is the ghost city,' he told me. 'It is the reflection of Amber within the sea. In it, everything in Amber is duplicated, as in a mirror. Llewella's people live there, and dwell as though in Amber. They hate me for a few past peccadilloes, so I cannot venture there with you, but if you would speak them fair and perhaps hint at your mission, I feel they will let you walk the Pattern of Rebma, which, while it is the reverse of that in Amber, should have the same effect. That is, it gives to a son of our father the power to walk among Shadows.'

'How will this power help me?'

'It should make you to know what you are.'

'Then I'm game,' I said.

'Good man. In this case, we'll keep heading south. It will take several days to reach the stairway . . . You will go with him, Deirdre?'

'I will go with my brother Corwin.'

I knew she would say that, and I was glad. I was afraid, but I was glad.

We walked all that night. We avoided three parties of armed troops, and in the morning we slept in a cave.

5

We spent two evenings making our way to the pink and sable sands of the great sea. It was on the morning of the third day that we arrived at the beach, having successfully avoided a small party the sundown before. We were loath to step out into the open until we had located the precise spot, Faiella-bionin, the Stairway to Rebma, and could cross quickly to it.

The rising sun cast billions of bright shards into the foaming swell of the waters, and our eyes were dazzled by their dance so that we could not see beneath the surface. We had lived on fruit and water for two days and I was ravenously hungry, but I forgot this as I regarded the wide, sloping tiger beach with its sudden twists and rises of coral, orange, pink, and red, and its abrupt caches of shells, driftwood, and small polished stones; and the sea beyond: rising and falling, splashing softly, all gold and blue and royal purple, and casting forth its life-song breezes like benedictions beneath dawn's violet skies.

The mountain that faces the dawn, Kolvir, which has held Amber like a mother her child for all of time, stood perhaps twenty miles to our left, the north, and the sun covered her with gold and made rainbow the veil above the city. Random looked upon it and gnashed his teeth, then looked away. Maybe I did, too.

Deirdre touched my hand, gestured with her head, and began to walk toward the north, parallel to the shore. Random and I followed. She had apparently spotted some landmark.

We'd advanced perhaps a quarter of a mile, when it seemed that the earth shook lightly.

'Hoofbeats!' hissed Random.

'Look!' said Deirdre, and her head was tilted back and she was pointing upward.

My eyes followed the gesture.

Overhead a hawk circled.

'How much farther is it?' I asked.

'That cairn of stones,' she said, and I saw it perhaps a hundred yards away, about eight feet in height, builded of head-sized, gray stones, worn by the wind, the sand, the water, standing in the shape of a truncated pyramid.

The hoofbeats came louder and then there were the notes of a horn, not Julian's call, though.

'Run!' said Random, and we did.

After perhaps twenty-five paces, the hawk descended. It swooped at Random, but he had his blade out and took a cut at it. Then it turned its attention to Deirdre.

I snatched my own blade from its sheath and tried a cut. Feathers flew. It rose and dropped again, and this time my blade hit something hard – and I think it fell, but I couldn't tell for sure, because I wasn't about to stop and look back. The sound of hoofbeats was quite steady now, and loud, and the horn notes were near at hand.

We reached the cairn and Deirdre turned at right angles to it and headed straight toward the sea.

I was not about to argue with someone who seemed to know what she was doing. I followed, and from the corner of my eye I saw the horsemen.

They were still off in the distance, but they were thundering along the beach, dogs barking and horns blowing, and Random and I ran like hell and waded out into the surf after our sister.

We were up to our waists when Random said, 'It's death if I stay and death if I go on.'

'One is imminent,' I said, 'and the other may be open to negotiation. Let's move!'

We did. We were on some sort of rocky surface which descended into the sea. I didn't know how we would breathe while we walked it, but Deirdre didn't seem worried about it, so I tried not to be.

But I was.

When the water swirled and swished about our heads, I was very worried. Deirdre walked straight ahead, though, descending, and I followed, and Random followed.

Each few feet there was a drop. We were descending an enormous staircase, and it was named Faiella-bionin, I knew.

67

One more step would bring the water above my head, but Deirdre had already dropped below the water line.

So I drew a deep breath and took the plunge.

There were more steps and I kept following them. I wondered why my body was not naturally buoyed above them, for I continued to remain erect and each step bore me downward as though on a natural staircase, though my movements were somewhat slowed. I began wondering what I'd do when I could hold my breath no longer.

There were bubbles about Random's head, and Deirdre's. I tried to observe what they were doing, but I couldn't figure it. Their breasts seemed to be rising and falling in a normal manner.

When we were about ten feet beneath the surface, Random glanced at me from where he moved at my left side, and I heard his voice. It was as though I had my ear pressed against the bottom of a bathtub and each of his words came as the sound of someone kicking upon the side.

They were clear, though:

'I don't think they'll persuade the dogs to follow, even if the horses do,' he said.

'How are you managing to breathe?' I tried saying, and I heard my own words distantly.

'Relax,' he said quickly. 'If you're holding your breath, let it out and don't worry. You'll be able to breathe so long as you don't venture off the stairway.'

'How can that be?' I asked.

'If we make it, you'll know,' he said, and his voice had a ringing quality to it, through the cold and passing green.

We were about twenty feet beneath the surface by then, and I exhaled a small amount of air and tried inhaling for perhaps a second.

There was nothing disturbing about the sensation, so I protracted it. There were more bubbles, but beyond that I felt nothing uncomfortable in the transition.

There was no sense of increasing pressure during the next ten feet or so, and I could see the staircase on which we moved as though through a greenish fog. Down, down, down it led. Straight. Direct. And there was some kind of light coming from below us.

'If we can make it through the archway, well be safe,' said my sister.

'*You'll* be safe,' Random corrected, and I wondered what he had done to be despised in the place called Rebma.

'If they ride horses which have never made the journey before, then they'll have to follow on foot,' said Random. 'In that case, well make it.'

'So they might not follow – if that is the case,' said Deirdre.

We hurried.

By the time we were perhaps fifty feet below the surface, the waters grew quite dark and chill, but the glow before us and below us increased, and after another ten steps, I could make out the source:

There was a pillar rising to the right. At its top was something globe-like and glowing. Perhaps fifteen steps lower, another such formation occurred to the left. Beyond that, it seemed there was another one on the right, and so on.

When we entered the vicinity of the thing, the waters grew warmer and the stairway itself became clear: it was white, shot through with pink and green, and resembled marble but was not slippery despite the water. It was perhaps fifty feet in width, and there was a wide banister of the same substance on either side.

Fishes swam past us as we walked it. When I looked back over my shoulder, there seemed to be no sign of pursuit.

It became brighter. We entered the vicinity of the first fight, and it wasn't a globe on the top of a pillar. My mind must have added that touch to the phenomenon, to try to rationalize it at least a bit. It appeared to be a flame, about two feet in height; dancing there, as atop a huge torch. I decided to ask about it later, and saved my – if you'll excuse the expression – breath, for the rapid descent we were making.

After we had entered the alley of light and had passed six more of the torches, Random said, 'They're after us,' and I looked back again and saw distant figures descending, four of them on horseback.

It is a strange feeling to laugh under water and hear yourself.

'Let them,' I said, and I touched the hilt of my blade, 'for now we have made it this far, I feel a power upon me!'

We hurried though, and off to our left and to our right the water grew black as ink. Only the stairway was illuminated, in our mad flight down it, and distantly I saw what appeared to be a mighty arch.

Deirdre was leaping down the stairs two at a time, and there came a vibration now, from the staccato beat of the horses' hooves behind us.

The band of armed men – filling the way from banister to banister – was far behind and above. But the four horsemen had gained on us. We followed Deirdre as she rushed downward; and my hand stayed upon my blade.

Three, four, five. We passed that many lights before I looked back again and saw that the horsemen were perhaps fifty feet above us. The footmen were now almost out of sight. The archway loomed ahead, perhaps two hundred feet distant. Big, shining like alabaster, and carved with Tritons, sea nymphs, mermaids, and dolphins, it was. And there seemed to be people on the other side of it.

'They must wonder why we have come here,' said Random.

'It will be an academic point if we don't make it,' I replied, hurrying, as another glance revealed that the horsemen had gained ten feet on us.

I drew my blade then, and it flashed in the torchlight. Random followed suit.

After another twenty steps or so, the vibrations were terrible within the green and we turned, so as not to be cut down as we ran.

They were almost upon us. The gates lay a hundred feet to our back, and it might have been a hundred miles, unless we could take the four horsemen.

I crouched, as the man who was headed toward me swung his blade. There was another rider to his right and slightly to his rear, so naturally I moved to his left, near to the rail. This required that he strike cross-body, as he held his blade in his right hand.

When he struck, I parried in *quarte* and riposted.

He was leaning far forward in the saddle, and the point of my blade entered his neck on the right side.

A great billow of blood, like crimson smoke, arose and swirled within the greenish light. Crazily, I wished Van Gogh were there to see it.

The horse continued past, and I leaped at the second rider from the rear.

He turned to parry the stroke, succeeded. But the force of his speed through the water and the strength of my blow removed him from the saddle. As he fell, I kicked, and he drifted. I struck at him, hovering there above me, and he parried again, but this carried him beyond the rail. I heard him scream as the pressure of the waters came upon him. Then he was silent.

I turned my attention then to Random, who had slain both a horse and a man and was dueling with a second man on foot. By the time I reached them, he had slain the man and was laughing. The blood billowed above them, and I suddenly realized that I *had* known mad, sad, bad Vincent Van Gogh, and it was really too bad that he couldn't have painted this.

The footmen were perhaps a hundred feet behind us, and we turned and headed toward the arches. Deirdre had already passed through them.

We ran and we made it. There were many swords at out sides, and the footmen turned back. Then we sheathed our blades, and Random said, 'I've had it,' and we moved to join with the band of people who had stood to defend us.

Random was immediately ordered to surrender his blade, and he shrugged and handed it over. Then two men came and stood on either side of him and a third at his back, and we continued on down the stair.

I lost all sense of time in that watery place, but I feel that we walked for somewhere between a quarter of an hour and half an hour before we reached our destination.

The golden gates of Rebma stood before us. We passed through them. We entered the city.

Everything was to be seen through a green haze. There were buildings, all of them fragile and most of them high, grouped in patterns and standing in colors that entered my eyes and tore through my mind, seeking after remembrance. They failed, the sole result of their digging being the now familiar ache that accompanies the half recalled, the unrecalled. I had walked these streets before, however, that I knew, or ones very much like them.

Random had not said a single word since he had been taken into custody. Deirdre's only conversation had been to inquire after our sister Llewella. She had been informed that Llewella was in Rebma.

I examined our escort. They were men with green hair, purple hair, and black hair, and all of them had eyes of green, save for one fellow whose were of a hazel color. All wore only scaled trunks and cloaks, cross-braces on their breasts, and short swords depending from sea-shell belts. All were pretty much lacking in body hair. None of them spoke to me, though some stared and some glared. I was allowed to keep my weapon.

Inside the city, we were conducted up a wide avenue, lighted by pillar flames set at even closer intervals than on Faiella-bionin, and people stared out at us from behind octagonal, tinted windows, and bright-bellied fishes swam by. There came a cool current, like a breeze, as we turned a corner; and after a few steps, a warm one, like a wind.

We were taken to the palace in the center of the city, and I knew it as my hand knew the glove in my belt. It was an image of the palace of Amber, obscured only by the green and confused by the many strangely placed mirrors which had been set within its walls, inside and out. A woman sat upon the throne in the glassite room I almost recalled, and her hair was green, though streaked with silver, and her eyes were round as moons of jade and her brows rose like the wings of olive gulls. Her mouth was small, her chin was small; her cheeks were high and wide and rounded. A circlet of white gold crossed her brow and there was a crystal necklace about her neck. At its tip there flashed a sapphire between her sweet bare breasts, whose nipples were also a pale green. She wore scaled trunks of blue and a silver belt, and she held a scepter of pink coral in her right hand and had a ring upon every finger, and each ring had a stone of a different blue within it. She did not smile as she spoke:

'What seek you here, outcasts of Amber?' she asked, and her voice was a lisping, soft, flowing thing.

Deirdre spoke in reply, saying: 'We flee the wrath of the prince who sits in the true city – Eric! To be frank, we wish to work his downfall. If he is loved here, we are lost, and we have delivered ourselves into the hands of our enemies. But I feel he is not loved here. So we come asking aid, gentle Moire—'

'I will not give you troops to assault Amber,' she replied. 'As you know, the chaos would be reflected within my own realm.'

'That is not what we would have of you, dear Moire,' Deirdre continued, 'but only a small thing, to be achieved at no pain or cost to yourself or your subjects.'

'Name it! For as you know, Eric is almost as disliked here as this recreant who stands at your left hand,' and with this she gestured at my brother, who stared at her in frank and insolent appraisal, a small smile playing about the corners of his lips.

If he was going to pay – whatever the price – for whatever he had done, I could see that he would pay it like a true prince of Amber – as our three dead brothers had done ages ago, I suddenly recalled. He would pay it, mocking them the while, laughing though his mouth was filled with the blood of his body, and as he died he would pronounce an irrevocable curse which would come to pass. I, too, had this power, I suddenly knew, and I would use it if circumstances required its use.

'The thing I would ask,' she said, 'is for my brother Corwin, who is also brother to the Lady Llewella, who dwells here with you. I believe that he has never given you offense . . .'

'That is true. But why does he not speak for himself?'

'That is a part of the problem, Lady. He cannot, for he does not know what to ask. Much of his memory has departed, from an accident which occurred when he dwelled among Shadows. It is to restore his remembrance that we have come here, to bring back his recollection of the old days, that he might oppose Eric in Amber.'

'Continue,' said the woman on the throne, regarding me through the shadows of her lashes on her eyes.

'In a place in this building,' she said, 'there is a room where few would go. In that room,' she continued, 'upon the floor, traced in fiery outline, there lies a duplicate of the thing we call the Pattern. Only a son or daughter of Amber's late liege may walk this Pattern and live; and it gives to such a person a power over Shadow.' Here Moire blinked several times, and I speculated as to the number of her subjects she had sent upon that path, to gain some control of this power for Rebma. Of course, she had failed. 'To walk the Pattern,' Deirdre went on, 'should, we feel, restore to Corwin his memory of himself as a prince of Amber. He cannot go to Amber to do it, and this is the only place I know where it is duplicated, other than Tir-na Nog'th, where of course we may not go at this time.'

Moire turned her gaze upon my sister, swept it over Random, returned it to me.

'Is Corwin willing to essay this thing?' she asked.

I bowed.

'Willing, m'lady,' I said, and she smiled then.

'Very well, you have my permission. I can guarantee you no guarantees of safety beyond my realm, however.'

'As to that, your majesty,' said Deirdre, 'we expect no boons, but will take care of it ourselves upon our departure.'

'Save for Random,' she said, 'who will be quite safe.'

'What mean you?' asked Deirdre, for Random would not, of course, speak for himself under the circumstances.

'Surely you recall,' she said, 'that one time Prince Random came into my realm as a friend, and did thereafter depart in haste with my daughter Morganthë.'

'I have heard this said, Lady Moire, but I am not aware of the truth or the baseness of the tale.'

'It is true,' said Moire, 'and a month thereafter was she returned to me. Her suicide came some months after the birth of her son Martin, What have you to say to that, Prince Random?'

'Nothing,' said Random.

'When Martin came of age,' said Moire, 'because he was of the blood of Amber, he determined to walk the Pattern. He is the only of my people to have succeeded. Thereafter, he walked in Shadow and I have not seen him since. What have you to say to that, Lord Random?'

'Nothing,' Random replied.

'Therefore, I will punish thee,' Moire continued. 'You shall marry the woman of my choice and remain with her in my realm for a year's time, or you will forfeit your life. What say you to that, Random?'

Random said nothing, but he nodded abruptly.

She struck her scepter upon the arm of her turquoise throne.

'Very well,' she said. 'So be it.'

And so it was.

We repaired to the chambers she had granted us, there to refresh ourselves. Subsequently she appeared at the door of my own.

'Hail, Moire,' I said.

'Lord Corwin of Amber,' she told me, 'often have I wished to meet thee.'

'And I thee,' I lied.

'Your exploits are legend.'

'Thank you, but I barely recall the high points.'

'May I enter here?'

'Certainly,' and I stepped aside.

She moved into the well-appointed suite she had granted me. She seated herself upon the edge of the orange couch.

'When would you like to essay the Pattern?'

'As soon as possible,' I told her.

She considered this, then said, 'Where have you been, among Shadows?'

'Very far from here,' I said, 'in a place that I learned to love.'

'It is strange that a lord of Amber should possess this capacity.'

'What capacity?'

'To love,' she replied.

'Perhaps I chose the wrong word.'

'I doubt it,' she said, 'for the ballads of Corwin do touch upon the strings of the heart.'

'The lady is kind.'

'But not wrong,' she replied.

'I'll give you a ballad one day.'

'What did you do when you dwelled in Shadow?'

'It occurs to me that I was a professional soldier, madam. I fought for whoever would pay me. Also, I composed the words and music to many popular songs.'

'Both these things occur to me as logical and natural.'

'Pray tell me, what of my brother Random?'

'He will marry with a girl among my subjects who is named Vialle. She is blind and has no wooers among our kind.'

'Are you certain,' said I, 'that you do the best thing for her?'

'She will obtain good status in this manner,' said Moire, 'though he depart after a year and never return. For whatever else may be said of him, he *is* a prince of Amber.'

'What if she comes to love him?'

'Could anyone really do this thing?'

'In my way, I love him, as a brother.'

'Then this is the first time a son of Amber has ever said such a thing, and I attribute it to your poetic temperament.'

'Whatever,' said I, 'be very sure that it is the best thing for the girl.'

'I have considered it,' she told me, 'and I am certain. She will recover from whatever pain he inflicts, and after his departure she will be a great lady of my court.'

'So may it be,' I said, and looked away, feeling a sadness come over me – for the girl, of course.

'What may I say to you?' I said. 'Perhaps you do a good thing. I hope so.' And I took her hand and kissed it.

'You, Lord Corwin, are the only prince of Amber I might support,' she told me, 'save possibly for Benedict. He is gone these twelve years and ten, however, and Lir knows where his bones may lie. Pity.'

'I did not know this,' I said. 'My memory is so screwed up. Please bear with me. I shall miss Benedict, an' he be dead. He was my Master of Arms and taught me of all weapons. But he was gentle.'

'As are you, Corwin,' she told me, taking my hand and drawing me toward her.

'No, not really,' I replied, as I seated myself on the couch at her side. Then she said, 'We've much time till we dine.' Then she leaned against me with the front of her shoulder which was soft.

'When do we eat?' I asked.

'Whenever I declare it,' she said, and she faced me more fully.

So I drew her upon me and found the catch to the buckle which covered the softness of her belly. There was more softness beneath, and her hair was green.

Upon the couch, I gave her her ballad. Her lips replied without words.

After we had eaten – and I had learned the trick of eating under water, which I might detail later on if circumstances really warrant – we rose from our places within the marble high hall, decorated with nets and ropes of red and brown, and we made our way back along a narrow corridor, and down, down, beneath the floor of the sea itself, first by means of a spiral staircase that screwed its way through absolute darkness and glowed. After about twenty paces, my brother said, 'Screw!' and stepped off the staircase and began swimming downward alongside it.

'It *is* faster that way,' said Moire.

'And it is a long way down,' said Deirdre, knowing the distance of the one in Amber.

So we all stepped off and swam downward through darkness, beside the glowing, twisting thing.

It took perhaps ten minutes to reach the bottom, but when our feet touched the floor, we stood, with no tendency to drift. There was light about us then, from a few feeble flames set within niches in the wall.

'Why is this part of the ocean, within the double of Amber, so different from waters elsewhere?' I asked.

'Because that is the way it is,' said Deirdre, which irritated me.

We were in an enormous cavern, and tunnels shot off from it in all directions. We moved toward one.

After walking along it for an awfully long while, we began to encounter side passages, some of which had doors or grills before them and some of which did not.

At the seventh of these we stopped. It was a huge gray door of some slate-like substance, bound in metal, towering to twice my height. I remembered something about the size of Tritons as I regarded that doorway. Then Moire smiled, just at me, and produced a large key from a ring upon her belt and set it within the lock.

She couldn't turn it, though. Perhaps the thing had been unused for too long.

Random growled and his hand shot forward, knocking hers aside.

He seized the key in his right hand and twisted.

There came a click.

Then he pushed the door open with his foot and we stared within.

In a room the size of a ballroom the Pattern was laid. The floor was black and looked smooth as glass. And on the floor was the Pattern.

It shimmered like the cold fire that it was, quivered, made the whole room seem somehow unsubstantial. It was an elaborate tracery of bright power, composed mainly of curves, though there were a few straight lines near its middle. It reminded me of a fantastically intricate, life-scale version of one of those maze things you do with a pencil (or ballpoint, as the case may be), to get you into or out of something. Like, I could almost see the words 'Start Here,' somewhere way to the back. It was perhaps a hundred yards across at its narrow middle, and maybe a hundred and fifty long.

It made bells ring within my head, and then came the throbbing. My mind recoiled from the touch of it. But if I were a prince of

Amber, then somewhere within my blood, my nervous system, my genes, this pattern was recorded somehow, so that I would respond properly, so that I could walk the bloody thing.

'Sure wish I could have a cigarette,' I said, and the girls giggled, though rather a little too rapidly and perhaps with a bit of a twist on the treble control.

Random took my arm and said, 'It's an ordeal, but it's not impossible or we wouldn't be here. Take it very slowly and don't let yourself be distracted. Don't be alarmed by the shower of sparks that will arise with each step. They can't hurt you. You'll feel a mild current passing through you the whole time, and after a while you'll start feeling high. But keep concentrating, and don't forget – keep walking! Don't stop, whatever you do, and don't stray from the path, or it'll probably kill you,' and as he spoke, we walked. We walked close to the right-hand wall and rounded the Pattern, heading toward its far end. The girls trailed behind us.

I whispered to him.

'I tried to talk her out of this thing she's planned for you. No luck.'

'I figured you would,' he said. 'Don't worry about it. I can do a year standing on my head, and they might even let me go sooner – if I'm obnoxious enough.'

'The girl she has lined up for you is named Vialle. She's blind.'

'Great,' he said. 'Great joke.'

'Remember that regency we spoke of?'

'Yeah.'

'Be kind to her then, stay the full year, and I will be generous.'

Nothing.

Then he squeezed my arm.

'Friend of yours, huh?' he chuckled. 'What's she like?'

'Is it a deal?' I said, slowly.

'It's a deal.'

Then we stood at the place where the Pattern began, near to the corner of the room.

I moved forward and regarded the line of inlaid fires that started near to the spot where I had placed my right foot. The Pattern constituted the only illumination within the room. The waters were chill about me.

I strode forward, setting my left foot upon the path. It was outlined by blue-white sparks. Then I set my right foot upon it, and I felt the current Random had mentioned. I took another step.

There was a crackle and I felt my hair beginning to rise. I took another step.

Then the thing began to curve, abruptly, back upon itself. I took ten more paces, and a certain resistance seemed to arise. It was as if a black barrier had grown up before me, of some substance which pushed back upon me with each effort that I made to pass forward.

I fought it. It was the First Veil, I suddenly knew.

To get beyond it would be an Achievement, a good sign, showing that I was indeed part of the Pattern. Each raising and lowering of my foot suddenly required a terrible effort, and sparks shot from my hair.

I concentrated on the fiery line. I walked it breathing heavily.

Suddenly the pressure was eased. The Veil had parted before me, as abruptly as it had occurred. I had passed beyond it and acquired something.

I had gained a piece of myself.

I saw the paper skins and the knobby, stick-like bones of the dead of Auschwitz. I had been present at Nuremberg, I knew. I heard the voice of Stephen Spender reciting 'Vienna,' and I saw Mother Courage cross the stage on the night of a Brecht premiere. I saw the rockets leap up from the stained hard places, Peenemunde, Vandenberg, Kennedy, Kyzyl Kum in Kazakhstan, and I touched with my hands the Wall of China. We were drinking beer and wine, and Shaxpur said he was drunk and went off to puke. I entered the green forests of the Western Reserve and took three scalps one day. I hummed a tune as we marched along and it caught on. It became 'Auprès de ma Blonde.' I remembered, I remembered . . . my life within the Shadow place its inhabitants had called the Earth. Three more steps, and I held a bloody blade and saw three dead men and my horse, on which I had fled the revolution in France. And more, so much more, back to—

I took another step.

Back to—

The dead. They were all about me. There was a horrible stink – the smell of decaying flesh – and I heard the howls of a dog who was being beaten to death. Billows of black smoke filled the sky, and an icy wind swept around me bearing a few small drops of rain. My throat was parched and my hands shook and my head was on fire. I staggered alone, seeing everything through the haze of the fever that burned me. The gutters were filled with garbage and dead cats and the emptyings of chamber pots. With a rattle and the ringing of a bell, the death wagon thundered by, splashing me with mud and cold water.

How long I wandered, I do not know, before a woman seized my arm and I saw a Death's Head ring upon her finger. She led me to her rooms, but discovered there that I had no money and was incoherent. A look of fear crossed her painted face, erasing the smile on her bright lips, and she fled and I collapsed upon her bed.

Later – again, how much later I do not know – a big man, the girl's Black Davy, came and slapped me across the face and dragged me to my feet. I seized his right biceps and hung on. He half carried, half pulled me toward the door.

When I realized that he was going to cast me out into the cold, I tightened my grip to protest it. I squeezed with all my remaining strength, mumbling half-coherent pleas.

Then through sweat and tear-filled eyes, I saw his face break open and heard a scream come forth from between his stained teeth.

The bone in his arm had broken where I'd squeezed it.

He pushed me away with his left hand and fell to his knees, weeping. I sat upon the floor, and my head cleared for a moment.

'I . . . am . . . staying here,' I said, 'until I feel better. Get out. If you come back – I'll kill you.'

'You've got the plague!' he cried. 'They'll come for your bones tomorrow!' and he spat then, got to his feet, and staggered out.

I made it to the door and barred it. Then I crawled back to the bed and slept.

If they came for my bones the next day, they were disappointed. For, perhaps ten hours later, in the middle of the night, I awoke in a cold sweat and realized my fever had broken. I was weak, but rational once more.

I realized I had lived through the plague.

I took a man's cloak I found in the wardrobe and took some money I found in a drawer.

Then I went forth into London and the Night, in a year of the plague, looking for something . . .

I had no recollection of who I was or what I was doing there.

That was how it had started.

I was well into the Pattern now, and the sparks flashed continually about my feet, reaching to the height of my knees. I no longer knew which direction I faced, or where Random and Deirdre and Moire stood. The currents swept through me, and it seemed my eyeballs were vibrating. Then came a pins-and-needles feeling in my cheeks and a coldness on the back of my neck. I clenched my teeth to keep them from chattering.

The auto accident had not given me my amnesia. I had been without full memory since the reign of Elizabeth I. Flora must have concluded that the recent accident had restored me. She had known of my condition. I was suddenly struck by the thought that she was on that Shadow Earth mainly to keep tabs on me.

Since the sixteenth century, then?

That I couldn't say. I'd find out, though.

I took six more rapid steps, reaching the end of an arc and coming to the beginning place of a straight line.

I set my foot upon it, and with each step that I took, another barrier began to rise against me. It was the Second Veil.

There was a right-angle turn, then another, then another.

I was a prince of Amber. It was true. There had been fifteen brothers and six were dead. There had been eight sisters, and two were dead, possibly four. We had spent much of our time in wandering in Shadow, or in our own universes. It is an academic, though valid philosophical question, as to whether one with power over Shadow could create his own universe. Whatever the ultimate answer, from a practical point we could.

Another curve began, and it was though I were walking in glue as I moved slowly along it.

One, two, three, four . . . I raised my fiery boots and let them down again.

My head throbbed and my heart felt as though it were fibrillating to pieces.

Amber!

The going was suddenly easy once more, as I remembered Amber.

Amber was the greatest city which had ever existed or ever would exist. Amber had always been and always would be, and every other city, everywhere, every other city that existed was but a reflection of a shadow of some phase of Amber. Amber, Amber, Amber . . . I remember thee. I shall never forget thee again. I guess, deep inside me, I never really did, through all those centuries I wandered the Shadow Earth, for often at night my dreams were troubled by images of thy green and golden spires and thy sweeping terraces. I remember thy wide promenades and the decks of flowers, golden and red. I recall the sweetness of thy airs, and the temples, palaces, and pleasances thou containest, contained, will always contain. Amber, immortal city from which every other city has taken its shape, I cannot forget thee, even now, nor forget that day on the Pattern of Rebma when I remembered thee within thy reflected walls, fresh from a meal after starvation and the loving of Moire, but nothing could compare with the pleasure and the love of remembering thee; and even now, as I stand contemplating the Courts of Chaos, telling this story to the only one present to hear, that perhaps he may repeat it, that it will not die after I have died within; even now, I remember thee with love, city that I was born to rule . . .

Ten paces, then a swirling filigree of fire confronted me. I essayed it, my sweat vanishing into the waters as fast as it sprang forth.

It was tricky, so devilish tricky, and it seemed that the waters of the room suddenly moved in great currents which threatened to sweep me from the Pattern. I struggled on, resisting them. Instinctively, I knew that to leave the Pattern before I'd completed it would mean my death. I dared not raise my eyes from the places of light that lay before me, to see how far I had come, how far I had yet to go.

The currents subsided and more of my memories returned, memories of my life as a prince of Amber . . . No, they are not yours for the asking; they are mine, some vicious and cruel, others perhaps noble – memories going back to my childhood in the great palace of Amber, with the green banner of my father Oberon flaring above it, white unicorn rampant, facing to the dexter.

Random had made it through the Pattern. Even Deirdre had made it. Therefore I, Corwin, would make it, no matter what the resistance.

I emerged from the filigree and marched along the Grand Curve. The forces that shape the universe fell upon me and beat me into their image.

I had an advantage over any other person who attempted the walk, however. I knew that I had done it before, so I knew that I could do it. This helped me against the unnatural fears which rose like black clouds and were gone again, only to return, their strength redoubled. I walked the Pattern and I remembered all, I remembered all the days before my centuries on the Shadow Earth and I remembered other places of Shadow, many of them special and dear to me, and one which I loved above all, save for Amber.

I walked three more curves, a straight line, and a series of sharp arcs, and I held within me once again a consciousness of the thing which I had never really lost: mine was the power over Shadows.

Ten turns which left me dizzy, another short arc, a straight line, and the Final Veil.

It was agony to move. Everything tried to beat me aside. The waters were cold, then boiling. It seemed that they constantly pushed against me. I struggled, putting one foot before the other. The sparks reached as high as my waist at this point, then my breast, my shoulders. They were into my eyes. They were all about me. I could barely see the Pattern itself.

Then a short arc, ending in blackness.

One, two . . . And to take the last step was like trying to push through a concrete wall.

I did it.

Then I turned slowly and looked back over the course I had come. I would not permit myself the luxury of sagging to my knees. I was a prince of Amber, and by God! Nothing could humble me in the presence of my peers. Not even the Pattern!

I waved jauntily in what I thought to be the right direction. Whether or not I could be made out very clearly was another matter.

Then I stood there a moment and thought.

I knew the power of the Pattern now. Going back along it would be no trick at all.

But why bother?

I lacked my deck of cards, but the power of the Pattern could serve me just as well . . .

They were waiting for me, my brother and sister and Moire with her thighs like marble pillars.

Deirdre could take care of herself from here on out – after all, we'd saved her life. I didn't feel obligated to go on protecting her on a day-by-day basis. Random was stuck in Rebma for a year, unless he had guts enough to leap forward and take the Pattern to this still center of power and perhaps escape. And as for Moire, it had been nice knowing her, and maybe I'd see her again some day, and like that. I closed my eyes and bowed my head.

Before I did so, though, I saw a fleeting shadow.

Random? Trying it? Whatever, he wouldn't know where I was headed. No one would.

I opened my eyes and I stood in the middle of the same Pattern, in reverse.

I was cold, and I was damn tired, but I was in Amber – in the real room, of which the one I had departed was but an image. From the Pattern, I could transfer myself to any point I wished within Amber.

Getting back would be a problem, however.

So I stood there and dripped and considered.

If Eric had taken the royal suite, then I might find him there. Or perhaps in the throne room. But then, I'd have to walk the Pattern again, in order to reach the escape point.

I transferred myself to a hiding place I knew of within the palace. It was a windowless cubicle into which some light trickled from observation slits high over head. I bolted its one sliding panel from the inside, dusted off a wooden bench set beside the wall, spread my cloak upon it and stretched out for a nap. If anyone came groping his way down from above, I'd hear him long before he reached me.

I slept.

After a while, I awakened. So I arose, dusted off my cloak and donned it once more. Then I began to negotiate the series of pegs which laddered then: way up into the palace.

I knew where it was, the third floor, by the markings on the walls.

I swung myself over to a small landing and searched for the peephole. I found it and gazed through. Nothing. The library was empty. So I slid back the panel and entered.

Within, I was stricken by the multitudes of books. They always do that to me. I considered everything, including the display cases, and finally moved toward the place where a crystal case contained everything that led up to a family banquet – private joke. It held four decks of the family cards, and I sought about for a means of obtaining one without setting off an alarm which might keep me from using it.

After maybe ten minutes, I succeeded in gimmicking the proper case. It was tricky. Then, pack in hands, I found a comfortable seat for the consideration thereof.

The cards were just like Flora's and they held us all under glass and were cold to the touch. Now, too, I knew why.

So I shuffled and spread them all out before me in the proper manner. Then I read them, and I saw that bad things were in store for the entire family; and I gathered them all together then.

Save for one.

It was the card depicting my brother Bleys.

I replaced the others in their case and tucked it into my belt. Then I considered Bleys.

At about that time there came a scratching in the lock of the great door to the library. What could I do? I loosened my blade in its scabbard and waited. I ducked low behind the desk, though.

Peering out, I saw that it was a guy named Dik, who had obviously come to clean the place, as he set out emptying the ashtrays and wastebaskets and dusting the shelves.

Since it would be demeaning to be discovered, I exposed myself.

I rose and said, 'Hello, Dik. Remember me?'

He turned three kinds of pale, half bolted, and said:

'Of course, Lord. How could I forget?'

'I suppose it would be possible, after all this time.'

'Never, Lord Corwin,' he replied.

'I suppose I'm here without official sanction, and engaged in a bit of illicit research,' I said, 'but if Eric doesn't like it when you tell him that you saw me, please explain that I was simply exercising my rights, and he will be seeing me personally – soon.'

'I'll do that, m'lord,' he said, bowing.

'Come sit with me a moment, friend Dik, and I'll tell you more.'

And he did, so I did.

'There was a time,' I said, addressing this ancient visage, 'when I was considered gone for good and abandoned forever. Since I still live, however, and since I maintain all my faculties, I fear that I must dispute Eric's claim to the throne of Amber. Though it's not a thing to be settled simply, as he is not the first-born, nor do I feel he would enjoy popular support if another were in sight. For these, among other reasons – most of them personal – I am about to oppose him. I have not yet decided how, nor upon what grounds, but by God! he deserves opposition! Tell him that. If he wishes to seek me, tell him that I dwell among Shadows, but different ones than before. He may know what I mean by that. I will not be easily destroyed, for I will guard myself at least as well as he does here. I will oppose him from hell to eternity, and I will not cease until one of us is dead. What say you to this, old retainer?'

And he took my hand and kissed it.

'Hail to thee, Corwin, Lord of Amber,' he said, and there was a tear in his eye.

Then the door cracked a crack behind him and swung open.

Eric entered.

'Hello,' said I, rising and putting a most obnoxious twang to my voice. 'I didn't expect to meet with you this early in the game. How go things in Amber?'

And his eyes were wide with amaze and his voice heavy with that which men call sarcasm, and I can't think of a better word, as he replied:

'Well, when it comes to things, Corwin. Poorly, on other counts, however.'

'Pity,' said I, 'and how shall we put things aright?'

'I know a way,' he said, and then he glared at Dik, who promptly departed and closed the door behind him. I heard it *snick* shut.

Eric loosened his blade in its scabbard.

'You want the throne,' he said.

'Don't we all?' I told him.

'I guess so,' he said, with a sigh. 'It's true, that uneasy-lies-the-head bit. I don't know why we are driven to strive so for this ridiculous position. But you must recall that I've defeated you twice, mercifully granting your life on a Shadow world the last occasion.'

'It wasn't that merciful,' I said. 'You know where you left me, to die of the plague. The first time, as I remember, it was pretty much a draw.'

'Then it is between the two of us now, Corwin,' he said. 'I am your elder and your better. If you wish to try me at arms, I find myself suitably attired. Slay me, and the throne will probably be yours. Try it. I don't think you can succeed, however. And I'd like to quit your claim right now. So come at me. Let's see what you learned on the Shadow Earth.'

And his blade was in his hand and mine in mine.

I moved around the desk.

'What an enormous *chutzpah* you possess,' I told him. 'What makes you better than the rest of us, and more fit to rule?'

'The fact that I was able to occupy the throne,' he replied. 'Try and take it.'

And I did.

I tried a head-cut, which he parried; and I parried his riposte to my heart and cut at his wrist.

He parried this and kicked a small stool between us. I set it aside, hopefully in the direction of his face, with my right toe, but it missed and he had at me again.

I parried his attack, and he mine. Then I lunged, was parried, was attacked, and parried again myself.

I tried a very fancy attack I'd learned in France, which involved a beat, a feint in *quarte*, a feint in *sixte*, and a lunge veering off into an attack on his wrist.

I nicked him and the blood flowed.

'Oh, damnable brother!' he said, retreating. 'Report has it Random accompanies thee.'

'This is true,' said I. 'More than one of us are assembled against you.'

And he lunged then and beat me back, and I felt suddenly that for all my work he was still my master. He was perhaps one of the greatest swordsmen I had ever faced. I suddenly had the feeling that I couldn't take him, and I parried like mad and retreated in the same fashion as he beat me back, step by step. We'd both had centuries under the greatest masters of the blade in business. The greatest alive, I knew, was brother Benedict, and he wasn't around to help, one way or the other. So I snatched things off the desk with my left hand and threw them at Eric. But he dodged everything and came on strong, and I circled to his left and all like that, but I couldn't draw the point of his blade from my left eye. And I was afraid. The man was magnificent. If I didn't hate him so, I would have applauded his performance.

I kept backing away, and the fear and the knowledge came upon me: I knew I still couldn't take him. He was a better man than I was, when it came to the blade. I cursed this, but I couldn't get around it. I tried three more elaborate attacks and was defeated on each occasion. He parried me and made me retreat before his own attacks.

Now don't get the wrong idea. I'm damn good. It's just that he seemed better.

Then there were some alarms and excursions in the hall outside. Eric's retainers were coming, and if he didn't kill me before they arrived, then I was confident that they'd do the job – probably with a bolt from a crossbow.

There was blood dripping from his right wrist. His hand was still steady but I had the feeling then that under other circumstances, by fighting a defensive fight, I just might be able to wear him down with that wrist injury going against him, and perhaps I could get through his guard at the proper moment when he began to slow.

I cursed softly and he laughed.

'You're a fool to have come here,' he said.

He didn't realize what I was doing until it was too late. (I'd been retreating until the door was at my back. It was risky, leaving myself with no room for retreat, but it was better than sure death.)

With my left hand, I managed to drop the bar. It was a big, heavy door and they'd have to knock it down now to get in. That gave me a few more minutes. It also gave me a shoulder wound, from an attack I could only partly parry as I dropped the bar. But it was my left shoulder. My sword arm remained intact.

I smiled, to put up a good front.

'Perhaps *you* were a fool, to enter *here*,' I said. 'You're slowing, you know,' and I tried a hard, fast, vicious attack.

He parried it, but he fell back two paces in doing so.

'That wound's getting to you,' I added. 'Your arm's weakening. You can feel the strength leaving it—'

'Shut up!' he said, and I realized I'd gotten through to him. This increased my chances by several percent, I decided, and I pressed him as hard as I could, realizing I couldn't keep that pace up very long.

But Eric didn't realize it.

I'd planted the seeds of fear, and he fell back before my sudden onslaught.

There was a banging on the door but I didn't have to worry about that for a while anyway.

'I'm going to take you, Eric,' I said. 'I'm tougher than I used to be, and you've had it, brother.'

I saw the fear begin in his eyes, and it spread over his face, and his style shifted to follow suit. He began fighting a completely defensive battle, backing away from my attack. I'm sure he wasn't faking either. I felt I had bluffed him, for he had always been better than I. But what if it had been partly psychological on my part too? What if I had almost beaten myself with this attitude, which Eric had helped to foster? What if I had bluffed myself all along? Maybe I was as good. With a strange sense of confidence, I tried the same attack I had used before and I scored, leaving another trail of red on his forearm.

'That was rather stupid, Eric,' I said, 'to fall for the same trick twice,' and he backed around a wide chair. We fought across it for a time.

The banging on the door stopped, and the voices which had been shouting inquiries through it fell silent.

'They've gone for axes,' Eric panted. 'They'll be in here in no time.'

I wouldn't drop my smile. I held it and said: 'It'll take a few minutes – which is more time than I'll need to finish this. You can hardly keep your guard now, and the blood keeps running – look at it!'

'Shut up!'

'By the time they get through, there will be only one prince in Amber, and it won't be you!'

Then, with his left arm, he swept a row of books from a shelf and they struck me and fell about me.

He didn't seize the opportunity to attack, however. He dashed across the room, picking up a small chair, which he held in his left hand.

He wedged himself into a corner and held the chair and his blade before him.

There were rapid footsteps in the hall outside, and then axes began to ring upon the door.

'Come on!' he said, 'Try and take me now!'

'You're scared,' I said.

He laughed.

'Academic,' he replied. 'You can't take me before that door falls, and then it will be all over for you.'

I had to agree. He could hold off any blade with that setup, at least for quite a few minutes.

I crossed the room quickly, to the opposite wall.

With my left hand, I opened the panel through which I had entered.

'Okay,' I said, 'it looks like you're going to live – for a time. You're lucky. Next time we meet, there won't be anyone to help you.'

He spat and called me a few traditional vile names, even putting down the chair to add an obscene gesture, as I ducked through the panel and closed it behind me.

There came a *thunk*, and eight inches of steel gleamed on my side of the panel as I was fastening it. He had thrown his blade. Risky, if I chose to return. But he knew I wouldn't, for the door sounded about ready to fall.

I descended the pegs as rapidly as I could, to the place where I had slept earlier. As I did, I considered my increased skill with the blade. At first, in the battle, I had been awed by the man who had beaten me before. Now, though, I wondered. Perhaps those centuries on the Shadow Earth were not a waste. Maybe I had actually gotten better during that time. Now I felt that I might be Eric's equal with the weapon. This made me feel good. If we met again, as I was sure we would, and there was no outside interference – who knew? I would court the chance, however. Today's encounter had scared him. I was certain. That might serve to slow his hand, to cause the necessary hesitation on the next occasion.

I let go and dropped the final fifteen feet, bending my knees as I landed. I was the proverbial five minutes ahead of the posse, but I was sure I could take advantage of it and escape.

For I had the cards in my belt.

I drew the card that was Bleys and stared at it. My shoulder hurt, but I forgot it, as the coldness came upon me.

There were two ways to depart directly from Amber into Shadow . . .

One was the Pattern, seldom used for this purpose.

Another was the Trumps, if you could trust a brother.

I considered Bleys. I could almost trust him. He *was* my brother, but he was in trouble and could use my help.

I stared at him, flame-crowned, dressed all in red and orange, with a sword in his right hand and a glass of wine in his left. The devil danced in his blue eyes, his beard blazed, and the tracery on his blade, I suddenly realized, flared with a portion of the Pattern. His rings flashed. He seemed to move.

The contact came like an icy wind.

The figure on the card seemed life-sized now and changed position into whatever stance he presently held. His eyes did not quite focus upon me, and his lips moved.

'Who is it?' they said, and I heard the words.

'Corwin,' said I, and he held forth his left hand, which no longer bore the goblet.

'Then come to me, if you would.'

I reached forth and our fingers met. I took a step.

I was still holding the card in my left hand, but Bleys and I stood together on a cliff and there was a chasm to our side and a high fortress to our other side. The sky above us was the color of flame.

'Hello, Bleys,' I said, tucking the card into my belt with the others. 'Thanks for the assistance.'

I suddenly felt weak and realized the blood was still flowing from my left shoulder.

'You're wounded!' he said, throwing an arm about my shoulder, and I started to nod but fainted instead.

Later that night, I sprawled in a big chair within the fortress and drank whisky. We smoked and passed the bottle and talked.

'So you were actually in Amber?'

'Yes, that's right.'

'And you wounded Eric in your duel?'

'Yes.'

'Damn! I wish you'd killed him!' Then he reflected. 'Well, maybe not. Then you'd have held the throne. I might have a better chance against Eric than I'd have had against you. I don't know. What are your plans?'

I decided upon complete honesty.

'We all want the throne,' I said, 'so there's no reason to lie to one another. I'm not about to try killing you for it – that would be foolish – but on the other hand, I'm not about to renounce my claim because I'm enjoying your hospitality. Random would like it, but he's pretty much out of the picture. No one has heard from Benedict for some time now. Gérard and Caine seem to be supporting Eric, rather than promoting their own claims. The same goes for Julian. That leaves Brand and our sisters. I don't know what the hell Brand is up to these days, but I do know that Deirdre is without power, unless she and Llewella can raise something in Rebma, and Flora is Eric's creature. I don't know what Fiona is up too.'

'And so that leaves us,' said Bleys, pouring us each another drink. 'Yes, you're right. I don't know what's going on in everyone's head right now, but I can assess our relative strengths and I think I'm in the best position. You made a wise choice in coming to me. Support me, and I'll give you a regency.'

'Bless your heart,' I said. 'We'll see.'

We sipped our whiskies.

'What else is there to do?' he asked, and I realized that the question was important.

'I might raise an army of my own, to lay siege to Amber,' I told him.

'Where among Shadows lies your army?' he inquired.

'That, of course, is my affair,' I said. 'I don't think I'd oppose you. When it comes to monarchs, I'd like to see either you, me, Gérard, or Benedict – if he still lives – upon the throne.'

'Preferably you, of course.'

'Of course.'

'Then we understand one another. So I think we can work together, for the time being.'

'And I,' I agreed, 'else I would not have delivered myself into your hands.'

He smiled within his beard.

'You needed someone,' he said, 'and I was the lesser evil.'

'True,' I agreed.

'I wish Benedict were here. I wish Gérard had not sold out.'

'Wishes, wishes,' I told him. 'Wish in one hand and do something else in the other, and squeeze them both and see which comes true.'

'Well taken,' he said.

We smoked a while in silence.

'How far can I trust you?' he asked.

'As far as I can trust you.'

'Then let's make a deal. Frankly, I had thought you dead for many years. I hadn't foreseen your showing up at a crucial time and pressing your own claim. But you're here, and that's that. Let's form an alliance – combine our forces and lay siege to Amber. Whichever of us lives through it winds up on top. If we both do, well – hell! – we can always fight a duel!'

I thought about it. It sounded like the best deal I'd get anywhere.

So I said, 'I'd like to sleep on it. Tell you in the morning, okay?'

'Okay.'

We finished our drinks then and fell to reminiscing. My shoulder throbbed a bit, but the whisky helped, and the salve which Bleys had supplied. After a time, we were almost maudlin.

It is strange, I guess, to have kin and to be without kinship, for as long as our lives had led us along our separate paths. Lord! We talked the moon out of the heavens before either of us grew tired. Then he clapped me upon my good shoulder and told me that he was beginning to feel his load and that a servant would be by in the morning to bring me breakfast. I nodded, we embraced, and he retired.

Then I moved to the window, and from that vantage I could see down far into the chasm.

The campfires below burned like stars. There were thousands of them. I could tell that Bleys had assembled a mighty force, and I was envious. But, on the other hand, it was a good thing. If anyone could take Eric, it was probably Bleys. He wouldn't be a bad thing in Amber; it was just that I preferred me.

Then I watched a while longer, and I saw that strange shapes moved among the lights. I wondered then as to the nature of his army.

Whatever, it was more than I possessed.

I made my way back to the table and poured me a final drink.

Before I quaffed it, however, I lighted a taper. In its light, I withdrew the pack of cards I had stolen.

I spread them before me and I came across the one depicting Eric. I laid it in the center of the table and put the rest away.

After a time, it came to life; and I saw Eric in his sleeping garments and I heard the words, 'Who is it?' His arm was bound.

'Me,' I said, 'Corwin. How are you?'

He cursed then, and I laughed. This was a dangerous game and maybe the whisky had contributed to it, but I continued: 'I just felt like telling you that all goes well with me. I also wanted to advise you that you were right when you spoke of the uneasy head. You won't be wearing it long, though. So cheerio! Brother! The day I come again to Amber is the day you die! Just thought I'd tell you – since that day is not too far off.'

'Come ahead,' he told me, 'and I'll not want for grace in the matter of your own passing.'

His eyes focused on me then and we were close.

I thumbed my nose at him and passed my palm over the card.

It was like hanging up a telephone, and I shuffled Eric in with all the rest.

I wondered though, as I approached sleep, concerning those troops of Bleys which occupied the defile below, and I thought upon Eric's defenses.

It would not be easy.

6

The land was known as Avernus, and the assembled troops were not quite men. I reviewed them the following morning, walking behind Bleys. They were all of them around seven feet in height, had very red skins and little hair, cat-like eyes, and six-digited hands and feet. They wore garments that looked as light as silk, but were woven of something else and were mainly gray or blue in color. Each bore two short blades, hooked at the end. Their ears were pointed and their many fingers clawed.

The climate was warm and the colors bewildering, and everyone thought we were gods.

Bleys had found a place where the religion involved brother-gods who looked like us and had their troubles. Invariably, in the terms of this *mythos*, an evil brother would seize power and seek to oppress the good brothers. And of course there was the legend of an Apocalypse where they themselves would be called upon to stand on the side of the surviving good brothers.

I wore my left arm in a black sling and considered those who were about to die.

I stood before a trooper and looked up at him. I asked him, 'Do you know who Eric is?'

'The Lord of Evil,' he replied.

I nodded and said, 'Very good,' and passed on.

Bleys had custom-made cannon fodder.

'How large is your army?' I asked him.

'Around fifty thousand,' he replied.

'I salute those who are about to Give Their All,' I told him. 'You can't take Amber with fifty thousand men, even providing you can get them all to the foot of Kolvir intact – and you can't. It's silly even to consider using these poor bastards against the immortal city, with their toy swords and all.'

'I know,' he said, 'but they're not all I've got.'

'You'll need a lot more.'

'Then how do three navies sound – half again the size of Caines and Gérard's fleets put together?

'I've a way.'

'Not yet enough,' said I, 'and barely a beginning.'

'I know. I'm still building,' he said.

'Well, we'd better build a lot more. Eric will sit in Amber and kill us as we march through Shadows. When the remaining forces finally reach the foot of Kolvir, he'll decimate them there. Then there will be the climb to Amber. How many hundred do you think will remain when we reach the city? Enough to be dispatched in five minutes, at almost no cost to Eric. If this is the best you've got, brother Bleys, I have misgivings concerning this expedition.'

'Eric has announced his coronation in three months' time,' he said. 'I can triple my forces by then – at least. Perhaps I can even have a quarter of a million Shadow troops to lead against Amber. There are other worlds like this one, and I will penetrate them. I will raise me such a force of holy crusaders as has never been sent against Amber before.'

'And Eric will have had the same time to intensify his defenses. I don't know, Bleys . . . it's almost a suicide run. I didn't know the full situation when I came here—'

'And what have you brought with you?' he asked. 'Nothing! It is rumored that you once commanded troops. Where are they?'

I turned away from him.

'They are no more,' I said. 'I am certain.'

'Could you not find a Shadow of your Shadow?'

'I don't want to try,' I said. 'I'm sorry.'

'Then what real good are you to me?'

'I'll go,' I told him, 'if that's all you had in mind, if that's all you really wanted me around for – more bodies.'

'Wait!' he cried out 'I spoke hastily. I don't want to lose your counsel, if nothing else. Stay with me, please. I will even apologize.'

'That is not necessary,' I said, knowing what this thing means to a prince of Amber. 'I'll stay. I think I can help you.'

'Good!' and he clapped me upon my good shoulder.

'And I'll get you more troops,' I added. 'Never fear.'

And I did.

I walked among Shadows, and found a race of furry creatures, dark and clawed and fanged, reasonably man-like, and about as intelligent as a freshman in the high school of your choice – sorry, kids, but what I mean is they were loyal, devoted, honest, and too easily screwed by bastards like me and my brother. I felt like the deejay of your choice.

Around a hundred thousand worshiped us to the extent of taking up arms.

Bleys was impressed and shut up. After a week my shoulder was healed. After two months we had our quarter million and more.

'Corwin, Corwin! You're still Corwin!' he said, and we took another drink.

But I was feeling kind of funny. Most of these troops were destined to die. I was the agent responsible for much of this. I felt some remorse, though I knew the difference between Shadow and Substance. Each death would be a real death; however, I knew that also.

And some nights I dwelled upon the playing cards. The missing Trumps had been restored to the pack I held. One of them was a portrait of Amber itself, and I knew it could bear me back into the city. The others were those of our dead or missing relatives. And one was Dad's, and I skipped it over quickly. He was gone.

I stared at each face for a long while to consider what might be gained from each. I cast the cards several times, and the same thing came up on each occasion.

His name was Caine.

He wore satin that was green and black, and a dark three-cornered hat with a green plume of feathers trailing down behind. At his belt there was an emerald-studded dagger. He was dark.

'Caine,' I said.

After a time, there came a reply.

'Who?' he asked.

'Corwin,' said I.

'Corwin! Is this a joke?'

'No.'

'What do you want?'

'What've you got?'

'You know that,' and his eyes shifted and lay upon me, but I watched his hand, which was near to his dagger.

'Where are you?'

'With Bleys.'

'There was a rumor you'd shown up in Amber recently – and I wondered at the bandages on Eric's arm.'

'You're looking at the reason,' I said. 'What's your price?'

'What do you mean?'

'Let us be frank and to the point. Do you think Bleys and I can take Eric?'

'No, that's why I'm with Eric. And I won't sell out my armada either, if that's what you're after – and I'd imagine you are.'

I smiled.

'Perceptive brother,' I replied. 'Well, it's been nice talking to you. See you in Amber – maybe.'

I moved my hand, and he cried out.

'Wait!'

'Why?'

'I don't even know your offer.'

'Yes, you do,' I said. 'You've guessed it, and you're not interested.'

'I didn't say that. It's just that I know where the equities lie.'

'You mean the power.'

'Okay, the power. What've you got to offer?'

We talked for maybe an hour, after which time the northern seaways were open to the three phantom fleets of Bleys, which might enter expecting reinforcements.

'If you fail, there'll be three beheadings in Amber,' said he.

'But you don't really expect that, do you?' I asked.

'No, I think either you or Bleys will sit upon the throne before too very long. I'll be satisfied to serve the winner. That regency should be nice. I'd still like Random's head as part of the price, though.'

'No deal,' I said. 'Take it as you've heard it or forget it.'

'I'll take it.'

I smiled and placed my palm upon the card and he was gone.

Gérard was a matter I'd leave for the morrow. Caine had exhausted me.

I rolled into bed and slept.

Gérard, when he learned the score, agreed to lay off us. Mainly because it was I who was asking, as he had considered Eric a lesser of potent evils.

I concluded the deal quickly, promising him everything he asked, as no heads were involved.

Then I reviewed the troops again and told them more of Amber. Strangely, they got along like brothers, the big red guys and the little hairy ones.

It was sad and it was true.

We were their gods, and that was that.

I saw the fleet, sailing on a great ocean the color of blood. I wondered. In the Shadow worlds through which they sailed, many of them would be lost.

I considered the troops of Avernus, and my recruits from the place called Ri'ik. Theirs was the task of marching to Earth and Amber.

I shuffled my cards and cast them. I picked up the one called Benedict. For a long while I searched it, but there was nothing but the cold.

Then I seized upon Brand's. For another long while there was nothing but the cold.

Then there came a scream. It was a horrible, tormented thing.

'Help me!' came the cry.

'How can I?' I asked.

'Who is that?' he asked, and I saw his body writhe.

'Corwin.'

'Deliver me from this place, brother Corwin! Anything you name shall be yours in return!'

'Where are you?'

'I—'

And there came a swirling of things my mind refused to conceive of, and another scream, torn forth as though in agony and ending in silence.

Then the coldness came in again.

I found that I was shaking. From what, I did not know.

I lit a cigarette and moved to the window to consider the night, leaving the cards where they had fallen upon the tabletop of my room within the garrison.

The stars were tiny and misted over. There were no constellations that I could recognize. A small blue moon dropped quickly through the darkness. The night had come on with a sudden, icy chill and I wrapped my cloak close about me. I thought back to the winter of our disastrous campaign in Russia. Gods! I'd almost frozen to death! And where did it all lead?

To the throne of Amber, of course.

For that was sufficient justification for anything.

But what of Brand? Where was he? What was happening about him, and who had done this thing to him?

Answers? None.

I wondered, though, as I stared up and out, tracing the path of that blue disk in its descent. Was there something I was missing in the whole picture, some factor I didn't quite dig?

No answer.

I seated myself at the table once more, a small drink at my hand.

I fingered my way through the pack and found Dad's card.

Oberon, Lord of Amber, stood before me in his green and his gold. High, wide, and thick, his beard black and shot with silver, his hair the same. Green rings in gold settings and a blade of golden color. It had once seemed to me that nothing could ever displace the immortal liege of Amber from his throne. What had happened? I still didn't know. But he was gone. How had my father met with his end?

I stared and concentrated.

Nothing, nothing—

Something?

Something.

There came a responding movement, though ever so weak, and the figure on the card turned in upon itself and shriveled to a shadow of the man he had been.

'Father?' I asked.

Nothing.

'Father?'

'Yes . . .' Very faint and distant, as though through a seashell, immersed in its monotone humming.

'Where are you? What has happened?'

'I . . .' Long pause.

'Yes? This is Corwin, your son. What came to pass in Amber, that you are gone?'

'My time,' he said, sounding even further away.

'Do you mean that you abdicated? None of my brothers has given me the tale, and I do not trust them sufficiently to ask them. I only know that the throne seems open to all grabbers. Eric now holds the city and Julian guards the Forest of Arden. Caine and Gérard maintain the seas. Bleys would oppose all and I am allied with him. What are your wishes in this matter?'

'You are the only one – who – has asked,' he gasped. 'Yes . . .'

' "Yes" what?'

'Yes, oppose – them . . .'

'What of you? How can I help you?'

'I am – beyond help. Take the throne . . .'

'I? Or Bleys and I?'

'You!' he said.

'Yes?'

'You have my blessing . . . Take the throne – and be quick – about it!'

'Why, Father?'

'I lack the breath – Take it!'

Then he, too was gone.

So Dad lived. That was interesting. What to do now?

I sipped my drink and thought about it.

He still lived, somewhere, and he was king in Amber. Why had he left? Where had he gone? What kind of, which, and how many? Like that.

Who knew? Not I. So there was no more to say, for now.

However . . .

I couldn't put the thing down. I want you to know that Dad and I never got along very well. I didn't hate him, like Random or some of the others. But I, sure as hell, had no reason to be especially fond of him. He had been big, he had been powerful, and he had been there. That was about it. He was also most of the history of Amber, as we knew it, and the history of Amber stretches back for so many millennia that you may as well stop counting. So what do you do?

As for me, I finished my drink and went to bed.

The following morning I attended a meeting of Bleys' general staff. He had four admirals, each in charge of roughly a quarter of his fleet, and a whole mess of army officers. Altogether there were about thirty of the high-ranking brass at the meeting, big and red or small and hairy, as the case might be.

The meeting lasted perhaps four hours, and then we all broke for lunch. It was decided that we would move three days hence. Since it would require one of the blood to open the way to Amber, I was to lead the fleet aboard the flagship, and Bleys would take his infantry through lands of Shadow.

I was troubled by this, and I asked him what would have happened had I not shown up to give this assistance. I was told two things in reply: one, if he had had to go it alone, he would have led the fleet through and left them at a great distance from shore, returned in a single vessel to Avernus and led his foot soldiers forward to a rendezvous at a given time; and two, he had purposely sought for a Shadow in which a brother would appear to give him aid.

I had some misgivings when I heard about the latter, though I knew I was really me. The former smacked of being a bit unworkable, since the fleet would be too far out to sea to receive any signals from the shore, and the chance of missing the date – allowing for mishaps when it came to a body that large – was too great, as I saw it, to encourage a whole big lot of faith in his general plan.

But as a tactician, I had always thought him brilliant; and when he laid out the maps of Amber and the outlying country which he himself had drawn, and when he had explained the tactics to be employed therein, I knew that he was a prince of Amber, almost matchless in his guile.

The only thing was, we were up against another prince of Amber, one who occupied what was definitely a stronger position. I was worried, but with the impending coronation, it seemed about the only course available to us, and I decided to go along for the whole ride. If we lost, we were creamed, but he held the biggest threat available and had a workable time schedule, which I didn't.

So I walked the land called Avernus and considered its foggy valleys and chasms, its smoking craters, its bright, bright sun against its crazy sky, its icy nights and too hot days, its many rocks and carloads of dark sand, its tiny, though vicious and poisonous beasts, and its big purple plants, like spineless cacti; and on the afternoon of the second day, as I stood on a cliff overlooking the sea, beneath a tower of massed vermilion clouds, I decided that I rather liked the place for all that, and if its sons would perish in the wars of the gods, I would immortalize them one day in song if I were able.

This mild balm in mind for what I feared, I joined the fleet and took command. If we made it, they would be feted forever in the halls of the immortals.

I was guide and opener of the way. I rejoiced.

So we set sail the following day, and I directed things from the lead ship. I led us into a storm, and we emerged that much nearer our destination. I led us past an enormous whirlpool, and we were so much to the good. I led us through a shallow rocky place, and the shade of the waters deepened afterward. Their colors began to approximate those of Amber. So I still knew how to do it. I could influence our fate in time and place. I could take us home. Home for me, that is.

I led us past strange islands where green birds cawed and green apes hung like fruit in the trees, swung, sometimes gibbered, and threw rocks into the sea, aimed, doubtless, at us.

I took us far out to sea, and then nosed the fleet around back in the direction of shore.

Bleys by now was marching across the plains of the worlds. Somehow, I knew he would make it, past whatever defenses Eric had set up. I kept in touch with him by means of the cards, and I learned of his encounters along the way. Like, ten thousand men dead in a plains battle with centaurs, five thousand lost in an earthquake of frightening proportions, fifteen hundred dead of a whirlwind plague that swept the camps, nineteen thousand dead or missing in action as they passed through the jungles of a place I didn't recognize, when the napalm fell upon them from the strange buzzing things that passed overhead, six thousand deserting in a place that looked like the heaven they had been promised, five hundred unaccounted for as they crossed a sand flat where a mushroom cloud burned and towered beside them, eighty-six hundred gone as they moved through a valley of suddenly militant machines that rolled forward on treads and fired fires, eight hundred sick and abandoned, two hundred dead from flash floods, fifty-four dying of duels among themselves, three hundred dead from eating poisonous native fruits, a thousand slain in a massive stampede of buffalo-like creatures, seventy-three gone when their tents caught fire, fifteen hundred carried away by the floods, two thousand slain by the winds that came down from the blue hills.

I was pleased that I'd lost only a hundred and eighty-six ships in that time.

To sleep, perchance to dream . . . Yeah, there's a thing that rubs. Eric was killing us by inches and hours. His proposed coronation was only a few weeks away, and he obviously knew we were coming against him, because we died and we died.

Now, it is written that only a prince of Amber may walk among Shadows, though of course he may lead or direct as many as he chooses along such courses. We led our troops and saw them die, but of Shadow I have this to say: there is Shadow and there is Substance, and this is the root of all things. Of Substance, there is only Amber, the real city, upon the real Earth, which contains everything. Of Shadow, there is an infinitude of things. Every possibility exists somewhere as a Shadow of the real. Amber, by its very existence, has cast such in all directions. And what may one say of it beyond? Shadow extends from Amber to Chaos, and all things are possible within it. There are only three ways of traversing it, and each of them is difficult.

If one is a prince or princess of the blood, then one may walk, crossing through Shadows, forcing one's environment to change as one passes, until it is finally in precisely the shape one desires it, and there stop. That Shadow world is then one's own, save for family intrusions, to do with as one would. In such a place had I dwelled for centuries.

The second means is the cards, cast by Dworkin, Master of the Line, who had created them in our image, to facilitate communications between members of the royal family. He was the ancient artist to whom space and perspective meant nothing. He had made up the family Trumps, which permitted the willer to touch his brethren wherever they might be. I had a feeling that these had not been used in full accord with their author's intention.

The third was the Pattern, also drawn by Dworkin, which could only be walked by a member of our family. It initiated the walker into the system of the cards, as it were, and at its ending gave its walker the power to stride across Shadows.

The cards and the Pattern made for instant transport from Substance through Shadow. The other way, walking, was harder.

I knew what Random had done in delivering me into the true world. As we had driven, he kept adding, from memory, that which he recalled of Amber, and subtracting that which did not agree. When everything corresponded, he knew we had arrived. It was no real trick, for had he the knowledge, any man could reach his own Amber. Even now, Bleys and I could find Shadow Ambers where each of us ruled, and spend all of time and eternity ruling there. But this would not be the same, for us. For none would be the true Amber, the city into which we were born, the city from which all others take their shapes.

So we were taking the hardest route, the walk through Shadow, for our invasion of Amber itself. Anyone knowing this and possessing the power could interpose obstacles. Eric had done so, and now we faced them as we died. What would come of this? No one knew.

But if Eric were crowned king, it would be reflected and shadowed everywhere.

All the surviving brothers, we princes of Amber, I am sure, felt it much better, each in his own simple way, personally to achieve this status and thereafter let the Shadows fall where they might.

We passed ghost fleets, the ships of Gérard, as we sailed – the Flying Dutchmen of this world/that world – and we knew we were coming near. I used them as reference points.

On the eighth day of our voyaging we were near to Amber. That is when the storm broke.

The sea turned dark, the clouds collected overhead, and the sails grew slack within the still that followed. The sun hid its face – an enormous blue one – and I felt that Eric had found us at last.

The the winds arose, and – if you'll excuse the expression – broke, upon the vessel I rode.

We were tempest-tossed and storm-torn, as the poets say, or said. My guts felt loose and watery as the first billows hit us. We were hurled from side to side like dice in a giant's hand. We were swept over the waters of the sea and the waters from the sky. The sky turned black, and there was sleet mixed in with the glassy bell ropes that pulled the thunder. Everyone, I'm sure, cried out. I know I did. I pulled my way along the shifting deck to seize the abandoned wheel. I strapped myself in place and held it. Eric had cut loose in Amber, that was for damn sure.

One, two, three, four, and there was no letup. Five hours, then. How many men had we lost? I dunno.

Then I felt and heard a tingling and a tinkling, and I saw Bleys as through a long gray tunnel.

'What's the matter?' he asked. 'I've been trying to reach you.'

'Life is full of vicissitudes,' I replied. 'We're riding out one of them.'

'Storm?' he said.

'You bet your sweet ass. Its the granddaddy of them all. I think I see a monster off to port. If he has any brains, he'll aim for the bottom . . . He just did.'

'We just had one ourselves,' Bleys told me.

'Monster or storm?'

'Storm,' he replied. Two hundred dead.'

'Keep the faith,' I said, 'hold the fort, and talk to me later. Of cay.'

He nodded, and there were lightnings at his back.

'Eric's got our number,' he added, before he cut off.

I had to agree.

It was three more hours before things let up, and many more later I learned that we had lost half of the fleet (and on my vessel – the flagship – we had lost forty of the crew of one hundred and twenty). It was a hard rain that fell.

Somehow, to the sea over Rebma, we made it.

I drew forth my cards and held Random's before me.

When he realized who was talking, the first thing he said was 'Turn back,' and I asked him why.

' 'Cause, according to Llewella, Eric can cream you now. She says wait a while, till he relaxes, and hit him then – like a year from now, maybe.'

I shook my head.

'Sorry,' said I. 'Can't. Too many losses involved in getting us this far. It's a now-or-never situation.'

He shrugged, wearing a 'Like, I warned you' expression.

'Why, though?' I asked him.

'Mainly because I just learned he can control the weather around here,' he said.

'We'll still have to chance it.'

He shrugged again.

'Don't say I didn't tell you.'

'He definitely knows we're coming?'

'What do you think? Is he a cretin?'

'No.'

'Then he knows. If I could guess it in Rebma, then he knows in Amber – and I *did* guess, from a wavering of Shadow.'

'Unfortunately,' I said, 'I have some misgivings about this expedition, but it's Bleys' show.'

'You cop out and let him get axed.'

'Sorry, but I can't take the chance. He might win. I'm bringing in the fleet.'

'You've spoken with Caine, with Gérard?'

'Yes.'

'Then you must think you have a chance upon the waters. But listen, Eric has figured a way to control the Jewel of Judgment, I gather, from court gossip about its double. He *can* use it to control the weather here. That's definite. God knows what else he might be able to do with it.'

'Pity,' I said 'We'll have to suffer it. Can't let a few storms demoralize us.'

'Corwin, I'll confess. I spoke with Eric himself three days ago.'

'Why?'

'He asked me. I spoke with him out of boredom. He went into great detail concerning his defenses.'

'That's because he learned from Julian that we came in together. He's sure it'll get back to me.'

'Probably,' he said. 'But that doesn't change what he said.'

'No,' I agreed.

'Then let Bleys fight his own war,' he told me. 'You can hit Eric later.'

'He's about to be crowned in Amber.'

'I know, I know. It's as easy to attack a king, though, as a prince, isn't it? What difference does it make what he calls himself at the time, so long as you take him? It'll still be Eric.'

'True,' I said, 'but I've committed myself.'

'Then uncommit yourself,' he said.

' 'Fraid I can't do that.'

'Then you're crazy, Corwin.'

'Probably.'

'Well, good luck, anyhow.'

'Thanks.'

'See you around.'

And that was that, and it troubled me.

Was I heading into a trap?

Eric was no fool. Perhaps he had a real death-gig lined up. Finally, I shrugged and leaned out over the rail, the cards once again behind my belt.

It is a proud and lonely thing to be a prince of Amber, incapable of trust I wasn't real fond of it just then, but there I was.

Eric, of course, had controlled the storm we'd just passed through, and it seemed in line with his being weather master in Amber, as Random had told me.

So I tried something myself.

I headed us toward an Amber lousy with snow. It was the most horrible blizzard I could conjure up.

The big flakes began to fall, out there on the ocean.

Let him stop them a normal enough Shadow offering, if he could. And he did.

Within a half hour's time the blizzard had died. Amber was virtually impervious – and it was really the only city. I didn't want to go off course, so I let things be. Eric *was* master of the weather in Amber.

What to do?

We sailed on, of course. Into the jaws of death.

What can one say?

The second storm was worse than the first, but I held the wheel. It was electrified, and focused only on the fleet. It drove us apart. It cost us forty vessels more.

I was afraid to call Bleys to see what had been done to him.

'Around two hundred thousand troops are left,' he said. 'Flash flood,' and I told him what Random had told me.

'I'll buy it,' he said. 'But let's not dwell on it. Weather or no, we'll beat him.'

'I hope so.'

I lit a cigarette and leaned across the bow.

Amber should be coming into sight soon. I knew the ways of Shadow now, and I know how to get there by walking.

But everyone had misgivings.

There would never be a perfect day, though . . .

So we sailed on, and the darkness came upon us like a sudden wave, and the worst storm of them all struck.

We managed to ride out its black lashings, but I was scared. It was all true, and we were in northern waters. If Caine had kept his word, all well and good. If he was getting us out, he was in an excellent position.

So I assumed he had sold us out. Why not? I prepared the fleet – seventy-three vessels remaining – for battle, when I saw him approach. The cards had lied – or else been very correct – when they'd pointed to him as the key figure.

The lead vessel headed toward my own, and I moved forward to meet it. We hove to, and side by side regarded one another. We could have communicated via the Trumps, but Caine didn't choose to; and he was in the stronger position. Therefore, family etiquette required that he choose his own means. He obviously wanted to be on record as he called out, through an amplifier:

'Corwin! Kindly surrender command of your fleet! I've got you outnumbered! You can't make it through!'

I regarded him across the waves and raised my own amplifier to my lips.

'What of our arrangement?' I asked.

'Null and void,' he said. 'Your force is far too weak to hurt Amber, so save lives and surrender it now.'

I looked over my left shoulder and regarded the sun.

'Pray hear me, brother Caine,' said I, 'and grant me this then: give me your leave to confer with my captains till the sun stands in high heaven.'

'Very well,' he replied, without hesitation. 'They appreciate their positions, I'm sure.'

I turned away then and ordered that the ship be turned about and headed back in the direction of the main body of vessels.

If I tried to flee, Caine would pursue me through the Shadows and destroy the ships, one by one. Gunpowder did not ignite on the real Earth, but if we moved very far away, it too would be employed to our undoing. Caine would find some, for it was probable, were I to depart, the fleet could not sail the Shadow seas without me, and would be left as sitting ducks upon the real waters here. So the crews were either dead or prisoners, whatever I did.

Random had been right.

I drew forth Bleys' Trump and concentrated till it moved.

'Yes?' he said, and his voice was agitated. I could almost hear the sounds of battle about him.

'We're in trouble,' I said. 'Seventy-three ships made it through, and Caine has called on us to surrender by noon.'

'Damn his eyes!' said Bleys. 'I haven't made it as far as you. We're in the middle of a fight now. An enormous cavalry force is cutting us to pieces. So I can't counsel you fairly. I've got my own problems. Do as you see fit. They're coming again!' And the contact was broken.

I drew forth Gérard's, and sought contact.

When we spoke it seemed I could see a shore line behind him. I seemed to recognize it. If my guess was correct, he was in southern waters. I don't like to remember our conversation. I asked him if he could help me against Caine, and if he would.

'I only agreed to let you by,' he said. 'That is why I withdrew to the south. I couldn't reach you in time if I wanted to. I did not agree to help you kill our brother.'

And before I could reply, be was gone. He was right, of course. He'd agreed to give me an opportunity, not to fight my battle for me.

What then did that leave me?

I lit a cigarette. I paced the deck. It was no longer morning. The mists had long vanished and the sun warmed my shoulders. Soon it would be noon. Perhaps two hours . . .

I fingered my cards, weighed the deck in my hand. I could try a contest of wills through them, with either Eric or Caine. There was that power present, and perhaps even others of which I knew nothing. They had been so designed, at the command of Oberon, by the hand of the mad artist Dworkin Barimen, that wild-eyed hunchback who had been a sorcerer, priest, or psychiatrist – the stories conflicted on this point – from some distant Shadow where Dad had saved him from a disastrous fate he had brought upon himself. The details were unknown, but he had always been a bit off his rocker since that time. Still, he was a great artist, and it was undeniable that he possessed some strange power. He had vanished ages ago, after creating the cards and tracing the Pattern in Amber. We had often speculated about him, but no one seemed to know his whereabouts. Perhaps Dad had done him in, to keep his secrets secret.

Caine would be ready for such an attack, and I probably couldn't break him, though I might be able to hold him. Even then, though, his captains had doubtless been given the order to attack.

Eric would surely be ready for anything, but if there was nothing else left to do, I might as well try it. I had nothing to lose but my soul.

Then there was the card for Amber itself. I could take my self there with it and try an assassination, but I figured the odds were about a million to one against my living to effect it.

I was willing to die fighting, but it was senseless for all these men to go down with me. Perhaps my blood was tainted, despite my power over the Pattern. A true prince of Amber should have had no such qualms. I decided then that my centuries on the Shadow Earth had changed me, softened me perhaps, had done something to me which made me unlike my brothers.

I decided to surrender the fleet and then transport myself to Amber and challenge Eric to a final duel. He'd be foolish to accept. But what the hell – I had nothing else left to do.

I turned to make my wishes known to my officers, and the power fell upon me, and I was stricken speechless.

I felt the contact and I finally managed to mutter 'Who?' through clenched teeth. There was no reply, but a twisting thing bored slowly within my mind and I wrestled with it there.

After a time when he saw that I could not be broken without a long struggle, I heard Eric's voice upon the wind:

'How goes the world with thee, brother?' he inquired.

'Poorly,' I said or thought, and he chuckled, though his voice seemed strained by the efforts of our striving.

'Too bad,' he told me. 'Had you come back and supported me, I would have done well by you. Now, of course, it is too late. Now, I will only rejoice when I have broken both you and Bleys.'

I did not reply at once, but fought him with all the power I possessed. He withdrew slightly before it, but he succeeded in holding me where I stood.

If either of us dared divert his attention for an instant, we could come into physical contact or one of us get the upper hand on the mental plane. I could see him now, clearly, in his chambers in the palace. Whichever of us made such a move, though, he would fall beneath the other's control.

So we glared at each other and struggled internally. Well, he had solved one of my problems, by attacking me first. He held my Trump in his left hand and his brows were furrowed. I sought for an edge, but couldn't find one. People were talking to me but I couldn't hear their words as I stood there backed against the rail.

What time was it?

All sense of time had departed since the beginning of the struggle. Could two hours have passed? Was that it? I couldn't be sure.

'I feel your troubled thought,' said Eric. 'Yes, I am coordinated with Caine. He contacted me after your parley. I can hold you thus while your fleet is demolished around you and sent down to Rehma to rot. The fishes will eat your men.'

'Wait,' I said. 'They are guiltless. Bleys and I have misled them, and they think we are in the right. Their deaths would serve no purpose. I was preparing to surrender the fleet.'

'Then you should not have taken so long,' he replied, 'for now it is too late. I cannot call Caine to countermand my orders, without releasing you, and the moment I release you I will fall beneath your mental domination or suffer physical assault. Our minds are too proximate.'

'Supposing I give you my word that I won't do this thing?'

'Any man would be forsworn to gain a kingdom,' said Eric.

'Can't you read the thought? Can't you feel it within my mind? I'll keep my word!'

'I feel there is a strange compassion for these men you have duped, and I know not what may have caused such a bond, but no. You know it yourself. Even if you are sincere at this moment – as you well may be – the temptation will be too great the instant the opportunity occurs. You know it yourself. I can't risk it.'

And I knew it. Amber burned too strongly in the blood of us.

'Your swordsmanship has increased remarkably,' he commented. 'I see that your exile has done you some good in that respect. You are closer to being my equal now than anyone save Benedict, who may well be dead.'

'Don't flatter yourself,' I said. 'I know I can take you now. In fact—'

'Don't bother. I won't duel with you at this late date,' and he smiled, reading my thought, which burned all too clearly.

'I more than half wish you had stood by me,' he said. 'I could have used you more than any of the others. Julian I spit upon. Caine is a coward. Gérard is strong, but stupid.'

I decided to put in the only good word I might.

'Listen,' I said. 'I conned Random into coming here with me. He wasn't hot on the idea. I think he would have supported you, had you asked him.'

'That bastard!' he said. 'I wouldn't trust him to empty chamber pots. One day I'd find a piranha in mine. No thanks. I might have pardoned him, save for your present recommendation. You'd like me to clasp him to my bosom and call him brother now, wouldn't you? Oh no! You leap too quickly to his defense. It reveals his true attitude, of which he has doubtless made you aware. Let us forget Random in the courts of clemency.'

I smelled smoke then and heard the sounds of metal on metal. That would mean that Caine had come upon us and was doing his job.

'Good,' said Eric, catching it from my mind.

'Stop them! Please! My men don't have a chance against that many!'

'Not even were you to yield—' and he bit it off and cursed. I caught the thought, then. He could have asked me to yield in return for their lives, and then let Caine continue with the slaughter. He would have liked to have done that, but he'd let those first words slip out in the heat of his passion.

I chuckled at his irritation.

'I'll have you soon, anyhow,' he said. 'As soon as they take the flagship.'

'Until then,' I said, 'try this!' And I hit him with everything I had, boring into his mind, hurting him with my hatred. I felt his pain and it drove me harder. For all the years of exile I'd spent, I lashed at him, seeking at least this payment. For his putting me through the plague, I beat at the barriers of his sanity, seeking this vengeance. For the auto accident, for which I knew he had been responsible, I struck at him, seeking some measure of anguish in return for my hurt.

His control began to slip and my frenzy increased. I bore down upon him and his hold upon me began to slacken.

Finally, 'You devil!' he cried, and moved his hand to cover the card that he held.

The contact was broken, and I stood there shaking.

I had done it. I had bested him in a contest of wills. No longer would I fear my tyrant brother in any form of single combat. I was stronger than he.

I sucked in several deep breaths and stood erect, ready for the moment the coldness of a new mental attack occurred. I knew that it wouldn't, though, not from Eric. I sensed that he feared my fury.

I looked about me and there was fighting. There was already blood on the decks. A ship had come alongside us and we were being boarded. Another vessel was attempting the same maneuver on the opposite side. A bolt whistled by my head.

I drew my blade and leaped into the fray.

I don't know how many I slew that day. I lost count somewhere after number twelve or thirteen. It was more than twice that, on that engagement alone, though. The strength with which a prince of Amber is naturally endowed, which had allowed me to lift a Mercedes, served me that day, so that I could raise a man with one hand and hurl him over the rail.

We slew everyone aboard both boarding ships and opened their hatches and sent them down to Rebma where Random would be amused by the carnage. My crew had been cut in half in the battle, and I had suffered innumerable nicks and scratches, but nothing serious. We went to the aid of a sister vessel and knocked off another of Caine's raiders.

The survivors of the rescued vessel came aboard the flagship and I had a full crew once more.

'Blood!' I called out. 'Give me blood and vengeance this day, my warriors, and you will be remembered in Amber forever!

And as a man, they raised their weapons and cried out, 'Blood!' And gallons – no, rivers – of it were let that day. We destroyed two more of Caine's raiders, replenishing our numbers from those of the survivors of our own fleet. As we headed toward a sixth, I climbed the mainmast and tried to take a quick count.

We looked to be outnumbered three to one. There seemed to be between forty-five and fifty-five remaining of my fleet.

We took the sixth, and we didn't have to look for the seventh and the eighth. They came to us. We took them too, but I received several wounds in the fighting that again left me with half a crew. My left shoulder and my right thigh had been cut deeply, and a slash along my right hip was hurting.

As we sent those ships to the bottom, two more moved toward us.

We fled and gained an ally in one of my own ships which had been victorious in its own recent battle. We combined crews once more, this time transferring the standard to the other vessel, which had been less damaged than my own, which had begun shipping water badly and was beginning to list to starboard.

We were allowed no breathing space, as another vessel neared and the men attempted to board.

My men were tired, and I was getting that way. Fortunately the other crew wasn't in such great shape either. Before the second of Caine's vessels came to its aid, we had overwhelmed it, boarded, and transferred the standard again. That ship had been in even better shape.

We took the next and I was left with a good ship, forty men, and gasping.

There was no one in sight to come to our aid now. All of my surviving ships were engaged by at least one of Caine's. A raider was heading toward us and we fled.

We gained perhaps twenty minutes this way. I tried to sail into Shadow, but it's a hard, slow thing that near to Amber. It's much easier to get this close than it is to depart, because Amber is the center, the nexus. If I'd had another ten minutes, I could have made it.

I did, though.

As the vessel hove nearer, I saw another one off in the distance turning in our direction. It bore the black and green standard beneath Eric's colors and the white unicorn. It was Caine's ship. He wanted to be there for the kill.

We took the first one and didn't even have time to open its hatches before Caine was upon us. I was left standing on the bloody deck, with a dozen men about me, and Caine moved to the bow of his ship and called upon me to surrender.

'Will you grant my men their lives if I do this thing?' I asked him.

'Yes,' he said. 'I'd lose a few crewmen myself if I didn't, and there's no need for that.'

'On your word as a prince?' I asked.

He thought about it a moment, then nodded.

'Very well,' he said. 'Have your men lay down their arms and board my vessel when I come alongside.'

I sheathed my blade and nodded about me.

'You have fought the good fight, and I love you for it,' I said. 'But we have lost in this place.' I dried my hands on my cloak as I spoke and wiped them carefully, as I'd hate to smudge a work of art. 'Lay down your arms and know that your exploits of this day will never be forgotten. One day I will praise you before the court of Amber.'

The men, the nine big red ones and the three remaining hairy ones, wept as they put down their arms.

'Do not fear that all is lost in the struggle for the city,' I said. 'We have lost only one engagement and the battle still continues elsewhere. My brother Bleys hacks his way toward Amber at this moment. Caine will keep his word to spare your lives when he sees that I have gone to join with Bleys upon the land, for he would not have knowledge that he was forsworn come into Amber. I am sorry that I cannot take you with me.'

And with this, I drew Bleys' Trump from the pack and held it low and before me, out of sight of the other vessel.

Just as Caine came alongside, there was movement beneath that cold, cold surface.

'Who?' Bleys asked.

'Corwin,' I said 'How fare your?'

'We won the battle, but lost many troops. We're resting now before we renew the march. How go things with you?'

'I think we've destroyed nearly half of Caine's fleet, but he's won the day. He's about to board me now. Give me escape.'

He held forth his hand and I touched it and collapsed into his arms.

'This is getting to be a habit,' I muttered, and then I saw that he was wounded too, about the head, and there was a bandage around his left hand. 'Had to grab the wrong end of a saber,' he remarked, as he saw my eyes fall upon it. 'It smarts.'

I caught my breath and then we walked to his tent, where he

opened a bottle of wine and gave me bread, cheese, and some dried meat. He still had plenty of cigarettes and I smoked one as a medical officer dressed my wounds.

He still had around a hundred and eighty thousand men behind him. As I stood on a hilltop and the evening began around me, it seemed as if I looked out over every camp I had ever stood within, stretching on and on over the miles and the centuries without end. I suddenly felt tears come into my eyes, for the men who are not like the lords of Amber, living but a brief span and passing into dust, that so many of them must meet their ends upon the battlefields of the world.

I returned to Bleys' tent and we finished the bottle of wine.

7

That night there was a bad storm. It hadn't let up when dawn struggled to cross the world's palm with silver, and it continued on through the day's march.

It is a very demoralizing thing to tramp along and be rained on, a cold rain at that. How I've always hated the mud, through which it seems I've spent centuries marching!

We sought after a Shadow way that was free of rain, but nothing we did seemed to matter.

We could march to Amber, but we would do it with our clothing sticking to us, to the drumbeat of the thunder, with the flashing of the lightning at our backs.

The next night the temperature plummeted, and in the morning I stared past the stiff flags and regarded a world gone white beneath a gray sky, filled with flurries. My breath went back in plumes behind me.

The troops were ill-equipped for this, save for the hairy ones, and we got them all moving quickly, to prevent frostbite. The big red guys suffered. Theirs had been a very warm world.

We were attacked by tiger, polar bear, and wolf that day. The tiger Bleys killed measured over fourteen feet from tail tip to nose.

We marched on well into the night, and the thaw began. Bleys pushed the troops to get them out of the cold Shadows. The Trump for Amber indicated that a warm, dry autumn prevailed there, and we were nearing the real Earth.

By midnight on that second night we'd marched through slush and sleet, cold rains, warm rains, and on into a dry world.

The orders were given to make camp then, with triple security cordons. Considering the tired condition of the men, we were ripe for an attack. But the troops were staggering and couldn't be pushed much further.

The attack came several hours later, and Julian led it, I learned later from the description given by survivors.

He headed commando raids against our most vulnerable campsites on the periphery of the main body. Had I known it to be Julian, I would have used his Trump to try to hold him, but I only knew it after the fact.

We'd lost perhaps two thousand men in the abrupt winter, and I didn't yet know how many Julian had accounted for.

It seemed the troops were beginning to get demoralized, but they followed when we ordered them ahead.

The next day was one continuous ambush. A body of men the size of ours could not be allowed to deviate sufficiently to try to deal with the harassing raids Julian led against our flanks. We got some of his men, but not enough – one for every ten of ours, perhaps.

By high noon we were crossing the valley that paralleled the sea-coast. The Forest of Arden was to the north and our left. Amber lay directly ahead. The breezes were cool and filled with the odors of earth and its sweet growing things. A few leaves fell. Amber lay eighty miles distant and was but a shimmer above the horizon.

That afternoon, with a gathering of clouds and but the lightest of rains, the bolts began to fall from the heavens. Then the storm ceased and the sun came forth to dry things off.

After a time, we smelled the smoke.

After another time, we saw it, flapping skyward all about us.

Then the sheets of flame began to rise and fall. They moved toward us, with their crunching, constant footsteps; and as they came nearer, we began to feel the heat, and somewhere, way back along the lines, a panic arose. There were cries, and the columns swelled and welled foward.

We began to run.

Flakes of ash were falling about us now and the smoke grew thicker. We sprinted ahead and the flames rushed even closer. The sheets of light and heat flapped a steady, welling thunder as we ran, and the waves of warmth beat upon us, washed over us. Soon they were right there alongside us, and the trees blackened and the leaves flaked down, and some of the smaller trees began to sway. For as far ahead as we could see, our way was an alley of fires.

We ran faster, for soon things would be worse.

And we were not mistaken.

Big trees began to topple across our path. We leaped over them, we circled around them. At least, we were on a trail . . .

The heat became stifling and the breath came heavy in our lungs. Deer and wolves and foxes and rabbits darted past us, fleeing with us, ignoring our presence and that of their natural enemies. The air above the smoke seemed filled with crying birds. Their droppings fell among us, went unnoticed.

To burn this ancient wood, as venerable as the Forest of Arden, seemed almost an act of sacrilege to me. But Eric was prince in Amber, and soon to be king. I suppose I might have, too . . .

My eyebrows and hair were singed. My throat felt like a chimney. How many would this assault cost us? I wondered.

Seventy miles of wooded valley lay between us and Amber, and over thirty behind us, going back to the forest's end.

'Bleys!' I gasped. 'Two or three miles ahead of us the trail forks! The right branch comes more quickly to the river Oisen, which goes down to the sea! I think it's our one chance! The whole Valley of Garnath is going to be burned! Our only hope lies in reaching the water!'

He nodded.

We raced on, but the fires outpaced us.

We made it to the fork, though, beating out flames on our smoldering clothing, wiping ashes from our eyes, spitting such from our mouths, running hands through our hair when the flamelets nested there.

'Only about a quarter mile more,' I said.

I had been struck several times by falling boughs. All the exposed areas of my skin pulsed with a more than feverish pain, and many of the covered areas as well. We ran through burning grasses, heading down a long slope, and when we reached the bottom we saw the water, and our speed increased, though we didn't think it possible. We plunged in and let the cold wetness embrace us.

Bleys and I contrived to float as near together as possible as the currents took us and we were swept along the twisting course of the Oisen. The interlocked branches of the trees overhead had become as the beams in a cathedral of fire. As they broke apart and collapsed in places, we had to turn onto our bellies and swim or dive for the deepest places, depending on how near we were. The waters about us were filled with hissing and blackened debris, and at our backs our surviving troops' heads in the river seemed as a strip of floating coconuts.

The waters were dark and cold and our wounds began to ache, and we shivered and our teeth chattered.

It was several miles before we left the burning wood and reached the low, flat, treeless place that led on to the sea. It would be a perfect place for Julian to be waiting, with archers, I decided. I mentioned this to Bleys and he agreed, but he didn't reckon there was much we could do about it. I was forced to agree.

The woods burned all around us, and we swam and we drifted.

It seemed like hours, but must have been less, before my fears began to materialize and the first volley of arrows descended.

I dove, and I swam underwater for a long distance. Since I was going with the current, I made it quite a way along the river before I had to surface once more.

As I did, more arrows fell about me.

The gods knew how long this gauntlet of death might be drawn, but I didn't want to stick around and find out.

I gulped air and dove once more.

I touched bottom, I felt my way among rocks.

I moved along for as far as I could, then headed toward the right bank, exhaling as I rose.

I burst through the surface, gasped, took a deep breath and went down again, without sticking around to get the lay of the land.

I swam on till my lungs were bursting, and surfaced then.

This time I wasn't quite so lucky. I took an arrow through my left biceps. I managed to dive and break off the shaft when I struck bottom. Then I pulled out the head and continued on by means of the frog kick and under-body sculling with my right hand. The next time up I'd be a sitting duck, I knew.

So I forced myself on, till the red flashes crossed my eyeballs and the blackness crept into my head. I must have stayed down for three minutes.

When I surfaced this time, though, nothing happened, and I trod water and gasped.

I made my way to the left bank and grabbed hold of the trailing undergrowth.

I looked all around me. We were running short on trees at this point, and the fires hadn't gotten this far. Both banks seemed empty, but so did the river. Could I have been the only survivor? It didn't seem possible. After all, there had been so many of us when the last march began.

I was half dead with fatigue and my entire body was laced with aches and pains. Every inch of my skin seemed to have been burned, but the waters were so cold that I was shaking and probably blue. I'd have to leave the river soon, if I wanted to live. I felt I could manage a few more underwater expeditions, and I decided to chance them before departing from the sheltering depths.

Somehow I managed four more laps, and I felt then that I might not come up again if I tried a fifth. So I hung onto a rock and caught my breath, then crawled ashore.

I rolled onto my back and looked all around. I didn't recognize the locale. The fires hadn't reached it yet, though. There was a thick clump of bushes off to my right and I crawled toward it, crawled into it, fell flat on my face and went to sleep.

When I awoke, I wished I hadn't. Every inch of me ached, and I was sick. I lay there for hours, half delirious, and finally managed to stagger back to the river for a long drink of water. Then I headed back for the thicket, made it, and slept again.

I was still sore when consciousness came once more, but a little bit stronger. I walked to the river and back, and by means of my icy Trump found that Bleys was still alive.

'Where are you?' he asked, when I had made the contact.

'Damned if I know,' I replied. 'Lucky to be anywhere at all. Near the sea, though. I can hear the waves and I know the smell.'

'You're near the river?'

'Yes.'

'Which bank?

'Left, as you'd face the sea. North.'

'Then stay put,' he told me, 'and I'll send someone after you. I'm assembling our forces now. I've already got over two thousand together, and Julian won't come near us. More keep straggling in every minute.'

'Okay,' I said, and that was it.

I stayed put. I slept as I did so.

I heard them bashing about in the bushes and was alert. I pushed some fronds aside and peered forth.

It was three of the big red guys.

So I straightened my gear and brushed all my garments, ran a hand through my hair, stood erect and swayed, took several deep breaths, and stepped forth.

'I am here,' I announced.

Two of them did double-takes, blades in their hands, as I said it.

But they recovered, smiled, paid me deference, and conducted me back to the camp. It was perhaps two miles distant. I made it without leaning.

Bleys appeared and said, 'We've got over three thousand now.' Then he called for a medical officer to take care of me again.

We were undisturbed all through the night, and the rest of our troops struggled in that night and the following day.

We had perhaps five thousand by then. We could see Amber in the distance.

We slept another night and on the following morning we set forth.

By afternoon we had made maybe fifteen miles. We marched along the beach, and there was no sign of Julian anywhere.

The feeling of pain from my burns began to subside. My thigh was healthy, but my shoulder and arm still hurt from here to hell and back again.

We marched along the beach, and there was no sign of Julian anywhere.

The feeling of pain from my burns began to subside. My thigh was healthy, but my shoulder and arm still hurt from here to hell and back again.

We marched on, and soon we were within forty miles of Amber. The weather stayed clement, and all of the wood to our left was a desolate, blackened ruin. The fire had destroyed most of the timber in the valley, so for once there was a thing in our favor. Julian nor anybody else could ambush us. We'd see them coming a mile off. We made another ten miles ere the sun fell and we bivouacked on the beach.

The next day, I remembered that Eric's coronation was near at hand and I reminded Bleys. We had almost lost count of the days, but realized we still had a few remaining.

We led a speed-march till noon, then rested. By then, we were twenty-five miles away from the foot of Kolvir. By twilight, the distance was ten.

And we kept on. We marched till midnight and we bivouacked once again. By that time, I was beginning to feel fairly alive once more. I practiced a few cuts with my blade and could almost manage them. The next day, I felt even better.

We marched until we came to the foot of Kolvir, where we were met by all of Julian's forces, combined with many from Caine's fleet who now stood as foot soldiers.

Bleys stood there and called things, like Robert E. Lee at Chancellorsville, and we took them.

We had maybe three thousand men when we had finished off everything Julian had to throw against us. Julian, of course, escaped.

But we had won. There was celebration that night. We had won.

I was very afraid by then, and I made my fears known to Bleys. Three thousand men against Kolvir.

I had lost the fleet, and Bleys had lost over ninety-eight percent of his foot soldiers. I did not look upon these as rejoiceable items.

I didn't like it.

But the next day we began the ascent. There was a stairway, allowing for the men to go two abreast along it. This would narrow soon, however, forcing us to go single file.

We made it a hundred yards up Kolvir, then two, then three.

Then the storm blew in from the sea, and we held tight and were lashed by it.

Afterward, a couple of hundred men were missing.

We struggled on and the rains came down. The way grew steeper, more slippery. A quarter of the way up Kolvir we met with a column of armed men descending. The first of these traded blows with the leader of our vanguard, and two men fell. Two steps were gained, and another man fell.

This went on for over an hour, and by then we were about a third of the way up and our line was wearing back toward Bleys and myself. It was good that our big red warriors were stronger than Eric's troops. There would come a clash of arms, a cry, and a man would be brought by. Sometimes he would be red, occasionally furry, but more often he wore Eric's colors.

We made it to the halfway point, fighting for every step. Once we reached the top, there would be the broad stair of which the one to Rebma had been but an image. It would lead up to the Great Arch, which was the eastern entranceway to Amber.

Perhaps fifty of our vanguard remained. Then forty, thirty, twenty, a dozen . . .

We were about two-thirds of the way up by then, and the stair zigged and zagged its way back and forth across the face of Kolvir. The eastern stair is seldom used. It is almost a decoration. Our original plans had been to cut through the now blackened valley and then circle, climbing, and to take the western way over the mountains and enter Amber from behind. The fire and Julian had changed all this. We'd never have made it up and around. It was now a frontal assault or nothing. And it wasn't going to be nothing.

Three more of Eric's warriors fell and we gained four steps. Then our front man made the long descent and we lost one.

The breeze was sharp and cool from off the sea, and birds were collecting at the foot of the mountain. The sun broke through the clouds, as Eric apparently put aside his weathermaking now that we were engaged with his force.

We gained six steps and lost another man.

It was strange and sad and wild . . .

Bleys stood before me, and soon his turn would come. Then mine, should he perish.

Six of the vanguard remained.

Ten steps . . .

Then five remained.

We pushed on, slowly, and there was blood on every step for as far back as I could see. There's a moral there, somewhere.

The fifth man slew four before he fell himself, so bringing us to another zig, or zag, as the case may be.

Onward and upward, our third man fighting with a blade in either hand. It was good that he fought in a holy war, for there was real zeal behind each blow. He took three before he died.

The next wasn't as zealous, or as good with his blades. He fell immediately, and then there were two.

Bleys drew his long, filigreed blade, and its edge sparkled in the sun.

'Soon, brother,' he said, 'we will see what they can do against a prince.'

'Only one, I hope,' I replied, and he chuckled.

I'd say we were three-quarters of the way there when Bleys' turn finally came.

He leaped forward, immediately dislodging the first man to face him. The point of his blade found the throat of the second, and the flat of it fell alongside the head of the third, dislodging him also. He dueled a moment with the fourth and dispatched him.

My own blade was in my hand, ready, as I watched and advanced.

He was good, even better than I remembered him to be. He advanced like a whirlwind, and his blade was alive with light. They fell before it – how they fell, my friend! Whatever else you might say of Bleys, on that day he acquitted himself as became his rank. I wondered how long he could keep going.

He'd a dagger in his left hand, which he used with brutal efficiency whenever he could manage a corps à corps. He left it in the throat of his eleventh victim.

I could see no end to the column which opposed us. I decided that it must stretch all the way to the landing at the top. I hoped my turn wouldn't come. I almost believed it.

Three more men plummeted past me and we came to a small landing and a turn. He cleared the landing and began the ascent. For half an hour I watched him, and they died and they died. I could hear the murmurs of awe from the men behind me. I almost thought he could make it to the top.

He used every trick available. He baffled blades and eyes with his cloak. He tripped the warriors. He seized wrists and twisted, with his full strength.

We made it to another landing. There was some blood on his sleeve by then, but he smiled constantly, and the warriors behind the warriors he killed were ashen. This helped him, too. And perhaps the fact that I stood ready to fill the gap also contributed to their fears and so slowed them, worked on their nerves. They'd heard of the naval engagement I later learned.

Bleys worked his way to the next landing, cleared it, turned again, began to ascend. I hadn't thought he could make it that far, then. I didn't think I could make it as far as he had. It was the most phenomenal display of swordsmanship and endurance I'd seen since Benedict had held the pass above Arden against the Moonriders out of Ghenesh.

He was tiring, though, I could see that too. If only there were some way for me to relieve him, to spell him for a time . . .

But there wasn't. So I followed, fearing every stroke might be his last.

I knew that he was weakening. We were within a hundred feet of the top at that point.

I suddenly felt for him. He was my brother and he'd done well by me. I don't think he thought he'd make it then, yet he was fighting on . . . in effect, giving me my chance for the throne.

He killed three more men, and his blade moved more slowly each time. He fought with the fourth for perhaps five minutes before he took him, I was certain that the next would be his last.

He wasn't, though.

As he slew that man, I transferred my blade from my right hand to my left, drew my dagger with my right and threw it.

It went in up to the hilt, in the throat of the next man.

Bleys sprang over two steps and hamstrung the man before him, casting him downward.

Then he cut upward, ripping open the belly of the one behind that one.

I rushed to fill the gap, to be right behind him and ready. He didn't need me yet, though.

He took the next two, with a new burst of energy. I called for another dagger and one was passed to me from somewhere along the line.

I kept it really till he slowed once more, and I used it on the man he fought.

The man was lunging as it spun in, so the hilt rather than the blade caught him. It struck against his head, though, and Bleys pushed against his shoulder and he fell. But the next man leaped forward, and though he impaled himself, he struck Bleys upon the shoulder and they went over the edge together.

By reflex, almost without knowing what I was doing, yet knowing fully in one of those microsecond decisions you justify after the fact, my left hand leaped to my belt, whipped out my pack of the Trumps and cast them toward Bleys as he seemed to hang there for an instant – so rapidly did my muscles and perceptions respond – and I cried out, 'Catch them, you fool!'

And he did.

I didn't have time to see what happened next, as I parried and thrust.

Then began the final lap of our journey up Kolvir.

Let's just say I made it and was gasping, as my troops came over the edge to support me there on the landing.

We consolidated our forces and pressed ahead.

It took us an hour to reach the Great Arch.

We passed through. We entered Amber.

Wherever Eric was, I'm sure he'd never guessed we'd make it this far.

And I wondered where Bleys was? Had he gotten a chance to grab a Trump and use it, before he reached the bottom? I guessed that I'd never know.

We had underestimated, all the way around. We were outnumbered now, and the only thing left to do was to fight on for as long as we could hold out. Why had I done such a foolish thing as throw Bleys my Trumps? I knew he had none of his own and that's what had dictated my response, conditioned perhaps by my years on the Shadow Earth. But I might have used them to escape, if things went badly.

Things went badly.

We fought on until twilight, and by then there was only a small band of us remaining.

We were surrounded at a point a thousand yards within Amber, and still far from the palace. We were fighting a defensive fight, and one by one we died. We were overwhelmed.

Llewella or Deirdre would have given me sanctuary. Why had I done it?

I killed another man and put the question out of my mind.

The sun went down and darkness filled the sky. We were down to a few hundred by then, and not much closer to the palace.

Then I saw Eric and heard him shouting orders. If only I could reach him!

But I couldn't.

I'd probably have surrendered, to save my remaining troops, who had served me far too well.

But there was no one to surrender to, no one asking for a surrender. Eric couldn't even hear me if I cried out. He was out of the way, directing.

So we fought on, and I was down to a hundred men.

Let's be brief.

They killed everyone but me.

At me they threw nets and unleashed blunted arrows.

Finally, I fell and was clubbed and hog-tied, and then everything went away but a nightmare which attached itself and wouldn't let go, no matter what.

We had lost.

I awoke in a dungeon far below Amber, sorry that I had made it that far.

The fact that I still lived meant that Eric had plans for me. I visualized racks and braces, flames and tongs. I foresaw my coming degradation as I lay there on the damp straw.

How long had I been unconscious? I did not know.

I searched my cell for a means of committing suicide. I found nothing that would serve this purpose.

All my wounds blazed like suns, and I was so very tired.

I lay me down and slept once more.

I awakened, and still no one came to me. There was none to buy, none to torture.

Also, there was nothing for me to eat.

I lay there, wrapped in my cloak, and I reviewed everything that had happened since I'd awakened in Greenwood and refused my hypo. Better, perhaps, if I hadn't.

I knew despair.

Soon Eric would be crowned king in Amber. This thing might already have occurred.

But sleep was so lovely a thing, and I so tired.

It was the first real chance I'd had to rest and forget my wounds.

The cell was so dark and smelly and damp.

8

How many times I awakened and returned to sleep, I do not know. Twice I found bread and meat and water on a tray by the door. Both times, I emptied the tray. My cell was almost pitch dark and very chilly. I waited there, and I waited.

Then they came for me.

The door swung open and a feeble light entered. I blinked at it as I was called forth.

The corridor without was fitted to overflowing with armed men, so I wasn't about to try anything.

I rubbed at the stubble on my chin and went where they took me.

After a long walk, we came to the hall of the spiral stair and began to ascend. I asked no questions as we moved, and no one offered me any information.

When we reached the top, I was conducted further into the palace proper. They took me to a warm, clean room and ordered me to strip, which I did. Then I entered a steaming tub of water, and a servant came forth and scrubbed me and shaved me and trimmed my hair.

When I was dry again, I was given fresh garments, of black and of silver.

I donned them, and a black cloak was hung about my shoulders, its clasp a silver rose.

'You are ready,' said the sergeant of the guard. 'Come this way.'

I followed him, and the guard followed me.

I was taken far to the back of the palace where a smith placed manacles about my wrists, fetters on my ankles, with chains upon them too heavy for me to break. Had I resisted, I knew I would have been beaten unconscious and the result would have been the same. I had no desire to be beaten unconscious again, so I complied.

Then the chains were taken up by several of the guards, and I was led back toward the front of the palace. I had no eyes for the magnificence that lay all about me. I was a prisoner. I would probably soon be dead or on the rack. There was nothing I could do right now. A glance out of the window showed me that it was early evening, and there was no place for nostalgia as I passed through rooms where we had played as children.

I was led up a long corridor and into the great dining room.

There were tables all over the place, and people seated all about them, many of whom I knew.

All the fine gowns and suits of Amber burned about me on the bodies of the nobles, and there was music beneath the torchlight and food already upon the tables, though no one was eating yet.

I saw faces that I recognized, like Flora's, and some strange faces. There was the minstrel, Lord Rein – yes, he had been knighted, by me – whom I had not seen in centuries. He turned his eyes away when my gaze fell upon him.

I was taken to the foot of the huge center table and seated there.

The guards stayed and stood behind me. They fastened the ends of the chains to rings fresh-set in the floor. The seat at the head of my table was as yet unoccupied.

I did not recognize the woman to my right, but the man to my left was Julian. I ignored him and stared at the lady, a little wisp of a blonde.

'Good evening,' I said. 'I don't believe we've been introduced. My name is Corwin.'

She looked at the man at her right for support, a heavy, redheaded guy with lots of freckles. He looked away and suddenly became engaged in an animated conversation with the woman to his right.

'It's all right to talk with me, honest,' I said. 'It's not contagious.'

She managed a weak smile and said, 'I'm Carmel. How are you, Prince Corwin?'

'That's a sweet name,' I replied, 'and I'm just fine. What's a nice girl like you doing in a place like this?'

She took a quick drink of water.

'Corwin,' said Julian, louder than necessary. 'I think the lady finds you offensive and obnoxious.'

'What's she said to you so far this evening?' and he didn't blush. He whitened.

'That will be enough from you.'

I stretched then, and rattled my chains on purpose. Outside of the effect it produced, it also showed me how much slack I had. Not enough, of course. Eric had been careful.

'Come closer and whisper me your objections, brother,' I said.

But he didn't.

I had been the last to be seated, so I knew the time was near at hand. And it was.

There came five trumpet notes from six trumpets and Eric entered the hall.

Everybody stood.

Except for me.

The guards had to drag me to my feet by means of the chains and hold me there.

Eric smiled and descended the stair to my right. I could barely see his own colors beneath the ermine robe that he wore.

He moved to the head of the table and stood before his chair. A servant came and stood behind him, and the wine stewards made their rounds, pouring.

When all the glasses were filled, he raised his.

'May you dwell forever in Amber,' he said, 'which endureth forever,' and everyone raised his glass.

Except for me.

'Pick it up!' said Julian.

'Shove it up,' said I.

He didn't, only glared. But I leaned forward quickly then and raised my glass.

There were a couple of hundred people between us, but my voice carried. And Eric's eyes were upon me all the while, as I said, 'To Eric, who sits at the foot of the table!'

No one moved to touch me as Julian emptied his glass upon the floor. All the others did the same, but I managed to quaff most of mine, before it was struck from my hand.

Eric seated himself then and the nobles followed suit, and I was released to fall into my chair.

The serving began, and since I was hungry I ate as well as the rest of them, and better than most.

There was constant music and the meal lasted for over two hours. No one said a word to me during the whole time, and I said nothing more myself. But my presence was felt, and our table was quieter than the others.

Caine sat farther up along the table. At Eric's right hand. I gathered that Julian was out of favor. Neither Random nor Deirdre was present. There were many other nobles whom I recognized, some of whom I had once counted as friends, but none of these would return my glances.

I gathered then that it only required a small formality for Eric to be king in Amber.

And this followed shortly.

After dinner, there were no speeches. Eric simply stood.

There came another flash of trumpets and a raucous sound upon the air.

Then there was a procession, leading all the way to the throne room of Amber.

I knew what was coming next.

Eric stood before the throne and everybody bowed.

Except for me, that is, and I was forced to my knees anyway.

Today was the day of his coronation.

There was silence. Then Caine bore in the cushion which held the crown, the crown of Amber. He knelt and froze in that position, offering it.

Then I was jerked to my feet and dragged forward. I knew what was about to happen. It came upon me in a flash, and I fought. But I was beaten down and brought to my knees at the foot of the stair before the throne.

The music rose up softly – it was 'Greensleeves' – and somewhere at my back Julian said, 'Behold the crowning of a new king in Amber!' Then to me, in a whisper, 'Take up the crown and hand it to Eric. He will crown himself.'

I stared at the crown of Amber upon the crimson cushion Caine held.

It was wrought of silver and had seven high points, each topped by a gem stone. It was studded with emeralds, and there were two huge rubies at either temple.

I didn't move, thinking of the times I had seen the face of our father beneath it.

'No,' I said simply, and I felt a blow upon my left cheek.

'Take it and give it to Eric,' he repeated.

I tried to strike at him, but my chains were drawn tight I was struck again.

I stared at the high sharp peaks.

'Very well,' I finally said, and reached for it.

I held it in both hands for a moment then quickly placed it on my own head and declared, 'I crown me, Corwin, king of Amber!'

It was removed immediately and replaced upon the cushion. Several blows fell upon my back. There came a murmuring throughout the hall.

'Now pick it up and try it again,' said Julian. 'Take it and hand it to Eric.'

Another blow fell.

'Okay,' I told him, feeling my shirt grow wet.

This time I hurled it, hoping to put out one of Eric's eyes.

He caught it in his right hand and smiled down at me as I was beaten.

'Thank you,' he said. 'Now hear me, all you present, and those of you who listen in Shadow. I assume the crown and throne this day. I take into my hand the scepter of the kingdom of Amber. I have won the throne fairly, and I take it and hold it by the right of my blood.'

'Liar!' I cried, and a hand was clapped over my mouth.

'I crown myself Eric the First, King of Amber.'

'Long live the king!' cried the nobles, three times.

Then he leaned forward and whispered to me, 'Your eyes have looked upon the fairest sight they will ever behold . . . Guards! Take Corwin away to the smithy, and let his eyes be burnt from out his head! Let him remember the sights of this day as the last he might ever see! Then cast him into the darkness of the deepest dungeon beneath Amber, and let his name be forgotten!'

I spat and was beaten.

I fought every step of the way, but was taken forth from the hall. No one would look upon me as I went, and the last thing I remember was the sight of Eric seated upon his throne, pronouncing his blessing upon the nobles of Amber, and smiling.

That which he said was done to me, and mercifully I fainted before it was finished.

*

I have no idea how much later it was that I awakened within absolute blackness and felt the terrible pains within my head. Perhaps it was then that I pronounced the curse, or perhaps it had been at the time that the white-hot irons had descended. I don't remember. But I knew that Eric would never rest easy upon the throne, for the curse of a prince of Amber, pronounced in a fullness of fury, is always potent.

I clawed at the straw, in the absolute blackness of my cell, and no tears came. That was the honor of it. After a time – only you and I, gods, know how long – sleep came again.

When I awakened, there was still the pain. I rose to my feet. I measured off the dimensions of my cell. Four paces in width, five in length. There was a lavatory hole in the floor and a straw-tick mattress in a corner. The door contained a small slot at the bottom, and behind it there was a tray which held a stale piece of bread and a bottle of water. I ate and I drank, but I was not refreshed.

My head ached so, and there was nothing of peace within me.

I slept as much as I could, and no one came to see me. I awakened and crossed my cell and felt for food and ate it when I found it. I slept as much as I could.

After seven sleeps, the pain was gone from out my eye sockets. I hated my brother who was king in Amber. Better he had killed me.

I wondered at the popular reaction, but could not guess.

When the darkness reached as far as Amber, however, I knew that Eric would have his regrets. This much I knew, and this comforted me.

Thus began my days of darkness, and I had no way of measuring their passage. Even if I had had eyes, I could not have distinguished day from night in that place.

Time went on its way, ignoring me. There were occasions when I broke into a sweat over this and shivered. Had I been there months? Only hours? Or weeks? Or had it been years?

I forgot all about time. I slept, I paced (I knew exactly where to place my feet and when to turn), and I reflected upon things I had done and hadn't done. Sometimes I would sit cross-legged and breathe slowly and deeply, and empty my mind and keep it that way for as long as I could. This helped – thinking of nothing.

Eric had been clever. Although the power lived within me, now it was useless. A blind man cannot walk among Shadows.

My beard had grown down to my chest and my hair was long. I was always hungry at first, but after a time my appetite waned. Sometimes I grew dizzy when I stood up too rapidly.

I could still see, in my nightmares, but this hurt me even more when I awakened.

Later, though, I felt somewhat distant from the events which had led up to this. It was almost as though they had happened to a different person. And this, too, was true.

I had lost a lot of weight. I could visualize myself, pallid and thin. I couldn't even cry, though I felt like it a couple of times. There was something wrong with my tear ducts. It was a dreadful thing that any man should be brought to this.

Then one day there came a light scratching upon the door. I ignored it.

It came again, and still I did not respond.

Then I heard my name whispered, in the interrogative.

I crossed the cell.

'Yes?' I replied.

'It's me, Rein,' he said. 'How are you?'

I laughed at that.

'Fine! Oh just fine!' I said. 'Steak and champagne every night, and dancing girls. God! You should make the scene sometime!'

'I'm sorry,' he said, 'that there is nothing I can do for you,' and I could feel the pain in his voice.

'I know,' I said.

'I would if I could,' he told me.

'I know that, too.'

'I brought you something. Here.'

The little gate at the bottom of the cell door creaked slightly as it swung inward several times.

'What is it?' I asked.

'Some clean clothes,' he said, 'and three loaves of fresh bread, a head of cheese, some beef, two bottles of wine, a carton of cigarettes, and a lot of matches.'

My voice caught in my throat.

'Thanks, Rein. You're all right. How did you arrange this?'

'I know the guard who's standing duty this shift. He won't talk. He owes me too much.'

'He might try to cancel his debts by squealing,' I said. 'So don't do it again – much as I appreciate it. Needless to say, I'll dispose of the evidence.'

'I wish it had turned out different, Corwin.'

'You and me both. Thanks for thinking of me when you were ordered not to.'

'That part was easy,' he said.

'How long have I been in this place?'

'Four months and ten days,' he said.

'So what's new in Amber?'

'Eric reigns. That's all.'

'Where's Julian.

'Back in the Forest of Arden with his guard.'

'Why?'

'Some strange things made it through Shadow recently.'

'I see. How about Caine?'

'He's still in Amber, enjoying himself. Wenching and drinking, mostly.'

'And Gérard.'

'He's admiral of the entire fleet.'

I sighed with a bit of relief. I was afraid his withdrawal during the naval engagement might have cost him something with Eric.

'And what of Random?'

'He's up the hall aways.'

'What? He was taken?'

'Yes. He walked the Pattern in Rebma and showed up here, with a cross bow. He wounded Eric before he was taken.'

'Really? Why wasn't he slain?'

'Well, rumor has it he's married a noblewoman of Rebma. Eric didn't want to court an incident with Rebma at this point. Moire has quite a kingdom, and there is talk that Eric is even considering asking her to be his queen. All gossip, of course. But interesting.'

'Yes,' I said.

'She liked you, didn't she?'

'Somewhat. How did you hear?'

'I was present when Random was sentenced. I got to speak with him for a moment. The Lady Vialle, who claims to be his wife, has asked to join him in prison. Eric is not yet certain how to reply.'

I thought upon the blind girl, whom I had never met, and I wondered at this.

'How long ago did all this happen?' I asked.

'Mm. Thirty-four days,' he replied. 'That was when Random showed up. A week later, Vialle made her request.'

'She must be a strange woman, if she really loves Random.'

'Those were my sentiments,' he replied. 'I can't think of a more unusual combination.'

'If you should get to see him again, give him my regards and my regrets.'

'Yes.'

'How fare my sisters?'

'Deirdre and Llewella remain in Rebma. The Lady Florimel has been enjoying Eric's favors and stands high in the present court. I do not know where Fiona is presently.

'Has anything more been heard of Bleys? I am sure that he died.'

'He must have died,' said Rein. 'His body was never recovered, though.'

'What of Benedict?'

'As absent as ever.'

'How about Brand?'

'No word.'

'Then I guess that covers the whole family tree, as it stands at present. Have you written any new ballads?'

'No,' he said. 'I'm still working on "The Siege of Amber," but it will be an underground hit, if at all.'

I reached my hand out through the tiny gate at the bottom of the door.

'I would clasp hands with thee,' I said, and I felt his hand touch mine.

'It was good of thee to do this thing for me. Don't do it again, though. It would be foolish to risk Eric's wrath.'

He squeezed my hand, muttered something, and was gone.

I found his care package and stuffed myself with the meat, which was the most perishable item. I ate a lot of the bread, to accompany it, and I realized that I had almost forgotten how good good food can taste. Then I grew drowsy and slept. I don't think I slept very long, and when I awoke I opened one of the bottles of wine.

It didn't take as much as usual, in my weakened condition, to get me kind of high. I had a cigarette, sat down on my mattress, leaned back against the wall, and mused.

I remembered Rein as a child. I was already full grown by then and he was a candidate for court jester. A thin, wise kid. People had kidded him too much. Me included. But I wrote music, composed ballads, and he'd picked up a lute somewhere and had taught himself how to use it. Soon we were singing with voices together raised and all like that, and before long I took a liking to him and we worked together, practicing the martial arts. He was lousy at them, but I felt kind of sorry for the way I had treated him earlier, what with the way he had dug my stuff, so I forced the fake graces upon him and also made him a passable saber man. I'd never regretted it, and I guess he didn't either. Before long, he became minstrel to the court of Amber. I had called him my page all that while, and when the wars beckoned, against the dark things out of Shadow called Weir-monken, I made him my squire and we had ridden off to the wars together. I knighted him upon the battlefield, at Jones Falls, and he had deserved it. After that, he had gone on to become my better when it came to the ways of words and music. His colors were crimson and his words golden. I loved him, as one of my two or three friends in Amber. I didn't think he'd take the risk he had to bring me a decent meal, though. I didn't think anyone would. I had another drink and smoked another cigarette, in his name, to celebrate him. He was a good man. I wondered how long he would survive.

I threw all the butts into the head and also – eventually – the empty bottle. I didn't want anything around to show that I had been 'enjoying' myself, should a sudden inspection be held. I ate all the good food he had brought me, and I felt surfeited for the first time since I had been in durance. I saved the last bottle for one massive spell of drunkenness and forgetfulness.

And after that time had passed, I returned to my cycle of recriminations.

I hoped, mainly, that Eric had no measure of our complete powers. He was long in Amber, granted, but he didn't know everything. Not yet. Not the way Dad had known. There was a million-in-one shot that might still work in my favor. So much so, and so different that at least it served to grant me my small purchase upon sanity, there in the grip of despair.

But maybe I did go mad for a time, I don't know. There are days that are great blanks to me now, as I stand here on the brink of Chaos. God knows what they held, and I'll never see a shrink to find out.

There are none of you, good doctors, who could cope with my family anyway.

I lay there and I paced there, within the numbing darkness. I grew quite sensitive to sounds. I listened to the scurry of rats' feet through straw, the distant moaning of other prisoners, the echoes of a guard's footsteps as he approached with a tray of food. I began estimating distances and direction from things like this.

I suppose I became more sensitive to odors also, but I tried not to think about them too much. Aside from the unimaginably nauseating ones there was, for a long while, what I would swear to be the odor of decaying flesh. I wondered. If I were to die, how long would it be before someone took notice? How many chunks of bread and bowls of slop would go uneaten before the guard thought to check within after my continued existence?

The answer to that one could be very important.

The death odor was around for a long while. I tried to think in terms of time again, and it seemed that it persisted for over a week.

Though I rationed myself carefully, resisting the compulsion, the handy temptation, for as long as I could, I finally found myself down to my final pack of cigarettes.

I tore it open and lit one. I had had a carton of Salems and I had smoked eleven packs. That was two hundred and twenty cigarettes. I had once timed myself with one, and it had taken me seven minutes to smoke it. That made for a total of one thousand five hundred and forty minutes spent smoking, or twenty-five hours and forty minutes. I was sure I had spent at least an hour between cigarettes, more like an hour and a half. Say an hour and a half. Now figure that I was sleeping six to eight hours per day. That left sixteen to eighteen waking hours. I guessed I was smoking ten or twelve per day. So that meant maybe three weeks had passed since Rein's visit. He had told me it was four months and ten days since the coronation, which meant that it was now around five months.

I nursed my last pack, enjoying each one like a love affair. When they were all gone, I felt depressed.

Then a lot more time must have passed.

I got to wondering about Eric. How was he making out as liege? What problems was he encountering? What was he up to right now? Why hadn't he been around to torment me? Could I ever truly be forgotten in Amber, even by imperial decree? Never, I decided.

And what of my brothers? Why had none of them contacted me? It would be so easy to draw forth my Trump and break Eric's decree.

No one did, though.

I thought for a long while upon Moire, the last woman I had loved. What was she doing? Did she think of me ever? Probably not. Maybe she was Eric's mistress by now, or his queen. Did she ever speak to him of me? Again, probably not.

And what of my sisters? Forget it. Bitches all, they.

I had been blinded once before, by a cannon flashback in the eighteenth century on the Shadow Earth. But it had only lasted for around a month and my sight had returned. Eric had had a permanent thing in mind, however, when he had given his order. I still perspired and shuddered, and sometimes woke up screaming, whenever memory of the white-hot irons returned to me – hung there before my eyes – and then the contact!

I moaned softly and continued to pace.

There was absolutely nothing I could do. That was the most horrible part of the whole thing. I was as helpless as an embryo. To be born again into sight and fury was a thing for which I would give my soul. Even for an hour, with a blade in my hand, to duel once again with my brother.

I lay back on my mat and slept. When I awakened, there was food, and I ate once again and paced. My fingernails and my toenails had grown long. My beard was very long and my hair fell across my eyes, constantly. I felt filthy, and I itched all the time. I wondered whether I had fleas.

That a prince of Amber could be brought to this state drew a terrible emotion from the center of my being, wherever that may be. I had been reared to think of us as invincible entities, clean and cool and diamond-hard, like our pictures on the Trumps. Obviously, we were not.

At least, we were enough like other men to have our resources.

I played mental games, I told myself stories, I reviewed pleasant memories – there were many of these. I recalled the elements: wind, rain, snow, the summer's warmth, and the spring's cool breezes. I had had a small airplane on the Shadow Earth, and when I flew it I had enjoyed the sensation. I recalled the glistening panoramas of color and distance, the miniaturization of cities, the broad blue sweep of sky, the herds of clouds (where were they now?) and the clean expanse of the ocean beneath my wings. I remembered women I had loved, parties, military engagements. And when all was done, and I could help it no longer, I thought of Amber.

One time, when I did so, my tear glands began to function again. I wept.

After an interminable time, a time filled with blackness and many sleeps, I heard footsteps which paused before the door to my cell, and I heard the sound of a key within the lock.

It was a time so long after Rein's visit that I had forgotten the taste of the wine and the cigarettes. I could not really estimate its span, but it had been long.

There were two men in the corridor. I could tell his from their footsteps even before I heard the sounds of their voices.

One of the voices I recognized.

The door swung open and Julian said my name.

I didn't answer right away, and he repeated it.

'Corwin? Come here.'

Since I didn't have much choice in the matter, I drew myself erect and advanced. I stopped when I knew I was near him.

'What do you want?' I asked.

'Come with me.' And he took my arm.

We walked along the corridor, and he said nothing and I'd be damned if I'd ask him any questions.

From the echoes, I could tell when we entered the big hall. Soon after, he guided me up the stair.

Up, and into the palace proper we went.

I was taken to a room and seated in a chair. A barber set to work cutting my hair and my beard. I didn't recognize his voice when he asked me if I wanted the beard trimmed or removed.

'Cut it off,' I said, and a manicurist set to work on my nails, all twenty of them.

Then I was bathed, and someone helped me to dress in clean garments. They hung loose on me. I was deloused also, but forget that.

Then I was led into another black place filled with music and the odors of good food and the sounds of many voices and some laughter. I recognized it to be the dining room.

The voices subsided a bit as Julian led me in and seated me.

I sat there until the trumpet notes, to which I was forced to rise.

I heard the toast called out:

'To Eric the First, King of Amber! Long live the king!'

I didn't drink to that, but no one seemed to notice. It was Caine's voice that had called out the toast, from far up along the table.

I ate as much as I could, because it was the best meal I had been offered since the coronation. I gathered from conversation overheard that today was the anniversary of Eric's coronation, which meant I had spent an entire year in the dungeons.

No one spoke to me, and I didn't make any overtures. I was present as a ghost only. To humiliate me, and to serve as a reminder to my brothers, no doubt, as to the price of defying our liege. And everyone had been ordered to forget me.

It went on well into the night. Someone kept me well provided with wine, which was something, and I sat there and listened to the music of all the dances.

The tables had been removed by this time, and I was seated off somewhere in a corner.

I got stinking drunk and was half dragged, half carried back to my cell in the morning, when the whole thing was over save for the cleaning up. My only regret was that I hadn't gotten sick enough to dirty the floor or someone's pretty garments.

Thus ended the first year of darkness.

9

I shall not bore you with repetition. My second year was pretty much like my first, with the same finale. Ditto for the third. Rein came twice that second year, with a basket of goodies and a mouthful of gossip. Both times I forbade him ever to come again. The third year he came down six times, every other month, and each time I forbade him anew and ate his food and heard what he had to say.

Something was wrong in Amber. Strange *things* walked through Shadow and presented themselves, with violence, to all and sundry. They were destroyed, of course. Eric was still trying to figure out how they had occurred. I did not mention my curse, though I later rejoiced in the fact that it had come to pass.

Random, like myself, was still a prisoner. His wife *had* joined him. The positions of my brothers and sisters remained unchanged. This bolstered me through the third anniversary of the coronation, and it made me feel almost alive again.

It . . .

It! One day it was there, and it made me feel so good that I immediately broke out the final bottle of wine Rein had brought me and opened the last pack of cigarettes, which I had been saving.

I smoked them and sipped and enjoyed the feeling that I had somehow beaten Eric. If he found this out, I felt it might be fatal. But I knew he didn't know.

So I rejoiced, smoking, drinking and reveling in the light of that which had occurred.

Yes, the *light*.

I'd discovered a tiny patch of brightness, off somewhere to my right.

Do you know what that meant to me?

Well, let's take it like this: I had awakened in a hospital bed and learned that I had recovered all too soon. Dig?

I heal faster than others who have been broken. All the lords and ladies of Amber have something of this capacity.

I'd lived through the Plague, I'd lived through the march on Moscow . . .

I regenerate faster and better than anybody I've ever known.

Napoleon had once made a remark about it. So had General Mac-Arthur.

With nerve tissue it takes me a bit longer, that's all.

My sight was returning to me, that's what it meant – that lovely patch of brightness, off somewhere to my right.

After a time, I knew that it was the little barred area in the door to my cell.

I had grown new eyes, my fingers told me. It had taken me over three years, but I had done it. It was the billion-in-one thing I spoke of earlier, the thing which even Eric could not properly assess, because of the variances of powers among the individual members of the family. I had beaten him to this extent: I had learned that I could grow new eyeballs. I had always known that I could regenerate nerve tissues, given sufficient time. I had been left paraplegic from a spine injury received during the Franco-Prussian wars. After two years, it had gone away. I had had my hope – a wild one, I'll admit – that I could do what I had done then, with my burned-out orbs. And I had been right. They felt intact, and the sight was returning, slowly.

How long till the next anniversary of Eric's coronation? I stopped pacing and my heart beat faster. As soon as someone saw that I'd recovered my eyes, I'd lose them again.

Therefore, I'd have to escape before the four years had passed.

How?

I hadn't thought about it much up to this time, because even if I could figure a way to get out of my cell, I'd never make it out of Amber – or out of the palace, for that matter – without eyes or aid, and neither were available to me.

Now, though . . .

The door of my cell was a big, heavy, brass-bound thing, with only a tiny grille at a height of about five feet for purposes of looking in to see whether I was still alive, if anyone cared. Even if I succeeded in removing it, I could tell that I couldn't reach out far enough to touch the lock. There was a little swinging gate at the bottom of the door, large enough to push my food through and that's about all. The hinges were either on the outside or in between the door and the jamb, I couldn't tell for sure. Either way, I couldn't get at them. There were no windows and no other doors.

It was still almost like being blind, save for that feeble reassuring light through the grille. I knew my sight hadn't returned fully. That was still a long way off. But even if it had, it was nearly pitch dark in there. I knew this because I knew the dungeons under Amber.

I lit a cigarette, paced some more, and assessed my possessions, seeking anything that might be of aid. There was my clothing, my sleeping mat, and all the damp straw I wanted. I also had matches, but I quickly rejected the notion of setting fire to the straw. I doubted anyone would come and open the door if I did. Most likely the guard would come and laugh, if he came at all. I had a spoon I'd picked up at the last banquet. I'd wanted a knife, really, but Julian had caught me trying to lift one and snatched it away. What he didn't know, though, was that that was my second attempt. I already had the spoon tucked inside my boot.

So what good was it?

I'd heard these stories of guys digging their way out of cells with the damnedest things – belt buckles (which I didn't have) – etc. But I didn't have time to try the Count of Monte Cristo bit. I needed out in a matter of months, or my new eyes wouldn't mean anything.

The door was mainly wood. Oak. It was bound with four metal strips. One went around it near the top, one near the bottom, right above the gate, and there were two which ran from top to bottom, passing along either side of the foot-wide grille. The door opened outward, I knew, and the lock was to my left. My memories told me the door was about two inches thick, and I recalled the approximate position of the lock, which I verified by leaning against the door and feeling the tension at that point. I knew that the door was also barred, but I could worry about that later. I might be able to raise it by sliding the handle of the spoon upward between the door's edge and the jamb.

I knelt on my sleeping mat and with the spoon I traced a box about that area which contained the lock. I worked until my hand was quite sore – maybe a couple of hours. Then I ran my fingernail over the surface of the wood. I hadn't scarred it much, but it was a beginning. I switched the spoon to my left hand and continued until it, too, began to ache.

I kept hoping that Rein would show up. I was sure I could talk him into giving me his dagger if I really pressed the matter. He didn't put in an appearance, though, so I just kept grinding away.

Day after day I worked, until I was perhaps half an inch into the wood. Each time I'd hear a guard's footsteps I'd move the pallet back to the far wall and lie on it with my back to the door. When he had passed, I'd resume work. Then I had to stop for a while, as much as I hated to. Even though I had wrapped them in cloth torn from my garments, my hands had blistered and the blisters had broken, and after a time the raw flesh underneath began to bleed. So I took a break to let them heal. I decided to devote the time to planning what I'd do after I got out.

When I'd worked my way far enough through the door, I'd raise the bar. The sound of it falling would probably bring a guard. By then, though, I'd be out. A couple of good kicks would break out the piece I was working on and the lock could stay right where it was if it wanted to. The door would swing open then and I would face the guard. He would be armed and I wouldn't. I'd have to take him.

He might be overconfident, thinking I couldn't see. On the other hand, he might be a bit afraid, if he recalled how I had entered into Amber. Either way he would die and I would then be armed. I gripped my right biceps with my left hand and my fingertips touched. Gods! I was emaciated. Whatever, I was of the blood of Amber, and I felt that even in that condition I could take any ordinary man. Maybe I was kidding myself, but I'd have to try it.

Then if I succeeded, with a blade in my hand, nothing could keep me from reaching the Pattern. I'd walk it, and when I made it to the center, I could transport myself to any Shadow world I chose. There I would recuperate, and this time I would not rush things. If it took me a century, I'd have everything letter-perfect before I moved against Amber again. After all, I was technically its liege. Hadn't I crowned myself in the presence of all, before Eric had done the same? I'd make good my claim to the throne!

If only it weren't impossible to walk into Shadow from Amber itself! Then I wouldn't have to fool around with the Pattern. But my Amber is the center of all, and you just don't depart it that easily.

After, say, a month my hands had healed and I was developing large callouses from my scraping activities. I heard a guard's footsteps and removed myself to the far side of the cell. There was a brief creak and my meal was slipped beneath the door. Then there were footsteps again, this time diminishing in the distance.

I returned to the door. Without looking, I knew what was on the tray: a chunk of stale bread, a crock of water, and a piece of cheese if I was lucky. I positioned the mat, knelt on it and felt at the groove. I was about halfway through.

Then I heard the chuckle.

It came from behind me.

I turned, not needing eyes to tell me that someone else was present. There was a man standing near the left wall, giggling.

'Who is it?' I asked, and my voice sounded strange. I realized then that these were the first words I had spoken in a long while.

'Escape,' he said. 'Trying to escape.' And he chuckled again.

'How did you get in here?'

'Walked,' he replied.

'From where? How?'

I struck a match and it hurt my eyes, but I held it.

He was a small man. Tiny, might be an even better word. He was around five feet tall and a hunchback. His hair and beard were as heavy as my own. The only distinguishing features in that great mass of fur were his long, hook nose and his almost black eyes, now squinted against the light.

'Dworkin! I said.

He chuckled again.

'That's my name. What's yours?'

'Don't you know me, Dworkin?' I struck another match and held it near my face. 'Look hard. Forget the beard and the hair. Add a hundred pounds to my frame. You drew me, in exquisite detail, on several packs of playing cards.'

'Corwin,' he said at last 'I remember you. Yes.'

'I had thought you were dead.'

'I'm not, though. See?' and he pirouetted before me. 'How is your father? Have you seen him recently? Did he put you here?'

'Oberon is no more,' I replied. 'My brother Eric reigns in Amber, and I am his prisoner.'

'Then I have seniority,' he told me, 'for I am Oberon's prisoner.'

'Oh? None of us knew that Dad had locked you up.'

I heard him weeping.

'Yes,' he said after a time. 'He didn't trust me.'

'Why not?'

'I told him I'd thought of a way to destroy Amber. I described it to him, and he locked me in.'

'That wasn't very nice,' I said.

'I know,' he agreed, 'but be did give me a pretty apartment and lots of things to do research with. Only he stopped coming to visit me after a time. He used to bring men who showed me splotches of ink and made me tell stories about them. That was fun, until I told a story I didn't like and turned the man into a frog. The king was angry when I wouldn't turn him back, and it's been so long since I've seen anybody that I'd even turn him back now, if he still wanted me to. Once—'

'How did you get here, into my cell?' I asked again.

'I told you. I walked.'

'Through the wall?'

'Of course not. Through the Shadow wall.'

'No man can walk through Shadows in Amber. There are no Shadows in Amber.'

'Well, I cheated,' he admitted.

'How?'

'I designed a new Trump and stepped through it, to see what was on this side of the wall. Oh my! – I just remembered . . . I can't get back without it. I'll have to make another. Have you got anything to eat? And something to draw with? And something to draw on?'

'Have a piece of bread,' I said, and handed it to him, 'and here's a piece of cheese to go along with it.'

'Thank you, Corwin,' and he wolfed them down and drank all my water afterward. 'Now, if you'll give me a pen and a piece of parchment, I'll be returning to my own rooms. I want to finish a book I was reading. It's been nice talking to you. Too bad about Eric, I'll stop back again some time and we'll talk some more. If you see your father, please tell him not to be angry with me because I'll—'

'I don't have a pen, or parchment,' I observed.

'Goodness,' he said, 'that's hardly civilized.'

'I know. But then, Eric isn't very.'

'Well, what have you got? I prefer my own apartment to this place. At least, it's better lighted.'

'You have dined with me,' I said, 'and now I am going to ask you a favor. If you will grant me this respect, I promise that I will do everything I can to make things right between you and Dad.'

'What is it that you want?' he asked.

'Long have I admired your work,' I said, 'and there is something I have always desired as a work of your hand. Do you recall the Lighthouse of Cabra?'

'Of course. I've been there many times. I know the keeper, Jopin. I used to play chess with him.'

'More than anything else I can think of,' I told him, 'for most of my adult life, I have longed to see one of your magical sketches of that great gray tower.'

'A very simple subject,' he said, 'and rather an appealing one, at that. I did some preliminary sketches in the past, but I never got beyond that point. Other work kept getting in the way. I'll fetch you one, if you'd like.'

'No,' I said. 'I'd like something more enduring, to keep me company here in my cell – to comfort me, and any others who may later occupy this place.'

'Commendable,' he said. 'What have you in mind as the medium.'

'I have a stylus here,' I told him (the spoon was fairly sharp by then), 'and I'd like to see it traced upon the far wall, so that I might look at it as I take my rest.'

He was silent a moment, then, 'The illumination is quite poor,' he remarked.

'I have several books of matches,' I replied. 'I'll light them and hold them for you. We might even burn some of this straw if we run low.'

'Those are hardly ideal working conditions . . .'

'I know,' I said, 'and I apologize for them, great Dworkin, but they are the best I have to offer. A work of art by your hand would brighten my humble existence beyond measure.'

He chuckled again.

'Very well. But you must promise me that you will provide light afterwards, so that I may sketch myself a way back to my own chambers.'

'Agreed,' I said, and I felt in my pocket.

I had three full packages of matches and part of a fourth.

I pressed the spoon into his hand and led him to the wall.

'Do you have the feel of the instrument?' I asked him.

'Yes, it's a sharpened spoon, isn't it?'

'Yes. I'll make a light as soon as you say you are ready. You'll have to sketch rapidly, because my supply of matches is limited. I'll allot half for the lighthouse and the other half for your own business.'

'All right,' he said, and I struck a match and he began to trace lines upon the moist gray wall.

First he did an upright rectangle to frame and contain the thing. Then with several deft strokes, the lighthouse began to appear. It was amazing, daft as he was, his skill was intact. I held each match at its barest base, spat on my left thumb and forefinger, and when I could hold it no longer in my right I took hold of the blackened end and inverted it, letting the match burn away completely before I struck another.

When the first book of matches was gone, he had finished the tower and was working on the sea and sky. I encouraged him, I murmured appreciation at every stroke.

'Great, really great,' I said, when it appeared to be almost finished. Then he made me waste another match while he signed it. I was almost through the second book by then.

'Now let's admire it,' he said.

'If you want to get back to your own apartments, you'll have to leave the admiring to me,' I told him. 'We're too low on matches to be art critics at this point.'

He pouted a bit, but moved to the other wall and began sketching as soon as I struck a light.

He sketched a tiny study, a skull on the desk, a globe beside it, walls full of books all around.

'Now that's good,' he said, when I had finished the third pack and was starting on the remaining partial pack.

It took him six more to finish up and one to sign it.

He gazed at it while the eighth match burned – there were only two remaining – then he took a step forward and was gone.

The match was burning my fingertips by then and I dropped it and it sizzled when it hit the straw and went out.

I stood there shaking, full of mixed feelings, and then I heard his voice and felt his presence at my side. He was back again.

'I just thought of something,' he said. 'How can you see the picture when it's so dark in here?'

'Oh. I can see in the dark,' I told him. 'I've lived with it so long that it has become my friend.'

'I see. I just wondered. Give me a light so I can go back now.'

'Very well,' I agreed, considering my second to last match. 'But you'd better bring your own illumination next time you stop around. I'll be out of matches after this.'

'All right.' And I struck a light and he considered his drawing, walked toward it, and vanished once more.

I turned quickly and considered the Lighthouse of Cabra before the match failed. Yes, the power was there. I could feel it.

Would my final match serve me, though?

No, I didn't think it would. A longer period of concentration than that was required for me to use a Trump as a gateway.

What could I burn? The straw was too damp and might not take fire. It would be horrible to have the gateway – my road to freedom – right there with me and not be able to use it.

I needed a flame that would last awhile.

My sleeping roll! It was a cloth liner stuffed with straw. That straw would be drier, and the cloth would burn, too.

I cleared half the floor, down to the bare stone. Then I sought the sharpened spoon, to use to cut the liner. I cursed then. Dworkin had carried it off with him.

I twisted and tore at the thing.

Finally, it came open and I pulled out the dry straw from the middle. I made a little heap of it and I set the liner nearby, to use as extra fuel if I needed it. The less smoke the better though. It would attract attention if a guard passed this way. This wasn't too likely, though, since I had just recently been fed, and I got one meal a day.

I struck my last match, then used it to set fire to the cardboard book that had contained it. When this got going. I used it on the straw.

It almost didn't take. The straw was damper than I'd thought, even though it came from the center of my mat. But finally there was a glow, and then a flame. It took two of the other empty matchbooks to achieve this, so I was glad I hadn't thrown them down the john.

I tossed on the third, held the liner in my left hand, and stood and faced the drawing.

The glow spread up the wall as the flames danced higher, and I concentrated on the tower and recalled it. I thought I heard the cry of a gull. I sniffed something like a salt breeze, and the place became more real as I stared.

I tossed the liner onto the fire, and the flames subsided for a moment, then sprang higher. I didn't remove my eyes from the drawing as I did this.

The magic was still there, in Dworkin's hand, for soon the lighthouse seemed as real to me as my cell. Then it seemed the only reality, and the cell but a Shadow at my back. I heard the splashing of the waves and felt something like the afternoon sun upon me.

I stepped forward, but my foot did not descend into the fire.

I stood upon the sandy, rock-strewn edge of the small island Cabra, which held the great gray lighthouse that lit a path for the ships of Amber by night. A flock of frightened gulls wheeled and screamed about me, and my laughter was one with the booming of the surf and the free song of the wind. Amber lay forty-three miles behind my left shoulder.

I had escaped.

10

I made my way to the lighthouse and climbed the stone stair that led to the door on its western face. It was high, wide, heavy, and watertight. Also, it was locked. There was a small quay about three hundred yards behind me. Two boats were moored at it. One was a row-boat and the other was a sailboat with a cabin. They swayed gently, and beneath the sun the water was mica behind them. I paused for a moment to regard them. It had been so long since I had seen anything that for an instant they seemed more than real, and I caught a sob within my throat and swallowed it.

I turned and knocked on the door.

After what seemed too long a wait, I knocked again.

Finally, I heard a noise within and the door swung open, creaking on its three dark hinges.

Jopin, the keeper, regarded me through bloodshot eyes and I smelled whisky upon his breath. He was about five and a half feet tall and so stooped that he reminded me somewhat of Dworkin. His beard was as long as mine, so of course it seemed longer, and it was the color of smoke, save for a few yellow stains near his dry-looking lips. His skin was as porous as an orange rind and the elements had darkened it to resemble a fine old piece of furniture. His dark eyes squinted, focused. As with many people who are hard of hearing, he spoke rather loudly.

'Who are you? What do you want?' he asked.

If I was that unrecognizable in my emaciated, hairy condition, I decided that I might as well maintain my anonymity.

'I am a traveler from the south and I was shipwrecked recently,' I said. 'I clung to a piece of wood for many days and was finally washed ashore here. I slept on the beach all morning. It was only recently that I recovered sufficient strength to walk to your light-house.'

He moved forward and took my arm. He threw his other arm around my shoulders.

'Come in, come in then,' he said. 'Lean on me. Take it easy. Come this way.'

He led me to his quarters, which were extraordinarily messy, being strewn with many old books, charts, maps, and pieces of nautical equipment. He wasn't any too steady himself, so I didn't lean too hard, just enough to maintain the impression of weakness I had tried to convey as I'd leaned against his doorframe.

He led me to a daybed, suggested I lie down, and left to secure the door and fetch me something to eat.

I removed my boots, but my feet were so filthy that I put them back on again. If I'd been drifting about very long, I wouldn't be dirty. I didn't want to give away my story, so I drew a blanket that was there over me and leaned back, really resting.

Jopin returned shortly with a pitcher of water, a pitcher of beer, a great slice of beef, and half a loaf of bread upon a square wooden tray. He swept clear the top of a small table, which he then kicked into a position beside the couch. The he set the tray down on it and bade me eat and drink.

I did. I stuffed myself. I glutted myself. I ate everything in sight. I emptied both pitchers.

Then I felt tremendously tired. Jopin nodded when he saw it come over me, and he told me to go to sleep. Before I knew it, I had.

When I awakened, it was night time and I felt considerably better than I had in many weeks. I got to my feet and retraced my earlier route and departed the building. It was chilly out there, but the sky was crystal clear and there seemed to be a million stars. The lens at the top of the tower blazed at my back, then went dark, blazed, then went dark. The water was cold, but I just had to cleanse myself. I bathed and washed my clothing and wrung it out. I must have spent an hour doing that. Then I went back to the lighthouse, hung my clothing over the back of an old chair to dry out, crawled beneath the blanket, slept again.

In the morning, when I awoke, Jopin was already up. He prepared me a hearty breakfast, and I treated it the same way as I had the dinner of the previous evening. Then I borrowed a razor, a mirror, and a pair of scissors and gave myself a shave and a sort of haircut. I bathed again afterward, and when I donned my salty, stiff, clean garments I felt almost human again.

Jopin stared at me when I returned from the sea and said, 'You look kinda familiar, fella,' and I shrugged.

'Now tell me about your wreck.'

So I did. Out of whole cloth. What a disaster I detailed! Down to the snapping of the mainmast, yet.

He patted me on the shoulder and poured me a drink. He lit the cigar he had given me.

'You just rest easy here,' he told me. 'I'll take you ashore any time you like, or I'll signal you a passing ship if you see one you recognize.'

I took him up on his offered hospitality. It was too much of a lifesaver not to. I ate his food and drank his drinks and let him give me a clean shirt which was too big for him. It had belonged to a friend of his who'd drowned at sea.

I stayed with him for three months, as I recovered my strength. I helped him around the place – tending the light on nights when he felt like getting smashed, and cleaning up all the rooms in the house – even to the extent of painting two of them and replacing five cracked windowpanes – and watching the sea with him on stormy nights.

He was apolitical, I learned. He didn't care who reigned in Amber. So far as he was concerned, the whole bloody crew of us was rotten. So long as he could tend his lighthouse and eat and drink of good food and brew, and consider his nautical charts in peace, he didn't give half a damn what happened ashore. I came to be rather fond of him, and since I knew something of old charts and maps also, we spent many a good evening correcting a few. I had sailed far into the north many years ago, and I gave him a new chart based on my recollections of the voyage. This seemed to please him immensely, as did my descriptions of those waters.

'Corey,' (that was how I'd named myself,) 'I'd like to sail with you one day,' he said. 'I hadn't realized you were skipper of your own vessel one time.'

'Who knows?' I told him. 'You were once a captain yourself, weren't you?'

'How'd you know?' he asked.

Actually, I'd remembered, but I gestured about me in reply.

'All these things you've collected,' I said, 'and your fondness for the charts. Also, you bear yourself like a man who once held a command.'

He smiled.

'Yes,' he told me, 'that's true. I had a command for over a hundred years. That seems long ago . . . Let's have another drink.'

I sipped mine and sort of put it aside. I must have gained over forty pounds in the months I had spent with him. Any day now, I was expecting him to recognize me as a member of the family. Maybe he would turn me in to Eric if he did – and maybe not. Now that we'd established this much of camaraderie, I had a feeling that he might not do it. I didn't want to take the chance and find out.

Sometimes as I sat tending the light I wondered, 'How long should I stay here?'

Not too much longer, I decided, adding a drop of grease to a swivel bearing. Not much longer at all. The time was drawing near when I should take to the road and walk among Shadows once again.

Then one day I felt the pressure, gentle and questing at first. I couldn't tell for sure who it was.

I immediately stood stock still, closed my eyes and made my mind go blank. It was about five minutes before the questing presence withdrew.

I paced then and wondered, and I smiled when I realized the shortness of my course. Unconsciously, I had been pacing out the dimensions of my cell back in Amber.

Someone had just tried to reach me, via my Trump. Was it Eric? Had he finally become aware of my absence and decided to try locating me in his manner? I wasn't sure. I felt that he might fear mental contact with me again. Julian, then? Or Gérard? Caine? Whoever it had been, I had closed him out completely, I knew that. And I would refuse such contact with any of my family. I might be missing some important news or a helpful call, but I couldn't afford to take the chance. The attempted contact and my blocking efforts left me with a chill. I shuddered. I thought about the thing all the rest of the day and decided that the time had come for me to move on. It wouldn't do for me to remain this close to Amber while I was so vulnerable. I had recovered sufficiently to make my way among Shadows, to seek for the place where I had to go if Amber were ever to be mine. I had been lulled into something close to peace by old Jopin's ministrations. It would be a pain to leave him, for in the months of our association I had come to like the old guy. So that evening, after we'd finished a game of chess, I told him of my plans to depart.

He poured us two drinks then raised his and said, 'Good luck to you, Corwin. I hope to see you again one day.'

I didn't question the fact that he had called me by my proper name, and he smiled as he realized that I hadn't let it slip by.

'You've been all right, Jopin,' I told him. 'If I should succeed in what I'm about to try, I won't forget what you did for me.'

He shook his head.

'I don't want anything,' he said. 'I'm happy right where I am, doing exactly what I'm doing. I enjoy running this damned tower. It's my whole life. If you should succeed in whatever you're about – no, don't tell me about it, please! I don't want to know! – I'll be hoping you'll stop around for a game of chess sometime.'

'I will,' I promised.

'You can take the *Butterfly* in the morning, if you'd like.'

'Thanks.'

The *Butterfly* was his sailboat.

'Before you go,' he said, 'I suggest you take my spyglass, climb the tower, and look back on the Vale of Garnath.'

'What's there to see?'

He shrugged.

'You'll have to make up your own mind about that.'

I nodded.

'Okay, I will.'

We then proceeded to get pleasantly high and turned in for the night. I'd miss old Jopin. With the exception of Rein, he was the only friend I'd found since my return. I wondered vaguely about the valley which had been a sheet of flame the last time I had crossed it. What could it be that was so unusual about it now, these four years later?

Troubled by dreams of werewolves and Sabbats, I slept, and the full moon rose above the world.

At the crack of dawn I did the same. Jopin was still sleeping, which was good, because I don't really like to say good-bye, and I had a funny feeling that I would never see him again.

I climbed the tower to the room that housed the big light, spyglass at my side. I moved to the window facing the shore and focused on the valley.

There was a mist hanging above the wood. It was a cold, gray, wet-looking thing that clung to the tops of the small, gnarly trees. The trees were dark, and their branches twisted together like the fingers of wrestling hands. Dark things darted among them, and from the patterns of their flight I knew they were not birds. Bats, probably. There was something evil present in that great wood, I knew, and then I recognized it. It was myself.

I had done this thing with my curse. I had transformed the peaceful Valley of Garnath into what it now represented: it was a symbol of my hate for Eric and for all those others who had stood by and let him get away with his power grab, let him blind me. I didn't like the looks of that forest, and as I stared at it I realized how my hate had objectified itself. I knew it because it was a part of me.

I had created a new entranceway into the real world. Garnath was now a pathway through Shadows. Shadows dark and grim. Only the dangerous, the malicious might walk that pathway. This was the source of the *things* Rein had mentioned, the things that troubled Eric. Good in a way – if they kept him occupied. But as I swung the glass, I couldn't escape the feeling that I had done a very bad thing indeed. At the time, I'd had no idea that I'd ever see the light of day's bright skies again. Now that I did, I realized that I'd unleashed a thing that would take an awful lot of undoing. Even now, strange shapes seemed to move within that place. I had done a thing which had never been done before, not during the whole of Oberon's reign: I had opened a new way to Amber. And I had opened it only to the worst. A day would come when the liege of Amber – whoever he might be – would be faced with the problem of closing that dreadful way. I knew this as I stared, realizing the thing to be a product of my own pain, anger, and hate. If I won out in Amber one day, I might have to cope with my own handiwork, which is always a devilish dung to attempt. I lowered the glass and sighed.

So be it, I decided. In the meantime, it would give Eric something to have insomnia over.

I grabbed a quick bite to eat, outfitted the *Butterfly* as rapidly as I could, hoisted some canvas, cast off, and set sail. Jopin was usually up by that hour, but maybe he didn't like good-byes either.

I headed her out to sea, knowing where I was going but not really certain how to get there. I'd be sailing through Shadow and strange waters, but it would be better than the overland route, what with my handiwork abroad in the realm.

I had set sail for a land near as sparkling as Amber itself, an almost immortal place, a place that did not really exist, not any longer. It was a place which had vanished into Chaos ages ago, but of which a Shadow must somewhere survive. All I had to do was find it, recognize it, and make it mine once again, as it had been in days long gone by. Then, with my own forces to back me up, I would do another thing Amber had never known. I didn't know how yet, but I promised myself that guns would blaze within the immortal city on the day of my return.

As I sailed into Shadow, a white bird of my desire came and sat upon my right shoulder, and I wrote a note and tied it to its leg and sent it on its way. The note said, 'I am coming,' and it was signed by me.

I would never rest until I held vengeance and the throne within my hand, and good night sweet prince to anybody who stood between me and these things.

The sun hung on my left and the winds bellied the sails and propelled me onward. I cursed once and then laughed.

I was free and I was running, but I had made it this far. I now had the chance I'd wanted all along.

A black bird of my desire came and sat on my left shoulder, and I wrote a note and tied it to its leg and sent it off into the west.

It said, 'Eric – I'll be back,' and it was signed: 'Corwin, Lord of Amber.'

A demon wind propelled me east of the sun.

THE GUNS OF AVALON

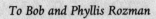

To Bob and Phyllis Rozman

1

I stood there on the beach and said, 'Good-bye, *Butterfly*,' and the ship slowly turned, then headed out toward deep water. It would make it back into port at the lighthouse of Cabra, I knew, for that place lay near to Shadow.

Turning away, I regarded the black line of trees near at hand, knowing that a long walk lay ahead of me. I moved in that direction, making the necessary adjustments as I advanced. A pre-dawn chill lay upon the silent forest, and this was good.

I was perhaps fifty pounds underweight and still occasionally experienced double vision, but I was improving. I had escaped the dungeons of Amber and recuperated somewhat, with the assistance of mad Dworkin and drunken Jopin, in that order. Now I had to find me a place, a place resembling another place – one which no longer existed. I located the path. I took it.

After a time, I stopped at a hollow tree that had to be there. I reached inside and drew forth my silvered blade and strapped it to my waist. It mattered not that it had been somewhere in Amber. It was here now, for the wood that I walked was in Shadow.

I continued for several hours, the unseen sun somewhere behind my left shoulder. Then I rested awhile, then moved on. It was good to see the leaves and the rocks and the dead tree trunks, the live ones, the grass, the dark earth. It was good to smell all the little smells of life, and to hear its buzzing/humming/chirping sounds. Gods! How I treasured my eyes! Having them back again after nearly four years of blackness was a thing for which I lacked words. And to be walking free . . .

I went on, my tattered cloak flapping in the morning breeze. I must have looked over fifty years old, my face creased, my form sparse, lean. Who would have known me for what I was?

As I walked, walked in Shadow, moved toward a place, I did not reach that place. It must be that I had grown somewhat soft. Here is what happened—

I came upon seven men by the side of the road, and six of them were dead, lying in various stages of red dismemberment. The seventh was in a semi-reclined position, his back against the mossy bole of an ancient oak. He held his blade across his lap and there was a large wet wound in his right side, from which the blood still flowed. He wore no armor, though some of the others did. His gray eyes were open, though glassy. His knuckles were skinned and his breathing was slow. From beneath shaggy brows, he watched the crows eat out the eyes of the dead. He did not seem to see me.

I raised my cowl and lowered my head to hide my face. I moved nearer.

I knew him, or someone very like him, once.

His blade twitched and the point rose as I advanced.

'I'm a friend,' I said. 'Would you like a drink of water?'

He hesitated a moment, then nodded.

'Yes.'

I opened my canteen and passed it to him.

He drank and coughed, drank some more.

'Sir, I thank you,' he said as he passed it back. 'I only regret it were not stronger. Damn this cut!'

'I've some of that, too. If you're sure you can handle it.'

He held out his hand and I unstoppered a small flask and gave it to him. He must have coughed for twenty seconds after a slug of that stuff Jopin drinks.

Then the left side of his mouth smiled and he winked lightly.

'Much better,' he said. 'Mind if I pour a drop of this onto my side? I hate to waste good whisky, but—'

'Use it all, if you have to. On second thought, though, your hand looks shaky. Maybe I'd better do the pouring.'

He nodded, and I opened his leather jacket and with my dagger cut away at his shirt until I had exposed the wound. It was nasty-looking, deep, running from front to back a couple inches above the top of his hip. He had other, less serious gashes on his arms, chest, and shoulders.

The blood kept oozing from the big one, and I blotted it a bit and wiped it clean with my kerchief.

His entire body jerked, one great spasm, and then he settled down to shivering. But he did not cry out. I had not thought he would. I folded the kerchief and pressed it in place on the wound. I tied it there, with a long strip I had torn from the bottom of my cloak.

'Want another drink?' I asked him.

'Of water,' he said. 'Then I fear I must sleep.'

He drank, then his head leaned forward until his chin was resting upon his breast. He slept, and I made him a pillow and covered him over with dead men's cloaks.

Then I sat there at his side and watched the pretty black birds.

He had not recognized me. But then, who would? Had I revealed myself to him, he might possibly have known me. We had never really met, I guess, this wounded man and I. But in a peculiar sense, we were acquainted.

I was walking in Shadow, seeking a place, a very special place. It had been destroyed once, but I had the power to re-create it, for Amber casts an infinity of shadows. A child of Amber may walk among them, and such was my heritage. You may call them parallel worlds if you wish, alternate universes if you would, the products of a deranged mind if you care to. I call them shadows, as do all who possess the power to walk among them. We select a possibility and we walk until we reach it. So, in a sense, we create it. Let's leave it at that for now.

I had sailed, had begun this walk toward Avalon.

Centuries before, I had lived there. It is a long, complicated, proud and painful story, and I may go into it later on, if I live to finish much more of this telling.

I was drawing nearer to my Avalon when I came upon the wounded knight and the six dead men. Had I chosen to walk on by, I could have reached a place where the six men lay dead and the knight stood unwounded – or a place where he lay dead and they stood laughing. Some would say it did not really matter, since all these things are possibilities, and therefore all of them exist somewhere in Shadow.

Any of my brothers and sisters – with the possible exceptions of

Gérard and Benedict – would not even have given a second glance. I have become somewhat chickenhearted, however. I was not always that way, but perhaps the shadow Earth, where I spent so many years, mellowed me a bit, and maybe my hitch in the dungeons of Amber reminded me somewhat of the quality of human suffering. I do not know. I only know that I could not pass by the hurt I saw on the form of someone much like someone who had once been a friend. If I were to speak my name in this man's ear, I might hear myself reviled, I would certainly hear a tale of woe.

So, all right. I would pay this much of the price: I would get him back on his feet, then I would cut out. No harm done, and perhaps some small good within this Other.

I sat there, watching him, and after several hours, he awakened.

'Hello,' I said, unstoppering my canteen. 'Have another drink?'

'Thank you.' He extended a hand.

I watched him drink, and when he handed it back he said, 'Excuse me for not introducing myself. I was not in good manner . . .'

'I know you,' I said, 'Call me Corey.'

He looked as if he were about to say, 'Corey of What?' but thought better of it and nodded.

'Very well, Sir Corey,' he demoted me. 'I wish to thank you.'

'I am thanked by the fact that you are looking better,' I told him. 'Want something to eat?'

'Yes, please.'

'I have some dried meat here and some bread that could be fresher,' I said. 'Also a big hunk of cheese. Eat all you want.'

I passed it to him and he did.

'What of yourself, Sir Corey?' he inquired.

'I've already eaten, while you were asleep.'

I looked about me, significantly. He smiled.

'. . . And you knocked off all six of them by yourself?' I said.

He nodded.

'Good show. What am I going to do with you now?'

He tried to see my face, failed.

'I do not understand,' he said.

'Where are you headed?'

'I have friends,' he said, 'some five leagues to the north. I was going in that direction when this thing happened. And I doubt very much that any man, or the Devil himself, could bear me on his back for one league. And if I could stand, Sir Corey, you'd a better idea as to my size.'

I rose, drew my blade, and felled a sapling – about two inches in diameter – with one cut. Then I stripped it and hacked it to the proper length.

I did it again, and with the belts and cloaks of dead men I rigged a stretcher.

He watched until I was finished, then commented:

'You swing a deadly blade, Sir Corey – and a silver one, it would seem . . .'

'Are you up to some traveling?' I asked him.

Five leagues is roughly fifteen miles.

'What of the dead?' he inquired.

'You want to maybe give them a decent Christian burial?' I said. 'Screw them! Nature takes care of its own. Let's get out of here. They stink already.'

I'd like at least to see them covered over. They fought well.'

I sighed.

'All right, if it will help you to sleep nights. I haven't a spade, so I'll build them a cairn. It's going to be a common burial, though.'

'Good enough,' he said.

I laid the six bodies out, side by side. I heard him mumbling something, which I guessed to be a prayer for the dead.

I ringed them around with stones. There were plenty of stones in the vicinity, so I worked quickly, choosing the largest so that things would go faster. That is were I made a mistake. One of them must have weighed around four hundred pounds, and I did not roll it. I hefted it and set it in place.

I heard a sharp intake of breath from his direction, and I realized that he had noted this.

I cursed then:

'Damn near ruptured myself on that one!' I said, and I selected smaller stones after that.

When I had finished, I said, 'All right. Are you ready to move?'

'Yes.'

I raised him in my arms and set him on the stretcher. He clenched his teeth as I did so.

'Where do we go?' I asked.

He gestured.

'Head back to the trail. Follow it to the left until it forks. Then go right at that place. How do you propose to . . . ?'

I scooped the stretcher up in my arms, holding him as you would a baby, cradle and all. Then I turned and walked back to the trail, carrying him.

'Corey?' he said.

'Yes?'

'You are one of the strongest men I have ever met – and it seems I should know you.'

I did not answer him immediately. Then I said, 'I try to keep in good condition. Clean living and all.'

'. . . And your voice sounds rather familiar.'

He was staring upward, still trying to see my face.

I decided to get off the subject fast.

'Who are these friends of yours I am taking you to?'

'We are headed for the Keep of Ganelon.'

'That ratfink!' I said, almost dropping him.

'While I do not understand the word you have used, I take it to be a term of opprobrium,' he said, 'from the tone of your voice. If such is the case, I must be his defender in—'

'Hold on,' I said. 'I've a feeling we're talking about two different guys with the same name. Sorry.'

Through the stretcher, I felt a certain tension go out of him.

'That is doubtless the case,' he said.

So I carried him until we reached the trail, and there I turned to the left.

He dropped off to sleep again, and I made better time after that, taking the fork he had told me about and sprinting while he snored. I began wondering about the six fellows who had tried to do him in and almost succeeded. I hoped that they did not have any friends beating about the bushes.

I slowed my pace back to a walk when his breathing changed.

'I was asleep,' he said.

'. . . And snoring,' I added.

'How far have you borne me?'

'Around two leagues, 'I'd say.'

'And you are not tired?'

'Some,' I said, 'but not enough to need rest just yet.'

'Mon Dieu!' he said. 'I am pleased never to have had you for an enemy. Are you certain you are not the Devil?'

'Yeah, sure,' I said. 'Don't you smell the brimstone? And my right hoof is killing me.'

He actually sniffed a couple times before he chuckled, which hurt my feelings a bit.

Actually, we had traveled over four leagues, as I reckoned it. I was hoping he would sleep again and not be too concerned about distances. My arms were beginning to ache.

'Who were those six men you slew?' I asked him.

'Wardens of the Circle,' he replied, 'and they were no longer men, but men possessed. Now pray to God, Sir Corey, that their souls be at peace.'

'Wardens of the Circle?' I asked. 'What Circle?'

'The dark Circle – the place of iniquity and loathsome beasts . . .' He took a deep breath. 'The source of the illness that lies upon the land.'

'This land doesn't look especially ill to me,' I said.

'We are far from that place, and the realm of Ganelon is still too strong for the invaders. But the Circle widens. I feel that the last battle will be fought here.'

'You have aroused my curiosity as to this thing.'

'Sir Corey, if you know not of it 'twere better you forgot it, skirted the Circle, and went your way. Though I should dearly love to fight by your side, this is not your fight – and who can tell the outcome?'

The trail began winding upward. Then, through a break in the trees, I saw a distant thing that made me pause and caused me to recall another, similar place.

'What . . . ?' asked my charge, turning. Then, 'Why, you moved much more quickly than I had guessed. That is our destination, the Keep of Ganelon.'

I thought then about a Ganelon. I did not want to, but I did. He had been a traitorous assassin and I had exiled him from Avalon centuries before. I had actually cast him through Shadow into another time and place, as my brother Eric had later done to me. I hoped it was not to this place that I had sent him. While not very likely, it was possible.

Though he was a mortal man with his allotted span, and I had exiled him from that place perhaps six hundred years ago, it was possible that it was only a few years past in terms of his world. Time, too, is a function of Shadow, and even Dworkin did not know all of its ins and outs. Or perhaps he did. Maybe that is what drove him mad. The most difficult thing about Time, I have learned, is doing it. In any case, I felt that this could not be my old enemy and former trusted aide, for *he* would certainly not be resisting any wave of iniquity that was sweeping across the land. He would be right in there pitching for the loathsome beasts, I felt sure.

A thing that caused me difficulty was the man that I carried. His counterpart had been alive in Avalon at the time of the exiling, meaning that the time lag could be just about right.

I did not care to encounter the Ganelon I had known and be recognized by him. He knew nothing of Shadow. He would only know that I had worked some dark magic on him, as an alternative to killing him, and while he had survived that alternative it might have been the rougher of the two.

But the man in my arms needed a place of rest and shelter, so I trudged forward.

I wondered, though . . .

There did seem to be something about me that lent itself to recognition by this man. If there were some memories of a shadow of myself in this place that was like yet not like Avalon, what form did they take? How would they condition a reception of the actual me should I be discovered?

The sun was beginning to sink. A cool breeze began, hinting of a chilly night to come. My ward was snoring once more, so I decided to sprint most of the remaining distance. I did not like the feeling that this forest after dark might become a place crawling with unclean denizens of some damned Circle that I knew nothing about, but who seemed to be on the make when it came to this particular piece of real estate.

So I ran through lengthening shadows, dismissing rising notions of pursuit, ambush, surveillance, until I could do so no longer. They had achieved the strength of a premonition, and then I heard the noises at my back: a soft pat-pat-pat, as of footfalls.

I set the stretcher down, and I drew my blade as I turned.

There were two of them, cats.

Their markings were precisely those of Siamese cats, only these were the size of tigers. Their eyes were of a solid, sun-bright yellow, pupilless. They seated themselves on their haunches as I turned, and they stared at me and did not blink.

They were about thirty paces away. I stood sideways between them and the stretcher, my blade raised.

Then the one to the left opened its mouth. I did not know whether to expect a purr or a roar.

Instead, it spoke. It said, 'Man, most mortal.'

The voice was not human-sounding. It was too high-pitched.

'Yet still it lives,' said the second, sounding much like the first.

'Slay it here,' said the first.

'What of the one who guards it with the blade I like not at all?'

'Mortal man?'

'Come find out,' I said, softly.

'It is thin, and perhaps it is old.'

'Yet it bore the other from the cairn to this place, rapidly and without rest. Let us flank it.'

I sprang forward as they moved, and the one to my right leaned toward me.

My blade split its skull and continued on into the shoulder. As I turned, yanking it free, the other swept past me, heading toward the stretcher. I swung wildly.

My blade fell upon its back and passed completely through its body. It emitted a shriek that grated like chalk on a blackboard as it fell in two pieces and began to burn. The other was burning also.

But the one I had halved was not yet dead. Its head turned toward me and those blazing eyes met my own and held them.

'I die the final death,' it said, 'and so I know you, Opener. Why do you slay us?'

And then the flames consumed its head.

I turned, cleaned my blade and sheathed it, picked up the stretcher, ignored all questions, and continued on.

A small knowledge had begun within me, as to what the thing was, what it had meant.

And I still sometimes see that burning cat head in dreams, and then

I awaken, wet and shivering, and the night seems darker, and filled with shapes I cannot define.

The Keep of Ganelon had a moat about it, and a drawbridge, which was raised. There was a tower at each of the four corners where its high walls met. From within those walls many other towers reaching even higher, tickling the bellies of low, dark clouds, occluding the early stars, casting shadows of jet down the high hill the place occupied. Several of the towers were already lighted, and the wind bore me the faint sound of voices.

I stood before the drawbridge, lowered my charge to the ground, cupped my hands about my mouth, and called out:

'Hola! Ganelon! Two travelers are stranded in the night!'

I heard the clink of metal on stone. I felt that I was being studied from somewhere above. I squinted upward, but my eyes were still far from normal.

'Who is there?' the voice came down, big and booming.

'Lance, who is wounded, and I, Corey of Cabra, who bore him here.'

I waited as he called this information to another sentry, and I heard more voices raised as the message was passed along the line.

After a pause of several minutes, a reply came back in the same manner.

Then the guard called down:

'Stay clear! We're going to lower the drawbridge! You may enter!'

The creaking began as he spoke, and in a brief time the thing banged to earth on our side of the moat. I raised my charge once more and walked across it.

Thus did I bear Sir Lancelot du Lac to the Keep of Ganelon, whom I trusted like a brother. That is to say, not at all.

There was a rush of people about me, and I found myself ringed by armed men. There was no hostility present, however, only concern. I had entered a large, cobbled courtyard, lit by torches and filled with bedrolls. I could smell sweat, smoke, horses, and the odors of cooking. A small army was bivouacked there.

Many had approached me and stood staring and murmuring, but

then there came up two who were fully arrayed, as for battle, and one of them touched my shoulder.

'Come this way,' he said.

I followed and they flanked me. The ring of people parted as we passed. The drawbridge was already creaking back into place. We moved toward the main complex of dark stone.

Inside, we walked along a hallway and passed what appeared to be a reception chamber. Then we came upon a stairway. The man to my right indicated that I should mount it. On the second floor, we stopped before a heavy wooden door and the guard knocked upon it.

'Come in,' called out a voice which unfortunately seemed very familiar.

We entered.

He sat at a heavy wooden table near a wide window overlooking the courtyard. He wore a brown leather jacket over a black shirt, and his trousers were also black. They were bloused over the tops of his dark boots. He had about his waist a wide belt which held a hoof-hilted dagger. A short sword lay on the table before him. His hair and beard were red, with a sprinkling of white. His eyes were dark as ebony.

He looked at me, then turned his attention to a pair of guards who entered with the stretcher.

'Put him on my bed,' he said. Then 'Roderick, tend to him.'

His physician, Roderick, was an old guy who didn't look as if he would do much harm, which relieved me somewhat. I had not fetched Lance all that distance to have him bled.

Then Ganelon turned to me once more.

'Where did you find him?' he asked.

'Five leagues to the south of here.'

'Who are you?'

'They call me Corey,' I said.

He studied me too closely, and his worm-like lips twitched toward a smile beneath his mustache.

'What is your part in this thing?' he asked.

'I don't know what you mean,' I said.

I had let my shoulders sag a bit. I spoke slowly, softly, and with a slight falter. My beard was longer than his, and lightened by dust. I imagined I looked like an older man. His attitude on appraisal tended to indicate that he thought I was.

'I am asking you why you helped him,' he said.

'Brotherhood of man, and all that,' I replied.

'You are a foreigner?'

I nodded.

'Well, you are welcome here for so long as you wish to stay.'

'Thanks. I will probably move on tomorrow.'

'Now join me in a glass of wine and tell me of the circumstances under which you found him.'

So I did.

Ganelon let me speak without interrupting, and those piercing eyes of his were on me all the while. While I had always felt laceration by means of the eyeballs to be a trite expression, it did not feel so that night. He stabbed at me with them. I wondered what he knew and what he was guessing concerning me.

Then fatigue sprang and seized me by the scuff of me neck. The exertion, the wine, the warm room – all of these worked together, and suddenly it was as if I were standing off in the corner somewhere and listening to myself, watching myself, feeling dissociated. While I was capable of great exertion in short bursts, I realized that I was still very low when it came to stamina. I also noticed that my hand was trembling.

'I'm sorry,' I heard myself saying. 'The day's labors are beginning to get to me . . .'

'Of course,' said Ganelon. 'I will talk with you more on the morrow. Sleep now. Sleep well.'

Then he called in one of the guards and ordered him to conduct me to a chamber. I must have staggered on the way, because I remember the guard's hand on my elbow, steering me.

That night I slept the sleep of the dead. It was a big, black thing, about fourteen hours long.

In the morning, I ached all over.

I bathed myself. There was a basin on the high dresser, and soap and a washcloth someone had thoughtfully set beside it. My throat felt packed with sawdust and my eyes were full of fuzz.

I sat down and assessed myself.

There had been a day when I could have carried Lance the entire distance without going to pieces afterward. There had been a day when I had fought my way up the face of Kolvir and into the heart of Amber itself.

Those days were gone. I suddenly felt like the wreck I must have looked.

Something would have to be done.

I had been putting on weight and picking up strength slowly. The process would have to be accelerated.

A week or two of clean living and violent exercise could help a lot, I decided. Ganelon had not given any real indication of having recognized me. All right. I would take advantage of the hospitality he had offered.

With that resolve, I sought out the kitchen and conned a hearty breakfast. Well, it was really around lunchtime, but let's call things by their proper names. I had a strong desire for a smoke and felt a certain perverse joy in the fact that I was out of tobacco. The Fates were conspiring to keep me true to myself.

I strolled out into the courtyard and a brisk, bright day. For a long while, I watched the men who were quartered there as they went through their training regime.

There were bowmen off at the far end, thwanging away at targets fastened to bales of hay. I noted that they employed thumb rings and an oriental grip on the bowstring, rather than the three-fingered technique with which I was more comfortable. It made me wonder a bit about his Shadow. The swordsmen used both the edges and points of their weapons, and there was a variety of blades and fencing techniques in evidence. I tried to estimate, and guessed there were perhaps eight hundred of them about – and I had no idea as to how many of them there might be out of sight. Their complexions, their hair, their eyes, varied from pale to quite dark. I heard many strange accents above the thwanging and the clanging, though most spoke the language of Avalon, which is of the tongue of Amber.

As I stood watching, one swordsman raised his hand, lowered his blade, mopped his brow, and stepped back. His opponent did not seem especially winded. This was my chance for some of the exercise I was seeking.

I moved forward, smiled, and said, 'I'm Corey of Cabra. I was watching you.'

I turned my attention to the big, dark man who was grinning at his resting buddy.

'Mind if I practice with you while your friend rests?' I asked him.

He kept grinning and pointed at his mouth and his ear. I tried several other languages, but none of them worked. So I pointed at the blade and at him and back to myself until he got the idea. His opponent seemed to think it was a good one, as the smaller fellow offered me his blade.

I took it into my hands. It was shorter and a lot heavier than Grayswandir. (That is the name of my blade, which I know I have not mentioned up until now. It is a story in itself, and I may or may not go into it before you learn what brought me to this final pass. But, should you hear me refer to it by name again, you will know what I am talking about.)

I swung my blade a few times to test it, removed my cloak, tossed it off to the side, and struck an *en garde*.

The big fellow attacked. I parried and attacked. He parried and riposted. I parried the riposte, feinted, and attacked. Et cetera. After five minutes, I knew that he was good. And I knew that I was better. He stopped me twice so that I could teach him a maneuver I had used. He learned both very quickly. After fifteen minutes, though, his grin widened. I guess that was around the point where he broke down most opponents by virtue of sheer staying power, if they were good enough to resist his attacks up until then. He had stamina, I'll say that. After twenty minutes, a puzzled look came onto his face. I just didn't look as if I could stand up that long. But then, what can any man really know of that which lies within a scion of Amber?

After twenty-five minutes, he was sheathed in sweat, but he continued on. My brother Random looks and acts, on occasion, like an asthmatic, teen-age hood – but once we had fenced together for over twenty-six hours, to see who would call it quits. (If you're curious, it was me. I had had a date lined up for the next day and had wanted to arrive in reasonably good condition.) We could have gone on. While I was not up to a performance like that just then, I knew that I could outlast the man I faced. After all, he was only human.

After about half an hour, when he was breathing heavily and

slowing down on his counterstrokes and I knew that in a few minutes he might guess that I was pulling mine, I raised my hand and lowered my blade as I had seen his previous opponent do. He ground to a halt also, then rushed forward and embraced me. I did not understand what he said, but I gathered that he was pleased with the workout. So was I.

The horrible thing was, I felt it. I found myself slightly heady.

But I needed more. I promised me I would kill myself with exercise that day, glut myself with food that night, sleep deeply, wake, and do it again.

So I went over to where the archers stood. After a time, I borrowed a bow, and in my three-fingered style unleashed perhaps a hundred arrows. I did not do too badly. Then, for a time, I watched the men on horseback, with their lances, shields, maces. I moved on. I watched some practice in hand-to-hand combat.

Finally, I wrestled three men in succession. Then I did feel beat. Absolutely. Entirely.

I sat down on a bench in the shade, sweating, breathing heavily. I wondered about Lance, about Ganelon, about supper. After perhaps ten minutes, I made my way back to the room I had been given and I bathed again.

By then I was ravenously hungry, so I set forth to find me dinner and information.

Before I had gone very far from the door, one of the guards whom I recognized from the previous evening – the one who had guided me to my chamber – approached and said, 'Lord Ganelon bids you dine with him in his quarters, at the ringing of the dinner bell.'

I thanked him, said I would be there, returned to my chamber, and rested on my bed until it was time. Then I made my way forth once again.

I was beginning to ache deeply and I had a few additional bruises. I decided this was a good thing, would help me to seem older. I banged on Ganelon's door and a boy admitted me, then dashed off to join another youth who was spreading a table near to the fireplace.

Ganelon wore a green shirt and trousers, green boots and belt, sat in a high-backed chair. He rose as I entered, walked forward to greet me.

'Sir Corey, I've heard report of your doings this day,' he said, clasping my hand. 'It makes your carrying Lance seem more believable. I must say you're more a man than you look – meaning no offense by that.'

I chuckled.

'No offense.'

He led me to a chair, handed me a glass of pale wine that was a bit too sweet for my taste, then said, 'Looking at you, I'd say I could push you over with one hand – but you carried Lance five leagues and killed two of those bastard cats on the way. And he told me about the cairn you built, of big stones—'

'How is Lance feeling today?' I interrupted.

'I had to place a guard in his chamber to be sure he rested. The muscle-bound clod wanted to get up and walk around. He'll stay there all week, though, by God!'

'Then he must be feeling better.'

He nodded.

'Here's to his health.'

'I'll drink to that.'

We drank. Then: 'Had I an army of men like you and Lance,' he said, 'the story might have been different.'

'What story?'

'The Circle and its Wardens,' he said. 'You've not heard of it?'

'Lance mentioned it. That's all.'

One boy tended an enormous chunk of beef on a spit above a low fire. Occasionally, he sloshed some wine over it as he turned the shaft. Whenever the odor drifted my way, my stomach would rumble and Ganelon would chuckle. The other boy left the room to fetch bread from the kitchen.

Ganelon was silent a long while. He finished his wine and poured himself another glass. I sipped slowly at my first.

'Have you ever heard of Avalon?' he finally asked.

'Yes,' I replied. 'There is a verse I heard long ago from a passing bard: "Beyond the River of the Blessed, there we sat down, yea, we wept, when we remembered Avalon. Our swords were shattered in our hands and we hung our shields on the oak tree. The silver towers were fallen, into a sea of blood. How many miles to Avalon? None, I say, and all. The silver towers are fallen".'

'Avalon fallen . . . ?' he said.

'I think the man was mad. I know of no Avalon. His verse stayed in my mind, though.'

Ganelon averted his face and did not speak again for several minutes. When he did, his voice was altered.

'There was,' he said. 'There was such a place. I lived there, years ago. I did not know it was fallen.'

'How came you here from that place?' I asked him.

'I was exiled by its sorcerer Lord, Corwin of Amber. He sent me through darkness and madness to this place, that I might suffer and die here – and I *have* suffered and come near to the final lay many a time. I've tried to find the way back, but nobody knows it. I've spoken with sorcerers, and even a captured creature of the Circle before we slew the thing. But none knew the road to Avalon. It is as the bard said, "No miles, and all",' he misquoted my lyric, 'Do you recall the bard's name?'

'I am sorry, but I do not.'

'Where is this Cabra place you hie from?'

'Far to the east, across the waters,' I said. 'Very far. It is an island kingdom.'

'Any chance they could furnish us with some troops? I can afford to pay quite a bit.'

I shook my head.

'It is a small place with a small militia, and it would be several months' travel both ways – sea and land. They have never fought as mercenaries, and for that matter they are not very warlike.'

'Then you seem to differ a great deal from your countrymen,' he said, looking at me once more.

I sipped my wine.

'I was an arms instructor,' I said, 'to the Royal Guard.'

'Then you might be inclined to hire out, to help train my troops?'

'I'll stay a few weeks and do that,' I said.

He nodded a tight-lipped microsecond of a smile, then, 'It saddens me to hear this indication that fair Avalon is gone,' he said. 'But if it is so, it means that my exiler is also likely dead.' He drained his wineglass. 'So even the demon came to a time when he could not defend his own,' he mused. 'That's a heartening thought. It means we might have a chance here, against these demons.'

'Begging your pardon,' I said, sticking my neck out for what I thought good reason, 'if you were referring to that Corwin of Amber, he did not die when whatever happened happened.'

The glass snapped in his hand.

'*You know Corwin?*' he said.

'No, but I know of him,' I replied. 'Several years ago, I met one of his brothers – a fellow named Brand. He told me of the place called Amber, and of the battle in which Corwin and a brother of his named Bleys led a horde against their brother Eric, who held the city. Bleys fell from the mountain Kolvir and Corwin was taken prisoner. Corwin's eyes were put out after Eric's coronation, and he was cast into the dungeons beneath Amber, where he may yet remain if he has not since died.'

Ganelon's face was drained of color as I spoke.

'All those names you mentioned – Brand, Bleys, Eric,' he said. 'I heard him mention them in days long gone by. How long ago did you hear of this thing?'

'It was about four years back.'

'He deserved better.'

'After what he did to you?'

'Well,' said the man, 'I've had a lot of time to think about it, and it is not as if I gave him no cause for what he did. He was strong – stronger than you or Lance, even – and clever. Also, he could be merry on occasion. Eric should have killed him quickly, not the way that he did. I've no love for him, but my hate's died down a bit. The demon deserved better than he got, that's all.'

The second boy returned with a basket of bread. The one who had prepared the meat removed it from the spit and set it on a platter in the center of the table.

Ganelon nodded toward it.

'Let's eat,' he said.

He rose and moved to the table.

I followed. We did not talk much during the meal.

After stuffing myself until my stomach would hold no more and soaking down its contents with another glass of too-sweet wine, I began to yawn. Ganelon cursed after the third one.

'Damn it, Corey! Stop that! It's contagious!'

He stifled a yawn of his own.

'Let's take some air,' he said, rising.

So we walked out along the walls, passing the sentries in their rounds. They would come to attention and salute Ganelon as soon as they saw who it was approaching, and he would give them a word of greeting and we would move on. We came to a battlement, where we paused to rest, seating ourselves on the stone, sucking in the evening air, cool and damp and full of the forest, and noting the appearance of the stars, one by one, in the darkening sky. The stone was cold beneath me. Far off in the distance, I thought I could detect the shimmer of the sea. I heard a night bird, from somewhere below us. Ganelon produced a pipe and tobacco from a pouch he wore at his belt. He filled it, tamped it, and struck a flame. His face would have been satanic in the spark light, save for whatever turned his mouth downward and drew the muscles in his cheeks up into that angle formed by the inner corners of his eyes and the sharp bridge of his nose. A devil is supposed to have an evil grin, and this one looked too morose.

I smelled the smoke. After a time, he began to speak, softly and very slowly at first:

'I remember Avalon,' he began. 'My birth there was not ignoble, but virtue was never one of my strong points. I went through my inheritance quickly and I took to the roads where I waylaid travelers. Later, I joined with a band of other men such as myself. When I discovered I was the strongest and most fit to lead, I became the leader. There were prices on all our heads. Mine was the highest.'

He spoke more rapidly now, and his voice grew more refined and his choice of words came as an echo from out of his past.

'Yes, I remember Avalon,' he said, 'a place of silver and shade and cool waters, where the stars shone like bonfires at night and the green of day was always the green of spring. Youth, love, beauty – I knew them in Avalon. Proud steeds, bright metal, soft lips, dark ale. Honor . . .'

He shook his head.

'One later day,' he said, 'when war commenced within the realm, the ruler offered full pardon to any outlaws who would follow him in battle against the insurgents. This was Corwin. I threw in with him and rode off to the wars. I became an officer, and then – later – a member of his staff. We won the battles, put down the uprising. Then Corwin ruled peacefully once more, and I remained at his court. Those were the good years. There later came some border skirmishes, but these we always won. He trusted me to handle such things for him. Then he granted a Dukedom to dignify the House of a minor noble whose daughter he desired in marriage. I had wanted that Dukedom, and he had long hinted it might one day be mine. I was furious, and I betrayed my command the next time I was dispatched to settle a dispute along the southern border, where something was always stirring. Many of my men died, and the invaders entered into the realm. Before they could be routed, Lord Corwin himself had to take up arms once more. The invaders had come through in great strength, and I thought they would conquer the realm. I hoped they would. But Corwin, again, with his foxy tactics, prevailed. I fled, but was captured and taken to him for sentencing. I cursed him and spat at him. I would not bow. I hated the ground he trod, and a condemned man has no reason not to put up the best front he can, to go out nice a man. Corwin said he would show me a measure of mercy for favors past. I told him to shove his mercy, and then I realized that he was mocking me. He ordered me released and he approached me. I knew he could kill me with his hands. I tried to fight with him, but to no avail. He stuck me once and I fell. When I awakened, I was strapped across his horse's rump. He rode along, jibing at me the while. I would not reply to anything he said, but we rode through wondrous lands and lands out of nightmare, which is one way I learned of his sorcerous power – for no traveler I have ever met has passed through the places I saw that day. Then he pronounced my exile, released me in this place, turned, and rode away.'

He paused to relight his pipe, which had gone out, puffed upon it for a time, went on: 'Many a bruising, cudgeling, biting, and beating did I take in this place at the hands of man and beast, only barely preserving my life. He had left me in the wickedest portion of the realm. But then one day my fortunes took a turn. An armored knight bade me depart the roadway that he might pass. At that point, I cared not whether I lived or died, so I called him a pock-marked whoreson and bade him go to the Devil. He charged me and I seized his lance and pushed its point into the ground, so unhorsing him. I drew him a smile beneath his chin with his own dagger, and thus obtained me mounting and weapons. Then did I set about paying back those who had used me poorly. I took up my old trade on the highways once again and I gained me another band of followers. We grew. When there were hundreds of us our needs were considerable. We would ride into a small town and make it ours. The local militia would fear us. This, too, was a good life, though not so splendid as the Avalon I never shall know again. All the roadside inns came to fear the thunder of our mounts, and travelers would soil their britches when they heard us coming. Ha! This lasted for several years. Large parties of armed men were sent to track us and destroy us, but always we evaded them or ambushed them. Then one day there was the dark Circle, and no one really knows why.'

He puffed more vigorously on his pipe, stared off into the distance.

'I am told it began as a tiny ring of toadstools, far to the west. A child was found dead in its center, and the man who found her – her father – died of convulsions several days later. The spot was immediately said to be accursed. It grew quickly in the months that followed, until it was half a league across. The grasses darkened and shone like metal within it, but did not die. The trees twisted and their leaves blackened. They swayed when there was no wind, and bats danced and darted among them. In the twilight, strange shapes could be seen moving – always *within* the Circle, mind you – and there were lights, as of small fires, throughout the night. The Circle continued to grow, and those who lived near it fled – mostly. A few remained. It was said that those who remained had struck some bargain with the dark things. And the Circle continued to widen, spreading like the ripple from a rock cast into a pond. More and more people remained, living, within it. I have spoken with these people, fought with them, slain them. It is as if there is something dead inside them all. Their voices lack the thrust and dip of men chewing over their words and tasting them. They seldom do much with their faces, but wear them like death masks. They began to leave the Circle in bands, marauding. They slew wantonly. They committed many atrocities and defiled places of worship. They put things to the torch when they left them. They never stole objects of silver. Then, after many months, other creatures than then began to come forth – strangely formed, like the hellcats you slew. Then the Circle slowed in its growth, almost halting, as though it were nearing some sort of limit. But now all manner of raiders emerged from it – some even faring forth during the day – laying waste to the countryside about its borders. When they had devastated the land about its entire circumference, the Circle moved to encompass those areas also. And so its growth began again, in this fashion. The old king, Uther, who had long hunted me forgot all about me and set his forces to patrolling that damned Circle. It was beginning to worry me, also, as I did not relish the notion of being seized by some hell-spawned bloodsucker as I slept. So I got together fifty-five of my men – that was all who would volunteer, and I wanted no cowards – and we rode into that place one afternoon. We came upon a pack of those dead-faced men burning a live goat on a stone altar and we lit into the lot of them. We took one prisoner and tied him to his own altar and questioned him there. He told us that the Circle would grow until it covered the entire land, from ocean to ocean. One day it would close with itself on the other side of the world. We had best join with them, if we wished to save our hides. Then one of my men stabbed him and he died. He really died, for I know a dead man when I see one. I've made it happen often enough. But as his blood fell upon the stone, his mouth opened and out came the loudest laugh I ever heard in my life. It was like thunder all about us. Then he sat up, unbreathing, and began to burn. As he burned, his form changed, until it was like that of the burning goat – only larger – there upon the altar. Then a voice came from the thing. It said, "Flee, mortal man! But you shall never leave this Circle!" And believe me, we fled! The sky grew black with bats and other – things. We heard the sound of hoofbeats. We rode with our blades in our hands, killing everything that came near us. There were cats such as you slew, and snakes and hopping things, and God knows what all else. As we neared the edge of the Circle, one of King Uther's patrols saw us and came to our aid. Sixteen of the fifty-five who had ridden in with me rode back out. And the patrol lost perhaps thirty men itself. When they saw who I was, they hustled me off to court. Here. This used to be Uther's palace. Told him what I had done, what I had seen and heard. He did with me as Corwin had. He offered full pardon to me and to my men if we would join with him against the Wardens of the Circle. Having gone through what I had gone through, I realized that the thing had to be stopped. So I agreed. Then I fell ill, I am told that I was delirious for three days. I was as weak as a child after my recovery, and I learned that everyone who had entered the Circle had been likewise taken. Three had died. I visited the rest of my men, told them the story, and they were enlisted. The patrols about the Circle were strengthened. But it would not be contained. In the years that followed, the Circle grew. We fought many skirmishes. I was promoted until I stood at Uther's right hand, as once I had at Corwin's. Then the skirmishes became more than skirmishes. Larger and larger parties emerged from that hellhole. We lost a few battles. They took some of our outposts. Then one night an army emerged, an army – a horde – of both men and the other things that dwelled there. That night we met the largest force we had ever engaged. King Uther himself rode to battle, against my advice – for he was advanced in years – and he fell that night and the land was without a ruler. I wanted my captain, Lancelot, to sit in stewardship, for I knew him to be a far more honorable man than myself . . . And it is strange here. I had known a Lancelot, just like him, in Avalon – but this man knew me not when first we met. It is strange . . . At any rate, he declined, and the position was thrust upon me. I hate it, but here I am. I have held them back for over three years now. All my instincts tell me to flee. What do I owe these damned people? What do I care if the bloody Circle widens? I could cross over the sea to some land it would never reach during my lifetime, and then forget the whole thing. Damn it! I didn't want this responsibility! Now it is mine, though!'

'Why?' I asked him, and the sound of my own voice was strange to me.

There was silence.

He emptied his pipe. He refilled it. He relit it. He puffed it.

There was more silence.

Then, 'I don't know,' he said. 'I'd stab a man in the back for a pair of shoes, if he had them and I needed them to keep my feet from freezing. I once did, that's how I know. But . . . this is different. This is a thing hurting everybody, and I'm the only one who can do the job. God damn it! I know they're going the bury me here one day, along with all the rest of them. But I can't pull out. I've got to hold that thing back as long as I can.'

My head was cleared by the cold night air, which gave my

consciousness a second wind, so to speak, though my body felt mildly anesthetized about me.

'Couldn't Lance lead them?' I asked.

'I'd say so. He's good man. But there is another reason. I think that goat-thing, whatever it was, on the altar, is a bit afraid of me. I had gone in there and it had told me I'd never make it back out again, but I did. I lived through the sickness that followed after. It knows it's me that has been fighting it all along. We won that great bloody engagement on the night Uther died, and I met the thing again in a different form and it knew me. Maybe this is a part of what is holding it back now.'

'What form?'

'A thing with a manlike shape, but with goat horns and red eyes. It was mounted on a piebald stallion. We fought for a time, but the tide of the battle swept us apart. Which was a good thing, too, for it was winning. It spoke again, as we swaggered swords, and I knew that head-filling voice. It called me a fool and told me I could never hope to win. But when morning came, the field was ours and we drove them back to the Circle, slaying them as they fled. The rider of the piebald escaped. There have been other sallyings forth since then, but none such as that night's. If I were to leave this land, another such army – one that is readying even now – would come forth. That thing would somehow know of my departure – just as it knew that Lance was bringing me another report on the disposition of troops within the Circle, sending those Wardens to destroy him as he returned. It knows of you by now, and surely it must wonder over this development. It must wonder who you are, for all your strength. I will stay here and fight it till I fall. I must. Do not ask me why. I only hope that before that day comes, I at least learn how this thing came to pass – *why* that Circle is out there.'

Then there came a fluttering near to my head. I ducked quickly to avoid whatever it was. It was not necessary, though. It was only a bird. A white bird. It landed on my left shoulder and stood there, making small noises. I held up my wrist and it hopped over onto it. There was a note tied to its leg. I unfastened it, read it, crumpled it in my hand. Then I studied invisible things distant.

'What is the matter, Sir Corey?' cried Ganelon.

The note, which I had sent on ahead to my destination, written in my own hand, transmitted by a bird of my desire, could only reach the place that had to be my next stop. This was not precisely the place that I had in mind. However, I could read my own omens.

'What is it?' he asked. 'What is it that you hold? A message?'

I nodded. I handed it to him. I could not very well throw it away, once he had seen me take it.

It read, 'I am coming,' and it bore my signature.

Ganelon puffed his pipe and read it in the glow.

'*He* lives? And he would come *here*?' he said.

'So it would seem.'

'This is very strange,' he said. 'I do not understand it at all . . .'

'It sounds like a promise of assistance,' I said, dismissing the bird, which cooed twice, then circled my head and departed.

Ganelon shook his head.

'I do not understand.'

'Why number the teeth of a horse you may receive for nothing?' I said. 'You have only succeeded in containing that thing.'

'True,' he said. 'Perhaps he could destroy it.'

'And perhaps it's just a joke,' I told him. 'A cruel one.'

He shook his head again.

'No. That is not his style. I wonder what he is after?'

'Sleep on it,' I suggested.

'There is little else that I can do, just now,' he said, stifling a yawn.

We rose then and walked the wall. We said our good nights, and I staggered off toward the pit of sleep and fell headlong into it.

2

Day. More aches. More pains.

Someone had left me a new cloak, a brown one, which I decided was a good thing. Especially if I put on more weight and Ganelon recalled my colors. I did not shave my beard, because he had known me in a slightly less hairy condition. I took pains to disguise my voice whenever he was about. I hid Grayswandir beneath my bed.

For all of the following week I drove myself ruthlessly. I worked and sweated and strove until the aches subsided and my muscles grew firm once more. I think I put on fifteen pounds that week. Slowly, very slowly, I began feeling like my old self.

The country was called Lorraine, and so was she. If I happened to be in the mood to hand you a line, I would tell you we met in a meadow behind the castle, she gathering flowers and me walking there for exercise and fresh air. Crap.

I guess a polite term would be camp follower. I met her at the end of a hard day's work, spent mainly with the saber and the mace. She was standing off on the side lines waiting for her date when I first caught sight of her. She smiled and I smiled back, nodded, winked, and passed her by. The next day I saw her again, and I said 'Hello' as I passed her. That's all.

Well, I kept running into her. By the end of my second week, when my aches were gone and I was over a hundred-eighty pounds and feeling that way again, I arranged to be with her one evening. By then, I was aware of her status and it was fine, so far as I was concerned. But we did not do the usual thing that night. No.

Instead, we talked, and then something else happened.

Her hair was rust-colored with a few strands of gray in it. I guessed she was under thirty, though. Eyes, very blue. Slightly pointed chin. Clean, even teeth inside a mouth that smiled at me a lot. Her voice was somewhat nasal, her hair was too long, her makeup laid on too heavily over too much tiredness, her complexion too freckled, her choice in clothing too bright and tight. But I liked her. I did not think I'd actually feel that way when I asked her out that night because, as I said, liking her was not what I had in mind.

There was no place to go but my chamber, so we had gone there. I had become a captain, and I took advantage of my rank by having dinner brought to us, and an extra bottle of wine.

'The men are afraid of you,' she said. 'They say you never grow tired.'

'I do,' I said, 'believe me.'

'Of course,' she said, shaking her too-long locks and smiling. 'Don't we all?'

'I daresay,' I replied.

'How old are you?'

'How old are *you*?'

'A gentlemen would not ask that question.'

'Neither would a lady.'

'When you first came here, they thought you were over fifty.'

'And . . . ?'

'And now they have no idea. Forty-five? Forty?'

'No,' I said.

'I didn't think so. But your beard fooled everyone.'

'Beards often do that.'

'You look better every day. Bigger . . .'

'Thanks. I feel better than I did when I arrived.'

'Sir Corey of Cabra,' she said. 'Where's Cabra? What's Cabra? Will you take me there with you, if I ask you nicely?'

'I'd tell you so,' I said, 'but I'd be lying.'

'I know. But it would be nice to hear.'

'Okay. I'll take you there with me. It's a lousy place.'

'Are you really as good as the men say?'

'I'm afraid not. Are you?'

'Not really. Do you want to go to bed now?'

'No. I'd rather talk. Have a glass of wine.'

'Thank you . . . Your health.'

'Yours.'

'Why is it you are such a good swordsman?'

'Aptitude and good teachers.'

'. . . And you carried Lance all that distance and slew those beasts . . .'

'Stories grow with the telling.'

'But I have watched you. You *are* better than the others. That is why Ganelon made you whatever deal he did. He knows a good thing when he sees it. I've had many friends who were swordsmen, and I've watched them at practice. You could cut them to pieces. The men say you are a good teacher. They like you, even if you do scare them.'

'Why do I frighten them? Because I am strong? There are many strong men in the world. Because I can stand up and swing a blade for a long while?'

'They think there is something supernatural involved.'

I laughed.

'No, I'm just the second-best swordsman around. Pardon me – maybe the third. But I try harder.'

'Who's better?'

'Eric of Amber, possibly.'

'Who is he?'

'A supernatural creature.'

'He's the best?'

'No.'

'Who is?'

'Benedict of Amber.'

'Is he one, too?'

'If he is still alive, he is.'

'Strange, that's what you are,' she said. 'And why? Tell me. *Are* you a supernatural creature?'

'Let's have another glass of wine.'

'It'll go to my head.'

'Good.'

I poured them.

'We are all going to die,' she said.

'Eventually.'

'I mean here, soon, fighting this thing.'

'Why do you say that?'

'It's too strong.'

'Then why stick around?'

'I've no place else to go. That's why I asked you about Cabra.'

'And why you came here tonight?'

'No. I came to see what you were like.'

'I am an athlete who is breaking training. Were you born around here?'

'Yes. In the wood.'

'Why'd you pick up with these guys?'

'Why not? It's better than getting pig shit on my heels every day.'

'Never have a man of your own? Steady, I mean?'

'Yes. He's dead. He's the one who found . . . the Fairy Ring.'

'I'm sorry.'

'I'm not. He used to get drunk whenever he could borrow or steal enough to afford it and then come home and beat me. I was glad when I met Ganelon.'

'So you think that the thing is too strong, that we are going to lose to it?'

'Yes.'

'You may be right. But I think you're wrong.'

She shrugged.

'You'll be fighting with us?'

'I'm afraid so.'

'Nobody knew for sure, or would say if they did. That might prove interesting. I'd like to see you fight with the goat-man.'

'Why?'

'Because he seems to be their leader. If you killed him, we'd have more of a chance. You might be able to do it.'

'I have to,' I said.

'Special reason?'

'Yes.'

'Private one?'

'Yes.'

'Good luck.'

'Thanks.'

She finished her wine, so I poured her another.

'I know *he* is a supernatural creature,' she said.

'Let's get off the subject.'

'All right. But will you do me a thing?'

'Name it.'

'Put on armor tomorrow, pick up a lance, get hold of a horse, and trounce that big cavalry officer Harald.'

'Why?'

'He beat me last week, just like Jarl used to. Can you do it?'

'Yes.'

'Will you?'

'Why not? Consider him trounced.'

She came over and leaned against me.

'I love you,' she said.

'Crap.'

'All right. How about, "I like you"?'

'Good enough. I—'

Then a chill and numbing wind blew along my spine. I stiffened and resisted what was to come by blanking my mind completely.

Someone was looking for me. It was someone of the House of Amber, doubtless, and he was using my Trump or something very like it. There was no mistaking the sensation. If it was Eric, then he had more guts than I gave him credit for, since I had almost napalmed his brain the last time we had been in contact. It could not be Random, unless he was out of prison, which I doubted. If it was Julian or Caine, they could go to hell. Bleys was probably dead. Possibly Benedict, too. That left Gérard, Brand, and our sisters. Of these, only Gérard might mean me well. So I resisted discovery, successfully. It took me perhaps five minutes, and when it was finished I was shaking and sweating and Lorraine was staring at me strangely.

'What happened?' she asked 'You aren't drunk yet, and neither am I.'

'Just a spell I sometimes get,' I said 'It's a disease I picked up in the islands.'

'I saw a face,' she said. 'Perhaps it was on the floor, maybe it was in my head. It was an old man. The collar of his garment was green and he looked a lot like you, except that his beard was gray.'

I slapped her then.

'You're lying! You couldn't have . . .'

'I'm just telling you what I saw! Don't hit me! I don't know what it meant! Who was he?'

'I think it was my father. God, it's strange . . .'

'What happened?' she repeated.

'A spell,' I said. I said. 'I sometimes get them, and people think they see my father on the castle wall or floor. Don't worry about it. It's not contagious.'

'Crap,' she said. 'You're lying to me.'

'I know. But please forget the whole thing.'

'Why should I?'

'Because you like me,' I told her. 'Remember? And because I'm going to trounce Harald for you tomorrow.'

'That's true,' she said, and I started shaking again and she fetched a blanket from the bed and put it about my shoulders.

She handed me my wine and I drank it. She sat beside me and rested her head on my shoulder, so I put my arm about her. A devil wind began to scream and I heard the rapid rattle of the rainfall that came with it. For a second, it seemed that something beat against the shutters. Lorraine whimpered slightly.

'I do not like what is happening tonight,' she said.

'Neither do I. Go bar the door. It's only bolted right now.'

As she did this, I moved our seat so that it faced my single window. I fetched Grayswandir out from beneath the bed and unsheathed it. Then I extinguished every light in the room, save for a single candle on the table to my right.

I reseated myself, my blade across my knees.

'What are we doing?' Lorraine asked, as she came and sat down at my left.

'Waiting,' I said.

'For what?'

'I am not positive, but this is certainly the night for it.'

She shuddered and drew near.

'You know, perhaps you had better leave,' I said.

'I know,' she said, 'but I'm afraid to go out. You'll be able to protect me if I stay here, won't you?'

I shook my head.

'I don't even know if I'll be able to protect myself.'

She touched Grayswandir.

'What a beautiful blade! I've never seen one like it.'

'There isn't another,' I said, and each time that I shifted a little, the light fell differently upon it, so that one moment it seemed filmed over with unhuman blood of an orange tint and the next it lay there cold and white as snow or a woman's breast, quivering in my hand each time a little chill took me.

I wondered how it was that Lorraine had seen something I had not during the attempted contact. She could not simply have imagined anything that close to home.

'There is something strange about *you*,' I said.

She was silent for four or five flickerings of the candle, then said, 'I've a touch of the second sight. My mother had more of it. People say my grandmother was a sorceress. I don't know any of that business, though. Well, not much of it. I haven't done it for years. I always wind up losing more than I gain.'

Then she was silent again, and I asked her, 'What do you mean?'

'I used a spell to get my first man,' she said, 'and look what he turned out to be. If I hadn't, I'd have been a lot better off. I wanted a pretty daughter, and I made that happen—'

She stopped abruptly and I realized she was crying.

'What's the matter? I don't understand . . .'

'I thought you knew,' she said.

'No, I'm afraid not.'

'She was the little girl in the Fairy Circle. I thought you knew . . .'

'I'm sorry.'

'I wish I didn't have the touch. I never use it any more. But it won't let me alone. It still brings me dreams and signs, and they are never over things I can do anything about. I wish it would go away and devil somebody else!'

'That's the one thing it will not do, Lorraine. I'm afraid you are stuck with it.'

'How do you know?'

'I've known people like you in the past, that's all.'

'You've a touch of it yourself, haven't you?'

'Yes.'

'Then you feel that there is something out there now, don't you?'

'Yes.'

'So do I. Do you know what it is doing?'

'It's looking for me.'

'Yes, I feel that, too. Why?'

'Perhaps to test my strength. It knows that I am here. If I am a new ally come to Ganelon, it must wonder what I represent, who I am . . .'

'Is it the horned one himself?'

'I don't know. I think not, though.'

'Why not?'

'If I am really he who would destroy it, it would be foolish to seek me out here in the keep of its enemy where I am surrounded by strength. I would say one of its minions is looking for me. Perhaps, somehow, that is what my father's ghost . . . I do not know. If its servant finds me and names me, it will know what preparations to make. If it finds me and destroys me, it will have solved the problem. If I destroy the servant, it will know that much more about my strength. Whichever way it works out, the horned one will be something ahead. So why should it risk its own pronged dome at this stage in the game?'

We waited, there in the shadow-clad chamber, as the taper burned away the minutes.

She asked me, 'What did you mean when you said, if it finds you and names you . . . ? Names you what?'

'The one who almost did not come here,' I said.

'You think that it might know you from somewhere, somehow?' she asked.

'I think it might,' I said.

She drew away from me then.

'Don't be afraid,' I said. 'I won't hurt you.'

'I am afraid, and you will hurt me!' she said. 'I know it! But I want you! Why do I want you?'

'I don't know,' I said.

'There is something out there now!' she said, sounding slightly hysterical. 'It's near! It's very near! Listen! Listen!'

'Shut up!' I said, as a cold, prickly feeling came to rest on the back of my neck and coiled about my throat. 'Get over on the far side of the room, behind the bed!'

'I'm afraid of the dark,' she said.

'Do it, or I'll have to knock you out and carry you. You'll be in my way here.'

I could hear a heavy flapping above the storm, and there came a scratching on the stone of the wall as she moved to obey me.

Then I was looking into two hot, red eyes which were looking back into my own. I dropped mine quickly. The thing stood there on the ledge outside the window and regarded me.

It was well over six feet in height, with great branches of antlers growing out of its forehead. Nude, its flesh was a uniform ash-gray in color. It appeared to be sexless, and it had gray, leathery wings extending far out behind it and joining with the night. It held a short, heavy sword of dark metal in its right hand, and there were runes carved all along the blade. With its left hand, it clutched at the lattice.

'Enter at your peril,' I said loudly, and I raised the point of Grayswandir to indicate its breast.

It chuckled. It just stood there and chuckled and giggled at me. It tried to meet my eyes once more, but I would not let it. If it looked into my eyes for long, it would know me, as the hellcat had known me.

When it spoke, it sounded like a bassoon blowing words.

'You are not the one,' it said, 'for you are smaller and older. Yet . . . That blade . . . It could be his. Who are you?'

'Who are you?' I asked.

'Strygalldwir is my name. Conjure with it and I will eat your heart and liver.'

'Conjure with it? I can't even pronounce it,' I said, 'and my cirrhosis would give you indigestion. Go away.'

'Who are you?' it repeated.

'*Misli, gammi gra'dil, Strygalldwir,*' I said, and it jumped as if given a hotfoot.

'You seek to drive me forth with such a simple spell?' it asked when it settled again, 'I am not one of the lesser ones.'

'It seemed to make you a bit uncomfortable.'

'Who are you?' it said again.

'None of your business, Charlie. Ladybird, Ladybird, fly away home—'

'Four times must I ask you and four times be refused before I may enter and slay you. Who are you?'

'No,' I said, standing. 'Come on in and burn!'

Then it tore away the latticework, and the wind that accompanied it into the chamber extinguished the candle.

I lunged forward, and there were sparks between us when

Grayswandir met the dark rune-sword. We clashed, then I sprang back. My eyes had adjusted to the half dark, so the loss of the light did not blind me. The creature saw well enough, also. It was stronger than a man, but then so am I. We circled the room. An icy wind moved about us, and when we passed the window again, cold droplets lashed my face. The first time that I cut the creature – a long slash across the breast – it remained silent, though tiny flames danced about the edges of the wound. The second time that I cut it – high upon the arm – it cried out, cursing me.

'Tonight I will suck the marrow from your bones!' it said. 'I will dry them and work them most cunningly into instruments of music! Whenever I play upon them, your spirit will writhe in bodiless agony!'

'You burn prettily,' I said.

It slowed for a fraction of a second and my opportunity was there.

I beat that dark blade aside and my lunge was perfect. The center of its breast was my target I ran it through.

It howled then, but did not fall. Grayswandir was torn from my grasp and flames bloomed about the wound. It stood there wearing them. It advanced a step toward me and I picked up a small chair and held it between us.

'I do not keep my heart where men do,' it said.

Then it lunged, but I blocked the blow with chair and caught it in the right eye with one of the legs. I threw the chair to the side then, and stepping forward, seized its right wrist and turned it over. I struck the elbow with the edge of my hand, as hard as I could. There came a sharp crack and the rune-sword clattered to the floor. Then its left hand struck my head and I fell.

It leaped for the blade, and I seized its ankle and jerked.

It sprawled, and I threw myself atop it and found its throat. I turned my head into the hollow of my shoulder, chin against my breast, as it clawed for my face with its left hand.

As my death grip tightened, its eyes sought mine, and this time I did not avoid them. There came a tiny shock at the base of my brain, as we both knew that we knew.

'You!' it managed to gasp, before I twisted my hands hard and the life went out of those red red eyes.

I stood, put my foot upon its carcass, and withdrew Grayswandir.

The thing burst into flames when my blade came free, and kept burning until there was nothing remaining but a charred spot upon the floor.

Then Lorraine came over and I put my arm about her and she asked me to take her back to her quarters and to bed. So I did, but we didn't do anything but lie there together until she had cried herself to sleep. That is how I met Lorraine.

Lance and Ganelon and I sat atop our mounts on a high hill, the late morning sun hitting us in the back, and we looked down into the place. Its appearance confirmed things for me.

It was akin to that twisted wood that filled the valley to the south of Amber.

Oh my father! What have I wrought? I said within my heart, but there was no answer other than the dark Circle that lay beneath me and spread for as far as the eye could see.

Through the bars of my visor, I looked down upon it – charred-seeming, desolate, and smelling of decay. I lived inside my visor these days. The men looked upon it as an affectation, but my rank gave me the right to be eccentric. I had worn it for over two weeks, since my battle with Strygalldwir. I had put it on the following morning before I trounced Harald to keep my promise to Lorraine, and I had decided that as my girth increased I had better keep my face concealed.

I weighed perhaps fourteen stone now, and felt like my old self again. If I could help clean up this mess in the land called Lorraine, I knew that I would have a chance at least to try what I most wanted, and perhaps succeed.

'So that's it,' I said. 'I don't see any troops mustering.'

'I believe we will have to ride north,' said Lance, 'and we will doubtless only see them after dark.'

'How far north?'

'Three or four leagues. They move about a bit.'

We had ridden for two days to reach the Circle. We had met a patrol earlier that morning and learned that the troops inside the thing continued to muster every night. They went through, various drills and then were gone – to someplace deeper inside – with the coming of morning. A perpetual thunderhead, I learned, rode above the Circle, though the storm never broke.

'Shall we breakfast here and then ride north?' I asked.

'Why not?' said Ganelon. 'I'm starved and we've time.'

So we dismounted and ate dried meat and drank from our canteen.

'I still do not understand that note,' said Ganelon, after belching, patting his stomach, and lighting his pipe. 'Will he stand beside us in the final battle, or will he not? Where is he, if he intends to help? The day of conflict draws nearer and nearer.'

'Forget him,' I said. 'It was probably a joke.'

'I can't, damn it!' he said. 'There is something passing strange about the whole business!'

'What is it?' asked Lance, and for the first time I realized that Ganelon had not told him.

'My old liege, Lord Corwin, sends an odd message by carrier bird, saying he is coming. I had thought him dead, but he sent this message,' Ganelon told him. 'I still do not know what to make of it.'

'Corwin?' said Lance, and I held my breath. 'Corwin of Amber?'

'Yes, Amber and Avalon.'

'Forget his message.'

'Why?'

'He is a man without honor, and his promise means nothing.'

'You know him?'

'I know of him. Long ago, he ruled in this land. Do you not recall the stories of the demon lordling? They are the same. That was Corwin, in days before my days. The best thing he did was abdicate and flee when the resistance grew too strong against him.'

That was not true!

Or was it?

Amber casts an infinity of shadows, and my Avalon had cast many of its own, because of my presence there. I might be known on many earths that I had never trod, for shadows of myself had walked them, mimicking imperfectly my deeds and my thoughts.

'No,' said Ganelon, 'I never paid heed to the old stories. I wonder if it *could* have been the same man, ruling here. That is interesting.'

'Very,' I agreed, to keep my hand in things. 'But if he ruled so long ago, surely he must be dead or decrepit by now.'

'He was a sorcerer,' said Lance.

'The one I knew certainly was,' said Ganelon, 'for he banished me from a land neither art nor artifice can discover now.'

'You never spoke of this before,' said Lance. 'How did it occur?'

'None of your business,' said Ganelon, and Lance was silent once again.

I hauled out my own pipe – I had obtained one two days earner – and Lance did the same. It was a clay job and drew hot and hard. We lit up, and the three of us sat there smoking.

'Well, he did the smart thing,' said Ganelon. 'Let's forget it now.'

We did not of course. But we stayed away from the subject after that.

If it had not been for the dark thing behind us, it would have been quite pleasant, just sitting there, relaxing. Suddenly, I felt close to the two of them. I wanted to say something, but I could not think what. Ganelon solved that by bringing up current business once more.

'So you want to hit them before they hit us?' he said.

'That's right,' I replied. 'Take the fight to their home territory.'

'The trouble is that it *is* their home territory,' he said. 'They know it better than we do now, and who knows what powers they might be able to call on there?'

'Kill the horned one and they will crumble,' I said.

'Perhaps. Perhaps not. Maybe you could do it,' said Ganelon. 'Unless I got lucky, though, I don't know whether I could. He's too mean to die easily. While I think I'm still as good a man as I was some years ago, I may be fooling myself. Perhaps I've grown soft. I never wanted this damn stay-at-home job!'

'I know,' I said.

'I know,' said Lance.

'Lance,' said Ganelon, 'should we do as our friend here says? Should we attack?'

He could have shrugged and equivocated. He did not.

'Yes,' he said. 'They almost had us last time. It was very close the night King Uther died. If we do not attack them now, I feel they may defeat us next time. Oh, it would not be easy, and we would hurt them badly. But I think they could do it. Let us see what we can see now, then make our plans for an attack.'

'All right,' said Ganelon. 'I am sick of waiting, too. Tell me that again after we return and I'll go along with it.'

So we did that thing.

We rode north that afternoon, and we hid ourselves in the hills and looked down upon the Circle. Within it, they worshipped, after their fashion, and they drilled. I estimated around four thousand troops. We had about twenty-five hundred. They also had weird flying, hopping, crawling things that made noises in the night. We had stout hearts. Yeah.

All that I needed was a few minutes alone with their leader, and it would be decided, one way or another. The whole thing down there. I had done it, and it was up to me to undo it, if I could.

I was afraid that I could not.

In a fit of passion, compounded of rage, horror, and pain, I had unleashed this thing, and it was reflected somewhere in every earth in existence. Such is the blood curse of a Prince of Amber.

We watched them all that night, the Wardens of the Circle, and in the morning we departed.

The verdict was, attack!

So we rode all the way back and nothing followed us. When we reached the Keep of Ganelon, we fell to planning. Our troops were ready – over-ready, perhaps – and we decided to strike within a fortnight.

As I lay with Lorraine, I told her of these things. For I felt that she should know. I possessed the power to spirit her away into Shadow – that very night, if she would agree. She did not.

'I'll stay with you,' she said.

'Okay.'

I did not tell her that I felt everything lay within my hands, but I have a feeling she knew and that for some reason she trusted me. I would not have, but that was her affair.

'You know how things might be,' I said.

'I know,' she said, and I knew that she knew and that was it.

We turned our attention to other subjects, and later we slept.

She'd had a dream.

In the morning, she said to me, 'I had a dream.'

'What about?' I asked.

'The coming battle,' she told me. 'I see you and the horned one locked in combat.'

'Who wins?'

'I don't know. But as you slept, I did a thing that might help you.'

'I wish you had not,' I said. 'I can take care of myself.'

'Then I dreamed of my own death, in this time.'

'Let me take you away to a place I know.'

'No, my place is here,' she told me.

'I don't pretend to own you,' I said, 'but I can save you from whatever you've dreamed. That much lies within my power, believe me.'

'I do believe you, but I will not go.'

'You're a damned fool.'

'Let me stay.'

'As you wish . . . Listen, I'll even send you to Cabra . . .'

'No.'

'You're a damned fool.'

'I know. I love you.'

'. . . And a stupid one. The word is "like". Remember?'

'You'll do it,' she said.

'Go to hell,' I said.

Then she wept, softly, until I comforted her once again.

That was Lorraine.

3

I thought back, one morning, upon all that had gone before. I thought of my brothers and sisters as though they were playing cards, which I knew was wrong. I thought back to the rest home where I had awakened, back to the battle for Amber, back to my walking the Pattern in Rebma, and back to that time with Moire, who just might be Eric's by now. I thought of Bleys and of Random, Deirdre, Caine, Gérard, and Eric, that morning. It was the morning of the battle, of course, and we were camped in the hills near the Circle. We had been attacked several times along the way, but they had been brief, guerrilla affairs. We had dispatched our assailants and continued. When we reached the area we had decided upon, we made our camp, posted guards, and retired. We slept undisturbed. I awoke wondering whether my brothers and sisters thought of me as I thought of them. It was a very sad thought.

In the privacy of a small grove, my helmet filled with soapy water, I shaved my beard. Then I dressed, slowly, in my private and tattered colors. I was as hard as stone, dark as soil, and mean as hell once more. Today would be the day. I donned my visor, put on chain mail, buckled my belt, and hung Grayswandir at my side. Then I fastened my cloak at my neck with a silver rose and was discovered by a messenger who had been looking for me to tell me that things were about ready.

I kissed Lorraine, who had insisted on coming along. Then I mounted my horse, a roan named Star, and rode off toward the front.

There I met with Ganelon and with Lance. They said, 'We are ready.'

I called for my officers and briefed them. They saluted, turned and rode away.

'Soon,' said Lance, lighting his pipe.

'How is your arm?'

'Fine, now,' he replied, 'after that workout you gave it yesterday. Perfect.'

I opened my visor and lit my own pipe.

'You've shaved your beard,' said Lance. 'I cannot picture you without it.'

'The helm fits better this way,' I said.

'Good fortune to us all,' said Ganelon. 'I know no gods, but if any care to be with us, I welcome them.'

'There is but one God,' said Lance. 'I pray that. He be with us.'

'Amen,' said Ganelon, lighting his pipe. 'For today.'

'It will be ours,' said Lance.

'Yes,' said I, as the sun stirred the east and the birds of morning the air, 'it has that feel to it.'

We emptied our pipes when we had finished and tucked them away at our belts. Then we secured ourselves with final tightenings and claspings of our armor and Ganelon said, 'Let us be about it.'

My officers reported back to me. My sections were ready.

We filed down the hillside, and we assembled outside the Circle. Nothing stirred within it, and no troops were visible.

'I wonder about Corwin,' Ganelon said to me.

'He is with us,' I told him, and he looked at me strangely, seemed to notice the rose for the first time, then nodded brusquely.

'Lance,' he said, when we had assembled. 'Give the order.'

And Lance drew his blade. His cried 'Charge!' echoed about us.

We were half a mile inside the Circle before anything happened. There were five hundred of us in the lead, all mounted. A dark cavalry appeared, and we met them. After five minutes, they broke and we rode on.

Then we heard the thunder.

There was lightning and the rain began to fall.

The thunderhead had finally broken.

A thin line of foot soldiers, pikemen mainly, barred our way, waiting stoically. Maybe we all smelled the trap, but we bore down upon them.

Then the cavalry hit our flanks.

We wheeled, and the fighting began in earnest.

It was perhaps twenty minutes later . . .

We held out, waiting for the main body to arrive.

Then the two hundred or so of us rode on . . .

Men. It was men that we slew, that slew us – gray-faced, dour-countenanced men. I wanted more. One more . . .

Theirs most have been a semi-metaphysical problem in logistics. How much could be diverted through this Gateway? I was not sure. Soon . . .

We topped a rise, and far ahead and below us lay a dark citadel.

I raised my blade.

As we descended, they attacked.

They hissed and they croaked and they flapped. They meant, to me, that he was running low on people. Grayswandir became a flame in my hand, a thunderbolt, a portable electric chair. I slew them as fast as they approached, and they burned as they died. To my right, I saw Lance draw a similar line of chaos, and he was muttering beneath his breath. Prayers for the dead, no doubt. To my left, Ganelon laid about him, and a wake of fires followed behind his horse's tail. Through the flashing lightning, the citadel loomed larger.

The hundred or so of us stormed ahead, and the abominations fell by the wayside.

When we reached the gate, we were faced by an infantry of men and beasts. We charged.

They outnumbered as, but we had little choice. Perhaps we had preceded our own infantry by too much. But I thought not. Time, as I saw it, was all important now.

'I've got to get through!' I cried. 'He's inside!'

'He's mine!' said Lance.

'You're both welcome to him!' said Ganelon, laying about him. 'Cross when you can! I'm with you!'

We slew and we slew and we slew, and then the tide turned in their favor. They pressed us, all the ugly things that were more or less than human, mixed in with human troops. We were drawn up into a tight knot, defending ourselves on all sides, when our bedraggled infantry arrived and began hacking. We pressed for the gate once more and made it this time, all forty or fifty of us.

We won through, and then there were troops in the courtyard to be slain.

The dozen or so of us who made it to the foot of the dark tower were faced by a final guard contingent.

'Go for it!' cried Ganelon, as we leaped from our horses and waded into them.

'Go for it!' cried Lance, and I guess they both meant me, or each other.

I took it to mean me, and I broke away from the fray and raced up the stairs.

He would be there, in the highest tower, I knew; and I would have to face him, and face him down. I did not know whether I could, but I had to try, because I was the only one who knew where he really came from – and I was the one who put him there.

I came to a heavy wooden door at the top of the stairs. I tried it but it was secured from the other side. So I kicked it as hard as I could.

It fell inward with a crash.

I saw him there by the window, a man-formed body dressed in light armor, goat head upon those massive shoulders.

I crossed the threshold and stopped.

He had turned to stare as the door had fallen, and now he sought my eyes through steel.

'Mortal man, you have come too far,' he said. 'Or *are* you mortal man?' and there was a blade in his hand.

'Ask Strygalldwir,' I said.

'You are the one who slew him,' he stated. 'Did he name you?'

'Maybe.'

There were footsteps on the stairs behind me. I stepped to the left of the doorway.

Ganelon burst into the chamber and I called 'Halt!' and he did.

'This is the thing,' he said. 'What is it?'

'My sin against a thing I loved,' I said. 'Stay away from it. It's mine.'

'You're welcome to it.'

He stood stock still.

'Did you really mean that?' asked the creature.

'Find out,' I said, and leaped forward.

But it did not fence with me. Instead, it did what any mortal fencer would consider foolish.

It hurled its blade at me, point forward, like a thunderbolt. And the sound of its passage came like a clap of thunder. The elements outside the tower echoed it, a deafening response.

With Grayswandir, I parried that blade as though it were an ordinary thrust. It embedded itself in the floor and burst into flame. Without, the lightning responded.

For an instant, the light was as blinding as a magnesium flare, and in that moment the creature was upon me.

It pinned my arms to my sides, and its horns struck against my visor, once, twice . . .

Then I threw my strength against those arms, and their grip began to weaken.

I dropped Grayswandir, and with a final heave broke the hold it had upon me.

In that moment, however, our eyes met.

Then we both struck, and we both reeled back.

'Lord of Amber,' it said then, 'why do you strive with me? It was you who gave us this passage, this way . . .'

'I regret a rash act and seek to undo it.'

'Too late – and this a strange place to begin.'

It struck again, so quickly that it got through my guard. I was slammed back against the wall. Its speed was deadly.

And then it raised its hand and made a sign, and I had a vision of the courts of Chaos come upon me – a vision that made my hackles rise, made a chill wind blow across my soul, to know what I had done.

'. . . You see?' it was saying. 'You gave us this Gateway. Help us now, and we will restore to you that which is yours.'

For a moment I was swayed. It was possible that it could do just what it had offered, if I would help.

But it would be a threat forever after. Allies briefly, we would be at each other's throats after we got what we wanted – and those dark forces would be much stronger by then. Still, if I held the city . . .

'Do we have a bargain?' came the sharp, near-bleat of the question.

I thought upon the shadows, and of the places beyond Shadow . . .

Slowly, I reached up and unbuckled my helm . . .

Then I hurled it, just as the creature seemed to relax. I think Ganelon was moving forward by then.

I leaped across the chamber and drove it back against the wall.

'No!' I cried.

Its manlike hands found my throat at about the same instant mine wrapped about its own.

I squeezed, with all my strength, and twisted. I guess it did the same.

I heard something snap like a dry stick. I wondered whose neck had broken. Mine sure hurt.

I opened my eyes and there was the sky. I was lying on my back on a blanket on the ground.

'I'm afraid he's going to live,' said Ganelon, and I turned my head, slowly, in the direction of his voice.

He was seated on the edge of the blanket, sword across his knees. Lorraine was with him.

'How goes it?' I said.

'We've won,' he told me. 'You've kept your promise. When you killed that thing, it was all over. The men fell senseless, the creatures burned.'

'Good.'

'I have been sitting here wondering why I no longer hate you.'

'Have you reached any conclusions?'

'No, not really. Maybe it's because we're a lot alike. I don't know.'

I smiled at Lorraine.

'I'm glad you're very poor when it comes to prophecy. The battle is over and you're still alive.'

'The death has already begun,' she said, not returning my smile.

'What do you mean?'

'They still tell stories of how the Lord Corwin had my grandfather executed – drawn and quartered publicly – for leading one of the early uprisings against him.'

'That wasn't me,' I said. 'It was one of my shadows.'

But she shook her head and said, 'Corwin of Amber, I am what I am,' and she rose and left me then.

'What was it?' asked Ganelon, ignoring her departure. 'What was the thing in the tower?'

'Mine,' I said; 'one of those things which was released when I laid my curse upon Amber. I opened the way then for that which lies beyond Shadow to enter the real world. The paths of least resistance are followed in these things, through the shadows to Amber. Here, the path was the Circle. Elsewhere, it might be some different thing. I have closed their way through this place now. You may rest easy here.'

'That is why you came here?'

'No,' I said. 'Not really. I was but passing on the road to Avalon when I came upon Lance. I could not let him lie there, and after I took him to you I became involved in this piece of my handiwork.'

'Avalon? Then you lied when you said it was destroyed?'

I shook my head.

'Not so. Our Avalon feel, but in Shadow I may find its like once more.'

'Take me with you.'

'Are you mad?'

'No, I would look once again on the land of my birth, no matter what the peril.'

'I do not go to dwell there,' I said, 'but to arm for battle. In Avalon there is a pink powder the jewelers use. I ignited a sample of it one time in Amber. I go there only to obtain it and to build guns that I may lay siege to Amber and gain the throne that is mine.'

'What of those things from beyond Shadow you spoke of.'

'I will deal with them afterwards. Should I lose this time, then they are Eric's problem.'

'You said that he had blinded you and cast you into the dungeons.'

'That is true. I grew new eyes. I escaped.'

'You *are* a demon.'

'This has often been said. I no longer deny it.'

'You will take me with you?'

'If you really wish to come. It will differ from the Avalon you knew, however.'

'To Amber!'

'You *are* mad!'

'No. Long have I wished to look upon that fabled city. After I have seen Avalon once again I will want to turn my hand to something new. Was I not a good general?'

'Yes.'

'Then you will teach me of these things you call guns, and I will help you in the greatest battle. I've not too many good years remaining before me, I know. Take me with you.'

'Your bones may bleach at the foot of Kolvir, beside my own.'

'What battle is certain? I will chance it.'

'As you would. You may come.'

'Thank you, Lord.'

We camped there that night, rode back to the keep in the morning. Then I sought after Lorraine. I learned that she had run off with one of her former lovers, an officer named Melkin. Although she had been upset, I resented the fact that she had not given me the opportunity to explain something of which she only knew rumors. I decided to follow them.

I mounted Star, turned my stiff neck in the direction they had supposedly taken, and rode on after. In a way, I could not blame her. I had not been received back at the keep as the slayer of the horned one might have been were he anyone else. The stories of their Corwin lingered on, and the demon tag was on all of them. The men I had worked with, fought beside, now looked at me with glances holding something more than fear – glances only, for they quickly dropped their eyes or turned them to another thing. Perhaps they feared that I wished to stay and reign over them. They might have been relieved, all save Ganelon, when I took to the trail. Ganelon, I think, feared that I would not return for him as I had promised. This, I feel, is the reason that he offered to ride with me. But it was a thing that I had to do by myself.

Lorraine had come to mean something to me, I was surprised to discover, and I found myself quite hurt by her action. I felt that she owed me a hearing before she went her way. Then if she still chose her mortal captain, they could have my blessing. If not, I realized that I wanted to keep her with me. Fair Avalon would be postponed for so long as it took me to resolve this to ending or continuance.

I rode along the trail and the birds sang in the trees about me. The day was bright with a sky-blue, tree-green peace, for the scourge had been lifted from the land. In my heart, there was something like a bit of joy that I had undone at least a small portion of the rottenness I had wrought Evil? Hell, I've done more of it than most men, but I had picked up a conscience too, somewhere along the way, and I let it enjoy one of its rare moments of satisfaction. Once I held Amber, I could allow it a little more leeway, I felt. Ha!

I was heading north, and the terrain was foreign to me. I followed a clearly marked trail, which bore the signs of two riders' recent passage. I followed all that day, through dusk and into evening, dismounting periodically to inspect the way. Finally, my eyes played too many tricks on me, so I located a small glen – several hundred yards to the left of the trail – and there I camped for the night. It was the pains in my neck, doubtless, that made me dream of the horned one and relive that battle. 'Help us now, and we will restore to you that which is yours,' it said. I awoke suddenly at that point, with a curse on my lips.

When morning paled the sky, I mounted and continued on. It had been a cold night, and the day still held me in hands out of the north. The grasses sparkled with a light frost and my cloak was damp from having been used as a bedroll.

By noon, something of warmth had returned to the world and the trail was fresher. I was gaining on them.

When I found her, I leaped down from my mount and ran to where she lay, beneath a wild rosebush without flowers, the thorns of which had scratched her cheek and shoulder. Dead, she had not been so for long, for the blood was still damp upon her breast where the blade had entered, and her flesh yet warm.

There were no rocks with which to build her a cairn, so I cut away the sod with Grayswandir and laid her there to rest. He had removed her bracelets, her rings, and her jeweled combs, which had held all she possessed of fortune. I had to close her eyes before I covered her over with my cloak, and here my hand faltered and my own eyes grew dim. It took me a long while.

I rode on, and it was not long before I overtook him, riding as though he were pursued by the Devil, which he was. I spoke not a word when I unhorsed him, nor afterward, and I did not use my blade, though he drew his own. I hurled his broken body into a high oak tree, and when I looked back it was dark with birds.

I replaced her rings, her bracelets, her combs, before I closed the grave, and that was Lorraine. All that she had ever been or wanted to be had come to this, and that is the whole story of how we met and how we parted, Lorraine and I, in the land called Lorraine, and it is like onto my life, I guess, for a Prince of Amber is part and party to all the rottenness that is in the world, which is why whenever I do speak of my conscience, something else within me must answer 'Ha!'. In the mirrors of the many judgments, my hands are the color of blood. I am a part of the evil which exists to oppose other evils. I destroy Melkins when I find them, and on that Great Day of which prophets speak but in which they do not truly believe, on that day when the world is completely cleansed of evil, then I, too, will go down into darkness, swallowing curses. Perhaps even sooner than that, I now judge. But whatever . . . Until that time, I shall not wash my hands nor let them hang useless.

Turning, I rode back to the Keep of Ganelon, who knew but would never understand.

4

Riding, riding, through the wild, weird ways that led to Avalon, we went, Ganelon and I, down alleys of dream and of nightmare beneath the brass bark of the sun and the hot, white isles of night, till these were gold and diamond chips and the moon swam like a swan. Day belled forth the green of spring, we crossed a mighty river and the mountains before us were frosted by night. I unleashed an arrow of my desire into the midnight and it took fire overhead, burned its way like a meteor into the north. The only dragon we encountered was lame and limped away quickly to hide, singeing daisies as it panted and wheezed. Migrations of bright birds arrowed our destination, and crystalline voices from lakes echoed our words as we passed. I sang as we rode, and after a time, Ganelon joined me. We had been traveling for over a week, and the land and the sky and the breezes told me we were near to Avalon now.

We camped in a wood near a lake as the sun slid behind stone and the day died down and ceased. I went off to the lake to bathe while Ganelon unpacked our gear. The water was cold and bracing. I splashed about in it for a long while.

I thought I heard several cries as I bathed, but I could not be certain. It was a weird wood and I was not overly concerned. However, I dressed quickly and hurried back to the camp.

As I walked, I heard it again: a whine, a plea. Drawing nearer, I realized that a conversation was in progress.

Then I entered the small clearing we had chosen. Our gear was spread about and the beginnings of a campfire had been laid.

Ganelon squatted on his haunches beneath an oak tree. The man hung from it.

He was young and fair of hair and complexion. Beyond that, it was hard to say at a glance. It is difficult, I discovered, to obtain a clear initial impression as to a man's features and size when he is hanging upside down several feet above the ground.

His hands had been tied behind his back and he hung from a low bough by a rope that had been knotted about his right ankle.

He was talking – brief, rapid phrases in response to Ganelon's questions – and his face was moist with spittle and sweat. He did not hang limply, but swung back and forth. There was an abrasion on his cheek and several spots of blood on his shirt front.

Halting, I restrained myself from interrupting for a moment and watched. Ganelon would not have put him where he was without a reason, so I was not immediately overwhelmed with sympathy for the fellow. Whatever it was that had prompted Ganelon to question him thus, I knew that I, too, would be interested in the information. I was also interested in whatever the session would show me concerning Ganelon, who was now something of an ally. And a few more minutes upside down could not do that much additional damage . . .

As his body slowed, Ganelon prodded him in the sternum with the tip of his blade and set him to swinging violently once again. This broke the skin lightly and another red spot appeared. At this, the boy cried out. From his complexion, I could see now that he was a youth. Ganelon extended his blade and held its point several inches beyond the place the boy's throat would come to on the backswing. At the last moment, he snatched it back and chuckled as the boy writhed and cried out, 'Please!'

'The rest,' said Ganelon. 'Tell me everything.'

'That's all!' said the other. 'I know no more!'

'Why not?'

'They swept on by me then! I could not see!'

'Why did you not follow?'

'They were mounted. I was on foot.'

'Why did you not follow on foot then?'

'I was dazed.'

'Dazed? You were afraid! You deserted!'

'No!'

Ganelon held his blade forth, snapped it away again at the final moment.

'No!' cried the youth.

Ganelon moved the blade again.

'Yes!' the boy screamed. 'I was afraid!'

'And you fled then?'

'Yes! I kept running! I've been fleeing ever since . . .'

'And you know nothing of how things went after that?'

'No.'

'You lie!'

He moved the blade again.

'No!' said the boy. 'Please . . .'

I stepped forward then.

'Ganelon,' I said.

He glanced at me and grinned, lowering the blade. The boy sought my eyes.

'What have we here?' I asked.

'Ha!' be said, slapping the inside of the youth's thigh so that he cried out. 'A thief, a deserter – with an interesting tale to tell.'

'Then cut him down and let me hear it,' I said.

Ganelon turned and cut through the cord with one swipe of his blade. The boy fell to the ground and began sobbing.

'I caught him trying to steal our supplies and thought to question him about the area,' Ganelon said. 'He's come from Avalon – quickly.'

'What do you mean?'

'He was a foot soldier in a battle that took place there two nights ago. He turned coward during the fighting and deserted.'

The youth began to mouth a denial and Ganelon kicked him.

'Silence!' he said. 'I'm telling it now – as you told me!'

The boy moved sideways like a crab and looked at me with wide, pleading eyes.

'Battle? Who was fighting?' I asked.

Ganelon smiled grimly.

'It sounds somewhat familiar,' he said. 'The forces of Avalon were engaged in what seems to have been the largest – and perhaps final – of a long series of confrontations with beings not quite natural.'

'Oh?'

I studied the boy and his eyes dropped, but I saw that fear was there before they fell.

'. . . Women,' Ganelon said. 'Pale furies out of some hell, lovely and cold. Armed and armored. Long, light hair. Eyes like ice. Mounted on white, fire-breathing steeds that fed on human flesh, they came forth by night from a warren of caves in the mountains an earthquake opened several years ago. They raided, taking young men back with them as captives, killing all others. Many appeared later as a soulless infantry, following their van. This sounds very like the men of the Circle we knew.'

'But many of those lived when they were freed,' I said. 'They did not seem soulless then, only somewhat as I once did – amnesiac. It seems strange,' I went on, 'that they did not block off these caves during the day, since the riders only came forth by night . . .'

'The deserter tells me this was tried,' said Ganelon, 'and they always burst forth after a time, stronger than before.'

The boy was ashen, but he nodded when I looked toward him inquiringly.

'Their General, whom he calls the Protector, routed them many times,' Ganelon continued. 'He even spent part of a night with their leader, a pale bitch named Lintra – whether in dalliance or parlay, I'm not certain. But nothing came of this. The raids continued and her forces grew stronger. The Protector finally decided to mass an all-out attack, in hopes of destroying them utterly. It was during that battle that this one fled,' he said, indicating the youth with a gesture of his blade, 'which is why we do not know the ending to the story.'

'Is that the way it was?' I asked him.

The boy looked away from the weapon's point, met my eyes for a moment, then nodded slowly.

'Interesting,' I said to Ganelon. 'Very. I've a feeling their problem is linked to the one we just solved. I wish I knew how their fight turned out.'

Ganelon nodded, shifted his grip on his weapon.

'Well, if we're finished with him now . . .' he said.

'Hold. I presume be was trying to steal something to eat?'

'Yes.'

'Free his hands. We'll feed him.'

'But he tried to steal from us.'

'Did you not say that you had once killed a man for a pair of shoes?'

'Yes, but that was different.'

'How so?'

'I got away with it.'

I laughed. It broke me up completely, and I could not stop laughing. He looked irritated, then puzzled. Then he began laughing himself.

The youth regarded us as if we were a pair of maniacs.

'All right,' said Ganelon finally, 'all right,' and he stooped, turned the boy with a single push, and severed the cord that bound his wrists.

'Come, lad,' he said. 'I'll fetch you something to eat,' and he moved to our gear and opened several food parcels.

The boy rose and limped slowly after him. He seized the food that was offered and began, eating quickly and noisily, not taking his eyes off Ganelon. His information, if true, presented me with several complications, the foremost being that it would probably be more difficult to obtain what I wanted in a war-ravaged land. It also lent weight to my fears as to the nature and extent of the disruption pattern.

I helped Ganelon build a small fire.

'How does this affect our plans?' he asked.

I saw no real choice. All of the shadows near to what I desired would be similarly involved. I could lay my course for one which did not possess such involvement, but in reaching it I would have achieved the wrong place. That which I desired would not be available there. If the forays of chaos kept occurring on my desire-walk through Shadow, then they were bound up with the nature of the desire and would have to be dealt with, one way or another, sooner or later. They could not be avoided. Such was the nature of the game, and I could not complain because I had laid down the rules.

'We go on,' I said. 'It is the place of my desire.'

The youth let out a brief cry, and then – perhaps from some feeling of indebtedness for my having prevented Ganelon from poking holes in him – warned, 'Do not go to Avalon, sir! There is nothing there that you could desire! You will be slain!'

I smiled to him and thanked him. Ganelon chuckled then and said, 'Let us take him back with us to stand a deserter's trial.'

At this, the youth scrambled to his feet and began running.

Still laughing, Ganelon drew his dagger and cocked his arm to throw it. I struck his arm and his cast went wide of its mark. The youth vanished within the wood and Ganelon continued to laugh.

He retrieved the dagger from where it had fallen and said, 'You should have let me kill him, you know.'

'I decided against it.'

He shrugged.

'If he returns and cuts our throats tonight you may find yourself feeling somewhat different.'

'I should imagine. But he will not, you know that.'

He shrugged again, skewering a piece of meat and warming it over the flames.

'Well, war has taught him to show a good pair of heels,' he acknowledged. 'Perhaps we *will* awaken in the morning.'

He took a bite and began to chew. It seemed like a good idea and I fetched some for myself.

Much later, I was awakened from a troubled sleep to stare at stars through a screen of leaves. Some omen-making portion of my mind had seized upon the youth and used us both badly. It was a long while before I could get back to sleep.

In the morning we kicked dirt over the ashes and rode on. We made it into the mountains that afternoon and passed through them the following day. There were occasional signs of recent passage on the trail we followed, but we encountered no one.

The following day we passed several farmhouses and cottages, not pausing at any of them. I had opted against the wild, demonic route I had followed when I exiled Ganelon. While quite brief, I knew that he would have found it massively disconcerting. I had wanted this time to think, so such a journeying was not called for. Now, however, the long route was nearing its end. We achieved Amber's sky that afternoon, and I admired it in silence. It might almost be the Forest of Arden through which we rode. There were no horn notes, however, no Julian, no Morgenstern, no stormhounds to harry us, as there had been in Arden when last I passed that way. There were only the bird notes in the great-boled trees, the complaint of a squirrel, the bark of a fox, the plash of a waterfall, the whites and blues and pinks of flowers in the shade.

The breezes of the afternoon were gentle and cool; they lulled me so that I was unprepared for the row of fresh graves beside the trail that came into sight when we rounded a bend. Near by, there was a torn and trampled glen. We tarried them briefly but learned nothing more than had been immediately apparent.

We passed another such place farther along, and several fire-charred groves. The trail was well worn by then and the side brush trampled and broken, as by the passage of many men and beasts. The smell of ashes was occasionally upon the air, and we hurried past the partly eaten carcass of a horse now well ripened where it lay.

The sky of Amber no longer heartened me, though the way was clear for a long while after that.

The day was running to evening and the forest had thinned considerably when Ganelon noted the smoke trails to the southeast. We took the first side path that seemed to lead in that direction, although it was tangent to Avalon proper. It was difficult to estimate the distance, but we could tell that we would not reach the place until after nightfall.

'Their army – still encamped?' Ganelon wondered.

'Or that of their conqueror.'

He shook his head and loosened his blade in its scabbard.

Toward twilight, I left the trail to follow a sound of running water to its source. It was a clear, clean stream that had made its way down from the mountains and still bore something of their chill within it. I bathed there, trimming my new beard and cleaning the dust of travel from my garments as well. As we were nearing this end of our journeying, it was my wish to arrive with what small splendor I could muster. Appreciating this, Ganelon even splashed water over his face and blew his nose loudly.

Standing on the bank, blinking my rinsed eyes at the heavens, I saw the moon resolve itself sharp and clear, the fuzziness fading from its edges. This was the first time it had happened. My breathing jerked to a halt and I kept staring. Then I scanned the sky for early stars, traced the edges of clouds, the distant mountains, the farthest trees. I looked back at the moon, and it still held clear and steady. My eyesight was normal once again.

Ganelon drew back at the sound of my laughter, and he never inquired as to its cause.

Suppressing an impulse to sing, I remounted and headed back toward the trail once again. The shadows deepened as we rode, and clusters of stars bloomed among the branches overhead. I inhaled a big piece of the night, held it a moment, released it. I was myself once again and the feeling was good.

Ganelon drew up beside me and said in a low voice, 'There will doubtless be sentries.'

'Yes,' I said.

'Then hadn't we better leave the trail?'

'No. I would rather not seem furtive. It matters not to me whether we arrive with an escort. We are simply two travelers.'

'They may require the reason for our travels.'

'Then let us be mercenaries who have heard of strife in the realm and come seeking employment.'

'Yes. We look the part. Let us hope they pause long enough to notice.'

'If they cannot see us that well, then we are poor targets.'

'True, but I am not fully comforted by the thought.'

I listened to the sounds of the horses' hoofs on the trail. The way was not straight. It twisted, curved, and wandered for a time, then took an upward turn. As we mounted the rise it followed, the trees thinned even more.

We came to the top of a hill then, and into a fairly open area. Advancing, we achieved a sudden view that covered several miles. We drew rein at an abrupt drop that curved its way into a gradual slope after ten or fifteen precipitous meters, sweeping downward to a large plain perhaps a mile distant, then continuing on through a hilly, sporadically wooded area. The plain was dotted with campfires and there were a few tents toward the center of things. A large number of horses grazed near by, and I guessed there were several hundred men sitting beside the fires or moving about the compound.

Ganelon sighed.

'At least they seem to be normal men,' he said.

'Yes.'

'. . . And if they are normal military men, we are probably being watched right now. This is too good a vantage to leave unposted.'

'Yes.'

There came a noise from behind us. We began to turn, just as a near by voice said, 'Don't move!'

I continued to turn my head, and I saw four men. Two of them held crossbows trained on us and the other two had blades in their hands. One of these advanced two paces.

'Dismount!' he ordered, 'On this side! Slowly!'

We climbed down from our mounts and faced him, keeping our hands away from our weapons.

'Who are you? Where are you from?' he asked.

'We are mercenaries,' I replied, 'from Lorraine. We heard there was fighting here, and we are seeking employment. We were headed for that camp below. It is yours, I hope?'

'. . . And if I said no, that we are a patrol for a force about to invade that camp?'

I shrugged. 'In that case, is your side interested in hiring a couple of men?'

He spat. 'The Protector has no need for your sort,' he said. Then, 'From what direction do you ride?'

'East,' I said.

'Did you meet with any – difficulty – recently?'

'No,' I said. 'Should we have?'

'Hard to say,' he decided. 'Remove your weapons. I'm going to send you down to the camp. They will want to question you about anything you may have seen in the east – anything unusual.'

'We've seen nothing unusual,' I said.

'Whatever, they will probably feed you. Though I doubt you will be hired. You have come a bit late for the fighting. Remove your weapons now.'

He called two more men from within the trees while we unbuckled our sword belts. He instructed them to escort us below, on foot. We were to lead our horses. The men took our weapons, and as we turned to go our interrogator cried out, 'Wait!'

I turned back toward him.

'You. What is your name?' he asked me.

'Corey,' I said.

'Stand still.'

He approached, drawing very near. He stared at me for perhaps ten seconds.

'What is the matter?' I asked.

Instead of replying, he fumbled with a pouch at his belt. He withdrew a handful of coins and held them close to his eyes.

'Damn! It's too dark,' he said, 'and we can't make a light.'

'For what?' I said.

'Oh, it is not of any great importance,' he told me. 'You struck me as familiar, though, and I was trying to think why. You look like the head stamped on some of our old coins. A few of them are still about.

'Doesn't he?' he addressed the nearest bowman.

The man lowered his crossbow and advanced. He squinted at me from a few paces' distance.

'Yes,' he said then, 'he does.'

'Who was it – the one we're thinking of?'

'One of those old men. Before my time. I don't remember.'

'Me neither. Well . . .' He shrugged. 'No importance. Go ahead, Corey. Answer their questions honestly and you'll not be harmed.'

I turned away and left him there in the moonlight, gazing after me and scratching the top of his head.

The men who guarded us were not the talkative sort. Which was just as well.

All the way down the hill I wondered about the boy's story and the resolution of the conflict he had described, for I had achieved the physical analogue of the world of my desire and would now have to operate within the prevailing situations.

The camp had the pleasant smell of man and beast, wood smoke, roasting meat, leather and oil, all intermingled in the firelight where men talked, honed weapons, repaired gear, ate, gamed, slept, drank, and watched us as we led our mounts through their midst escorted in the direction of a nearly central trio of tattered tents. A sphere of silence expanded about us as we went.

We were halted before the second-largest tent and one of our guards spoke with a man who was pacing the area. The man shook his head several times and gestured in the direction of the largest tent. The exchange lasted for several minutes, then our guard returned and spoke with the other guard who waited at our left. Finally, our man nodded and approached me while the other summoned a man from the nearest campfire.

'The officers are all at a meeting in the Protector's tent,' he said. 'We are going to hobble your horses and put them to graze. Unstrap your things and set them here. You will have to wait to see the captain.'

I nodded, and we set about unstowing our belongings and rubbing the horses down. I patted Star on the neck and watched a small man with a limp lead him and Ganelon's mount Firedrake off toward the other horses. We sat on our packs then and waited. One of the guards brought us some hot tea and accepted a pipeful of my tobacco. They moved then to a spot somewhat to our rear.

I watched the big tent, sipped my tea, and thought of Amber and a small night club in the Rue de Char et Pain in Brussels, on the shadow Earth I had so long inhabited. Once I obtained the jewelers rouge I needed from here, I would be heading for Brussels to deal with the arms merchants of the Gun Bourse once again. My order would be complicated and expensive, I realized, because some ammunition manufacturer would have to be persuaded to set up a special production line. I knew dealers on that Earth other than Interarmco, thanks to my itinerant military background in that place, and I estimated that it would only take me a few months to get outfitted there. I began considering the details and time passed quickly and pleasantly.

After what was probably an hour and a half, the shadows stirred within the large tent. It was several minutes after that before the entrance flap was thrown aside and men began to emerge, slowly, talking among themselves, glancing back within. The last two tarried at the threshold, still talking with someone who remained inside. The rest of them passed into the other tents.

The two at the entrance edged their way outside, still facing the interior. I could hear the sounds of their voices, although I could not make out what was being said. As they drifted farther outside, the man with whom they were speaking moved also and I caught a glimpse of him. The light was at his back and the two officers blocked most of my view, but I could see that he was thin and very tall.

Our guards had not yet stirred, indicating to me that one of the two officers was the captain mentioned earlier. I continued to stare, willing them to move farther and grant me a better look at their superior.

After a time they did, and a few moments later he took a step forward.

At first, I could not tell whether it was just a play of light and shadow . . . But no! He moved again and I had a clear view for a moment. He was missing his right arm, from a point just below the elbow. It was so heavily bandaged that I guessed the loss to have been quite recent.

Then his large left hand made a downward, sweeping gesture and hovered a good distance out from his body. The stump twitched at the same moment, and so did something at the back of my mind. His hair was long and straight and brown, and I saw the the way that his jaw jutted . . .

He stepped outside then, and a breeze caught the cloak he wore and caused it to flare to his right. I saw that his shirt was yellow, his trousers brown. The cloak itself was a flame-like orange, and he caught its edge with an unnaturally rapid movement of his left hand and drew it back to cover his stump.

I stood quickly, and his head snapped in my direction.

Our gazes met, and neither of us moved for several heartbeats after that.

The two officers turned and stared, and then he pushed them aside and was striding toward me. I heard Ganelon grunt and climb quickly to his feet. Our guards were taken by surprise, also.

He halted several paces before me and his hazel eyes swept over me. He seldom smiled, but he managed a faint one this time.

'Come with me,' he said, and he turned back toward his tent.

We followed him, leaving our gear where it lay.

He dismissed the two officers with a glance, halted beside the tent's entrance and motioned us in. He followed and let the flap fall behind him. My eyes took in his bedroll, a small table, benches, weapons, a campaign chest. There was an oil lamp on the table, as well as books, maps, a bottle, and some cups. Another lamp flickered atop the chest.

He clasped my hand and smiled again.

'Corwin,' he said, 'and still alive.'

'Benedict,' I said, smiling myself, 'and breathing yet. It has been devilish long.'

'Indeed. Who is your friend?'

'His name is Ganelon.'

'Ganelon,' he said, nodding toward him but not offering to clasp hands.

He moved to the table then and poured three cups of wine. He passed one to me, another to Ganelon, raised the third himself.

'To your health, brother,' he said.

'To yours.'

We drank.

Then, 'Be seated,' he said, gesturing toward the nearest bench and seating himself at the table, 'and welcome to Avalon.'

'Thank you – Protector.'

He grimaced.

'The sobriquet is not unearned,' he said flatly, continuing to study my face. 'I wonder whether their earlier protector could say the same?'

'It was not really his place,' I said, 'and I believe that he could.'

He shrugged.

'Of course,' he said. 'Enough of that! Where have you been? What have you been doing? Why have you come here? Tell me of yourself. It has been too long.'

I nodded. It was unfortunate, but family etiquette as well as the balance of power required that I answer his questions before asking any of my own. He was my elder, and I had – albeit unknowing – intruded in his sphere of influence. It was not that I begrudged him the courtesy. He was one of the few among my many relatives whom I respected and even liked. It was that I was itching to question him. It had been, as he had said, too long.

And how much should I tell him now? I had no notion where his sympathies might lie. I did not desire to discover the reasons for his self-imposed exile from Amber by mentioning the wrong things. I would have to begin with something fairly neutral and sound him out as I went along.

'There must be a beginning,' he said then. 'I care not what face you put upon it.'

'There are many beginnings,' I said. 'It is difficult . . . I suppose I should go all the way back and take it from there.'

I took another sip of the wine.

'Yes,' I decided. 'That seems simplest – though it was only comparatively recently that I recalled much of what had occurred.

'It was several years after the defeat of the Moonriders out of Ghenesh and your departure that Eric and I had a major falling out,' I began. 'Yes, it was a quarrel over the succession. Dad had been making abdication noises again, and he still refused to name a successor. Naturally, the old arguments were resumed as to who was more legitimate. Of course, you and Eric are both my elders, but while Faiella, mother to Eric and myself, was his wife after the death of Clymnea, they—'

'Enough!' cried Benedict, slapping the table so hard that it cracked.

The lamp danced and sputtered, but by some small miracle was not upset. The tent's entrance flap was immediately pushed aside and a concerned guard peered in. Benedict glanced at him and he withdrew.

'I do not wish to sit in on our respective bastardy proceedings,' Benedict said softly. 'That obscene pastime was one of the reasons I initially absented myself from felicity. Please continue your story without the benefit of footnotes.'

'Well – yes,' I said, coughing lightly. 'As I was saying, we had some rather bitter arguments concerning the whole matter. Then one evening it went beyond there words. We fought.'

'A duel?'

'Nothing that formal. A simultaneous decision to murder one another is more like it. At any rate, we fought for a long while and Eric finally got the upper hand and proceeded to pulverize me. At the risk of getting ahead of my story, I have to add that all of this was only recalled to me about five years ago.'

Benedict nodded, as though he understood.

'I can only conjecture as to what occurred immediately after I lost consciousness,' I went on. 'But Eric stopped short of killing me himself. When I awakened, I was on a shadow Earth in a place called London. The plague was rampant at the time, and I had contracted it. I recovered with no memory of anything prior to London. I dwelled on that shadow world for centuries, seeking some clue as to my identity. I traveled all over it, often as part of some military campaign. I attended their universities, I spoke with some of their wisest men, I consulted famous physicians. But nowhere could I find the key to my past. It was obvious to me that I was not like other men and I took great pains to conceal this fact. I was furious because I could have anything that I wanted except what I wanted most – my own identity, my memories.

'The years passed, but this anger and this longing did not. It took an accident that fractured my skull to set off the changes that led to the return of my first recollections. This was approximately five years ago, and the irony of it is that I have good reason to believe Eric was

228

responsible for the accident. Flora had apparently been resident on that shadow Earth all along, keeping watch over me.

'To return to conjecture, Eric must have stayed his hand at the last moment, desiring my death, but not wanting it traceable to him. So he transported me through Shadow to a place of sudden, almost certain death – doubtless to return and say that we had argued and I had ridden off in a huff, muttering something about going away again. We had been hunting in the Forest of Arden that day – just the two of us, together.'

'I find it strange,' Benedict interrupted, 'that two rivals such as yourselves should elect to hunt together under such circumstances.'

I took a sip of wine and smiled.

'Perhaps it was a trifle more contrived than I made it sound,' I said. 'Perhaps we both welcomed the opportunity to hunt together – just the two of us.'

'I see,' he said. 'So it is possible that your situations could have been reversed?'

'Well,' I said, 'that is difficult to say. I do not believe I would have gone that far. I am talking as of now, of course. People do change, you know. Back then . . . ? Yes, I might have done the same thing to him. I cannot say for certain, but it is possible.'

He nodded again, and I felt a flash of anger which passed quickly into amusement.

'Fortunately, I am not out to justify my own motives for anything,' I continued. 'To go on with my guesswork, I believe that Eric kept tabs on me after that, doubtless disappointed at first that I had survived, but satisfied as to my harmlessness. So he arranged to have Flora keep an eye on me, and the world turned peacefully for a long while. Then, presumably, Dad abdicated and disappeared without the question of the succession having been settled—'

'The hell he did!' said Benedict. 'There was no abdication. He just vanished. One morning he simply was not in his chambers. His bed had not even been slept in. There were no messages. He had been seen entering the suite the evening before, but no one saw him depart. And even this was not considered strange for a long while. At first it was simply thought that he was sojourning in Shadow once again, perhaps to seek another bride. It was a long while before anyone dared suspect foul play or chose to construe this as a novel form of abdication.'

'I was not aware of this,' I said. 'Your sources of information seem to have been closer to the heart of things than mine were.'

He only nodded, giving rise to uneasy speculations on my part as to his contact in Amber. For all I knew, he could be pro-Eric these days.

'When was the last time you were back there yourself?' I ventured.

'A little over twenty years ago,' he replied, 'but I keep in touch.'

Not with anyone who had cared to mention it to me! He must have known that as he said it, so did he mean me to take it as a caution – or a threat? My mind raced. Of course he possessed a set of the Major Trumps. I fanned them mentally and went through them like mad. Random had professed ignorance as to his whereabouts. Brand had been missing a long while. I had had indication that he was still alive, imprisoned in some unpleasant place or other and in no position to report on the happenings in Amber. Flora could not have been his contact, as she had been in virtual exile in Shadow herself until recently. Llewella was in Rebma. Deirdre was in Rebma also, and had been out of favor in Amber when last I saw her. Fiona? Julian had told me she was 'somewhere to the south'. He was uncertain as to precisely where. Who did that leave?

Eric himself, Julian, Gérard, or Caine, as I saw it. Scratch Eric. He would not have passed along the details of Dad's non-abdication in a manner that would allow things to be taken as Benedict had taken them. Julian supported Eric, but was not without personal ambitions of the highest order. He would pass along information if it might benefit him to do so. Ditto for Caine. Gérard, on the other hand, had always struck me as more interested in the welfare of Amber itself than in the question of who sat on its throne. He was not over-fond of Eric, though, and had once been willing to support either Bleys or myself over him. I believed he would have considered Benedict's awareness of events to be something in the nature of an insurance policy for the realm. Yes, it was almost certainly one of these three. Julian hated me, Caine neither liked nor disliked me especially, and Gérard and I shared fond memories that went all the way back to my childhood. I would have to find out who it was, quickly – and he was not yet ready to tell me, of course, knowing nothing of my present motives. A liaison with Amber could be used to hurt me or benefit me in short order, depending upon his desire and the person on the other end. It was therefore both sword and shield to him, and I was somewhat hurt that he had chosen to display these accoutrements so quickly. I chose to take it that his recent injury had served to make him abnormally wary, for I had certainly never given him cause for distress. Still, this caused me to feel abnormally wary also, a sad thing to know when meeting one's brother again for the first time in many years.

'It is interesting,' I said, swirling the wine within my cup. 'In this light, then, it appears that everyone may have acted prematurely.'

'Not everyone,' he said.

I felt my face redden.

'Your pardon,' I said.

He nodded curtly.

'Please continue your telling.'

'Well, to continue my chain of assumptions,' I said, 'when Eric decided that the throne had been vacant long enough and the time had come to make his move, he must also have decided that my amnesia was not sufficient and that it would be better to see my claim quitted entirely. At this time, he arranged for me to have an accident off on that shadow Earth, an accident which should have proven fatal but did not.'

'How do you know this? How much of it is guesswork?'

'Flora as much as admitted it to me – including her own complicity in the thing – when I questioned her later.'

'Very interesting. Go on.'

'The bash on my head provided what even Sigmund Freud had been unable to obtain for me earlier,' I said. 'There returned to me small recollections that grew stronger and stronger – especially after I encountered Flora and was exposed to all manner of things that stimulated my memory. I was able to convince her that it had fully returned, so her speech was open as to people and things. Then Random showed up, fleeing from something—'

'Fleeing? From what? Why?'

'From some strange creatures out of Shadow. I never found out why.'

'Interesting,' he said, and I had to agree. I had thought of it often, back in the cell, wondering just why Random had entered, stage left, pursued by Furies, in the first place. From the moment we met until the moment we parted, we had been in some sort of peril; I had been preoccupied with my own troubles and he had volunteered nothing concerning his abrupt appearance. It had crossed my mind, of course, at the time of his arrival, but I was uncertain as to whether it was something of which I might be expected to have knowledge, and I let it go at that. Events then submerged it until later in my cell and again the present moment. Interesting? Indeed. Also, troubling.

'I managed to take in Random as to my condition,' I continued. 'He believed I was seeking the throne, when all that I was consciously seeking was my memory. He agreed to help me return to Amber, and he succeeded in getting me back. Well, almost,' I corrected. 'We wound up in Rebma. By then, I had told Random my true condition, and he proposed my walking the Pattern again as a means of restoring it fully. The opportunity was there, and I took it. It proved effective, and I used the power of the Pattern to transport myself into Amber.'

He smiled.

'At this point, Random must have been a very unhappy man,' he said.

'He was not exactly singing with glee,' I said. 'He had accepted Moire's judgment, that he wed a woman of her choosing – a blind girl named Vialle – and remain there with her for at least a year. I left him behind, and I later learned that he had done this thing. Deirdre was also there. We had encountered her along the way, in flight from Amber, and the three of us had entered Rebma together. She remained behind, also.'

I finished my wine and Benedict nodded toward the bottle. It was almost empty, though, so he fetched a fresh bottle from his chest and we refilled our cups. I took a long swallow. It was better wine than the previous. Must have been his private stock.

'In the palace,' I went on, 'I made my way to the library, where I obtained a pack of the Tarots. This was my main reason for venturing there. I was surprised by Eric before I could do much else and we fought, there in the library. I succeeded in wounding him and believe I could have finished him, save that reinforcements arrived and I was forced to flee. I contacted Bleys then, who gave me passage to him in Shadow. You may have heard the rest from your own sources. How Bleys and I threw in together, assaulted Amber, lost. He fell from the face of Kolvir. I tossed him my Tarots and he caught them. I understand that his body was never found. But it was a long way down – though I believe the tide was high by then. I do not know whether he died that day or not.'

'Neither do I,' said Benedict.

'So I was imprisoned and Eric was crowned. I was prevailed upon to assist in the coronation, despite a small demurrer on my part. I did succeed in crowning myself before that bastard – genealogically speaking – had it back and placed it on his own head. Then he had me blinded and sent to the dungeons.'

He leaned forward and studied my face.

'Yes,' he said, 'I had heard that. How was it done?'

'Hot irons,' I said, wincing involuntarily and repressing an impulse to clutch at my eyes. 'I passed out partway through the ordeal.'

'Was there actual contact with the eyeballs?'

'Yes,' I said. 'I think so.'

'And how long did the regeneration take?'

'It was close to four years before I could see again,' I said, 'and my vision is just getting back to normal now. So – about five years altogether, I would say.'

He leaned back, sighed, and smiled faintly.

'Good,' he said. 'You give me some small hope. Others of us have lost portions of their anatomy and experienced regeneration also, of course, but I never lost anything significant – until now.'

'Oh yes,' I said. 'It is a most impressive record. I reviewed it regularly for years. A collection of bits and pieces, many of them forgotten I daresay, but by the principals and myself: fingertips, toes, ear lobes. I would say that there is hope for your arm. Not for a long while, of course.

'It is a good thing that you are ambidextrous,' I added.

His smile went on and off and he took a drink of wine. No, he was not ready to tell me what had happened to him.

I took another sip of my own. I did not want to tell him about Dworkin as something of an ace in the hole. None of us understood the man's full power, and he was obviously mad. But he could be manipulated. Even Dad had apparently come to fear him after a time, and had had him locked away. What was it that he had told me back in my cell? That Dad had had him confined after he had announced his discovery of a means for destroying all of Amber. If this was not just the rambling of a psychotic and was the real reason for his being where he was, then Dad had been far more generous than I would have been. The man was too dangerous to let live. On the other hand, though, Dad had been trying to cure him of his condition. Dworkin had spoken of doctors, men he had frightened away or destroyed when he had turned his powers against them. Most of my memories of him were of a wise, kindly old man, quite devoted to Dad and the rest of the family. It would be difficult readily to destroy someone like that if there was some hope. He had been confined to what should have been inescapable quarters. Yet when he had grown bored one day, he had simply walked out. No man can walk through Shadow in Amber, the very absence of Shadow, so he had done something I did not understand, something involving the principle behind the Trumps, and had left his quarters. Before he returned to them, I managed to persuade him to provide me with a similar exit from my own cell, one that transported me to the lighthouse of Cabra, where I recovered somewhat, then set out upon the voyage that took me to Lorraine. Most likely he was still undetected. As I understood it, our family had always possessed special powers, but it was he who analyzed them and formalized their functions by means of the Pattern and the Tarots. He had often tried to discuss the matter, but it had seemed awfully abstract and boring to most of us. We are a very pragmatic family, damn it! Brand was the only one who seemed to have had any interest in the subject. And Fiona. I had almost forgotten. Sometimes Fiona would listen. And Dad. Dad knew an awful lot of things that he never discussed. He never had much time for us, and there were so many things about him that we did not know. But he was probably as well versed as Dworkin in whatever principles were involved. Their main difference was one of application. Dworkin was an artist. I do not really know what Dad was. He never encouraged intimacy, though he was not an unkind father. Whenever he took note of us, he was quite lavish with gifts and diversions. But he left our upbringing to various members of his court. He tolerated us, I feel, as occasionally inevitable consequences of passion. Actually, I am quite surprised that the family is not much larger. The thirteen of us, plus two brothers and a sister I knew who were now dead, represent close to fifteen hundred years of parental production. There had been a few others also, of whom I had heard, long before us, who had not survived. Not a tremendous batting average for so lusty a liege, but then none of us had proved excessively fertile either. As soon as we were able to fend for ourselves and walk in Shadow, Dad had encouraged us to do so, find places where we would be happy and settle there. This was my connection with the Avalon which is no more. So far as I knew, Dad's own origins were known only to himself. I had never encountered anyone whose memory stretched back to a time when there had been no Oberon. Strange? Not to know where one's own father comes from, when one has had centuries in which to exercise one's curiosity? Yes. But he was secretive, powerful, shrewd – traits we all possess to some degree. He wanted us well situated and satisfied, I feel – but never so endowed as to present a threat to his own reign. There was in him, I guessed, an element of uneasiness, a not unjustifiable sense of caution with respect to our learning too much concerning himself and times long gone by. I do not believe that he had ever truly envisioned a time when he would not rule in Amber. He occasionally spoke jokingly or grumblingly, of abdication. But I always felt this to be a calculated thing, to see what responses it would provoke. He must have realized the state of affairs his passing would produce, but refused to believe that the situation would ever occur. And no one of us really knew all of his duties and responsibilities, his secret commitments. As distasteful as I found the admission, I was coming to feel that none of us was really fit to take the throne. I would have liked to blame Dad for this inadequacy, but unfortunately I had known Freud too long not to feel self-conscious about it. Also, I was now beginning to wonder about the validity of any of our claims. If there had been no abdication and he did indeed still live, then the best any of us could really hope to do was sit in regency. I would not look forward – especially from the throne – to his returning and finding things otherwise. Let's face it, I was afraid of him, and not without cause. Only a fool does not fear a genuine power that he does not understand. But whether the title be king or regent, my claim on it was stronger than Eric's and I was still determined to have it. If a power out of Dad's dark past, which none of us really understood, could serve to secure it, and if Dworkin did represent such a power, then he must remain hidden until he could be employed on my behalf.

Even, I asked myself, if the power he represented was the power to destroy Amber itself, and with it to shatter the shadow worlds and capsize all of existence as I understood it?

Especially then, I answered myself. For who else could be trusted with such power?

We are indeed a very pragmatic family.

More wine, and then I fumbled with my pipe, cleaning it, repacking it.

'That, basically, is my story to date,' I said, regarding my handiwork, rising and taking a light from the lamp. 'After I recovered my sight, I managed to escape, fled Amber, tarried for a time in a place called Lorraine, whare I encountered Ganelon, then came here.'

'Why?'

I reseated myself and looked at him again.

'Because it is near to the Avalon I once knew,' I said.

I had purposely refrained from mentioning any earlier acquaintanceship with Ganelon, and hoped that he would take a cue from it. This shadow was near enough to our Avalon so that Ganelon should be familiar with its topography and most of its customs. For whatever it was worth, it seemed politic to keep this information from Benedict.

He passed over it as I thought he might, buried there where it was beside more interesting digging.

'And of your escape?' he asked. 'How did you manage that?'

'I had help, of course,' I admitted, 'in getting out of the cell. Once out – well, there are still a few passages of which Eric is unaware.'

'I see,' he said, nodding – hoping, naturally, that I would go on to mention my partisans' names, but knowing better than to ask.

I puffed my pipe and leaned back, smiling.

'It is good to have friends,' he said, as if in agreement with some unvoiced thought I might be entertaining.

'I guess that we all have a few of them in Amber.'

'I like to think so,' he said. Then, 'I understand you left the partly whittled cell door locked behind you, had set fire to your bedding, and had drawn pictures on the wall.'

'Yes,' I said. 'Prolonged confinement does something to a man's mind. At least, it did to mine. There are long periods during which I know I was irrational.'

'I do not envy you the experience, brother,' he said. 'Not at all. What are your plans now?'

'They are still uncertain.'

'Do you feel that you might wish to remain here?'

'I do not know,' I said. 'What is the state of affairs here?'

'I am in charge,' he said – a simple statement of fact, not a boast, 'I believe I have just succeeded in destroying the only major threat to the realm. If I am correct, then a reasonably tranquil period should be at hand. The price was high' – he glanced at what remained of his arm – 'but will have been worth it – as shall be seen before very long, when things have returned to normal.'

He then proceeded to relate what was basically the same situation the youth had described, going on to tell how they had won the battle. The leader of the hellmaids slain, her riders had bolted and fled. Most of them were also slain, then, and the caverns had been sealed once more. Benedict had decided to maintain a small force in the field for mopping-up purposes, his scouts the while combing the area for survivors.

He made no mention of the meeting between himself and their leader, Lintra.

'Who slew their leader?' I asked him.

'I managed it,' he said, making a sudden movement with his stump, 'though I hesitated a moment too long on my first blow.'

I glanced away and so did Ganelon. When I looked back, his face had returned to normal and he had lowered his arm.

'We looked for you. Did you know that, Corwin?' he asked. 'Brand searched for you in many shadows, as did Gérard. You guessed correctly as to what Eric said after your disappearance that day. We were inclined to look farther than his word, however. We tried your Trump repeatedly, but there was no response. It must be that brain damage can block it. That is interesting. Your failure to respond to the Trump led us to believe you had died. Then Julian, Caine, and Random joined the search.'

'All that? Really? I am astonished.'

He smiled.

'Oh,' I said then, and smiled myself.

Their joining the hunt at that point meant that it was not my welfare that concerned them, but the possibility of obtaining evidence of fratricide against Eric, so as to displace him or blackmail him.

'I sought for you in the vicinity of Avalon,' he continued, 'and I found this place and was taken by it. It was in a pitiful condition in those days, and for generations I worked to restore it to its former glory. While I began this in memory of you, I developed a fondness for this land and its people. They came to consider me their protector, and so did I.'

I was troubled as well as touched by this. Was he implying that I had fouled things up terribly and that he had tarried here to put them in order – so as to clean up after his kid brother this one last time? Or did he mean that he realized I had loved this place – or a place very much like it – and that he had worked to set it in good order as something I might have wished done? Perhaps I was becoming oversensitive.

'It is good to know that I was sought,' I said, 'and it is very good to know that you are the defender of this land. I would like to see this place, for it does remind me of the Avalon that I knew. Would you have any objections to my visiting here?'

'That is all that you wish to do? Visit?'

'That is all that I had in mind.'

'Know then that what is remembered of the shadow of yourself that once reigned here is not good. Children are not named Corwin in his place, nor am I brother to any Corwin here.'

'I understand,' I said. 'My name is Corey. Can we be old friends?'

He nodded.

'Old friends of mine are always welcome to visit here,' he said.

I smiled and nodded. I felt insulted that he would entertain the notion that I had designs upon this shadow of a shadow: I, who had – albeit but for an instant – felt the cold fire of Amber's crown upon my brow.

I wondered what his attitude would have been had he known of my responsibility, when it came down to basics, for the raids. For that matter, I suppose, I was also responsible for the loss of his arm. I preferred to push things one step farther back, however, and hold Eric responsible. After all, it was his action that had prompted my curse.

Still, I hoped that Benedict would never find out.

I wanted very badly to know where he stood with respect to Eric.

Would he support him, throw his weight behind me, or just stay out of the way when I made my move? Conversely, I was certain that he wondered whether my ambitions were dead or still smoldering – and if the latter, what my plans were for stoking them. So . . .

Who was going to raise the matter?

I took several good puffs on my pipe, finished my wine, poured some more, puffed again. I listened to the sounds of the camp, the wind, my stomach . . .

Benedict took a sip of wine.

Then, 'What are your long-range plans?' he asked me, almost casually.

I could say that I had not made up my mind yet, that I was simply happy to be free, alive, seeing . . . I could tell him that that was enough for me, for now, that I had no special plans . . .

. . . And he would know that I lied in my teeth. For he knew me better than that.

So, 'You know what my plans are,' I said.

'If you were to ask for my support,' he said, 'I would deny it. Amber is in bad enough shape without another power grab.'

'Eric is a usurper.'

'I choose to look upon him as regent only. At this time, any of us who claims the throne is guilty of usurpation.'

'Then you believe Dad still lives?'

'Yes. Alive and distressed. He has made several attempts to communicate.'

I succeeded in keeping my face from showing anything. So I was not the only one, then. To reveal my experiences at this point would sound hypocritical, opportunistic, or a flat lie – since in our seeming contact of five years ago he had given me the go-ahead to take the throne. Of course, he could have been referring to a regency then . . .

'You did not lend support to Eric when he took the throne,' I said. 'Would you give it to him now that he holds it, if an attempt were made to unseat him?'

'It is as I said,' he told me. 'I look upon him as regent. I do not say that I approve of this, but I desire no further strife in Amber.'

'Then you *would* support him?'

'I have said all that I have to say on the matter. You are welcome to visit my Avalon, but not to use it as a staging area for an invasion of

Amber. Does that clarify matters with respect to anything you may have in mind?'

'It clarifies matters,' I said.

'This being the case, do you still wish to visit here?'

'I do not know,' I said. 'Does your desire to avoid strife in Amber work both ways?'

'What do you mean?'

'I mean that if I were returned to Amber against my will, I would damn well create as much strife as I could to prevent a recurrence of my previous situation.'

The lines went out of his face and he slowly lowered his eyes.

'I did not mean to imply that I would betray you. Do you think that I am without feelings, Corwin? I would not see you imprisoned again, blinded – or worse. You are always welcome to visit here, and you may leave your fears along with your ambitions at the border.'

'Then I would still like to visit,' I said. 'I have no army, nor did I come here to recruit one.'

'Then you know that you are most welcome.'

'Thank you, Benedict. While I did not to expect to find you here, I am glad that I did.'

He reddened faintly and nodded.

'It pleases me, also,' he said. 'Am I the first of us you have seen – since your escape?'

I nodded.

'Yes, and I am curious as to how everyone is faring. Any major reports?'

'No new deaths,' he said.

We both chuckled, and I knew that I would have to turn up the family gossip on my own. It had been worth the attempt, though.

'I am planning on remaining in the field for a time,' he said, 'and continuing my patrols until I am satisfied that none of the invaders remain. It could be another week before we withdraw.'

'Oh? Then it was not a total victory?'

'I believe that it was, but I never take unnecessary chances. It is worth a little more time to be certain.'

'Prudent,' I said, nodding.

'. . . So unless you have a strong desire to remain here in camp, I see no reason why you should not proceed on toward town and get near the center of things. I maintain several residences about Avalon. I have in mind for your use a small manor house that I have found pleasant. It is not far from town.'

'I look forward to seeing it.'

'I will provide you with a map and a letter to my steward in the morning.'

'Thank you, Benedict.'

'I will join you there as soon as I have finished here,' he said, 'and in the meantime, I have messengers passing that way daily. I will keep in touch with you through them.'

'Very good.'

'Then find yourselves a comfortable piece of ground,' he said. 'You'll not miss the breakfast call, I'm sure.'

'I seldom do,' I said. 'Is it all right if we sleep at that spot where we left our gear?'

'Certainly,' he said, and we finished the wine.

As we left his tent, I seized the flap up high when I opened it and was able to squeeze it several inches to the side when I cast it before me. Benedict bade us good night and turned away as he let it fall, not noticing the gap of several inches that I had created along its one side.

I made my bed up a good distance to the right of our equipment, facing in the direction of Benedict's tent, and I moved the gear itself as I rummaged through it. Ganelon shot me a quizzical look, but I simply nodded and made a movement with my eyes toward the tent. He glanced that way, retained the nod, and proceeded to spread his own blankets farther to the right.

I measured it with my eyes, walked over, and said, 'You know, I'd much rather sleep here. Would you mind switching with me?' I added a wink for emphasis.

'Makes no difference to me,' he said, shrugging.

The campfires had died or were dying, and most of the company had turned in. The guard only paid us heed a couple of times around. The camp was very quiet and there were no clouds to obscure the brilliance of the stars. I was tired, and the smells of the smoke and the damp earth came pleasantly to my nostrils, reminding me of other times and places such as this and the rest at the day's end.

Instead of closing my eyes, however, I fetched my pack and propped my back against it, filled my pipe again, and struck it to life.

I adjusted my position twice as he paced within the tent. Once, he vanished from my field of vision and remained hidden for several moments. But the far light moved then, and I knew that be had opened the chest. Then he came into sight once more and cleared the table, dropped back for an instant, returned and reseated himself in his earlier position. I moved so that I could keep sight of his left arm.

He was paging through a book, or sorting something of about that size.

Cards, maybe?

Naturally.

I would have given a lot for one glimpse of the Trump that he finally settled upon and held before him. I would have given a lot to have Grayswandir beneath my hand, in case another person suddenly came into the tent by means other than the entrance through which I spied. My palms and the soles of my feet tingled, in anticipation of flight or combat.

But he remained alone.

He sat there unmoving for perhaps a quarter of an hour, and when he finally stirred it was only to replace the cards somewhere in his chest and to extinguish the lamps.

The guard continued on his monotonous rounds and Ganelon began to snore.

I emptied my pipe and rolled over onto my side.

Tomorrow, I told myself. If I wake up here tomorrow, everything will be all right . . .

5

I sucked on a blade of grass and watched the mill wheel turn. I was lying on my stomach on the stream's opposite bank, my head propped in my hands. There was a tiny rainbow in the mist above the froth and boil at the foot of the waterfall, an occasional droplet found its way to me. The steady splashing and the sound of the wheel drowned out all other noises in the wood. The mill was deserted today, and I contemplated it because I had not seen its like in ages. Watching the wheel and listening to the water were more than just relaxing. It was somewhat hypnotic.

It was our third day at Benedict's place, and Ganelon was off in town seeking amusement. I had accompanied him on the previous day and learned what I wanted to know at that time. Now I had no time for sight-seeing. I had to think and act quickly. There had been no difficulty at the camp. Benedict had seen us fed and had furnished us with the map and the letter he had promised. We had departed at sunrise and arrived at the manor around midday. We were well received, and after settling into the quarters we were shown, we had made our way into town, where we had spent the balance of the day.

Benedict was planning to remain in the field for several more days. I would have to be done with the task I had set myself before he came home. So a hellride was in order. There was no time for leisurely journeying. I had to remember the proper shadows and be under way soon.

It would have been refreshing, being in this place that was so like my Avalon, except that my thwarted purposes were reaching the point of obsession. Realizing this was not tantamount to controlling it, however. Familiar sights and sounds had diverted me only briefly, then I had turned once more to my planning.

It should work out neatly, as I saw it. This one journey should solve two of my problems, if I could manage it without arousing suspicion.

243

It meant that I would definitely be gone overnight, but I had anticipated this and had already instructed Ganelon to cover for me.

My head nodding with each creak of the wheel, I forced everything else from my mind and set about remembering the necessary texture of the sand, its coloration, the temperature, the winds, the touch of salt in the air, the clouds . . .

I slept then and I dreamed, but not of the place that I sought.

I regarded a big roulette wheel, and we were all of us on it – my brothers, my sisters, myself, and others whom I knew or had known – rising and falling, each with his allotted section. We were all shouting for it to stop for us and wailing as we passed the top and headed down once more. The wheel had begun to slow and I was on the rise. A fair-haired youth hung upside down before me, shouting pleas and warnings that were drowned in the cacophony of voices. His face darkened, writhed, became a horrible thing to behold, and I slashed at the cord that bound his ankle and he fell from sight. The wheel slowed even more as I neared the top, and I saw Lorraine then. She was gesturing, beckoning frantically, and calling my name. I leaned toward her, seeing her clearly, wanting her, wanting to help her. But as the wheel continued its turning she passed from, my sight.

'Corwin!'

I tried to ignore her cry, for I was almost to the top. It came again, but I tensed myself and prepared to spring upward. If it did not stop for me, I was going to try gimmicking the damned thing, even though falling off would mean my total ruin. I readied myself for the leap. Another click . . .

'Corwin!'

It receded, returned, faded, and I was looking toward the water wheel again with my name echoing in my ears and mingling, merging, fading into the sound of the stream.

I blinked my eyes and ran my fingers through my hair. A number of dandelions fell about my shoulders as I did so, and I heard a giggle from somewhere behind me.

I turned quickly and stared.

She stood about a dozen paces from me, a tall, slender girl with dark eyes and close-cropped brown hair. She wore a fencing jacket and held a rapier in her right hand, a mask in her left. She was looking at me and laughing. Her teeth were white, even, and a trifle long; a band of freckles crossed her small nose and the upper portions of her well-tanned cheeks. There was that air of vitality about her which is attractive in ways different from there comeliness. Especially, perhaps, when viewed from the vantage of many years.

She saluted me with her blade.

'*En garde*, Corwin!' she said.

'Who the Devil are you?' I asked, just then noticing a jacket, mask, and rapier beside me in the grass.

'No questions, no answers,' she said. 'Not till we've fenced.'

She fitted her mask over her head then and waited.

I rose and picked up the jacket. I could see that it would be easier to fence than argue with her. The fact that she knew my name disturbed me, and the more that I thought of it the more she seemed somehow familiar. It was best to humor her, I decided, shrugging into the jacket and buckling it.

I picked up the blade, pulled on the mask.

'All right,' I said, sketching a brief salute and advancing. 'All right.'

She moved forward then and we met. I let her carry the attack.

She came on very fast with a beat-feint-feint-thrust My riposte was twice as fast, but she was able to parry it and come back with equal speed. I began a slow retreat then, drawing her out. She laughed and came on, pressing me hard. She was good and she knew it. She wanted to show off. She almost got through twice, too, in the same way – low-line – which I did not like at all. I caught her with a stop-thrust as soon as I could after that. She cursed softly, good-naturedly, as she acknowledged it and came right back at me. I do not ordinarily like to fence with women, no matter how good they are, but this time I discovered that I was enjoying myself. The skill and grace with which she carried the attacks and bore them gave me pleasure to behold and respond to, and I found myself contemplating the mind that lay behind that style. At first, I had wanted to tire her quickly, to conclude the match and question her. Now I found myself desiring to prolong the encounter.

She did not tire readily. There was small cause for concern on that count. I lost track of time as we stamped back and forth along the bank of the stream, our blades clicking steadily.

A long while must have passed, though, before she stamped her heel and threw up her blade in a final salute. She tore off her mask then and gave me another smile.

'Thank you!' she said, breathing heavily.

I returned the salute and drew off the bird cage. I turned and fumbled with the jacket buckles, and before I realized it she had approached and kissed me on the cheek. She had not had to stand tiptoe to do it either. I felt momentarily confused, but I smiled. Before I could say anything, she had taken my arm and turned me back in the direction from which we had come.

'I've brought us a picnic basket,' she said.

'Very good. I am hungry. I am also curious . . .'

'I will tell you anything that you want to hear,' she said merrily.

'How about telling me your name?' I said.

'Dara,' she replied. 'My name is Dara, after my grandmother.'

She glanced at me as she said it, as though hoping for a reaction. I almost hated to disappoint her, but I nodded and repeated it, then, 'Why did you call me Corwin?' I asked.

'Because that is your name,' she said. 'I recognized you.'

'From where?'

She released my arm.

'Here it is,' she said, reaching behind a tree and raising a basket that had been resting upon the ridges of exposed roots.

'I hope the ants didn't get to it,' she said, moving to a shaded area beside the stream and spreading a cloth upon the ground.

I hung the fencing gear on a nearby shrub.

'You seem to carry quite a few things around with you,' I observed.

'My horse is back that way,' she said, gesturing downstream with her head.

She returned her attention to weighting down the cloth and unpacking the basket.

'Why way back there?' I asked.

'So that I could sneak up on you, of course. If you'd heard a horse clomping around you'd have been awake sure as hell.'

'You're probably right,' I said.

She paused as though pondering deeply, then spoiled it with a giggle.

'But you didn't the first time, though. Still . . .'

'The first time?' I said, seeing she wanted me to ask it.

'Yes, I almost rode over you awhile back,' she said. 'You were sound asleep. When I saw who it was, I went back for a picnic basket and the fencing gear.'

'Oh. I see.'

'Come and sit down now,' she said. 'And open the bottle, will you?'

She put a bottle beside my place and carefully unwrapped two crystal goblets, which she then set in the center of the cloth.

I moved to my place and sat down.

'That is Benedict's best crystal,' I noted, as I opened the bottle.

'Yes,' she said. 'Do be careful not to upset them when you pour – and I don't think we should clink them together.'

'No, I don't think we should,' I said, and I poured.

She raised her glass.

'To the reunion,' she said.

'What reunion?'

'Ours.'

'I have never met you before.'

'Don't be so prosaic,' she said, and took a drink.

I shrugged.

'To the reunion.'

She began to eat then, so I did too. She was so enjoying the air of mystery she had created that I wanted to co-operate, just to keep her happy.

'Now where could I have met you?' I ventured. 'Was it some great court? A harem, perhaps . . . ?'

'Perhaps it was in Amber,' she said. 'There you were . . .'

'Amber?' I said, remembering that I was holding Benedict's crystal and confining my emotions to my voice. 'Just who are you, anyway?'

'. . . There you were – handsome, conceited, admired by all the ladies,' she continued, 'and there I was – a mousy little thing, admiring you from afar. Gray, or pastel – not vivid – little Dara – a late bloomer, I hasten to add – eating her heart out for you—'

I muttered a mild obscenity and she laughed again.

'That wasn't it?' she asked.

'No,' I said, taking another bite of beef and bread. 'More likely it was that brothel where I sprained by back. I was drunk that night—'

'You remember!' she cried. 'It was a part-time job. I used to break horses during the day.'

'I give up,' I said, and I poured more wine.

The really irritating thing was that there *was* something damnably familiar about her. But from her appearance and her behavior, I guessed her age at about seventeen. This pretty much precluded our paths ever having crossed.

'Did Benedict teach you your fencing?' I asked.

'Yes.'

'What is he to you?'

'My lover, of course,' she replied. 'He keeps me in jewels and furs – and he fences with me.'

She laughed again.

I continued to study her face.

Yes, it was possible . . .

'I am hurt,' I said, finally.

'Why?' she asked.

'Benedict didn't give me a cigar.'

'Cigar?'

'You are his daughter, aren't you?'

She redened, but she shook her head.

'No,' she said. 'But you are getting close.'

'Granddaughter?' I said.

'Well . . . sort of.'

'I am afraid that I do not understand.'

'Grandfather is what he likes me to call him. Actually, though, he was my grandmother's father.'

'I see. Are there any others at home like you?'

'No, I am the only one.'

'What of your mother – and your grandmother?'

'Dead, both of them.'

'How did they die?'

'Violently. Both times it happened while he was back in Amber. I believe that is why he has not returned there for a long while now. He does not like to leave me unprotected – even though he knows that I can take care of myself. You know that I can, too, don't you?'

I nodded. It explained several things, one of them being why he was Protector here. He had to keep her somewhere, and he certainly would not want to take her back to Amber. He would not even want her existence known to the rest of us. She could be made into an easy armlock. And it would be out of keeping to make me aware of her so readily.

So, 'I do not believe that you are supposed to be here,' I said, 'and I feel that Benedict would be quite angry if he knew that you were.'

'Yon are just the same as he is! I am an adult, damn it!'

'Have you heard me deny it? You *are* supposed to be someplace else, though, aren't you?'

She filled her mouth instead of answering. So I did, too. After several uncomfortable minutes of chewing, I decided to start on a fresh subject.

'How did you recognize me?' I asked.

She swallowed, took a drink of wine, grinned.

'From your picture, of course,' she said.

'What picture?'

'On the card,' she said. 'We used to play with them when I was very small. I learned all my relatives that way. You and Eric are the other good swordsmen, I knew that. That is why I—'

'You have a set of the Trumps?' I interrupted.

'No,' she said, pouting. 'He wouldn't give me a set – and I know he has several, too.'

'Really? Where does he keep them?'

She narrowed her eyes, focusing them on my own. Damn! I hadn't meant to sound that eager.

But, 'He has a set with him most of the time,' she said, 'and I have no idea where he keeps the others. Why? Won't he let you see them?'

'I haven't asked him,' I told her. 'Do you understand their significance?'

'There were certain things I was not allowed to do when I was near them. I gather that they have a special use, but he never told me what it is. They are quite important, aren't they?'

'Yes.'

'I thought so. He is always so careful with them. Do you have a set?'

'Yes, but it's out on loan just now.'

'I see. And you would like to use them for something complicated and sinister.'

I shrugged.

'I would like to use them, but for very dull, uncomplicated purposes.'

'Such as?'

I shook my head.

'If Benedict does not want you to know their function yet, I am not about to tell you.'

She made a small growling noise.

'You're afraid of him,' she said.

'I have considerable respect for Benedict, not to mention some affection.'

She laughed.

'Is he a better fighter than you, a better swordsman?'

I looked away. She must have just gotten back from someplace fairly removed from things. The townspeople I'd met had all known about Benedict's arm. It was not the sort of news that traveled slowly. I certainly was not going to be the first to tell her.

'Have it as you would,' I said. 'Where have you been?'

'The village,' she said, 'in the mountains. Grandpa took me there to stay with some friends of his called Tecys. Do you know the Tecys?'

'No, I don't.'

'I've been here before,' she said. 'He always takes me to stay with them in the village when there is any sort of trouble here. The place has no name. I just call it the village. It is quite strange – the people, as well as the village. They seem to – sort of – worship us. They treat me as if I were something holy, and they never tell me anything I want to know. It is not a long ride, but the mountains are different, the sky is different – everything! – and it is as if there were no way back, once I am there. I had tried coming back on my own before, but I just got lost Grandpa always had to come for me, and then the way was easy. The Tecys follow all of his instructions concerning me. They treat him as if he were some sort of god.'

'He is,' I said, 'to them.'

'You said that you do not know them.'

'I don't have to. I know Benedict.'

'How does he do it? Tell me.'

I shook my head.

'How did you do it?' I asked her. 'How did you get back here this time?'

She finished her wine and held out the glass. When I looked up from refilling it, her head was cocked toward her right shoulder, her brows were furrowed, and her eyes were focused on something far away.

'I do not really know,' she said, raising the glass and sipping from it automatically. 'I am not quite certain how I went about it . . .'

With her left hand, she began to toy with her knife, finally picking it up.

'I was mad, mad as hell for having been packed off again,' she said. 'I told him that I wanted to stay here and fight, but he took me riding with him and after a time we arrived at the village. I do not know how. It was not a long ride, and suddenly we were there. I know this area. I was born here, I grew up here. I've ridden all over, hundreds of leagues in all directions. I was never able to find it when I went looking. But it seemed only a brief while that we rode, and suddenly we were at the Tecys' again. But it had been several years, and I can be more determined about things now that I am grown. I resolved to return by myself.'

With the knife, she began scraping and digging at the ground beside her, not seeming to notice what she was doing.

'I waited till nightfall,' she went on, 'and studied the stars to take my direction. It was an unreal feeling. The stars were all different I didn't recognize any of the constellations. I went back inside and thought about it. I was a little bit afraid and did not know what to do. I spent the next day trying to get more information out of the Tecys and the other people in the village. But it was like a bad dream. Either they were stupid or they were purposely trying to confuse me. Not only was there no way to get from here to there, they had no idea where "here" was and were none too certain about "there". That night I checked the stars again, to be sure about what I had seen, and I was about ready to begin believing them.'

She moved the knife back and forth as if honing it now, smoothing the soil and packing it flat. Then she began to trace designs.

'For the next several days, I tried to find my way back,' she continued. 'I thought I could locate our trail and backtrack along it, but it just sort of vanished. Then I did the only other thing I could think of. Each morning I struck out in a different direction, rode until noon, then headed back. I came across nothing that was familiar. It was totally bewildering. Each night I went to sleep more angry and upset over the way things were turning out – and more determined to find my own way back to Avalon. I had to show Grandpa that he could no longer dump me like a child and expect me to stay put.

'Then, after about a week, I began having dreams. Nightmares, sort of. Did you ever dream that you were running and running and not going anyplace? That is sort of what it was like – with the burning spider web. Only it wasn't really a spider web, there was no spider and it wasn't burning. But I was caught in his thing, going around it and through it. But I wasn't really moving. That is not completely right, but I do not know how else to put it. And I had to keep trying – actually, I wanted to – to move about it. When I woke up I was tired, as if I had actually been exerting myself all night long. This went on for many nights, and each night it seemed stronger and longer and more real.

'Then this morning I got up, the dream still dancing in my head, and I knew that I could ride home. I set out, still half dreaming, it seemed. I rode the entire distance without stopping once, and this time I paid no special heed to my surroundings, but kept thinking of Avalon – and as I rode, things kept getting more and more familiar until I was here again. Only then did it seem as if I were fully awake. Now the village and the Tecys, that sky, those stars, the woods, the mountains, they all seem like a dream to me. I am not at all certain that I could find my way back there. Is that not strange? Can you tell me what happened?'

I rose and circled the remains of our lunch. I sat down beside her.

'Do you remember the looks of the burning spider web that really wasn't a spider web, or burning?' I asked her.

'Yes – sort of,' she said.

'Give me that knife,' I said.

She passed it to me.

With its point, I began adding to her doodling in the dirt, extending lines, rubbing some out, adding others. She did not say a word the entire time, but she watched every move that I made. When I had finished, I put the knife aside and waited for a long, silent while.

Then, finally, she spoke very softly.

'Yes, that is it,' she said turning away from the design to stare at me. 'How did you know? How did you know what I had dreamed?'

'Because' I said, 'you dreamed a thing that is inscribed in your very genes. Why, how, I do not know. It demonstrates, however, that you are indeed a daughter of Amber. What you did was walk in Shadow. What you dreamed was the Great Pattern of Amber. By its power do those of the blood royal hold dominion over shadows. Do you understand what I am talking about?'

'I am not certain,' she said. 'I do not think so. I haw heard Grandpa cursing shadows, but I never understood what be meant.'

'Then you do not know where Amber truly lies.'

'No. He was always evasive. He told me of Amber and of the family. But I do not even know the direction in which Amber lies. I only know that it is far.'

'It lies in all directions,' I said, 'or any direction one chooses. One need but—'

'Yes!' she interrupted. 'I had forgotten, or thought he was just being mysterious or humoring me, Brand said exactly the same thing a long while ago. What does it mean, though?'

'Brand! When was Brand here?'

'Years ago,' she said, 'when I was just a little girl. He used to visit here often. I was very much in love with him and I pestered him mercilessly. He used to tell me stories, teach me games . . .'

'When was the last time you saw him?'

'Oh, eight or nine years ago, I'd say.'

'Have you met any of the others?'

'Yes,' she said. 'Julian and Gérard were here not too long ago. Just a few months back.'

I suddenly felt very insecure. Benedict had certainly been quiet about a lot of things. I would rather have been ill advised than kept totally ignorant of affairs. It makes it easier for you to be angry when you find out. The trouble with Benedict was that he was too honest, though. He would rather tell me nothing than lie to me. I felt something unpleasant coming my way, however, and knew that there could be no dawdling now, that I would have to move as quickly as possible. Yes, it had to be a hard hellride for the stones. Still, there was more to be learned here before I essayed it. Time . . . Damn!

'Was that the first time that you met them?' I asked.

'Yes,' she said, 'and my feelings were very hurt.' She paused, sighed. 'Grandpa would not let me speak of our being related. He introduced me as his ward. And he refused to tell me why. Damn it!'

'I'm sure he had some very good reasons.'

'Oh, I am too. But it does not make you feel any better, when you have been waiting all your life to meet your relatives. Do *you* know why he treated me like that?'

'These are trying times in Amber,' I said, 'and things will get worse before they get better. The fewer people who know of your existence, the less chance there is of your getting involved and coming to harm. He did it only to protect you.'

She made a spitting noise.

'I do not need protecting,' she said. 'I can take care of myself.'

'You are a fine fencer,' I said. 'Unfortunately, life is more complicated than a fair dueling situation.'

'I know that. I'm not a child. But—'

' "But" nothing! He did the same thing I'd do if you were mine. He's protecting himself as well as you. I'm surprised he let Brand know about you. He's going to be damned mad that I found out.'

Her head jerked and she stared at me, eyes wide.

'But you wouldn't do anything to hurt us,' she said. 'We – we're related . . .'

'How the hell do you know why I'm here or what I'm thinking?' I said. 'You might have just stuck both your necks in nooses!'

'You *are* joking, aren't you?' she said, slowly raising her left hand between us.

'I don't know,' I said. 'I need not be – and I wouldn't be talking about it if I did have something rotten in mind, would I?'

'No . . . I guess not,' she said.

'I am going to tell you something Benedict should have told you long ago,' I said. 'Never trust a relative. It is far worse than trusting strangers. With a stranger there is a possibility that you might be safe.'

'You really mean that, don't you?'

'Yes.'

'Yourself included?'

I smiled.

'Of course it does not apply to me. I am the soul of honor, kindness, mercy, and goodness. Trust me in all things.'

'I will,' she said, and I laughed.

'I will,' she insisted, 'You would not hurt us. I know that.'

'Tell me about Gérard and Julian,' I said, feeling uncomfortable, as always, in the presence of unsolicited trust. 'What was the reason for their visit?'

She was silent for a moment, still studying me, then, 'I have been telling you quite a few things,' she said, 'haven't I? You are right. One can never be too careful. I believe that it is your turn to talk again.'

'Good. You are learning how to deal with us. What do you want to know?'

'Where is the village, really? And Amber? They are somehow alike, aren't they? What did you mean when you said that Amber lies in all directions, or any? What are shadows?'

I got to my feet and looked down at her. I held out my hand. She looked very young and more than a little frightened then, but she took it.

'Where . . . ?' she asked, rising.

'This way,' I said, and I took her to stand at the place where I had slept and regarded the falls and the water wheel.

She began to say something, but I stopped her.

'Look. Just look,' I said.

So we stood there looking at the rushing, the splashing, the turning while I ordered my mind. Then, 'Come,' I said, turning her by the elbow and walking her toward the wood.

As we moved among the trees, a cloud obscured the sun and the shadows deepened. The voices of the birds grew more shrill and a dampness came up out of the ground. As we passed from tree to tree, their leaves became longer and broader. When the sun appeared again, its light came more yellow, and beyond a turning of the way we encountered hanging vines. The bird cries grew hoarser, more numerous. Our trail took an upward turn, and I led her past an outcropping of flint and onto higher ground. A distant, barely perceptible ramble seemed to come from behind us. The sky was a different blue as we moved through an open place, and we frightened a large, brown lizard that had been sunning itself on a rock. As we took a turn about another mass of stone, she said, 'I did not know this was here. I have never been this way before.' But I did not answer her, for I was busy shifting the stuff of Shadow.

Then we faced the wood once more, but now the way led uphill through it. Now the trees were tropical giants, interspersed with ferns, and new noises – barks, hisses, and buzzes – were to be heard. Moving up this trail, the rumble grew louder about us, the very ground beginning to vibrate with it. Dara held tightly to my arm, saying nothing now, but searching everything with her eyes. There were big, flat, pale flowers and puddles where the moisture dripped from overhead. The temperature had risen considerably and we were perspiring quite a bit. Now the rumble grew to a mighty roar, and when at length we emerged from the wood again, it was a sound like steady thunder that fell against us. I guided her to the edge of the precipice and gestured outward and down.

It plunged for over a thousand feet: a mighty cataract that smote the gray river like an anvil. The currents were rapid and strong, bearing bubbles and flecks of foam a great distance before they finally dissolved. Across from us, perhaps half a mile distant, partly screened by rainbow and mist, like an island slapped by a Titan, a gigantic wheel slowly rotated, ponderous and gleaming. High overhead, enormous birds rode like drifting crucifixes the currents of the air.

We stood there for a fairly long while. Conversation was impossible, which was just as well. After a time, when she turned from it to look at me, narrow-eyed, speculative, I nodded and gestured with my eyes toward the wood. Turning then, we made our way back in the direction from which we had come.

Our return was the same process in reverse, and I managed it with greater ease. When conversation became possible once more, Dara still kept her silence, apparently realizing by then that I was a part of the process of change going on around us.

It was not until we stood beside our own stream once more, watching the small mill wheel in its turning that she spoke.

'Was that place like the village?'

'Yes. A shadow.'

'And like Amber?'

'No. Amber casts Shadow. It can be sliced to any shape, if you know how. That place was a shadow, your village was a shadow – and *this* place is a shadow. Any place that you can imagine exists somewhere in Shadow.'

'. . . And you and Grandpa and the others can go about in these shadows, picking and choosing what you desire?'

'Yes.'

'That is what I did, then coming back from the village.'

'Yes.'

Her face became a study in realization. Her almost-black eyebrows dropped half an inch and her nostrils flared with a quick inhalation.

'I can do it, too . . .' she said. 'Go anywhere, do anything I want!'

'The ability lies within you,' I said.

She kissed me then, a sudden, impulsive thing, then rotated away, her hair bobbing on her slim neck as she tried to look at everything at once.

'Then I can do anything,' she said, coming to a standstill.

'There are limitations, dangers . . .'

'That is life,' she said. 'How do I learn to control it?'

'The Great Pattern of Amber is the key. You must walk it in order to gain the ability. It is inscribed on the floor in a chamber beneath the palace in Amber. It is quite large. You must begin on the outside and walk it to its center without stopping. There is considerable resistance and the feat is quite an ordeal. If you stop, if you attempt to depart the Pattern before completing it, it will destroy you. Complete it, though, and your power over Shadow will be subject to your conscious control.'

She raced to our picnic site and studied the pattern we had drawn on the ground there.

I followed more slowly. As I drew near, she said, 'I must go to Amber and walk it!'

'I am certain that Benedict plans for you to do so, eventually,' I said.

'Eventually?' she said 'Now! I must walk it now! Why did he never tell me of these things?'

'Because you cannot do it yet. Conditions in Amber are such that it would be dangerous to both of you to allow your existence to become known there. Amber is barred to you, temporarily.'

'It is not fair!' she said, turning to glare at me.

'Of course not,' I said. 'But that is the way things stand just now. Don't blame me.'

The words came somewhat stickily to my lips. Part of the blame, of course, was mine.

'It would almost be better if you had not told me of these things,' she said, 'if I cannot have them.'

'It is not as bad as all that,' I said. 'The situation in Amber will become stable again – before too very long.'

'How will I learn of it?'

'Benedict will know. He will tell you then.'

'He has not seen fit to tell me much of anything!'

'To what end? Just to make you feel bad? You know that he has been good to you, that he cares for you. When the time is ready, he will move on your behalf.'

'And if he does not? Will you help me then?'

'I will do what I can.'

'How will I able to find you? To let you know?'

I smiled. It had gotten to this point without my half trying. No need to tell her the really important part. Just enough to be possibly useful to me later . . .

'The cards,' I said, 'the family Trumps. They are more than a mere sentimental affectation. They are means of communication. Get hold of mine, stare at it, concentrate on it, try to keep all other thoughts out of your mind, pretend that it is really me and begin talking to me then. You will find that it really is, and that I am answering you.'

'Those are all the things Grandpa told me not to do when I handle the cards!'

'Of course.'

'How does it work?'

'Another time,' I said. 'A thing for a thing. Remember? I have told you now of Amber and of Shadow. Tell me of the visit here by Gérard and Julian.'

'Yes,' she said. 'There is not really much to tell, though. One morning, five or six months ago, Grandpa simply stopped what he was doing. He was pruning some trees back in the orchard – he likes to do that himself – and I was helping him. He was up on a ladder, snipping away, and suddenly he just stopped, lowered the clippers, and did not move for several minutes. I thought that he was just resting, and I kept on with my raking. Then I heard him talking – not just muttering – but talking as though he were carrying on a conversation. At first, I thought he was talking to me, and I asked him what he had said. He ignored me, though. Now that I know about the

Trumps, I realize that he must have been talking to one of them just then. Probably Julian. Anyway, he climbed down from the ladder quite quickly after that, told me he had to go away for a day or so, and started back toward the manor. He stopped before he had gone very far, though, and returned. That was when he told me that if Julian and Gérard were to visit here that I was to be introduced as his ward, the orphaned daughter of a faithful servant. He rode away a short while later, leading two spare horses. He was wearing his blade.

'He returned in the middle of the night, bringing both of them with him. Gérard was barely conscious. His left leg was broken, and the entire left side of his body was badly bruised. Julian was quite battered also, but he had no broken bones. They remained with us for the better part of a month, and they healed quickly. Then they borrowed two horses and departed. I have not seen them since.'

'What did they say as to how they had been injured?'

'Only that they had been in an accident. They would not discuss it with me.'

'Where? Where did it happen?'

'On the black road. I overheard them talking about it several times.'

'Where is this black road?'

'I do not know.'

'What did they say about it?'

'They cursed it a lot. That was all.'

Looking down, I saw that there was some wine left in the bottle. I stooped and poured two final drinks, passed her one.

'To the reunion,' I said, and smiled.

'. . . The reunion,' she agreed, and we drank.

She began cleaning the area and I assisted her, my earlier sense of urgency upon me once again.

'How long should I wait before I try to reach you?' she asked.

'Three months. Give me three months.'

'Where will you be then?'

'In Amber, I hope.'

'How long will you be staying here?'

'Not very. In fact, I have to take a little trip right now. I should be back tomorrow, though. I will probably only be staying for a few days after that.'

'I wish you would stay longer.'

'I wish that I could. I would like to, now that I have met you.'

She reddened and turned what seemed all of her attention to repacking the basket I gathered up the fencing gear.

'Are you going back to the manor now?' she said.

'To the stables. I'll be leaving immediately.'

She picked up the basket.

'We will go together then. My horse is this way.'

I nodded and followed her toward a footpath to our right.

'I suppose,' she said, 'that it would be best for me not to mention any of this to anybody, Grandpa in particular?'

'That would be prudent.'

The splash and gargle of the stream, as it flowed to the river, on its way to the sea, faded, faded, was gone, and only the creak of the land-locked wheel that cut it as it went, remained for a time in the air.

6

Steady movement is more important than speed, much of the time. So long as there is a regular progression of stimuli to get your mental hooks into, there is room for later movement. Once this begins, its rate is a matter of discretion.

So I moved slowly, but steadily, using my discretion. No sense in tiring Star unnecessarily. Rapid shifts are hard enough on people. Animals, who are not so good at lying to themselves, have a rougher time of it, sometimes going completely berserk.

I crossed the stream at a small wooden bridge and moved parallel to it for a time. My intention was to skirt the town itself, but to follow the general direction of the watercourse until I reached the vicinity of the coast. It was midafternoon. My way was shaded, cool. Grayswandir hung at my side.

I bore west, coming at length to the hills that rose there. I refrained from beginning the shift until after I had reached a point that looked down upon the city that represented the largest concentration of population in this realm that was like my Avalon. The city bore the same name, and several thousand people lived there, worked there. Several of the silver towers were missing, and the stream cut the city at a somewhat different angle farther south, having widened or been widened eightfold by men. There was some smoke from the smithies and the public houses, stirred lightly by breezes from the south; people, mounted, afoot, driving wagons, driving coaches, moved through the narrow streets, entered and departed shops, hostels, residences; flocks of birds wheeled, descended, rose about the place where horses were tethered; a few bright pennons and banners stirred listlessly; the waters sparkled and there was a haze in the air. I was too far away to hear the sounds of voices, and of clanking, hammering, sawing, rattling, and creaking as anything other than a generalized hum. While I could distinguish no individual odors, had I still been blind I would have known by sniffing the air that a city was near.

Seeing it from up there, a certain nostalgia came over me, a wistful rag-tail of a dream accompanied by a faint longing for the place that was this place's namesake to me in a vanished shadow and of long ago, where life had been just as simple and I happier than I was at that moment.

But one does not live as long as I have lived without achieving that quality of consciousness which strips naïve feelings as they occur and is generally loathe to participate in the creation of sentimentality.

Those days were passed, that thing done with, and it was Amber now that held me completely. I turned and continued southward, confirmed in my desire to succeed. Amber, I do not forget . . .

The sun became a dazzling, bright blister above my head and the winds began to scream about me. The sky grew more and more yellow and glaring as I rode, until it was as if a desert stretched from horizon to horizon overhead. The hills grew rockier as I descended toward the lowlands, exhibiting wind-sculpted forms of grotesque shape and somber coloration. A dust storm struck me as I emerged from the foothills, so that I had to muffle my face with my cloak and narrow my eyes to slits. Star whinnied, snuffled repeatedly, plodded on. Sand, stone, winds, and the sky more orange then, a slate-like crop of clouds toward which the sun was heading . . .

Then long shadows, the dying of the wind, stillness . . . Only the click of hoof on rock and the sounds of breathing . . . Dimness, as they rush together and the sun is foiled by clouds . . . The walls of the day shaken by thunder . . . An unnatural clarity of distant objects . . . A cool, blue, and electric feeling in the air . . . Thunder again . . .

Now, a rippling, glassy curtain to my right as the rain advances . . . Blue fracture lines within the clouds . . . The temperature plummeting, our pace steady, the world a monochromatic backdrop now . . .

Gonging thunder, flashing white, the curtain flaring toward us now . . . Two hundred meters . . . One-fifty . . . Enough!

Its bottommost edge plowing, furrowing, frothing . . . The moist smell of the earth . . . Star's whinny . . . A burst of speed . . .

Small rivulets of water creeping outward, sinking, staining the ground . . . Now bubbling muddily, now trickling . . . Now a steady flow . . . Streamlets all about us, splashing . . .

High ground ahead, and Star's muscles bunching and relaxing, bunching and relaxing beneath me, as he leaps the rills and freshets, plunges through a racing, roiling sheet, and strikes the slope, hoofs sparking against stones as we mount higher, the voice of the gurgling, eddying flow beneath us deepening to a steady roar . . .

Higher, then, and dry, pausing to wring out the corners of my cloak . . . Below, behind, and to the right a gray, storm-tossed sea laps at the foot of the cliff we hold . . .

Inland now toward clover fields and evenings, the boom of the surf at my back . . .

Pursuing falling stars into the darkening east and eventual silence and night . . .

Clear the sky and bright the stars, but a few small wisps of cloud . . .

A howling pack of red-eyed things, twisting along our trail . . . Shadow . . . Green-eyed . . . Shadow . . . Yellow . . . Shadow . . . Gone . . .

But dark peaks with skirts of snow, jostling one another about me . . . Frozen snow, as dry as dust, lifted in waves by the icy blasts of the heights . . . Powdery snow, flour-like . . . Memory here, of the Italian Alps, of skiing . . . Waves of snow drifting across stone faces . . . A white fire within the night air . . . My feet rapidly numbing within my wet boots . . . Star bewildered and snorting, testing each step and shaking his head as if in disbelief . . .

So shadows beyond the rock, a gentler slope, a dying wind, less snow . . .

A twisting trail, a corkscrew trail, an adit into warmth . . . Down, down, down the night, beneath the changing stars . . .

Far the snows of an hour ago, now scrubby plants and level plain . . . Far, and the night birds stagger into the air, wheeling above the carrion feast, shedding hoarse notes of protest as we pass . . .

Slow again, to the place where the grasses wave, stirred by the less cold breeze . . . The cough of a hunting cat . . . The shadowy flight of a bounding, deer-like beast . . . Stars sliding into place and feelings in my feet once more . . .

Star rearing, neighing, racing ahead from some unseen thing . . . A long time in the soothing then, and longer still till the shivers go . . .

Now icicles of a partial moon falling on distant treetops . . . Moist earth exhaling a luminescent mist . . . Moths dancing in the night light . . .

The ground momentarily buckling and swaying, as if mountains were shifting their feet . . . To every star its double . . . A halo round the dumbbell moon . . . The plain, the air above it, filled with fleeing shapes . . .

The earth, a wound-down clock, ticks and grows still . . . Stability . . . Inertia . . . The stars and the moon reunited with their spirits . . .

Skirting the growing fringe of trees, west . . . Impressions of a sleeping jungle: delirium of serpents under oilcloth . . .

West, west . . . Somewhere a river with broad, clean banks to ease my passage to the sea . . .

Thud of hoofs, shuttling of shadows . . . The night air upon my face . . . A glimpse of bright beings on high, dark walls, shining towers . . . The air is sweetened . . . Vision swims . . . Shadows . . .

We are merged, centaur-like, Star and I, under a single skin of sweat . . . We take the air and give it back in mutual explosions of exertion . . . Neck clothed in thunder, terrible the glory of the nostrils . . . Swallowing the ground . . .

Laughing, the smell of the waters upon us, the trees very near to our left . . .

Then among them . . . Sleek bark, hanging vines, broad leaves, droplets of moisture . . . Spider web in the moonlight, struggling shapes within . . . Spongy turf . . . Phosphorent fungus on fallen trees . . .

A clear space . . . Long grasses rustling . . .

More trees . . .

Again, the riversmell . . .

Sounds, later . . . Sounds . . . The glassy chuckling of water . . .

Closer, louder, beside it at last . . . The heavens buckling and bending in its belly, and the trees . . . Clean, with a cold, damp tang . . . Leftward beside it pacing it now . . . Easy and flowing, we follow . . .

To drink . . . Splashing in its shallows, then hock-high with head depressed, Star, in it, drinking like a pump, blasting spray from his nostrils . . . Upriver, it laps at my boots . . . Dripping from my hair running down my arms . . . Star's head turning, at the laughter . . .

Then downriver again, clean, slow, winding . . . Then straight, widening, slowing . . .

Trees thickening then thinning . . .

Long, steady, slow . . .

A faint light in the east . . .

Sloping downward now and fewer trees . . . Rockier, and the darkness made whole once again . . .

The first, dim hint of the sea, lost an odor later . . . Clicking, on, in the nightsend chill . . . Again, an instant's salt . . .

Rock, and an absence of trees . . . Hard, steep, bleak, down . . . Ever-increasing precipitousness . . .

Flashing between walls of stone . . . Dislodged pebbles vanishing in the now racing current their splashes drowned in the roar's echoes . . . Deeper the defile, widening . . .

Down, down . . .

Farther still . . .

Now pale once more the east, gentler the slope . . . Again, the touch of salt, stronger . . .

Shale and grit . . . Around a corner, down, and brighter still . . .

Steady, soft and loose the footing . . .

The breese and the light, the breeze and the light . . . Beyond a crop of rock . . .

Draw rein.

Below me lay the stark seaboard, where rank upon rank of rolling dunes, harassed by the winds out of the southwest, tossed spumes of sand that partly obliterated the distant outlines of the bleak morning sea.

I watched the pink film spread across the water from the east. Here and there, the shifting sands revealed dark patches of gravel. Rugged masses of rock reared above the swell of the waves. Between the massive dunes – hundreds of feet in height – and myself, there high above that evil coast, lay a smashed and pitted plain of angular rocks and gravel, just now emerging from hell or night into dawn's first glow, and alive with shadows.

Yes, it was right.

I dismounted and watched the sun force a bleak and glaring day upon the prospect. It was the hard, white light I had sought. Here, *sans* humans, was the necessary place, just as I had seen it decades earlier on the shadow Earth of my exile. No bulldozers, sifters, broom-wielding blacks; no maximum-security city of Oranjemund. No X-ray machines, barbed wire, or armed guards. None of these things here. No. For this shadow had never known a Sir Ernest Oppenheimer, and there had never been a Consolidated Diamond Mines of South West Africa, nor a government to approve their amalgamation of coastal mining interests. Here was the desert called Namib in that place some four hundred miles to the northwest of Cape Town, a strip of dunes and rock ranging from a couple to a dozen miles in width and running along that forsaken coast line for perhaps three hundred miles on the seaward side of the Richtersveld Mountains, within whose shadow I now stood. Here, unlike any conventional mine, the diamonds were scattered as casually as bird droppings across the sand. I, of course, had brought along a rake and a sieve.

I broke out the rations and prepared breakfast. It was going to be a hot, dusty day.

As I worked the dunes, I thought of Doyle, the little wispy-haired jeweler with the brick-red complexion and wens on his cheeks, back in Avalon. Jewelers rouge? Why did I want all that jewelers rouge – enough to supply an army of jewelers for a dozen lifetimes? I had shrugged. What was it to him what I wanted it for, so long as I was able to pay for it? Well, if there was some new use of the stuff and good money to be made, a man would be a fool . . . In other words, he would be unable to furnish me with such a quantity within a week? Small, square chuckles had escaped through the gaps in his smile. A week? Oh, no! Of course not! That was ridiculous, out of the question . . . I saw. Well, a quick thanks and perhaps his competitor up the way might be able to produce the stuff, and might also be interested in a few uncut diamonds I was expecting in a matter of days . . . Diamonds, did I say? Wait. He was always interested in diamonds himself . . . Yes, but he was sadly deficient in the jewelers rouge department. A raised hand. It might be that he had spoken nastily with respect to his ability to produce the polishing material. It was the quantity that had disturbed him. But the ingredients were plentiful and the formula fairly simple. Yes, there was no real reason why something could not be worked out. Within a week, at that. Now, about the diamonds . . .

Before I left his shop, something had been worked out.

I have met many persons who thought that gunpowder explodes, which of course is incorrect. It burns rapidly, building up gas pressure which ejects a bullet from the mouth of a shell and drives it through the barrel of a weapon, after having been ignited by the primer, which does the actual exploding when the firing pin is driven into it. Now, with typical family foresight, I had experimented with a variety of combustibles over the years. My disappointment at the discovery that gunpowder would not ignite in Amber, and that all of the primers I tested were equally inert there, was a thing mitigated only by the knowledge that none of my relatives could bring firearms into Amber either. It was much later, during a visit to Amber, after polishing a bracelet I had brought for Deirdre, that I discovered this wonderful property of jewelers rouge from Avalon when I disposed of the polishing cloth in a fireplace. Fortunately, the quantity involved was small, and I was alone at the time.

It made an excellent primer, straight from the container. When cut with a sufficient quantity of inert material, it could also be made to burn properly.

I kept this bit of information to myself, feeling that one day it would be used to decide certain basic issues in Amber. Unfortunately, Eric and I had our run-in before that day arrived and it went into storage along with all my other memories. When things finally did clear for me, my fortunes were quickly cast with those of Bleys, who was preparing an assault on Amber. He had not really needed me then, but had taken me in on the enterprise, I feel, so that he could keep an eye on me. Had I furnished him with guns, he would have been invincible and I would have been unnecessary. More important, had we succeeded in seizing Amber in accordance with his plans, the situation would have become strained indeed, with the bulk of the occupying forces, as well as the officers' loyalty, his. Then I would have required something to adjust the balance of power more equitably. A few bombs and automatic weapons, say.

Had I been my whole self even a month earlier, things would have been quite different. I could have been sitting in Amber, rather than being scorched, abraded, and desiccated, with another hellride before me and a knot of troubles to be worked out after that.

I spat sand so that I would not choke when I laughed. Hell, we make our own ifs. I had better things to think about than what could have happened. Like Eric . . .

I remember that day, Eric. I was in chains and I had been forced to my knees before the throne. I had already crowned myself, to mock you, and been beaten for it. The second time I had the crown in my hands, I threw it at you. But you caught it and smiled. I was glad that it was not damaged when it failed to damage you. Such a beautiful thing . . . All of silver, with its seven high points, and studded with emeralds to beat all diamonds. Two large rubies at either temple . . . You crowned yourself that day, all arrogance and hasty pomp. The first words that you spoke then were whispered to me, before the echoes of 'Long live the king!' had died within the hall. I remember every one of them. 'Your eyes have looked upon the fairest sight they ever will behold,' you said. Then, 'Guards!' you ordered. 'Take Corwin away to the smithy, and let his eyes be burnt from out his head! Let him remember the sights of this day as the last he might ever see! Then cast him into the darkness of the deepest dungeon beneath Amber, and let his name be forgotten!'

'Now you reign in Amber,' I said aloud. 'But I have my eyes, and I have neither forgotten nor been forgotten.'

No, I thought. Wrap yourself in the kingship, Eric. The walls of Amber are high and thick. Stay behind them. Ring yourself with the futile steel of blades. Ant-like, you armor your house in dust. You know now that you will never be secure so long as I live, and I have told you that I will be back. I am coming, Eric. I will bring me up guns out of Avalon, and I will break down your doors and smite your defenders. Then it will be as it was, briefly, another time, before your men came to you and saved you. That day I had only a few drops of your blood. This time, I will have it all.

I uncovered another rough diamond, the sixteenth or so, and flipped it into the sack at my waist.

As I faced the setting sun, I wondered about Benedict, Julian, and Gérard. What was the connection? Whatever, I did not like any combination of interests which involved Julian. Gérard was all right.

I had been able to sleep back at the camp when I had thought that it was he whom Benedict was contacting. If he was now allied with Julian, though, it was cause for increased uneasiness. If anyone hated me even more than Eric, it was Julian. If he knew where I was, then my danger was great. I was not yet ready for a confrontation.

I supposed Benedict could find a moral justification for selling me out at this point. After all, he knew that whatever I did – and he knew that I was going to do something – would result in strife in Amber. I could understand, even sympathize with his feelings. He was dedicated to the preservation of the realm. Unlike Julian, he was a man of principle, and I regretted having to be at odds with him. My hope was that my coup would be as quick and painless as a tooth extraction under gas, and that we would be back on the same side again soon afterward. Having met Dara now, I also wanted it this way for her sake.

He had told me too little for comfort. I had no way of knowing whether he really intended to remain in the field the entire week, or whether he was even now co-operating with the forces of Amber in the laying of my trap, the walling of my prison, the digging of my grave. I had to hurry though I longed to linger in Avalon.

I envied Ganelon, in whatever tavern or brothel he drank, whored, or fought, on whatever hillside he hunted. He had come home. Should I leave him to his pleasures, despite his offer to accompany me to Amber? But no, he would be questioned on my departure – used badly, if Julian had anything to do with it – and then become an outcast in what must seem his own land to him, if they let him go at all. Then he would doubtless become an outlaw again, and the third time would probably prove his undoing. No, I would keep my promise. He would come with me, if that was what he still wanted. If he had changed his mind, well – I even envied him the prospect of outlawry in Avalon. I would have liked to remain longer, to ride with Dara in the hills, tramp about the countryside, sail upon the rivers . . .

I thought about the girl. The knowledge of her existence changed things somewhat. I was not certain how. Despite our major hatreds and petty animosities, we Amberites are a very family-conscious bunch, always eager for news of one another, desirous to know everyone's position in the changing picture. A pause for gossip has doubtless stayed a few death blows among us. I sometimes think of us as a gang of mean little old ladies in a combination rest home and obstacle course.

I could not fit Dara into things yet because she did not know where she fit herself. Oh, she would learn eventually. She would receive superb tutelage once her existence became known. Now that I had brought her awareness of her uniqueness it would only be a matter of time before this occurred and she joined in the games. I had felt somewhat serpent-like at points during our conversation in the grove – but hell, she had a right to know. She was bound to find out sooner or later, and the sooner she did the sooner she could start shoring up her defenses. It was for her own benefit.

Of course, it was possible – even likely – that her mother and grandmother had lived their lives in ignorance of their heritage . . .

And where had it gotten them? They died violently, she had said.

Was it possible, I wondered, that the long arm of Amber had reached for them out of Shadow? And that it might strike again?

Benedict could be a tough and mean and nasty as any of us when he wanted to be. Tougher, even. He would fight to protect his own, doubtless even kill one of us if he thought it necessary. He must have assumed that keeping her existence a secret and keeping her ignorant would protect her. He would be angry with me when he found out what I had done, which was another reason for clearing out in a hurry. But I had not told her what I had out of sheer perverseness. I wanted her to survive, and I did not feel he was handling things property. When I returned, she would have had time to think things over. She would have many questions and I would seize the opportunity to caution her at length and to give specifics.

I gnashed my teeth.

None of this should be necessary. When I ruled in Amber, things would be different. They had to be . . .

Why had no one ever come up with a way to change the basic nature of man? Even the erasure of all my memories and a new life in a new world had resulted in the same old Corwin. If I were not happy with what I was it could be a proposition worthy of despair.

In a quiet part of the river, I washed away the dust, the sweat, wondering the while about the black road which had so injured my brothers. There were many things that I needed to know.

As I bathed, Grayswandir was never far from my hand. One of us is capable of tracking another through Shadow, when the trail is still warm. As it was, my bath was undisturbed, though I used Grayswandir three times on the way back, on less mundane things than brothers.

But this was to be expected, as I had accelerated the pace considerably . . .

It was still dark, though dawn was not too far away, when I entered the stables at my brother's manor. I tended Star, who had grown somewhat wild, talking to him and soothing him as I rubbed him down, then putting out a good supply of food and water. Ganelon's Firedrake greeted me from the opposite stall. I cleaned up at the pump to the rear of the stable, trying to decide where I was going to catch a little sleep.

I needed some rest. A few hours' worth would hold me for a time, but I refused to take them beneath Benedict's roof. I would not be taken that easily, and while I had often said that I wanted to die in bed, what I really meant was that in my old age I wanted to be stepped on by an elephant while making love.

I was not averse to drinking his booze, though, and I wanted a belt of something strong. The manor was dark; I entered quietly and I found the sideboard.

I poured a stiff one, tossed it off, poured another, and carried it to the window. I could see for a great distance. The manor stood on a hillside and Benedict had landscaped the place well.

' "White in the moon the long road lies," ' I recited, surprised at the sound of my own voice. ' "The moon stands blank above . . ." '

'So it does. So it does, Corwin my lad,' I heard Ganelon say.

'I didn't see you sitting there,' I said softly, not turning from the window.

'That's because I'm sitting so still,' he said.

'Oh,' I said. 'How drunk are you?'

'Hardly at all,' he said, 'now. But if you would care to be a good fellow and fetch me a drink . . .'

I turned.

'Why can't you get your own?'

'It hurts to move.'

'All right.'

I went and poured him one, carried it to him. He raised it slowly, nodded his thanks, took a sip.

'Ah, that's good!' he sighed. 'May it numb things a bit.'

'You were in a fight,' I decided.

'Aye,' he said. 'Several.'

'Then bear your wounds like a good trooper and let me save my sympathy.'

'But I won!'

'God! Where did you leave the bodies?'

'Oh, they are not that bad off. 'Twas a girl did this to me.'

'Then I'd say you got your money's worth.'

''Twas not that sort of thing at all. I believe I've embarrassed us.'

'Us? How?'

'I did not know she was the lady of the house. I came in feeling jolly, and I thought her some serving wench . . .'

'Dara?' I said, tensing.

'Aye, the same. I slapped her on the rump and went for a kiss or two—' He groaned. 'Then she picked me up. She raised me off the ground and held me up over her head. Then she told me she was the lady of the house. Then she let me fall . . . I'm eighteen stone if I'm a pebble, man, and it was a long way down.'

He took another drink, and I chuckled.

'She laughed, too,' he said ruefully. 'She helped me up then and was not unkind, and of course I apologized – That brother of yours must be quite a man. I never met a girl that strong. The things she could do to a man . . .' There was awe in his voice. He shook his head slowly and tossed back the rest of his drink. 'It was frightening – not to mention embarrassing,' he concluded.

'She accepted your apology?'

'Oh, yes. She was quite gracious about the whole thing. She told me to forget all about it, and said that she would, too.'

'Then why are you not in bed sleeping it off?'

'I was waiting up, in case you came in at an odd hour. I wanted to catch you right away.'

'Well, you have.'

He rose slowly and picked up his glass.

'Let's go outside,' he said.

'Good idea.'

He picked up the brandy decanter on the way out, which I also thought was a good idea, and we followed a path through the garden behind the house. Finally he heaved himself onto an old stone bench at the foot of a large oak tree, where he refilled both our glasses and took a drink from his own.

'Ah! He has good taste in liquor, too, your brother,' he said.

I seated myself beside him and filled my pipe.

'After I told her I was sorry and introduced myself, we got to talking for a time,' he said. 'As soon as she learned I was with you, she wanted to know all sorts of things about Amber and shadows and you and the rest of your family.'

'Did you tell her anything?' I said, striking a light.

'Couldn't have if I wanted to,' he said. 'I had none of the answers.'

'Good.'

'It got me to thinking, though. I do not believe Benedict tells her too much, and I can see why. I would be careful what I say around her, Corwin. She seems over-curious.'

I nodded, puffing.

'There is a reason for it,' I said. 'A very good reason. I am glad to know, though, that you keep your wits about you even when you have been drinking. Thanks for telling me.'

He shrugged and took a drink.

'A good bashing is a sobering thing. Also, your welfare is my welfare.'

'True. Does this version of Avalon meet with your approval?'

'Version? It *is* my Avalon,' he said. 'A new generation of people is in the land, but it is the same place. I visited the Field of Thorns today, where I put down Jack Hailey's bunch in your service. It was the same place.'

'The Field of Thorns . . .' I said, remembering.

'Yes, this is my Avalon,' he continued, 'and I'll be coming back here for my old age, if we live through Amber.'

'You still want to come along?'

'All my life I've wanted to see Amber – well, since I first heard of it. That was from you, in happier times.'

'I do not really remember what I said. It must have been a good telling.'

'We were both wonderfully drunk that night, and it seemed but a brief while that you talked – weeping some of the time – telling me of the mighty mountain Kolvir and the green and golden spires of the city, of the promenades, the decks, the terrace, the flowers, the fountains . . . It seemed but a brief while, but it was most of the night for before we staggered off to bed the morning had begun. God! I could almost draw you a map of the place! I must see it before I die.'

'I do not remember that night,' I said slowly. 'I must have been very, very drunk.'

He chuckled.

'We had some good times here in the old days,' he said. 'And they do remember us here. But as people who lived very long ago – and they have many of the stories wrong. But hell! How many people get their stories right from day to day?'

I said nothing, smoking, thinking back.

'. . . All of which leads me to a question or two,' he said.

'Shoot.'

'Will your attack on Amber put you at great odds with your brother Benedict?'

'I really wish that I knew the answer to that one,' I said. 'I think that it will, initially. But my move should be completed before he can reach Amber from here, in response to any distress call that goes out. That is, reach Amber with reinforcements. He could get there in no time at all, personally, if someone on the other end were helping. But that would serve little purpose. No. Rather than tear Amber apart, he will support whoever can hold it together, I am certain. Once I have ousted Eric, he will want the strife to stop right there and he will go along with my holding the throne, just to put an end to it. He will not really approve of the seizure in, the first place, of course.'

'That is what I am getting at. Will there be bad blood between you afterward as a result of that?'

'I do not believe so. This is purely a matter of politics, and we have known one another most of our lives, he and I, and have always been on better terms with each other than either of us with Eric.'

'I see. Since you and I are in his together and Avalon seems to be Benedict's now, I was wondering what his feelings would be about my returning here one day. Would he hate me for having helped you?'

'I doubt that very much. He has never been that sort of person.'

'Then let me carry things a step further. God knows I am an experienced military man, and if we succeed in taking Amber he will have ample evidence of the fact. With his right arm injured the way that it is and all, do you think he might consider taking me on as a field commander for his militia? I know this area so well. I could take him to the Field of Thorns and describe that battle. Hell! I would serve him well – as well as I served you.'

He laughed then.

'Pardon me. Better than I served you.'

I chuckled, sipped my drink.

'It would be tricky,' I said. 'Of course I like the idea. But I am not too certain that you could ever enjoy his trust. It would seem too obvious a ploy on my part.'

'Damn politics! That is not what I meant! Soldiering is all that I know, and I love Avalon!'

'I believe you. But would he?'

'With only one aim be will be needing a good man about. He could—'

I began to laugh and restrained myself quickly, for the sound of laughter seems to carry for a good distance. Also, Ganelon's feelings were involved.

'I am sorry,' I said. 'Excuse me, please. You do not understand. You do not really understand who it was we talked with in the tent that night. He may have seemed an ordinary man to you – a handicapped one, at that. But this is not so. I fear Benedict. He is unlike any other being in Shadow or reality. He is the Master of Arms for Amber. Can you conceive of a millennium? A thousand years? Several of them? Can you understand a man who, for almost every day of a lifetime like that, has spent some time dwelling with weapons, tactics, strategies? Because you see him in a tiny kingdom, commanding a small militia, with a well-pruned orchard in his back yard, do not be deceived. All that there is of military science thunders in his head. He has often journeyed from shadow to shadow, witnessing variation after variation on the same battle, with but slightly altered circumstances, in order to test his theories of warfare. He has commanded armies so vast that you could watch them march by day after day and see no end to the columns. Although he is inconvenienced by the loss of his arm, I would not wish to fight with him either with weapons or barehanded. It is fortunate that he has no designs upon the throne, or he would be occupying it right now. If he were, I believe that I would give up at this moment and pay him homage. I fear Benedict.'

Ganelon was silent for a long while, and I took another drink for my throat had become dry.

'I did not realize this, of course,' he said then. 'I will be happy if he just lets me come back to Avalon,'

'That much he will do. I know.'

'Dara told me she had a message from him today. He has decided to cut short his stay in the field. He will probably be returning tomorrow.'

'Damn!' I said, standing. 'We will have to move soon, then. I hope Doyle has that stuff ready. We must go to him in the morning and expedite matters. I want to be away from here before Benedict gets back!'

'You have the pretties then?'

'Yes.'

'May I see them?'

I undid the sack at my belt and passed it to him. He opened it and withdrew several stones, holding them in the palm of his left hand and turning them slowly with his fingertips.

'They do not look like much,' he said, 'from what I can see of them in this light. Wait! There's a glimmer! No . . .'

'They are in the rough, of course. You are holding a fortune in your hands.'

'Amazing,' he said, dropping them back in the sack and refastening it. 'It was so easy for you.'

'It was not all that easy.'

'Still, to gather a fortune so quickly seems somehow unfair.'

He passed it back.

'I will see that you are provided with a fortune when our labors are done,' I said. 'That should prove some compensation, should Benedict not offer you a position.'

'Now that I know who he is, I am more determined than ever to work for him one day.'

'We will see what can be done.'

'Yes. Thank you, Corwin. How shall we work our departure?'

'I want you to go and get some rest, for I will roust you out of bed early. Star and Firedrake will take unkindly to the notion of draft duty, I fear, but we will then borrow one of Benedict's wagons and head into town. Before this, I will try to arrange a good smoke screen here for our orderly withdrawal. We will then hurry Doyle the jeweler about his task, obtain our cargo, and depart into Shadow as quickly as possible. The greater our head start, the more difficult it will be for Benedict to track us. If I can get half a day's lead into Shadow, it will be practically impossible for him.'

'Why should he be so eager to come after us in the first place?'

'He does no trust me worth a damn – and justly so. He is waiting for me to make my move. He knows there is something I need here, but he does not know what. He wants to find out, so that he can seal off another threat to Amber. As soon as he realizes we have gone for good, he will know what we have it and he will come looking.'

Ganelon yawned, stretched, finished his drink.

'Yes,' he said then. 'We'd best rest now, to be in condition for the hurrying. Now that you have told me more about Benedict, I am less surprised by the other thing I meant to tell you – though no less discomfited.'

'That being . . . ?'

He rose to his feet, pitied up the decanter carefully, then pointed down the path.

'If you continue on in that direction,' he said, 'passing the hedge that marks the end of this bower and entering the woods that lie below – and then go on for another two hundred paces or so – you come to a place where there is a little grove of saplings off to the left, standing in a sudden declivity perhaps four feet lower than the level of the trail itself. Down in it, stamped down and strewn over with leaves and twigs, there is a fresh grave. I found it while taking the air earlier, when I paused to relieve myself down there.'

'How do you know it is a grave?'

He chuckled.

'When holes have bodies in them that is how they are generally called. It was quite shallow, and I poked around a bit with a stick. There are four bodies in there – three men and a woman.'

'How recently dead?'

'Very. A few days, I'd judge.'

'You left it as you found it?'

'I'm not a fool, Corwin.'

'Sorry. But this troubles me considerably, because I don't understand it at all.'

'Obviously they gave Benedict some trouble and he returned the favor.'

'Perhaps. What were they like? How did they die?'

'Nothing special about them. They were in their middle years, and their throats had been cut – save for one fellow who got it in the guts.'

'Strange. Yes, it is good that we are leaving soon. We have enough problems of our own without getting involved in the local ones.'

'Agreed. So let us be off to bed.'

'You go ahead. I am not quite ready yet.'

'Take your own advice and get some rest,' he said, turning back toward the manor. 'Don't sit up and worry.'

'I won't.'

'Good night, then.'

'See you in the morning.'

I watched him return along the path. He was right, of course, but I was not yet ready to surrender my consciousness. I went over my plans again, to be certain there was nothing I was overlooking, finished my drink and set the glass on the bench. I rose then and strolled, trailing wisps of tobacco smoke about me. There was a bit of moonlight from over my shoulder and dawn was still a few hours' distant, as I reckoned it. I was firm in my resolve to spend the rest of the night out of doors, and I thought to find me a good place to sack out.

Of course, I evenually wandered down the path and into the grove of saplings. A little poking around showed me that there had been some recent digging, but I was in no mood to exhume bodies by moonlight and was perfectly willing to take Ganelon's word as to what he had found there. I am not even certain why I went there. Morbid streak, I guess. I did decide against sleeping in the vicinity, though.

I made my way into the northwest corner of the garden, finding an area that was out of line of sight from the manor. There were high hedgerows and the grass was long, soft, and sweet-smelling. I spread my cloak, sat down upon it, and pulled off my boots. I put my feet down into the cool grass and sighed.

Not too much longer, I decided. Shadows to diamonds to guns to Amber. I was on my way. A year ago I had been rotting in a cell, crossing and recrossing the line between sanity and madness so many times that I had all but rubbed it out. Now I was free, strong, sighted, and had a plan. Now I was a threat seeking fulfillment once again, a deadlier threat than I had been previously. This time I did not have my fortunes tied up with the plans of another. Now I was responsible for my own success or failure.

The feeling was good, as was the grass, as was the alcohol which had now seeped through my system and warmed me with a pleasant flame. I cleaned my pipe, put it away, stretched, yawned, and was about to recline.

I detected a distant movement, propped myself on my elbows and watched for it again. I did not have long to wait. A figure was passing slowly along the path, pausing frequently, moving quietly. It vanished beneath the tree where Ganelon and I had been sitting, and did not emerge again for a long while. Then it continued on for several dozen paces, stopped and seemed to be staring in my direction. Then it advanced toward me.

Passing about a clump of shrubbery and emerging from the shadows, her face was suddenly touched by the moonlight. Apparently aware of this, she smiled in my direction, slowing as she came near, stopping when she stood before me.

She said, 'I take it your quarters are not to your liking, Lord Corwin.'

'Not at all,' I said. 'It is such a beautiful night that it appealed to the outdoorsman in me.'

'Something must have appealed to you last night, also,' she said, 'despite the rain,' and she seated herself beside me on my cloak. 'Did you sleep indoors or out?'

'I spent it out,' I said. 'But I did not sleep. In fact, I have not slept since I saw you last.'

'Where have you been?'

'Down by the seaside, sifting sand.'

'Sounds depressing.'

'It was.'

'I have been doing a lot of thinking, since we walked in Shadow.'

'I would imagine.'

'I have not done too much sleeping either. That was why I heard you come in, heard you talking with Ganelon, knew you were out here somewhere when he came back alone.'

'You were right.'

'I must get to Amber, you know. And walk the Pattern.'

'I know. You will.'

'Soon, Corwin. Soon!'

'You are young, Dara. There is plenty of time.'

'Damn it! I have been waiting all my life – without even knowing about it! Is there no way I can go now?'

'No.'

'Why not? You could take me on a quick journey through shadows, take me to Amber, let me walk the Pattern . . .'

'If we are not slain immediately, we might be fortunate enough to be given adjoining cells for a time – or racks – before we are executed.'

'Whatever for? You are a Prince of the City. You have a right to do as you please.'

I laughed.

'I am an outlaw, dear. If I return to Amber I will be executed, if I am lucky. Or something much worse if I am not. But seeing as how things turned out last time, I should think they would kill me quickly. This courtesy would doubtless also be extended to my companions.'

'Oberon would not do such a thing.'

'Given sufficient provocation, I believe that he would. But the question does not really arise. Oberon is no more, and my brother Eric sits on the throne and calls himself liege.'

'When did this occur?'

'Several years ago, as time is measured in Amber.'

'Why would he want to kill you?'

'To keep me from killing him, of course.'

'Would you?'

'Yes, and I will. Soon, too, I think.'

She turned to face me then.

'Why?'

'So that I can occupy the throne myself. It is rightly mine, you see. Eric has usurped it. I am just recently escaped from torture and several years' imprisonment at his hands. He made the mistake, however, of allowing himself the luxury of keeping me alive so that he could contemplate my wretchedness. He never thought that I would get free and return to challenge him again. Neither did I, for that matter. But since I have been fortunate enough to obtain a second chance, I shall be careful not to make the same mistake he did.'

'But he is your brother.'

'Few are more aware of that fact than he and I, I assure you.'

'How soon do you expect to accomplish – your objectives?'

'As I said the other day, if you can get hold of the Trumps, contact me in about three months. If you cannot, and things come about according to my plans, I will get in touch with you fairly early in my reign. You should have your chance to take the Pattern before another year passes.'

'And if you fail?'

'Then you will have a longer wait ahead of you. Until Eric has assured the permanency of his own reign, and until Benedict has acknowledged him king. You see, Benedict is not willing to do this. He has remained away from Amber for a long while, and for all Eric knows, he is no longer among the living. Should he put in an appearance now, he is going to have to take a position either for or against Eric. Should he come out for him, then the continuance of Eric's reign will be assured – and Benedict does not want to be responsible for that. Should be come out against him, there will be strife – and he does not want to be responsible for that either. He has no desire for the crown himself. Only by remaining out of the picture entirely can he assure the measure of tranquility that does prevail. Were he to appear and refuse to take either position, *he* could possibly get away with it, but it would be tantamount to denying Eric's kingship and would still lead to trouble. Were he to appear with you, he would be surrendering his will, for Eric would put pressure on him through you.'

'Then if you lose I might never get to Amber!'

'I am only describing the situation as I see it. There are doubtless many factors of which I am unaware. I have been out of circulation for a long while.'

'You *must* win!' she said. Then, suddenly, 'Would Grandpa support you?'

'I doubt it. But the situation would be quite different. I am aware of his existence, and of yours. I will not ask his support. So long as he does not oppose me, I will be satisfied. And if I am quick, efficient, and successful, he will not oppose me. He will not like my having found out about you, but when he sees that I mean you no harm all will be well on that count.'

'Why would you not use me? It seems the logical thing to do.'

'It is. But I've discovered I like you,' I said, 'so that's out of the question.'

She laughed.

'I've charmed you!' she said.

I chuckled.

'In your own delicate way, at sword's point, yes.'

Abruptly, she sobered.

'Grandpa is coming back tomorrow,' she said. 'Did your man Ganelon tell you?'

'Yes.'

'How does that affect whatever you are about?'

'I intend to be hell and gone out of here before he returns.'

'What will he do?'

'The first thing that he will do will be to get very angry with you for being here. Then he will want to know how you managed your return and how much you have told me about yourself.'

'What should I tell him?'

'Tell him the truth about how you got back. That will give him something to think about. As to your status, your woman's intuition cautioned you concerning my trustworthiness, and you took the same line with me as you did with Julian and Gérard. As to my where-abouts, Ganelon and I borrowed a wagon and headed into town, saying that we would not be back until quite late.'

'Where will you really be going?'

'Into town, briefly. But we will not be coming back. I want as much of a head start as possible because he can track me through Shadow, up to a point.'

'I will delay him as best I can for you. Were you not going to see me before you left?'

'I was going to have this talk with you in the morning. You got it ahead of time by being restless.'

'Then I am glad that I was – restless. How are you going to conquer Amber?'

I shook my head. 'No, dear Dara. All scheming princes must keep a few small secrets. That's one of mine.'

'I am surprised to learn there is so much distrust and plotting in Amber.'

'Why? The same conflicts exist everywhere, in various forms. They are all about you, always, for all places take their form from Amber.'

'It is difficult to understand . . .'

'One day you will. Leave it at that for now.'

'Then tell me another thing. Since I am able to negotiate shadows somewhat, even without having taken the Pattern, tell me more precisely how you go about it. I want to get better at it.'

'No!' I said. 'I will not have you fooling with Shadow until you are ready. It is dangerous even after you have taken the Pattern. To do it before is foolhardy. You were lucky, but do not try it again. I'll even help, by not telling you anything more about it.'

'All right!' she said. 'Sorry. I guess I can wait.'

'I guess you can. No hard feelings?'

'No. Well—' She laughed. 'They wouldn't do me any good, I guess. You must know what you are talking about. I am glad that you care what happens to me.'

I grunted, and she reached out and touched my cheek. At this, I turned my head again and her face was moving slowly toward my own, smile gone and lips parting, eyes almost closed. As we kissed, I felt her arms slide about my neck and shoulders and mine found their way into a similar position around her. My surprise was lost in the sweetness, gave way to warmth and a certain excitement.

If Benedict ever found out, he was going to be more than just irritated with me . . .

7

The wagon creaked, monotonously, and the sun was already well into the west, though it still poured hot streams of daylight upon us. Back among the cases, Ganelon snored, and I envied him his noisy occupation. He had been sleeping for several hours, and this was my third day without rest.

We were perhaps fifteen miles out of the city, and heading into the northeast. Doyle had not had my order completely ready, but Ganelon and I had persuaded him to close up his shop and accelerate his production. This involved several additional hours' curse-worthy delay. I had been too keyed-up to sleep then and was unable to do so now, so I was edging my way through shadows.

I forced back the fatigue and the evening and found some clouds to shade me. We moved along a dry, deeply rutted, clay road. It was an ugly shade of yellow, and it cracked and crumbled as we went. Brown grasses hung limply on either side of the way, and the trees were short, twisted things, their barks thick and shaggy. We passed numerous outcrops of shale.

I had paid Doyle well for his compounds, and had also purchased a handsome bracelet to be delivered to Dara the following day. My diamonds were at my belt, Grayswandir near to my hand. Star and Plredrake walked steadily, strongly. I was on my way to having it made.

I wondered whether Benedict had returned yet. I wondered how long he would remain deceived as to my whereabouts. I was by no means out of danger from him. He could follow a trail for a great distance through Shadow, and I was leaving him a good one. I had little choice in the matter, though. I needed the wagon, I was stuck with our present speed, and I was in no condition to manage another hellride. I handled the shifts slowly and carefully, very conscious of my dulled senses and growing weariness counting on the gradual accumulation of change and distance to build up a barrier between Benedict and myself, hoping that it would soon become an impenetrable one.

I found my way from late afternoon back to noontide within the next two miles, but kept it a cloudy noon, for it was only its light that I desired, not its heat. Then I managed to locate a small breeze. It increased the probability of rain, but it was worth it. You can't have everything.

I was fighting back drowsiness by then, and the temptation was great to awaken Ganelon and simply add more miles to our distance by letting him drive while I slept. But I was afraid to try it this early in the journey. There were still too many things to do.

I wanted more daylight, but I also wanted a better road, and I was sick of that goddamned yellow clay, and I had to do something about those clouds, and I had to keep in mind where we were headed . . .

I rubbed my eyes, I took several deep breaths. Things were starting to jump around inside my head, and the steady clop-clop of the horses' hoofs and the creaking of the wagon were starting to have a soporific effect. I was already numb to the jolting and the swaying. The reins hung loosely in my hands, and I had already nodded and let them slip once. Fortunately, the horses seemed to have a good idea as to what was expected of them.

After a time, we mounted a long, easy slope that led down into mid-morning. By then, the sky was quite dark, and it took several miles and half a dozen twistings of the road to dissipate the cloud cover somewhat. A storm could turn our way into a river of mud quite quickly. I winced at the thought, let the sky alone and concentrated on the road once more.

We came to a dilapidated bridge leading across a dry stream bed. On its other side, the road was smoother, less yellow. As we proceeded, it grew darker, fatter, harder, and the grass came green beside it.

By then though, it had begun raining.

I fought with this for a time determined not to surrender my grass and the dark, easy road. My head ached, but the shower ended within a quarter of a mile and the sun came out once more.

The sun . . . oh yes, the sun.

We rattled on, finally coming to a dip in the road that kept twisting its way down among brighter trees. We descended into a cool valley, where we eventually crossed another small bridge, this one with a narrow band of water drifting along the middle of the bed beneath it. I had wrapped the reins about my wrist by then, because I kept nodding. As from a great distance, I focused my concentration, straightening, sorting . . .

Birds queried the day, tentatively, from within the woods to my right. Glistening droplets of dew clung to the grass, the leaves. A chill came into the air, and the rays of the morning sun slanted down through the trees . . .

But my body was not fooled by the awakening within tin's shadow, and I was relieved finally to hear Ganelon stir and curse. If he had not come around before much longer I would have had to awaken him.

Good enough. I tugged gently on the reins and the horses got the idea and halted. I put on the brake, as we were still on an incline, and located a water bottle.

'Here!' said Ganelon, as I drank. 'Leave a drop for me!'

I passed the bottle back to him.

'You are taking over now,' I told him. 'I have to get some sleep.'

He drank for half a minute, then let out an explosive exhalation.

'Right,' he said, swinging himself over the edge of the wagon and down. 'But bide a moment. Nature summons.'

He stepped off the road, and I crawled back onto the bed of the wagon and stretched out where he had lain, folding my cloak into a pillow.

Moments later, I heard him climb onto the driver's seat, and there was a jolt as he released the brake. I heard him cluck his tongue and snap the reins lightly.

'Is it morning?' he called back to me.

'Yes.'

'God! I've slept all day and all night!'

I chuckled.

'No. I did a little shadow-shifting,' I said. 'You only slept six or seven hours.'

'I don't understand. But never mind, I believe you. Where are we now?'

'Still heading northeast,' I said, 'around twenty miles out of the city and maybe a dozen or so from Benedict's place. We have moved through Shadow, also.'

'What am I to do now?'

'Just keep following the road. We need the distance.'

'Could Benedict still reach us?'

'I think so. That's why we can't give the horses their rest yet.'

'All right. Is there anything special I should be alert for?'

'No.'

'When should I rouse you?'

'Never.'

He was silent then, and as I waited for my consciousness to be consumed, I thought of Dara, of course. I had been thinking of her on and off all day.

The thing had been quite unpremeditated on my part. I had not even thought of her as a woman until she came into my arms and revised my thinking on the subject. A moment later, and my spinal nerves took over, reducing much of what passes for cerebration down to its basics, as Freud had once said to me. I could not blame it on the alcohol, as I had not had that much and it had not affected me especially. Why did I want to blame it on anything? Because I felt somewhat guilty, that was why. She was too distant a relation for me to really think of her as one. That was not it. I did not feel I had taken unfair advantage of her, for she had known what she was doing when she came looking for me. It was the circumstances that made me question my own motives, even in the midst of things. I had wanted to do more than simply win her confidence and a measure of friendship when I had first spoken with her and taken her on that walk into Shadow. I was trying to alienate some of her loyalty, trust, and affection from Benedict and transfer it to myself. I had wanted her on my side, as a possible ally in what might become an enemy camp. I had hoped to be able to use her, should the need arise when the going got rough. All this was true. But I did not want to believe that I had had her as I did just to further this end. I suspected there was some truth to it, though, and it made me uncomfortable and more than a little ignoble. Why? I had done plenty of things in my time that many would consider much worse, and I was not especially troubled by these. I wrestled with it, not liking to admit it but already knowing the answer. I cared for the girl. It was as simple as that. It was different from the friendship I had felt for Lorraine, with its element of world-weary understanding between two veterans about it, or the air of casual sensuality that had existed briefly between Moire and myself, back before I had taken the Pattern for the second time. It was quite different. I had known her so briefly that it was most illogical. I was a man with centuries behind me. Yet . . . I had not felt this way in centuries. I had forgotten the feeling, until now. I did not want to be in love with her. Not now. Later, perhaps. Better yet, not at all. She was all wrong for me. She was a child. Everything that she would want to do, everything that she would find new and fascinating, I had already done. No, it was all wrong. I had no business falling in love with her. I should not let myself . . .

Ganelon hummed some bawdy tune, badly. The wagon jounced and creaked, took a turn uphill. The sun fell upon my face, and I covered my eyes with my forearm. Somewhere thereabout, oblivion fixed its grip and squeezed.

When I awoke, it was past noon and I was feeling grimy. I took a long drink of water, poured some in the palm of my hand, and rubbed it in my eyes. I combed my hair with my fingers. I took a look at our surroundings.

There was greenery about us, small stands of trees and open spaces where tall grasses grew. It was till a dirt road that we traveled, hard-packed and fairly smooth. The sky was clear, but for a few small clouds, and shade alternated with sunlight fairly regularly. There was a light breeze.

'Back among the living. Good!' said Ganelon, as I climbed over the front wall and took a seat beside him.

'The horses are getting tired, Corwin, and I'd like to stretch my legs a bit,' he said. 'I'm also getting very hungry. Aren't you?'

'Yes. Pull off into that shady place to the left and well stop awhile.'

'I would like to go on a bit farther than that,' he said.

'For any special reason?'

'Yes. I want to show you something.'

'Go ahead.'

We clopped along for perhaps half a mile, then came to a bend in the road that took us in a more northerly direction. Before very long we came to a hill, and when we had mounted it there was another hill, leading even higher.

'How much farther do you want to go?' I said.

'Let's take this next hill,' he replied. 'We might be able to see it from up there.'

'All right.'

The horses strained against the steepness of that second hill, and I got out and pushed from behind. When we finally reached the top, I felt even grimier from the mixture of sweat and dust, but I was fully awake once more. Ganelon reined in the horses and put on the brake. He climbed back in the wagon and up onto a crate then. He stood, facing to the left, and shaded his eyes.

'Come up here, Corwin,' he called.

I climbed over the tailgate and he squatted and extended a hand. I took it, and he helped me up onto the crate, where I stood beside him. He pointed, and I followed the gesture.

Perhaps three-quarters of a mile distant, running from left to right for as far as I could see, was a wide, black band. We were several hundred yards higher than the thing and had a decent view of, I would say, half a mile of its length. It was several hundred feet across, and though it curved and turned twice that I could see, its width appeared to remain constant. There were trees within it, and they were totally black. There seemed to be some movement. I could not say what it was. Perhaps it was only the wind rippling the black grasses near its edge. But there was also a definite sensation of flowing within it, like current in a flat, dark river.

'What is it?' I said.

'I thought perhaps you could tell me,' Ganelon replied. 'I had thought it a part of your shadow-sorceries.'

I shook my head slowly.

'I was quite drowsy, but I would remember if I had arranged for anything that strange to occur. How did you know it was there?'

'We skirted it several times as you slept, then edged away again. I did not like the feeling at all. It was a very familiar one. Does it not remind you of something?'

'Yes. Yes, it does. Unfortunately.'

He nodded.

'It's like that damned Circle back in Lorraine. That's what it's like.'

'The black road . . .' I said.

'What?'

'The black road,' I repeated. 'I did not know what she was referring to when she mentioned it, but now I begin to understand. This is not good at all.'

'Another ill omen?'

'I am afraid so.'

He cursed, then, 'Will it cause us any immediate trouble?' he asked.

'I don't believe so, but I am not certain.'

He climbed down from the crate and I followed.

'Let's find some forage for the horses then,' he said, 'and tend to our own bellies as well.'

'Yes.'

We moved forward and he took the reins. We found a good spot at the foot of the hill.

We tarried there for the better part of an hour, talking mainly of Avalon. We did not speak again of the black road, though I thought of it quite a bit. I had to get a closer look at the thing, of course.

When we were ready to move on, I took the reins again. The horses, somewhat refreshed, moved out at a good pace.

Ganelon sat beside me on the left, still in a talkative mood. I was only just then beginning to realize how much this strange homecoming had meant to him. He had revisited many of his old haunts from the days of his outlawry, as well as four battlefields where he had distinguished himself greatly after he had achieved respectability. I was in many ways moved by his reminiscences. An unusual mixture of gold and clay, this man. He should have been an Amberite.

The miles slid by quickly and we were drawing near to the black road again when I felt a familiar mental jab. I passed the reins to Ganelon.

'Take them!' I said. 'Drive!'

'What is it?'

'Later! Just drive!'

'Should I hurry?'

'No. Keep it normal. Don't say anything for a while.'

I closed my eyes and rested my head in my hands, emptying my mind and building a wall around the emptiness. No one home. Out to lunch. No solicitors. This property is vacant. Do not disturb.

Trespassers will be prosecuted. Beware of dog. Falling rock. Slippery when wet. To be razed for urban renewal . . .

It eased, then came on again, hard, and I blocked it again. There followed a third wave. I stopped that one, too.

Then it was gone.

I sighed, massaged my eyeballs.

'It's all right now,' I said.

'What happened?'

'Someone tried to reach me by a very special means. It was almost certainly Benedict. He must just now have found out any of a number of things that could make him want to stop us. I'll take the reins again now. I fear he will be on our trail soon.'

Ganelon handed them over.

'What are our chances of escaping him?'

'Pretty fair now, I'd say, that we've got more distance behind us. I am going to shuffle some more shadows as soon as my head stops spinning.'

I guided us on, and our way twisted and wound, paralleling that black road for a time, then heading in closer to it Finally, we were only a few hundred yards away from it.

Ganelon studied it in silence for a long while, then said, 'It reminds me too much of that other place. The little tongues of mist that lick about things, the feeling that something is always moving just at the corner of your eye . . .'

I bit my lip. I began to perspire heavily. I was trying to shift away from the thing now and there was some sort of resistance. It was not the same feeling of monolithic immovability as occurs when you try to move through Shadow in Amber. It was altogether different. It was a feeling of – inescapability.

We moved through Shadow all right. The sun drifted higher in the heavens, heading back toward noonday – for I did not relish the thought of nightfall beside that black strip – and the sky lost something of its blue and the trees shot higher about us and mountains appeared in the distance.

Was it that the road cut through Shadow itself?

It must. Why else would Julian and Gérard have located it and been sufficiently intrigued to explore the thing?

It was unfortunate, but I feared we had much in common, that road and I.

Damn it!

We moved beside it for a long while, gradually moving closer together, also. Soon, only about a hundred feet separated us. Fifty . . .

. . . And, as I had felt they eventually must, our paths finally intersected.

I drew rein. I packed my pipe and lit it, smoked as I studied the thing. Star and Firedrake obviously did not approve of the black area that cut across our way. They had whinnied and tried to pull off to the side.

It was a long, diagonal cut across the black place if we wanted to keep to the road. Also, part of the terrain was hidden from our sight by a series of low, stone hills. There were heavy grasses at the edge of the black and patches of it, here and there, about the foot of the hills. Bits of mist scudded among them and faint, vaporous clouds hovered in all the hollows. The sky, seen through the atmosphere that hung about the place, was several shades darker, with a smeared, sooty tone to it. A silence that was not the same as stillness lay upon it, almost as though some unseen entity were poised, holding its breath.

Then we heard a scream. It was a girl's voice. The old lady in distress trick?

It came from somewhere to the right, beyond those hills. It smelled fishy. But hell! It could be real.

I tossed the reins to Ganelon and jumped to the ground, taking Grayswandir into my hand.

'I'm going to investigate,' I said, moving off to the right and leaping the gulley that ran beside the road.

'Hurry back.'

I plowed through some brush and scrambled up a rocky slope. I pushed my way through more shrubbery on its down side and mounted another, higher slope. The scream came again as I was climbing it, and this time I heard other sounds as well.

Then I reached the top and was able to see for a good distance.

The black area began about forty feet below me, and the scene I sought was laid about a hundred-fifty feet within it.

It was a monochromatic sight, save for the flames. A woman, all in white, black hair hanging loose, down to her waist, was bound to one of those dark trees, smoldering branches heaped around her feet. Half a dozen hairy, albino men, almost completely naked and continuing the process of undressing as they moved, shuffled about, muttering and chuckling, poking at the woman and the fire with sticks that they carried and clutching at their loins repeatedly. The flames were high enough now to singe the woman's garments, causing them to smolder. Her long dress was sufficiently torn and disarrayed so that I could see she possessed a lovely, voluptuous form, though the smoke wrapped her in such a manner that I was unable to see her face.

I rushed forward, entering the area of the black road, leaping over the long, twining grasses, and charged into the group, beheading the nearest man and running another through before they knew I was upon them. The others turned and flailed at me with their sticks, shouting as they swung them.

Grayswandir ate off big chunks of them, until they fell apart and were silent. Their juices were black.

I turned, holding my breath, and kicked away the front of the fire. Then I moved in close to the lady and cut her bonds. She fell into my arms, sobbing.

It was only then that I noticed her face – or, rather, her lack of once. She wore a full, ivory mask, oval and curving, featureless, save for two tiny rectangular grilles for her eyes.

I drew her away from the smoke and the gore. She clung to me, breathing heavily, thrusting her entire body against me. After what seemed an appropriate period of time, I attempted to disentangle myself. But she would not release me, and she was surprisingly strong.

'It is all right now,' I said, or something equally trite and apt, but she did not reply.

She kept shifting her grip upon my body, with rough caressing movements and a rather disconcerting effect. Her desirability was enhanced, from instant to instant. I found myself stroking her hair, and the rest of her as well.

'It is all right now,' I repeated. 'Who are you? Why were they burning you? Who were they?'

But she did not reply. She had stopped sobbing, but her breathing was still heavy, although in a different way.

'Why do you wear this mask?'

I reached for it and she jerked her head back.

This did not seem especially important though. While some cold, logical part of me knew that the passion was irrational, I was as powerless as the gods of the Epicureans. I wanted her and I was ready to have her.

Then I heard Ganelon cry out my name and I tried to turn in that direction.

But she restrained me. I was amazed at her strength.

'Child of Amber,' came her half-familiar voice. 'We owe you this for what you have given us, and we will have all of you now.'

Ganelon's voice came to me again, a steady stream of profanities.

I exerted all my strength against that grip and it weakened. My hand shot forward and I tore away the mask.

There came a brief cry of anger as I freed myself, and four final, fading words as the mask came away:

'Amber must be destroyed!'

There was no face behind the mask. There was nothing there at all.

Her garment collapsed and hung limply over my arm. She – or it – had vanished.

Turning quickly, I saw that Ganelon was sprawled at the edge of the black, his legs twisted unnaturally. His blade rose and fell slowly, but I could not see at what he was striking. I ran toward him.

The black grasses, over which I had leaped, were twined about his ankles and legs. Even as he hacked at them, others lashed about as though seeking to capture his sword arm. He had succeeded in partly freeing his right leg, and I leaned far forward and managed to finish the job.

I moved to a position behind him, out of reach of the grasses, and tossed away the mask, which I just then realized I was still clutching. It fell to earth beyond the edge of the black and immediately began to smolder.

Catching him under the arms, I strove to drag Ganelon back. The stuff resisted fiercely, but at last I tore him free. I carried him then, leaping over the remaining dark grasses that separated us from the more docile, green variety beyond the road.

He regained his footing and continued to lean heavily against me, bending forward and slapping at his leggings.

'They're numb,' he said. 'My legs are asleep.'

I helped him back to the wagon. He transferred his grip to its side and began stamping his feet.

'They're tingling,' he announced, 'It's starting to come back . . . Oow!'

Finally, he limped to the front of the wagon. I helped him climb onto the seat and followed him up.

He sighed.

'That's better,' he said. 'They're coming along now. That stuff just sucked the strength out of them. Out of the rest of me, too. What happened?'

'Our bad omen made good on its promise.'

'What now?'

I picked up the reins and released the brake.

'We go across,' I said. 'I have to find out more about this thing. Keep your blade handy.'

He grunted and laid the weapon across his knees. The horses did not like the idea of going on, but I flicked their flanks lightly with the whip and they began to move.

We entered the black area, and it was like riding into a World War II newsreel. Remote though near at hand, stark, depressing, grim. Even the creaking and the hoof falls were somehow muffled, made to seem more distant. A faint, persistent ringing began in my ears. The grasses beside the road stirred as we passed, though I kept well away from them. We passed through several patches of mist. They were odorless, but our breathing grew labored on each occasion. As we neared the first hill, I began the shift that would take us through Shadow.

We rounded the hill.

Nothing.

The dark, miasmal prospect was unaltered.

I grew angry then. I drew the Pattern from memory and held it blazing before my mind's eye. I essayed the shift once more.

Immediately, my head began to ache. A pain shot from my forehead to the back of my skull and hung there tike a hot wire. But this only fanned my anger and caused me to try even harder to shift the black road into nothingness.

Things wavered. The mists thickened, rolled across the road in billows. Outlines grew indistinct. I shook the reins. The horse moved after. My head began to throb, felt as if were about to come apart.

Instead, momentarily, everything else did . . .

The ground shook, cracking in places, but it was more than just that. Everything seemed to undergo a spasmodic shudder, and the cracking was more than there fracture lines in the ground.

It was as though someone had suddenly kicked the leg of a table on which a loosely assembled jigsaw puzzle lay. Gaps appeared in the entire prospect: here, a green bough; there, a sparkle of water, a glimpse of blue sky, absolute blackness, white nothingness, the front of a brick building, faces behind a window, fire, a piece of star-filled sky . . .

The horses were galloping by then, and I had all I could do to keep from screaming for the pain.

A babble of mixed noises – animal, human, mechanical – washed over us. It seemed that I could hear Ganelon cursing, but I could not be certain.

I thought that I would pass out from the pain, but I determined, out of sheer stubbornness and anger, to persist until I did. I concentrated on the Pattern as a dying man might cry out to his God, and I threw my entire will against the existence of the black road.

Then the pressure was off and the horses were plunging wildly, dragging us into a green field. Ganelon snatched at the reins, but I drew on them myself and shouted to the horses until they halted.

We had crossed the black road.

I turned immediately and looked back. The scene had the wavering quality of something seen through troubled waters. Our path through it stood clean and steady, however, like a bridge or a dam, and the grasses at its edge were green.

'That was worse,' Ganelon said, 'than the ride you took me on when you exiled me.'

'I think so, too,' I said, and I spoke to the horses gently, finally persuading them to return to the dirt road and continue on along it.

The world was brighter here, and the trees that we soon moved among were great pines. The air was fresh with their fragrance. Squirrels and birds moved within them. The soil was darker, richer. We seemed to be at a higher altitude than we had been before the crossing. It pleased me that we had indeed shifted – and in the direction I had desired.

Our way curved, ran back a bit, straightened. Every now and then we caught a glimpse of the black road. It was not too far off to our right. We were still running roughly parallel to it. The thing definitely cut through Shadow. From what we saw of it, it appeared to have settled back down to being its normal, sinister self once more.

My headache faded and my heart grew somewhat lighter. We achieved higher ground and a pleasant view over a large area of hills and forest, reminding me of parts of Pennsylvania I had enjoyed driving through years earlier.

I stretched; then, 'How are your legs now?' I asked.

'All right,' Ganelon said, looking back along our trail. 'I can see for a great distance, Corwin . . .'

'Yes?'

'I see a horseman, coming very fast.'

I stood and turned. I think I might have groaned as I dropped back into the seat and shook the reins.

He was still too far to tell for certain – on the other side of the black road. But who else could it be, pushing along at that speed on our trail?

I cursed then.

We were nearing the crest of the rise. I turned to Ganelon and said, 'Get ready for another hellride.'

'It's Benedict?'

'I think so. We lost too much time back there. He can move awfully fast – especially through Shadow – all alone like that.'

'Do you think you can still lose him?'

'We'll find out,' I said. 'Real soon now.'

I clucked to the horses and shook the reins again. We reached the top and a blast of icy air struck us. We leveled off and the shadow of a boulder to our left darkened the sky. When we had passed it, the darkness remained and crystals of fine-textured snow stung our faces and hands.

Within a few moments, we were heading downward once more and the snowfall became a blinding buzzard. The wind screamed in our ears and the wagon rattled and skidded. I leveled us quickly.

There were drifts all about by then and the road was white. Our breath fumed and ice glistened on trees and rocks.

Motion and temporary bafflement of the senses. That was what it took . . .

We raced on, and the wind slammed and bit and cried out. Drifts began to cover the road.

We rounded a bend and emerged from the storm. The world was still a glaceed-over thing and an occasional flake flitted by, but the sun pulled free of the clouds, pouring light upon the land, and we headed downward once more . . .

. . . Passing through a fog and emerging in a barren, though snowless waste of rock and pitted land . . .

. . . We bore to the the right, regained the sun, followed a twisted course on a level plain, winding among tall, featureless stands of blue-gray stone . . .

. . . Where far off to our right the black road paced us.

Waves of heat washed over us and the land steamed. Bubbles popped in boiling stews that filled the craters, adding their fumes to the dank air. Shallow puddles lay like a handful of old, bronze corns.

The horses raced, half-maddened now, as geysers began to erupt along the trail. Scalding waters spewed across the roadway, narrowly missing us, running in steaming, slick sheets. The sky was brass and the sun was a mushy apple. The wind was a panting dog with bad breath.

The ground trembled, and far off to our left a mountain blew its top toward the heavens and hurled fires after it. An ear-splitting crash temporarily deafened us and concussion waves kept beating against our bodies. The wagon swayed and shimmied.

The ground continued to shake and the winds slammed us with near-hurricane force as we rushed toward a row of black-topped hills. We left what there was of a roadway when it turned in the wrong direction and headed, bumping and shuddering, across the plain itself. The hills continued to grow, dancing in the troubled air.

I turned when I felt Ganelon's hand on my arm. He was shouting something, but I could not hear him. Then he pointed back and I followed his gesture. I saw nothing that I had not expected to see. The air was turbulent, filled with dust, debris, ashes. I shrugged and returned my attention to the hills.

A greater darkness occurred at the base of the nearest hill. I made for it.

It grew before me as the ground slanted downward once more, an enormous cavern mouth, curtained by a steady fall of dust and gravel.

I cracked the whip in the air and we raced across the final five or six hundred yards and plunged into it.

I began slowing the horses immediately, letting them relax into a walk.

We continued to move downward, turned a corner, and came into a wide, high grotto. Light leaked down from holes high above, dappling stalactites and falling upon quivering green pools. The ground continued to shake, and my hearing took a turn for the better as I saw a massive stalagmite crumble and heard the faint tinkle of its fall.

We crossed a black-bottomed chasm on a bridge that might have been limestone, which shattered behind us and vanished.

Bits of rock rained down from overhead and sometimes large stones fell. Patches of green and red fungus glowed in corners and cracks, streaks of minerals sparkled and bent, large crystals and flat flowers of pale stone added to the moist, eerie beauty of the place. We wheeled through caverns like chains of babbles and coursed a white-crested torrent until it vanished into a black hole.

A long, corkscrew gallery took us upward once more, and I heard Ganelon's voice, faint and echoing, 'I thought that I glimpsed move-ment – that might be a rider – at the crest of the mountain – just for an instant – back there.'

We moved into a slightly brighter chamber.

'If it was Benedict, he's got a hard act to follow,' I shouted, and there came the tremors and muffled crashings as more things collapsed behind us.

We proceeded onward and upward, until finally openings began to occur overhead, giving upon patches of clear blue sky. The hoof clicks and the sounds of the wagon gradually assumed a normal volume and their echoes came to us also. The tremors ceased, small birds darted above us, and the light increased in intensity.

Then another twisting of the way, and our exit lay before us, a wide, low opening onto day. We had to duck our heads as we passed beneath the jagged lintel.

We bounced up and over a jutting lip of moss-covered stone, then looked upon a bed of gravel that lay like a scythed track upon the hillside, passing among gigantic trees, vanishing within them, below. I made a clicking noise with my tongue, encouraging the horses on their way.

'They are very tired now,' Ganelon remarked.

'I know. Soon they will get to rest, one way or another.'

The gravel crunched beneath our wheels. The smell of the trees was good.

'Have you noticed it? Down there, off to the right?'

'What . . .' I began, turning my head. Then, 'Oh,' I finished.

The infernal black road was with us still, perhaps a mile distant.

'How many shadows does it cut across?' I mused.

'All of them, it would seem,' Ganelon suggested.

I shook my head slowly.

'I hope not,' I said.

We proceeded downward, beneath a blue sky and a golden sun westering in a normal way.

'I was almost afraid to come out of that cave,' Ganelon said after a time. 'No telling what would be on this side.'

'The horses couldn't take much more. I had to let up. If that was Benedict we saw, his horse had better be in very good condition. He was pushing it hard. Then to have it face all that . . . I think he would fall back.'

'Maybe it's used to it,' Ganelon said, as we crunched around a bend to the right, losing sight of the cave mouth.

'There is always that possibility,' I said, and I thought of Dara again, wondering what she was doing at that moment.

We wove our way steadily downward, shifting slowly and imperceptibly. Our trail kept drifting to the right, and I cursed when I realized we were nearing the black road.

'Damn! It's as persistent as an insurance salesman!' I said, feeling my anger turn to something like hatred. 'When the time is right, I am going to destroy that thing!'

Ganelon did not reply. He was taking a long drink of water. He passed me the bottle and I did, too.

At length, we achieved level terrain, and the trail continued to twist and curve at the least excuse. It allowed the horses to take it easy and it would slow a mounted pursuer.

About an hour later, I began to feel comfortable and we stopped to eat. We had just about finished our meal when Ganelon – who had not removed his gaze from the hillside – stood and shaded his eyes.

'No,' I said, leaping to my feet. 'I don't believe it.'

A lone rider had emerged from the mouth of the cave. I watched as he halted for a moment, then continued on down the trail.

'What do we do now?' Ganelon asked.

'Let's pick up our stuff and get moving again. We can at least delay the inevitable a little longer. I want more time to think.'

We rolled once more, still moving at a moderate pace, though my mind was racing at full speed. There had to be a way to stop him. Preferably, without killing him.

But I couldn't think of any.

Except for the black road, which was edging nearer once more, we had come into a lovely afternoon in a beautiful place. It was a shame to dampen it with blood, particularly if it might be my blood. Even with his blade in his left hand, I was afraid to face him. Ganelon would be of no use to me. Benedict would barely notice him.

I shifted as we took another turning. Moments later, a faint smell of smoke came to my nostrils. I shifted slightly again.

'He's coming fast!' Ganelon announced. 'I just saw – There's smoke! Flames! The woods are on fire!'

I laughed and looked back. Half the hillside swam under smoke and an orange thing raced through the green, its crackling just then reaching my ears. Of their own accord, the horses increased their pace.

'Corwin! Did you—'

'Yes! If it were steeper and there were no trees, I'd have tried an avalanche.'

The air was momentarily filled with birds. We drew nearer the black way. Firedrake tossed his head and whinnied. There were flecks of foam on his muzzle. He tried to bolt, then reared and pawed the air. Star made a frightened noise and pulled to the right. I fought a moment, regained control, decided to let them run a bit.

'He's still coming!' cried Ganelon.

I cursed and we ran. Eventually, our path brought us alongside the black road. We were on a long straightaway, and a glance back showed me that the whole hillside was ablaze, the trail running like a nasty scar down its middle. It was then that I saw the rider. He was almost halfway down and moving like something in the Kentucky Derby. God! What a horse that had to be! I wondered what shadow had borne him.

I drew on the reins, gently at first, then harder, until finally we began to slow. We were only a few hundred feet from the black road by then, and I had seen to it that there was a place not too far ahead where the gap narrowed to thirty or forty. I managed to rein in the horses when we reached it, and they stood there quivering. I handed the reins to Ganelon, drew Grayswandir, and stepped down to the road.

Why not? It was a good, clear, level area, and perhaps that black, blasted slice of land, contrasting with the colors of life and growth immediately beside it, appealed to some morbid instinct in me.

'What now?' Ganelon asked.

'We cannot shake him,' I said, 'and if he makes it through the fire he will be here in a few minutes. There is no sense to running any farther. I'll meet him here.'

Ganelon twisted the reins around a side bar and reached for his blade.

'No,' I said. 'You cannot affect the outcome one way or the other. Here is what I want you to do: take the wagon on up the road and wait there with it. If things are resolved to my satisfaction, we will be continuing on. If they are not, surrender immediately to Benedict. It is me that he wants, and he will be the only one left who can take you back to Avalon. He will do it, too. You will at least retire to your homeland that way.'

He hesitated.

'Go on,' I told him. 'Do as I said.'

He looked down at the ground. He unwound the reins. He looked at me.

'Good luck,' he said, and he shook the horses forward.

I backed off the trail, moved to a position before a small stand of saplings, and waited. I kept Grayswandir in my hand, glanced once at the black road, then fixed my eyes on the trail.

Before long, be appeared up near the flame line, smoke and fire all about him, burning branches falling. It was Benedict all right, his face partly muffled, the stump of his right arm upraised to shield his eyes, coming like some ghastly escapee from hell. Bursting through a shower of sparks and cinders, he came into the clear and plunged on down the trail.

Soon, I could hear the hoofbeats. A gentlemanly thing to do would be to sheathe my blade while I waited. If I did that, though, I might not have a chance to draw it again.

I found myself wondering how Benedict would be wearing his blade and what sort it would be. Straight? Curved? Long? Short? He could use them all with equal facility. He had taught me how to fence . . .

It might be smart as well as gentlemanly to sheathe Grayswandir. He might be willing to talk first – and this way I was asking for trouble. As the hoofbeats grew louder, though, I realized I was afraid to put it away.

I wiped my palm only before he came into view. He had slowed for the turn, and he must have seen me at the same instant I saw him. He rode straight toward me, slowing. But halting did not appear to be his immediate aim.

It was almost a mystical experience. I do not know how else to put it. My mind outran time as he neared, and it was as though I had an eternity to ponder the approach of this man who was my brother. His garments were filthy, his face blackened, the stump of his right arm raised, gesturing anywhere. The great beast that he rode was striped, black and red, with a wild red mane and tail. But it really was a horse, and its eyes rolled and there was foam at its mouth and its breathing was painful to hear. I saw then that he wore his blade slung across his back, for its shaft protruded high above his right shoulder. Still slowing, eyes fixed upon me, he departed the road, bearing slightly toward my left, jerked the rents once and released them, keeping control of the horse with his knees. His left hand went up in a salute-like movement that passed above his head and seized the hilt of his weapon. It came free without a sound, describing a beautiful arc above him and coming to rest in a lethal position out from his minuscule line of edge that gleamed like a filament of mirror. The picture he presented was burned into my mind with a kind of magnificence, a certain splendor that was strangely moving. The blade was a long, scythe-like affair that I had seen him use before. Only then we had stood as allies against a mutual foe I had begun to believe unbeatable. Benedict has proved otherwise that night. Now that I saw it raised against me I was overwhelmed with a sense of my own mortality, which I had never experienced before in this fashion. It was as though a layer had been stripped from the world and I had a sudden, full understanding of death itself.

The moment was gone. I backed into the grove. I had stood there so that I could take advantage of the trees. I dropped back about twelve feet among them and took two steps to my left. The horse reared at the last possible moment and snorted and whinnied, moist nostrils flaring. It turned aside, tearing up turf. Benedict's arm moved with near-invisible speed, like the tongue of a toad, and his blade passed through a sapling I'd guess at three inches in diameter. The tree continued to stand upright for a moment, then slowly toppled.

His boots struck the earth and he strode toward me. I had wanted the grove for this reason, also, to make him come to me in a place where a long blade would be hampered by branches and boles.

But as he advanced, he swung the weapon, almost casually, back and forth, and the trees fell about him as he passed. If only he were not so infernally competent If only he were not Benedict . . .

'Benedict,' I said, in a normal voice, 'she is an adult now, and she is capable of making up her own, mind about things.'

But he gave no sign of having heard me. He just kept coming, swinging that great blade from side to side. It made an almost ringing sound as it passed through the air, followed by a soft *thukk*! as it bit through another tree, slowing only slightly.

I raised Grayswandir to point at his breast.

'Come no farther, Benedict,' I said. 'I do not wish to fight with you.'

He moved his blade into an attack position and said one word: 'Murderer!'

His hand twitched then and my blade was almost simultaneously beaten aside. I parried the ensuing thrust and he brushed my riposte aside and was at me again.

This time I did not even bother to riposte. I simply parried, retreated, and stepped behind a tree.

'I don't understand,' I said, beating down his blade as it slid by the trunk and nearly skewered me. 'I have not murdered anyone recently. Certainly not in Avalon.'

Another *thukk*! and the tree was falling toward me. I got out of its way and retreated, parrying.

'Murderer,' he said again.

'I don't know what you are talking about, Benedict.'

'Liar!'

I stood my ground then and held it. Damn it! It was senseless to die for the wrong reason! I riposted as fast as I could, seeking openings everywhere. There were none.

'At least tell me!' I shouted. 'Please!'

But he seemed to be finished with talking. He pressed forward and I had to fall back once more. It was like trying to fence with a glacier. I became convinced then that he was out of his mind, not that that helped me any. With anybody else, an insane madness would cause the loss of some control in a fight. But Benedict had hammered out his reflexes over the centuries, and I seriously believed that the removal of his cerebral cortex would not have altered his movements from their state of perfection.

He drove me steadily back, and I dodged among trees and he cut them down and kept coming. I made the mistake of attacking and barely stopped his counterthrusts inches from my breast. I fought down the first wave of panic that came to me when I saw that he was driving me back toward the edge of the grove. Soon he would have me in the open, with no trees to slow him.

My attention was focused on him so completely that I did not realize what was then to occur until it did.

With a mighty cry, Ganelon sprang from somewhere, wrapping his arms about Benedict and pinning his sword arm to his side.

Even had I really wanted to, though, I did not have the opportunity to kill him then. He was too fast, and Ganelon was not aware of the man's strength.

Benedict twisted to his right, interposing Ganelon between us, and at the same time brought the stump of his arm around like a club, striking Ganelon in the left temple. Then he pulled his left arm free, seized Ganelon by his belt, swept him off his feet, and threw him at me. As I stepped aside, he retrieved his blade from where it had fallen near his feet and came at me again. I barely had time to glance and see that Ganelon had landed in a heap some ten paces to my rear.

I parried and resumed my retreat. I only had one trick remaining, and it saddened me that if it failed Amber would be deprived of its rightful liege.

It is somewhat more difficult to fence with a good left-hander than a good right-hander, and this worked against me also. But I had to experiment a bit. There was something I had to learn, even if it meant taking a chance.

I took a long step back, moving momentarily out of range, then leaned forward and attacked. It was a very calculated thing, and very fast.

One unexpected result, which I am certain was at least partly luck, was that I got through, even though I missed my target. For an instant, Grayswandir rode high off one of his parries and nicked his left ear. This slowed him slightly for a few moments, but not enough to matter. If anything, it served to strengthen his defense. I continued to press my attack, but there was simply no getting through then. It was only a small cut, but the blood ran down to his ear lobe and spattered off, a few drops at a time. It could even be distracting, if I permitted myself to do more than take note of it.

Then I did what I feared, but had to try. I left him a small opening, just for a moment, knowing that he would come right through it toward my heart.

He did, and I parried it at the last instant. I do not like to think about how close he came that time.

Then I began to yield once more, giving ground, backing out of the grove. Parrying and retreating, I moved past the spot where Ganelon lay. I fell back another fifteen feet or so, fighting defensively, conservatively.

Then I gave Benedict another opening.

He drove in, as he had before, and I managed to stop him again. He pressed the attack even harder after that, pushing me back to the edge of the black road.

There, I stopped and held my ground, shifting my position to the spot I had chosen. I would have to hold him just a few moments longer, to set him up . . .

They were very rough moments, but I fought furiously and readied myself.

Then I gave him the same opening again.

I knew he would come in the same as before, and my right leg was across and back behind my left, then straightening, as he did. I gave his blade but the barest beat to the side as I sprang backward onto the black road, immediately extending my arm full length to discourage a balaestra.

Then he did what I had hoped. He beat at my blade and advanced normally when I dropped it into quarte . . .

. . . causing him to step into the patch of black grasses over which I had leaped.

I dared not look down at first. I simply stood my ground and gave the flora a chance.

It only took a few moments. Benedict became aware of it the next time that he tried to move. I saw the puzzled expression flash across his face, then the strain. It had him, I knew.

I doubted, though, that it could hold him very long, so I moved immediately.

I danced to the right, out of range of his blade, rushed forward and sprang across the grasses, off the black road once again. He tried to turn, but they had twined themselves about his legs all the way up to his knees. He swayed for a moment, but retained his balance.

I passed behind him and to his right. One easy thrust and he was a dead man, but of course there was no reason to do it now.

He swung his arm back behind his neck and turned his head, pointing the blade at me. He began pulling his left leg free.

But I feinted toward his right, and when he moved to parry it I slapped him across the back of the neck with the flat of Grayswandir.

It stunned him, and I was able to move in and punch him in the kidney with my left hand. He bent slightly and I blocked his sword arm and struck him in the back of the neck again, this time with my fist, hard. He fell, unconscious, and I removed his blade from his hand and cast it aside. The blood from his left ear lobe trailed down his neck like some exotic earring.

I put Grayswandir aside, seized Benedict under the armpits, and dragged him back from the black road. The grasses resisted mightily, but I strained against them and finally had him free.

Ganelon had gotten to his feet by then. He limped up and stood beside me, looking down at Benedict.

'What a fellow he is,' he said. 'What a fellow he is . . . What are we going to do with him?'

I picked him up in a fireman's carry and stood.

'Take him back toward the wagon right now,' I said. 'Will you bring the blades?'

'All right.'

I headed up the road and Benedict remained unconscious – which was good, because I did not want to have to hit him again if I could help it. I deposited him at the base of a sturdy tree beside the road near the wagon.

I resheathed our blades when Ganelon came up, and set him to stripping ropes from several of the cases. While he did this, I searched Benedict and found what I was looking for.

I bound him to the tree then, while Ganelon fetched his horse. We tethered it to a nearby bush, upon which I also hung his blade.

Then I mounted to the driver's seat of the wagon and Ganelon came up alongside.

'Are you just going to leave him there?' he asked.

'For now,' I said.

We moved on up the road. I did not look back, but Ganelon did.

'He hasn't moved yet,' he reported. Then, 'Nobody ever just took me and threw me like that, With one hand yet.'

'That's why I told you to wait with the wagon, and not to fight with him if I lost.'

'What is to become of him now?'

'I will see that he is taken care of, soon.'

'He will be all right, though?'

I nodded.

'Good.'

We continued on for perhaps two miles and I halted the horses. I climbed down.

'Don't be upset by anything that happens,' I said. 'I am going to make arrangements for Benedict now.'

I moved off the road and stood in the shade, taking out the deck of Trumps Benedict had been carrying. I riffled through them, located Gérard, and removed him from the pack. The rest I returned to the silk-lined, wooden case, inlaid with bone, in which Benedict had carried them.

I held Gérard's Trump before me and regarded it.

After a time, it grew warm, real, seemed to stir. I felt Gérard's actual presence. He was in Amber. He was walking down a street that I recognized. He looks a lot like me, only larger, heavier. I saw that he still wore his beard.

He halted and stared.

'Corwin!'

'Yes, Gérard. You are looking well.'

'Your eyes! You can see?'

'Yes, I can see again.'

'Where are you?'

'Come to me now and I will show you.'

His gaze tightened.

'I am not certain that I can do that, Corwin. I am very involved just now.'

'It is Benedict,' I said. 'You are the only one I can trust to help him.'

'Benedict? He is in trouble?'

'Yes.'

'Then why does he not summon me himself?'

'He is unable to. He is restrained.'

'Why? How?'

'It is too long and involved to go into now. Believe me, he needs your help, right away.'

He raked his beard with his upper teeth.

'And you cannot handle it yourself?'

'Absolutely not.'

'And you think I can?'

'I know you can.'

He loosened his blade in its scabbard.

'I would not like to think this is some sort of trick, Corwin.'

'I assure you it is not. With all the time I have had to think, I would have come up with something a little more subtle.'

He sighed. Then he nodded.

'All right. I'm coming to you.'

'Come ahead.'

He stood for a moment, then took a step forward.

He stood beside me. He reached out and clasped my shoulder. He smiled.

'Corwin,' he said. 'I'm glad you've your eyes back.'

I looked away.

'So am I. So am I.'

'Who is that in the wagon?'

'A friend. His name is Ganelon.'

'Where is Benedict? What is the problem?'

I gestured.

'Back there,' I said. 'About two miles down the road. He is bound to a tree. His horse is tethered near by.'

'Then why are you here?'

'I am fleeing.'

'From what?'

'Benedict I'm the one who bound him.'

He wrinkled his brow.

'I do not understand . . .'

I shook my head.

'There is a misunderstandmg between us. I could not reason with him and we fought. I knocked him unconscious and I tied him up. I cannot free him, or he would attack me again. Neither can I leave him as he is. He may come to some harm before he can free himself. So I summoned you. Please go to him, release him, and see him home.'

'What will you be doing the while?'

'Getting the hell out of here, losing myself in Shadow. You will be doing both of us a favor to keep him from trying to follow me again. I do not want to have to fight him a second time.'

'I see. Now will you tell me what happened?'

'I am not certain. He called me a murderer. I give you my word I slew no one the whole time I was in Avalon. Please tell him I said that. I have no reason to lie to you, and I swear that it is true. There is another matter which may have disturbed him somewhat. If he mentions it, tell him that he will have to rely on Dara's explanation.'

'And what is it?'

I shrugged.

'You will know if he mentions it. If he does not, forget it.'

'Dara, you say?'

'Yes.'

'Very well, I shall do as you have asked . . . Now, will you tell me how you managed your escape from Amber?'

I smiled.

'Academic interest? Or do you feel you might have need of the route yourself one day?'

He chuckled.

'It strikes me as a handy piece of information to have.'

'I regret, dear brother, that the world is not yet ready for this knowledge. If I had to tell anyone, I would tell you – but there is no way it could benefit you, whereas its secrecy may serve me in the future.'

'In other words, you have a private way into and out of Amber. What are you planning, Corwin?'

'What do you think?'

'The answer is obvious. But my feelings on the matter are mixed.'

'Care to tell me about them?'

He gestured toward a section of the black road that was visible from where we stood.

'That thing,' he said. 'It runs to the foot of Kolvir now. A variety of menaces travel it to attack Amber. We defend, we are always victorious. But the attacks grow stronger and they come more frequently. Now would not be a good time for you to move, Corwin.'

'Or it might be the perfect time,' I said.

'For you then, but not necessarily for Amber.'

'How has Eric been handling the situation?'

'Adequately. As I said, we are always victorious.'

'I do not mean the attacks. I mean the entire problem – its cause.'

'I have traveled the black road myself, going a great distance along it.'

'And?'

'I was unable to go the entire distance. You know how the shadows grow wilder and stranger the farther you get from Amber?'

'Yes.'

'. . . Until the mind itself is twisted and turned toward madness?'

'Yes.'

'. . . And somewhere beyond this lie the Courts of Chaos. The road goes on, Corwin. I am convinced that it runs the entire distance.'

'Then it is as I feared,' I said.

'That is why, whether I sympathize with you or not, I do not recommend the present time for your efforts. The security of Amber must come before all else.'

'I see. Then there is nothing more to be said just now.'

'And your plans?'

'Since you do not know what they are, it is meaningless to tell you that they are unchanged. But they are unchanged.'

'I do not know whether to wish you luck, but I wish you well. I am glad that you have your sight back.' He clasped my hand. 'I had best get on to Benedict now. I take it he is not badly hurt?'

'Not by me. I only hit him a few times. Do not forget to give him my message.'

'I won't.'

'And take him back to Avalon.'

'I will try.'

'Then good-bye for now, Gérard.'

'Good-bye, Corwin,'

He turned then and walked on down the road. I watched until he was out of sight before I returned to the wagon. Then I replaced his Trump in the deck and continued on my way to Antwerp.

8

I stood on the hilltop and looked down at the house. There was shrubbery all about me, so I was not especially obtrusive.

I do not really know what I expected to see. A burned-out shell? A car in the driveway? A family scattered about the redwood patio furniture? Armed guards?

I saw that the roof could use some new slate, that the lawn had long ago returned to a natural condition. I was surprised that I could see only one broken window there in the rear.

So the place was supposed to look deserted. I wondered.

I spread my jacket on the ground and seated myself on it. I lit a cigarette. There were no other houses for quite a distance.

I had gotten close to seven hundred thousand dollars for the diamonds. It had taken me a week and a half to make the deal. From Antwerp we had traveled to Brussels, spending several evenings at a club on the Rue de Char et Pain before the man I wanted found me.

Arthur was quite puzzled by the arrangement. A slight, white-haired man with a neat mustache, ex-RAF officer, Oxonian, he had begun shaking his head after the first two minutes and kept inter-rupting me with questions about delivery. While he was no Sir Basil Zaharoff, he became genuinely concerned when a client's ideas sounded too half-baked. It troubled him if something went sour too soon after delivery. He seemed to think it reflected back on him in some way. For this reason, he was often more helpful then the others when it came to shipment. He was concerned about my plans for transportation because I did not seem to have any.

What one generally requires in an arrangement of this sort is an end-use certificate. What it is, basically, is a document affirming that country X has ordered the weapons in question. You need the thing in order to get an export permit from the manufacturer's country. This keeps them looking honest, even if the shipment should be recon-signed to country Y once it has crossed their border. The customary thing to do is to buy the assistance of an ambassadorial representative of country X – preferably one with relatives or friends connected with the Defense Department back home – in order to get the papers. They come high, and I believe Arthur had a list of all the going rates in his head.

'But how are you going to ship them?' he had kept asking. 'How will you get them where you want them?'

'That,' I said, 'will be my problem. Let me worry about it.'

But he kept shaking his head.

'It is no good trying to cut corners that way, Colonel,' he said. (I had been a colonel to him since we had first met, some dozen years before. Why, I am not certain.) 'No good at all. Try to save a few dollars that way and you might lose the whole shipment and wind up in real trouble. Now I can fix you up through one of these young African nations quite reasonably—'

'No. Just fix me up with the weapons.'

During our talk, Ganelon just sat there drinking beer, as red-bearded and sinister-looking as ever, and nodding to everything that I said. As he spoke no English, he had no idea as to the state of negotiations. Nor, for that matter, did he really care. He followed my instructions, though, and spoke to me periodically in Thari and we would chat briefly in that language about nothing in particular. Sheer perversity. Poor old Arthur was a good linguist and he wanted to know the destination of the pieces. I could feel him straining to identify the language each time that we spoke. Finally, he began nodding as though he had.

After some more discussion, he stuck his neck out and said, 'I read the newspapers. I am certain his crowd can afford the insurance.'

That was almost worth the price of admission to me.

But, 'No,' I said. 'Believe me, when I take possession of those automatic rifles, they are going to vanish off the face of the Earth.'

'Neat trick, that,' he said, 'considering I don't even know where we will be picking them up yet.'

'It does not matter.'

'Confidence is a fine thing. Then there is foolhardiness . . .' He shrugged. 'Have it as you say then – your problem.'

Then I told him about the ammo and he must have been convinced as to my mental deterioration. He just stared at me for a long while, not even shaking his head this time. It was a good ten minutes before I could even get him to look at the specifications. It was then that he began shaking his head and mumbling about silver bullets and inert primers.

The ultimate arbiter, cash, convinced him we would do it my way, however. There was no trouble on the rifles or the trucks, but persuading an arms factory to produce my ammo was going to be expensive, he told me. He was not even certain he could find one that would be willing. When I told him that the cost was no object, it seemed to upset him even more. If I could afford to indulge in weird, experimental ammo, an end-use certificate would not come to that much—

No, I told him no. My way, I reminded him.

He sighed and tugged at the fringe of his mustache. Then he nodded. Very well, we would do it my way.

He overcharged me, of course. Since I was rational in all other matters, the alternative to psychosis would be that I was party to an expensive boondoggle. While the ramifications must have intrigued him, he apparently decided not to look too far into such a sticky-seeming enterprise. He was willing to seize every opportunity I extended for dissociating himself from the project. Once he found the ammo people – a Swiss outfit, as it turned out – he was quite willing to put me into contact with them and wash his hands of everything but the money.

Ganelon and I went to Switzerland on fake papers. He was a German and I was Portuguese. I did not especially care what my papers showed, so long as the forgery was of good quality, but I had settled on German as the best language for Ganelon to learn, since he had to learn one and German tourists have always seemed to be all over the place. He picked it up quite rapidly. I had told him to tell any real Germans and any Swiss who asked that he had been raised in Finland.

We spent three weeks in Switzerland before I was satisfied with the quality controls on my ammo. As I had suspected, the stuff was totally inert in this shadow. I had worked out the formula, though, which was all that really mattered at that point. The silver came high, of course. Perhaps I was being over-cautious. Still, there are some things about Amber that are best dispatched with that metal and I could afford it. For that matter, what better bullet – short of gold – for a king? Should I wind up shooting Eric there would be no *lése-majesté* involved. Indulge me, brothers.

Then I left Ganelon to shift for himself for a time, since he had thrown himself into his tourist role in a true Stanislavskian fashion. I saw him off to Italy, camera about his neck and a faraway look in his eyes, and I flew back to the States.

Back? Yes. That run-down place on the hillside below me had been my home for the better part of a decade. I had been heading toward it when I was forced off the road and into the accident which led to everything which has since occurred.

I drew on my cigarette and regarded the place. It had not been run-down then. I had always kept it in good shape. The place had been completely paid for. Six rooms and an attached two-car garage. Around seven acres. The whole hillside, actually. I had lived there alone most of the time. I had liked it. I had spent much of my time in the den and in my workshop. I wondered whether the Mori woodcut still hung in my study. *Face to face* it was called, and it depicted two warriors in mortal combat. It would be nice to have it back. It would be gone, though, I felt. Probably everything that had not been stolen had been sold for back taxes. I imagined that was what the State of New York would do. I was surprised that the house itself seemed not to have acquired new occupants. I kept watching, to make certain. Hell, I was in no hurry. There was no place else I had to be.

I had contacted Gérard shortly after my arrival in Belgium. I had decided against trying to talk with Benedict for the time being. I was afraid that he would simply try to attack me, one way or the other, if I did.

Gérard had studied me quite carefully. He was out somewhere in open country and he seemed to be alone.

'Corwin?' he had said, then, 'Yes . . .'

'Right. What happened with Benedict?'

'I found him as you said he would be and I released him. He was set to pursue you once again, but I was able to persuade him that a considerable time had passed since I had seen you. Since you said you had left him unconscious, I figured that was the best line to take.

Also, his horse was very tired. We went back to Avalon together. I remained with him through the funerals, then borrowed a horse. I am on my way back to Amber now.'

'Funerals? What funerals?'

Again, that calculating look.

'You really do not know?' he said.

'If I knew, damn it, I would not ask!'

'His servants. They were murdered. He says you did it.'

'No,' I said. 'No. That is ridiculous. Why should I want to murder his servants? I do not understand . . .'

'It was not long after his return that he went looking for them, as they were not on hand to welcome him. He found them murdered and you and your companion gone.'

'Now I see how it looked,' I said. 'Where were the bodies?'

'Buried, but not too deeply, in the little wood behind the garden to the rear of the house.'

Just so, just so . . . Better not to mention I had known about the grave.

'But what possible reason does he think I could have for doing such a thing?' I protested.

'He is puzzled, Corwin. Very puzzled, now. He could not understand why you did not kill him when you had the chance, and why you sent for me when you could have just left him there.'

'I see now why he kept calling me a murderer as we fought, but – Did you tell him what I said about not having slain anyone?'

'Yes. At first he shrugged it off as a self-serving statement. I told him you sounded sincere, and very puzzled yourself. I believe it bothered him a bit that you should be so insistent. He asked me several times whether I believed you.'

'Do you?'

He dropped his eyes.

'Damn it, Corwin! What am I supposed to believe? I came into the middle of this. We have been apart for so long . . .'

He met my gaze.

'There is more to it,' he said.

'What is that?'

'Why did you call me to help him? That was a complete deck you took. You could have called any of us.'

'You must be joking,' I said.

'No, I want an answer.'

'Very well. You are the only other one I trust.'

'Is that all?'

'No. Benedict does not want his whereabouts known back in Amber. You and Julian are the only two I know for certain to be aware of his location, I don't like Julian, I don't trust him. So I called you.'

'How did you know that Julian and I knew about him?'

'He helped you both out when you ran into trouble on the black road awhile back, and he put you up while you recuperated. Dara told me about it.'

'Dara? Who is this Dara anyway?'

'The orphaned daughter of a couple who once worked for Benedict,' I said. 'She was around when you and Julian were there.'

'And you sent her a bracelet. You also mentioned her to me by the road, back when you summoned me.'

'Correct. What is the matter?'

'Nothing. I do not really remember her, though. Tell me, why did you leave so suddenly? You have to admit, it seemed the act of a guilty man.'

'Yes,' I said, 'I was guilty – but not of murder. I went to Avalon to obtain something that I wanted, I got it, and I cleared out. You saw that wagon, and you saw that I had a cargo in it. I got out before he retained to keep from answering questions Benedict might ask me about it. Hell! If I just wanted to run, I wouldn't go dragging a wagon along behind me! I'd have traveled on horseback, fast and light.'

'What was in the wagon?'

'No,' I said. 'I did not want to tell Benedict and I do not want to tell you. Oh, he can find out, I suppose. But let him do it the hard way, if he must. It is immaterial though. The fact I went there for something and really obtained it should be sufficient. It is not especially valuable there, but is in another place. Fair enough?'

'Yes,' he said. 'It does make a kind of sense.'

'Then answer my question. Do you think I murdered them?'

'No,' he said. 'I believe you.'

'What about Benedict, now? What does he think?'

'He would not attack you again without talking first. There is doubt in his mind, I know that.'

'Good. That's something, anyway. Thank you, Gérard. I am going away now.'

I moved to break the contact.

'Wait, Corwin! Wait!'

'What is it?'

'How did you cut the black road? You destroyed a section of it at the place you crossed over. How did you do it?'

'The Pattern,' I said. 'If you ever get in trouble with that thing, hit it with the Pattern. You know how you have to sometimes hold it in your mind if shadows begin to run away from you and things start going wild?'

'Yes. I tried that and it didn't work. All I got was a headache. It is not of Shadow.'

'Yes and no,' I said. 'I know what it is. You did not try hard enough. I used the Pattern until my head felt as if it were being torn apart, until I was half blind from the pain and about ready to pass out. Then the road came apart about me instead. It was no fun, but it did work.'

'I will remember,' he said. 'Are you going to talk to Benedict now?'

'No,' I said. 'He already has everything we've gone over. Now that he is cooling off, he will begin pushing the facts around some more. I would just as soon he do it on his own – and I do not want to risk another fight. When I close this time I will be silent for a long while. I will resist all efforts to communicate with me, also.'

'What of Amber, Corwin? What of Amber?'

I dropped my eyes.

'Don't get in my way when I come back, Gérard. Believe me, it will be no contest.'

'Corwin . . . Wait. I'd like to ask you to reconsider. Do not hit Amber now. She is weak in all the wrong ways.'

'I am sorry, Gérard. But I am certain I have given the matter more thought during the past five years than all the rest of you put together.'

'I am sorry, too, then.'

'I guess I had better be going now.'

He nodded.

'Good-bye, Corwin.'

'Good-bye, Gérard.'

After waiting several hours for the sun to disappear behind the hill, leaving the house in a premature twilight, I mashed a final cigarette, shook out my jacket and donned it, rose to my feet. There had been no signs of life about the place, no movement behind the dirty windows, the broken window. Slowly, I descended the hill.

Flora's place out in Westchester had been sold some years before, which came as no surprise to me. I had checked merely as a matter of curiosity, since I was back in town. Had even driven past the place once. There was no reason for her to remain on this shadow Earth. Her long wardenship having ended successfully, she was being rewarded in Amber the last time I had seen her. To have been so near for as long as I had without even realizing her presence was a thing I found somewhat galling.

I had debated contacting Random, decided against it. The only way he could possibly benefit me would be with information as to current affairs in Amber. While this would be nice to have, it was not absolutely essential. I was fairly certain that I could trust him. After all, he had been of some assistance to me in the past. Admitted, it was hardly altruism – but still, he had gone a bit further than he had had to. It was five years ago, though, and a lot had happened since. He was being tolerated around Amber again, and he had a wife now. He might be eager to gain a little standing. I just did not know. But weighing the possible benefits against the possible losses, I thought it better to wait and see him personally the next time I was in town.

I had kept my word and resisted all attempts to make contact with me. They had come almost daily during my first two weeks back on the shadow Earth. Several weeks had passed, though, and I had not been troubled since. Why should I give anyone a free shot at my thinking machinery? No thanks, brothers.

I advanced upon the rear of the house, sidled up to a window, wiped it with my elbow. I had been watching the place for three days, and it struck me as very unlikely that anyone was inside. Still . . .

I peered in.

It was a mess, of course, and a lot of my stuff was missing. But some of it was still there. I moved to my right and tried the door. Locked. I chuckled.

I walked around to the patio. Ninth brick in, fourth brick up. The key was still beneath it. I wiped it on my jacket as I walked back. I let myself in.

There was dust on everything, but it had been disturbed in some places. There were coffee containers, sandwich wrappers, and the remains of a petrified hamburger in the fireplace. A lot of weather had found its way down that chimney in my absence. I crossed over and closed the damper.

I saw that the front door had been broken about the lock. I tried it. It seemed to be nailed shut. There was an obscenity scrawled on the wall in the foyer. I walked on into the kitchen. It was a total mess. Anything that had survived plunder was on the floor. The stove and the refrigerator were gone, the floor scarred where they had been pushed along.

I backed away, went and checked my workshop. Yes, it had been stripped. Completely. Passing on, I was surprised to find my bed, still unmade, and two expensive chairs all intact in my bedroom.

My study was a more pleasant surprise. The big desk was covered with litter and muss, but then it always had been. Lighting a cigarette, I went and sat behind it. I guess it was just too heavy and bulky for anyone to make off with. My books were all on their shelves. Nobody steals books but your friends. And there—

I could not believe it. I got to my feet again and crossed the room to stare at close range.

Yoshitoshi Mori's beautiful woodcut hung right where it had always been, clean, stark, elegant, violent. To think that no one had made off with one of my most prized possessions . . .

Clean?

I scrutinized it. I ran my finger along the frame.

Too clean. It bore none of the dust and grit which covered everything else in the house.

I checked it for trip wires, found none, removed it from its hook, lowered it.

No, the wall was no lighter behind it. It matched the rest of the wall perfectly.

I put Mori's work on the window seat and returned to my desk. I was troubled, as someone doubtless intended me to be. Someone had obviously removed it and taken good care of it – a thing for which I was not ungrateful – and then only just recently restored it. It was as if my return had been anticipated.

Which should be adequate reason for immediate flight, I suppose. But that was silly. If it was part of some trap, it had already been sprung. I jerked the automatic from my jacket pocket and tucked it behind my belt. I had not even known that I would be coming back myself. It was just something I had decided to do since I had had some time on my hands. I was not even certain as to why I had wanted to see the place again.

So this was some sort of contingency arrangement. If I should come by the old homestead, it might be to obtain the only thing in the place worth having. So preserve it and display it so that I will have to take notice. All right, I had. I had not been attacked yet, so it did not seem a trap. What then?

A message. Some sort of a message.

What? How? And who?

The safest place in the house, had it remained unravaged, should still be the safe. It was not beyond any of my siblings' skill. I moved to the rear wall, pressed the panel loose, and swung it out. I spun the dial through its combination, stepped back, opened the door with my old swagger stick.

No explosion. Good. Not that I had expected any.

There had been nothing of any great value inside – a few hundred dollars in cash, some bonds, receipts, correspondence.

An envelope. A fresh, white envelope lay in plain sight. I did not remember it.

My name upon it, written in an elegant hand. Not with ballpoint either.

It contained a letter and a card.

Brother Corwin, the letter said, *If you are reading this, then we still think enough alike for me to be able to anticipate you somewhat. I thank you for the loan of the woodcut – one of two possible reasons, as I see it, for your returning to this squalid shadow. I am loathe to relinquish it, as our tastes are also somewhat akin and it has graced my chambers for several years now. There is something to the subject that strikes a familiar chord. Its return is to be taken as evidence of my good will and a bid for your attention. In that I must be honest with you if I am to stand a chance of convincing you of anything, I will not apologize for what has been done. My only regret, actually, is that I did not kill you when I should have. Vanity it was, that played me for a fool. While time may have healed your eyes, I doubt it will ever significantly alter our feelings for one another. Your letter – 'I'll be back' – lies upon my writing table at this moment. Had I written it, I know that I would be back. Some things being equal between us, I anticipate your return, and not without somewhat of apprehension. Knowing you for no fool, I contemplate your arriving in force. And here is where vanity is paid of present pride. I would have peace between us, Corwin, for the sake of the realm, not my own. Strong forces out of Shadow have come to beset Amber regularly, and I do not fully understand their nature. Against these forces, the most formidable in my memory ever to assail Amber, the family has united behind me. I would like to have your support in this struggle. Failing that, I request that you forbear invading me for a time. If you elect to assist, I will require no homage of you, simply acknowledgment of my leadership for the duration of the crisis. You will be accorded your normal honors. It is important that you contact me to see the truth of what I say. As I have failed to reach you by means of your Trump, I enclose my own for your use. While the possibility that I am lying to you is foremost in your mind, I give you my word that I am not. – Eric, Lord of Amber.*

I reread it and chuckled. What did he think curses were for, anyway?

No good, my brother. It was kind of you to think of me in your moment of need – and I believe you, never doubt it, for we are all of us honorable men – but our meeting will come according to my schedule, not yours. As for Amber, I am not unmindful of her needs, and I will deal with them in my own time and fashion. You make the mistake, Eric, of considering yourself necessary. The graveyards are fitted with men who thought they could not be replaced. I will wait though, to tell you this, face to face.

I tucked his letter and the Trump in my jacket pocket. I killed my cigarette in the dirty ashtray on my desk. Then I fetched some linen from the bedroom to wrap my combatants. They would wait for me in a safer place, this time.

As I passed through the house again, I wondered why I had come back, really. I thought of some of the people I had known when I had lived there, and wondered whether they ever thought of me, whether they wondered what had become of me. I would never know, of course.

Night had begun and the sky was clear and its first stars bright as I stepped outside and locked the door behind me. I went around to the side and returned the key to its place beneath, the patio. Then I mounted the hill.

When I looked back from the top, the house seemed to have shrunken there in the darkness, to have become a piece of the desolation, like an empty beer can tossed beside the road. I crossed over and down, heading across a field toward the place where I had parked, wishing I had not looked back.

9

Ganelon and I departed Switzerland in a pair of trucks. We had driven them there from Belgium, and I had taken the rifles in mine. Figuring ten pounds per piece, the three hundred had come to around a ton and a half, which was not bad. After we took on the ammo, we still had plenty of room for fuel and other supplies. We had taken a short cut through Shadow, of course, to avoid the people who wait around borders to delay traffic. We departed in the same fashion, with me in the lead to open the way, so to speak.

I led us through a land of dark hills and narrow villages, where the only vehicles we passed were horse-drawn. When the sky grew bright lemon, the beasts of burden were striped and feathered. We drove for hours, finally encountering the black road, paralleling it for a time, then heading off in another direction. The skies went through a dozen shiftings, and the contours of the land melted and merged from hill to plain and back again. We crept along poor roads and skidded on flats as smooth and hard as glass. We edged our way across a mountain's face and skirted a wine-dark sea. We passed through storms and fogs.

It took me half a day to find them again, or a shadow so close that it made no difference. Yes, those whom I had exploited once before. They were short fellows, very hairy, very dark, with long incisors and retractable claws. But they had trigger fingers, and they worshiped me. They were overjoyed at my return. It little mattered that five years earlier I had sent the cream of their manhood off to die in a strange land. The gods are not to be questioned, but loved, honored, and obeyed. They were quite disappointed that I only wanted a few hundred. I had to turn away thousands of volunteers. The morality of it did not especially trouble me this time. One way of looking at it might be that by employing this group I was seeing to it that the others had not died in vain. Of course I did not look at it that way, but

I enjoy exercises in sophistry. I suppose I might also consider them mercenaries being paid in spiritual coin. What difference did it make whether they fought for money or for a belief? I was capable of supplying either one when I needed troops.

Actually, though, these would be pretty safe, being the only ones in the place with fire power. My ammo was still inert in their homeland, however, and it took several days of marching through Shadow to reach a land sufficiently like Amber for it to become functional. The only catch was that shadows follow a law of congruency of correspondences, so that the place actually was close to Amber. This kept me somewhat on edge throughout their training. It was unlikely that a brother would blunder through that shadow. Still, worse coincidences have occurred.

We drilled for close to three weeks before I decided we were ready. Then, on a bright, crisp morning, we broke camp and moved on into Shadow, the columns of troops following behind the trucks. The trucks would cease to function when we neared Amber – they were already giving us some trouble – but they might as well be used to haul the equipment as far along as possible.

This time, I intended to go over the top of Kolvir from the north, rather than essay its seaward face again. All of the men had an understanding of the layout, and the disposition of the rifle squads had already been determined and run through in practice.

We halted for lunch, ate well, and continued on, the shadows slowly slipping away about us. The sky became a dark but brilliant blue, the sky of Amber. The earth was black among rocks and the bright green of the grass. The trees and the shrubs had a moist lucency to their foliage. The air was sweet and clean.

By nightfall, we were passing among the massive trees at the fringes of Arden. We bivouacked there, posting a very heavy guard. Ganelon, now wearing khakis and a beret, sat with me long into the night, going over the maps I had drawn. We still had about forty miles to go before we hit the mountains.

The trucks gave out the following afternoon. They went through several transformations, stalled repeatedly, and finally refused to start at all. We pushed them into a ravine and cut branches to cover them over. We distributed the ammo and the rest of the rations and continued on.

We departed the hard, dirt roadway after that and worked our way through the woods themselves. As I still knew them well, it was less of a problem than it might have been. It slowed us, naturally, but lessened chances of surprise by one of Julian's patrols. The trees were quite large, as we were well into Arden proper, and the topography sprang back into mind as we moved.

We encountered nothing more menacing than foxes, deer, rabbits, and squirrels that day. The smells of the place and its green, gold, and brown brought back thoughts of happier times. Near sunset, I scaled a forest giant and was able to make out the range that held Kolvir. A storm was playing about its peaks just then and its clouds hid their highest portions.

The following noon we ran into one of Julian's patrols. I do not really know who surprised whom, or who was more surprised. The firing broke out almost immediately. I shouted myself hoarse stopping it, as everyone seemed anxious to try out his weapon on a live target. It was a small group – a dozen and a half men – and we got all of them. We suffered only one minor casualty, from one of our men wounding another – or perhaps the man had wounded himself. I never got the story straight. We moved on quickly then, because we had made a hell of a racket and I had no idea as to the disposition of other forces in the vicinity.

We gained considerable distance and altitude by nightfall, and the mountains were in sight whenever there was a clear line of vision. The storm clouds still clung to their peaks. My troops were excited over the day's slaughter and took a long while getting to sleep that night.

The next day we reached the foothills, successfully avoiding two patrols. I pushed us on and up well after nightfall, to reach a place of cover I had had in mind. We bedded down at an altitude perhaps half a mile higher than we had the previous night. We were under the cloud cover, but there was no rainfall, despite a constant atmospheric tension of the sort that precedes a storm. I did not sleep well that night. I dreamed of the burning cat head, and of Lorraine.

In the morning, we moved out under gray skies, and I pushed the troops remorselessly, heading steadily upward. We heard the sounds of distant thunder, and the air was alive and electric.

About mid-morning, as I led our file up a twisted, rocky route, I heard a shout from behind me, followed by several bursts of gunfire. I headed back immediately.

A small knot of men, Ganelon among them, stood staring down at something, talking in low voices. I pushed my way through.

I could not believe it. Never in my memory had one been seen this near to Amber. Perhaps twelve feet in length, bearing that terrible parody of a human face on the shoulders of a lion, eagle-like wings folded above its now bloody sides, a still-twitching tail like that of a scorpion, I had glimpsed the manticora once in isles far to the south, a frightful beast that had always held a spot near the top of my unclean list.

'It tore Rall in half, it tore Rall in half,' one of the men kept repeating.

About twenty paces away, I saw what was left of Rall. We covered him over with a tarp and weighted it down with rocks. That was really about all that we could do. If nothing else, it served to restore a quality of wariness that had seemed to vanish after the previous day's easy victory. The men were silent and cautious as we continued on our way.

'Quite a thing, that,' Ganelon said. 'Has it the intelligence of a man?'

'I do not really know.'

'I've a funny, nervous feeling, Corwin. As though something terrible is about to happen. I don't know how else to put it.'

'I know.'

'You feel it, too?'

'Yes.'

He nodded.

'Maybe it's the weather,' I said.

He nodded again, more slowly.

The sky continued to darken as we climbed, and the thunder never ceased. Flashes of heat lightning occurred in the west, and the winds grew stronger. Looking up, I could see great masses of clouds about the higher peaks. Black, bird-like shapes were constantly outlined against them.

We encountered another manticora later, but we dispatched it with no damage to ourselves. About an hour later, we were attacked by a flock of large, razor-beaked birds, the like of which I had never seen before. We succeeded in driving them off, but this, too, disturbed me.

We kept climbing, wondering when the storm was going to begin. The winds increased in velocity.

It grew quite dark, though I knew the sun had not yet set. The air took on a misty, hazy quality as we neared the cloud clusters. A feeling of dampness worked its way into everything. The rocks were more slippery. I was tempted to call a halt, but we were still a good distance from Kolvir and I did not want to strain the rations situation, which I had calculated quite carefully.

We achieved perhaps another four miles and several thousand feet in elevation before we were forced to stop. It was pitch black by men, the only illumination at all coming from the intermittent flashes of lightning. We camped in a large circle on a hard, bare slope, sentries all about the perimeter. The thunder came like long flourishes of martial music. The temperature plummeted. Even had I permitted fires, there was nothing burnable about. We settled down for a cold, clammy, dark time.

The manticoras attacked several hours later, sudden and silent. Seven men died and we killed sixteen of the beasts. I have no idea how many others fled. I cursed Eric as I bound my wounds and wondered from what shadow he had drawn the things.

During what passed for morning, we advanced perhaps five miles toward Kolvir before bearing off to the west. It was one of three possible routes we could follow, and I had always considered it the best for a possible attack. The birds came to plague us again, several times, with greater numbers and persistency. Shooting a few of them, though, was all it took to rout the entire flock.

Finally, we rounded the base of a huge escarpment, our way taking us outward and upward through thunder and mist, until we were afforded a sudden vista, sweeping down and out for dozens of miles across the Valley of Garnath that lay to our right.

I called a halt and moved forward to observe.

When last I had seen that once lovely valley, it had been a twisted wilderness. Now, things were even worse. The black road cut through it, running to the base of Kolvir itself, where it halted. A battle was raging within the valley. Mounted forces swirled together, engaged, wheeled away. Lines of foot soldiers advanced, met, fell back. The lightning kept flashing and striking among them. The dark birds swept about them like ashes on the wind.

The dampness lay like a cold blanket. The echoes of the thunder bounced about the peaks. I stared, puzzling, at the conflict below.

The distance was too great for me to determine the combatants. At first it occurred to me that someone else might be about the same thing I was – that perhaps Bleys had survived and returned with a new army.

But no. These were coming in from the west, along the black road. And I saw now that the birds accompanied them, and bounding forms that were neither horses nor men. The manticoras, perhaps.

The lightings fell upon them as they came, scattering, burning, blasting. As I realized that they never strode near the defenders, I recalled that Eric had apparently gained some measure of control over that device known as the Jewel of Judgment, with which Dad had exercised his will upon the weather about Amber. Eric had employed it against us with considerable effect five years earlier.

So the forces from Shadow about which I had been hearing reports, were even stronger than I had thought. I had envisioned harassment, but not a pitched battle at the foot of Kolvir. I looked down at the movements within the blackness. The road seemed almost to writhe from the activity about it.

Ganelon came and stood beside me. He was silent for a long while.

I did not want him to ask me, but I felt powerless to say it except as answer to a question.

'What now, Corwin?'

'We most increase the pace,' I said. 'I want to be in Amber tonight.'

We moved again. The going was better for a time, and that helped. The storm without rain continued, its lightnings and thunders increasing in brilliance and volume. We moved through a constant twilight.

When we came to a safe-seeming place later that afternoon – a place within five miles of the northern skirts of Amber – I halted us again, for rest and a final meal. We had to scream at one another in order to be heard, so I could not address the men. I simply passed the word along concerning our proximity and the need for readiness.

I took my rations with me and scouted on ahead while the others rested. About a mile farther along, I mounted a steep upturn, pausing when I achieved its crest. There was a battle of some sort in progress on the slopes ahead.

I kept out of sight and observed. A force out of Amber was engaged with a larger body of attackers which must have either preceded us up the slope or arrived by different means. I suspected the latter, inasmuch as we had seen no signs of recent passage. The engagement explained our own good fortune in not encountering defensive patrols on the way up.

I moved nearer. While the attackers could have come up by one of the two other routes, I saw additional evidence that this need not have been the case. They swept in from the west like great gusts of wind-blown leaves. The aerial movement I had witnessed from the distance had been of greater variety than the belligerent bird life. The attackers came in on winged, two-legged, dragon-like creatures, the closest parallel with which I was familiar being a heraldic beast, the wyvern. I had never seen a non-decorative wyvern before, but then I had never felt any great desire to go looking for one.

Among the defenders were numerous archers, who took a deadly toll of those in flight. Sheets of pure hell erupted among them also, as the lightnings flashed and flared, sending them like cinders toward the ground. But still they came on, landing, so that both man and beast could attack those entrenched. I looked for and located the pulsating glow given off by the Jewel of Judgment when it has been tuned to operate. It came from the midst of the largest body of defenders, dug in near the base of a high cliff.

I stared and studied, focusing on the wearer of the gem. Yes, there could be no doubt. It was Eric.

On my belly now, I crawled even farther. I saw the leader of the nearest party of defenders behead a landing wyvern with a single sword stroke. With his left hand, he seized the harness of its rider and hurled him over thirty feet, out beyond the lip-like brink of the place. As he turned then to shout an order, I saw that it was Gérard. He appeared to be leading a flanking assault on a mass of the attackers who were assailing the forces at the foot of the cliff. On its far side, a similar body of troops was doing likewise. Another of my brothers?

I wondered how long the battle had been in progress, both in the valley and here above. Quite a while, I guess, considering the duration of the unnatural storm.

I moved to the right, turning my attention to the west. The battle in the valley continued unabated. From this distance, it was impossible to tell who was who, let alone who was winning. I could see, though, that no new forces were arriving from out of the west to supplement the attackers.

I was perplexed as to my own best course of action. Clearly, I could not attack Eric when he was engaged in anything this crucial to the defense of Amber herself. Waiting to pick up the pieces afterward might be wisest. However, I could already feel the rat teeth of doubt at work on that idea.

Even without reinforcements for the attackers, the outcome of the encounter was by no means clear-cut. The invaders were strong, numerous. I had no idea as to what Eric might have in reserve. At that moment, it was impossible for me to gauge whether war bonds for Amber would be a good investment. If Eric lost, it would then be necessary for me to take on the invaders myself, after much of Amber's manpower had been wasted.

If I were to move in now with automatic weapons, there was little doubt in my mind that we would crush the wyvern-riders quickly. For that matter, one or more of my brothers had to be down in the valley. A gateway for some of my troops could be set up by means of the Trumps. It would surprise whatever was down there for Amber suddenly to come up with riflemen.

I returned my attention to the conflict nearer at hand. No, it was not going well. I speculated as to the results of my intervening. Eric would certainly be in no position to turn on me. Besides any sympathy that might be mine for what he had put me through, I would be responsible for pulling his nuts out of the fire. While he would be grateful for the relief, he would not be too happy over the general sentiment this would arouse. No, indeed. I would be back in Amber with a very deadly personal bodyguard and a lot of good will going for me. An intriguing thought. It would provide a far smoother route to my objective than the brutal frontal assault culminating in regicide that I had had in mind.

Yes.

I felt myself smiling. I was about to become a hero.

I must grant myself a small measure of grace, however. Given the choice only between Amber with Eric on the throne and Amber fallen, there is no question but that my decision would have been the same, to attack. Things were not going well enough to be certain, and while it would work to my advantage to save the day, my own advantage was not, ultimately, essential. I could not hate thee, Eric, so much, loved I not Amber more.

I withdrew and hurried back down the slope, flashes of lightning hurling my shadow in every which direction.

I halted at the periphery of my encampment. At its farther edge, Ganelon stood in shouting converse with a lone horseman, and I recognized the horse.

I advanced, and at a sign from its rider the horse moved forward, winding its way among the troops, heading in my direction. Ganelon shook his head and followed.

The rider was Dara. As soon as she was within earshot, I shouted at her.

'What the hell are you doing here?'

She dismounted, smiling, and stood before me.

'I wanted to come to Amber,' she said. 'So I did.'

'How did you get here?'

'I followed Grandpa,' she said. 'It is easier to follow someone through Shadow, I discovered, than to do it yourself.'

'Benedict is here?'

She nodded.

'Down below. He is directing the forces in the valley. Julian is there, too.'

Ganelon came up and stood near.

'She said that she followed us up here,' he shouted. 'She has been behind us for a couple days.'

'Is that true?' I asked.

She nodded again, still smiling.

'It was not hard to do.'

'But why did you do it?'

'To get into Amber, of course! I want to walk the Pattern! That is where you are going, isn't it?'

'Of course it is. But there happens to be a war in the way!'

'What are you going to do about it?'

'Win it, of course!'

'Good. I'll wait.'

I cursed for a few moments to give myself time to think, then, 'Where were you when Benedict returned?' I asked.

The smile went away.

'I do not know,' she said. 'I went out riding after you left, and I stayed away the entire day. I wanted to be alone to think. When I returned in the evening, he was not there. I rode again the following day. I traveled quite a distance, and when it grew dark I decided to camp out I do that often. The next afternoon, as I was returning home, I came to the top of a hill and saw him passing below, heading to the east. I decided to follow him. The way led through Shadow, I understand that now – and you were right about it being easier to follow. I do not know how long it took. Time got all mixed up. He came here, and I recognized it from the picture on one of the cards. He met with Julian in a wood to the north, and they returned together to that battle below.' She gestured toward the valley. 'I remained in the forest for several days, not knowing what to do. I was afraid of getting lost if I tried to backtrack. Then I saw your force climbing the mountains. I saw you and I saw Ganelon at their head. I knew that Amber lay that way, and I followed. I waited until now to approach, because I wanted you to be too near to Amber to send me back when I did.'

'I don't believe you are telling me the whole truth,' I said, 'but I haven't the time to care. We are going ahead now, and there will be fighting. The safest thing for you will be to remain here. I will assign you a couple of bodyguards.'

'I do not want them!'

'I don't care what you want. You are going to have them. When the fighting is over I will send for you.'

I turned then and selected two men at random, ordering them to remain behind and guard her. They did not seem overjoyed at the prospect.

'What are those weapons your men bear?' Dara asked.

'Later,' I said. 'I'm busy.'

I relayed a sketchy briefing and ordered my squads.

'You seem to have a very small number of men,' she said.

'They are sufficient,' I replied. 'I will see you later.'

I left her there with her guards.

We moved back along the route I had taken. The thunder ceased as we advanced, and the silence became less a thing of relief than of suspense to me. The twilight resettled about us, and I perspired within the damp blanket of the air.

I called a halt before we reached the first point from which I had observed the action. I returned to it then, accompanied by Ganelon.

The wyvern-riders were all over the place and their beasts fought along with them. They were pressing the defenders back against the cliff face. I sought for but could not locate Eric or the glow of his jewel.

'Which ones are the enemy?' Ganelon asked me.

'The beast-riders.'

They were all of them landing now that heaven's artillery had let up. As soon as they struck the solid surface, they charged forward. I searched among the defenders, but Gérard was no longer in sight.

'Bring up the troops,' I said, raising my rifle. 'Tell them to get the beasts and the riders both.'

Ganelon withdrew, and I took aim at a descending wyvern, fired, and watched its swoop turn into a sudden flurry of pinions. It struck against the slope and began to flop about. I fired again.

The beast began to burn as it died. Soon I had three bonfires going. I crawled up to my second previous position. Secure, I took aim and fired once more.

I got another, but by then some of them were turning in my direction. I fired the rest of my ammo and hastened to reload. Several of them had begun moving toward me by then. They were quite fast.

I managed to stop them and was reloading again when the first rifle squad arrived. We put down a heavier fire, and began to advance as the others came up.

It was all over within ten minutes. Within the first five they had apparently realized that they hadn't a chance, and they began to flee back toward the ledge, launching themselves into space, becoming airborne again. We shot them down as they ran, and burning flesh and smoldering bones lay everywhere about us.

The moist rock rose sheer to our left, its summit lost in the clouds, so that it seemed as if it might tower endlessly above us. The winds still whipped the smoke and the mist, and the rocks were smeared and splotched with blood. As we had advanced, firing, the forces of Amber quickly realized that we represented assistance and began to push forward from their position at the base of the cliff. I saw that they were being led by my brother Caine. For a moment our eyes locked together across the distance, then he plunged ahead into the fray.

Scattered groups of Amberites united into a second force as the attackers fell back. Actually, they limited our field of fire when they attacked the far flank of the wizened beast-men and their wyverns, but I had no way of getting word of this to them. We drew closer, and our firing was accurate.

A small knot of men remained at the base of the cliff. I had a feeling they were guarding Eric, and that he had possibly been wounded, since the storm effects had ceased abruptly. I worked my own way off in that direction.

The firing was already beginning to die down as I drew near the group, and I was hardly aware of what happened next until it was too late.

Something big came rushing up from behind and was by me in an instant. I hit the ground and rolled, bringing my rifle to bear automatically. My finger did not tighten on the trigger, however. It was Dara, who had just plunged past me on horseback. She turned and laughed as I screamed at her.

'Get back down there! Damn you! You'll be killed!'

'I'll see you in Amber!' she cried, and she shot on across the grisly rock and made it up the trail that lay beyond.

I was furious. But there was nothing I could do about it just then. Snarling, I got back to my feet and continued on.

As I advanced upon the group, I heard my name spoken several times. Heads turned in my direction. People moved aside to let me pass. I recognized many of them, but I paid them no heed.

I think that I saw Gérard at about the same time that he saw me. He had been kneeling in their midst, and he rose to his feet and waited. His face was expressionless.

As I drew nearer, I saw that it was as I had suspected. He had been kneeling to tend an injured man who rested upon the ground. It was Eric.

I nodded to Gérard as I came up beside him, and I looked down at Eric. My feelings were quite mixed. The blood from his several chest wounds was very bright and there was a lot of it. The Jewel of Judgment, which still hung on a chain about his neck, was covered with it. Eerily, it continued its faint, glowing pulsation, heart-like beneath the gore. Eric's eyes were closed, his head resting upon a rolled-up cloak. His breathing was labored.

I knelt, unable to take my eyes off that ashen face. I tried to push my hate aside just a little, since he was obviously dying, so that I might have a better chance to understand this man who was my brother for the moments that remained to him. I found that I could muster up something of sympathy by considering all that he was losing along with his life and wondering whether it would have been me lying there if I had come out on top five years earlier. I tried to think of something in his favor, and all I could come up with were the epitaph-like words, *He died fighting for Amber.* That was something, though. The phrase kept running through my mind.

His eyes tightened, flickered, opened. His face remained without expression as his eyes focused on mine. I wondered whether he even recognized me.

But he said my name, and then, 'I knew that it would be you.' He paused for a couple of breaths and went on, 'They saved you some trouble, didn't they?'

I did not reply. He already knew the answer.

'Your turn will come one day,' he continued. 'Then we will be peers.' He chuckled and realized too late that he should not have. He went into an unpleasant spasm of moist coughing. When it passed he glared at me.

'I could feel your curse,' he said. 'All around me. The whole time. You didn't even have to die to make it stick.'

Then, as if reading my thoughts, he smiled faintly and said, 'No, I'm not going to give you my death curse. I've reserved that for the enemies of Amber – out there.' He gestured with his eyes. He pronounced it then, in a whisper, and I shuddered to overhear it.

He returned his gaze to my face and stared for a moment. Then he plucked at the chain about his neck.

'The Jewel . . .' he said. 'You take it with you to the center of the Pattern. Hold it up. Very close – to an eye. Stare into it – and consider it a place. Try to project yourself – inside. You don't go. But there is – experience . . . Afterward, you know how to use it . . .'

'How—?' I began, but stopped. He had already told me how to attune to it. Why ask him to waste his breath on how he had figured it out?

But he caught it and managed, 'Dworkin's notes . . . under fireplace . . . my—'

Then he was taken with another coughing spell and the blood came out of his nose and his mouth. He sucked in a deep breath and heaved himself into a sitting position, eyes rolling wildly.

'Acquit yourself as well as I have – bastard!' he said, then fell into my arms and heaved out his final, bloody breath.

I held him for several moments, then lowered him into his former position. His eyes were still open, and I reached out and closed them. Almost automatically, I put his hands together atop the now lifeless gem. I had no stomach to take it from him at that moment. I stood then, removed my cloak, and covered him with it.

Turning, I saw that all of them were staring at me. Familiar faces, many of than. Some strange ones mixed in. So many who had been there that night when I had come to dinner in chains . . .

No. It was not the time to think of that. I pushed it from my mind. The shooting had stopped, and Ganelon was calling the troops back and ordering some sort of formation.

I walked forward.

I passed among the Amberites. I passed among the dead. I walked by my own troops and moved to the edge of the cliff.

In the valley below me, the fighting continued, the cavalry flowing like turbulent waters, merging, eddying, receding, the infantry still swarming like insects.

I drew forth the cards I had taken from Benedict. I removed his own from the deck. It shimmered before me, and after a time there was contact.

He was mounted on the same red and black horse on which he had pursued me. He was in motion and there was fighting all about him. Seeing that he confronted another horseman, I remained still. He spoke but a single word.

'Bide,' he said.

He dispatched his opponent with two quick movements of his blade. Then he wheeled his mount and began to withdraw from the fray. I saw that his horse's reins had been lengthened and were looped and tied loosely about the remainder of his right arm. It took him over ten minutes to remove himself to a place of relative calm. When he had, he regarded me, and I could tell that he was also studying the prospect that lay at my back.

'Yes, I am on the heights,' I told him. 'We have won. Eric died in the battle.'

He continued to stare, waiting for me to go on. His face betrayed no emotion.

'We won because I brought riflemen,' I said. 'I finally found an explosive agent that functions here.'

His eyes narrowed and he nodded. I felt that he realized immediately what the stuff was and where it had come from.

'While there are many things I want to discuss with you,' I continued, 'I want to take care of the enemy first. If you will hold the contact, I will send you several hundred riflemen.'

He smiled.

'Hurry,' he said.

I shouted for Ganelon, and he answered me from only a few paces away. I told him to line the troops up, single file. He nodded and went off, shouting orders.

As we waited, I said, 'Benedict, Dara is here. She was able to follow you through Shadow when you rode in from Avalon. I want—'

He bared his teeth and shouted: 'Who the hell is this Dara you keep talking about? I never heard of her till you came along! Please tell me! I would really like to know!'

I smiled faintly.

'It's no good,' I said, shaking my head. 'I know all about her, though I have told no one else that you've a great granddaughter.'

His lips parted involuntarily and his eyes were suddenly wide.

'Corwin,' he said, 'you are either mad or deceived. I've no such descendant that I know of. As for anyone following me here through Shadow, I came in on Julian's Trump.'

Of course. My only excuse for not tripping her up immediately was my preoccupation with the conflict. Benedict would have been notified of the battle by means of the Trumps. Why should he waste time traveling when an instant means of transport was at hand?

'Damn!' I said. 'She is in Amber by now! Listen, Benedict! I am going to get Gérard or Caine over here to handle the transfer of the troops to you. Ganelon will come through, also. Give them their orders through him.'

I looked around, saw Gérard talking with several of the nobles. I shouted for him with a desperate urgency. His head turned quickly. Then he began running in my direction.

'Corwin! What is it?' Benedict was shouting.

'I don't know! But something is very wrong!'

I thrust the Tramp at Gérard as he came up.

'See that the troops get through to Benedict!' I said. 'Is Random in the palace?'

'Yes.'

'Free or confined?'

'Free – more or less. There will be some guards about. Eric still doesn't – didn't trust him.'

I turned.

'Ganelon,' I called out. 'Do what Gérard here tells you. He is going to send you to Benedict – down there.' I gestured. 'See that the men follow Benedict's orders. I have to get into Amber now.'

'All right,' he called back.

Gérard headed in his direction, and I fanned the Trumps once more. I located Random's and began to concentrate. At that moment, it finally began to rain.

I made contact almost immediately.

'Hello, Random,' I said, as soon as his image came to life. 'Remember me?'

'Where are you?' he asked.

'In the mountains,' I told him. 'We just won this part of the battle, and I am sending Benedict the help he needs to clean up in the valley. Now, though, I need your help. Bring me across.'

'I don't know, Corwin. Eric—'

'Eric is dead.'

'Then who is in charge?'

'Who do you think? Bring me across!'

He nodded quickly and extended his hand. I reached out and clasped it. I stepped forward. I stood beside him on a balcony overlooking one of the courtyards. The railing was of white marble, and not much was blooming down below. We were two stories up.

I swayed and he seized my arm.

'You're hurt!' he said.

I shook my head, only just then realizing how tired I was. I had not slept very much the past few nights. That, and everything else . . .

'No,' I said, glancing down at the gory mess that was my shirt front 'Just tired. The blood is Eric's.'

He ran a hand through his straw-colored hair and pursed his lips.

'So you *did* finally nail him . . .' he said softly.

I shook my head again.

'No. He was already dying when I got to him. Come with me now! Hurry! It is important!'

'Where to? What is the matter?'

'To the Pattern,' I said. 'Why? I am not certain, but I know that it is important. Come on!'

We entered the palace, moving toward the nearest stairwell. There were two guards at its head, but they came to attention as we approached and did not attempt to interfere with our passage.

'I'm glad it's true about your eyes,' Random said as we headed down. 'Do you see all right?'

'Yes. I hear that you are still married.'

'Yes. I am.'

When we reached the ground floor, we hurried to the right. There had been another pair of guards at the foot of the stair, but they did not move to stop us.

'Yes,' he repeated, as we headed toward the center of the palace. 'You are surprised, aren't you?'

'Yes. I thought you were going to get the year over with and be done with it.'

'So did I,' he said. 'But I fell in love with her. I really did.'

'Stranger things have happened.'

We crossed the marble dining hall and entered the long, narrow corridor that led far back through shadows and dust. I suppressed a shudder as I thought of my condition the last time I had come this way.

'She really cares for me,' he said. 'Like nobody else ever has before.'

'I'm glad for you,' I said.

We reached the door that opened onto the platform heading the long, spiral stairway down. It was open. We passed through and began the descent.

'I'm not,' he said, as we hurried around and around. 'I didn't want to fall in love. Not then. We've been prisoners the whole time, you know. How can she be proud of that?'

'That is over now,' I said. 'You became a prisoner because you followed me and tried to kill Eric, didn't you?'

'Yes. Then she joined me here.'

'I will not forget,' I said.

We rushed on. I was a great distance down, and there were only lanterns every forty feet or so. It was a huge, natural cavern. I wondered whether anyone knew how many tunnels and corridors it contained. I suddenly felt myself overwhelmed with pity for any poor wretches rotting in its dungeons, for whatever reasons. I resolved to release them all or find something better to do with them.

Long minutes passed. I could see the flickering of the torches and the lanterns below.

'There is a girl,' I said, 'and her name is Dara. She told me she was Benedict's great-granddaughter and gave me reason to believe it. I told her somewhat concerning Shadow, reality, and the Pattern. She does possess some power over Shadow, and she was anxious to walk the Pattern. When last I saw her, she was headed this way. Now Benedict swears she is not his. Suddenly I am fearful. I want to keep her from the Pattern. I want to question her.'

'Strange,' he said. 'Very. I agree with you. Do you think she might be there now?'

'If she is not, then I feel she will be along soon.'

We finally reached the floor, and I began to raise through the shadows toward the proper tunnel.

'Wait!' Random cried.

I halted and turned. It took me a moment to locate him, as he was back behind the stairs. I returned.

My question did not reach my lips. I saw that he knelt beside a large, bearded man.

'Dead,' he said. 'A very thin blade. Good thrust. Just recently.'

'Come on!'

We both ran to the tunnel and turned up it. Its seventh side passage was the one we wanted. I drew Grayswandir as we neared it, for that great, dark, metal-bound door was standing ajar.

I sprang through. Random was right behind me. The floor of that enormous room is black and looks to be smooth as glass, although it is not slippery. The Pattern burns upon it, within it, an intricate, shimmering maze of curved lines, perhaps a hundred and fifty yards long. We halted at its edge, staring.

Something was out there, walking it. I felt that old, tingling chill the thing always gives me as I watched. Was it Data? It was difficult for me to make out the figure within the fountains of sparks that spewed constantly about it. Whoever it was had to be of the blood royal, for it was common knowledge that anyone else would be destroyed by the Pattern, and this individual had already made it past the Grand Curve and was negotiating the complicated series of arcs that led toward the Final Veil.

The firefly form seemed to change shape as it moved. For a time, my senses kept rejecting the tiny subliminal glimpses that I knew must be coming through to me. I heard Random gasp beside me, and it seemed to breach my subconscious dam. A horde of impressions flooded my mind.

It seemed to tower hugely in that always unsubstantial-seeming chamber. Then shrink, die down, almost to nothing. It seemed a slim woman for a moment – possibly Dara, her hair lightened by the glow, streaming, crackling with static electricity. Then it was not hair, but great, curved horns from some wide, uncertain brow, whose crooklegged owner struggled to shuffle hoofs along the blazing way. Then something else . . . An enormous cat . . . A faceless woman . . . A bright-winged thing of indescribable beauty . . . A tower of ashes . . .

'Dara!' I cried out 'Is that you?'

My voice echoed back, and that was all. Whoever/whatever it was struggled now with the Final Veil. My muscles strained forward in unwilling sympathy with the effort.

Finally, it burst through.

Yes, it was Dara! Tall and magnificent now. Both beautiful and somehow horrible at the same time. The sight of her tore at the fabric of my mind. Her arms were upraised in exultation and an inhuman laughter flowed from her lips. I wanted to look away, yet I could not move. Had I truely held, caressed, made move to – that? I was mightily repelled and simultaneously attracted as I had never been before. I could not understand this overwhelming ambivalence.

Then she looked at me.

The laughter ceased. Her altered voice rang out.

'Lord Corwin, are you liege of Amber now?'

From somewhere, I managed a reply.

'For all practical purposes,' I said.

'Good! Then behold your nemesis!'

'Who are you? *What* are you?'

'You will never know,' she said. 'It is just exactly too late now.'

'I do not understand. What do you mean?'

'Amber,' she said, 'will be destroyed.'

And she vanished.

'What the hell,' said Random then, 'was that?'

I shook my head.

'I do not know. I really do not know. And I feel that it is the most important thing in the world that we find out.'

He gripped my arm.

'Corwin,' he said. 'She – it – meant it. And it may be possible, you know.'

I nodded.

'I know.'

'What are we going to do now?'

I resheathed Grayswandir and turned back toward the door.

'Pick up the pieces,' I said. 'I have what I thought I always wanted within my grasp now, and I must secure it. And I cannot wait for what is to come. I must seek it out and stop it before it ever reaches Amber.'

'Do you know where to seek it?' he asked.

We turned up the tunnel.

'I believe it lies at the other end of the black road,' I said.

We moved on through the cavern to the stairs where the dead man lay and went round and round above him in the dark.

SIGN OF THE UNICORN

For Jadawin and his Demiurge,
not to forget Kickaha.

1

I ignored the questions in the eyes of the groom as I lowered the grisly parcel and turned the horse in for care and maintenance. My cloak could not really conceal the nature of its contents as I slung the guts over my shoulder and stamped off toward the rear entrance to the palace. Hell would soon be demanding its paycheck.

I skirted the exercise area and made my way to the trail that led toward the southern end of the palace gardens. Fewer eyes along that route. I would still be spotted, but it would be a lot less awkward than going in the front way, where things are always busy. Damn.

And again, damn. Of troubles I considered myself amply possessed. But those who have do seem to get. Some spiritual form of compound interest, I suppose.

There were a few idlers beside the fountain at the far end of the garden. Also, a couple of guards were passing among the bushes near the trail. The guards saw me coming, held a brief discussion, and looked the other way. Prudent.

Me, back less than a week. Most things, still unresolved. The court of Amber, full of suspicion and unrest. This, now: a death to further jeopardize the brief, unhappy pre-reign of Corwin I: me.

Time now to do something I should have done right away. But there had been so many things to do, from the very first. It was not as if I had been nodding, as I saw it. I had assigned priorities and acted on them. Now, though . . .

I crossed the garden, out of the shade and into the slanting sunlight. I swung up the wide, curving stair. A guard snapped to attention as I entered the palace. I made for the rear stairway, then up to the second floor. Then the third.

From the right, my brother Random stepped out of his suite and into the hallway.

'Corwin!' he said, studying my face. 'What's the matter? I saw you from the balcony and—'

'Inside,' I said, gesturing with my eyes. 'We are going to have a private conference. Now.'

He hesitated, regarding my burden.

'Let's make it two rooms up,' he said. 'Okay? Vialle's in here.'

'All right.'

He led the way, opened the door. I entered the small sitting room, sought a likely spot, dropped the body.

Random stared at the bundle.

'What am I supposed to do?' he asked.

'Unwrap the goodies,' I said, 'and take a look.'

He knelt and undid the cloak. He folded it back.

'Dead all right,' he observed. 'What's the problem?'

'You did not look closely enough,' I said. 'Peel back an eyelid. Open the mouth and look at the teeth. Feel the spurs on the backs of the hands. Count the joints in the fingers. Then you tell me about the problem.'

He began doing these things. As soon as he looked at the hands he stopped and nodded.

'All right,' he said. 'I remember.'

'Remember out loud.'

'It was back at Flora's place . . .'

'That was where I first saw anyone like this,' I said. 'They were after you, though. I never did find out why.'

'That's right,' he said. 'I never got a chance to tell you about it. We weren't together all that long. Strange . . . Where did this one come from?'

I hesitated, torn between pushing him for his story and telling him mine. Mine won out because it was mine and very immediate.

I sighed and sank into a chair.

'We've just lost us another brother,' I said. 'Caine is dead. I got there a bit too late. That thing – person – did it. I wanted it alive, for obvious reasons. But it put up quite a fight. I didn't have much of a choice.'

He whistled softly, seated himself in the chair opposite me.

'I see,' he said very softly.

I studied his face. Was that the faintest of smiles waiting in the wings to enter and meet my own? Quite possibly.

'No,' I said flatly. 'If it were otherwise, I would have arranged for a lot less doubt as to my innocence. I'm telling you what really happened.'

'All right,' he said. 'Where is Caine?'

'Under a layer of sod, near the Grove of the Unicorn.'

'That looks suspicious right there,' he said. 'Or will. To the others.'

I nodded.

'I know. I had to hide the body and cover it in the meantime, though. I couldn't just bring him back and start parrying questions. Not when there were important facts waiting for me, in your head.'

'Okay,' he said. 'I don't know how important they are, but they're yours. But don't leave me hanging, huh? How did this thing happen?'

'It was right after lunch,' I said. 'I had eaten down at the harbor with Gérard. Afterward, Benedict brought me topside through his Trump. Back in my rooms, I found a note which apparently had been slipped in under the door. It requested a private meeting, later in the afternoon, at the Grove of the Unicorn. It was signed "Caine".'

'Have you still got the note?'

'Yes.' I dug it out of my pocket and passed it to him. 'Here.'

He studied it and shook his head.

'I don't know,' he said. 'It *could* be his writing – if he were in a hurry – but I don't think it is.'

I shrugged. I took the note back, folded it, put it away.

'Whatever, I tried to reach him with his Trump, to save myself the ride. But he wasn't receiving. I guessed it was to maintain secrecy as to his whereabouts, if it was all that important. So I got a horse and rode on down.'

'Did you tell anyone where you were going?'

'Not a soul. I did decide to give the horse a workout, though, so I rode along at a pretty good clip. I didn't see it happen, but I saw him lying there as I came into the wood. His throat had been cut, and there was a disturbance off in the bushes some distance away. I rode the guy down, jumped him, fought with him, had to kill him. We didn't engage in any conversation while this was going on.'

'You're sure you got the right guy?'

'As sure as you can be under such circumstances. His trail went back to Caine. He had fresh blood on his garments.'

'Might have been his own.'

'Look again. No wounds. I broke his neck. Of course I remembered where I had seen his like before, so I brought him right to you. Before you tell me about it, though, there was one more thing – just for a clincher.' I withdrew the second note, passed it over. 'The creature had this on its person. I presume it had removed it from Caine.'

Random read it, nodded, and handed it back.

'From you, to Caine, asking to be met there. Yes, I see. Needless to say . . .'

'Needless to say,' I finished. 'And it does look a bit like my writing – at first glance, anyway.'

'I wonder what would have happened if you had gotten there first?'

'Probably nothing,' I said. 'Alive and looking bad – that seems how they wanted me. The trick was to get us there in the proper order, and I didn't hurry quite enough to miss what was bound to follow.'

He nodded.

'Granting the tight scheduling,' he said, 'it had to be someone on the scene, here in the palace. Any ideas?'

I chuckled and reached for a cigarette. I lit it and chuckled again.

'I'm just back. You have been here all along,' I said. 'Which one hates me the most these days?'

'That is an embarrassing question, Corwin,' he stated. 'Everyone's down on you for something. Ordinarily, I would nominate Julian. Only it doesn't seem to hold up here.'

'Why not?'

'He and Caine got along very well. For years now. They had been looking out for each other, hanging around together. Pretty thick. Julian is cold and petty and just as nasty as you remember. But if he liked anybody, he liked Caine. I don't think he'd do it to him, not even to get at you. After all, he probably could have found plenty of other ways if that was all he wanted,'

I sighed.

'Who's next?'

'I don't know. I just don't know.'

'Okay. How do you read the reactions to this?'

'You're screwed, Corwin. Everyone is going to think you did it, no matter what you say.'

I nodded at the corpse. Random shook his head.

'That could easily be some poor clod you dug up out of Shadow to take the blame.'

'I know,' I said. 'Funny, coming back to Amber as I did, I arrived at an ideal time for positioning myself advantageously.'

'A perfect time,' Random agreed. 'You didn't even have to kill Eric to get what you wanted. That was a stroke of luck.'

'Yes. Still, it is no secret that that is what I came to do, and it is only a matter of time before my troops – foreign, specially armed, and quartered here – are going to start provoking some very bad feelings. Only the presence of an external threat has saved me from that so far. And then there are the things I am suspected of having done before my return – like murdering Benedict's retainers. Now this . . .'

'Yes,' Random said, 'I saw it coming as soon as you told me. When you and Bleys attacked years ago, Gérard deployed part of the fleet so that it was out of your way. Caine, on the other hand, engaged you with his vessels and scuttled you. Now that he is gone, I imagine you will put Gérard in command of the entire fleet.'

'Who else? He is the only man for the job.'

'Nevertheless . . .'

'Nevertheless. Admitted. If I were going to kill any one person to strengthen my position, Caine would be the logical choice. That's the real, damning truth.'

'How do you propose handling this?'

'Tell everyone what happened and try to discover who was behind it. Have you any better suggestions?'

'I've been trying to think how I could alibi you. But it does not look promising.'

I shook my head.

'You are too close to me. No matter how good we made it sound, it would probably have the opposite effect.'

'Have you considered admitting to it?'

'Yes. But self-defense is out. With a cut throat, it had to be a matter of surprise. And I have no stomach for starting off with the alternative: hoke up some evidence that he was up to something rotten and say I did it for the good of Amber. I flatly refuse to take on fake guilt under those terms. I'd wind up with a bad odor that way, too.'

'But with a real tough reputation.'

'It's the wrong kind of tough for the sort of show I want to run. No, that's out.'

'That covers everything, then – just about.'

'What do you mean "just about"?'

He studied his left thumbnail through slitted eyes.

'Well, it occurs to me that if there is anyone else you are anxious to get out of the picture, now is the time to consider that a frame can often be shifted.'

I thought about it and finished my cigarette.

'Not bad,' I said, 'but I can't spare any more brothers at the moment. Not even Julian. Anyhow, he's the least frameable.'

'It need not be family,' he said, 'Plenty of noble Amberites around with possible motives. Take Sir Reginald—'

'Forget it, Random! The reframing is out, too.'

'Okay. I've exhausted my little gray cells, then.'

'Not the ones in charge of memory, I hope.'

'All right.'

He sighed. He stretched. He got to his feet, stepped over the room's other occupant, and made his way to the window. Drawing back the drapes, he stared out for a time.

'All right,' he repeated. 'There's a lot to tell . . .'

Then he remembered out loud.

2

While sex heads a great number of lists, we all have other things we like to do in between. With me, Corwin, it's drumming, being up in the air, and gambling – in no special order. Well, maybe soaring has a little edge – in gliders, balloons, and certain variations – but mood has a lot to do with that too, you know. I mean, ask me another time and I might say one of the others. Depends on what you want most at the moment.

Anyway, I was here in Amber some years ago. Not doing much of anything. Just visiting and being a nuisance. Dad was still around, and when I noticed that he was getting into one of his grumpy moods, I decided it was time to take a walk. A long one. I had often noticed that his fondness for me tended to increase as an inverse function of my proximity. He gave me a fancy riding crop for a going-away present – to hasten the process of affection, I suppose. Still, it was a very nice crop – silver-chased, beautifully tooled – and I made good use of it. I had decided to go looking for an assemblage of all my simple pleasures in one small nook of Shadow.

It was a long ride – I will not bore you with the details – and it was pretty far from Amber, as such things go. This time, I was not looking for a place where I would be especially important. That can get either boring or difficult fairly quickly, depending on how responsible you want to be. I wanted to be an irresponsible nonentity and just enjoy myself.

Texorami was a wide open port city, with sultry days and long nights, lots of good music, gambling around the clock, duels every morning and in-between mayhem for those who couldn't wait. And the air currents were fabulous. I had a little red sail plane I used to go sky surfing in, every couple of days. It was the good life. I played drums till all hours in a basement spot up the river where the walls sweated almost as much as the customers and the smoke used to wash around the lights like streams of milk. When I was done playing I'd go find some action, women, or cards, usually. And that was it for the rest of the night. Damn Eric, anyway! That reminds me again . . . He once accused me of cheating at cards, did you know that? And that's about the only thing I wouldn't cheat at. I take my card playing seriously. I'm good and I'm also lucky. Eric was neither. The trouble with him was that he was good at so many things he wouldn't admit even to himself that there were some things other people could do better. If you kept beating him at anything you had to be cheating. He started a nasty argument over it one night – could have gotten serious – but Gérard and Caine broke it up. Give Caine that. He took my part that time. Poor guy . . . Hell of a way to go, you know? His throat . . . Well, anyhow, there I was in Texorami, making music and women, winning at cards and jockeying around the sky. Palm trees and night-blooming wallflowers. Lots of good port smells – spices, coffee, tar, salt – you know. Gentlefolk, merchants, and peons – the same straights as in most other places. Sailors and assorted travelers passing in and out. Guys like me living around the edges of things. I spent a little over two years in Texorami, happy. Really. Not much contact with the others. Sort of postcardlike hellos via the Trumps every now and then, and that was about it. Amber was pretty much off my mind. All this changed one night when I was sitting there with a full house and the guy across from me was trying to make up his mind whether or not I was bluffing.

The Jack of Diamonds began talking to me.

Yes, that is how it started. I was in a weird frame of mind anyway. I had just finished a couple hot sets and was still kind of high. Also, I was physically strung out from a long day's gliding and not much sleep the night before. I decided later it must be our mental quirk associated with the Trumps that made me see it that way when someone was trying to reach me and I had cards in my hand – any cards. Ordinarily, of course, we get the message empty-handed, unless we are doing the calling. It could have been that my subconscious – which was kind of footloose at the time – just seized on the available props out of habit. Later, though, I had cause to wonder. Really, I just don't know.

The Jack said, 'Random'. Then its face blurred and it said, 'Help me'. I began getting a feel of the personality by then, but it was weak.

The whole thing was very weak. Then the face rearranged itself and I saw that I was right. It was Brand. He looked like hell, and he seemed to be chained or tied to something. 'Help me,' he said again.

'I'm here,' I said. 'What's the matter?'

'. . . prisoner,' he said, and something else that I couldn't make out.

'Where?' I asked.

He shook his head at that.

'Can't bring you through,' he said. 'No Trumps, and I am too weak. You will have to come the long way around . . .'

I did not ask him how he was managing it without my Trump. Finding out where he was seemed of first importance. I asked him how I could locate him.

'Look very closely,' he said. 'Remember every feature. I may only be able to show you once. Come armed, too . . .'

Then I saw the landscape – over his shoulder, out a window, over a battlement. I can't be sure. It was far from Amber, somewhere where the shadows go mad. Farther than I like to go. Stark, with shifting colors. Fiery. Day without a sun in the sky. Rocks that glided like sailboats across the land. Brand there in some sort of tower – a small point of stability in that flowing scene. I remembered it, all right. And I remembered the presence coiled about the base of that tower. Brilliant. Prismatic. Some sort of watch-thing, it seemed – too bright for me to make out its outline, to guess its proper size. Then it all just went away. Instant off. And there I was, staring at the Jack of Diamonds again, with the guy across from me not knowing whether to be mad at my long distraction or concerned that I might be having some sort of sick spell.

I closed up shop with that hand and went home. I lay stretched out on my bed, smoking and thinking. Brand had still been in Amber when I had departed. Later, though, when I had asked after him, no one had any idea as to his whereabouts. He had been having one of his melancholy spells, had snapped out of it one day and ridden off. And that was that. No messages either – either way. He wasn't answering, he wasn't talking.

I tried to figure every angle. He was smart, damn smart. Possibly the best mind in the family. He was in trouble and he had called me. Eric and Gérard were more the heroic types and would probably have welcomed the adventure. Caine would have gone out of curiosity, I think. Julian, to look better than the rest of us and to score points with Dad. Or, easiest of all, Brand could have called Dad himself. Dad would have done something about it. But he had called me. Why?

It occurred to me then that maybe one or more of the others had been responsible for his circumstances. If, say, Dad was beginning to favor him . . . Well. You know. Eliminate the positive. And if he did call Dad, he would look like a weakling.

So I suppressed my impulse to yell for reinforcements. He had called me, and it was quite possible that I would be cutting his throat by letting anyone back in Amber in on the fact that he had gotten the message out. Okay. What was in it for me?

If it involved the succession and he had truly become fairhaired, I figured that I could do a lot worse than give him this to remember me by. And if it did not . . . There were all sorts of other possibilities. Perhaps he had stumbled onto something going on back home, something it would be useful to know about I was even curious as to the means he had employed for bypassing the Trumps. So it was curiosity, I'd say, that made me decide to go it alone and try to rescue him.

I dusted off my own Trumps and tried reaching him again. As you might expect, there was no response. I got a good night's sleep then and tried one more time in the morning. Again, nothing. Okay, no sense waiting any longer.

I cleaned up my blade, ate a big meal, and got into some rugged clothes. I also picked up a pair of dark, Polaroid goggles. Didn't know how they would work there, but that warden-thing had been awfully bright – and it never hurts to try anything extra you can think of. For that matter, I also took a gun. I had a feeling it would be worthless, and I was right. But like I said, you never know till you try.

The only person I said good-bye to was another drummer, because I stopped to give him my set before I left. I knew he'd take good care of them.

Then I went on down to the hangar, got the sail plane ready, went aloft, and caught a proper current. It seemed a neat way to do it.

I don't know whether you've ever glided through Shadow, but – No? Well, I headed out over the sea till the land was only a dim line to the north. Then I had the waters go cobalt beneath me, rear up and snake sparkly beards. The wind shifted. I turned. I raced the waves shoreward beneath a darkening sky. Texorami was gone when I returned to the rivermouth, replaced by miles of swamp. I rode the currents inward, crossing and recrossing the river at new twists and kinks it had acquired. Gone were the piers, the trails, the traffic. The trees were high.

Clouds massed in the west pink and pearl and yellow. The sun phased from orange through red to yellow. You shake your head? The sun was the price of the cities, you see. In a hurry, I depopulate – or, rather, go the elemental route. At that altitude artifacts would have been distracting. Shading and texture becomes everything for me. That's what I meant about gliding it being a bit different.

So, I bore to the west till the woods gave way to surface green, which quickly faded, dispersed, broke to brown, tan, yellow. Light and crumbly then, splotched. The price of that was a storm. I rode it out as much as I could, till the lightnings forked nearby and I feared that the gusts were getting to be too much for the little glider. I toned it down fast then, but got more green below as a result. Still, I pulled it out of the storm with a yellow sun firm and bright at my back. After a time, I got it to go desert beneath me again, stark and rolling.

Then the sun shrank and strands of cloud whipped past its face, erasing it bit by bit. That was the shortcut that took me farther from Amber than I had been in a long while.

No sun then, but the light remained, just as bright but eerie now, directionless. It tricked my eyes, it screwed up perspective. I dropped lower, limiting my range of vision. Soon large rocks came into view, and I fought for the shapes I remembered. Gradually, these occurred.

The buckling, flowing effect was easier to achieve under these conditions, but its production was physically disconcerting. It made it even more difficult to judge my effectiveness in guiding the glider. I got lower than I thought I was and almost collided with one of the rocks. Finally, though, the smokes rose and flames danced about as I remembered them – conforming to no particular pattern, just emerging here and there from crevasses, holes, cave mouths. Colors began to misbehave as I recalled from my brief view. Then came the actual motion of the rocks – drifting, sailing, like rudderless boats in a place where they wring out rainbows.

By then, the air currents had gone crazy. One updraft after another, like fountains. I fought them as best I could, but knew I could not hold things together much longer at that altitude. I rose a considerable distance, forgetting everything for a time while trying to stabilize the craft. When I looked down again, it was like viewing a free-form regatta of black icebergs. The rocks were racing around, clashing together, backing off, colliding again, spinning, arcing across the open spaces, passing among one another. Then I was slammed about, forced down, forced up – and I saw a strut give way. I gave the shadows their final nudge, then looked again. The tower had appeared in the distance, something brighter than ice or aluminum stationed at its base.

That final push had done it. I realized that just as I felt the winds start a particularly nasty piece of business. Then several cables snapped and I was on my way down – like riding a waterfall. I got the nose up, brought it in low and wild, saw where we were headed, and jumped at the last moment. The poor gilder was pulverized by one of those peripatetic monoliths. I felt worse about that than I did about the scrapes, rips, and lumps I collected.

Then I had to move quickly, because a hill was racing toward me. We both veered, fortunately in different directions. I hadn't the faintest notion as to their motive force, and at first I could see no pattern to their movements. The ground varied from warm to extremely hot underfoot, and along with the smoke and occasional jets of flame, nasty-smelling gases were escaping from numerous openings in the ground. I hurried toward the tower, following a necessarily irregular course.

It took a long while to cover the distance. Just how long, I was uncertain, as I had no way of keeping track of the time. By then, though, I was beginning to notice some interesting regularities. First, the larger stones moved at a greater velocity than the smaller ones. Second, they seemed to be orbiting one another – cycles within cycles within cycles, larger about smaller, none of them ever still. Perhaps the prime mover was a dust mote or a single molecule – somewhere. I had neither time nor desire to indulge in any attempt to determine the center of the affair. Keeping this in mind, I did manage to observe as I went, though, enough so that I was able to anticipate a number of their collisions well in advance.

So Childe Random to the dark tower came, yeah, gun in one hand, blade in the other. The goggles hung about my neck. With all the smoke and confused lighting, I wasn't about to don them until it became absolutely necessary.

Now, whatever the reason, the rocks avoided the tower. While it seemed to stand on a hill, I realized as I approached that it would be more correct to say that the rocks had scooped out an enormous basin just short of it I could not tell from my side, however, whether the effect was that of an island or a peninsula.

I dashed through the smoke and rubble, avoiding the jets of flame that leaped from the cracks and holes. Finally I scrambled up the slope, removing myself from the courseway. Then for several moments I clung at a spot just below any line of sight from the tower. I checked my weapons, controlled my breathing, and put on the goggles. Everything set, I went over the top and came up into a crouch.

Yes, the shades worked. And yes, the beast was waiting.

It was a fright all right, because in some ways it was kind of beautiful. It had a snake body as big around as a barrel, with a head sort of like a massive claw hammer, but kind of tapered to the snout end. Eyes of a very pale green. And it was clear as glass, with very faint, fine lines seeming to indicate scales. Whatever flowed in its veins was reasonably clear, also. You could look right into it and see its organs – opaque or cloudy as the case might be. You could almost be distracted by watching the thing function. And it had a dense mane, like bristles of glass, about the head and collaring its gullet. Its movement when it saw me, raised that head and slithered forward, was like flowing water – living water, it seemed, a bedless river without banks. What almost froze me, though, was that I could see into its stomach. There was a partly digested man in it.

I raised the gun, aimed at the nearest eye, and squeezed the trigger.

I already told you it didn't work. So I threw the gun, leaped to my left, and sprang in on its right side, going for its eye with my blade.

You know how hard it can be to kill things built along reptilian lines. I decided immediately to try to blind the thing and hack off its tongue as the first order of business. Then, being more than a little fast on my feet, I might have any number of chances to lay in some good ones about the head until I decapitated it. Then let it tie itself in knots till it stopped. I was hoping, too, that it might be sluggish because it was still digesting someone.

If it was sluggish then, I was glad that I hadn't stopped by earlier. It drew its head out of the path of my blade and snapped down over it while I was still off balance. That snout glanced across my chest, and it did feel as if I had been hit by a massive hammer. It knocked me sprawling.

I kept on rolling to get out of range, coming up short near the edge of the embankment. I recovered my footing there while it unwound itself, dragged a lot of weight in my direction, and then reared up and cocked its head again, about fifteen feet above me.

I know damn well that Gérard would have chosen that moment to attack. The big bastard would have strode forward with that monster blade of his and cut the thing in half. Then it probably would have fallen on him and writhed all over him, and he'd have come away with a few bruises. Maybe a bloody nose. Benedict would not have missed the eye. He would have had one in each pocket by then and be playing football with the head while composing a footnote to Clausewitz. But they are genuine hero types. Me, I just stood there holding the blade point upward, both hands on the hilt, my elbows on my hips, my head as far back out of the way as possible. I would much rather have run and called it a day. Only I knew that if I tried it, that head would drop down and smear me.

Cries from within the tower indicated that I had been spotted, but I was not about to look away to see what was going on. Then I began cursing the thing. I wanted it to strike and get it over with, one way or the other.

When it finally did, I shuffled my feet, twisted my body, and swung the point into line with my target.

My left side was partly numbed by the blow, and I felt as if I had been driven a foot into the ground. Somehow I managed to remain upright. Yes, I had done everything perfectly. The maneuver had gone exactly as I had hoped and planned.

Except for the beast's part. It wasn't co-operating by producing the appropriate death throes.

In fact, it was beginning to rise.

It took my blade with it, too. The hilt protruded from its left eye socket, the point emerged like another bristle amid the mane on the back of its head. I had a feeling that the offensive team had had it.

At that moment, figures began to emerge – slowly, cautiously – from an opening at the base of the tower. They were armed and ugly-looking, and I had a feeling that they were not on my side of the disagreement.

Okay. I know when it is time to fold and hope for a better hand another day.

'Brand!' I shouted. 'It's Random! I can't get through! Sorry!'

Then I turned, ran, and leaped back over the edge, down into the place where the rocks did their unsettling things. I wondered whether I had chosen the best time to descend.

Like so many things, the answer was yes and no.

It was not the sort of jump I would make for many reasons other than those which prevailed. I came down alive, but that seemed the most that could be said for it. I was stunned, and for a long while I thought I had broken my ankle.

The thing that got me moving again was a rustling sound from above and the rattle of gravel about me. When I readjusted the goggles and looked up, I saw that the beast had decided to come down and finish the job. It was winding its phantom way down the slope, the area about its head having darkened and opaqued since I had skewered it upstairs.

I sat up. I got to my knees. I tried my ankle, couldn't use it. Nothing around to serve as a crutch, either. Okay. I crawled then. Away. What else was there to do? Gain as much ground as I could and think hard while I was about it.

Salvation was a rock – one of the smaller, slower ones, only about the size of a moving van. When I saw it approaching, it occurred to me that here was transportation if I could make it aboard. Maybe some safety, too. The faster, really massive ones appeared to get the most abuse.

This in mind, I watched the big ones that accompanied my own, estimated their paths and velocities, tried to gauge the movement of the entire system, readied myself for the moment, the effort. I also listened to the approach of the beast, heard the cries of the troops from the edge of the bluff, wondered whether anyone up there was giving odds on me and what they might be if they were.

When the time came, I went. I got past the first big one without any trouble, but had to wait for the next one to go by. I took a chance in crossing the path of the final one. Had to, to make it in time.

I made it to the right spot at the right moment, caught on to the holds I had been eyeing, and was dragged maybe twenty feet before I could pull myself up off the ground. Then I hauled my way to its uncomfortable top, sprawled there, and looked back.

It had been close. Still was, for that matter, as the beast was pacing me, its one good eye following the spinning big ones.

From overhead I heard a disappointed wail. Then the guys started down the slope, shouting what I took to be encouragement to the creature. I commenced massaging my ankle. I tried to relax. The brute crossed over, passing behind the first big rock as it completed another orbit.

How far could I shift through Shadow before it reached me? I wondered. True, there was constant movement, a changing of textures . . .

The thing waited for the second rock, slithered by behind it, paced me again, drew nearer.

Shadow, Shadow, on the wing—

The men were almost to the base of the slope by then. The beast was waiting for its opening – the next time around – past the inner satellite. I knew that it was capable of rearing high enough to snatch me from my perch.

—Come alive and smear that thing!

As I spun and glided I caught hold of the stuff of Shadow, sank into the feel of it, worked with the textures, possible to probable to actual, felt it coming with the finest twist, gave it that necessary fillip at the appropriate moment . . .

It came in from the beast's blind side, of course. A big mother of a rock, careening along like a semi out of control . . .

It would have been more elegant to mash it between two of them. However, I hadn't the time for finesse. I simply ran it over and left it there, thrashing in the granite traffic.

Moments later, however, inexplicably, the mashed and mangled body rose suddenly above the ground and drifted skyward, twisting. It kept going, buffeted by the winds, dwindling, dwindling, gone.

My own rock bore me away, slowly, steadily. The entire pattern was drifting. The guys from the tower then went into a huddle and decided to pursue me. They moved away from the base of the slope, began to make their way across the plain. But this was no real problem, I felt. I would ride my stony mount through Shadow, leaving them worlds away. This was by far the easiest course of action open to me. They would doubtless have been more difficult to take by surprise than the beast. After all, this was their land; they were wary and unmaimed.

I removed the goggles and tested my ankle again. I stood for a moment. It was very sore, but it bore my weight. I reclined once more and turned my thoughts to what had occurred. I had lost my blade and I was now in less than top shape. Rather than go on with the venture under these conditions, I knew that I was doing the safest wisest thing by getting the hell out. I had gained enough knowledge of the lay-out and the conditions for my chances to be better next time around. All right . . .

The sky brightened above me, the colors and shadings lost something of their arbitrary, meandering habit. The flames began to subside about me. Good. Clouds started to find their ways across the sky. Excellent. Soon a localized glow began behind a cloudbank. Superb. When it went away, a sun would hang once again in the heavens.

I looked back and was surprised to see that I was still being pursued. However, it could easily be that I had not dealt properly with their analogues for this slice of Shadow. It is never good to assume that you have taken care of everything when you are in a hurry. So . . .

I shifted again. The rock gradually altered its course, shifted its shape, lost its satellites, moved in a straight line toward what was to become the west. Above me, the clouds dispersed and a pale sun shone down. We picked up speed. That should have taken care of everything right there. I had positively come into a different place.

But it had not. When I looked again, they were still coming. True, I had gained some distance on them. But the party trooped right along after me.

Well, all right. Things like that can sometimes happen.

There were of course two possibilities. My mind still being more than a little disturbed from all that had just occurred, I had not performed ideally and had drawn them along with me. Or, I had maintained a constant where I should have suppressed a variable – that is, shifted into a place and unconsciously required that the pursuit element be present. Different guys then, but still chasing me.

I rubbed my ankle some more. The sun brightened toward orange. A wind out of the north raised a screen of dust and sand and hung it at my back, removing the gang from my sight. I raced on into the west, where a line of mountains had now grown up. Time was in a distortion phase. My ankle felt a little better.

I rested a while. Mine was reasonably comfortable, as rocks go. No sense turning it into a hellride when everything seemed to be proceeding smoothly. I stretched out, hands behind my head, and watched the mountains draw nearer. I thought about Brand and the tower. That was the place all right. Everything was just as it had been in the glimpse he had given me. Except for the guards, of course. I decided that I would cut through the proper piece of Shadow, recruit a cohort of my own, then go back and give them hell. Yes, then everything would be fine . . .

After a time, I stretched, rolled over onto my stomach, and looked back. Damned if they weren't still following me! They had even gained some.

Naturally, I got angry. To hell with flight! They were asking for it, and it was time they got it.

I rose to my feet. My ankle was only half sore, a little numb. I raised my arms and looked for the shadows I wanted. I found them.

Slowly the rock swung out from its straight course into an arc, turning off to the right. The curve tightened. I swung through a parabola and headed back toward them, my velocity gradually increasing as I went. No time to raise a storm at my back, though I thought that would have been a nice touch if I could have managed it.

As I swept down upon them – there were maybe two dozen – they pudently began to scatter. A number of them didn't make it, though. I swung through another curve and returned as soon as I could.

I was shaken by the sight of several corpses rising into the air, dripping gore, two of them already high above me.

I was almost upon them on that second pass when I realized that a few of them had jumped aboard as I had gone through. The first one over the edge drew his blade and rushed me. I blocked his arm, took the weapon away from him, and threw him back down. I guess it was then that I became aware of those spurs on the backs of their hands. I had been slashed by his.

By that time I was the target of a number of curiously shaped missiles from below, two more guys were coming over the edge, and it looked as if several more might have made it aboard.

Well, even Benedict sometimes retreats. I had at least given the survivors something to remember.

I let go of the shadows, tore a barbed wheel from my side, another from my thigh, hacked off a guy's swordarm and kicked him in the stomach, dropped to my knees to avoid a wild swing from the next one, and caught him across the legs with my riposte. He went over, too.

There were five more on the way up and we were sailing westward once again, leaving perhaps a dozen live ones to regroup on the sand at my back, a sky full of oozing drifters above them.

I had the advantage with the next fellow because I caught him just partway over the edge. So much for him, and then there were four.

While I had been dealing with him, though, three more had arisen, simultaneously, at three different points.

I rushed the nearest and dispatched him, but the other two made it over and were upon me while I was about it. As I defended myself from, their attack, the final one came up and joined them.

They were not all that good, but it was getting crowded and there were a lot of points and sharp edges straying about me. I kept parrying and moving, trying to get them to block one another, get in each other's way. I was partly successful, and when I had the best lineup I thought I was going to get, I rushed them, taking a couple of cuts – I had to lay myself open a bit to do it – but splitting one skull for my pains. He went over the edge and took the second one with him in a tangle of limbs and gear.

Unfortunately, the inconsiderate lout had carried off my blade, snagged in some bony cleft or other he had chosen to interpose when I swung. It was obviously my day for losing blades, and I wondered if my horoscope would have mentioned it if I had thought to look before I'd set out.

Anyhow, I moved quickly to avoid the final guy's swing. In doing so, I slipped on some blood and went skidding toward the front of the rock. If I went down that way, it would plow right over me, leaving a very flat Random there, like an exotic rug, to puzzle and delight future wayfarers.

I clawed for handholds as I slid, and the guy took a couple of quick steps toward me, raising his blade to do unto me as I had his buddy.

I caught hold of his ankle, though, and it did the trick of braking me very nicely – and damned if someone shouldn't choose that moment to try to get hold of me via the Trumps.

'I'm busy!' I shouted. 'Call back later!' and my own motion was arrested as the guy toppled, clattered, and went sliding by.

I tried to reach him before he fell to rugdom, but I was not quite quick enough. I had wanted to save him for questioning. Still, my unegged beer was more than satisfactory. I headed back top and center to observe and muse.

The survivors were still following me, but I had a sufficient lead. I did not at the moment have to worry about another boarding party. Good enough. I was headed toward the mountains once again. The sun I had conjured was beginning to bake me. I was soaked with sweat and blood. My wounds were giving me trouble. I was thirsty. Soon, soon, I decided, it would have to rain. Take care of that before anything else.

So I began the preliminaries to a shift in that direction: clouds massing, building, darkening . . .

I drifted off somewhere along the line, had a disjointed dream of someone trying to reach me again but not making it. Sweet darkness.

I awakened to the rain, sudden and hard-driving. I could not tell whether the darkness in the sky was from storm, evening, or both. It was cooler, though, and I spread my cloak and just lay there with my mouth open. Periodically I wrung moisture from the cloak. My thirst was eventually slaked and I began feeling clean again. The rock had also become so slick-looking that I was afraid to move about on it. The mountains were much nearer, their peaks limned by frequent lightnings. Things were too dark in the opposite direction for me to tell whether my pursuers were still with me. It would have been pretty rough trekking for them to have kept up, but then it is seldom good policy to rely on assumptions when traveling through strange shadows. I was a bit irritated with myself for going to sleep, but since no harm had come of it I drew my soggy cloak about me and decided to forgive myself. I felt around for some cigarettes I had brought along and found that about half of them had survived. After the eighth try, I juggled shadows enough to get a light. Then I just sat there, smoking and being rained on. It was a good feeling and I didn't move to change anything else, not for hours.

When the storm finally let up and the sky came clear, it was a night full of strange constellations. Beautiful though, the way nights can be on the desert. Much later, I detected a gentle upward sloping and my rock started to slow. Something began happening in terms of whatever physical rules controlled the situation. I mean, the slope itself did not seem so pronounced that it would affect our velocity as radically as it had. I did not want to tamper with Shadow in a direction that would probably take me out of my way. I wanted to get back onto more familiar turf as soon as possible – find my way to a place where my gut anticipations of physical events had more of a chance of being correct.

So I let the rock grind to a halt, climbed down when it did, and continued on up the slope, hiking. As I went, I played the Shadow game we all learned as children. Pass some obstruction – a scrawny tree, a stand of stone – and have the sky be different from one side to the other. Gradually I restored familiar constellations. I knew that I would be climbing down a different mountain from the one I ascended. My wounds still throbbed dully, but my ankle had stopped bothering me except for a little stiffness. I was rested. I knew that I could go for a long while. Everything seemed to be all right again.

It was a long hike, up the gradually steepening way. But I hit a trail eventually, and that made things easier. I trudged steadily upward under the now familiar skies, determined to keep moving and make it across by morning. As I went, my garments altered to fit the shadow – denim trousers and jacket now, my wet cloak a dry serape. I heard an owl nearby, and from a great distance below and behind came what might have been the yipyip-howl of a coyote. These signs of a more familiar place made me feel somewhat secure, exorcised any vestiges of desperation that remained with my flight.

An hour or so later, I yielded to the temptation to play with Shadow just a bit. It was not all that improbable for a stray horse to be wandering in these hills, and of course I found him. After ten or so minutes of becoming friendly, I was mounted bareback and moving toward the top in a more congenial fashion. The wind sowed frost in our path. The moon came and sparked it to life.

To be brief, I rode all night, passing over the crest and commencing my downward passage well before dawn. As I descended, the mountain grew even more vast above me, which of course was the best time for this to occur. Things were green on this side of the range, and divided by neat highways, punctuated by occasional dwellings. Everything therefore was proceeding in accordance with my desire.

Early morning. I was into the foothills and my denim had turned to khaki and a bright shirt. I had a light sport jacket slung before me. At a great height, a jetliner poked holes in the air, moving from horizon to horizon. There were birdsongs about me, and the day was mild, sunny.

It was about then that I heard my name spoken and felt the touch of the Trump once more. I drew up short and responded.

'Yes?'

It was Julian.

'Random, where are you?' he asked.

'Pretty far from Amber,' I replied. 'Why?'

'Have any of the others been in touch with you?'

'Not recently,' I said. 'But someone did try to get hold of me yesterday. I was busy though, and couldn't talk.'

'That was me,' he said. 'We have a situation here that you had better know about.'

'Where are you?' I asked.

'In Amber. A number of things have happened recently.'

'Like what?'

'Dad has been gone now for an unusually long time. No one knows where.'

'He's done that before.'

'But not without leaving instructions and making delegations. He always provided them in the past.'

'True,' I said. 'But how long is "Long"?'

'Well over a year. You weren't aware of this at all?'

'I knew that he was gone. Gérard mentioned it some time back.'

'Then add more time to that.'

'I get the idea. How have you been operating?'

'That is the problem. We have simply been dealing with affairs as they arise. Gérard and Caine had been running the navy anyway, on Dad's orders. Without him, they have been making all their own decisions. I took charge of the patrols in Arden again. There is no central authority though, to arbitrate, to make policy decisions, to speak for all of Amber.'

'So we need a regent. We can cut cards for it, I suppose.'

'It is not that simple. We think Dad is dead.'

'Dead? Why? How?'

'We have tried to raise him on his Trump. We have been trying every day for over half a year now. Nothing. What do you think?'

I nodded.

'He may be dead,' I said. 'You'd think he would have come across with something. Still, the possibility of his being in some trouble – say, a prisoner somewhere – is not precluded.'

'A cell can't stop the Trumps. Nothing can. He would call for help the minute we made contact.'

'I can't argue with that,' I said. But I thought of Brand as I said it. 'Perhaps he is deliberately resisting contact, though.'

'What for?'

'I have no idea, but it is possible. You know bow secretive he is about some things.'

'No,' Julian said, 'it doesn't hold up. He would have given some operating instructions, somewhere along the line.'

'Well, whatever the reasons, whatever the situation, what do you propose doing now?'

'Someone has to occupy the throne,' he said.

I had seen it coming throughout the entire dialogue, of course – the opportunity it had long seemed would never come to pass.

'Who?' I asked.

'Eric seems the best choice,' he replied. 'Actually, he has been acting in that capacity for months now. It simply becomes a matter of formalizing it.'

'Not just as regent?'

'Not just as regent.'

'I see . . . Yes, I guess that things have been happening in my absence. What about Benedict as a choice?'

'He seems to be happy where he is, off somewhere in Shadow.'

'What does he think of the whole idea?'

'He is not entirely in favor of it. But we do not believe he will offer resistance. It would disrupt things too much.'

'I see,' I said again. 'And Bleys?'

'He and Eric had some rather heated discussions of the issue, but the troops do not take their orders from Bleys. He left Amber about three months ago. He could cause some trouble later. But then, we are forewarned.'

'Gérard? Caine?'

'They will go along with Eric. I was wondering about yourself.'

'What about the girls?'

He shrugged.

'They tend to take things lying down. No problem.'

'I don't suppose Corwin . . .'

'Nothing new. He's dead. We all know it. His monument has been gathering dust and ivy for centuries. If not, then he has intentionally divorced himself from Amber forever. Nothing there. Now I am wondering where you stand.'

I chuckled.

'I am hardly in a position to possess forceful opinions,' I said.

'We need to know now.'

I nodded.

'I have always been able to detect the quarter of the wind,' I said. 'I do not sail against it.'

He smiled and returned my nod.

'Very good,' he said.

'When is the coronation? I assume that I am invited.'

'Of course, of course. But the date has not yet been set. There are still a few minor matters to be dealt with. As soon as the affair is calendared, one of us will contact you again.'

'Thank you, Julian.'

'Good-bye for now, Random.'

And I sat there being troubled for a long while before I started on downward again. How long had Eric spent engineering it? I wondered. Much of the politicking back in Amber could have been done pretty quickly, but the setting up of the situation in the first place seemed the product of long-term thinking and planning. I was naturally suspicious as to his involvement in Brand's predicament. I also could not help but give some thought to the possibility of his having a hand in Dad's disappearance. That would have taken some doing and have required a really foolproof trap. But the more I thought of it, the less I was willing to put it past him. I even dredged up some old speculations as to his part in your own passing, Corwin. But, offhand, I could not think of a single thing to do about any of it. Go along with it, I figured, if that's where the power was. Stay in his good graces.

Still . . . One should always get more than one angle on a story. I tried to make up my mind as to who would give me a good one. While I was thinking along these lines, something caught my eye as I glanced back and up, appreciating anew the heights from which I had not quite descended.

There were a number of riders up near the top. They had apparently traversed the same trail I had taken. I could not get an exact nose count, but it seemed suspiciously close to a dozen – a fairly sizable group to be out riding at just that place and time. As I saw that they were proceeding on down the same way that I had come, I had a prickly feeling along the base of my neck. What if . . . ? What if they were the same guys? Because I felt that they were.

Individually, they were no match for me. Even a couple of them together had not made that great a showing. That was not it. The real chiller was that if that's who it was, then we were not alone in our ability to manipulate Shadow in a very sophisticated fashion. It meant that someone else was capable of a stunt that for all my life I had thought to be the sole property of our family. Add to this the fact that they were Brand's wardens, and their designs on the family – at least part of it – did not look all that clement. I perspired suddenly at the notion of enemies who could match our greatest power.

Of course, they were too far off for me to really know just then whether that was truly who it was. But you have to explore every contingency if you want to keep winning the survival game. Could Eric have found or trained or created some special beings to serve him in this particular capacity? Along with you and Eric, Brand had one of the firmest claims on the succession . . . not to take anything away from your case, damn it! Hell! You know what I mean. I have to talk about it to show you how I was thinking at the time. That's all. So, Brand had had the basis for a pretty good claim if he had been in a position to press it. You being out of the picture, he was Eric's chief rival when it came to adding a legal touch to things. Putting that together with his plight and the ability of those guys to traverse Shadow, Eric came to look a lot more sinister to me. I was more scared by that thought than I was by the riders themselves, though they did not exactly fill me with delight. I decided that I had better do several things quickly: talk to someone else in Amber, and have him take me through the Trump.

Okay. I decided quickly. Gérard seemed the safest choice. He is reasonably open, neutral. Honest about most things. And from what Julian had said, Gérard's role in the whole business seemed kind of passive. That is, he was not going to resist Eric's move actively. He would not want to cause a lot of trouble. Didn't mean he approved. He was probably just being safe and conservative old Gérard. That decided, I reached for my deck of Trumps and almost howled. They were gone.

I searched every pocket in every garment about me. I had taken them along when I'd left Texorami. I could have lost them at any point in the previous day's action. I had certainly been battered and thrown about a lot. And it had been a great day for losing things. I composed a complicated litany of curses and dug my heels into the horse's sides. I was going to have to move fast and think faster now. The first thing would be to get into a nice, crowded, civilized place where an assassin of the more primitive sort would be at a disadvantage.

As I hurried downhill, heading for one of the roads, I worked with the stuff of Shadow – quite subtly this time, using every bit of skill I could muster. There were just two things I desired at the moment: a final assault on my possible trackers and a fast path to a place of sanctuary.

The world shimmered and did a final jig, becoming the California I had been seeking. A rasping, growling noise reached my ears, for the final touch I had intended. Looking back, I saw a section of cliff face come loose, almost in slow motion, and slide directly toward the horsemen. A while later, I had dismounted and was walking in the direction of the road, my garments even fresher and of better quality. I was uncertain as to the time of year, and I wondered what the weather was like in New York.

Before very long, the bus that I had anticipated approached and I flagged it down. I located a window seat, smoked for a while, and watched the countryside. After a time, I dozed.

I did not wake until early afternoon, when we pulled into a terminal. I was ravenous by then, and decided I had better have something to eat before getting a cab to the airport. So I bought three cheeseburgers and a couple of malts with a few of my quondam Texorami greenbacks. Getting served and eating took me maybe twenty minutes. Leaving the snack bar, I saw that there were a number of taxis standing idle at the stand out front. Before I picked one up, though, I decided to make an important stop in the men's room.

At the very damnedest moment you can think of, six stalls flew open behind my back and their occupants rushed me. There was no mistaking the spurs on the backs of their hands, the oversized jaws, the smoldering eyes. Not only had they caught up with me, they were now clad in the same acceptable garb as anyone else in the neighborhood. Gone were any remaining doubts as to their power over Shadow.

Fortunately, one of them was faster than the others. Also, perhaps because of my size, they still might not have been fully aware of my strength. I seized that first one high up on the arm, avoiding those hand bayonets he sported, pulled him over in front of me, picked him up, and threw him at the others. Then I just turned and ran. I broke the door on the way out. I didn't even pause to zip up until I was in a taxi and had the driver burning rubber.

Enough. It was no longer simple sanctuary that I had in mind. I wanted to get hold of a set of Trumps and tell someone else in the family about those guys. If they were Eric's creatures, the others ought to be made aware of them. If they were not, then Eric ought to be told, too. If they could make their way through Shadow like that, perhaps others could, also. Whatever they represented might one day constitute a threat to Amber herself. Supposing – just supposing – that no one back home was involved? What if Dad and Brand were the victims of a totally unsuspected enemy? Then there was something big and menacing afoot, and I had stepped right into it. That would be an excellent reason for their hounding me this thoroughly. They would want me pretty badly. My mind ran wild. They might even be harrying me toward some sort of a trap. No need for the visible ones to be the only ones about.

I brought my emotions to heel. One by one, you must deal with those things that come to hand, I told myself. That is all. Divorce the feelings from the speculations, or at least provide for separate maintenance. This is sister Flora's shadow. She lives on the other edge of the continent in a place called Westchester. Get to a phone, get hold of information, and call her. Tell her it is urgent and ask for sanctuary. She can't refuse you that, even if she does hate your guts. Then jump a jet and get the hell over there. Speculate on the way if you want, but keep cool now.

So I telephoned from the airport and you answered it, Corwin. That was the variable that broke all the possible equations I had been juggling – you suddenly showing up at that time, that place, that point in events. I grabbed for it when you offered me protection, and not just because I wanted protection. I could probably have taken those six guys out by myself. But that was no longer it. *I thought they were yours*. I figured you had been lying low all along, waiting for the right moment to move in. Now, I thought, you were ready. This explains everything. You had taken out Brand and you were about to use your Shadow-walking zombies for purposes of going back and catching Eric with his pants down. I wanted to be on your side because I hated Eric and because I knew you were a careful planner and you usually get what you go after. I mentioned the pursuit by guys out of Shadow to see what you would say. The fact that you said nothing didn't really prove anything, though. Either you were being cagey, I figured, or you had no way of knowing where I had been. I also thought of the possibility of walking into a trap of your devising, but I was already in trouble and did not see that I was so important to the balance of power that you would want to dispose of me. Especially if I offered my support, which I was quite willing to do. So I flew on out. And damned if those six didn't board later and follow me. Is he giving me an escort? I wondered. Better not start making more assumptions. I shook them again when we landed, and headed for Flora's place. Then I acted as if none of my guesses had occurred, waiting to see what you would do. When you helped me dispose of the guys, I was really puzzled. Were you genuinely surprised, or was it a put-on, with you sacrificing a few of the troops to keep me ignorant of something?

All right, I decided, be ignorant, co-operate, see what he has in mind. I was a perfect setup for that act you pulled to cover the condition of your memory. When I did learn the truth, it was simply too late. We were headed for Rebma and none of this would have meant anything to you. Later, I didn't care to tell Eric anything after his coronation. I was his prisoner then and not exactly kindly disposed toward him. It even occurred to me that my information might be worth something one day – at least, my freedom again – if that threat ever materialized. As for Brand, I doubt anyone would have believed me; and even if someone did, I was the only one who knew how to reach that shadow. Could you see Eric buying that as a reason for releasing me? He would have laughed and told me to come up with a better story. And I never heard from Brand again. None of the others seem to have heard from him either. Odds are he's dead by now – I'd say. And that is the story I never got to tell you. You figure out what it all means.

3

I studied Random, remembering what a great card player he was. By looking at his face, I could no more tell whether he was lying, in whole or in part, than I could learn by scrutinizing the Jack of, say, Diamonds. Nice touch, that part, too. There was enough of that kind of business to his story to give it some feel of verisimilitude.

'To paraphrase Oedipus, Hamlet, Lear, and all those guys,' I said, 'I wish I had known this some time ago.'

'This was the first chance I really had to tell you,' he said.

'True,' I agreed. 'Unfortunately, it not only fails to clarify things, it complicates the puzzle even more. Which is no mean trick. Here we are with a black road running up to the foot of Kolvir. It passes through Shadow, and things have succeeded in traversing it to beset Amber. We do not know the exact nature of the forces behind it, but they are obviously malign and they seem to be growing is strength. I have been feeling guilty about it for some while now, because I see it as being tied in with my curse. Yes, I laid one on us. Curse or no curse, though, everything eventually resolves into some sort of tangibility that can be combatted. Which is exactly what we are going to do. But all week long I have been trying to figure out Dara's part in things. Who is she really? What is she? Why was she so anxious to try the Pattern? How is it that she managed to succeed? And that final threat of hers . . . "Amber will be destroyed," she said. It seems more than coincidental that this occurred at the same time as the attack over the black road. I do not see it as a separate thing, but as a part of the same cloth. And it all seems to be tied in with the fact that there is a traitor somewhere here in Amber – Caine's death, the notes . . . Someone here is either abetting an external enemy or is behind the whole thing himself. Now you link it all up with Brand's disappearance, by way of this guy.' I nudged the corpse with my foot. 'It makes it look as if Dad's death or absence is also a part of it. If that is the case, though, it makes for a major conspiracy – with detail after detail having been carefully worked out over a period of years.'

Random explored a cupboard in the corner, produced a bottle and a pair of goblets. He filled them and brought me one, then returned to his chair. We drank a silent toast to futility.

'Well,' he said, 'plotting is the number-one pastime around here, and everyone *has* had plenty of time, you know. We are both too young to remember brothers Osric and Finndo, who died for the good of Amber. But the impression I get from talking with Benedict—'

'Yes,' I said, '—that they had done more than wishful thinking about the throne, and it became necessary that they die bravely for Amber. I've heard that, too. Maybe so, maybe not. We'll never know for sure. Still . . . Yes, the point is well taken, though almost unnecessary. I do not doubt that it has been tried before. I do not put it past a number of us. Who, though? We will be operating under a severe handicap until we find out. Any move that we make externally will probably only be directed against a limb of the beast. Come up with an idea.'

'Corwin,' he said, 'to be frank about it, I could make a case for it being anyone here – even myself, prisoner status and all. In fact, something like that would be a great blind for it. I would have taken genuine delight in looking helpless while actually pulling the strings that made all the others dance. Any of us would, though. We all have our motives, our ambitions. And over the years we all have had time and opportunity to lay a lot of groundwork. No, that is the wrong way to go about it, looking for suspects. Everyone here falls into that category. Let us decide instead what it is that would distinguish such an individual, aside from motives, apart from opportunities. I would say, let's look at the methods involved.'

'All right. Then you start.'

'Some one of us knows more than the rest of us about the workings of Shadow – the ins and the outs, the whys and the hows. He also has allies, obtained from somewhere fairly far afield. This is the combination he has brought to bear upon Amber. Now, we have no way of looking at a person and telling whether he possesses such special knowledge and skills. But let us consider where he could have obtained them. It could be that he simply learned something off in

Shadow somewhere, on his own. Or he could have been studying all along, here, while Dworkin was still alive and willing to give lessons.'

I stared down into my glass. Dworkin could *still* be living. He had provided my means of escape from the dungeons of Amber – how long ago? I had told no one this, and was not about to. For one thing, Dworkin was quite mad – which was apparently why Dad had had him locked away. For another, he had demonstrated powers I did not understand, which convinced me he could be quite dangerous. Still, he had been kindly disposed toward me after a minimum of flattery and reminiscence. If he were still around, I suspected that with a bit of patience I might be able to handle him. So I had kept the whole business locked away in my mind as a possible secret weapon. I saw no reason for changing that decision at this point.

'Brand did hang around him a lot,' I acknowledged, finally seeing what he was getting at. 'He was interested in things of that sort.'

'Exactly,' Random replied. 'And he obviously knew more than the rest of us, to be able to send me that message without a Trump.'

'You think he made a deal with outsiders, opened the way for them, then discovered that they no longer needed him when they hung him out to dry?'

'Not necessarily. Though. I suppose that is possible, too. My thinking runs more like this – and I don't deny my prejudice in his favor: I think he had learned enough about the subject so that he was able to detect it when someone did something peculiar involving the Trumps, the Pattern, or that area of Shadow most adjacent to Amber. Then he slipped up. Perhaps he underestimated the culprit and confronted him directly, rather than going to Dad or Dworkin. What then? The guilty party subdued him and imprisoned him in that tower. Either he thought enough of him not to want to kill him if he did not have to, or he had some later use of him in mind.'

'You make that sound plausible, too,' I said, and I would have added, 'and it fits your story nicely' and watched his poker face again, except for one thing. Back when I was with Bleys, before our attack on Amber, I had had a momentary contact with Brand while fooling with the Trumps. He had indicated distress, imprisonment, and then the contact had been broken. Random's story did fit, to that extent. So, instead, I said, 'If he can point the finger, we have got to get him back and set him to pointing.'

'I was hoping you would say that,' Random replied. 'I hate to leave a bit of business like that unfinished.'

I went and fetched the bottle, refilled our glasses. I sipped, I lit another cigarette.

'Before we get into that, though,' I said, 'I have to decide on the best way of breaking the news about Caine. Where is Flora, anyway?'

'Down in town, I think. She was here this morning. I can find her for you, I'm pretty sure.'

'Do it, then. She is the only other one I know of who has seen one of these guys, back when they broke into her place in Westchester. We might as well have her handy for that much corroboration as to their nastiness. Besides, I have some other filings I want to ask her.'

He swallowed his drink and rose.

'All right I'll go do that now. Where should I bring her?'

'My quarters. If I'm not there, wait.'

He nodded.

I rose and accompanied him into the hall.

'Have you got the key to this room?' I asked.

'It's on a hook inside.'

'Better get it and lock up. We wouldn't want a premature un-veiling.'

He did that and gave me the key. I walked with him as far as the first landing and saw him on his way. Then I headed for my own quarters.

From my safe, I removed the Jewel of Judgment, a ruby pendant which had given Dad and Eric control over the weather in the vicinity of Amber. Before he died, Eric had told me the procedure to be followed in tuning it to my own use. I had not had time to do it, though, and did not really have the time now. But during my conversation with Random I had decided that I was going to have to take the time. I had located Dworkin's notes, beneath a stone near Eric's fireplace. He had given me that much information also, that last time. I would have liked to know where he had come across the notes in the first place, though, for they were incomplete. I fetched them from the rear of the safe and regarded them once again. They did agree with Eric's explanation as to how the attunement was to be managed.

But they also indicated that the stone had other uses, that the control of meteorological phenomena was almost an incidental, though spectacular, demonstration of a complex of principles which underlay the Pattern, the Trumps, and the physical integrity of Amber herself, apart from Shadow. Unfortunately, the details were lacking. Still, the more I searched my memory, the more something along these lines did seem indicated. Only rarely had Dad produced the stone; and though he had spoken of it as a weather changer, the weather had not always been especially altered on those occasions when he had sported it. And he had often taken it along with him on his little trips. So I was ready to believe that there was more to it than that. Eric had probably reasoned the same way, but he had not been able to hunt out its other uses either. He had simply taken advantage of its obvious powers when Bleys and I had attacked Amber; and he had used it the same way this past week when the creatures had made their assault from the black road. It had served him well on both occasions, even if it had not been sufficient to save his life. So I had better get hold of its power myself, I decided, now. Any extra edge was important. And it would be good to be seen wearing the thing, too, I judged. Especially now.

I put the notes back into the safe, the jewel in my pocket. I left then and headed downstairs. Again, as before, to walk those halls made me feel as if I had never been away. This was home, this was what I wanted. Now I was its defender. I did not even wear the crown, yet all its problems had become my own. It was ironic. I had come back to claim the crown, to wrest it from Eric, to hold the glory, to reign. Now, suddenly, things were falling apart. It had not taken long to realize that Eric had behaved incorrectly. If he had indeed done Dad in, he had no right to the crown. If he had not, then he had acted prematurely. Either way, the coronation had served only to fatten his already obese ego. Myself, I wanted it and I knew that I could take it. But it would be equally irresponsible to do so with my troops quartered in Amber, suspicion of Caine's murder about to descend upon me, first signs of a fantastic plot suddenly displayed before me, and the continuing possibility that Dad was still alive. On several occasions it seemed we had been in contact, briefly – and at one such time, years ago, that he had okayed my succession. But there was so much deceit and trickery afoot that I did not know what to believe. He had not abdicated. Also, I had had a head injury, and I was well aware of my own desires. The mind is a funny place. I do not even trust my own. Could it be that I had manufactured that whole business? A lot had happened since. The price of being an Amberite, I suppose, is that you cannot even trust yourself. I wondered what Freud would have said. While he had failed to pierce my amnesia, he had come up with some awfully good guesses as to what my father had been like, what our relationship had been, even though I had not realized it at the time. I wished that I could have one more session with him.

I made my way through the marble dining hall and into the dark, narrow corridor that lay behind. I nodded to the guard and walked on back to the door. Through it men, out onto the platform, across and down. The interminable spiral stairway that leads into the guts of Kolvir. Walking. Lights every now and then. Blackness beyond.

It seemed that a balance had shifted somewhere along the way, and that I was no longer acting but being acted upon, being forced to move, to respond. Being herded. And each move led to another. Where had it all begun? Maybe it had been going on for years and I was only just now becoming aware of it. Perhaps we were all victims, in a fashion and to a degree none of us had realized. Great victuals for morbid thought. Sigmund, where are you now? I had wanted to be king – still wanted to be king – more than anything else. Yet the more I learned and the more I thought about what I had learned, the more all of my movements actually seemed to amount to Amber Pawn to King Four. I realized then that this feeling had been present for some time, growing, and I did not like it at all. But nothing that has ever lived has gotten by without making some mistake, I consoled myself. If my feeling represented actuality, my personal Pavlov was getting closer to my fangs with each ringing of the bell. Soon now, soon, I felt that it had to be soon, I would have to see that he came very near. Then it would be mine to see that he neither went away nor ever came again.

Turning, turning, around and down, light here, light there, these my thoughts, like thread on a spool, winding or unwinding, hard to be sure. Below me the sound of metal against stone. A guard's scabbard, the guard rising. A ripple of light from a lantern raised.

'Lord Corwin . . .'

'Jamie.'

At bottom, I took a lantern from the shelf. Putting a light to it, I turned and headed toward the tunnel, pushing the darkness on ahead of me, a step at a time.

Eventually the tunnel, and so up it, counting side passages. It was the seventh that I wanted. Echoes and shadows. Must and dust.

Coming to it, then. Turning there. Not too much farther.

Finally, that great, dark, metal-bound door. I unlocked it and pushed hard. It creaked, resisted, finally moved inward.

I set down the lantern, just to the right, inside. I had no further need of it, as the Pattern itself gave off sufficient light for what I had to do.

For a moment I regarded the Pattern – a shining mass of curved hues that tricked the eye as it tried to trace them – imbedded there, huge, in the floor's slick blackness. It had given me power over Shadow, it had restored most of my memory. It would also destroy me in an instant if I were to essay it improperly. What gratitude the prospect did arouse in me was therefore not untinged with fear. It was a splendid and cryptic old family heirloom which belonged right where it was, in the cellar.

I moved off to the corner where the tracery began. There I composed my mind, relaxed my body, and set my left foot upon the Pattern. Without pausing, I strode forward then and felt the current begin. Blue sparks outlined my boots. Another step. There was an audible crackling this time and the beginning of resistance. I took the first curvelength, striving to hurry, wanting to reach the First Veil as quickly as possible. By the time I did, my hair was stirring and the sparks were brighter, longer.

The strain increased. Each step required more effort than the previous one. The crackling grew louder and the current intensified. My hair rose and I shook off sparks. I kept my eyes on the fiery line and did not stop pushing.

Suddenly the pressure abated. I staggered but kept moving. I was through the First Veil and into the feeling of accomplishment that that entailed. I recalled the last time that I had come this way, in Rebma, the city under the sea. The maneuver I had just completed was what had started the return of my memories. Yes. I pushed ahead and the sparks grew and the currents rose once again, setting my flesh to tingling.

The Second Veil . . . The angles . . . It always seemed to tax the strength to its limits, to produce the feeling that one's entire being was transformed into pure Will. It was a driving, relentless sensation. At the moment, the negotiation of the Pattern was the only thing in the world that meant anything to me. I had always been there, striving, never been away, always would be there, contending, my will against the maze of power. Time had vanished. Only the tension held.

The sparks were up to my waist. I entered the Grand Carve and fought my way along it. I was continually destroyed and reborn at every step of its length, baked by the fires of creation, chilled by the cold at entropy's end.

Out and onward, turning. Three more curves, a straight line, a number of arcs. Dizziness, a sensation of fading and intensifying as though I were oscillating into and out of existence. Turn after turn after turn after turn . . . A short, sharp arc . . . The line that led to the Final Veil . . . I imagine I was gasping and drenched with sweat by then. I never seem to remember for sure. I could hardly move my feet. The sparks were up to my shoulders. They came into my eyes and I lost sight of the Pattern itself between bunks. In, out, in, out . . . There it was. I dragged my right foot forward, knowing how Benedict must have felt, his legs snared by the black grass. Right before I rabbit-punched him. I felt bludgeoned myself – all over. Left foot, forward . . . So slowly it was hard to be certain it was actually moving. My hands were blue flames, my legs pillars of fire. Another step. Another. Yet another.

I felt like a slowly animated statue, a thawing snowman, a buckling girder . . . Two more . . . Three . . . Glacial, my movements, but I who directed them had all of eternity and a perfect constancy of will that would be realized . . .

I passed through the Veil. A short arc followed. Three steps to cross it into blackness and peace. They were the worst of all.

A coffee break for Sisyphus! That was my first thought as I departed the Pattern. *I've done it again!* was my second. And, *Never again!* was my third.

I allowed myself the luxury of a few deep breaths and a little shaking. Then I unpocketed the jewel and raised it by its chain. I held it before my eye.

Red inside, of course – a deep cherry-red, smoke-shot, fulgent. It seemed to have picked up something extra of light and glitter during the trip through the Pattern. I continued to stare, thinking over the instructions, comparing them with things I already knew.

Once you have walked the Pattern and reached this point, you can cause it to transport you to any place that you can visualize. All that it takes is the desire and an act of will. Such being the case, I was not without a moment's trepidation. If the effect proceeded as it normally did, I could be throwing myself into a peculiar sort of trap. But Eric had succeeded. He had not been locked into the heart of a gem somewhere off in Shadow. The Dworkin who had written those notes had been a great man, and I had trusted him.

Composing my mind, I intensified my scrutiny of the stone's interior.

There was a distorted reflection of the Pattern within it, surrounded by winking points of light, tiny flares and flashes, different curves and paths. I made my decision, I focused my will . . .

Redness and slow motion. Like sulking into an ocean of high viscosity. Very slowly, at first. Drifting and darkening, all the pretty lights far, far ahead. Faintly, my apparent velocity increased. Flakes of light, distant, intermittent. A trifle faster then, it seemed. No scale. I was a point of consciousness of indeterminate dimensions. Aware of movement, aware of the configuration toward which I advanced, now almost rapidly. The redness was nearly gone, as was the consciousness of any medium. Resistance vanished. I was speeding. All of this, now, seemed to have taken but a single instant, was still taking that same instant. There was a peculiar, timeless quality to the entire affair. My velocity relative to what now seemed my target was enormous. The little, twisted maze was growing, was resolving into what appeared a three-dimensional variation of the Pattern itself. Punctuated by flares of colored light, it grew before me, still reminiscent of a bizarre galaxy half raveled in the middle of the ever-night, haloed with a pale shine of dust, its streamers composed of countless flickering points. And it grew or I shrank, or it advanced or I advanced, and we were near, near together, and it filled all of space now, top to bottom, this way to that, and my personal velocity still seemed, if anything, to be increasing. I was caught, overwhelmed by the blaze, and there was a stray streamer which I knew to be the beginning. I was too close – lost, actually – to apprehend its over-all configuration any longer, but the buckling, the flickering, the weaving of all that I could see of it, everywhere about me, made me wonder whether three dimensions were sufficient to account for the senses-warping complexities with which I was confronted. Rather than my galactic analogy, something in my mind shifted to the other extreme, suggesting the infinitely dimensioned Hilbert space of the subatomic. But then, it was a metaphor of desperation. Truly and simply, I did not understand anything about it. I had only a growing feeling – Pattern-conditioned? Instinctive? – that I had to pass through this maze also to gain the new degree of power that I sought.

Nor was I incorrect I was swept on into it without any slackening of my apparent velocity. I was spun and whirled along blazing ways, passing through substanceless clouds of glitter and shine. There were no areas of resistance, as in the Pattern itself, my initial impetus seeming sufficient to bear me throughout. A whirlwind tour of the Milky Way? A drowning man swept among canyons of coral? An insomniac sparrow passing over an amusement park of a July Fourth evening? These my thoughts as I recapitulated my recent passage in this transformed fashion.

. . . And out, through, over, and done, in a blaze of ruddy light that found me regarding myself holding the pendant beside the Pattern, then regarding the pendant, Pattern within it, within me, everything within me, me within it, the redness subsiding, down, gone. Then just me, the pendant, the Pattern, alone, subject-object relationships reestablished – only an octave higher, which I feel is about the best way there is to put it. For a certain empathy now existed. It was as though I had acquired an extra sense, and an additional means of expression. It was a peculiar sensation, satisfying.

Anxious to test it, I summoned my resolve once again and commanded the Pattern to transport me elsewhere.

I stood then in the round room, atop the highest tower in Amber. Crossing it, I passed outside, onto a very small balcony. The contrast was powerful, coining so close to the supersensory voyage I had just completed. For several long moments I simply stood there, looking.

The sea was a study in textures, as the sky was partly overcast and getting on toward evening. The clouds themselves showed patterns of soft brightness and rough shading. The wind made its way seaward, so that the salt smell was temporarily denied me. Dark birds dotted the air, swinging and hovering at a great distance out over the water. Below me, the palace yards and the terraces of the city lay spread in enduring elegance out to Kolvir's rim. People were tiny on the thoroughfares, their movements discountable. I felt very alone.

Then I touched the pendant and called for a storm.

4

Random and Flora were waiting in my quarters when I returned. Random's eyes went first to the pendant, then to my own. I nodded.

I turned toward Flora, bowing slightly.

'Sister,' I said, 'it has been a while, and then a while.'

She looked somewhat frightened, which was all to the good. She smiled and took my hand, though.

'Brother,' she said. 'I see that you have kept your word.'

Pale gold, her hair. She had cut it, but retained the bangs. I could not decide whether I liked it that way or not. She had very lovely hair. Blue eyes, too, and tons of vanity to keep everything in her favorite perspective. At times she seemed to behave quite stupidly, but then at other times I have wondered.

'Excuse me for staring,' I said, 'but the last time that we met I was unable to see you.'

'I am very happy that the situation has been corrected,' she said. 'It was quite – there was nothing that I could do, you know.'

'I know,' I said, recalling the occasional lilt of her laughter from the other side of the darkness on one of the anniversaries of the event. 'I know.'

I moved to the window and opened it, knowing that the rain would not be coming in. I like the smell of a storm.

'Random, did you learn anything of interest with regard to a possible postman?' I asked.

'Not really,' he said. 'I made some inquiries. No one seems to have seen anyone else in the right place at the right time.'

'I see,' I said. 'Thank you. I may see you again later.'

'All right,' he said. 'I'll be in my quarters all evening, then.'

I nodded, turned, leaned back against the sill, watched Flora. Random closed the door quietly as he left. I listened to the rain for half a minute or so.

'What are you going to do with me?' she said finally.

'Do?'

'You are in a position to call for a settlement on old debts. I assume that things are about to begin.'

'Perhaps,' I said. 'Most things depend on other things. This thing is no different.'

'What do you mean?'

'Give me what I want, and we'll see. I have even been known to be a nice guy on occasion.'

'What is it that you want?'

'The story, Flora. Let's start with that. Of how you came to be my shepherdess there on that shadow, Earth. All pertinent details. What was the arrangement? What was the understanding? Everything. That's all.'

She sighed.

'The beginning . . .' she said. 'Yes . . . It was in Paris, a party, at a certain Monsieur Focault's. This was about three years before the Terror—'

'Stop,' I said. 'What were you doing there?'

'I had been in that general area of Shadow for approximately five of their years,' she said. 'I had been wandering, looking for something novel, something that suited my fancy. I came upon that place at that time in the same way we find anything. I let my desires lead me and I followed my instincts.'

'A peculiar coincidence.'

'Not in light of all the time involved – and considering the amount of travel in which we indulge. It was, if you like, my Avalon, my Amber surrogate, my home away from home. Call it what you will, I was there, at that party, that October night, when you came in with the little redheaded girl – Jacqueline, I believe, was her name.'

That brought it back, from quite a distance, a memory I hadn't called for in a long, long while. I remembered Jacqueline far better than I did Focault's party, but there had been such an occasion.

'Go ahead.'

'As I said,' she went on, 'I was there. You arrived later. You caught my attention immediately, of course. Still, if one exists for a sufficiently long period of time and travels considerably, one does occasionally encounter a person greatly resembling someone else one has known. That was my first thought after the initial excitement faded. Surely it had to be a double. So much time had passed without a whisper. Yet we all have secrets and good reasons for having them. This could be one of yours. So I saw that we were introduced and then had a devil of a time getting you away from that little redheaded piece for more than a few minutes. And you insisted your name was Fenneval – Cordell Fenneval. I grew uncertain. I could not tell whether it was a double or you playing games. The third possibility did cross my mind, though – that you had dwelled in some adjacent area of Shadow for a sufficient time to cast shadows of yourself. I might have departed still wondering had not Jacqueline later boasted to me concerning your strength. Now this is not the commonest subject of conversation for a woman, and the way in which she said it led me to believe that she had actually been quite impressed by some things you had done. I drew her out a bit and realized that they were all of them feats of which you were capable. That eliminated the notion of it being a double. It had to be either you or your shadow. This in mind, even if Cordell was not Corwin he was a clue, a clue that you were or had been in that shady neighborhood – the first real clue I had come across concerning your whereabouts. I had to pursue it I began keeping track of you then, checking into your past. The more people I questioned, the more puzzling it became. In fact, after several months I was still unable to decide. There were enough smudgy areas to make it possible. Things were resolved for me the following summer, though, when I revisited Amber for a time. I mentioned the peculiar affair to Eric . . .'

'Yes?'

'Well . . . he was – somewhat – aware – of the possibility.'

She paused and rearranged her gloves on the seat beside her.

'Uh-huh,' I said. 'Just what did he tell you?'

'That it might be the real you,' she said. 'He told me there had been – an accident.'

'Really?'

'Well, no,' she admitted. 'Not an accident. He said there had been a fight and he had injured you. He thought you were going to die, and he did not want the blame. So he transported you off into Shadow and left you there, in that place. After a long while, he decided that you must be dead, that it was finally all over between you. My news naturally disturbed him. So he swore me to secrecy and sent me back to keep you under surveillance. I had a good excuse for being there, as I had already told everyone how much I liked the place.'

'You didn't promise to keep silent for nothing, Flora. What did he give you?'

'He gave me his word that should he ever come into power here in Amber, I would not be forgotten.'

'A little risky,' I said. 'After all, that would still leave you with something on him – knowledge of the whereabouts of a rival claimant, and of his part in putting him there.'

'True. But things sort of balanced out, and I would have to admit having become an accomplice in order to talk about it.'

I nodded.

'Tight, but not impossible,' I agreed. 'But did you think he would let me continue living if he ever did get a chance at the throne?'

'That was never discussed. Never.'

'It must have crossed your mind, though.'

'Yes, later,' she said, 'and I decided that he would probably do nothing. After all, it was beginning to seem likely that you had been deprived of your memory. There was no reason to do anything to you so long as you were harmless.'

'So you stayed on to watch me, to see that I remained harmless?'

'Yes.'

'What would you have done had I shown signs of recovering my memory?'

She looked at me, then looked away.

'I would have reported it to Eric.'

'And what would he have done then?'

'I don't know.'

I laughed a little, and she blushed. I could not remember the last time I had seen Flora blush.

'I will not belabor the obvious,' I said. 'All right, you stayed on, you watched me. What next? What happened?'

'Nothing special. You just went on leading your life and I went on keeping track of it.'

'All of the others knew where you were?'

'Yes. I'd made no secret of my whereabouts. In fact, all of them came around to visit me at one time or another.'

'That includes Random?'

She curled her lip.

'Yes, several times,' she said.

'Why the sneer?'

'It is too late to start pretending I like him,' she said. 'You know. I just don't like the people he associates with – assorted criminals, jazz musicians . . . I had to show him family courtesy when be was visiting my shadow, but he put a big strain on my nerves, bringing those people around at all hours – jam sessions, poker parties. The place usually reeked for weeks afterward and I was always glad to see him go. Sorry. I know you like him, but you wanted the truth.'

'He offended your delicate sensibilities. Okay. I now direct your attention to the brief time when I was your guest. Random joined us rather abruptly. Pursuing him were half a dozen nasty fellows whom we dispatched in your living room.'

'I recall the event quite vividly.'

'Do you recall the guys responsible – the creatures we had to deal with?'

'Yes.'

'Sufficiently well to recognize one if you ever saw another?'

'I think so.'

'Good. Had you ever seen one before?'

'No.'

'Since?'

'No.'

'Had you ever heard them described anywhere?'

'Not that I can remember. Why?'

I shook my head.

'Not yet. This is my inquisition, remember? Now I want you to think back for a time before that evening. Back to the event that put me in Greenwood. Maybe even a little earlier. What happened, and how did you find out about it? What were the circumstances? What was your part in things?'

'Yes,' she said, 'I knew you would ask me that sooner or later. What happened was that Eric contacted me the day after it occurred – from Amber, via my Trump.' She glanced at me again, obviously to see how I was taking it, to study my reactions. I remained expressionless. 'He told me you had been in a bad accident the previous evening, and that you were hospitalized. He told me to have you transferred to a private place, one where I could have more say as to the course of your treatment.'

'In other words, he wanted me to stay a vegetable.'

'He wanted them to keep you sedated.'

'Did he or did he not admit to being responsible for the accident?'

'He did not say that he had had someone shoot out your tire, but he did know that that was what had happened. How else could he have known? When I learned later that he was planning to take the throne, I assumed that he had finally decided it was best to remove you entirely. When the attempt failed, it seemed logical that he would do the next most effective thing: see that you were kept out of the way until after the coronation.'

'I was not aware that the tire had been shot out,' I said.

Her face changed. She recovered.

'You told me that you knew it was not an accident – that someone had tried to kill you. I assumed you were aware of the specifics.'

I was treading on slightly mucky ground again for the first time in a long while. I still had a bit of amnesia, and I had decided I probably always would. My memories of the few days prior to the accident were still spotty. The Pattern had restored the lost memories of my entire life up until then, but the trauma appeared to have destroyed recollection of some of the events immediately preceding it. Not an uncommon occurrence. Organic damage rather than simple functional distress, most likely. I was happy enough to have all the rest back, so those did not seem especially lamentable. As to the accident itself, and my feelings that it had been more than an accident, I did recall the gunshots. There had been two of them. I might even have glimpsed the figure with the rifle – fleetingly, too late. Or maybe that was pure fantasy. It seemed that I had, though. I had had something like that in mind when I had headed out for Westchester. Even at this late time, though, when I held the power in Amber, I was loath to admit this single deficiency. I had faked my way with Flora before with a lot less to go on. I decided to stick with a winning combination.

'I was in no position to get out and see what had been hit,' I said. 'I heard the shots. I lost control. I had assumed that it was a tire, but I never knew for sure. The only reason I raised the question was because I was curious as to how you knew it was a tire.'

'I already told you that Eric told me about it.'

'It was the way that you said it that bothered me. You made it sound as if you already knew all the details before he contacted you.'

She shook her head.

'Then pardon my syntax,' she said. 'That sometimes happens when you look at things after the fact. I am going to have to deny what you are implying. I had nothing to do with it and I had no prior knowledge that it had occurred.'

'Since Eric is no longer around to confirm or deny anything, we will simply have to let it go,' I said, 'for now,' and I said it to make her look even harder to her defense, to direct her attention away from any possible slip, either in word or expression, from which she might infer the small flaw which still existed in my memory. 'Did you later become aware of the indentity of the person with the gun?' I asked.

'Never,' she said. 'Most likely some hired thug. I don't know.'

'Have you any idea how long I was unconscious before someone found me, took me to a hospital?'

She shook her head again.

Something was bothering me and I could not quite put my finger on it.

'Did Eric say what time I had been taken into the hospital?'

'No.'

'When I was with you, why did you try walking back to Amber rather than using Eric's Trump?'

'I couldn't raise him.'

'You could have called someone else to bring you through,' I said. 'Flora, I think you are lying to me.'

It was really only a test, to observe her reaction. Why not?

'About what?' she asked. 'I couldn't raise anyone else. They were all otherwise occupied. Is that what you mean?'

She studied me.

I raised my arm and pointed at her and the lightning flashed at my back, just outside the window. I felt a tingle, a mild jolt. The thunderclap was also impressive.

'You sin by omission,' I tried.

She covered her face with her hands and began to weep.

'I don't know what you mean!' she said. 'I answered all your questions! What do you want? I don't know where you were going or who shot at you or what time it occurred! I just know the facts I've given you, damn it!'

She was either sincere or unbreakable by these means, I decided. Whichever, I was wasting my time and could get nothing more this way. Also, I had better switch us away from the accident before she began thinking too much about its importance to me. If there was something there that I was missing, I wanted to find it first.

'Come with me,' I said.

'Where are we going?'

'I have something I want you to identify. I will tell you why after you see it.'

She rose and followed me. I took her up the hall to see the body before I gave her the story on Caine. She regarded the corpse quite dispassionately. She nodded.

'Yes,' she said, and, 'Even if I did not know it I would be glad to say that I did, for you.'

I grunted a noncommittal. Family loyalty always touches me, somewhere. I could not tell whether she believed what I had said about Caine. But things sort of equal to equal things sort of being equal to each other, it didn't much seem to matter. I did not tell her anything about Brand and she did not seem to possess any new information concerning him. Her only other comment when everything I'd had to say was said, was, 'You wear the jewel well. What about the headpiece?'

'It is too soon to talk of such things,' I told her.

'Whatever my support may be worth . . .'

'I know,' I said. 'I know.'

My tomb is a quiet place. It stands alone in a rocky declivity, shielded on three sides against the elements, surrounded by transported soil wherein a pair of scrubby trees, miscellaneous shrubs, weeds, and great ropes of mountain ivy are rooted, about two miles down, in back of the crest of Kolvir. It is a long, low building with two benches in front, and the ivy has contrived to cover it to a great extent, mercifully masking most of a bombastic statement graven on its face beneath my name. It is, understandably, vacant most of the time.

That evening, however, Ganelon and I repaired thither, accompanied by a good supply of wine and some loaves and cold cuts.

'You weren't joking!' he said, having dismounted, crossed over, and parted the ivy, able to read by the moon's light the words that were rendered there.

'Of course not,' I said, climbing down and taking charge of the horses. 'It's mine all right.'

Tethering our mounts to a nearby shrub, I unslung our bags of provisions and carried them to the nearest bench. Ganelon joined me as I opened the first bottle and poured us a dark, deep pair.

'I still don't understand,' he said, accepting his.

'What's there to understand? I'm dead and buried there,' I said. 'It's my cenotaph, is what it is – the monument that gets set up when the body has not been recovered. I only just learned about mine recently. It was raised several centuries ago, when it was decided I wasn't coming back.'

'Kind of spooky,' he said, 'What's inside then?'

'Nothing. Though they did thoughtfully provide a niche and a casket, just in case my remains put in an appearance. You cover both bets that way.'

Ganelon made himself a sandwich.

'Whose idea was it?' he asked.

'Random thinks it was Brand's or Eric's. No one remembers for sure. They all seemed to feel it was a good idea at the time.'

He chuckled, an evil noise that perfectly suited his creased, scarred, and red-bearded self.

'What's to become of it now?'

I shrugged.

'I suppose some of them think it's a shame to waste it this way and would like to see me fill it. In the meantime, though, it's a good place to come and get drunk. I hadn't really paid my respects yet.'

I put together a pair of sandwiches and ate them both. This was the first real breather I had had since my return, and perhaps the last for some time to come. It was impossible to say. But I had not really had a chance to speak with Ganelon at any length during the past week, and he was one of the few persons I trusted. I wanted to tell him everything. I had to. I had to talk with someone who was not a part of it in the same way as the rest of us. So I did.

The moon moved a considerable distance and the shards of broken glass multiplied within my crypt.

'So how did the others take it?' he asked me.

'Predictably,' I answered. 'I could tell that Julian did not believe a word of it even though he said that he did. He knows how I feel about him, and he is in no position to challenge me. I don't think Benedict believes me either, but he is a lot harder to read. He is biding his time, and I hope giving me the benefit of the doubt while he is about it. As for Gérard, I have the feeling that this was the final weight, and whatever trust he had left for me has just collapsed. Still, he will be returning to Amber early tomorrow, to accompany me to the grove to recover Caine's body. No sense in turning it into a safari, but I did want another family member present. Deirdre now – she seemed happy about it. Didn't believe a word, I'm sure. But no matter. She has always been on my side, and she has never liked Caine. I'd say she is glad that I seem to be consolidating my position. I can't really tell whether Llewella believed me or not. She doesn't much give a damn what the rest of us do to one another, so far as I can see. As to Fiona, she simply seemed amused at the whole business. But then, she has always had this detached, superior way of regarding things. You can never be certain what represents her real thinking.'

'Did you tell them the business about Brand yet?'

'No. I told them about Caine and I told them I wanted them all to be in Amber by tomorrow evening. That is when the subject of Brand will be raised. I've an idea I want to try out.'

'You contacted all of them by means of the Trumps?'

'That's right.'

'There is something I have been meaning to ask you about that. Back on the shadow world we visited to obtain the weapons, there are telephones . . .'

'Yes?'

'I learned about wiretaps and such while we were there. Is it possible, do you think, that the Trumps could be bugged?'

I began to laugh, then caught myself as some of the implications of his suggestion sank in. Finally, 'I don't really know,' I said. 'So much concerning Dworkin's work remains a mystery – the thought just never occurred to me. I've never tried it myself. I wonder, though . . .'

'Do you know how many sets there are?'

'Well, everyone in the family has a pack or two and there were a dozen or so spares in the library. I don't really know whether there are any others.'

'It seems to me that a lot could be learned just by listening in.'

'Yes. Dad's deck, Brand's, my original pack, the one Random lost – Hell! There are quite a number unaccounted for these days. I don't know what to do about it. Start an inventory and try some experiments, I guess. Thanks for mentioning it.'

He nodded and we both sipped for a while in silence.

Then, 'What are you going to do, Corwin?' he asked.

'About what?'

'About everything. What do we attack now, and in what order?'

'My original intention was to begin tracing the black road toward its origin as soon as things were settled here in Amber,' I said. 'Now, though, I have shifted my priorities. I want Brand retained as soon as possible, if he is still living. If not, I want to find out what happened to him.'

'But will the enemy give you the breathing time? He might be preparing a new offensive right now.'

'Yes, of course. I have considered that. I feel we have some time, since they were defeated so recently. They will have to pull themselves together again, beef up their forces, reassess the situation in light of our new weapons. What I have in mind for the moment is to establish a series of lookout stations along the road to give us advance warning of any new movements on their part. Benedict has already agreed to take charge of the operation.'

'I wonder how much time we have.'

I poured him another drink, as it was the only answer I could think of.

'Things were never this complicated back in Avalon – *our* Avalon, I mean.'

'True,' I said. 'You are not the only one who misses those days. At least, they seem simpler now.'

He nodded. I offered him a cigarette, but he declined in favor of his pipe. In the flamelight, he studied the Jewel of Judgment which still hung about my neck.

'You say you can really control the weather with that thing?' he asked.

'Yes,' I said.

'How do you know?'

'I've tried it. It works.'

'What did you do?'

'That storm this afternoon. It was mine.'

'I wonder . . .'

'What?'

'I wonder what I would have done with that sort of power. What I would do with it.'

'The first thing that crossed my mind,' I said, slapping the wall of my tomb, 'was to destroy this place by lightning – strike it repeatedly and reduce it to rubble. Leave no doubt in anyone's mind as to my feelings, my power.'

'Why didn't you?'

'Got to thinking about it a bit more then. Decided – hell! They might really have a use for the place before too long, if I'm not smart enough or tough enough or lucky enough. Such being the case, I tried to decide where I would like them to dump my bones. It caught me then that this is really a pretty good spot – up high, clean, where the elements still walk naked. Nothing in sight but rock and sky. Stars, clouds, sun, moon, wind, rain . . . better company than a lot of other stiffs. Don't know why I should have to lie beside anyone I wouldn't want next to me now, and there aren't many.'

'You're getting morbid, Corwin. Or drunk. Or both. Bitter, too. You don't need that.'

'Who the hell are you to say what I need?'

I felt him stiffen beside me, then relax.

'I don't know,' he finally said. 'Just saying what I see.'

'How are the troops holding up?' I asked.

'I think they are still bewildered, Corwin. They came to fight a holy war on the slopes of heaven. They think that's what the shooting was all about last week. So they are happy on that count, seeing as we won. But now this waiting, in the city . . . They don't understand the place. Some of the ones they thought to be enemies are now friends. They are confused. They know they are being kept ready for combat, but they have no idea against whom, or when. As they have been restricted to the billets the whole time, they have not yet realized the extent to which their presence is resented by the regulars and the population at large. They will probably be catching on fairly soon, though. I had been waiting to raise the subject, but you've been so busy lately . . .'

I sat smoking for a time.

Then, 'I guess I had better have a talk with them,' I said. 'Won't have a chance tomorrow, though, and something should be done soon. I think they should be moved – to a bivouac area in the Forest of Arden. Tomorrow, yes. I'll locate it for you on the map when we get back. Tell them it is to keep them close to the black road. Tell them that another attack could come that way at any time – which is no less that the truth. Drill them, maintain their fighting edge. I'll come down as soon as I can and talk to them.'

'That will leave you without a personal force in Amber.'

'True. It may prove a useful risk, though, both as a demonstration of confidence and a gesture of consideration. Yes, I think it will turn out to be a good move. If not . . .' I shrugged.

I poured and tossed another empty into my tomb.

'By the way,' I said, 'I'm sorry.'

'What for?'

'I just noticed that I am morbid and drunk and bitter. I don't need that.'

He chuckled and clicked his glass against my own.

'I know,' he said. 'I know.'

So we sat there while the moon fell, till the last bottle was interred among its fellows. We talked for a time of days gone by. At length we fell silent and my eyes drifted to the stars above Amber. It was good that we had come to this place, but now the city was calling me back. Knowing my thoughts, Ganelon rose and stretched, headed for the horses. I relieved myself beside my tomb and followed him.

5

The Grove of the Unicorn lies in Arden to the southwest of Kolvir, near to that jutting place where the land begins its final descent into the valley called Garnath. While Garnath had been cursed, burned, invaded, and fought through in recent years, the adjacent highlands stood unmolested. The grove where Dad claimed to have seen the unicorn ages before and to have experienced the peculiar events which led to his adopting the beast as the patron of Amber and placing it on his coat of arms, was, as near as we could tell, a spot now but slightly screened from the long view across Garnath to the sea – twenty or thirty paces in from the upper edge of things: an asymmetrical glade where a small spring trickled from a mass of rock, formed a clear pool, brimmed into a tiny creek, made its way off toward Garnath and on down.

It was to this place that Gérard and I rode the following day, leaving at an hour that found us halfway down our trail from Kolvir before the sun skipped flakes of light across the ocean, then cast its whole bucketful against the sky. Gérard drew rein as it was doing this. He dismounted then and motioned to me to do the same. I did, leaving Star and the pack horse I was leading there beside his own huge piebald. I followed him off perhaps a dozen paces into a basin half-filled with gravel. He halted and I came up beside him.

'What is it?' I asked.

He turned and faced me and his eyes were narrow and his jaw clamped tight. He unfastened his cloak, folded it, and placed it on the ground. He unclasped his swordbelt and lay it atop the cloak.

'Get rid of your blade and your cloak,' he said. 'They will only get in the way.'

I had an inkling of what was coming, and I decided I had better go along with it. I folded my cloak, placed the Jewel of Judgment beside Grayswandir, and faced him once again. I said only one word.

'Why?'

'It has been a long time,' he said, 'and you might have forgotten.'

He came at me slowly, and I got my arms out in front of me and backed away. He did not swing at me. I used to be faster than he was. We were both crouched, and he was making slow, pawing movements with his left hand, his right hand nearer to his body, twitching slightly.

If I had had to choose a place to fight with Gérard, this would not have been it. He, of course, was aware of this. If I had to fight with Gérard at all, I would not have chosen to do so with my hands. I am better than Gérard with a blade or a quarterstaff. Anything that involved speed and strategy and gave me a chance to hit him occasionally while keeping him at bay would permit me to wear him down eventually and provide openings for heavier and heavier assaults. He, of course, was aware of this also. That is why he had trapped me as he had. I understood Gérard, though, and I had to play by his rules now.

I brushed his hand away a couple of times as he stepped up his movements, pressing nearer to me with every pace. Finally I took a chance, ducked and swung. I landed a fast, hard left just a little above his middle. It would have broken a stout board or ruptured the insides of a lesser mortal Unfortunately, time had not softened Gérard. I heard him grunt, but he blocked my right, got his right hand under my left arm, and caught my shoulder from behind.

I closed with him fast then, anticipating a shoulder lock I might not be able to break; and, turning, driving forward, catching his left shoulder in a similar fashion, I hooked my right leg behind his knee and was able to cast him backward to the ground.

He maintained his grip, though, and I came down atop him. I released my own hold and was able to drive my right elbow into his left side as we hit. The angle was not ideal and his left hand went up and across, reaching to grasp his right somewhere behind my head.

I was able to duck out of it, but he still had my arm. For a moment I had a clear shot at his groin with my right, but I restrained myself. It is not that I have any qualms about hitting a man below his belt. I knew that if I did it to Gérard just then his reflexes would probably cause him to break my shoulder. Instead, scraping my forearm on the gravel, I managed to twist my left arm up behind his head, while at the same time sliding my right arm between his legs and catching him about the left thigh. I rolled back as I did this, attempting to straighten my legs as soon as my feet were beneath me. I wanted to raise him off the ground and slam him down again, driving my shoulder into his middle for good measure.

But Gérard scissored his legs and rolled to the left, forcing me to somersault across his body. I let go my hold on his head and pulled my left arm free as I went over. I scrambled clockwise then, dragging my right arm away and going for a toehold.

But Gérard would have none of that. He had gotten his arms beneath him by then. With one great heave he tore himself free and twisted his way back to his feet. I straightened myself and leaped backward. He began moving toward me immediately, and I decided that he was going to maul the hell out of me if I just kept grappling with him. I had to take a few chances.

I watched his feet, and at what I judged to be the best moment I dove in beneath his extended arms just as he was shifting his weight forward onto his left foot and raising his right. I was able to catch hold of his right ankle and hoist it about four feet high behind him. He went over and down, forward and to his left.

He scrambled to get to his feet and I caught him on the jaw with a left that knocked him down again. He shook his head and blocked with his arms as he came up once more. I tried to kick him in the stomach, but missed as he pivoted, catching him on the hip. He maintained his balance and advanced again.

I threw jabs at his face and circled. I caught him twice more in the stomach and danced away. He smiled. He knew I was afraid to close with him. I snapped a kick at his stomach and connected. His arms dropped sufficiently for me to chop him alongside the neck, just above the collarbone. At that moment, however, his arms shot forward and locked about my waist. I slammed his jaw with the heel of my hand, but it did not stop him from tightening his grip and raising me above the ground. Too late to hit him again. Those massive arms were already crushing my kidneys. I sought his carotids with my thumbs, squeezed.

But he kept raising me, back, up over his head. My grip loosened, slipped away. Then he slammed me down on my back in the gravel, as peasant women do their laundry on rocks.

There were exploding points of light and the world was a jittering, half-real place as he dragged me to my feet again. I saw his fist—

The sunrise was lovely, but the angle was wrong . . . By about ninety degrees . . .

Suddenly I was assailed by vertigo. It canceled out the beginning awareness of a roadmap of pains that ran along my back and reached the big city somewhere in the vicinity of my chin.

I was hanging high in the air. By turning my head slightly I could see for a very great distance, down.

I felt a set of powerful clamps affixed to my body – shoulder and thigh. When I turned to look at them, I saw that they were hands. Twisting my neck even farther, I saw that they were Gérard's hands. He was holding me at full arm's length above his head. He stood at the very edge of the trail, and I could see Garnath and the terminus of the black road far below. If he let go, part of me might join the bird droppings that smeared the cliff face and the rest would come to resemble washed-up jellyfish I had known on beaches past.

'Yes. Look down, Corwin,' he said, feeling me stir, glancing up, meeting my eyes. 'All that I need to do is open my hands.'

'I hear you,' I said softly, trying to figure a way to drag him along with me if he decided to do it.

'I am not a clever man,' he said. 'But I had a thought – a terrible thought. This is the only way that I know to do something about it. My thought was that you had been away from Amber for an awfully long while. I have no way of knowing whether the story about your losing your memory is entirely true. You have come back and you have taken charge of things, but you do not yet truly rule here. I was troubled by the deaths of Benedict's servants, as I am troubled now by the death of Caine. But Eric has died recently also, and Benedict is maimed. It is not so easy to blame you for this part of things, but it has occurred to me that it might be possible – if it should be that you are secretly allied with our enemies of the black road.'

'I am not,' I said.

'It does not matter, for what I have to say,' he said. 'Just hear me out. Things will go the way that they will go. If, during your long absence, you arranged this state of affairs – possibly even removing

Dad and Brand as part of your design – then I see you as out to destroy all family resistence to your usurpation.'

'Would I have delivered myself to Eric to be blinded and imprisoned if this were the case?'

'Hear me out!' he repeated. 'You could easily have made mistakes that led to that. It does not matter now. You may be as innocent as you say or as guilty as possible. Look down, Corwin. That is all. Look down at the black road. Death is the limit of the distance you travel if that is your doing. I have shown you my strength once again, lest you have forgotten. I can kill you, Corwin. Do not even be certain that your blade will protect you, if I can get my hands on you but once. And I will, to keep my promise. My promise is only that if you are guilty I will kill you the moment I learn of it. Know also that my life is insured, Corwin, for it is linked now to your own.'

'What do you mean?'

'All of the others are with us at this moment, via my Trump, watching, listening. You cannot arrange my removal now without revealing your intentions to the entire family. That way, if I die forsworn, my promise can still be kept.'

'I get the point,' I said. 'And if someone else kills you? They remove me, also. That leaves Julian, Benedict, Random, and the girls to man the barricades. Better and better – for whoever it is. Whose idea was this, really?'

'Mine! Mine alone!' he said, and I felt his grip tighten, his arms bend and grow tense. 'You are just trying to confuse things! Like you always do!' he groaned. 'Things didn't go bad till you came back! Damn it, Corwin! I think it's your fault!'

Then he hurled me into the air.

'Not guilty, Gérard!' was all I had time to shout.

Then he caught me – a great, shoulder-wrenching grab – and snatched me back from the precipice. He swung me in and around and set me on my feet. He walked off immediately, heading back to the gravelly area where we had fought. I followed him and we collected our things.

As he was clasping his big belt he looked up at me and looked away again.

'We'll not talk about it any more,' he said.

'All right.'

I turned and walked back to the horses. We mounted and continued on down the trail.

The spring made its small music in the grove. Higher now, the sun strung fines of light through the trees. There was still some dew on the ground. The sod that I had cut for Caine's grave was moist with it.

I fetched the spade that I had packed and opened the grave. Without a word, Gérard helped me move the body onto a piece of sailcloth we had brought for that purpose. We folded it about him and closed it with big, loose stitches.

'Corwin! Look!' It was a whisper, and Gérard's hand closed on my elbow as he spoke.

I followed the direction of his gaze and froze. Neither of us moved as we regarded the apparition: a soft, shimmering white encompassed it, as if it were covered with down rather than fur and maning; its tiny, cloven hooves were golden, as was the delicate, whorled horn that rose from its narrow head. It stood atop one of the lesser rocks, nibbling at the lichen that grew there. Its eyes, when it raised them and looked in our direction, were a bright, emerald green. It joined us in immobility for a pair of instants. Then it made a quick, nervous gesture with its front feet, pawing the air and striking the stone, three times. And then it blurred and vanished like a snowflake, silently, perhaps in the woods to our right.

I rose and crossed to the stone. Gérard followed me. There, in the moss, I traced its tiny hoofmarks.

'Then we really did see it,' Gérard said.

I nodded.

'We saw something. Did you ever see it before?'

'No. Did you?'

I shook my head.

'Julian claims he once saw it,' he said, 'in the distance. Says his hounds refused to give chase.'

'It was beautiful. That long, silky tail, those shiny hooves . . .'

'Yes. Dad always took it as a good omen.'

'I'd like to myself.'

'Strange time for it to appear . . . All these years . . .'

I nodded again.

'Is there a special observance? It being our patron and all . . . is there something we should do?'

'If there is, Dad never told me about it,' I said. I patted the rock on which it had appeared. 'If you herald some turn in our fortunes, if you bring us some measure of grace – thanks, unicorn,' I said. 'And even if you do not, thanks for the brightness of your company at a dark time.'

We went and drank from the spring then. We secured our grim parcel on the back of the third horse. We led our mounts until we were away from the place, where, save for the water, things had become very still.

6

Life's incessant ceremonies leap everlasting, humans spring eternal on hope's breast, and frying pans without fires are often far between: the sum of my long life's wisdom that evening, tendered in a spirit of creative anxiety, answered by Random with a nod and a friendly obscenity.

We were in the library, and I was seated on the edge of the big desk. Random occupied a chair to my right. Gérard stood at the other end of the room, inspecting some weapons that hung on the wall. Or maybe it was Rein's etching of the unicorn he was looking at. Whichever, along with ourselves, he was also ignoring Julian, who was slouched in an easy chair beside the display cases, right center, legs extended and crossed at the ankles, arms folded, staring down at his scaley boots. Fiona – five-two, perhaps, in height – green eyes fixed on Flora's own blue as they spoke, there beside the fireplace, hair more than compensating for the vacant hearth, smoldering, reminded me, as always, of something from which the artist had just drawn back, setting aside his tools, questions slowly forming behind his smile. The place at the base of her throat where his thumb had notched the collarbone always drew my eyes as the mark of a master craftsman, especially when she raised her head, quizzical or imperious, to regard us taller others. She smiled faintly, just then, doubtless aware of my gaze, an almost clairvoyant faculty the acceptance of which has never deprived of its ability to disconcert. Llewella, off in a corner, pretending to study a book, had her back to the rest of us, her green tresses bobbed a couple of inches above her dark collar. Whether her withdrawal involved animus, self-consciousness in her alienation, or simple caution, I could never be certain. Probably something of all these. Hers was not that familiar a presence in Amber.

. . . And the fact that we constituted a collection of individuals rather than a group, a family, at a time when I wanted to achieve some over-identity, some will to co-operate, was what led to my observations and Random's acknowledgment.

I felt a familiar presence, heard a 'Hello, Corwin' and there was Deirdre, reaching toward me. I extended my hand, clasped her own, raised it. She took a step forward, as if to the first strain of some formal dance, and moved close, facing me. For an instant a grilled window had framed her head and shoulders and a rich tapestry had adorned the wall to her left. Planned and posed, of course. Still, effective. She held my Trump in her left hand. She smiled. The others glanced our way as she appeared and she hit them all with that smile, like the Mona Lisa with a machine gun, turning slowly.

'Corwin,' she said, kissing me briefly and withdrawing, 'I fear I am early.'

'Never,' I replied, turning toward Random, who had just risen and who anticipated me by seconds.

'May I fetch you a drink, sister?' he asked, taking her hand and nodding toward the sideboard.

'Why, yes. Thank you,' and he led her off and poured her some wine, avoiding or at least postponing, I suppose, her usual clash with Flora. At least, I assumed most of the old frictions were still alive as I remembered them. So if it cost me her company for the moment it also maintained the domestic-tranquility index, which was important to me just then. Random can be good at such things when he wants to.

I drummed the side of the desk with my fingertips, I rubbed my aching shoulder, I uncrossed and recrossed my legs, I debated lighting a cigarette . . .

Suddenly he was there. At the far end of the room, Gérard had turned to his left, said something, and extended his hand. An instant later, he was clasping the left and only hand of Benedict, the final member of our group.

All right. The fact that Benedict had chosen to come in on Gérard's Trump rather than mine was his way of expressing his feelings toward me. Was it also an indication of an alliance to keep me in check? It was at least calculated to make me wonder. Could it have been Benedict who had put Gérard up to our morning's exercise? Probably.

At that moment Julian rose to his feet, crossed the room, gave

Benedict a word and a handclasp. This activity attracted Llewella. She turned, closing her book and laying it aside. Smiling then, she advanced and greeted Benedict, nodded to Julian, said something to Gérard. The impromptu conference warmed, grew animated. All right again, and again.

Four and three. And two in the middle . . .

I waited, staring at the group across the room. We were all present, and I could have asked them for attention and proceeded with what I had in mind. However . . .

It was too tempting. All of us could feel the tension, I knew. It was as if a pair of magnetic poles had suddenly been activated within the room. I was curious to see how all the filings would fall.

Flora gave me one quick glance. I doubted that she had changed her mind overnight – unless, of course, there had been some new development. No, I felt confident that I had anticipated the next move.

Nor was I incorrect. I overheard her mentioning thirst and a glass of wine. She turned partway and made a move in my direction, as if expecting Fiona to accompany her. She hesitated for a moment when this did not occur, suddenly became the focus of the entire company's attention, realized this fact, made a quick decision, smiled, and moved in my direction.

'Corwin,' she said, 'I believe I would like a glass of wine.'

Without turning my head or removing my gaze from the tableau before me, I called back over my shoulder, 'Random, pour Flora a glass of wine, would you?'

'But of course,' he replied, and I heard the necessary sounds.

Flora nodded, unsmiled, and passed beyond me to the right.

Four and four, leaving dear Fiona burning brightly in the middle of the room. Totally self-conscious and enjoying it, she immediately turned toward the oval mirror with the dark, intricately carved frame, hanging in the space between the two nearest tiers of shelves. She proceeded to adjust a stray strand of hair in the vicinity of her left temple.

Her movement produced a flash of green and silver among the red and gold geometries of the carpet, near to the place where her left foot had rested.

I had simultaneous desires to curse and to smile. The arrant bitch was playing games with us again. Always remarkable, though . . . Nothing had changed. Neither cursing nor smiling, I moved forward, as she had known I would.

But Julian too approached, and a trifle more quickly than I. He had been a bit nearer, may have spotted it a fraction of an instant sooner.

He scooped it up and dangled it gently.

'Your bracelet, sister,' he said pleasantly. 'It seems to have forsaken your wrist, foolish thing. Here – allow me.'

She extended her hand, giving him one of those lowered-eyelash smiles while he refastened her chain of emeralds. Completing the business, he folded her hand within both of his own and began to turn back toward his corner, from whence the others were casting sidelong glances while attempting to seem locally occupied.

'I believe you would be amused by a witticism we are about to share,' he began.

Her smile grew even more delightful as she disengaged her hand.

'Thank you, Julian,' she replied. 'I am certain that when I hear it I will laugh. Last as usual, I fear.' She turned and took my arm. 'I find that I feel a greater desire,' she said, 'for a glass of wine.'

So I took her back with me and saw her refreshed. Five and four.

Julian, who dislikes showing strong feelings, reached a decision a few moments later and followed us over. He poured himself a glass, sipped from it studied me for ten or fifteen seconds, then said, 'I believe we are all present now. When do you plan to proceed with whatever you have in mind?'

'I see no reason for further delay,' I said, 'now that everyone has had his turn.' I raised my voice then and directed it across the room. 'The time has come. Let us get comfortable.'

The others drifted over. Chairs were dragged up and settled into. More wine was poured. A minute later we had an audience.

'Thank you,' I said when the final stirrings had subsided. 'I have a number of things I would like to say, and some of them might even get said. The course of it all will depend on what goes before, and we will get into that right now. Random, tell them what you told me yesterday.'

'All right.'

I withdrew to the seat behind the desk and Random moved to occupy the edge of it. I leaned back and listened again to the story of his communication with Brand and his attempt to rescue him. It was a condensed version, bereft of the speculations which had not really strayed from my consciousness since Random had put them there. And despite their ommission, a tacit awareness of the implications was occurring within all the others. I knew that. It was the main reason I had wanted Random to speak first. Had I simply come out with an attempt to make a case for my suspicions, I would almost certainly have been assumed to be engaged in the time-honored practice of directing attention away from myself – an act to be followed immediately by the separate, sharp, metallic clicks of minds snapping shut against me. This way, despite any thoughts that Random would say whatever I wanted him to say, they would hear him out, wondering the while. They would toy with the ideas, attempting to foresee the point of my having called the assembly in the first place. They would allow the time that would permit the premises to take root contingent upon later corroboration. And they would be wondering whether we could produce the evidence. I was wondering that same thing myself.

While I waited and wondered I watched the others, a fruitless yet inevitable exercise. Simple curiosity, more than suspicion even, required that I search these faces for reactions, clues, indications – the faces that I knew better than any others, to the limits of my understanding such things. And of course they told me nothing. Perhaps it is true that you really only look at a person the first time you see him, and after that you do a quick bit of mental shorthand each time you recognize him. My brain is lazy enough to give that its likelihood, using its abstracting powers and a presumption of regularity to avoid work whenever possible. This time I forced myself to see, though, and it still did not help. Julian maintained his slightly bored, slightly amused mask. Gérard appeared alternately surprised, angry, and wistful. Benedict just looked bleak and suspicious. Llewella seemed as sad and inscrutable as ever. Deirdre looked distracted, Flora acquiescent, and Fiona was studying everyone else, myself included, assembling her own catalog of reactions.

The only thing that I could tell, after some time, was that Random was making an impression. While no one betrayed himself, I saw the boredom vanish, the old suspicion abate, the new suspicion come to life. Interest rose among my kin. Fascination, almost. Then everyone had questions. At first a few, then a barrage.

'Wait,' I finally interrupted. 'Let him finish. The whole thing. Some of these will answer themselves. Get the others afterward.'

There were nods and growls, and Random proceeded through to the real end. That is, he carried it on to our fight with the beastmen at Flora's, indicating that they were of the same ilk as the one who had slain Caine. Flora endorsed this part.

Then, when the questions came, I watched them carefully. So long as they dealt with the matter of Random's story, they were all to the good. But I wanted to cut things short of speculation as to the possibility of one of us being behind it all. As soon as that came out, talk of me and the smell of red herring would also drift in. This could lead to ugly words and the emergence of a mood I was not anxious to engender. Better to go for the proof first, save on later recriminations, corner the culprit right now if possible, and consolidate my position on the spot.

So I watched and waited. When I felt that the vital moment had ticked its way too near I stopped the clock.

'None of this discussion, this speculation, would be necessary,' I said, 'if we had all of the facts right now. And there may be a way to get them – right now. That is why you are here.'

That did it. I had them Attentive. Ready. Maybe even willing.

'I propose we attempt to reach Brand and bring him home,' I said, 'now.'

'How?' Benedict asked me.

'The Trumps.'

'It has been tried,' said Julian. 'He cannot be reached that way. No response.'

'I was not referring to the ordinary usage,' I said. 'I asked you all to bring full sets of Trumps with you. I trust that you have them?'

There were nods.

'Good,' I said. 'Let us shuffle out Brand's Trump now. I propose that all nine of us attempt to contact him simultaneously.'

'An interesting thought,' Benedict said.

'Yes,' Julian agreed, producing his deck and riffling through it. 'Worth trying, at least. It may generate additional power. I do not really know.'

I located Brand's Trump. I waited until all the others had found it. Then, 'Let us coordinate things,' I said. 'Is everyone ready?'

Eight assents were spoken.

'Then go ahead. Try. Now.'

I studied my card. Brand's features were similar to my own, but he was shorter and slenderer. His hair was like Fiona's. He wore a green riding suit. He rode a white horse. How long ago? How long ago was that? I wondered. Something of a dreamer, a mystic, a poet, Brand was always disillusioned or elated, cynical or wholly trusting. His feelings never seemed to find a middle ground. Manic-depressive is too facile a term for his complex character, yet it might serve to indicate a direction of departure, multitudes of qualifications lining the roadway thereafter. Pursuant to this state of affairs, I must admit that there were times when I found him so charming, considerate, and loyal that I valued him above all my other kin. Other times, however, he could be so bitter, sarcastic, and downright savage that I tried to avoid his company for fear that I might do him harm. Summing up, the last time I had seen him had been one of the latter occasions, just a bit before Eric and I had had the falling out that led to my exile from Amber.

. . . And those were my thoughts and feelings as I studied his Trump, reaching out to him with my mind, my will, opening the vacant place I sought him to fill. About me, the others shuffled their own memories and did the same.

Slowly the card took on a dream-dust quality and acquired the illusion of depth. There followed that familiar blurring, with the sense of movement which heralds contact with the subject. The Trump grew colder beneath my fingertips, and then things flowed and formed, achieving a sudden verity of vision, persistent, dramatic, full.

He seemed to be in a cell. There was a stone wall behind him. There was straw on the floor. He was manacled, and his chain ran back through a huge ring bolt set in the wall above and behind him. It was a fairly long chain, providing sufficient slack for movement, and at the moment he was taking advantage of this fact, lying sprawled on a heap of straw and rags off in the corner. His hair and beard were quite long, his face thinner than I had ever before seen it. His clothes were tattered and filthy. He seemed to be sleeping. My mind went back to my own imprisonment – the smells, the cold, the wretched fare, the dampness, the loneliness, the madness that came and went. At least he still had his eyes, for they flickered and I saw them when several of us spoke his name; green they were, with a flat, vacant look.

Was he drugged? Or did he believe himself to be hallucinating?

But suddenly his spirit returned. He raised himself. He extended his hand.

'Brothers!' he said. 'Sisters . . .'

'I'm coming!' came a shout that shook the room.

Gérard had leaped to his feet, knocking over his chair. He dashed across the room and snatched a great battle ax from its pegs on the wall. He slung it at his wrist, holding the Trump in that same hand. For a moment he froze, studying the card. Then he extended his free hand and suddenly he was there, clasping Brand, who chose that moment to pass out again. The image wavered. The contact was broken.

Cursing, I sought through the pack after Gérard's own Trump. Several of the others seemed to be doing the same thing. Locating it, I moved for contact. Slowly, the melting, the turning, the re-forming occurred. There!

Gérard had drawn the chain taut across the stones of the wall and was attacking it with the ax. It was a heavy thing, however, and resisted his powerful blows for a long while. Eventually several of the links were mashed and scarred, but by then he had been at it for almost two minutes, and the ringing, chopping sounds had alerted the jailers.

For there were noises from the left – a rattling sound, the sliding of bolts, the creaking of hinges. Although my field of perception did not extend that far, it seemed obvious that the cell's door was being opened. Brand raised himself once more. Gérard continued to hack at the chain.

'Gérard! The door!' I shouted.

'I know!' he bellowed, wrapping the chain about his arm and yanking it. It did not yield.

Then he let go of the chain and swung the ax, as one of the horny-handed warriors rushed him, blade upraised. The swordsman fell, to be replaced by another. Then a third and a fourth crowded by them. Others were close on their heels.

There was a blur of movement at that moment and Random knelt within the tableau, his right hand clasped with Brand's, his left holding his chair before him like a shield, its legs pointing outward. He sprang to his feet and rushed the attackers, driving the chair like a battering ram amid them. They fell back. He raised the chair and swung it. One lay dead on the floor, felled by Gérard's ax. Another had drawn off to one side, clutching at the stump of his right arm. Random produced a dagger and left it in a nearby stomach, brained two more with the chair, and drove back the final man. Eerily, while this was going on, the dead man rose above the floor and slowly drifted upward, spilling and dripping the while. The one who had been stabbed collapsed to his knees, clutching at the blade.

In the meantime, Gérard had taken hold of the chain with both hands. He braced one foot against the wall and commenced to pull. His shoulders rose as the great muscles tightened across his back. The chain held. Ten seconds, perhaps. Fifteen . . .

Then, with a snap and a rattle, it parted. Gérard stumbled backward, catching himself with an outflung hand. He glanced back, apparently at Random, who was out of my line of sight at the moment. Seemingly satisfied, he turned away, stooped and raised Brand, who had fallen unconscious again. Holding him in his arms, he turned and extended one hand from beneath the limp form. Random leaped back into sight beside them, *sans* chair, and gestured to us also.

All of us reached for them, and a moment later they stood amid us and we crowded around.

A sort of cheer had gone up as we rushed to touch him, to see him, our brother who had been gone these many years and just now snatched back from his mysterious captors. And at last, hopefully, finally, some answers might also have been liberated. Only he looked so weak, so thin, so pale . . .

'Get back!' Gérard shouted. 'I'm taking him to the couch! Then you can look all you—'

Dead silence. For everyone had backed off, and then turned to stone. This was because there was blood on Brand, and it was dripping. And this was because there was a knife in his left side, to the rear. It had not been there moments before. Some one of us had just tried for his kidney and possibly succeeded. I was not heartened by the fact that the Random-Corwin Conjecture that it was One Of Us

Behind It All had just received a significant boost. I had an instant during which to concentrate all my faculties in an attempt to mentally photograph everyone's position. Then the spell was broken. Gérard bore Brand to the couch and we drew aside; and we all knew that we all realized not only what had happened, but what it implied.

Gérard set Brand down in a prone position and tore away his filthy shirt.

'Get me clean water to bathe him,' he said. 'And towels. Get me saline solution and glucose and something to hang them from. Get me a whole medical kit.'

Deirdre and Flora moved toward the door.

'My quarters are closest,' said Random. 'One of you will find a medical kit there. But the only IV stuff is in the lab on file third floor. I'd better come and help.'

They departed together.

We all had had medical training somewhere along the line, both here and abroad. That which we learned in Shadow, though, had to be modified in Amber. Most antibiotics from the shadow worlds, for example, were ineffectual here. On the other hand, our personal immunological processes appear to behave differently from those of any other peoples we have studied, so that it is much more difficult for us to become infected – and if infected we deal with it more expeditiously. Then, too, we possess profound regenerative abilities.

All of which is as it must be, of course, the ideal necessarily being superior to its shadows. And Amberites that we are, and aware of these facts from an early age, all of us obtained medical training relatively early in life. Basically, despite what is often said about being your own physician, it goes back to our not unjustified distrust of virtually everyone, and most particularly of those who might hold our lives in their hands. All of which partly explains why I did not rush to shoulder Gérard aside to undertake Brand's treatment myself, despite the fact that I had been through a med school on the shadow Earth within the past couple of generations. The other part of the explanation is that Gérard was not letting anyone else near Brand. Julian and Fiona had both moved forward, apparently with the same thing in mind, only to encounter Gérard's left arm like a gate at a railway crossing.

'No,' he had said. 'I know that I did not do it, and that is all that I know. There will be no second chance for anyone else.'

With any one of us sustaining that sort of wound while in an otherwise sound condition, I would say that if he made it through the first half hour he would make it. Brand, though . . . The shape he was in . . . There was no telling.

When the others returned with the materials and equipment, Gérard cleaned Brand, sutured the wound, and dressed it. He hooked up the IV, broke off the manacles with a hammer and chisel Random had located, covered Brand with a sheet and a blanket, and took his pulse again.

'How is it?' I asked.

'Weak,' he said, and he drew up a chair and seated himself beside the couch. 'Someone fetch me my blade – and a glass of wine. I didn't have any. Also, if there is any food left over there, I'm hungry.'

Llewella headed for the sideboard and Random got him his blade from the rack behind the door.

'Are you just going to camp there?' Random asked, passing him the weapon.

'I am.'

'What about moving Brand to a better bed?'

'He is all right where he is. I will decide when he can be moved. In the meantime, someone get a fire going. Then put out a few of those candles.'

Random nodded.

'I'll do it,' he said. Then he picked up the knife Gérard had drawn from Brand's side, a thin stiletto, its blade about seven inches in length. He held it across the palm of his hand.

'Does anyone recognize this?' he asked.

'Not I,' said Benedict.

'Nor I,' said Julian.

'No,' I said.

The girls shook their heads.

Random studied it.

'Easily concealed – up a sleeve, in a boot or bodice. It took real nerve to use it that way . . .'

'Desperation,' I said.

'. . . And a very accurate anticipation of our mob scene. Inspired, almost.'

'Could one of the guards have done it?' Julian asked. 'Back in the cell?'

'No,' Gérard said. 'None of them came near enough.'

'It looks to be decently balanced for throwing,' Deirdre said.

'It is,' said Random, shifting it about his fingertips, 'Only none of them had a clear shot or the opportunity. I'm positive.'

Llewella returned, bearing a tray containing slabs of meat, half a loaf of bread, a bottle of wine, and a goblet. I cleared a small table and set it beside Gérard's chair. As Llewella deposited the tray, she asked, 'But why? That only leaves us. Why would one of us want to do it?'

I sighed.

'Whose prisoner do you think he might have been?' I asked.

'One of us?'

'If he possessed knowledge which someone was willing to go to this length to suppress, what do you think? The same reason also served to put him where he was and keep him there.'

Her brows tightened.

'That does not make sense either. Why didn't they just kill him and be done with it?'

I shrugged.

'Must have had some use for him,' I said. 'But there is really only one person who can answer that question adequately. When you find him, ask him.'

'Or her,' Julian said. 'Sister, you seem possessed of a super-abundance of naïveté, suddenly.'

Her gaze locked with Julian's own, a pair of icebergs reflecting frigid infinities.

'As I recall,' she said, 'you rose from your seat when they came through, turned to the left, rounded the desk, and stood slightly to Gérard's right. You leaned pretty far forward. I believe your hands were out of sight, below.'

'And as I recall,' he said, 'you were within striking distance yourself, off to Gérard's left – and leaning forward.'

'I would have had to do it with my left hand – and I am right-handed.'

'Perhaps he owes what life he still possesses to that fact.'

'You seem awfully anxious, Julian, to find that it was someone else.'

'All right,' I said. 'All right! You know this is self-defeating. Only one of us did it, and this is not the way to smoke him out.'

'Or her,' Julian added.

Gérard rose, towered, glared.

'I will not have you disturbing my patient,' he said. 'And, Random, you said you were going to see to the fire.'

'Right away,' Random said, and moved to do it.

'Let us adjourn to the sitting room off the main hall,' I said, 'downstairs. Gérard, I will post a couple of guards outside the door here.'

'No,' Gérard said. 'I would rather that anyone who wishes to try it get this far. I will hand you his head in the morning.'

I nodded.

'Well, you can ring for anything you need – or call one of us on the Trumps. We will fill you in in the morning on anything that we learn.'

Gérard seated himself, grunted, and began eating. Random got the fire going and extinguished some lights. Brand's blanket rose and fell, slowly but regularly. We filed quietly from the room and headed for the stairway, leaving them there together with the flare and the crackle, the tubes and the bottles.

Many are the times I have awakened, sometimes shaking, always afraid, from the dream that I occupied my old cell, blind once more, in the dungeons beneath Amber. It is not as if I were unfamiliar with the condition of imprisonment. I have been locked away on a number of occasions, for various periods of time. But solitary, plus blindness with small hope of recovery, made for a big charge to the sensory-deprivation counter in the department store of the mind. That, with the sense of finality to it all, had left its marks. I generally keep these memories safely tucked away during waking hours, but at night, sometimes, they come loose, dance down the aisles and frolic round the notions counter, one, two, three. Seeing Brand there in his cell had brought them out again, along with an unseasonal chill; and that final thrust served to establish a more or less permanent residence for them. Now, among my kin in the shield-hung sitting room, I could not avoid the thought that one or more of them had done unto Brand as Eric had done unto me. While this capacity was in itself hardly a surprising discovery, the matter of occupying the same room with the culprit and having no idea as to his identity was more than a little disturbing. My only consolation was that each of the others, according to his means, must be disturbed also. Including the guilty, now that the existence theorem had shown a positive. I knew then that I had been hoping all along that outsiders were entirely to blame. Now, though . . . On the one hand I felt even more restricted than usual in what I could say. On the other, it seemed a good time to press for information, with everyone in an abnormal state of mind. The desire to co-operate for purposes of dealing with the threat could prove helpful. And even the guilty party would want to behave the same as everyone else. Who knew but that he might slip up while making the effort?

'Well, have you any other interesting little experiments you would care to conduct?' Julian asked me, clasping his hands behind his head and leaning back in my favorite chair.

'Not at the moment,' I said.

'Pity,' he replied. 'I was hoping you would suggest we go looking for Dad now in the same fashion. Then, if we are lucky, we find him and someone puts him out of the way with more certainty. After that, we could all play Russian roulette with those fine new weapons you've furnished – winner take all.'

'Your words are ill-considered,' I said.

'Not so. I considered every one of them,' he answered. 'We spend so much time lying to one another that I decided it might be amusing to say what I really felt. Just to see whether anyone noticed.'

'Now you see that we have. We also notice that the real you is no improvement over the old one.'

'Whichever you prefer, both of us have been wondering whether you have any idea what you are going to do next.'

'I do,' I said. 'I now intend to obtain answers to a number of questions dealing with everything that is plaguing us. We might as well start with Brand and his troubles.' Turning toward Benedict, who was sitting gazing into the fire, I said, 'Back in Avalon, Benedict, you told me that Brand was one of the ones who searched for me after my disappearance.'

'That is correct,' Benedict answered.

'All of us went looking,' Julian said.

'Not at first,' I replied. 'Initially, it was Brand, Gérard, and yourself, Benedict. Isn't that what you told me?'

'Yes,' he said. 'The others did have a go at it later, though. I told you that, too.'

I nodded.

'Did Brand report anything unusual at that time?' I asked.

'Unusual? In what way?' said Benedict.

'I don't know. I am looking for some connection between what happened to him and what happened to me.'

'Then you are looking in the wrong place,' Benedict said. 'He returned and reported no success. And he was around for ages after that, unmolested.'

'I gathered that much,' I said. 'I understand from what Random has told me, though, that his final disappearance occurred approximately a month before my own recovery and return. That almost strikes me as peculiar. If he did not report anything special after his return from the search, did he do so prior to his disappearance? Or in the interim? Anyone? Anything? Say it if you've got it!'

There followed some mutual glancing about. The looks seemed more curious than suspicious or nervous, though.

Finally, then, 'Well,' Llewella said, 'I do not know. Do not know whether it is significant, I mean.'

All eyes came to rest upon her. She began to knot and unknot the ends of her belt cord, slowly, as she spoke.

'It was in the interim, and it may have no bearing,' she went on. 'It is just something that struck me as peculiar. Brand came to Rebma long ago—'

'How long ago?' I asked.

She furrowed her brow.

'Fifty, sixty, seventy years . . . I am not certain.'

I tried to summon up the rough conversion factor I had worked out during my long incarceration. A day in Amber, it seemed, constituted a bit over two and a half days on the shadow Earth where I had spent my exile. I wanted to relate events in Amber to my own time-scale whenever possible, just in case any peculiar correspondences turned up. So Brand had gone to Rebma sometime in what was, to me, the nineteenth century.

'Whatever the date,' she said, 'he came and visited me. Stayed for several weeks.' She glanced at Random then. 'He was asking about Martin.'

Random narrowed his eyes and cocked his head.

'Did he say why?' he asked her.

'Not exactly,' she said. 'He implied that he had met Martin somewhere in his travels, and he gave the impression that he would like to get in touch with him again. I did not realize until some time after his departure that finding out everything he could concerning Martin was probably the entire reason for his visit. You know how subtle Brand can be, finding out things without seeming to be after them. It was only after I had spoken with a number of others whom he had visited that I began to see what had occurred, I never did find out why, though.'

'That is – most peculiar,' Random observed. 'For it brings to mind something to which I had never attached any significance. He once questioned me at great length concerning my son – and it may well have been at about the same time. He never indicated that he had met him, however – or that he had any desire to do so. It started out as a bit of banter on the subject of bastards. When I took offense he apologized and asked a number of more proper questions about the boy, which I assumed he then put for the sake of politeness – to leave me with a softer remembrance. As you say, though, he had a way of drawing admissions from people. Why is it you never told me of this before?'

She smiled prettily.

'Why should I have?' she said.

Random nodded slowly, his face expressionless.

'Well, what did you tell him?' he said. 'What did he learn? What do you know about Martin that I don't?'

She shook her head, her smile fading.

'Nothing – actually,' she said. 'To my knowledge, no one in Rebma ever heard from Martin after he took the Pattern and vanished. I do not believe that Brand departed knowing any more than he did when he arrived.'

'Strange . . .' I said. 'Did he approach anyone else on the subject?'

'I don't remember,' Julian said.

'Nor I,' said Benedict.

The others shook their heads.

'Then let us note it and leave it for now,' I said. 'There are other things I also need to know. Julian, I understand that you and Gérard attempted to follow the black road a while back, and that Gérard was injured along the way. I believe you both stayed with Benedict for a time after that, while Gérard recuperated. I would like to know about that expedition.'

'It seems as if you already do,' Julian replied. 'You have just stated everything that occurred.'

'Where did you learn of this, Corwin,' Benedict inquired.

'Back in Avalon,' I said.

'From whom?'

'Dara,' I said.

He rose to his feet, came over, stood before me, glared down.

'You still persist in that absurd story about the girl!'

I sighed.

'We have been round and round on this too many times,' I said. 'By now I have told you everything that I know on the subject. Either you accept it or you do not. She is the one who told me, though.'

'Apparently, then, there were some things you did not tell me. You never mentioned that part before.'

'Is it true or isn't it? About Julian and Gérard.'

'It is true,' he said.

'Then forget the source for now and let us get on with what happened.'

'Agreed,' Benedict said. 'I may speak candidly, now that the reason for secrecy is no longer with us. Eric, of course. He was unaware of my whereabouts, as were most of the others. Gérard was my main source of news in Amber. Eric grew more and more apprehensive concerning the black road and finally decided to send scouts to trace it through Shadow to its source. Julian and Gérard were selected. They were attacked by a very strong party of its creatures at a point near Avalon. Gérard called to me, via my Trump, for assistance and I went to their aid. The enemy was dispatched. As Gérard had sustained a broken leg in the fighting and Julian was a bit battered himself, I took them both home with me. I broke my silence with Eric at that time, to tell him where they were and what had become of them. He ordered them not to continue their journey, but to return to Amber after they had recovered. They remained with me until they did. Then they went back.'

'That is all?'

'That is all.'

But it wasn't. Dara had also told me something else. She had mentioned another visitor. I remembered it quite distinctly. That day, beside the stream, a tiny rainbow in the mist above the waterfall, the mill wheel turning round and round, delivering dreams and grinding them, that day we had fenced and talked and walked in Shadow, had passed through a primordial wood, coming to a spot beside a mighty torrent where turned a wheel fit for the granary of the gods, that day we had picnicked, flirted, gossiped, she had told me many things, some of them doubtless false. But she had not lied concerning the journey of Julian and Gérard, and I believed it possible that she had

426

also spoken truly when she said that Brand had visited Benedict in Avalon. 'Frequently' was the word she had used.

Now, Benedict made no secret of the fact that he distrusted me. I could see this alone as sufficient reason for his withholding information on anything he judged too sensitive to become my business. Hell, buying his story, I would not have trusted me either if our situations were reversed. Only a fool would have called him on it at that moment, though. Because of the other possibilities.

It could be that he planned to tell me later, in private, of the circumstances surrounding Brand's visits. They could well have involved something he did not wish to discuss before the group, and especially before Brand's would-be killer.

Or – there was, of course, the possibility that Benedict himself was behind it all. I did not even like to think about the consequences. Having served under Napoleon, Lee, and MacArthur, I appreciated the tactician as well as the strategist. Benedict was both, and he was the best I had ever known. The recent loss of his right arm had in no way diminished him in this, or for that matter impaired his personal fighting skills. Had I not been very lucky recently he could easily have turned me into a pile of scallops over our misunderstanding. No, I did not want it to be Benedict, and I was not about to grope after whatever he had at that moment seen fit to conceal. I only hoped that he was just saving it for later.

So I settled for his, 'That is all,' and decided to move on to other matters.

'Flora,' I said, 'back when I first visited you, after my accident, you said something which I still do not quite understand. In that I had ample time relatively soon thereafter in which to review many things, I came across it in my memories and occasionally puzzled over it. I still do not understand it. So would you please tell me what you meant when you said that the shadows contained more horrors than any had thought?'

'Why, I do not properly recall saying it,' Flora said. 'But I suppose that I must have, if it made such an impression. You know the effect that I was referring to: that Amber seems to act as something of a magnet on adjacent shadows, drawing things across from them; the nearer you get to Amber the easier the road becomes, even for shadow-things. While there always seems to be some exchange of materials among adjacent shadows themselves, the effect is more forceful and also more of a one-way process when it comes to Amber. We have always been alert for peculiar things slipping through. Well, for several years prior to your recovery, more such things than usual seemed to be showing up in the vicinity of Amber. Dangerous things, almost invariably. Many were recognizable creatures from nearby realms. After a time, though, things kept coming in from farther and farther afield. Eventually, some which were totally unknown made it through. No reason could be found for this sudden transportation of menaces, although we sought fairly far for disturbances which might be driving them this way. In other words, highly improbable penetrations of Shadow were occurring.'

'This actually began while Dad was still around?'

'Oh yes. It started several years before your recovery – as I said.'

'I see. Did anyone consider the possibility of there being a connection between this state of affairs and Dad's departure?'

'Certainly,' Benedict replied. 'I still feel that that was the reason for it. He went off to investigate, or to seek a remedy.'

'But that is purely conjecture,' Julian said. 'You know how he was. He gave no reasons.'

Benedict shrugged.

'It is a reasonable inference, though,' he said. 'I understand that he had spoken of his concern over the – monster migrations, if you like – on numerous occasions.'

I withdrew my cards from their case, having recently gotten into the habit of carrying a set of Trumps with me at all times. I raised Gérard's Trump and regarded it. The others were silent, watching me as I did this. Moments later, there was contact.

Gérard was still seated in his chair, his blade across his knees. He was still eating. He swallowed when he felt my presence and said, 'Yes, Corwin? What do you want?'

'How is Brand?'

'Sleeping,' he said. 'His pulse is a little stronger. His breathing is the same – regular. It's still too early—'

'I know,' I said. 'I mainly wanted to check your recollection of something: near the end there, did you get the impression from anything he might have said or done that Dad's going away might have been connected with the increased number of Shadow beings that were slipping through into Amber?'

'That,' said Julian, 'is what is known as a leading question.'

Gérard wiped his mouth.

'There could have been a connection, yes,' he said. 'He seemed disturbed, preoccupied with something. And he did talk about the creatures. But he never really said that that was his main concern – or whether it was something entirely different.'

'Like what?'

He shook his head.

'Anything. I – yes . . . yes, there is something you probably ought to know, for whatever it is worth. Some time after his disappearance, I did make an effort to find out one thing. That was, whether I was indeed the last person to see him before his departure. I am fairly certain that I was. I had been here in the palace all evening, and I was preparing to return to the flagship. Dad had retired about an hour earlier, but I had stayed on in the guard room, playing draughts with Captain Thoben. As we were sailing the following morning, I decided to take a book with me. So I came up here to the library. Dad was seated at the desk.' He gestured with his head. 'He was going through some old books, and he had not yet changed his garments. He nodded to me when I entered, and I told him I had just come up for a book. He said, "You've come to the right place," and he kept on reading. While I was looking over the shelves, he said something to the effect that he could not sleep. I found a book, told him good night, he said, "Good sailing," and I left.' He lowered his eyes again. 'Now I am positive he was wearing the Jewel of Judgment that night, that I saw it on him then as plainly as I see it on you now. I am equally certain that he had not had it on earlier that evening. For a long while after, I thought that he had taken it along with him, wherever he went. There was no indication in his chambers that he had later changed his clothing. I never saw the stone again until you and Bleys were defeated in your assault on Amber. Then, Eric was wearing it. When I questioned him he claimed that he had found it in Dad's chambers. Lacking evidence to the contrary, I had to accept his story. But I was never happy with it. Your question – and seeing you wearing it – has brought it all back. So I thought you had better know about it.'

'Thanks,' I said, and another question occurred to me but I decided against asking it at that moment. For the benefit of the others, I closed off by saying, 'So do you think he needs any more blankets? Or anything else?'

Gérard raised his glass to me, then took a drink.

'Very good. Keep up the good work,' I said, and I passed my hand over his card.

'Brother Brand seems to be doing all right,' I said, 'and Gérard does not recollect Dad's saying anything that would directly connect Shadow slippage and his departure. I wonder how Brand will recall things, when he comes around?'

'*If* he comes around,' Julian said.

'I think that he will,' I said. 'We have all taken some pretty bad beatings. Our vitality is one of the few things we have come to trust. My guess is that he will be talking by morning.'

'What do you propose doing with the guilty party,' he asked, 'if Brand names him?'

'Question him,' I said.

'Then I would like to do the questioning. I am beginning to feel that you may be right this time, Corwin, and that the person who stabbed him may also be responsible for our intermittent state of siege, for Dad's disappearance, and for Caine's killing. So I would enjoy questioning him before we cut his throat, and I would like to volunteer for that last part also.'

'We will keep it in mind,' I said.

'You are not excluded from the reckoning, Corwin.'

'I was aware of that.'

'I have something to say,' said Benedict, smothering a rejoinder from Julian. 'I find myself troubled both by the strength and the apparent objective of the opposition, I have encountered them now on several occasions, and they *are* out for blood. Accepting for the moment your story of the girl Dara, Corwin, her final words do seem to sum up their attitude: "Amber will be destroyed". Not conquered, subjugated, or taught a lesson. Destroyed. Julian, you wouldn't mind ruling here, would you?'

Julian smiled.

'Perhaps next year this time,' he said. 'Not today, thank you.'

'What I am getting at is that I could see you – or any of us – employing mercenaries or obtaining allies to effect a takeover. I cannot see you employing a force so powerful that it would represent a grave problem itself afterward. Not a force that seems bent on destruction rather than conquest I cannot see you, me, Corwin, the others as actually trying to destroy Amber, or willing to gamble with forces that would. That is the part I do not like about Corwin's notion that one of us is behind this.'

I had to nod. I was not unaware of the weakness of that link in my chain of speculations. Still, there were so many unknowns . . . I could offer alternatives, such as Random then did, but guesses prove nothing.

'It may be,' Random said, 'that one of us made the deal but underestimated his allies. The guilty party may now be sweating this thing as much as the rest of us. He may not be in a position to turn things off now, even if he wants to.'

'We could offer him the opportunity,' Fiona said, 'to betray his allies to us now. If Julian could be persuaded to leave his throat uncut and the rest of us were willing to do the same, he might come around – if Random's guess is correct. He would not claim the throne, but he was obviously not about to have it before. He would have his life and he could save Amber quite a bit of trouble. Is anyone willing to commit himself to a position on this?'

'I am,' I said. 'I will give him his life if he will come across, with the understanding that it will be spent in exile.'

'I will go along with that.' Benedict said.

'So will I,' said Random.

'On one condition,' Julian said. 'If he was not personally responsible for Caine's death, I will go along with it. Otherwise, no. And there would have to be evidence.'

'Life, in exile,' Deirdre said. 'All right I agree.'

'So do I,' said Flora.

'And I,' Llewella followed.

'Gérard will probably agree too,' I said. 'But I really wonder whether Brand will feel the same as the rest of us. I've a feeling he may not.'

'Let us check with Gérard,' Benedict said. 'If Brand makes it and proves the only holdout, the guilty party will know he has only one enemy to avoid – and they can always work out their own terms on that count.'

'All right,' I said, smothering a few misgivings, and I recontacted Gérard, who agreed also.

So we rose to our feet and swore that much by the Unicorn of Amber – Julian's oath having an extra clause to it – and swore to enforce exile on any of our own number who violated the oath. Frankly, I did not think it would net us anything, but it is always nice to see families doing things together.

After that, everyone made a point of mentioning that he would be remaining in the palace overnight, presumably to indicate that no one feared anything Brand might have to say in the morning – and especially to indicate that no one had a desire to get out of town, a thing that would not be forgotten, even if Brand gave up the ghost during the night. In that I had no further questions to put to the group and no one had sprung forward to own up to the misdeeds covered by the oath, I leaned back and listened for a time after that. Things came apart, falling into a series of conversations and exchanges, one of the main topics being an attempted reconstruction of the library tableau, each of us in his own place and, invariably, why each of us was in a position to have done it, except for the speaker. I smoked; I said nothing on the subject. Deirdre did spot an interesting possibility, however. Namely, that Gérard could have done the stabbing himself while we were all crowded around, and that his heroic efforts were not prompted by any desire to save Brand's neck, but rather to achieve a position where he could stop his tongue – in which case Brand would never make it through the night. Ingenious, but I just couldn't believe it. No one else bought it either. At least, no one volunteered to go upstairs and throw Gérard out.

After a time Fiona drifted over and sat beside me.

'Well, I've tried the only thing I could think of,' she said. 'I hope some good comes of it.'

'It may,' I said.

'I see that you have added a peculiar piece of ornamentation to your wardrobe,' she said, raising the Jewel of Judgment between her thumb and forefinger and studying it.

Then she raised her eyes.

'Can you make it do tricks for you?' she asked.

'Some,' I said.

'Then you knew how to attune it. It involves the Pattern, doesn't it?'

'Yes. Eric told me how to go about it, right before he died.'

'I see.'

She released it, settled back into her seat, regarded the flames.

'Did he give you any cautions to go along with it?' she asked.

'No,' I said.

'I wonder whether that was a matter of design or circumstance?'

'Well, he was pretty busy dying at the time. That limited our conversation considerably.'

'I know. I was wondering whether his hatred for you outweighed his hopes for the realm, or whether he was simply ignorant of some of the principles involved.'

'What do you know about it?'

'Think again of Eric's death, Corwin. I was not there when it occurred, but I came in early for the funeral. I was present when his body was bathed, shaved, dressed – and I examined his wounds. I do not believe that any of them were fatal, in themselves. There were three chest wounds, but only one looked as if it might have run into the mediastinal area—'

'One's enough, if—'

'Wait,' she said. 'It was difficult, but I tried judging the angle of the puncture with a thin glass rod. I wanted to make an incision, but Caine would not permit it. Still, I do not believe that his heart or arteries were damaged. It is still not too late to order an autopsy, if you would like me to check further on this. I am certain that his injuries and the general stress contributed to his death, but I believe it was the jewel that made the difference.'

'Why do you think this?'

'Because of some things that Dworkin said when I studied with him – and things that I noticed afterward, because of this. He indicated that while it conferred unusual abilities, it also represented a drain on the vitality of its master. The longer you wear it, the more it somehow takes out of you. I paid attention after that, and I noticed that Dad wore it only seldom and never kept it on for long periods of time.'

My thoughts returned to Eric, the day he lay dying on the slopes of Kolvir, the battle raging about him I remembered my first look at him, his face pale, his breath labored, blood on his chest . . . And the Jewel of Judgment, there on its chain, was pulsing, heartlike, among the moist folds of his garments. I had never seen it do that before, or since. I recalled that the effect had grown fainter, weaker. And when he died and I folded his hands atop it, the phenomenon had ceased.

'What do you know of its function?' I asked her.

She shook her head.

'Dworkin considered that a state secret. I know the obvious – weather control – and I inferred from some of Dad's remarks that it has something to do with a heightened perception, or a higher perception. Dworkin had mentioned it primarily as an example of the pervasiveness of the Pattern in everything that gives us power – even the Trumps contain the Pattern, if you look closely, look long enough – and he cited it as an instance of a conservation principle: all of our special powers have their price. The greater the power, the larger the investment. The Trumps are a small matter, but there is still an element of fatigue involved in their employment. Walking through Shadow, which is an exercise of the image of the Pattern which exists within us, is an even greater expenditure. To essay the Pattern itself, physically, is a massive drain on one's energies. But the jewel, he said, represents an even higher octave of the same thing, and its cost to its employer is exponentially greater.'

Thus, if correct, another ambiguous insight into the character of my late and least favored brother. If he were aware of this phenomenon and had donned the jewel and worn it overlong anyhow, in the defense of Amber, it made him something of a hero. But then, seen in this light, his passing it along to me, without warnings, became a deathbed effort at a final piece of vengeance. But he had exempted me from his curse, he'd said, so as to spend it properly on our enemies in the field. This, of course, only meant that he hated them a little more than he hated me and was deploying his final energies as strategically as possible, for Amber. I thought then of the partial character of Dworkin's notes, as I had recovered them from the hiding place Eric had indicated. Could it be that Eric had acquired them intact and had purposely destroyed that portion containing the cautions so as to damn his successor? That notion did not strike me as quite adequate, for he had had no way of knowing that I would return when I did, as I did, that the course of battle would run as it had, and that I would indeed be his successor. It could just as easily have been one of his favorites that followed him to power, in which case he would certainly not have wanted him to inherit any booby traps. No. As I saw it, either Eric was not really aware of this property of the stone, having acquired only partial instructions for its use, or someone had gotten to those papers before I had and removed sufficient material to leave me with a mortal liability. It may well have been the hand of the real enemy, once again.

'Do you know the safety factor?' I asked.

'No,' she said. 'I can give you only two pointers, for whatever they may be worth. The first is that I do not recall Dad's ever wearing it for long periods of time. The second, I pieced together from a number of things that he said, beginning with a comment to the effect that "when people turn into statues you are either in the wrong place or in trouble." I pressed him quite a bit on that over a long period of time, and I eventually got the impression that the first sign of having worn it too long is some sort of distortion of your time sense. Apparently it begins speeding up the metabolism – everything – with a net effect that the world seems to be slowing down around you. This must take quite a toll on a person. That is everything that I know about it, and I admit that a large part of the last is guesswork. How long have you been wearing it?'

'A while now,' I said, taking my mental poke and glancing about to see whether things seemed to be slowing down any.

I could not really tell, though of course I did not feel in the best of shape. I had assumed it was totally Gérard's doing, though. I was not about to yank it off, however, just because another family member had suggested it, even if it was clever Fiona in one of her friendlier moods. Perversity, cussedness . . . No, independence. That was it. That and purely formal distrust. I had only put it on for the evening a few hours before, anyway. I'd wait.

'Well, you have made your point in wearing it,' she was saying. 'I simply wanted to advise you against prolonged exposure until you know more about it.'

'Thanks, Fi. I'll have it off soon, and I appreciate your telling me. By the way, whatever became of Dworkin?'

She tapped her temple.

'His mind finally went, poor man. I like to think that Dad had him put away in some restful retreat in Shadow.'

'I see what you mean,' I said. 'Yes, let us think that. Poor fellow.'

Julian rose to his feet, concluding a conversation with Llewella. He stretched, nodded to her, and strolled over.

'Corwin, have you thought of any more questions for us?' he said.

'None that I'd care to ask just now.'

He smiled.

'Anything more that you want to tell us?'

'Not at the moment.'

'Any more experiments, demonstrations, charades?'

'No.'

'Good. Then I'm going to bed. Good night.'

'Night.'

He bowed to Fiona, waved to Benedict and Random, nodded to Flora and Deirdre as he passed them on the way to the door. He paused on the threshold, turned back and said, 'Now you can all talk about me,' and went on out.

'All right,' Fiona said. 'Let's. I think he's the one.'

'Why?' I asked.

'I'll go down the list, subjective, intuitive, and biased as it is. Benedict, in my opinion, is above suspicion. If he wanted the throne, he'd have it by now, by direct, military methods. With all the time he has had, he could have managed an attack that would have succeeded, even against Dad. He is that good, and we all know it. You, on the other hand, have made a number of blunders which you would not have made had you been in full possession of your faculties. That is why I believe your story, amnesia and all. No one gets himself blinded as a piece of strategy. Gérard is well on the way to establishing his own innocence. I almost think he is up there with Brand now more for that reason than from any desire to protect Brand. At any rate, we will know for sure before long – or else have some new suspicions. Random has simply been watched too closely these past years to have had the opportunity to engineer everything that has been happening. So he is out. Of us more delicate sorts, Flora hasn't the brains, Deirdre lacks the guts, Llewella hasn't the motivations, as she is happy elsewhere but never here, and I, of course, am innocent of all but malice. That leaves Julian. Is he capable? Yes. Does he want the throne? Of course. Has he had time and opportunity? Again, yes. He is your man.'

'Would he have killed Caine?' I asked. 'They were buddies.'

She curled her lip.

'Julian has no friends,' she said. 'That icy personality of his is thawed only by thoughts of himself. Oh, in recent years he *seemed* closer to Caine than to anyone else. But even that . . . even that could have been a part of it. Shamming a friendship long enough to make it seem believable, so that he would not be suspect at this time. I can believe Julian capable of that because I cannot believe him capable of strong emotional attachments.'

I shook my head.

'I don't know,' I said. 'His friendship with Caine is something that occurred during my absence, so everything I know concerning it is secondhand. Still, if Julian were looking for friendship in the form of another personality close to his own, I can see it. They were a lot alike. I tend to think it was real, because I don't think anybody is capable of deceiving someone about his friendship for years. Unless the other party is awfully stupid, which is something Caine was not. And – well, you say your reasoning was subjective, intuitive, and biased. So is mine, on something like this. I just don't like to think anybody is such a miserable wretch that he would use his only friend that way. That's why I think there is something wrong with your list.'

She sighed.

'For someone who has been around for as long as you have, Corwin, you say some silly things. Were you changed by your long stay in that funny little place? Years ago you would have seen the obvious, as I do.'

'Perhaps I have changed, for such things no longer seem obvious. Or could it be that you have changed, Fiona? A trifle more cynical than the little girl I once knew. It might not have been all that obvious to you, years ago.'

She smiled softly.

'Never tell a woman she has changed, Corwin. Except for the better. You used to know that, too. Could it be that you are really only one of Corwin's shadows, sent back to suffer and intimidate here on his behalf? Is the real Corwin somewhere else, laughing at us all?'

'I am here, and I am not laughing,' I said.

She laughed.

'Yes, that is it!' she said. 'I have just decided that you are not yourself!'

'Announcement, everybody!' she cried, springing to her feet. 'I have just noticed that this is not really Corwin! It has to be one of his shadows! It has just announced a belief in friendship, dignity, nobility of spirit, and those other things which figure prominently in popular romances! I am obviously onto something!'

The others stared at her. She laughed again, then sat down abruptly.

I heard Flora mutter 'drunk' and return to her conversation with Deirdre. Random said, 'Let's hear it for shadows,' and turned back to a discussion with Benedict and Llewella.

'See?' she said.

'What?'

'You're insubstantial,' she said, patting my knee. 'And so am I, now that I think about it. It has been a bad day, Corwin.'

'I know. I feel like hell, too. I thought I had such a fine idea for getting Brand back. Not only that, it worked. A lot of good it did him.'

'Don't overlook those bits of virtue you've acquired,' she said. 'You're not to blame for the way it turned out.'

'Thanks.'

'I believe that Julian might have had the right idea,' she said. 'I don't feel like staying awake any longer.'

I rose with her, walked her to the door.

'I'm all right,' she said. 'Really.'

'Sure?'

She nodded sharply.

'See you in the morning then.'

'I hope so,' she said. 'Now you can talk about me.'

She winked and went out.

I turned back, saw that Benedict and Llewella were approaching.

'Turning in?' I asked.

Benedict nodded.

'Might as well,' Llewella said, and she kissed me on the cheek.

'What was that for?'

'A number of things,' she said. 'Good night.'

'Good night.'

Random was crouched on the hearth, poking at the fire. Deirdre turned to him and said, 'Don't throw on more wood just for us. Flora and I are going too.'

'Okay.' He set the poker aside and rose. 'Sleep well,' he called after them.

Deirdre gave me a sleepy smile and Flora a nervous one. I added my good night and watched them leave.

'Learn anything new and useful?' Random asked.

I shrugged.

'Did you?'

'Opinions, conjectures. No new facts,' he said. 'We were trying to decide who might be next on the list.'

'And . . . ?'

'Benedict thinks it's a toss-up. You or him. Providing you are not behind it all, of course. He also thinks your buddy Ganelon ought to watch his step.'

'Ganelon . . . Yes, that's a thought – and it should have been mine. I think he is right about the toss-up, too. It may even be slightly weighted against him, since they know I'm alert because of the attempted frameup.'

'I would say that all of us are now aware that Benedict is alert himself. He managed to mention his opinion to everyone. I believe that he would welcome an attempt.'

I chuckled.

'That balances the coin again. I guess it *is* a toss-up.'

'He said that, too. Naturally, he knew I would tell you.'

'Naturally, I wish he would start talking to me again. Well . . . not much I can do about it now,' I said. 'The hell with everything. I'm going to bed.'

He nodded.

'Look under it first.'

We left the room, headed up the hall.

'Corwin, I wish you'd had the foresight to bring some coffee back with you, along with the guns,' he said. 'I could use a cup.'

'Doesn't it keep you awake?'

'No. I like a couple of cups in the evening.'

'I miss it mornings. We'll have to import some when this mess is all settled.'

'Small comfort, but a good idea. What got into Fi, anyhow?'

'She thinks Julian is our man.'

'She may be right.'

'What about Caine?'

'Supposing it was not a single individual,' he said as we mounted the stair. 'Say it was two, like Julian *and* Caine. They finally had a falling out, Caine lost, Julian disposed of him and used the death to weaken your position as well. Former friends make the worst enemies.'

'It's no use,' I said. 'I get dizzy when I start sorting the possibilities. We are either going to have to wait for something more to happen, or make something happen. Probably the latter. But not tonight—'

'Hey! Wait up!'

'Sorry.' I paused at the landing. 'Don't know what got into me. Finishing spurt, I guess.'

'Nervous energy,' he said, coming abreast of me once more. We continued on up, and I made an effort to match his pace, fighting down a desire to hurry.

'Well, sleep well,' he said finally.

'Good night, Random.'

He continued on up the stair and I headed off along the corridor toward my quarters. I was feeling jittery by then, which must be why I dropped my key.

I reached and plucked it out of the air before it had fallen very far. Simultaneously, I was struck by the impression that its motion was somewhat slower than it should have been. I inserted it in the lock and turned it.

The room was dark, but I decided against lighting a candle or an oil lamp. I had gotten used to the dark a long time ago. I locked and bolted the door. My eyes were already half adjusted to the gloom, from the dim hallway. I turned. There was some starlight leaking in about the drapes, too. I crossed the room, unfastening my collar.

He was waiting in my bed chamber, to the left of the entrance. He was perfectly positioned and he did nothing to give himself away. I walked right into it. He had the ideal station, he held the dagger ready, he had the element of total surprise going for him. By rights I should have died – not in my bed, but just there at its foot.

I caught a glimpse of the movement, realized the presence and its significance as I stepped over the threshold.

I knew that it was too late to avoid the thrust even as I raised my arm to try to block it. But one peculiarity struck me before the blade itself did: my assailant seemed to be moving too slowly. Quick, with all the tension of his wait behind it, that is how it should have been. I should never have known it was occurring until after the act, if then. I should not have had time to turn partway and swing my arm as far as I did. A ruddy haze filled my vision and I felt my forearm strike the side of the outflung arm at about the same moment as the steel touched my belly and bit. Within the redness there seemed a faint tracing of that cosmic version of the Pattern I had followed earlier in the day. As I doubled and fell, unable to think but still for a moment conscious, it came clearer, came nearer, the design. I wanted to flee, but horse my body stumbled. I was thrown.

8

Out of every life a little blood must spill. Unfortunately, it was my turn again, and it felt like more than a little. I was lying, doubled up, on my right side, both arms clutching at my middle. I was wet, and every now and then something trickled along the creases of my belly. Front, lower left, just above the beltline, I felt like a casually opened envelope. These were my first sensations as consciousness came around again. And my first thought was, 'What is he waiting for?' Obviously, the *coup de grâce* had been withheld. Why?

I opened my eyes. They had taken advantage of whatever time had elapsed to adjust themselves to the darkness. I turned my head. I did not see anyone else in the room with me. But something peculiar had occurred and I could not quite place it I closed my eyes and let my head fall back to the mattress once more.

Something was wrong, yet at the same time right . . .

The mattress . . . Yes, I was lying on my bed. I doubted my ability to have gotten there unassisted. But it would be absurd to knife me and then help me to bed.

My bed . . . It was my bed, yet it was not.

I squeezed my eyes tight. I gritted my teeth. I did not understand. I knew that my thinking could not be normal there on the fringes of shock, by blood pooling in my guts and then leaking out. I tried to force myself to think clearly. It was not easy.

My bed. Before you are fully aware of anything else, you are aware whether you are awakening in your own bed. And I was, but—

I fought down an enormous impulse to sneeze, because I felt it would tear me apart I compressed my nostrils and breathed in short gasps through my mouth. The taste, smell, and feel of dust was all about me.

The nasal assault subsided and I opened my eyes. I knew then where I was. I did not understand the why and how of it, but I had come once more to a place I had never expected to see again.

I lowered my right hand, used it to raise myself.

It was my bedroom in my house. The old one. The place which had been mine back when I was Carl Corey. I had been returned to Shadow, to that world where I had spent the years of my exile. The room was heavy with dust. The bed had not been made up since the last time I had slept in it, over half a decade before. I knew the state of the house fully, having looked in on it only a few weeks earlier.

I pushed myself further, managed to slide my feet out over the edge of the bed and down. Then I doubled up again and sat there. It was bad.

While I felt temporarily safe from further assault, I knew that I required more than safety just then. I had to have help, and I was in no position to help myself. I was not even certain how much longer I might remain conscious. So I had to get down and get out. The phone would be dead, the nearest house was not too close by. I would have to get down to the road, at least. I reflected grimly that one of my reasons for locating where I had was that it was not a well-traveled road. I enjoy my solitude, at least some of the time.

With my right hand I drew up the nearest pillow and supped off its case. I turned it inside out, tried to fold it, gave up, wadded it, slipped it beneath my shirt, and pressed it against my wound. Then I sat there, just holding it in place. It had been a major exertion and I found it painful to take too deep a breath.

After a time, though, I drew the second pillow to me, held it across my knees and let it slip out of its case. I wanted the pillowslip to wave at a passing motorist, for my garments, as usual, were dark. Before I could draw it through my belt though, I was confounded by the behavior of the pillow itself. It had not yet reached the floor. I had released it, nothing was supporting it, and it *was* moving. But it was moving quite slowly, descending with a dreamlike deliberation.

I thought of the fall of the key as I had dropped it outside my room. I thought of my unintended quickness on mounting the stair with Random. I thought of Fiona's words, and of the Jewel of Judgment, which still hung about my neck, now pulsating in time with me throbbing of my side. It might have saved my life, at least for the moment; yes, it probably had, if Fiona's notions were correct. It had probably given me a moment or so more than would otherwise have been my due when the assailant struck, letting me turn, letting me swing my arm. It might, somehow, even have been responsible for my sudden transportation. But I would have to think about such things at another time, should I succeed in maintaining a meaningful relationship with the future. For now, the jewel had to go – in case Fiona's fears concerning it were also correct – and I had to get moving.

I tucked away the second pillow cover, then tried to stand, holding on to the footboard. No good! Dizziness and too much pain. I lowered myself to the floor, afraid of passing out on the way down. I made it. I rested. Then I began to move, a slow crawl.

The front door, as I recalled, was now nailed shut. All right. Out the back, then.

I made it to the bedroom door and halted, leaning against its frame. As I rested there I removed the Jewel of Judgment from my neck and wrapped its chain about my wrist. I had to cache it someplace, and the safe in my study was too far out of the way. Besides, I believed that I was leaving a trail of blood. Anyone finding and following it might well be curious enough to investigate and spring the small thing. And I lacked the time and the energy . . .

I made my way out, around, and through. I had to rise and exert myself to get the back door open. I made the mistake of not resting first.

When I regained consciousness, I was lying across the threshold. The night was raw and clouds filled much of the sky. A mean wind rattled branches above the patio. I felt several drops of moisture on the back of my outflong hand.

I pushed up and crawled out. The snow was about two inches deep. The icy air helped to revive me. With something near panic, I realized just how foggy my mind had been during much of my course from the bedroom. It was possible that I might go under at any time.

I started immediately for the far corner of the house, deviating only to reach the compost heap, tear my way into it drop the jewel, and reposition the clump of dead grasses I had broken loose. I brushed snow over it and continued on.

Once I made it about the corner, I was shielded from the wind and headed down a slight incline. I reached the front of the house and rested once more. A car had just passed and I watched its taillights dwindle. It was the only vehicle in sight.

Icy crystals stung my face as I moved again. My knees were wet and burning cold. The front yard sloped, gently at first, then dropped sharply toward the road. There was a dip about a hundred yards to the right, where motorists generally hit their brakes. It seemed that this might give me a few moments more in the headlights of anyone coming from that direction – one of those small assurances the mind always seeks when things get serious, an aspirin for the emotions. With three rest stops, I made it down to the roadside, then over to the big rock that bore my house number. I sat on it and leaned back against the icy embankment. I hauled out the second pillow case and draped it across my knees.

I waited. I knew that my mind was fuzzy. I believe that I drifted into and out of consciousness a number of times. Whenever I caught myself at it, I attempted to impose some version of order on my thoughts, to assess what had happened in the light of everything else that had just happened, to seek other safety measures. The former effort proved too much, however. It was simply too difficult to think beyond the level of responding to circumstance. With a sort of numb enlightenment, though, it occurred to me that I was still in possession of my Trumps. I could contact someone in Amber, have him transport me back.

But who? I was not so far gone that I failed to realize I might be contacting the one responsible for my condition. Would it be better to gamble that way, or to take my chances here? Still, Random or Gérard—

I thought that I heard a car. Fault, distant . . . The wind and my pulsebeat were competing with perception, though. I turned my head. I concentrated.

There . . . Again. Yes. It was an engine. I got ready to wave the cloth.

Even then, my mind kept straying. And one thought that flitted through was that I might already be unable to muster sufficient concentration to manipulate the Trumps.

The sound grew louder. I raised the cloth. Moments later, the farthest visible point along the road to my right was touched with light. Shortly after, I saw the car at the top of the rise. I lost sight of it once more as it descended the hill. Then it climbed again and came on, snowflakes flashing through its headbeams.

I began waving as it approached the dip. The lights caught me as it came up out of it, and the driver could not have missed seeing me. He went by, though, a man in a late model sedan, a woman in the passenger seat. The woman turned and looked at me, but the driver did not even slow down.

A couple of minutes later another car came by, a bit older, a woman driving, no visible passengers. It did slow down, but only for a moment. She must not have liked my looks. She stepped on the gas and was gone in an instant.

I sagged back and rested. A prince of Amber can hardly invoke the brotherhood of roan for purposes of moral condemnation. At least not with a straight face, and it hurt too much to laugh just then.

Without strength, concentration, and some ability to move, my power over Shadow was useless. I would use it first, I decided, to get to some warm place . . . I wondered whether I could make it back up the hill, to the compost heap. I had not thought of trying to use the jewel to alter the weather. Probably I was too weak for that too, though. Probably the effort would kill me. Still . . .

I shook my head. I was drifting off, more than half a dream. I had to stay awake. Was that another car? Maybe. I tried to raise the cloth and dropped it. When I leaned forward to retrieve it, I just had to rest my head on my knees for a moment. Deirdre . . . I would call my dear sister. If anyone would help me, Deirdre would. I would get out her Trump and call her. In a minute. If only she weren't my sister . . . I had to rest. I am a knave, not a fool. Perhaps, sometimes, when I rest, I am even sorry for things. Some things. If only it were warmer . . . But it wasn't too bad, bent over this way . . . Was that a car? I wanted to raise my head but found that I could not. It would not make that much difference in being seen, though, I decided.

I felt light on my eyelids and I heard the engine. Now it was neither advancing nor retreating. Just a steady cycling of growls. Then I heard a shout. Then the click-pause-chunk of a car door opening and closing. I felt that I could open my eyes but I did not want to. I was afraid that I would look only on the dark and empty road, that the sounds would resolve into pulsebeats and wind once more. It was better to keep what I had than to gamble.

'Hey! What's the matter? You hurt?'

Footsteps . . . This was real.

I opened my eyes. I forced myself up once again.

'Corey! My God! It's *you!*'

I forced a grin, cut my nod short of a topple.

'It's me, Bill. How've you been?'

'What happened?'

'I'm hurt,' I said. 'Maybe bad. Need a doctor.'

'Can you walk if I help? Or should I carry you?'

'Let's try walking,' I said.

He got me to my feet and I leaned on him. We started for his car. I only remember the first few steps.

When that low-swinging sweet chariot turned sour and swung high once more, I tried to raise my arm, realized that it was restrained, settled for a consideration of the tube affixed thereto, and decided that I was going to live. I had sniffed hospital smells and consulted my internal clock. Having made it this far, I felt that I owed it to myself to continue. And I was warm, and as comfortable as recent history allowed. That settled, I closed my eyes, lowered my head, and went back to sleep.

Later, when I came around again, felt more fit and was spotted by a nurse, she told me that it was seven hours since I had been brought in and that a doctor would be by to talk with me shortly. She also got me a glass of water and told me that it had stopped snowing. She was curious as to what had happened to me.

I decided that it was time to start plotting my story. The simpler the better. All right. I was coming home after an extended stay abroad. I had hitchhiked out, gone on in, and been attacked by some vandal or drifter I had surprised inside. I crawled back out and sought help. Finis.

When I told it to the doctor I could not tell at first whether he believed me. He was a heavy man whose face had sagged and set long ago. His name was Bailey, Morris Bailey, and he nodded as I spoke and then asked me, 'Did you get a look at the fellow?'

I shook my head.

'It was dark,' I said.

'Did he rob you too?'

'I don't know.'

'Were you carrying a wallet?'

I decided I had better say yes to that one.

'Well, you didn't have it when you came in here, so he must have taken it.'

'Must have,' I agreed.

'Do you remember me at all?'

'Can't say that I do. Should I?'

'You seemed vaguely familiar to me when they brought you in. That was all, at first . . .'

'And . . . ?' I asked.

'What sort of garments were you wearing? They seemed something like a uniform.'

'Latest thing, Over There, these days. You were saying that I looked familiar?'

'Yes,' he agreed. 'Where is Over There, anyway? Where did you come from? Where have you been?'

'I travel a lot,' I said. 'You were going to tell me something a moment ago.'

'Yes,' he said. 'We are a small clinic, and some time ago a fast-talking salesman persuaded the directors to invest in a computerized medical-records system. If the area had developed more and we had expanded a lot, it might have been worthwhile. Neither of these things happened, though, and it is an expensive item. It even encouraged a certain laziness among the clerical help. Old files just don't get purged the way they used to, even for the emergency room. Space there for a lot of useless backlog. So, when Mr Roth gave me your name and I ran a routine check on you, I found something and I realized why you looked familiar. I had been working the emergency room that night too, around seven years ago, when you had your auto accident. I remembered working on you then – and how I thought you weren't going to make it. You surprised me, though, and you still do. I can't even find the scars that *should* be there. You did a nice job of healing up.'

'Thanks. A tribute to the physician, I'd say.'

'May I have your age, for the record?'

'Thirty-six,' I said. That's always safe.

He jotted it somewhere in the folder he held across his knees.

'You know, I would have sworn – once I got to checking you over and remembering – that that's about what you looked the last time I saw you.'

'Clean living.'

'Do you know about your blood type?'

'It's an exotic. But you can treat it as an AB Positive for all practical purposes. I can take anything, but don't give mine to anybody else.'

He nodded.

'The nature of your mishap is going to require a police report, you know.'

'I had guessed that.'

'Just thought you might want to be thinking about it.'

'Thanks,' I said. 'So you were on duty that night, and you patched me up? Interesting. What else do you recall about it?'

'What do you mean?'

'The circumstances under which I was brought in that time. My own memory is a blank from right before the accident until some time after I had been transferred up to the other place – Greenwood. Do you recall how I arrived?'

He frowned, just when I had decided he had one face for all occasions.

'We sent an ambulance,' he said.

'In response to what? Who reported the accident? How?'

'I see what you mean,' he said. 'It was the State Patrol that called for the ambulance. As I recollect, someone had seen the accident and phoned then: headquarters. They then radioed a car in the vicinity. It went to the lake, verified the report, gave you first aid, and called for the ambulance. And that was it.'

'Any record of who called in the report in the first place?'

He shrugged.

'That's not the sort of thing we keep track of,' he said.

'Didn't your insurance company investigate? Wasn't there a claim? They could probably—'

'I had to leave the country right after I recovered,' I said. 'I never pursued the matter. I suppose there would have been a police report, though.'

'Surely. But I have no idea how long they keep them around.' He chuckled. 'Unless, of course, that same salesman got to them, too . . .

It is rather late to be talking about that though, isn't it? It seems to me there is a statue of limitations on things of that sort. Your friend Roth will tell you for sure—'

'It isn't a claim that I have in mind,' I said. 'Just a desire to know what really happened. I have wondered about it on and off for a number of years now. You see, I have this touch of retrograde amnesia going.'

'Have you ever talked it over with a psychiatrist?' he said, and there was something about the way he said it that I did not like. Came one of those little flashes of insight then: Could Flora have managed to get me certified insane before my transfer to Greenwood? Was that on my record here? And was I still on escape status from that place? A lot of time had passed and I knew nothing of the legalities involved. If this was indeed the case, however, I imagined they would have no way of knowing whether I had been certified sane again in some other jurisdiction. Prudence, I guess it was, cautioned me to lean forward and glance at the doctor's wrist. I seemed possessed of a subliminal memory that he had consulted a calendar watch when taking my pulse. Yes, he had. I squinted. All right. Day and month: November 28. I did a quick calculation with my two-and-a-half-to-one conversion and had the year. It *was* seven, as he had indicated.

'No, I haven't,' I said. 'I just assumed it was organic rather than functional and wrote the time off as a loss.'

'I see,' he said. 'You use such phrases rather glibly. People who've been in therapy sometimes do that.'

'I know,' I said. 'I've read a lot about it.'

He sighed. He stood.

'Look,' he said. 'I am going to call Mr Roth and let him know you are awake. It is probably best.'

'What do you mean by that?'

'I mean that with your friend being an attorney, there might be things you want to discuss with him before you talk to the police.'

He opened the folder wherein he had somewhere jotted my age, raised his pen, furrowed his brow, and said, 'What's the date, anyway?'

I wanted my Trumps. I imagined my belongings would be in the drawer of the bedside table, but getting at it involved too much twisting and I did not want to put the strain on my sutures. It was not all that urgent, though. Eight hours' sleep in Amber would come to around twenty hours here, so everyone should still have been respectably retired back home. I wanted to get hold of Random, though, to come up with some sort of cover story for my not being there in the morning. Later.

I did not want to look suspicious at a time like this. Also, I wanted to know immediately whatever Brand had to say. I wanted to be in a position to act on it I did a quick bit of mental juggling. If I could do the worst of my recovering here in Shadow, it would mean less wasted time for me back in Amber. I would have to budget my time carefully and avoid complications on this end. I hoped that Bill would arrive soon. I was anxious to know what the picture was in his place.

Bill was a native of the area, had gone to school in Buffalo, come back, married, joined the family firm, and that was that. He had known me as a retired Army officer who sometimes traveled on vague business. We both belonged to the country club, which was where I had met him. I had known him for over a year without our exchanging more than a few words. Then one evening I happened to be next to him in the bar and it had somehow come out that he was hot on military history, particularly the Napoleonic Wars. The next thing we knew, they were closing up the place around us. We were close friends from then on, right up until the time of my difficulties. I had occasionally wondered about him since. In fact, the only thing that had prevented me from seeing him the last time I had passed through was that he would doubtless have had all sorts of questions as to what had become of me, and I had had too many things on my mind to deal with them all that gracefully and still enjoy myself. I had even thought once or twice of coming back and seeing him if I could, when everything was finally settled in Amber. Next to the fact that this was not the case, I regretted not being able to meet him in the club lounge.

He arrived within the hour, short, heavy, ruddy, a bit grayer on the sides, grinning, nodding. I had propped myself up by then, already tried a few deep breaths and decided they were premature. He clasped my hand and took the bedside chair. He had his briefcase with him.

'You scared the hell out of me last night, Carl. Thought I was seeing a ghost,' he said.

I nodded.

'A bit later, and I might have been one,' I said. 'Thanks. How have you been?

Bill sighed.

'Busy. You know. The same old stuff, only more of it.'

'And Alice?'

'She's fine. And we've got two new grandsons – Bill Jr's – twins. Wait a minute.'

He fished out his wallet and located a photo.

'Here.'

I studied it, noted the family resemblances.

'Hard to believe,' I said.

'You don't took much worse for the years.'

I chuckled and patted my abdomen.

'Subtracting that, I mean,' he said. 'Where have you been?'

'God! Where haven't I been!' I said. 'So many places I've lost count.'

He remained expressionless, caught my eyes and stared.

'Carl, what kind of trouble are you in?' he asked.

I smiled.

'If you mean am I in trouble with the law, the answer is no. My troubles actually involve another country, and I am going to have to go back there shortly.'

His face relaxed again, and there was a small glint behind his bifocals.

'Are you some sort of military adviser in that place?'

I nodded.

'Can you tell me where?'

I shook my head.

'Sorry.'

'That I can sort of understand,' he said. 'Dr Roth told me what you said had happened last night. Off the record now, was it connected with whatever you have been doing?'

I nodded again.

'That makes things a little clearer,' he said. 'Not much, but enough. I won't even ask you which agency, or even if there is one. I have always known you to be a gentleman, and a rational one at that. That was why I grew curious at the time of your disappearance and did some investigating. I felt a bit officious and self-conscious about it. But your civil status was quite puzzling, and I wanted to know what had happened. Mainly, because I was concerned about you. I hope that doesn't disturb you.'

'Disturb me?' I said. 'There aren't that many people who care what happens to me. I'm grateful. Also, curious what you discovered. I never had the time to look into it, you know, to straighten things out. How about telling me what you learned?'

He opened the briefcase and withdrew a manila folder. Spreading it across his knees, he shuffled out several sheets of yellow paper covered with neat handwriting. Raising the first of these, he regarded it a moment, then said, 'After you escaped from the hospital in Albany and had your accident, Brandon apparently dropped out of the picture and—'

'Stop!' I said, raising my hand, trying to sit up.

'What?' he asked.

'You have the order wrong, also the place,' I said. 'First came the accident, and Greenwood is not in Albany.'

'I know,' he said. 'I was referring to the Porter Sanitarium, where you spent two days and then escaped. You had your accident that same day, and you were brought here as a result of it. Then your sister Evelyn entered the picture. She had you transferred to Greenwood, where you spent a couple of weeks before departing on your own motion once again. Right?'

'Partly,' I said. 'Namely, the last part. As I was telling the doctor earlier, my memory is shot for a couple of days prior to the accident. This business about a place in Albany *does* sort of seem to ring a bell, but only very faintly. Do you have more on it?'

'Oh yes,' he said. 'It may even have something to do with the state of your memory. You were committed on a bum order—'

'By whom?'

He shook the paper and peered.

' "Brother, Brandon Corey; attendant physician, Hillary B. Rand, psychiatrist",' he read. 'Hear any more bells?'

'Quite possibly,' I said. 'Go ahead.'

'Well, an order got signed on that basis,' he said. 'You were duly certified, taken into custody, and transported. Then, concerning your memory . . .'

'Yes?'

'I don't know that much about the practice and its effects on the memory, but you were subjected to electroshock therapy while you were at Porter. Then, as I said, the record indicates that you escaped after the second day. You apparently recovered your car from some unspecified locale and were heading back this way when you had the accident.'

'That seems right,' I said. 'It does.' For a moment when he had begun talking, I had had a wild vision of having been returned to the wrong shadow – one where everything was similar, but not congruent. Now, though, I did not believe this to be the case. I was responding to this story on some level.

'Now, about that order,' he said. 'It was based on false evidence, but there was no way of the court's knowing it at the time. The real Dr Rand was in England when everything happened, and when I contacted him later he had never heard of you. His office had been broken into while he was away, though. Also, peculiarly, his middle initial is not B. He had never heard of Brandon Corey either.'

'What did become of Brandon?'

'He simply vanished. Several attempts were made to contact him at the time of your escape from Porter, but he could not be found. Then you had the accident, were brought here and treated. At that time, a woman named Evelyn Flaumel, who represented herself as your sister, contacted this place, told them you had been probated and that the family wanted you transferred to Greenwood. In the absence of Brandon, who had been appointed your guardian, her instructions were followed, as the only available next of kin. That was how it came about that you were sent to the other place. You escaped again, a couple of weeks later, and that is where my chronology ends.'

'Then what is my legal status right now?' asked.

'Oh, you've been made whole,' he said. 'Dr Rand went down after I talked with him and gave the court an affidavit reciting these facts. The order was vacated.'

'Then why is the doctor here acting as if I might be a psycho case?'

'Oh my! That *is* a thought. It hadn't occurred to me. All their records here would show is that one time you apparently were. I had better see him on the way out I have a copy of the journal entry in here, too. I can show it to him.'

'How long was it after I left Greenwood that things were set right with the court?'

'The following month,' he said. 'It was several weeks before I could bring myself to get nosy.'

'You couldn't know how happy I am that you did,' I said. 'And you have given me several pieces of information I think are going to prove extremely important.'

'It is nice to be able to help a friend sometime,' he said, closing the folder and replacing it in his briefcase. 'One thing . . . When this is all over – whatever you are doing – if you are permitted to talk about it, I would like to hear the story.'

'I can't promise,' I said.

'I know. Just thought I'd mention it. By the way, what do you want to do about the house?'

'Mine? Do I still hold title to it?'

'Yes, but it will probably be sold this year for back taxes if you don't do anything about it.'

'I'm surprised that hasn't already happened.'

'You gave the bank power of attorney for paying your bills.'

'I never thought of that. I'd just set it up for utilities and my charge accounts. Stuff like that.'

'Well, the account is nearly empty now,' he said. 'I was talking to McNally over there the other day. That means the house will go next year if you don't do anything.'

'I've got no use for it now,' I said. 'They can do whatever they want with it.'

'Then you might as well sell it and realize what you can.'

'I won't be around that long.'

'I could handle it for you. Send the money wherever you want.'

'All right,' I said. 'I'll sign anything necessary. Pay my hospital bill out of it and keep the rest.'

'I couldn't do that.'

I shrugged.

'Do whatever you think best, but be sure and take a good fee.'

'I'll put the balance in your account.'

'All right. Thanks. By the way, before I forget, would you look in the drawer of that table and see if there is a deck of cards there? I can't reach it yet, and I'll be wanting them later.'

'Surely.'

He readied over, opened it.

'A big brown envelope,' he said. 'Kind of bulgy. They probably put whatever was in your pockets in it.'

'Open it.'

'Yes, here's a pack of cards,' he said, reaching inside. 'Say! That's a beautiful case! May I?'

'I—' What could I say?

He slipped the case.

'Lovely . . .' he murmured. 'Some kind of tarots . . . Are they antique?'

'Yes.'

'Cold as ice . . . I never saw anything like these. Say, that's you! Dressed up like some kind of knight! What's their purpose?'

'A very complicated game,' I said.

'How could that be you if they are antique?'

'I didn't say it was me. You did.'

'Yes, so I did. Ancestor?'

'Sort of.'

'Now that's a good-looking gal! But so is the redhead . . .'

'I think . . .'

He squared the deck and replaced it in the case. He passed it to me.

'Nice unicorn, too,' he added. 'I shouldn't have looked at them, should I?'

'That's an right.'

He sighed and leaned back in the chair, clasping his hands behind his head.

'I couldn't help it,' he said. 'It is just that there is something very strange about you, Carl, beyond any hush-hush work you may be doing – and mysteries intrigue me. I've never been this close to a real puzzler before.'

'Because you just slipped yourself a cold deck of tarots?' I asked.

'No, that just adds atmosphere,' he said. 'While what you have been doing all these years is admittedly none of my business, there is one recent incident I am unable to comprehend.'

'What is that?'

'After I brought you here and took Alice home last night, I went back to your place, hoping to get some sort of idea as to what had happened. The snow had let up by then, though it started in again later, and your track was still clearly visible, going around the house and down the front yard.'

I nodded.

'But there were no tracks going in – nothing to indicate your arrival. And for that matter, there were no other tracks departing – nothing to show the flight of your assailant.'

I chuckled.

'You think the wound was self-inflicted?'

'No, of course not. There wasn't even a weapon in sight I followed the bloodstains back to the bedroom, to your bed. I had only my flashlight to see by, of course, but what I saw gave me an eerie feeling. It seemed as if you had just suddenly appeared there on the bed, bleeding, and then gotten up and made your way out.'

'Impossible, of course.'

'I wonder about the lack of tracks, though.'

'The wind must have blown snow over them.'

'And not the others?' He shook his head. 'No, I don't think so. I just want to go on the record as interested in the answer to that one too, if you ever do want to tell me about things.'

'I will remember.' I said.

'Yes,' he said. 'But I wonder . . . I've a peculiar feeling that I may never see you again. It is as if I were one of those minor characters in a melodrama who gets shuffled offstage without ever learning how things turn out.'

'I can appreciate the feeling,' I said. 'My own role sometimes makes me want to strangle the author. But look at it this way: inside stories seldom live up to one's expectations. Usually they are grubby little things, reducing down to the basest of motives when all is known. Conjectures and illusions are often the better possessions.'

He smiled.

'You talk the same as always,' he said, 'yet I have known occasions when you have been tempted to virtue. Several of them . . .'

'How did we get from the footprints to me?' I said. 'I was about to tell you that I suddenly recalled having approached the house by exactly the same route as I left it. My departure obviously obliterated the signs of my arrival.'

'Not bad,' he said. 'And your attacker followed the same route?'

'Must have.'

'Pretty good,' he acknowledged. 'You know how to raise a reasonable doubt. But I still feel that the preponderance of evidence indicates the weird.'

'Weird? No. Peculiar, perhaps. A matter of interpretation.'

'Or semantics. Have you read the police report on your accident?'

'No. Have you?'

'Uh-huh. What if *it* was more than peculiar? Then will you grant me my word, as I used it: "weird"?'

'Very well.'

'. . . And answer one question?'

'I don't know . . .'

'A simple yes-or-no question. That's all.'

'Okay, it's a deal. What did it say?'

'It said that they received report of the accident and a patrol car proceeded to the scene. There they encountered a strangely garbed man in the process of giving you first aid. He stated that he had pulled you from the wrecked car in the lake. This seemed believable in that he was also soaking wet. Average height, light build, red hair. He had on a green outfit that one of the officers said looked lite something out of a Robin Hood movie. He refused to identify himself, to accompany them or to give a statement of any sort. When they insisted that he do so, he whistled and a white horse came trotting up. He leaped onto its back and rode off. He was not seen again.'

I laughed. It hurt, but I couldn't help it.

'I'll be damned!' I said. 'Things are starting to make sense.'

Bill just stared at me for a moment. Then, 'Really?' he said.

'Yes, I think so. It may well have been worth getting stabbed and coming back for what I learned today.'

'You put the two in peculiar order,' he said, massaging his chin.

'Yes, I do. But I am beginning to see some order where I had seen nothing before. This one may have been worth the price of admission, all unintended.'

'All because of a guy on a white horse?'

'Partly, partly . . . Bill, I am going to be leaving here soon.'

'You are not going anywhere for a while.'

'Just the same – those papers you mentioned . . . I think I had better get them signed today.'

'All right. I'll get them over this afternoon. But I don't want you doing anything foolish.'

'I grow more cautious by the moment,' I said, 'believe me.'

'I hope so,' he said, snapping his briefcase shut and rising. 'Well, get your rest. I'll clear things up with the doctor and have those papers sent over today.'

'Thanks again.'

I shook his hand.

'By the way,' he said, 'you did agree to answer a question.'

'I did, didn't I? What is it?'

'Are you human?' he asked, still gripping my hand, no special expression on his face.

I started in on a grin, then threw it away.

'I don't know. I – I like to think so. But I don't really— Of course I am! That's a silly . . . Oh hell! You really mean it, don't you? And I said I'd be honest . . .' I chewed my lip and thought for a moment. Then, 'I don't think so,' I said.

'Neither do I,' he said, and he smiled. 'It doesn't make any real difference to me, but I thought it might to you – to know that someone knows you are different and doesn't care.'

'I'll remember that, too,' I said.

'Well . . . see you around.'

'Right.'

9

It was just after the state patrolman left . . . Late afternoon. I was lying there feeling better, and feeling better that I felt better. Lying there, reflecting on the hazards involved in living in Amber. Brand and I were both laid up by means of the family's favorite weapon. I wondered who had gotten it worse. Probably he had. It might have reached his kidney, and he was in poor condition to begin with.

I had stumbled across the room and back again twice before Bill's clerk came over with the papers for me to sign. It was necessary that I know my limits. It always is. Since I tended to heal several times faster than those about me in that shadow, I felt that I ought to be able to stand and walk some, to perform in the same fashion as one of these after, say, a day and a half, maybe two. I established that I could. It did hurt, and I was dizzy the first time, less dizzy the second. That was something, anyway. So I lay there feeling better.

I had fanned the Trumps dozens of times, dealt private solitaires, read ambiguous fortunes among familiar faces. And each time I had restrained myself, suppressing my desire to contact Random, to tell him what had happened, to inquire after new developments. Later, I kept telling myself. Each additional hour they sleep is two and a half for you, here. Each two and a half for you, here, is the equivalent of seven or eight for some lesser mortal, here. Abide. Think, Regenerate.

And so it came to pass that a little after dinnertime, just as the sky was darkening again, I was beaten to the punch. I had already told a well-starched young member of the State Patrol everything that I was going to tell him. I have no idea whether he believed me, but he was polite and he did not stay long. In fact, it was only moments after he left that things began to happen.

Lying there, feeling better, I was waiting for Dr Bailey to stop by and check whether I was still oriented. Lying there, assessing all of the things Bill had told me, trying to fit them together with other things that I knew or had guessed at . . .

Contact! I had been anticipated. Someone in Amber was an early riser.

'Corwin!'

It was Random, agitated.

'Corwin! Get up! Open the door! Brand's come around, and he's asking for you.'

'Have you been pounding on that door, trying to get me up?'

'That's right.'

'Are you alone?'

'Yes.'

'Good. I am not inside. You have reached me in Shadow.'

'I do not understand.'

'Neither do I. I am hurt, but I will live. I will give you the story later. Tell me about Brand.'

'He woke up just a little while ago. Told Gérard he had to talk to you right away. Gérard rang up a servant, sent him to your room. When he couldn't rouse you, he came to me. I just sent him back to tell Gérard I'd be bringing you along shortly.'

'I see,' I said, stretching slowly and sitting up. 'Get in some place where you can't be seen, and I'll come through. I will need a robe or something. I am missing some clothes.'

'It would probably be best if I went back to my rooms, then.'

'Okay. Go ahead.'

'A minute, then.'

And silence.

I moved my legs slowly. I sat on the edge of the bed. I gathered up my Trumps and replaced them in their case. I felt it important that I mask my injury back in Amber. Even in normal times one never advertises one's vulnerability.

I took a deep breath and stood, holding on to the bed frame. My practice had paid off. I breathed normally and relaxed my grip. Not bad, if I moved slowly, if I did not exert myself beyond the barest essentials required for appearances' sake . . . I might be able to carry it until my strength really returned.

Just then I heard a footfall, and a friendly nurse was framed in the doorway, crisp, symmetrical, differing from a snowflake mainly in that they are all of them alike.

'Get back in that bed, Mr Corey! You are not supposed to be up!'

'Madam,' I said, 'it is quite necessary that I be up. I have to go.'

'You could have rung for a pan,' she said, entering the room and advancing.

I gave my head a weary shake just as Random's presence reached me once more. I wondered how she would report this one – and if she would mention my prismatic afterimage as I trumped out. Another entry, I suppose, for the growing record of folklore I tend to leave behind.

'Think of it this way, my dear,' I told her. 'Ours has been a purely physical relationship all along. There will be others . . . many others. *Adieu!*'

I bowed and blew her a kiss as I stepped forward into Amber, leaving her to clutch at rainbows as I caught hold of Random's shoulder and staggered.

'Corwin! What the hell—'

'If blood be the price of admiralty, I've just bought me a naval commission,' I said. 'Give me something to wear.'

He draped a long, heavy cloak about my shoulders and I fumbled to clasp it at my throat.

'All set,' I said. 'Take me to him.'

He led me out the door, into the hall, toward the stair. I leaned on him heavily as we went.

'How bad is it?' he asked me.

'Knife,' I said, and laid my hand on the spot, 'Someone attacked me in my room last night.'

'Who?'

'Well, it couldn't have been you, because I had just left you,' I said, 'and Gérard was up in the library with Brand. Subtract the three of you from the rest and start guessing. That is the best—'

'Julian,' he said.

'His stock is definitely bearish,' I said. 'Fiona was just running him down for me the other night, and of course it is no secret that he is not my favorite.'

'Corwin, he's gone. He cut out during the night. The servant who came to get me told me that Julian had departed. What does that took like to you?'

We reached the stair. I kept one hand on Random and the other on the banister. I called a halt at the first landing and rested there briefly.

'I don't know,' I said. 'It can sometimes be just as bad to extend the benefit of the doubt too far as not to grant it at all. But it does occur to me that if he thought he had disposed of me, he would look a lot better by staying here and acting surprised to learn of it than by getting the hell out. That *does* look suspicious. I am inclined to think be might have departed because he was afraid of what Brand would have to say when be came around.'

'But you lived, Corwin. You got away from whoever attacked you, and he could not be certain that he had done you in. If it were me, I would be worlds away by now.'

'There is that,' I acknowledged, and we started on down again. 'Yes, you might well be right Let us leave it academic for now. And no one is to know I have been injured.'

He nodded.

'As you say. Silence beats a chamber pot in Amber.'

'How's that?'

' 'Tis gilt, m'lord, like a royal flush.'

'Your wit pains both wounded and unwounded parts, Random. Spend some figuring how the assailant entered my room.'

'Your panel?'

'It secures from the inside. I keep it that way now. And the door's lock is a new one. Tricky.'

'All right, I have it. My answer requires that it be a family member, too.'

'Tell me.'

'Someone was willing to psyche himself up and tough it through the Pattern again for a shot at you. He went below, walked it, projected himself into your room, and attacked you.'

'That would be perfect except for one thing. We all left at pretty much the same time. The attack did not occur later on in the evening. It happened immediately on my entering. I do not believe there was sufficient time for one of us to get down to the chamber, let alone negotiate the Pattern. The attacker was already waiting. So if it was one of us, he had gotten in by some other means.'

463

'Then he picked your lock, tricks and all.'

'Possibly,' I said as we reached the landing and continued on. 'We will rest at the corner so that I can go into the library unassisted.'

'Sure thing.'

We did that. I composed myself, drew the cloak completely about me, squared my shoulders, advanced, and knocked on the door.

'Just a minute.' Gérard's voice.

Footsteps approaching the door . . .

'Who is it?'

'Corwin,' I said. 'Random's with me.'

I heard him call back, 'You want Random, too?' and I heard a soft 'No,' in reply.

The door opened.

'Just you, Corwin,' Gérard said.

I nodded and turned to Random.

'Later,' I told him.

He returned my nod and headed back in the direction from which we had come. I entered the library.

'Open your cloak, Corwin,' Gérard ordered.

'That is not necessary,' Brand said, and I looked over and saw that he was propped up by a number of cushions and showing a yellow-toothed smile.

'Sorry, I am not as trusting as Brand,' Gérard said, 'and I will not have my work wasted. Let's have a look.'

'I said that it is not necessary,' Brand repeated. 'He is not the one who stabbed me.'

Gérard turned quickly.

'How do you know he isn't?' he asked.

'Because I know who did, of course. Don't be an ass, Gérard, I wouldn't have asked for him if I had reason to fear him.'

'You were unconscious when I brought you through. You couldn't know who did it.'

'Are you certain of that?'

'Well . . . Why didn't you tell me, then?'

'I have my reasons, and they are valid ones. I want to speak with Corwin alone now.'

Gérard lowered his head.

'You had better not be delirious,' he said. He stepped to the door, opened it again. 'I'll be within hailing distance,' he added, and closed it behind him.

I moved nearer. Brand reached up and I clasped his hand.

'Good to see that you made it back,' he said.

'Vice versa,' I said, and then I took Gérard's chair, trying not to collapse into it.

'How do you feel now?' I asked.

'Rotten, in one sense. But better than I have in years, in another. It's all relative.'

'Most things are.'

'Not in Amber.'

I sighed.

'All right. I wasn't getting technical. What the hell happened?'

His gaze was most intense. He was studying me, looking for something. What? Knowledge, I'd guess. Or, more correctly, ignorance. Negatives being harder to gauge, his mind had to be moving fast, must have been from the moment he had come around. Knowing him, he was more interested in what I did not know than in what I knew. He wasn't going to give away anything if he could help it. He wanted to know the minimum enlightenment he need shed in order to get what he wanted. Not a watt more would he willingly spend. For this was his way, and of course he wanted something. Unless . . . More strongly in recent years than ever before I have tried to convince myself that people do change, that the passage of time does not serve merely to accentuate that which is already there, that qualitative changes do sometimes occur in people because of things they have done, seen, thought, and felt. It would provide some small solace in times such as these when everything else seems to be going wrong, not to mention pepping up my mundane philosophy no end. And Brand had probably been responsible for saving my life and my memory, whatever his reasons. Very well. I resolved to give him the doubt's benefit without exposing my back. A small concession here, my move against the simple psychology of humors which generally governs the openings of our games.

'Things are never what they seem, Corwin,' he began. 'Your friend today is your enemy tomorrow, and—'

'Cut it out!' I said. 'Cards-on-the-table time is here. I do appreciate what Brandon Corey did for me, and it was my idea to try the trick we used to locate you and bring you back.'

He nodded.

'I fancy there were good reasons for a recrudescence of fraternal sentiment after all this time.'

'I might suppose you had additional reasons for helping me, also.'

He smiled again, raised his right hand and lowered it.

'Then we are either even or in each other's debt, depending upon how one looks at these things. As it would seem we now have need of each other, it would be well to regard ourselves in the most flattering light.'

'You are stalling, Brand. You are trying to psych me. You are also spoiling my day's effort at idealism. You got me out of bed to tell me something. Be my guest.'

'Same old Corwin,' he said, chuckling. Then he looked away. 'Or are you? I wonder . . . Did it change you, do you think? Living all that while in Shadow? Not knowing who you really were? Being a part of something else?'

'Maybe,' I said. 'I don't know. Yes, I guess I did. I know that it shortened my temper when it comes to family politics.'

'Plain-speaking, blunt, plain-dealing? You miss some of the fun that way. But then there is a value to such novelty. Keep everyone unbalanced with it . . . revert when they least expect it . . . Yes, it might prove valuable. Refreshing, too. All right! Panic not. Thus end my preliminaries. All pleasantries are now exchanged. I'll bare the basics, bridle the beast Unreason, and wrest from murky mystery the pearl of sweetest sense. But one thing first, if you would. Have you anything smokable with you? It has been a number of years, and I'd like some foul weed or other – to celebrate my homecoming.'

I started to say no. But I was sure there were some cigarettes in the desk, left there by me. I did not really want the exercise, but, 'Just a minute,' I said.

I tried to make my movements look casual rather than stiff as I rose and crossed the room. I attempted to make it seem as if I were resting my hand naturally upon the desktop as I rummaged through it, rather than leaning as heavily as I was. I masked my movements with my body and my cloak as much as possible.

I located the package and returned as I had come, stopping to light a pair at the hearth. Brand was slow in taking his from me.

'Your hand is rather shaky,' he said. 'What is the matter?'

'Too much partying last night,' I said, returning to my chair.

'I hadn't thought of that. I imagine there would have been, wouldn't there? Of course. Everyone together in one room . . . Unexpected success in finding me, bringing me back . . . A desperate move on the part of a very nervous, very guilty person . . . Half success there. Me injured and mum, but for how long? Then—'

'You said that you knew who did it. Were you kidding?'

'No, I was not.'

'Who then?'

'In its place, dear brother. In its place. Sequence and order, time and stress – they are most important in this matter. Allow me to savor the drama of the event in safe retrospect. I see me punctured and all of you gathered round. Ah! what would I not give to witness that tableau! Could you possibly describe for me the expression on each face?'

'I'm afraid their faces were my least concern at the time.'

He sighed and blew smoke.

'Ah, that is good,' he said. 'Never mind, I can see their faces. I've a vivid imagination, you know. Shock, distress, puzzlement – shading over into suspicion, fear. Then all of you departed, I'm told, and gentle Gérard my nursemaid here.' He paused, stared into the smoke, and for a moment the note of mockery was absent. 'He is the only decent one among us, you know.'

'He's high on my list,' I said.

'He took good care of me. He's always looked out for the rest of us.' He chuckled suddenly. 'Frankly, I can't see why he bothers. As I was musing, though – prompted by your recuperating self – you must have adjourned to talk things over. There is another party I'm sad I missed. All those emotions and suspicions and lies bouncing off one another – and no one wanting to be the first to say good night. It must have gotten shrill after a time. Everyone on his own best behavior, with an eye out to blacken the rest. Attempts to intimidate the one guilty person. Perhaps a few stones shied at scapegoats. But, all in all, nothing much really accomplished. Am I right?'

I nodded, appreciative of the way his mind worked, and resigned to letting him tell it his way.

'You know you're right,' I said.

He gave me a sharp look at that, then went on. 'But everyone did finally go off, to lie awake worrying, or to get together with an accomplice, to scheme. There were hidden turmoils in the night. It is flattering to know that my well-being was on everyone's mind. Some, of course, were for it, others against. And in the midst of it all, I rallied – nay, flourished – not wishing to disappoint my supporters. Gérard spent a long while bringing me up to date on recent history. When I had enough of this, I sent for you.'

'In case you haven't noticed, I'm here. What did you want to tell me?'

'Patience, brother! Patience! Consider all the years you spent in Shadow, not even remembering – this.' He gestured widely with his cigarette. 'Consider all that time you waited, unknowing, until I succeeded in locating you and tried to remedy your plight. Surely a few moments now are not so priceless by contrast.'

'I was told that you had sought me,' I said. 'I wondered at that, for we had not exactly parted on the best of terms the last time we were together.'

He nodded.

'I cannot deny it,' he said. 'But I always get over such things, eventually.'

I snorted.

'I have been deciding how much to tell you, and what you would believe,' he continued. 'I doubted you would accept it if I had simply come out and said that, save for a few small items, my present motives are almost entirely altruistic.'

I snorted again.

'But this is true,' he went on, 'and to lay your suspicions, I add that it is because I have small choice in it. Beginnings are always difficult. Wherever I begin, something preceded it. You were gone for so long. If one must name a single thing, however, then let it be the throne. There. I have said it. We had thought of a way to take it, you see. This was just after your disappearance, and in some ways, I suppose, prompted by it. Dad suspected Eric of having slain you. But there was no evidence. We worked on this feeling, though – a word here and there, every now and then. Years passed, with you unreachable by any means, and it seemed more and more likely that you were indeed dead. Dad looked upon Eric with growing disfavor. Then, one night, pursuant to a discussion I had begun on a totally neutral matter – most of us present at the table – he said that no fratricide would ever take the throne, and he was looking at Eric as he said it. You know how his eyes could get. Eric grew bright as a sunset and could not swallow for a long while. But then Dad took things much further than any of us had anticipated or desired. In fairness to you, I do not know whether he spoke solely to vent his feelings, or whether he actually meant what he said. But he told us that he had more than half decided upon you as his successor, so that he took whatever misadventure had befallen you quite personally. He would not have spoken of it, but that he was convinced as to your passing. In the months that followed, we reared you a cenotaph to give some solid form to this conclusion, and we made certain that no one forgot Dad's feelings toward Eric. All along, after yourself, Eric was the one we felt had to be gotten around to reach the throne.'

'We! Who were the others?'

'Patience, Corwin. Sequence and order, time and stress! Accent, emphasis . . . listen.' He took another cigarette, chain-lit it from the butt, stabbed the air with its burning tip.

'The next step required that we get Dad out of Amber. This was the most crucial and dangerous part of it, and it was here that we disagreed. I did not like the idea of an alliance with a power I did not fully understand, especially one that gave them some hold on us. Using shadows is one thing; allowing them to use you is ill-considered, whatever the circumstances. I argued against it, but the majority had it otherwise.' He smiled. 'Two to one. Yes, there were three of us. We went ahead then. The trap was set and Dad went after the bait—'

'Is he still living?' I asked.

'I do not know,' Brand said. 'Things went wrong afterward, and then I'd troubles of my own to concern me. After Dad's departure, though, our next move was to consolidate our position while waiting a respectable period of time for a presumption of death to seem warranted. Ideally, all that we required was the co-operation of one person. Either Caine or Julian – it did not matter which. You see,

Bleys had already gone off into Shadow and was in the process of putting together a large military force—'

'Bleys! He was one of you?'

'Indeed. We intended him for the throne – with sufficient strings on him, of course, so that it would have amounted to a *de facto* triumvirate. So, he went off to assemble troops, as I was saying. We hoped for a bloodless takeover, but we had to be ready in the event that words proved insufficient to will our case. If Julian gave us the land route in, or Caine the waves, we could have transported the troops with dispatch and held the day by force of arms, should that have proven necessary. Unfortunately, I chose the wrong man. In my estimate, Caine was Julian's superior in matters of corruption. So, with measured delicacy I sounded him on the matter. He seemed willing to go along with things, at first. But he either reconsidered subsequently or deceived me quite skillfully from the beginning. Naturally, I prefer to believe that it was the former. Whatever, at some point he came to the conclusion that he stood to benefit more by supporting a rival claimant. To wit, Eric. Now Eric's hopes had been somewhat dashed by Dad's attitude toward him – but Dad was gone, and our intended move gave Eric the chance to act as defender of the throne. Unfortunately for us, such a position would also put him but a step away from the throne itself. To make matters darker, Julian went along with Caine in pledging the loyalty of his troops to Eric, as defender. Thus was the other trio formed. So Eric took a public oath to defend the throne, and the lines were thereby drawn. I was naturally in a somewhat embarrassing position at this time. I bore the brunt of their animosity, as they did not know who my fellows were. Yet they could not imprison or torture me, for I would immediately be trumped out of their hands. And if they were to kill me, they realized there might well be a reprisal by parties unknown. So it had to stand as a stalemate for a time. They also saw that I could no longer move directly against them. They kept me under heavy surveillance. So a more devious route was charted. Again I disagreed and again I lost, two to one. We were to employ the same forces we had called upon to deal with Dad, this time for purposes of discrediting Eric. If the job of defending Amber, so confidently assumed, were to prove too much for him and Bleys then came onto the scene and handled the situation with dispatch, why Bleys would even have popular support as he moved on to assume the role of defender himself and – after a fit period of time – suffered the thrusting of sovereignty upon him, for the good of Amber.'

'Question,' I interrupted. 'What about Benedict? I know he was off being discontent in his Avalon, but if something really threatened Amber . . .'

'Yes,' he said, nodding, 'and for that reason, a part of our deal was to involve Benedict with a number of problems of his own.'

I thought of the harassment of Benedict's Avalon by the hellmaids. I thought of the stump of his right arm. I opened my mouth to speak again, but Brand raised his hand.

'Let me finish in my own fashion, Corwin. I am not unmindful of your thought processes as you speak. I feel the pain in your side, twin to my own. Yes, I know these things and many more.' His eyes burned strangely as he took another cigarette into his hand and it lit of its own accord. He drew heavily upon it and spoke as he exhaled. 'I broke with the others over this decision. I saw it as involving too great a peril, as placing Amber herself in jeopardy. Broke with them . . .' He watched the smoke for several moments before he continued. 'But things were too far advanced that I might simply walk away. I had to oppose them, in order to defend myself as well as Amber. It was too late to swing over to Eric's side. He would not have protected me if he could have – and besides, I was certain he was going to lose. It was then that I decided to employ certain new abilities I had acquired. I had often wondered at the strange relationship between Eric and Flora, off on that shadow Earth she pretended so to enjoy. I had had a slight suspicion that there was something about that place which concerned him, and that she might be his agent there. While I could not get close enough to him to achieve any satisfaction on this count, I felt confident that it would not take too much in the way of investigation, direct and otherwise, to learn what Flora was about. And so I did. Then suddenly the pace accelerated. My own party was concerned as to my whereabouts. Then when I picked you up and shocked back a few memories, Eric learned from Flora that something was suddenly quite amiss. Consequently, both sides were soon looking for me. I had decided that your return would throw everyone's plans out the window and get me out of the pocket I was in long enough to come up with an alternative to the way things were going.

Eric's claim would be clouded once again, you would have had supporters of your own, my party would have lost the purpose for its entire maneuver and I had assumed you would not be ungrateful to me for my part in things. Then you went and escaped from Porter, and things really got complicated. All of us were looking for you, as I later learned, for different reasons. But my former associates had something very extra going for them. They learned what was happening, located you, and got there first. Obviously, there was a very simple way to preserve the status quo, where they would continue to hold the edge. Bleys fired the shots that put you and your car into the lake. I arrived just as this was occurring. He departed almost immediately, for it looked as if he had done a thorough job. I dragged you out, though, and there was enough left to start treating. It was frustrating now that I think back on it, not knowing whether the treatment had really been effective, whether you would awaken as Corwin or Corey. It was frustrating afterward, also, still not knowing . . . I hellrode out when help arrived. My associates caught up with me somewhat later and put me where you found me. Do you know the rest of the story?'

'Not all of it.'

'Then stop me whenever we've caught up on this. I only obtained it later, myself. Eric's crowd learned of the accident, got your location, and had you transferred to a private place, where you could be better protected, and kept you heavily sedated, so that *they* could be protected.'

'Why should Eric protect me, especially if my presence was going to wreck his plans?'

'By then seven of us knew you were still living. That was too many. It was simply too late to do what he would have liked to do. He was still trying to live down Dad's words. If anything had happened to you once you were in his power, it would have blocked his movement to the throne. If Benedict ever got word of it, or Gérard . . . No, he'd not have made it. Afterward, yes. Before, no. What happened was that general knowledge of the fact of your existence forced his hand. He scheduled his coronation and resolved to keep you out of the way until it had occurred. An extremely premature bit of business, not that I see he had much of a choice. I guess you know what happened after that, since it happened to you.'

'I fell in with Bleys, just as he was making his move. Not too fortunate.'

He shrugged.

'Oh, it might have been – if you had won, and if you had been able to do something about Bleys. You hadn't a chance, though, not really. My grasp of their motivations begins to dissolve at this point, but I believe that that entire assault really constituted some sort of feint.'

'Why?'

'As I said, I do not know. But they already had Eric just abont where they wanted him. It should not have been necessary to call that attack.'

I shook my head. Too much, too fast . . . Many of the facts sounded true, once I subtracted the narrator's bias. But still . . .

'I don't know . . .' I began.

'Of course,' he said. 'But if you ask me I will tell you.'

'Who was the third member of your group?'

'The same person who stabbed me, of course. Would you care to venture a guess?'

'Just tell me.'

'Fiona. The whole thing was her idea.'

'Why didn't you tell me that right away?'

'Because you would not have sat still long enough to hear the rest of what I had to say. You would have dashed off to put her under restraint, discovered that she was gone, roused all the others, started an investigation, and wasted a lot of valuable time. You still may, but it at least provided me with your attention for a sufficient time for me to convince you that I know what I am about. Now, when I tell you that time is essential and that you must hear the rest of what I have to say as soon as possible – if Amber is to have any chance at all – you might listen rather than chase a crazy lady.'

I had already half risen from my chair.

'I shouldn't go after her?' I said.

'The hell with her, for now. You've got bigger problems. You had better sit down again.'

So I did.

10

A raft of moonbeams . . . the ghostly torchlight, like fires in black-and-white films . . . stars . . . a few fine filaments of mist . . .

I leaned upon the rail, I looked across the world . . . Utter silence held the night, the dream-drenched city, the entire universe from here. Distant things – the sea, Amber, Arden, Garnath, the Lighthouse of Cabra, the Grove of the Unicorn, my tomb atop Kolvir . . . Silent, far below, yet clear, distinct . . . A god's eye view, I'd say, or that of a soul cut loose and drifting high . . . In the middle of the night . . .

I had come to the place where the ghosts play at being ghosts, where the omens, portents, signs, and animate desires thread the nightly avenues and palace high halls of Amber in the sky, Tir-na Nog'th . . .

Turning, my back to the rail and dayworld's vestiges below, I regarded the avenues and dark terraces, the halls of the lords, the quarters of the low . . . The moonlight is intense in Tir-na Nog'th, silvers over the facing sides of all our imaged places . . . Stick in hand, I passed forward, and the strangelings moved about me, appeared at windows, on balconies, on benches, at gates . . . Unseen I passed, for truly put, in this place I was the ghost to whatever their substance . . .

Silence and silver . . . Only the tapping of my stick, and that mostly muted . . . More mists adrift toward the heart of things . . . The palace a white bonfire of it . . . Dew, like drops of mercury on the finely sanded petals and stems in the gardens by the walks . . . The passing moon as painful to the eye as the sun at midday, the stars outshone, dimmed by it . . . Silver and silence . . . The shine . . .

I had not planned on coming, for its omens – if that they truly be – are deceitful, its similarities to the lives and places below unsettling, its spectacle often disconcerting. Still, I had come . . . A part of my bargain with time . . .

After I had left Brand to continue his recovery in the keeping of

Gérard, I had realized that I required additional rest myself and sought to obtain it without betraying my disability. Fiona was indeed flown, and neither she nor Julian could be reached by means of the Trumps. Had I told Benedict and Gérard what Brand had told me, I was certain that they would have insisted we begin efforts at tracking her down, at tracking both of them. I was equally certain that such efforts would prove useless.

I had sent for Random and Ganelon and retired to my quarters, giving out that I intended to pass the day in rest and quiet thought in anticipation of spending the night in Tir-na Nog'th – reasonable behavior for any Amberite with a serious problem. I did not put much stock in the practice, but most of the others did. As it was the perfect time for me to be about such a thing, I felt that it would make my day's retirement believable. Of course, this obliged me to follow through on it that night. But this, too, was good. It gave me a day, a night, and part of the following day in which to heal sufficiently to carry my wound that much the better. I felt that it would be time well spent.

You've got to tell someone, though. I told Random and I told Ganelon. Propped in my bed, I told them of the plans of Brand, Fiona, and Bleys, and of the Eric-Julian-Caine cabal. I told them what Brand had said concerning my return and his own imprisonment by his fellow conspirators. They saw why the survivors of both factions – Fiona and Julian – had run off: doubtless to marshal their forces, hopefully to expend them on one another, but probably not. Not immediately, anyhow. More likely, one or the other would move to take Amber first.

'They will just have to take numbers and wait their turns, like everyone else,' Random had said.

'Not exactly,' I remembered saying. 'Fiona's allies and the things that have been coming in on the black road are the same guys.'

'And the Circle in Lorraine?' Ganelon had asked.

'The same. That was how it manifested itself in that shadow. They came a great distance.'

'Ubiquitous bastards,' Random had said.

Nodding, I had tried to explain . . .

And so I came to Tir-na Nog'th. When the moon rose and the apparition of Amber came faintly into the heavens, stars showing through it, pale halo about its towers, tiny flecks of movement upon its walls, I waited, waited with Ganelon and Random, waited on the highest crop of Kolvir, there where the three steps are fashioned, roughly, out of the stone . . .

When the moonlight touched them, the outline of the entire stairway began to take shape, spanning the great gulf to that point above the sea the vision city held. When the moonlight fell fall upon it, the stair had taken as much of substance as it would ever possess, and I set my foot on the stone . . . Random held a full deck of Trumps and I'd mine within my jacket. Grayswandir, forged upon this very stone by moonlight, held power in the city in the sky, and so I bore my blade along. I had rested all day, and I held a staff to lean upon. Illusion of distance and time . . . The stairs through the Corwin-ignoring sky escalate somehow, for it is not a simple arithmetic progression up them once motion has commenced. I was here, I was there, I was a quarter of the way up before my shoulder had forgotten the clasp of Ganelon's hand . . . If I looked too hard at any portion of the stair, it lost its shimmering opacity and I saw the ocean far below as through a translucent lens . . . I lost track of time, though it seems it's never long, afterward . . . As far beneath the waves as I'd soon be above them, off to my right, glittering and curling, the outline of Rebma appeared within the sea. I thought of Moire, wondered how she fared. What would become of our deep-water double should Amber ever fall? Would the image remain unshattered in its mirror? Or would building blocks and bones be taken and shaken alike, dice in the deepwater casino canyons our fleets fly over? No answer in the man-drowning, Corwin-confounding waters, though I felt a twinge in my side.

At the head of the stair, I entered, coming into the ghost city as one would enter Amber after mounting the great forestall up Kolvir's seaward face.

I leaned upon the rail, looked across the world.

The black road led off to the south. I could not see it by night. Not that it mattered. I knew now where it led. Or rather where Brand said that it led. As he appeared to have used up a life's worth of reasons for lying, I believed that I knew where it led.

All the way.

From the brightness of Amber and the power and clean-shining splendor of adjacent Shadow, off through the progressively darkening slices of image that lead away in any direction, farther, through the twisted landscapes, and farther still, on through places seen only when drunk, delirious, or dreaming illy, and farther yet again, running beyond the place where I stop . . . Where *I* stop . . .

How to put simply that which is not a simple thing . . . ? Solipsism, I suppose, is where we have to begin – the notion that nothing exists but the self, or, at least, that we cannot truly be aware of anything but our own existence and experience. I can find, somewhere, off in Shadow, anything I can visualize. Any of us can. This, in good faith, does not transcend the limits of the ego. It may be argued, and in fact has, by most of us, that we create the shadows we visit out of the stuff of our own psyches, that we alone truly exist, that the shadows we traverse are but projections of our own desires . . . Whatever the merits of his argument, and there are several, it does go far toward explaining much of the family's attitude toward people, places, and things outside of Amber. Namely, we are toymakers and they, our playthings – sometimes dangerously animated to be sure; but this, too, is part of the game. We are impresarios by temperament, and we treat one another accordingly. While solipsism does tend to leave one slightly embarrassed on questions of etiology, one can easily avoid the embarrassment by refusing to admit the validity of the questions. Most of us are, as I have often observed, almost entirely pragmatic in the conduct of our affairs. Almost . . .

Yet – yet there is a disturbing element in the picture. There is a place where the shadows go mad . . . When you purposely push yourself through layer after layer of Shadow, surrendering – again, purposely – a piece of your understanding every step of the way, you come at last to a mad place beyond which you cannot go. Why do this? In hope of an insight, I'd say, or a new game . . . But when you come to this place, as we all have, you realize that you have reached the limit of Shadow or the end of yourself – synonymous terms, as we had always thought. Now, though . . .

Now I know that it is not so, now as I stand, waiting, without the Courts of Chaos, telling you what it was like, I know that it is not so. But I knew well enough then, that night, in Tir-na Nog'th, had known earlier, when I had fought the goat-man in the Black Circle of Lorraine, had known that day in the Lighthouse of Cabra, after my escape from the dungeons of Amber, when I had looked upon ruined Garnath . . . I knew that that was not all there was to it. I knew because I knew that the black road ran beyond that point. It passed through madness into chaos and kept going. The things that traveled across it came from somewhere, but they were not my things. I had somehow helped to grant them this passage, but they did not spring from my version of reality. They were their own, or someone else's – small matter there – and they tore holes in that small metaphysic we had woven over the ages. They had entered our preserve, they were not of it, they threatened it, they threatened us. Fiona and Brand had reached beyond everything and found something, where none of the rest of us had believed anything to exist. The danger released was, on some level, almost worth the evidence obtained: we were not alone, nor were shadows truly our toys. Whatever our relationship with Shadow, I could nevermore regard it in the old light . . .

All because the black road headed south and ran beyond the end of the world, where I stop.

Silence and silver . . . Walking away from the rail, leaning on my stick, passing through the fog-spun, mist-woven, moonlight-brushed fabric of vision within the troubling city . . . Ghosts . . . Shadows of shadows . . . Images of probability . . . Might-bes and might-have-beens . . . Probability lost . . . Probability regained . . .

Walking, across the promenade now . . . Figures, faces, many of them familiar . . . What are they about? Hard to say . . . Some lips move, some faces show animation. There are no words there for me. I pass among them, unnoted.

There . . . One such figure . . . Alone, but waiting . . . Fingers unknottmg minutes, casting them away . . . Face averted, and I wish to see it . . . A sign that I will or should . . . She sits on a stone bench beneath a gnarly tree . . . She gazes in the direction of the palace . . . Her form is quite familiar . . . Approaching, I see that it is Lorraine . . . She continues to regard a point far beyond me, does not hear me say that I have avenged her death.

But mine is the power to be heard here . . . It hangs in the sheath at my side.

Drawing Grayswandir, I raise my blade overhead where moonlight tricks its patterns into a kind of motion. I place it on the ground between us.

'Corwin!'

Her head snaps back, her hair rusts in the moonlight her eyes focus.

'Where did you come from? You're early.'

'You wait for me?'

'Of course. You told me to—'

'How did you come to this place?'

'This bench . . . ?'

'No. This city.'

'Amber? I do not understand. You brought me yourself. I—'

'Are you happy here?'

'You know that I am, so long as I am with you.'

I had not forgotten the evenness of her teeth, the hint of freckles beneath the soft light's veil . . .

'What happened? It is very important. Pretend for a moment that I do not know, and tell me everything that happened to us after the battle of the Black Circle in Lorraine.'

She frowned. She stood. She turned away.

'We had that argument,' she said. 'You followed me, drove away Melkin, and we talked. I saw that I was wrong and I went with you to Avalon. There, your brother Benedict persuaded you to talk with Eric. You were not reconciled, but you agreed to a trace because of something that he told you. He swore not to harm you and you swore to defend Amber, with Benedict to witness both oaths. We remained in Avalon while you obtained chemicals, and we went to another place later, a place where you purchased strange weapons. We won the battle, but Eric lies wounded now.' She stood and faced me. 'Are you thinking of ending the truce? Is that it Corwin?'

I shook my head, and though I knew better I reached to embrace her. I wanted to hold her, despite the fact that one of us did not exist could not exist when that tiny gap of space between our skins was crossed, to tell her that whatever had happened or would happen—

The shock was not severe, but it caused me to stumble. I lay across Grayswandir . . . My staff had fallen to the grass several paces away. Rising to my knees, I saw that the color had gone out of her face, her eyes, her hair. Her mouth shaped ghost words as her head turned, searching. Sheathing Grayswandir, recovering my staff, I rose once again. Her seeing passed through me and focused. Her face grew smooth, she smiled, started forward. I moved aside and turned, watching her run toward the man who approached, seeing her clasped in his arms, glimpsing his face as he bent her toward her own, lucky ghost, silver rose at the throat of his garment, kissing her, this man I would never know, silver on silence, and silver . . .

Walking away . . . Not looking back . . . Crossing the promenade . . .

The voice of Random: 'Corwin, are you all right?'

'Yes.'

'Anything interesting happening?'

'Later, Random.'

'Sorry.'

And sudden, the gleaming stair before the palace grounds . . . Up it, and a turn to the right . . . Slow and easy now, into the garden . . . Ghost flowers throb on their stalks all about me, ghost shrubs spill blossoms like frozen firework displays. *Sans* colors, all . . . Only the essentials sketched in, degrees of luminosity in silver the terms of their claim on the eye. Only the essentials here. Is Tir-na Nog'th a special sphere of Shadow in the real world, swayed by the promptings of the id – a full-sized projective test in the sky, perhaps even a therapeutic device? Despite the silver, I'd say, if this is a piece of the soul, the night is very dark . . . And silent . . .

Walking . . . By fountains, benches, groves, cunning alcoves in mazes of hedging . . . Passing along the waits, up an occasional step, across small bridges . . . Moving past ponds, among trees, by an odd piece of statuary, a boulder, a sundial (moondial, here?), bearing to my right, pressing steadily ahead, rounding, after a time, the northern end of the palace, swinging left then, past a courtyard overhung by balconies, more ghosts here and there upon them, behind them, within . . .

Circling around to the rear, just to see the back gardens this way, again, for they are lovely by normal moonlight in the true Amber.

A few more figures, talking, standing . . . No motion but my own is apparent.

. . . And feel myself drawn to the right. As one should never turn down a free oracle, I go.

. . . Toward a mass of high hedging, a small open area within, if it is not overgrown . . . Long ago there was . . .

Two figures, embracing, within. They part as I begin to turn away.

None of my affair, but . . . Deirdre . . . One of them is Deirdre. I know who the man will be before he turns. It is a cruel joke by whatever powers rule that silver, that silence . . . Back, back, away from that hedge . . . Turning, stumbling, rising again, going, away, now, quickly . . .

The voice of Random: 'Corwin? Are you all right?'

'Later! Damn it! Later!'

'It is not too long till sunrise, Corwin. I felt I had better remind you—'

'Consider me reminded!'

Away, now, quickly . . . Time, too, is a dream in Tir-na Nog'th. Small comfort, but better than none. Quickly, now, away, going, again . . .

. . . Toward the palace, bright architecture of the mind or spirit, more clearly standing now than the real ever did . . . To judge perfection is to render a worthless verdict, but I must see what lies within . . . This must be an end of sorts, for I am driven. I had not paused to recover my staff from where it had fallen this time, among the sparkling grasses. I know where I must go, what I must do. Obvious now, though the logic which has seized me is not that of the waking mind.

Hurrying, climbing, up to the rearward portal . . . The side-biting soreness comes home again . . . Across the threshold, in . . .

Into an absence of starshine and moonlight. The illumination is without direction, seeming almost to drift and to pool, aimlessly. Wherever it misses, the shadows are absolute, occluding large sections of room, hallway, closet, and stair.

Among them, through them, almost running now . . . Monochrome of my home . . . Apprehension overtakes me . . . The black spots seem like holes in this piece of reality now . . . I fear to pass too near. Fall in and be lost . . .

Turning . . . Crossing . . . Finally . . . Entering . . . The throne room . . . Bushels of blackness stacked where my eyes would drive down lines of seeing to the throne itself . . .

There, though, is movement.

A drifting, to my right, as I advance.

A lifting, with the drifting.

The boots on feet on legs come into view as forward pressing I near the place's base.

Grayswandir comes into my hand, finding its way into a patch of light, renewing its eyetricking, shapeshifting stretch, acquiring a glow of its own . . .

I place my left foot on the step, rest my left hand on my knee. Distracting but bearable, the throb of my healing gut. I wait for the blackness, the emptiness, to be drawn, appropriate curtain for the theatrics with which I am burdened this night.

And it slides aside, revealing a hand, an arm, a shoulder, the arm a glinting, metallic thing, its planes like the facets of a gem, its wrist and elbow wondrous weaves of silver cable, pinned with flecks of fire, the hand, stylized, skeletal, a Swiss toy, a mechanical insect, functional, deadly, beautiful in its way . . .

And it slides aside, revealing the rest of the man . . .

Benedict stands relaxed beside the throne, his left and human hand laid lightly upon it. He leans toward the throne. His lips are moving.

And it slides aside, revealing the throne's occupant . . .

'Dara!'

Turned toward her right she smiles, she nods to Benedict, her lips move. I advance and extend Grayswandir till its point rests lightly in the concavity beneath her sternum . . .

Slowly, quite slowly, she turns her head and meets my eyes. She takes on color and life. Her lips move again, and this time her words reach me.

'What are you?'

'No. That is my question. You answer it. Now.'

'I am Dara. Dara of Amber, Queen Dara. I hold this throne by right of blood and conquest. Who are you?'

'Corwin. Also of Amber. Don't move! I did not ask *who* you are—'

'Corwin is dead these many centuries. I have seen his tomb.'

'Empty.'

'Not so. His body lies within.'

'Give me your lineage!'

Her eyes move to her right where the shade of Benedict still stands. A blade has appeared in his new hand, seeming almost an extension of it but he holds it loosely, casually. His left hand now rests on her arm.

His eyes seek me in back of Grayswandir's hilt. Failing, they go again to that which is visible – Grayswandir – recognizing its design . . .

'I am the great-granddaughter of Benedict and the hellmaid Lintra, whom he loved and later slew.' Benedict winces at this, but she continues. 'I never knew her. My mother and my mother's mother were born in a place where time does not run as in Amber. I am the first of my mother's line to bear all the marks of humanity. And you, Lord Corwin, are but a ghost from a long dead past albeit a dangerous shade. How you came here, I do not know. But it was wrong of you. Return to your grave. Trouble not the living.'

My hand wavers. Grayswandir strays no more than half an inch. Yet that is sufficient.

Benedict's thrust is below my threshold of perception. His new arm drives the new hand that holds the blade that strikes Grayswandir, as his old arm draws his old hand, which has seized upon Dara, back across the arm of the throne . . . This subliminal impression reaches me moments later, as I fall back, cutting air, recover and strike an *en garde*, reflexively . . . It is ridiculous for a pair of ghosts to fight. Here, it is uneven. He cannot even reach me, whereas Grayswandir—

But no! His blade changes hands as he releases Dara and pivots, bringing them together, old hand and new. His left wrist rotates as he slides it forward and down, moving into what would be *corps à corps*, were we two facing mortal bodies. For a moment our guards are locked. That moment is enough . . .

That gleaming, mechanical hand comes forward, a thing of moon-light and fire, blackness and smoothness, all angles, no curves, fingers slightly flexed, palm silver-scribbled with a half-familiar design, comes forward, comes forward and catches at my throat . . .

Missing the fingers catch my shoulder and the thumb goes hooking – whether for clavicle or larynx, I do not know. I throw one punch with my left, toward his midsection, and there is nothing there . . .

The voice of Random: 'Corwin! The sun is about to rise! You've got to come down now!'

I cannot even answer. A second or two and that hand would tear away whatever it held. That hand . . . Grayswandir and that hand, which strangely resembles it, are the only two things which seem to coexist in my world and the city of ghosts . . .

'I see it Corwin! Pull away and reach for me! The Trump—'

I spin Grayswandir out of the bind and bring it around and down in a long, slashing arc . . .

Only a ghost could have beaten Benedict or Benedict's ghost with that maneuver. We stand too close for him to block my blade, but his countercut perfectly placed, would have removed my arm, had there been an arm there to meet it . . .

As there is not, I complete the stroke, delivering the blow with the full force of my right arm, high upon that lethal device of moonlight and fire, blackness and smoothness, near to the point where it is joined with him.

With an evil tearing at my shoulder, me arm comes away from Benedict and grows still . . . We both fall.

'Get up! By the unicorn, Corwin, get up! The sun is rising! The city will come apart about you!'

The floor beneath me wavers to and from a misty transparency. I glimpse a light-scaled expanse of water. I roll to my feet, barely avoiding the ghost's rush to clutch at the arm he has lost. It clings like a dead parasite and my side is hurting again . . .

Suddenly I am heavy and the vision of ocean does not fade. I begin to sink through the floor. Color returns to the world, wavering stripes of pink. The Corwin-spurning floor parts and the Corwin-killing gulf is opened . . .

I fall . . .

'This way, Corwin! Now!'

Random stands on a mountaintop and reaches for me. I extend my hand . . .

11

. . . And frying pans without fires are often far between . . .

We untangled ourselves and rose. I sat down again immediately, on the bottommost stair. I worked the metal hand loose from my shoulder – no blood there, but a promise of bruises to come – then cast it and its arm to the ground. The light of early morning did not detract from its exquisite and menacing appearance.

Ganelon and Random stood beside me.

'You all right, Corwin?'

'Yes. Just let me catch my breath.'

'I brought food,' Random said. 'We could have breakfast right here.'

'Good idea.'

As Random began unpacking provisions, Ganelon nudged the arm with the toe of his boot.

'What the hell,' he asked, Is that?'

I shook my head.

'I lopped it off the ghost of Benedict,' I told him. 'For reasons I do not understand, it was able to reach me.'

He stooped and picked it up, studied it.

'A lot lighter than I thought it would be,' he observed. He raked the air with it. 'You could do quite a job on someone, with a hand like that.'

'I know.'

He worked the fingers.

'Maybe the real Benedict could use it.'

'Maybe,' I said. 'My feelings are quite mixed when it comes to offering it to him but, possibly you're right . . .'

'How's the side?'

I prodded it gently.

'Not especially bad, everything considered. I'll be able to ride after breakfast, so long as we take it nice and easy.'

'Good. Say, Corwin, while Random is getting things ready, I have a question that may be out of order, but it has been bothering me all along.'

'Ask it.'

'Well, let me put it this way: I am all for you, or I would not be here. I will fight for you to have your throne, no matter what. But every time talk of the succession occurs, someone gets angry and breaks it off or the subject gets changed. Like Random did, while you were up there. I suppose that it is not absolutely essential for me to know the basis of your claim to the throne, or that of any of the others, but I cannot help being curious as to the reasons for all the friction.'

I sighed, then sat silent for a time.

'All right,' I said after a while, and then I chuckled. 'All right. If we cannot agree on these things ourselves, I would guess that they must seem pretty confused to an outsider. Benedict is the eldest. His mother was Cymnea. She bore Dad two other sons, also – Osric and Finndo. Then – how does one put these things? – Faiella bore Eric. After that, Dad found some defect in his marriage with Cymnea and had it dissolved – *ab initio*, as they would say in my old shadow – from the beginning. Neat trick, that. But he was the king.'

'Didn't that make all of them illegitimate?'

'Well, it left their status less certain. Osric and Finndo were more than a little irritated, as I understand it, but they died shortly thereafter. Benedict was either less irritated or more politic about the entire affair. He never raised a fuss. Dad then married Faiella.'

'And that made Eric legitimate?'

'It would have, if he had acknowledged Eric as his son. He treated him as if he were, but he never did anything formal in that regard. It involved the smoothing-over process with Cymnea's family, which had become a bit stronger around that time.'

'Still, if he treated him as his own . . .'

'Ah! But he later *did* acknowledge Llewella formally. She was born out of wedlock, but he decided to recognize her, poor girl. All of Eric's supporters hated her for its effect on his status. Anyway, Faiella was later to become my mother. I was born safely in wedlock, making me the first with a clean claim on the throne. Talk to one of the others and you may get a different line of reasoning, but those are the facts it will have to be based on. Somehow it does not seem quite as important as it once did, though, with Eric dead and Benedict not really interested . . . But that is where I stand.'

'I see – sort of,' he said. 'Just one more thing, then . . .'

'What?'

'Who is next? That is to say, if anything were to happen to you . . . ?'

I shook my head.

'It gets even more complicated there, now. Caine would have been next. With him dead, I see it as swinging over to Clarissa's brood – the redheads. Bleys would have followed, then Brand.'

'Clarissa? What become of your mother?'

'She died in childbirth. Deirdre was the child. Dad did not remarry for many years after mother's death. When he did, it was a redheaded wench from a far southern shadow. I never liked her. He began feeling the same way after a time and started fooling around again. They had one reconciliation after Llewella's birth in Rebma, and Brand was the result. When they were finally divorced, he recognized Llewella to spite Clarissa. At least, that is what I think happened.'

'So you are not counting the ladies in the succession?'

'No. They are neither interested nor fit. If I were, though, Fiona would precede Bleys and Llewella would follow him. After Clarissa's crowd, it would swing over to Julian, Gérard, and Random, in that order. Excuse me – count Flora before Julian. The marriage data is even more involved, but no one will dispute the final order. Let it go at that.'

'Gladly,' he said. 'So now Brand gets it if you die, right?'

'Well . . . He is a self-confessed traitor and he rubs everybody the wrong way. I do not believe the rest of them would have him, as he stands now. But I do not believe he has by any means given up.'

'But the alternative is Julian.'

I shrugged.

'The fact that I do not like Julian does not make him unfit. In fact, he might even be a very effective monarch.'

'So he knifed you for the chance to prove it,' Random called out. 'Come on and eat.'

'I still don't think so,' I said, getting to my feet and heading for the food. 'First, I don't see how he could have gotten to me. Second, it would have been too damned obvious. Third, if I die in the near future Benedict will have the real say as to the succession. Everyone knows that. He's got the seniority, he's got the wits, and he's got the power. He could simply say, for example, "The hell with all this bickering, I am backing Gérard," and that would be it.'

'What if he decided to reinterpret his own status and take it himself?' Ganelon asked.

We seated ourselves on the ground and took the tin dishes Random had filled.

'He could have had it long before this, had he wanted it,' I said. 'There are several ways of regarding the offspring of a void marriage, and the most favorable one would be the most likely in his case. Osric and Finndo rushed to judgment, taking the worst view. Benedict knew better. He just waited. So . . . It is possible. Unlikely, though, I'd say.'

'Then – in the normal course of affairs – if anything happened to you, it could still be very much up in the air?'

'Very much.'

'But why was Caine killed?' Random asked. Then, between mouthfuls, he answered his own question. 'So that when they got you, it would swing over to Clarissa's kids immediately. It has occurred to me that Bleys is probably still living, and be is next in line. His body was never found. My guess is this: he trumped off to Fiona during your attack and returned to Shadow to rebuild his forces, leaving you to what he hoped would be your death at the hands of Eric. He is finally ready to move again. So they killed Caine and tried for you. If they are really allied with the black-road horde, they could have arranged for another assault from that quarter. Then he could have done the same thing you did – arrive at the last hour, turn back the invaders, and move on in. And there he would be, next in line and first in force. Simple. Except that you survived and Brand has been returned. If we are to believe Brand's accusation of Fiona – and I see no reason why we should not – then it follows from their original program.'

I nodded.

'Possibly,' I said. 'I asked Brand just those things. He admitted their possibility, but he disavowed any knowledge as to whether Bleys was still living. Personally, I think he was lying.'

'Why?'

'It is possible that he wishes to combine revenge for his imprisonment and the attempt on his life with the removal of the one impediment, save for myself, to his own succession. I think he feels that I will be expended in a scheme he is evolving to deal with the black road. The destruction of his own cabal and the removal of the road could make him look pretty decent, especially after all the penance he has had thrust upon him. Then, maybe then, he would have a chance – or thinks that he would.'

'Then you think Bleys is still living, too?'

'Just a feeling,' I said. 'But yes, I do.'

'What is their strength, anyway?'

'An endorsement of higher education,' I said. 'Fiona and Brand paid attention to Dworkin while the rest of us were off indulging our assorted passions in Shadow. Consequently, they seem to have obtained a better grasp of principles than we possess. They know more about Shadow and what lies beyond it, more about the Pattern, more about the Trumps than we do. That is why Brand was able to send you his message.'

'An interesting thought . . .' Random mused. 'Do you think they might have disposed of Dworkin after they felt they had learned enough from him? It would certainly help to keep things exclusive, if anything happened to Dad.'

'That thought had not occurred to me.' I said.

And I wondered, could they have done something that had affected his mind? Something that left him as he was when last. I had seen him? If so, were they aware that he was possibly still living somewhere? Or might they have assumed his total destruction?

'Yes, an interesting thought,' I said. 'I suppose that it is possible.'

The sun inched its way upward, and the food restored me. No trace of Tir-na Nog'th remained in the morning's light. My memories of it had already taken on the quality of images in a dim mirror. Ganelon fetched its only other token, the arm, and Random packed it away along with the dishes. By daylight, the first three steps looked less like stairs and more like jumbled rock.

Random gestured with his head.

'Take the same way back?' he asked.

'Yes,' I said, and we mounted.

We had come by way of a trail that wound about Kolvir to the south. It was longer but less rugged than the route across the crest. I'd a humor to pamper myself so long as my side protested.

So we bore to the right, moving single file, Random in the lead, Ganelon to the rear. The trail ran gently upward, then cut back down again. The air was cool, and it bore the aromas of verdure and moist earth, a thing quite unusual in that stark place, at that altitude. Straying air currents, I reasoned, from the forest far below.

We let the horses pick their own casual pace down through the dip and up the next rise. As we neared its crest, Random's horse whinnied and began to rear. He controlled it immediately, and I glanced about but saw nothing that might have startled it.

When he reached its summit, Random slowed and called back, 'Take a look at that sunrise now, will you?'

It would have been rather difficult to avoid doing so, though I did not remark on the fact. Random was seldom given to sentimentality over vegetation, geology, or illumination.

I almost drew rein myself as I topped the rise, for the sun was a fantastic golden ball. It seemed half again its normal size, and its peculiar coloration was unlike anything I remembered having seen before. It did marvelous things to the band of ocean that had come into view above the next rise, and the tints of cloud and sky were indeed singular. I did not halt, though, for the sudden brightness was almost painful.

'You're right,' I called out, following him down into the next declivity. Behind me, Ganelon snorted an appreciative oath.

When I had blinked away the aftereffects of that display I noticed that the vegetation was heavier than I had remembered in this little pocket in the sky. I had thought there were several scrubby trees and some patches of lichen, but there were actually several dozen trees, larger than I recalled, and greener, with a clutch of grasses here and there and a vine or two softening the outlines of the rocks. However, since my return I had only passed this way after dark. And now that I thought of it, it was probably the source of the aromas that had come to me earlier.

Passing through, it seemed that the little hollow was also wider than I recalled it. By the time we had crossed and were ascending once more, I was certain of it.

'Random,' I called out, 'has this place changed recently?'

'Hard to say,' he answered. 'Eric didn't let me out much. It seems to have grown up a bit.'

'It seems bigger – wider.'

'Yes, it does. I had thought that that was just my imagination.'

When we reached the next crest I was not dazzled again because the sun was blocked by foliage. The area ahead of us contained many more trees than the one we had just departed – and they were larger and closer together. We drew rein.

'I don't remember this,' he said. 'Even passing through at night, it would have registered. We must have taken a wrong turn.'

'I don't see how. Still, we know about where we are. I would rather go ahead than go back and start again. We should keep aware of conditions around Amber, anyway.'

'True.'

He headed down toward the wood. We followed.

'It's kind of unusual, at this altitude – a growth like this,' he called back.

'There also seems to be a lot more soil than I recall.'

'I believe you are right.'

The trail curved to the left as we entered among the trees. I could see no reason for this deviation from the direct route. We stayed with it, however, and it added to the illusion of distance. After a few moments it swung suddenly to the right again. The prospect on cutting back was peculiar. The trees seemed even taller and were now so dense as to puzzle the eye that sought their penetration. When it turned once more it broadened, and the way was straight for a great distance ahead. Too great, in fact. Our little dell just wasn't that wide.

Random halted again.

'Damn it, Corwin! This is ridiculous!' he said. 'You are not playing games, are you?'

'I couldn't if I would,' I said. 'I have never been able to manipulate Shadow anywhere on Kolvir. There isn't supposed to be any to work with here.'

'That has always been my understanding, too. Amber casts Shadow but is not of it. I don't like this at all. What do you say we turn back?'

'I've a feeling we might not be able to retrace our way,' I said. 'There has to be a reason for this, and I want to know it.'

'It occurs to me that it might be some sort of a trap.'

'Even so,' I said.

He nodded and we rode on, down that shaded way, under trees now grown more stately. The wood was silent about us. The ground remained level, the trail straight. Half consciously, we pushed the horses to a greater pace.

About five minutes passed before we spoke again. Then Random said, 'Corwin, this can't be Shadow.'

'Why not?'

'I have been trying to influence it and nothing happens. Have you tried?'

'No.'

'Why don't you?'

'All right.'

A rock could jut beyond the coming tree, a morning glory twine and bell within that shrubby stand . . . There ought a patch of sky come clear, a wispy cloud upon it . . . Then let there be a fallen limb, a stair of fungus up its side . . . A scummed-over puddle . . . A frog . . . Falling feather, drifting seed . . . A limb that twists just so . . . Another trail upon our way, fresh-cut, deep-marked, past the place the feather should have fallen . . .

'No good,' I said.

'If it is not Shadow, what is it?'

'Something else, of course.'

He shook his head and checked again to see that his blade was loose in its scabbard. Automatically, I did the same. Moments later, I heard Ganelon's make a small clicking noise behind me.

Ahead, the trail began to narrow, and shortly thereafter it commenced to wander. We were forced to slow our pace once again, and the trees pressed nearer with branches sweeping lower than at any time before. The trail became a path. It jogged, it curved, it gave a final twist and then quit.

Random ducked a limb, then raised his hand and halted. We came up beside him. For as far as I could see ahead there was no indication of the trail's picking up again. Looking back, I failed to locate any sign of it either.

'Suggestions,' he said, 'are now in order. We do not know where we have been or where we are going, let alone where we are. My suggestion is the hell with curiosity. Let's get out of here the fastest way we know how.'

'The Trumps?' Ganelon asked.

'Yes. What do you say, Corwin?'

'Okay. I don't like it either, and I can't think of anything better to try. Go ahead.'

'Who should I try for?' he asked, producing his deck and uncasing it 'Gérard?'

'Yes.'

He shuffled through his cards, located Gérard's, stared at it. We stared at him. Time went its way.

'I can't seem to reach him,' he finally announced.

'Try Benedict.'

'Okay.'

Repeat performance. No contact.

'Try Deirdre,' I said, drawing forth my own deck and searching out her Trump. 'I'll join you. We will see whether it makes a difference with two of us trying.'

And again. And again.

'Nothing,' I said after a long effort.

Random shook his head.

'Did you notice anything unusual about your Trumps?' he asked.

'Yes, but I don't know what it is. They do seem different.'

'Mine seem to have lost that quality of coldness they once possessed,' he said.

I shuffled mine slowly. I ran my fingertips across them.

'Yes, you are right,' I said. 'That's it. But let us try again. Say, Flora.'

'Okay.'

The results were the same. And with Llewella. And Brand.

'Any idea what could be wrong?' Random asked.

'Not the slightest. They couldn't all be blocking us. They couldn't all be dead . . . Oh, I suppose they could. But it is highly unlikely. Something seems to have affected the Trumps themselves, is what it is. And I never knew of anything that could do that.'

'Well, they are not guaranteed one hundred percent,' Random said, 'according to the manufacturer.'

'What do you know that I don't?'

He chuckled.

'You never forget the day you come of age and walk the Pattern,' he said. 'I remember it as though it were last year. When I had succeeded – all flushed with excitement, with glory – Dworkin presented me with my first set of Trumps and instructed me in their use. I distinctly recall asking him whether they worked everywhere. And I remember his answer: "No," he said. "But they should serve in any place you will ever be." He never much liked me, you know.'

'But did you ask him what he meant by that?'

'Yes, and he said, "I doubt that you will ever achieve a state where they will fail to serve you. Why don't you run along now?", and I did. I was anxious to go play with the Trumps all by myself.'

' "Achieve a state?" He didn't say "reach a place"?'

'No. I have a very good memory for certain things.'

'Peculiar – though not much help that I can see. Smacks of the metaphysical.'

'I'd wager Brand would know.'

'I've a feeling you're right, for all the good that does us.'

'We ought to do something other than discuss metaphysics,' Ganelon commented. 'If you can't manipulate Shadow and you can't work the Trumps, it would seem that the next thing to do is determine where we are. And then go looking for help.'

I nodded.

'Since we are not in Amber, I think it is safe to assume that we are in Shadow – a very special place, quite near to Amber, since the changeover was not abrupt. In that we were transported without active co-operation on our part, there had to be some agency and presumably some intent behind the maneuver. If it is going to attack us, now is as good a time as any. If there is something else it wants, then it is going to have to show us, because we aren't even in a position to make a good guess.'

'So you propose we do nothing?'

'I propose we wait. I don't see any value in wandering about, losing ourselves further.'

'I seem to remember your once telling me that adjacent shadows tend to be somewhat congruent,' Ganelon said.

'Yes, I probably did. So what?'

'Then, if we are as near to Amber as you suppose, we need but ride toward the rising sun to come to a spot that parallels the city itself.'

'It is not quite that simple. But supposing it were, what good would it do us?'

'Perhaps the Trumps would function again at the point of maximum congruity.'

Random looked at Ganelon, looked at me.

'That may be worth trying,' he said. 'What have we got to lose?'

'Whatever small orientation we still possess,' I said. 'Look, it is not a bad idea. If nothing develops here, we will try it. However, looking back, it seems that the road behind us closes in direct proportion to the distance we advance. We are not simply moving in space. Under these circumstances, I am loath to wander until I am satisfied that we have no other option. If someone desires our presence at a particular location, it is up to him now to phrase the invitation a little more legibly. We wait.'

They both nodded. Random began to dismount, then froze, one foot in the stirrup, one on the ground.

'After all these years,' he said, and, 'I never really believed it . . .'

'What is it?' I whispered.

'The option,' he said, and he mounted again.

He persuaded his horse to move very slowly forward. I followed, and a moment later I glimpsed it, white as I had seen it in the grove, standing, half hidden, amid a clump of ferns: the unicorn.

It turned as we moved, and seconds later flashed ahead, to stand partly concealed once more by the trunks of several trees.

'I see it!' Ganelon whispered. 'To think there really is such a beast . . . Your family's emblem, isn't it?'

'Yes.'

'A good sign, I'd say.'

I did not answer, but followed, keeping it in sight. That it was meant to be followed I did not doubt.

It had a way of remaining partly concealed the entire while – looking out from behind something, passing from cover to cover, moving with an incredible swiftness when it did move, avoiding open areas, favoring glade and shade. We followed, deeper and deeper into the wood which had given up all semblance of anything to be found on Kolvir's slopes. It resembled Arden now, more than anything else near Amber, as the ground was relatively level and the trees grew more and more stately.

An hour had passed, I guessed, and another had followed it, before we came to a small, clear stream and the unicorn turned and headed up it. As we rode along the bank, Random commented, 'This is starting to look sort of familiar.'

'Yes,' I said, 'but only sort of. I can't quite say why.'

'Nor I.'

We entered upon a slope shortly thereafter, and it grew steeper before very long. The going became more difficult for the horses, but the unicorn adjusted its pace to accommodate them. The ground became rockier, the trees smaller. The stream curved in its splashing course. I lost track of its twists and tarns, but we were finally nesting the top of the small mount up which we had been traveling.

We achieved a level area and continued along it toward the wood from which the stream issued. At this point I caught an oblique view – ahead and to the right, through a place where the land fell away – of an icy blue sea, quite far below us.

'We're pretty high up,' Ganelon said. 'It seemed like lowland, but—'

'The Grove of the Unicorn!' Random interrupted. 'That's what it looks like. See!'

Nor was he incorrect. Ahead lay an area strewn with boulders. Amid them a spring uttered the stream we followed. This place was larger and more lush, its situation incorrect in terms of my internal compass. Yet the similarity had to be more than coincidental. The unicorn mounted the rock nearest the spring, looked at us, then turned away. It might have been staring down at the ocean.

Then, as we continued, the grove, the unicorn, the trees about us, the stream beside us took on an unusual clarity, all, as though each were radiating some special illumination, causing it to quiver with the intensity of its color while at the same time wavering, slightly, just at the edges of perception. This produced in me an incipient feeling like the beginning of the emotional accompaniment to a hellride.

Then, then and then, with each stride of my mount, something went out of the world about us. An adjustment in the relationships of objects suddenly occurred, eroding my sense of depth, destroying perspective, rearranging the display of articles within my field of vision, so that everything presented its entire outer surface without simultaneously appearing to occupy an increased area: angles predominated, and relative sizes seemed suddenly ridiculous. Random's horse reared and neighed, massive, apocalpytic, instantly recalling *Guernica* to my mind. And to my distress I saw that we ourselves had not been untouched by the phenomenon – but that Random, straggling with his mount, and Ganelon, still managing to control Firedrake, had, like everything else, been transfigured by this cubist dream of space.

But Star was a veteran of many a hellride; Firedrake, also, had been through a lot. We clung to them and felt the movements that we could not accurately gauge. And Random succeeded, at last, in imposing his will upon his mount, though the prospect continued to alter as we advanced.

Light values shifted next. The sky grew black, not as night, but like a flat, nonreflecting surface. So did certain vacant areas between objects. The only light left in the world seemed to originate from things themselves, and all of it was gradually bleached. Various intensities of white emerged from the planes of existence, and brightest of all, immense, awful, the unicorn suddenly reared, pawing at the air, filling perhaps ninety percent of creation with what became a slow-motion gesture I feared would annihilate us if we advanced another pace.

Then there was only the light.

Then absolute stillness.

Then the light was gone and there was nothing. Not even blackness. A gap in existence, which might have lasted an instant or an eternity . . .

Then the blackness returned, and the light. Only they were reversed. Light filled the interstices, outlining voids that must be objects. The first sound that I heard was the rushing of water, and I knew somehow that we were halted beside the spring. The first thing that I felt was Star's quivering. Then I smelled the sea.

Then the Pattern came into view, or a distorted negative of it . . .

I leaned forward and more light leaked around the edges of things. I leaned back; it went away. Forward again, this time farther than before . . .

The light spread, introduced various shades of gray into the scheme of things. With my knees then, gently, I suggested that Star advance.

With each pace, something returned to the world. Surfaces, textures, colors . . .

Behind me, I heard the others begin to follow. Below me, the Pattern surrendered nothing of its mystery, but it acquired a context which, by degrees, found its place within the larger reshaping of the world about us.

Continuing downhill, a sense of depth reemerged. The sea, now plainly visible off to the right, underwent a possibly purely optical separation from the sky, with which it seemed momentarily to have been joined in some sort of *Urmeer* of the waters above and the waters below. Unsettling upon reflection, but unnoted while in effect. We were heading down a steep, rocky incline which seemed to have taken its beginning at the rear of the grove to which the unicorn had led us. Perhaps a hundred meters below us was a perfectly level area which appeared to be solid, unfractured rock – roughly oval in shape, a couple of hundred meters along its major axis. The slope down which we rode swung off to the left and returned, describing a vast arc, a parenthesis, half cupping the smooth shelf. Beyond its rightward jutting there was nothing – that is to say the land fell away in steep descent toward that peculiar sea.

And, continuing, all three dimensions seemed to reassert themselves once more. The sun was that great orb of molten gold we had seen earlier. The sky was a deeper blue than that of Amber, and there were no clouds in it. That sea was a matching blue, unspecked by sail or island. I saw no birds, and I heard no sounds other than our own. An enormous silence lay upon this place, this day. In the bowl of my suddenly clear vision, the Pattern at last achieved its disposition upon the surface below. I thought at first that it was inscribed in the rock, but as we drew nearer I saw that it was contained within it – gold-pink swirls, like veining in an exotic marble, natural-seeming despite the obvious purpose to the design.

I drew rein and the others came up beside me, Random to my right, Ganelon to my left.

We regarded it in silence for a long while. A dark, rough-edged smudge had obliterated an area of the section immediately beneath us, running from its outer rim to the center.

'You know,' Random finally said, 'it is as if someone had shaved the top off Kolvir, cutting at about the level of the dungeons.'

'Yes,' I said.

'Then – looking for congruence – that would be about where our own Pattern lies.'

'Yes,' I said again.

'And that blotted area is to the south, from whence comes the black road.'

I nodded slowly as the understanding arrived and forged itself into a certainty.

'What does it mean?' he asked. 'It seems to correspond to the true state of affairs, but beyond that I do not understand its significance. Why have we been brought here and shown this thing?'

'It does not correspond to the true state of affairs,' I said. 'It *is* the true state of affairs.'

Ganelon turned toward us.

'On that shadow Earth we visited – where you had spent so many years – I heard a poem about two roads that diverged in a wood,' he said. 'It ends, "I took the one less traveled by, and that has made an the difference". When I heard it, I thought of something you had once said – "All roads lead to Amber" – and I wondered then, as I do now, at the difference the choice may make, despite the end's apparent inevitability to those of your blood.'

'You know?' I said. 'You understand?'

'I think so.'

He nodded, then pointed.

'That is the real Amber down there, isn't it?'

'Yes,' I said. 'Yes, it is.'

THE HAND OF OBERON

To Jay Haldeman,
of fellowship and artichokes.

1

A bright flash of insight, to match that peculiar sun . . .

There it was . . . Displayed within that light, a thing I had only seen self-illuminated in darkness up until then: the Pattern, the great Pattern of Amber cast upon an oval shelf beneath/above a strange sky-sea.

. . . And I knew, perhaps by that within me which bound us, that this had to be the real one. Which meant that the Pattern in Amber was but its first shadow. Which meant—

Which meant that. Amber itself was but a shadow, albeit a special one, for the Pattern was not carried over into places beyond the realm of Amber, Rebma, and Tir-na Nog'th. Meaning, then, that this place to which we had come was, by the law of precedence and configuration, the real Amber.

I turned to a smiling Ganelon, his beard and wild hair molten in the merciless light.

'How did you know?' I asked him.

'You know I am a very good guesser, Corwin,' he replied, 'and I recall everything you ever told me about how things work in Amber: how its shadow and those of your struggles are cast across the worlds. I often wondered, in thinking of the black road, whether anything could have cast such a shadow into Amber itself. And I imagined that such a something would have to be extremely basic, powerful, and secret.' He gestured at the scene before us. 'Like that.'

'Continue,' I said.

His expression changed and he shrugged.

'So there had to be a layer of reality deeper than your Amber,' he explained, 'where the dirty work was done. Your patron beast led us to what seems to be such a place, and that blot on the Pattern looks to be the dirty work. You agreed.'

I nodded.

'It was your perceptiveness rather than the conclusion itself which stunned me so,' I said.

'You beat me to it,' admitted Random, off to my right, 'but the feeling has found its way into my intestines – to put it delicately. I do believe that somehow that is the basis of our world down there.'

'An outsider can sometimes see things better than one who is part of them,' Ganelon offered.

Random glanced at me and returned his attention to the spectacle.

'Do you think things will change any more,' he asked, 'If we go down for a closer look?'

'Only one way to find out,' I said.

'Single file, then,' Random agreed. 'I'll lead.'

'All right.'

Random guided his mount to the right, the left, the right, in a long series of switchbacks which zigged us and zagged us across most of the face of the wall. Continuing in the order we had maintained all day, I followed him and Ganelon came last.

'Seems stable enough now,' Random called back.

'So far,' I said.

'Some sort of opening in the rocks below.'

I leaned forward. There was a cave mouth back to the right, on level with the oval plain. Its situation was such that it had been hidden from sight when we had occupied our higher position.

'We pass fairly near it,' I said.

'—quickly, cautiously, and silently,' Random added, drawing his blade.

I unsheathed Grayswandir, and one turn back above me Ganelon drew his own weapon.

We did not pass the opening, but turned leftward once more before we came to it. We moved within ten or fifteen feet of it, however, and I detected an unpleasant odor which I could not identify. The horses must have done a better job of it, though, or been pessimists by nature, because they flattened their ears, widened their nostrils, and made alarmed noises while turning against the reins. They calmed, however, as soon as we had made the turn and begun moving away once again. They did not suffer a relapse until we reached the end of our descent and moved to approach the damaged Pattern. They refused to go near it.

504

Random dismounted. He advanced to the edge of the design, paused and stared. After a time, he spoke without looking back.

'It follows that the damage was deliberate,' he said, 'from everything else that we know.'

'It seems to follow,' I said.

'It is also obvious that we were brought here for a reason.'

'I'd say so.'

'Then it does not take too much imagination to conclude that our purpose for being here is to determine how the Pattern was damaged and what might be done to repair it.'

'Possibly. What is your diagnosis?'

'Nothing yet.'

He moved along the perimeter of the figure, off to the right where the smear-effect began. I resheathed my blade and prepared to dismount Ganelon reached over and took hold of my shoulder.

'I can make it myself—' I began.

But, 'Corwin,' he said, ignoring my words, 'there does appear to be a small irregularity out toward the middle of the Pattern. It does not look like something that belongs . . .'

'Where?'

He pointed and I followed the gesture.

There was some foreign object near the center. A stick? A stone? A stray bit of paper . . . ? It was impossible to tell from this distance.

'I see it,' I said.

We dismounted and headed toward Random, who by then was crouched at the extreme right of the figure, examining the discoloration.

'Ganelon's spotted something out toward the center,' I said.

Random nodded.

'I've noticed it,' he replied. 'I was just trying to decide on the best way to head out for a better look. I do not relish the notion of walking a broken Pattern. On the other hand, I was wondering what I would be laying myself open to if I tried heading in across the blackened area. What do you think?'

'Walking what there is of the Pattern would take some time,' I said, 'if the resistance is on par with what it is at home. Also, we have been taught that it is death to stray from it – and his setup would force me to leave it when I reach the blot. On the other hand, as you say, I might be alerting our enemies by treading on the black. So—'

'So neither of you is going to do it,' Ganelon interrupted. 'I am.'

Then, without waiting for a reply, he took a running leap into the black sector, raced along it toward the center, paused long enough to pick up some small object, turned and headed back.

Moments later, he stood before us.

'That was a risky thing to do,' Random said.

He nodded.

'But you two would still be debating it if I hadn't.' He raised his hand and extended it. 'Now, what do you make of this?'

He was holding a dagger. Impaled on it was a rectangle of stained pasteboard. I took them from him.

'Looks like a Trump,' Random said.

'Yes.'

I worked the card loose, smoothed down the torn sections. The man I regarded upon it was half familiar – meaning of course that he was also half strange. Light, straight hair, a trifle sharp-featured, a small smile, somewhat slight of build.

I shook my head.

'I do not know him,' I said.

'Let me see.'

Random took the card from me, frowned at it.

'No,' he said after a time. 'I don't either. It almost seems as though I should, but . . . No.'

At that moment, the horses renewed their complaints much more forcefully. And we needed but turn part way to learn the cause of their discomfort, in that it had chosen that moment to emerge from the cave.

'Damn,' said Random.

I agreed with him.

Ganelon cleared his throat, took forth his blade.

'Anyone know what it is?' he asked quietly.

My first impression of the beast was that it was snakelike, both from its movements and because of the fact that its long thick tail seemed more a continuation of its long thin body man a mere appendage. It moved on four double-jointed legs, however, large-footed and wickedly clawed. Its narrow head was beaked, and it swung from side to side as it advanced, showing us one pale blue eye and then the other. Large wings were folded against its sides, purple and leathery. It possessed neither hair nor feathers, though there were scaled areas across its breast, shoulders, back, and along the length of its tail. From beak-bayonet to twisting tail-tip it seemed a little over three meters. There was a small tinkling sound as it moved, and I caught a flash of something bright at its throat.

'Closest thing I know,' said Random, 'is a heraldic beast – the griffin. Only this one is bald and purple.'

'Definitely not our national bird,' I added, drawing Grayswandir and swinging its point into line with the creature's head.

The beast darted a red, forked tongue. It raised its wings a few inches, then let them fall. When its head swung to the right its tail moved to the left, then left and right, right and left – producing a near-hypnotic, flowing effect as it advanced.

It seemed more concerned with the horses than with us, however, for its course was directed well past us toward the spot where our mounts stood quivering and stamping. I moved to interpose myself.

At that point, it reared.

Its wings went up and out, spreading like a pair of slack sails suddenly caught by a gust of wind. It was back on its hind legs and towering above us, seeming to occupy at least four times the space it had previously. And then it shrieked, a god-awful, hunting scream or challenge that left my ears ringing. With that, it snapped those wings downward and sprang, becoming temporarily airborne.

The horses bolted and ran. The beast was beyond our reach. It was only then that I realized what the bright flash and the tinkling had represented. The thing was tethered, by means of a long chain running back into the cave. The exact length of its leash was immediately a question of more than academic interest.

I turned as it passed, hissing, flapping, and falling, beyond us. It had not possessed sufficient momentum to obtain true flight in that brief rush upward. I saw that Star and Firedrake were retreating toward the far end of the oval. Random's mount Iago, on the other hand, had bolted in the direction of the Pattern.

The beast touched ground again, turned as if to pursue Iago, appeared to study us once more, and froze. It was much nearer this time – under four meters – and it cocked its head, showing us its right eye, then opened its beak and made a soft cawing noise.

'What say we rush it now?' said Random.

'No. Wait. There is something peculiar about its behavior.'

It had dropped its head while I was speaking, spreading its wings downward. It struck the ground three times with its beak and looked up again. Then it drew its wings part way back toward its body. Its tail twitched once, then swung more vigorously from side to side. It opened its beak and repeated the cawing sound.

At that moment we were distracted.

Iago had entered the Pattern, well to the side of the darkened area. Five or six meters into it, standing obliquely across the lines of power, he was caught near one of the Veil points like an insect on a piece of flypaper. He cried loudly as the sparks came up about him and his mane rose and stood erect.

Immediately, the sky began to darken directly overhead. But it was no cloud of water vapor which had begun to coalesce. Rather, it was a perfectly circular formation which had appeared, red at the center, yellow nearer the edges, turning in a clockwise direction. A sound like a single bell chime followed by the growl of a bull-roarer suddenly came to our ears.

Iago continued his struggles, first freeing his right front foot, then entangling it again as he freed the left, neighing wildly the while. The sparks were up to his shoulders by then, and he shook them like raindrops from his body and neck, his entire form taking on a soft, buttery glow.

The roaring increased in volume and small lightnings began to play at the heart of the red thing above us. A rattling noise caught my attention at that moment, and I glanced downward to discover that the purple griffin had slithered past and moved to interpose itself between us and the loud red phenomenon. It crouched like a gargoyle, facing away from us, watching the spectacle.

Just then, Iago freed both front feet and reared. There was something insubstantial about him by then, what with his brightness and the spark-shot indistinctness of his outline. He might have neighed at that moment, but all other sounds were submerged by the incessant roar from above.

A funnel descended from the noisy formation – bright, flashing, wailing now, and tremendously fast. It touched the rearing horse, and for a moment his outline expanded enormously, becoming increasingly tenuous in direct proportion to this effect. And then he was gone. For a brief interval, the funnel remained stationary, like a perfectly balanced top. Then the sound began to diminish.

The trunk raised itself, slowly, to a point but a small distance – perhaps the height of a man – above the Pattern. Then it snapped upward as quickly as it had descended.

The wailing ceased. The roaring began to subside. The miniature lightnings faded within the circle. The entire formation began to pale and slow. A moment later, it was but a bit of darkness; another moment and it was gone.

No trace of Iago remained anywhere that I could see.

'Don't ask me,' I said when Random turned toward me. 'I don't know either.'

He nodded, then directed his attention toward our purple companion, who was just then rattling his chain.

'What about Charlie here?' he asked, fingering his blade.

'I had the distinct impression he was trying to protect us,' I said, taking a step forward. 'Cover me. I want to try something.'

'You sure you can move fast enough?' he asked. 'With that side . . .'

'Don't worry,' I said, a trifle more heartily than necessary, and I kept moving.

He was correct about my left side, where the healing knife wound still ached dully and seemed to exercise a drag on my movements. But Grayswandir was still in my right hand and this was one of those occasions when my trust in my instincts was running high. I had relied on this feeling in the past with good results. There are times when such gambles just seem to be in order.

Random moved ahead and to the right I turned sidewise and extended my left hand as you would in introducing yourself to a strange dog, slowly. Our heraldic companion had risen from its crouch and was turning.

It faced us again and studied Ganelon, off to my left. Then it regarded my hand. It lowered its head and repeated the ground-striking movement, cawed very softly – a small, bubbling sound – raised its head and slowly extended it. It wagged its great tail, touched my fingers with its beak, then repeated the performance. Carefully, I placed my hand on its head. The wagging increased; its head remained motionless. I scratched it gently about the neck and it turned its head slowly then, as if enjoying it I withdrew my hand and dropped back a pace.

'I think we're friends,' I said softly. 'Now you try it, Random.'

'Are you kidding?'

'No, I'm sure you're safe. Try it.'

'What will you do if you are wrong?'

'Apologize.'

'Great.'

He advanced and offered his hand. The beast remained friendly.

'All right,' he said half a minute or so later, still stroking its neck, 'what have we proved?'

'That he is a watchdog.'

'What is he watching?'

'The Pattern, apparently.'

'Offhand then,' said Random, moving back, 'I would say that his work leaves something to be desired.' He gestured at the dark area. 'Which is understandable, if he is this friendly to anyone who doesn't eat oats and whinny.'

'My guess is that he is quite selective. It is also possible that he was set here after the damage was done, to defend against further unappreciated activity.'

'Who set him?'

'I'd like to know myself. Someone on our side, apparently.'

'You can now test your theory farther by letting Ganelon approach him.'

Ganelon did not move.

'It may be you have a family smell about you,' he finally said, 'and he only favors Amberites. So I will pass, thank you.'

'All right. It is not that important. Your guesses have been good so far. How do you interpret events?'

'Of the two factions out for the throne,' he said, 'that composed of Brand, Fiona, and Bleys was, as you said, more aware of the nature of the forces that play about Amber. Brand did not supply you with particulars – unless you omitted some incidents he might have related – but my guess is that this damage to the Pattern represents the means by which their allies gained access to your realm. One or more of them did that damage, which provided the dark route. If the watchdog here responds to a family smell or some other identifying information you all possess, then he could actually have been here all along and not seen fit to move against the despoilers.'

'Possibly,' Random observed. 'Any idea how it was accomplished?'

'Perhaps,' he replied. 'I will let you demonstrate it for me, if you are willing.'

'What does it involve?'

'Come this way,' he said, turning and heading over to the edge of the Pattern.

I followed him. Random did the same. The watchgriffin slunk at my side.

Ganelon turned and extended his hand.

'Corwin, may I trouble you for that dagger I fetched us?'

'Here,' I said, drawing it from my belt and passing it over.

'I repeat, what does it involve?' Random inquired.

'The blood of Amber,' Ganelon replied.

'I am not so sure I like this idea,' Random said.

'All you have to do is prick your finger with it,' he said, extending the blade, 'and let a drop fall upon the Pattern.'

'What will happen?'

'Let's try it and see.'

Random looked at me.

'What do you say?' he asked.

'Go ahead. Let's find out I'm intrigued.'

He nodded.

'Okay.'

He received the blade from Ganelon and nicked the tip of his left little finger. He squeezed the finger then, holding it above the Pattern. A tiny red bead appeared, grew larger, quivered, fell.

Immediately, a wisp of smoke rose from the spot where it struck, accompanied by a tiny crackling noise.

'I'll be damned,' said Random, apparently fascinated.

A tiny stain had come into being, gradually spreading to about the size of a half dollar.

'There you are,' said Ganelon. 'That is how it was done.'

The stain was indeed a miniature counterpart of the massive blot further to our right. The watchgriffin gave forth a small shriek and drew back, rapidly turning his head from one of us to the other.

'Easy, fellow. Easy,' I said, reaching out and calming him once more.

'But what could have caused such a large—' Random began, and then he nodded slowly.

'What indeed?' said Ganelon. 'I see no mark to show where your horse was destroyed.'

'The blood of Amber,' Random said. 'You are just full of insights today, aren't you?'

'Ask Corwin to tell you of Lorraine, the place where I dwelled for so long,' he said, 'the place where the dark circle grew. I am alert to the effects of these powers, though I knew them then only at a distance. These matters have become clearer to me with each new thing I have learned from you. Yes, I have insights now that I know more of these workings. Ask Corwin of the mind of his general.'

'Corwin,' Random said, 'give me the pierced Trump.'

I withdrew it from my pocket and smoothed it. The stains seemed more ominous now. Another thing also struck me. I did not believe that it had been executed by Dworkin, sage, mage, artist, and one-time mentor to the children of Oberon. It had not occurred to me until that moment that anyone else might be capable of producing one. While the style of this one did seem somehow familiar, it was not his work. Where had I seen that deliberate line before, less spontaneous than the master's, as though every movement had been totally intellectualized before the pen touched the paper? And there was something else wrong with it – a quality of idealization of a different order from that of our own Trumps, almost as if the artist had been working with old memories, glimpses, or descriptions rather than a living subject.

'The Trump, Corwin. If you please,' Random said.

There was that about the way in which he said it to make me hesitate. It gave rise to the feeling that he was somehow a jump ahead of me on something important, a feeling which I did not like at all.

'I've petted old ugly here for you, and I've just bled for the cause, Corwin. Now let's have it.'

I handed it over, my uneasiness increasing as he held it in his hand

and furrowed his brow. Why was I suddenly the stupid one? Does a night in Tir-na Nog'th slow cerebration? Why—

Random began to curse, a string of profanities unsurpassed by anything encountered in my long military career.

Then, 'What is it?' I said. 'I don't understand,'

'The blood of Amber,' he finally said. 'Whoever did it walked the Pattern first, you see. Then they stood there at the center and contacted him via this Trump. When he responded and a firm contact was achieved, they stabbed him. His blood flowed upon the Pattern, obliterating that part of it, as mine did here.'

He was silent for the space of several deep breaths.

'It smacks of a ritual,' I said.

'Damn rituals!' he said. 'Damn all of them! One of them is going to die, Corwin. I am going to kill him – or her.'

'I still do not—'

'I am a fool,' he said, 'for not seeing it right away. Look! Look closely!'

He thrust the pierced Trump at me. I stared. I still did not see.

'Now look at me!' he said. 'See me!'

I did. Then I looked back at the card.

I realized what he meant.

'I was never anything to him but a whisper of life in the darkness. But they used my son for this,' he said. 'That has to be a picture of Martin.'

2

Standing there beside the broken Pattern, regarding a picture of the man who may or may not have been Random's son, who may or may not have died of a knife wound received from a point within the Pattern, I turned and took a giant step back within my mind for an instant replay of the events which had brought me to this point of peculiar revelation. I had learned so many new things recently that the occurrences of the past few years seemed almost to constitute a different story than they had while I was living them. Now this new possibility and a number of things it implied had just shifted the perspective again.

I had not even been aware of my name when I had awakened in Greenwood, that private hospital in upstate New York where I had spent two totally blank weeks subsequent to my accident. It was only recently that I had been told that the accident itself had been engineered by my brother Bleys, immediately following my escape from the Porter Sanitarium in Albany. I got this story from my brother Brand, who had railroaded me into Porter in the first place, by means of fake psychiatric evidence. At Porter, I had been subjected to electroshock therapy over the span of several days, results ambiguous but presumably involving the return of a few memories. Apparently, this was what had scared Bleys into making the attempt on my life at the time of my escape, shooting out a couple of my tires on a curve above a lake. This doubtless would have resulted in my death, had Brand not been a step behind Bleys and out to protect his insurance investment, me. He said he had gotten word to the cops, dragged me out of the lake, and administered first aid until help arrived. Shortly after that, he was captured by his former partners – Bleys and our sister Fiona – who confined him in a guarded tower in a distant place in Shadow.

There had been two cabals, plotting and counterplotting after the throne, treading on one another's heels, breathing down one another's necks, and doing anything else to one another that might suggest itself at that range. Our brother Eric, backed by brothers Julian and Caine, had been preparing to take the throne, long left vacant by the unexplained absence of our father, Oberon, Unexplained to Eric, Julian, and Caine, that is. To the other group, consisting of Bleys, Fiona, and – formerly – Brand, it was not unexplained because they were responsible for it. They had arranged for this state of affairs to come into being in order to open the way for Bleys's accession to the throne. But Brand had committed a tactical error in attempting to obtain Caine's assistance in their play for the throne, in that Caine decided a better deal obtained in upholding Eric's part. This left Brand under close scrutiny, but did not immediately result in the betrayal of his partners' identities. At about that time, Bleys and Fiona decided to employ their secret allies against Eric. Brand had demurred in this, fearing the strength of those forces, and as a result had been rejected by Bleys and Fiona. With everyone on his back then, he had sought to upset the balance of powers completely by journeying to the shadow Earth where Eric had left me to die centuries before. It was only later that Eric had learned that I had not died but was possessed of total amnesia, which was almost as good, but set sister Flora to watch over my exile, and hoped that that was the last of it. Brand later told me he had gotten me committed to Porter in a desperate move to restore my memory as a preliminary to my return to Amber.

While Fiona and Bleys had been dealing with Brand, Eric had been in touch with Flora. She had arranged for my transfer to Greenwood from the clinic to which the police had taken me, with instructions to keep me narcotized, while Eric began arrangements for his coronation in Amber. Shortly thereafter, our brother Random's idyllic existence in Texorami was broken when Brand managed to send him a message outside the normal family channels – i.e., the Trumps – requesting deliverance. While Random, who was blissfully nonpartisan in the power struggle, was about this business, I managed to deliver myself from Greenwood, still relatively un-memoried. Having obtained Flora's address from Greenwood's frightened director, I betook myself to her place in Westchester, engaged in some elaborate bluffing, and moved in as a house guest. Random, in the meantime, had been less than successful in his attempt to rescue Brand. Slaying the snaky warden of the tower, he had had to flee its inner guards, utilizing one of the region's strangely mobile rocks. The guards, a hardy band of not quite human guys, had succeeded in pursuing him through Shadow, however, a feat normally impossible for most non-Amberites. Random had fled then to the shadow Earth where I was guiding Flora along the paths of misunderstanding while attempting to locate the proper route to enlightenment as to my own circumstances. Crossing the continent in response to my assurance that he would be under my protection, Random had come believing that his pursuers were my own creatures. When I helped him destroy them he was puzzled but unwilling to raise the issue while I seemed engaged in some private maneuver throneward. In fact, he had easily been tricked into conveying me back to Amber through Shadow.

This venture had proved beneficial in some respects while much less satisfactory in others. When I had finally revealed the true state of my personal situation, Random and our sister Deirdre, whom we had encountered along the way, conducted me to Amber's mirror-city within the sea, Rebma. There I had walked the image of the Pattern and recovered the bulk of my memories as a result – thereby also settling the issue as to whether I was the real Corwin or merely one of his shadows. From Rebma I had traveled into Amber, utilizing the power of the Pattern to effect an instantaneous journey home. After fighting an inconclusive duel with Eric, I had fled via the Trumps into the keeping of my beloved brother and would-be assassin, Bleys.

I joined with Bleys in an attack on Amber, a mismanaged affair which we had lost. Bleys vanished during the final engagement, under circumstances which looked likely to prove fatal but the more that I learned and thought about it, probably had not. This left me to become Eric's prisoner and an unwilling party to his coronation, after which he had had me blinded and locked away. A few years in the dungeons of Amber had seen a regeneration of my eyes, in direct proportion to the deterioration of my state of mind. It was only the accidental appearance of Dad's old adviser Dworkin, worse off mentally than myself, which had led to a way of escape.

After that, I set about recovering and I resolved to be more prudent the next time I went after Eric. I journeyed through Shadow toward an old land where I had once reigned – Avalon – with plans to obtain there a substance of which I alone among Amberites was aware, a chemical unique in its ability to undergo detonation in Amber. En route, I had passed through the land of Lorraine, there encountering my old exiled Avalonian general Ganelon, or someone very much like him. I remained because of a wounded knight, a girl, and a local menace peculiarly similar to a thing occurring in the vicinity of Amber herself – a growing black circle somehow related to the black road our enemies traveled, a thing for which I held myself partly responsible because of a curse I had pronounced at the time of my blinding. I won the battle, lost the girl, and traveled on to Avalon with Ganelon.

The Avalon we reached, we quickly learned, was under the protection of my brother Benedict, who had been having troubles of his own with a situation possibly akin to the black circle/black road menaces. Benedict had lost his right arm in the final engagement, but had been victorious in his battle with the hellmaids. He had warned me to keep my intentions toward Amber and Eric pure, and had then allowed us the hospitality of his manor while he remained for a few days more in the field. It was at his place that I met Dara.

Dara told me she was Benedict's great-granddaughter, whose existence had been kept secret from Amber. She drew me out as far as she could on Amber, the Pattern, the Trumps, and our ability to walk in Shadow. She was also an extremely skilled fencer. We indulged in a bit of casual lovemaking on my return from a hellride to a place where I obtained a sufficient quantity of rough diamonds to pay for the things I was going to need for my assault on Amber. The following day, Ganelon and I picked up our supply of the necessary chemicals and departed for the shadow Earth where I had spent my exile, there to obtain automatic weapons and ammunition manufactured to my specifications.

En route, we had some difficulties along the black road, which seemed to have extended its scope of influence among the worlds of Shadow. We were equal to the troubles it presented, but I almost perished in a duel with Benedict, who had pursued as through a wild hellride. Too angry for argument, he had fought me through a small wood – still a better man than I, even wielding his blade lefthanded. I had only managed to best him by means of a trick involving a property of the black road of which he was unaware. I had been convinced that he wanted my blood because of the affair with Dara.

But no. In the few words that passed between us he denied any knowledge of the existence of such a person. Instead, he had come after us convinced that I had murdered his servants. Now, Ganelon had indeed located some fresh corpses in the wood at Benedict's place, but we had agreed to forget about them, having no idea as to their identities and no desire to complicate our existence any further.

Leaving Benedict in the care of brother Gérard, whom I had summoned via his Trump from Amber, Ganelon and I proceeded to the shadow Earth, armed ourselves, recruited a strike force in Shadow, and headed off to attack Amber. But upon our arrival we discovered that Amber was already under attack by creatures which had come in along the black road. My new weapons quickly turned the tide in Amber's favor, and my brother Eric died in that battle, leaving me his problems, his ill will, and the Jewel of Judgment – a weather-controlling weapon he had used against me when Bleys and I had attacked Amber.

At that point, Dara showed up, swept on by us, rode into Amber, found her way to the Pattern, and proceeded to walk it – prima-facie evidence that we were indeed somehow related. During the course of this ordeal, however, she had exhibited what appeared to be peculiar physical transformations. Upon completion of the Pattern, she announced that Amber would be destroyed. Then she had vanished.

About a week later, brother Caine was murdered, under conditions arranged to show me as the culprit. The fact that I had slain his slayer was hardly satisfactory evidence of my innocence, in that the guy was necessarily in no condition to talk about it. Realizing, however, that I had seen his like before, in the persons of those creatures who had pursued Random into Flora's home, I finally found time to sit down with Random and hear the story of his unsuccessful attempt to rescue Brand from his tower.

Random, subsequent to my leaving him in Rebma years before, when I had journeyed to Amber to fight my duel with Eric, had been forced by Rebma's queen, Moire, to marry a woman of her court: Vialle, a lovely blind girl. This was partly intended as a punishment for Random, who years before had left Moire's late daughter Morganthe pregnant with Martin, the apparent subject of the damaged Trump Random now held in his hands. Strangely, for Random, he appeared to have fallen in love with Vialle, and he now resided with her in Amber.

After I left Random, I fetched the Jewel of Judgment and took it down to the chamber of the Pattern. There, I followed the partial instructions I had received for purposes of attuning it to my use. I underwent some unusual sensations during the process and was successful in obtaining control of its most obvious function: the ability to direct meteorological phenomena. After that, I questioned Flora concerning my exile. Her story seemed reasonable and jibed with those facts I did possess, although I had the feeling she was holding back somewhat on events at the time of my accident. She did promise to identify Caine's slayer as one of the same sort as those individuals Random and I had fought at her home in Westchester, however, and she assured me of her support in anything I might currently be about.

At the time I had heard Random's story, I was still unaware of the two factions and their machinations. I decided then that if Brand were still living, his rescue was of first importance, if for no other reason than the fact that he obviously possessed information that someone did not want circulated. I hit on a scheme for achieving this, the trial of which was only postponed for the time required by Gérard and myself for returning Caine's body to Amber. Part of this time, however, was appropriated by Gérard for purposes of beating me unconscious, just in case I had forgotten he was capable of the feat, to add weight to his words when he informed me that he would personally kill me should it turn out that I was the author of Amber's present woes. It was the most exclusive closed circuit fight I knew of, viewed by the family via Gérard's Trump – an act of insurance should I actually be the culprit and have a mind to erase his name from the list of the living because of his threat. We journeyed on to the Grove of the Unicorn then and exhumed Caine. At that time, we actually caught a brief glimpse of the legendary unicorn of Amber.

That evening we met in the library of the palace in Amber – we being Random, Gérard, Benedict, Julian, Deirdre, Fiona, Flora, Llewella, and myself. There we tested my idea for finding Brand. It amounted to all nine of us simultaneously attempting to reach him via his Trump. And we succeeded.

We contacted him and were successful in transporting him back to Amber. In the midst of the excitement, however, with all of us crowded about as Gérard bore him through, someone planted a dagger in Brand's side. Gérard immediately elected himself attending physician and cleared the room.

The rest of us moved to a downstairs sitting room, there to backbite and discuss events. During this time, Fiona advised me that the Jewel of Judgment might represent a hazard in situations of prolonged exposure, suggesting the possibility that it, rather than his wounds, might have been the cause of Eric's death. One of the first signs, she believed, was a distortion of one's time-sense – an apparent slowdown of temporal sequence, actually representing a speed-up of physiological events. I resolved to be more cautious with it, in that she was more conversant with these matters than the rest of us, having once been an advanced pupil of Dworkin's.

And perhaps she was correct. Perhaps there was such an effect in operation later that evening when I returned to my own quarters. At least, it seemed as if the person who attempted to kill me was moving a trifle more slowly than I would have myself under similar circumstances. At that, the stroke was almost successful. The blade caught me in the side and the world went away.

Leaking life, I awoke in my old bed in my old home on the shadow Earth where I had dwelled for so long as Carl Corey. How I had been returned, I had no idea. I crawled outside and into a blizzard. Clinging precariously to consciousness, I cached the Jewel of Judgment in my old compost heap, for the world did indeed seem to be slowing down about me. Then I made it to the road, to try flagging down a passing motorist.

It was a friend and former neighbor, Bill Roth, who found me there and drove me to the nearest clinic. There, I was treated by the same doctor who had attended me years before, at the time of my accident. He suspected I might be a psychiatric case, as the old record did reflect that faked state of affairs.

Bill showed up later, however, and set a number of things right. An attorney, he had grown curious at the time of my disappearance and done some investigating. He had learned about my fake certification and my successive escapes. He even possessed details on these matters and on the accident itself. He still felt there was something strange about me, but it did not really bother him that much.

Later, Random contacted me via my Trump and advised me that

Brand had come around and was asking for me. With Random's assistance, I returned to Amber. I went to see Brand. It was then that I learned of the nature of the power struggle which had been going on about me, and the identities of the participants. His story, together with what Bill had told me back on the shadow Earth, finally brought some sense and coherence to occurrences of the past several years. He also told me more concerning the nature of the danger we currently faced.

I did nothing the following day, ostensibly for purposes of preparing myself for a visit to Tir-na Nog'th, actually to buy additional time in which to recover from my injury. This commitment made, however, it had to be kept. I did journey to the city in the sky that night, encountering a confusing collection of signs and portents, signifying perhaps nothing, and collecting a peculiar mechanical arm from the ghost of my brother Benedict while I was about it.

Returned from this excursion on high, I breakfasted with Random and Ganelon before setting out across Kolvir to return home. Slowly, bewilderingly, the trail began to change about us. It was as though we were walking in Shadow, a well-nigh impossible feat this near to Amber. When we reached this conclusion, we tried to alter our course, but neither Random nor I were able to affect the changing scene. About that time, the unicorn put in an appearance. It seemed to want us to follow it. We did.

It had led us through a kaleidoscopic series of changes, until finally we arrived at this place, where it abandoned us to our present devices. Now, with this entire sequence of events tumbling though my head, my mind moved about the peripheries, pushed its way forward, returned to the words Random had just spoken. I felt that I was slightly ahead of him once more. For how long this state of affairs might last, I did not know, but I realized where I had seen work by the same hand which had executed the pierced Trump.

Brand had often painted when he was entering one of his melancholy periods, and his favorite techniques came to mind as I recalled canvas after canvas he had brightened or darkened. Add to this his campaign of years before to obtain recollections and descriptions from everyone who had known Martin. While Random had not recognized his style, I wondered how long it might be before he began thinking as I just had about the possible ends of Brand's information gathering. Even if his hand had not actually propelled the blade, Brand was party to the act by providing the means. I knew Random well enough to know that he meant what he had said. He would try to kill Brand as soon as he saw the connection. This was going to be more than awkward.

It had nothing to do with the fact that Brand had probably saved my life. I figured I had squared accounts with him by getting him out of that damned tower. No. It was neither indebtedness nor sentiment that caused me to cast about for ways to mislead Random or slow him down. It was the naked, frigid fact that I needed Brand. He had seen to that. My reason for saving him was no more altruistic than his had been in dragging me out of the lake. He possessed something I needed now: information. He had realized this immediately and he was rationing it – his life's union dues.

'I do see the resemblance,' I said to Random, 'and you may well be right about what happened.'

'Of course I am right.'

'It is the card that was pierced,' I said.

'Obviously. I don't—'

'He was not brought through on the Trump, then. The person who did it therefore made contact, but was unable to persuade him to come across.'

'So? The contact had progressed to a point of sufficient solidity and proximity that he was able to stab him anyway. He was probably even able to achieve a mental lock and hold him where he was while he bled. The kid probably hadn't had much experience with the Trumps.'

'Maybe yes, maybe no,' I said, 'Llewella or Moire might be able to tell us how much he knew about the Trumps, But what I was getting at was the possibility that contact could have been broken before death. If he inherited your regenerative abilities he might have survived.'

'Might have? I don't want guesses! I want answers!'

I commenced a balancing act within my mind. I believed I knew something that he did not, but then my source was not the best. Also, I wanted to keep quiet about the possibility because I had not had a chance to discuss it with Benedict. On the other hand, Martin was

Random's son, and I did want to direct his attention away from Brand.

'Random, I may have something,' I said.

'What?'

'Right after Brand was stabbed,' I said, 'when we were talking together in the sitting room, do you remember when the conversation turned to the subject of Martin?'

'Yes. Nothing new came up.'

'I had something I might have added at that time, but I restrained myself because everyone was there. Also, because I wanted to pursue it in private with the party concerned.'

'Who?'

'Benedict.'

'Benedict? What has he to do with Martin?'

'I do not know. That is why I wanted to keep it quiet until I found out. And my source of information was a touchy one, at that.'

'Go ahead.'

'Dara. Benedict gets mad as hell whenever I mention her name, but so far a number of things she told me have proved correct – things like the journey of Julian and Gérard along the black road, their injury, their stay in Avalon, Benedict admitted these things had happened.'

'What did she say about Martin?'

Indeed. How to phrase it without giving away the show on Brand . . . ? Dara had said that Brand had visited Benedict a number of times in Avalon, over a span of years. The time differential between Amber and Avalon is such that it seemed likely now that I thought about it that the visits fell into the period when Brand was so actively seeking information on Martin. I had wondered what kept drawing him back there, since he and Benedict had never been especially chummy.

'Only that Benedict had had a visitor named Martin, whom she thought was from Amber,' I lied.

'When?'

'Some while back. I'm not sure.'

'Why didn't you tell me this before?'

'It is not really very much – and besides, you had never seemed especially interested in Martin.'

Random shifted his gaze to the griffin, crouched and gurgling on my right, then nodded.

'I am now,' he said. 'Things change. If he is still alive, I would like to get to know him. If he is not . . .'

'Okay,' I said. 'The best way to be about either one is to start figuring a way to get home. I believe we have seen what we were supposed to see and I would like to clear out.'

'I was thinking about that,' he said, 'and it occurred to me that we could probably use this Pattern for that purpose. Just head out to the center and transfer back.'

'Going in along the dark area?' I asked.

'Why not? Ganelon has already tried it and he's okay.'

'A moment,' said Ganelon. 'I did not say that it was easy, and I am positive you could not get the horses to go that route.'

'What do you mean?' I said.

'Do you remember that place where we crossed the black road – back when we were fleeing Avalon?'

'Of course.'

'Well, the sensations I experienced in retrieving the card and the dagger were not unlike the upset that came over us at that time. It is one of the reasons I was running so fast. I would favor trying the Trumps again first, under the theory that this point is congruent with Amber.'

I nodded.

'All right. We might as well try making it as easy as we can. Let's collect the horses first.'

We did this, learning the length of the griffin's leash while we were about it. He was drawn up short about thirty meters from the cave mouth, and immediately set up a bleating complaint. This did not make the job of pacifying the horses any easier, but it did give rise to a peculiar notion which I decided to keep to myself.

Once we had things under control, Random located his Trumps and I brought out my own.

'Let's try for Benedict,' he said.

'All right. Any time now.'

I noticed immediately that the cards felt cold again, a good sign. I shuffled out Benedict's and began the preliminaries. Beside me, Random did the same.

Contact came almost at once.

'What is the occasion?' Benedict asked, his eyes moving over Random, Ganelon, and the horses, then meeting with my own.

'Will you bring us through?' I said.

'Horses, too?'

'The works.'

'Come ahead.'

He extended his hand and I touched it. We all moved toward him. Moments later, we stood with him in a high, rocky place, a chill wind ruffling our garments, the sun of Amber past midday in a sky full of clouds. Benedict wore a stiff leather jacket and buckskin leggings. His shirt was a faded yellow. An orange cloak concealed the stump of his right arm. He tightened his long jaw and peered down at me.

'Interesting spot you hie from,' he said. 'I glimpsed something of the background.'

I nodded.

'Interesting view from this height, also,' I said, noting the spyglass at his belt at the same time that I realized we stood on the wide ledge of rock from which Eric had commanded battle on the day of his death and my return. I moved to regard the dark swath through Garnath, far below and stretching off to the horizon.

'Yes,' he said. 'The black road appears to have stabilized its boundaries at most points. At a few others though, it is still widening. It is almost as if it is nearing a final conformity with some – pattern . . . Now tell me, from what point have you journeyed?'

'I spent last night in Tir-na Nog'th,' I said, 'and this morning we went astray in crossing Kolvir.'

'Not an easy thing to do,' he said. 'Getting lost on your own mountain. You keep heading east, you know. That is the direction from which the sun has been known to take its course.'

I felt my face flush.

'There was an accident,' I said, looking away. 'We lost a horse.'

'What sort of accident?'

'A serious one – for the horse.'

'Benedict,' said Random, suddenly looking up from what I realized to be the pierced Trump, 'what can you tell me concerning my son Martin?'

Benedict studied him for several moments before he spoke. Then, 'Why the sudden interest?' he asked.

'Because I have reason to believe he may be dead,' he said. 'If that is the case, I want to avenge it. If it is not the case – well, the thought that it might be has caused me some upset. If he is still living, I would like to meet him and talk with him.'

'What makes you think he might be dead?'

Random glanced at me. I nodded.

'Start with breakfast,' I said.

'While he is doing that, I'll find us lunch,' said Ganelon, rummaging in one of the bags.

'The unicorn showed us the way . . .' Random began.

3

We sat in silence. Random had finished speaking and Benedict was staring skyward over Garnath. His face betrayed nothing. I had long ago learned to respect his silence.

At length, he nodded, once, sharply, and turned to regard Random.

'I have long suspected something of this order,' he stated, 'from things that Dad and Dworkin let fall over the years. I had the impression there was a primal Pattern which they had either located or created, situating our Amber but a shadow away to draw upon its forces. I never obtained any notion as to how one might travel to that place, however.' He turned back toward Garnath, gesturing with his chin. 'And that, you tell me, corresponds to what was done there?'

'It seems to,' Random replied.

'. . . Brought about by the shedding of Martin's blood?'

'I think so.'

Benedict raised the Trump Random had passed him during his narration. At that time, Benedict had made no comment.

'Yes,' he said now, 'this is Martin. He came to me after he departed Rebma. He stayed with me a long while.'

'Why did he go to you?' Random asked.

Benedict smiled faintly.

'He had to go somewhere, you know,' he said. 'He was sick of his position in Rebma, ambivalent toward Amber, young, free, and just come into his power through the Pattern. He wanted to get away, see new things, travel in Shadow – as we all did. I had taken him to Avalon once when he was a small boy, to let him walk on dry land of a summer, to teach him to ride a horse, to have him see a crop harvested. When he was suddenly in a position to go anywhere he would in an instant, his choices were still restricted to the few places of which he had knowledge. True, he might have dreamed up a place in that instant and gone there – creating it, as it were. But he was also aware that he still had many things to learn, to ensure his safety in Shadow. So he elected to come to me, to ask me to teach him. And I did. He spent the better part of a year at my place. I taught him to fight, taught him of the ways of the Trumps and of Shadow, instructed him in those things an Amberite must know if he is to survive.'

'Why did you do all these things?' Random asked.

'Someone had to. It was me that he came to, so it was mine to do,' Benedict replied. 'It was not as if I were not very fond of the boy, though,' he added.

Random nodded.

'You say that he was with you for almost a year. What became of him after that?'

'That wanderlust you know as well as I. Once he had obtained some confidence in his abilities, he wanted to exercise them. In the course of instructing him, I had taken him on journeys in Shadow myself, had introduced him to people of my acquaintance at various places. But there came a time when he wanted to make his own way. One day then, he bade me good-bye and fared forth.'

'Have you seen him since?' Random asked.

'Yes. He returned periodically, staying with me for a time, to tell me of his adventures, his discoveries. It was always clear that it was just a visit. After a time, he would get restless and depart again.'

'When was the last time you saw him?'

'Several years ago, Avalon time, under the usual circumstances. He showed up one morning, stayed for perhaps two weeks, told me of the things he had seen and done, talked of the many things he wanted to do. Later, he set off once more.'

'And you never heard from him again?'

'On the contrary. There were messages left with mutual friends when he would pass their way. Occasionally, he would even contact me via my Trump—'

'He had a set of the Trumps?' I broke in.

'Yes, I made him a gift of one of my extra decks.'

'Did you have a Trump for him?'

He shook his head.

'I was not even aware that such a Trump existed, until I saw this one,' he said, raising the card, glancing at it, and passing it back to

Random. 'I haven't the art to prepare one. Random, have you tried reaching him with this Trump?'

'Yes, any number of times since we came across it. Just a few minutes ago, as a matter of fact. Nothing.'

'Of course that proves nothing. If everything occurred as you guessed and he did survive it, he may have resolved to block any future attempts at contact. He does know how to do that.'

'Did it occur as I guessed? Do you know more about it?'

'I have an idea,' Benedict said. 'You see, he did show up injured at a friend's place – off in Shadow – some years ago. It was a body wound, caused by the thrust of a blade. They said he came to them in very bad shape and did not go into details as to what had occurred. He remained for a few days – until he was able to get around again – and departed before he was really fully recovered. That was the last they heard of him. The last that I did, also.'

'Weren't you curious?' Random asked. 'Didn't you go looking for him?'

'Of course I was curious. I still am. But a man should have the right to lead his own life without the meddling of relatives, no matter how well-intentioned. He had pulled through the crisis and he did not attempt to contact me. He apparently knew what he wanted to do. He did leave a message for me with the Tecys, saying that when I learned of what had happened I was not to worry, that he knew what he was about.'

'The Tecys?' I said.

'That's right. Friends of mine off in Shadow.'

I refrained from saying the things that I might. I had thought them just another part of Data's story, for she had so twisted the truth in other areas. She had mentioned the Tecys to me as if she knew them, as if she had stayed with them – all with Benedict's knowledge. The moment did not seem appropriate, however, to tell him of my previous night's vision in Tir-na Nog'th and the things it had indicated concerning his relationship to the girl. I had not yet had sufficient time to ponder the matter and all that it implied.

Random stood, paced, paused near the ledge, his back to us, fingers knotted behind him. After a moment, he turned and stalked back.

'How can we get in touch with the Tecys?' he asked Benedict.

'No way,' said Benedict, 'except to go and see them.'

Random turned to me.

'Corwin, I need a horse. You say that Star's been through a number of hellrides . . .'

'He's had a busy morning.'

'It wasn't that strenuous. It was mostly fright, and he seems okay now. May I borrow him?'

Before I could answer, he turned toward Benedict.

'You'll take me, won't you?' he said.

Benedict hesitated.

'I do not know what more there is to learn—' he began.

'Anything! Anything at all they might remember – possibly something that did not really seem important at the time but is now, knowing what we know.'

Benedict looked to me. I nodded.

'He can ride Star, if you are willing to take him.'

'All right,' Benedict said, getting to his feet. 'I'll fetch my mount.'

He turned and headed off toward the place where the great striped beast was tethered.

'Thanks, Corwin,' Random said.

'I'll let you do me a favor in return.'

'What.'

'Let me borrow Martin's Trump.'

'What for?'

'An idea just hit me. It is too complicated to get into if you want to get moving. No harm should come of it, though.'

He chewed his lip.

'Okay. I want it back when you are done with it.'

'Of course.'

'Will it help find him?'

'Maybe.'

He passed me the card.

'You heading back to the palace now?' he asked.

'Yes.'

'Would you tell Vialle what has happened and where I have gone? She worries.'

'Sure. I'll do that.'

'I'll take good care of Star.'

'I know that Good luck.'

'Thanks.'

I rode Firedrake. Ganelon walked. He had insisted. We followed the route I had taken in pursuing Dara on the day of the battle. Along with recent developments, that is probably what made me think of her again. I dusted off my feelings and examined them carefully. I realized then that despite the games she had played with me, the killings she had doubtless been privy or party to, and her stated designs upon the realm, I was still attracted to her by something more than curiosity. I was not really surprised to discover this. Things had looked pretty much the same the last time I had pulled a surprise inspection in the emotional barracks. I wondered then how much of truth there might have been to my final vision of the previous night, wherein her possible line of descent from Benedict had been stated. There was indeed a physical resemblance, and I was more than half convinced. In the ghost city, of course, the shade of Benedict had conceded as much, raising his new, strange arm in her defense . . .

'What's funny?' Ganelon asked, from where he strode to my left.

'The arm,' I said, 'that came to me from Tir-na Nog'th – I had worried over some hidden import, some unforeseen force of destiny to the thing, coming as it had into our world from that place of mystery and dream. Yet it did not even last the day. Nothing remained when the Pattern destroyed Iago. The entire evening's visions come to nothing.'

Ganelon cleared his throat.

'Well, it wasn't exactly the way you seem to think,' he said.

'What do you mean?'

'That arm device was not in Iago's saddlebag. Random stowed it your bag. That's where the food was, and after we had eaten he returned the utensils to where they had been in his own bag, but not the arm. There was no space.'

'Oh,' I said. 'Then—'

Ganelon nodded.

'—So he has it with him now,' he finished.

'The arm and Benedict both. Damn! I've small liking for that thing. It tried to kill me. No one has ever been attacked in Tir-na Nog'th before.'

'But Benedict, Benedict's okay. He's on our side, even if you have some differences at the moment Right?'

I did not answer him.

He reached up and took Firedrake's reins, drawing him to a halt. He stared up then, studying my face.

'Corwin, what happened up there, anyway? What did you learn?'

I hesitated. In truth, what had I learned in the city in the sky? No one was certain as to the mechanism behind the visions of Tir-na Nog'th. It could well be, as we have sometimes suspected, that the place simply served to objectify one's unspoken fears and desires, mixing them perhaps with unconscious guesswork. Sharing conclusions and reasonably based conjectures was one thing. Suspicions engendered by something unknown were likely better retained than given currency. Still, that arm was solid enough . . .

'I told you,' I said, 'that I had knocked that arm off the ghost of Benedict. Obviously, we were fighting.'

'You see it then as an omen that you and Benedict will eventually be in conflict?'

'Perhaps.'

'You were shown a reason for it, weren't you?'

'Okay,' I said, finding a sigh without trying. 'Yes. It was indicated that Dara was indeed related to Benedict – a thing which may well be correct. It is also quite possible, if it is true, that he is unaware of it. Therefore, we keep quiet about it until we can verify it or discount it Understood?'

'Of course. But how could this thing be?'

'Just as she said.'

'Great-granddaughter?'

I nodded.

'By whom?'

'The hellmaid we knew only by reputation – Lintra, the lady who cost him his arm.'

'But that battle was only a recent thing.'

'Time flows differently in different realms of Shadow, Ganelon. In the farther reaches— It would not be impossible.'

He shook his head and relaxed his grip on the reins.

'Corwin, I really think Benedict should know about this,' he said. 'If it is true, you ought to give him a chance to prepare himself rather than let him discover it of a sudden. You people are such an infertile lot that paternity seems to hit you harder than it does others. Look at Random. For years, he had disowned his son, and now – I've a feeling he'd risk his life for him.'

'So do I,' I said. 'Now forget the first part but carry the second one a step farther in the case of Benedict.'

'You think he would take Dora's side against Amber?'

'I would rather avoid presenting him with the choice by not letting him know that it exists – if it exists.'

'I think you do him a disservice. He is hardly an emotional infant Get hold of him on the Trump and tell him your suspicions. That way, at least, he can be thinking about it, rather than have him risk some sudden confrontation unprepared.'

'He would not believe me. You have seen how he gets whenever I mention Dara.'

'That in itself may say something. Possibly he suspects what might have happened and rejects it so vehemently because he would have it otherwise.'

'Right now it would just widen a rift I am trying to heal.'

'Your holding back on him now may serve to rupture it completely when he finds out.'

'No. I believe I know my brother better than you do.'

He released the reins.

'Very well,' be said. 'I hope you are right.'

I did not answer, but started Firedrake to moving once more. There was an unspoken understanding between us that Ganelon could ask me anything he wanted, and it also went without saying that I would listen to any advice he had to offer me. This was partly because his position was unique. We were not related. He was no Amberite. The struggles and problems of Amber were his only by choice. We had been friends and then enemies long ago, and finally, more recently, friends again and allies in a battle in his adopted land. That matter concluded, he had asked to come with me, to help me deal with my own affairs and those of Amber. As I saw it, he owed me nothing now, nor I him – if one keeps a scoreboard tally on such matters. Therefore, it was friendship alone that bound us, a stronger thing than bygone debts and points of honor: in other words, a thing which gave him the right to bug me on matters such as this, where I might have told even Random to go to hell once I had made up my mind. I realized I should not be irritated when everything that he said was tendered in good faith. Most likely it was an old military feeling, going back to our earliest relationship as well as being tied in with the present state of affairs: I do not like having my decisions and orders questioned. Probably, I decided, I was irritated even more by the fact that he had made some shrewd guesses of late, and some fairly sound suggestions based upon them – things I felt I ought to have caught myself. No one likes to admit to a resentment based on something like that. Still . . . was that all? A simple projection of dissatisfaction over a few instances of personal inadequacy? An old army reflex as to the sanctity of my decisions? Or was it something deeper that had been bothering me and was just now coming to the surface?

'Corwin,' Ganelon said, 'I've been doing some thinking . . .'

I sighed.

'Yes?'

'. . . about Random's son. The way your crowd heals, I suppose it is possible that he might have survived and still be about.'

'I would like to think so.'

'Do not be too hasty.'

'What do you mean?'

'I gather he had very little contact with Amber and the rest of the family, growing up in Rebma the way that he did.'

'That is the way I understand it too.'

'In fact outside of Benedict – and Llewella, back in Rebma – the only other one he apparently had contact with would have been the one who stabbed him – Bleys, Brand, or Fiona. It has occurred to me that he probably has a pretty distorted view of the family.'

'Distorted,' I said, 'but maybe not unwarranted, if I see what you are getting at.'

'I think you do. It seems conceivable that he is not only afraid of the family, but may have it in for the lot of you.'

'It is possible,' I said.

'Do you think he could have thrown in with the enemy?'

I shook my head.

'Not if he knows they are the tools of the crowd that tried to kill him.'

'But are they? I wonder . . . ? You say Brand got scared and tried to back out of whatever arrangement they had with the black road gang. If they are that strong, I wonder whether Fiona and Bleys might not have become *their* tools? If this were the case, I could see Martin angling for something which gave him power over them.'

'Too elaborate a structure of guesses,' I said.

'The enemy seems to know a lot about you.'

'True, but they had a couple traitors to give them lessons.'

'Could they have given them everything you say Dara knew?'

'That is a good point,' I said, 'but it is hard to say.' Except for the business about the Tecys, which occurred to me immediately, I decided to keep that to myself for the moment though, to find out what he was leading up to, rather than going off on a tangent. So, 'Martin was hardly in a position to tell them much about Amber,' I said.

Ganelon was silent for a moment. Then, 'Have you had a chance to check on the business I asked you about that night at your tomb?' he said.

'What business?'

'Whether the Trumps could be bugged,' he said. 'Now that we know Martin had a deck . . .'

It was my turn to be silent while a small family of moments crossed my path, single file, from the left, sticking their tongues out at me.

'No,' I said then. 'I haven't had a chance.'

We proceeded on for quite a distance before he said, 'Corwin, the night you brought Brand back . . . ?'

'Yes?'

'You say you accounted for everyone later, in trying to figure out who it was that stabbed you, and that any of them would have been hard put to pull the stunt in the time involved.'

'Oh,' I said, 'and oh.'

He nodded.

'Now you have another relative to think about. He may lack the family finesse only because he is young and unpracticed.'

Sitting there in my mind, I gestured back at the silent parade of moments that crossed between Amber and then.

4

She asked who it was when I knocked and I told her.

'Just a moment.'

I heard her footsteps and then the door swung in. Vialle is only a little over five feet tall and quite slim. Brunette, fine featured, very soft-spoken. She was wearing red. Her sightless eyes looked through me, reminding me of darkness past, of pain.

'Random,' I said, 'asked me to tell you that he would be delayed a little longer, but that there was nothing to worry about.'

'Please come in,' she said, stepping aside and drawing the door the rest of the way open.

I did. I did not want to, but I did. I had not intended to take Random's request literally – that I tell her what had happened and where he had gone. I had meant simply to tell her what I had already said, nothing more. It was not until we had ridden our separate ways that I realized exactly what Random's request had amounted to: he had just asked me to go tell his wife, to whom I had never spoken more than half a dozen words, that he had taken off to go looking for his illegitimate son – the lad whose mother, Morganthe, had committed suicide, a thing for which Random had been punished by being forced to marry Vialle. The fact that the marriage had somehow worked beautifully was something which still amazed me. I had no desire to dispense a load of awkward tidings, and as I moved into the room I sought alternatives.

I passed a bust of Random set on a high shelf on the wall to my left. I had actually gone by before it registered that my brother was indeed the subject. Across the room, I saw her workbench. Turning back, I studied the bust.

'I did not realize that you sculpted,' I said.

'Yes.'

Casting my gaze about the apartment, I quickly located other examples of her work.

536

'Quite good,' I said.

'Thank you. Won't you sit down?'

I lowered myself into a large, high-armed chair, which proved more comfortable than it had looked. She seated herself on a low divan to my right, curling her legs beneath her.

'May I get you something to eat, or to drink?'

'No thanks. I can only stay a short while. What it is, is that Random, Ganelon, and I had gotten a bit sidetracked on the way home, and after that delay we met with Benedict for a time. The upshot of it was that Random and Benedict had to make another small journey.'

'How long will be be away?'

'Probably overnight. Maybe a bit longer. If he is going to be much longer he will probably call back on someone's Trump, and we'll let you know.'

My side began to throb and I rested my hand upon it, massaging it gently.

'Random has told me many things about you,' she said.

I chuckled.

'Are you certain you would not care for something to eat? It would be no trouble.'

'Did he tell you that I am always hungry?'

She laughed.

'No. But if you have been as active as you say, I would guess that you did not take time for lunch.'

'In that you would be only half-correct. All right. If you've a spare piece of bread lying about it might do me some good to gnaw on it.'

'Fine. Just a moment.'

She rose and departed into the next room. I took the opportunity to scratch heartily all about my wound where it was suddenly itching fit to kill. I had accepted her hospitality partly for this reason and partly because of the realization that I actually was hungry. Only a little later it struck me that she could not have seen me attacking my side as I was. Her sure movements, her confident manner, had relaxed my awareness of her blindness. Good. It pleased me that she was able to carry it so well.

I heard her humming a tune: 'The Ballad of the Water Crossers', the song of Amber's great merchant navy. Amber is not noted for manufacture, and agriculture has never been our forte. But our ships sail the shadows, plying between anywhere and anywhere, dealing in anything. Just about every male Amberite, noble or otherwise, spends some time in the fleet. Those of the blood laid down the trade routes long ago that other vessels might follow, the seas of a double dozen worlds in every captain's head. I had assisted in this in times gone by, and though my involvement had never been so deep as Gérard's or Caine's, I had been mightily moved by the forces of the deep and the spirit of the men who crossed it.

After a while, Vialle came in bearing a tray heavy with bread, meat, cheese, fruit, and a flask of wine. She set it upon a table near at hand.

'You mean to feed a regiment?' I asked.

'Best to be safe.'

'Thanks. Won't you join me?'

'A piece of fruit, perhaps,' she said.

Her fingers sought for a second, located an apple. She returned to the divan.

'Random tells me you wrote that song,' she said.

'That was a very long time ago, Vialle.'

'Have you composed any recently?'

I began to shake my head, caught myself, said, 'No. That part of me is . . . resting.'

'Pity. It is lovely.'

'Random is the real musician in the family.'

'Yes, he is very good. But performance and composition are two different things.'

'True. One day when things have eased up . . . Tell me, are you happy here in Amber? Is everything to your liking? Is there anything that you need?'

She smiled.

'All that I need is Random. He is a good man.'

I was strangely moved to hear her speak of him in this fashion.

'Then I am happy for you,' I said. And, 'Younger, smaller . . . he might have had it a bit rougher than the rest of us,' I went on. 'Nothing quite as useless as another prince when there is already a crowd of them about. I was as guilty as the rest Bleys and I once stranded him for two days on an islet to the south of here . . .'

'. . . And Gérard went and got him when he learned of it,' she said.

'Yes, he told me. It must bother you if you remember it after all this time.'

'It must have made an impression on him, too.'

'No, he forgave you long ago. He told it as a joke. Also, he drove a spike through the heel of your boot – pierced your foot when you put it on.'

'Then it *was* Random! I'll be damned! I had always blamed Julian for that one.'

'That one bothers Random.'

'How long ago all of this was . . .' I said.

I shook my head and continued eating. Hunger seized me and she gave me several minutes of silence in which to get the upper hand on it. When I had, I felt compelled to say something.

'That is better. Much better,' I began. 'It was a peculiar and trying night that I spent in the sky-city.'

'Did you receive omens of a useful nature?'

'I do not know how useful they might prove. On the other hand, I suppose I'd rather have had them than not. Have there been any interesting happenings hereabouts?'

'A servant tells me your brother Brand continues to rally. He ate well this morning, which is encouraging.'

'True,' I said. 'True. It would seem he is out of danger.'

'Likely. It – it is a terrible series of happenings to which you have all been subjected. I am sorry. I was hoping you might obtain some indication of an upturn in your affairs during the night you spent in Tir-na Nog'th.'

'It does not matter,' I said. 'I am not that sure of the value of the thing.'

'Then why – oh.'

I studied her with renewed interest. Her face still betrayed nothing, but her right hand twitched, tapping and plucking at the material of the divan. Then, as with a sudden awareness of its eloquence, she stilled it. She was obviously a person who had answered her own question and wished now she had done it in silence.

'Yes,' I said, 'I was stalling. You are aware of my injury.'

She nodded.

'I am not angry with Random for having told you,' I said. 'His judgment has always been acute and geared to defense. I see no reason not to rely on it myself. I must inquire as to how much he has told you, however, both for your own safety and my peace of mind. For there are things I suspect but have not yet spoken.'

'I understand. It is difficult to assess a negative – the things he might have left out, I mean – but he tells me most things. I know your story and most of the others'. He keeps me aware of events, suspicions, conjectures.'

'Thank you,' I said, taking a sip of the wine. 'It makes it easier for me to speak then, seeing how things are with you. I am going to tell you everything that happened from breakfast till now . . .'

So I did.

She smiled occasionally as I spoke, but she did not interrupt. When I had finished, she asked, 'You thought that mention of Martin would upset me?'

'It seemed possible,' I told her.

'No,' she said. 'You see, I knew Martin in Rebma, when he was but a small boy. I was there while he was growing up. I liked him then. Even if he were not Random's son he would still be dear to me. I can only be pleased with Random's concern and hope that it has come in time to benefit them both.'

I shook my head.

'I do not meet people like you too often,' I said. 'I am glad that I finally have.'

She laughed, then said, 'You were without sight for a long while.'

'Yes.'

'It can embitter a person, or it can give him a greater joy in those things which he does have.'

I did not have to think back over my feelings from those days of blindness to know that I was a person of the first sort, even discounting the circumstances under which I had suffered it I am sorry, but that is the way that I am, and I am sorry.

'True,' I said. 'You are fortunate.'

'It is really only a state of mind – a thing a Lord of Shadow can easily appreciate.'

She rose.

'I have always wondered as to your appearance,' she said. 'Random has described you, but that is different. May I?'

'Of course.'

She approached and placed her finger tips upon my face. Delicately, she traced my features.

'Yes,' she said, 'you are much as I had thought you would be. And I feel the tension in you. It has been there for a long while, has it not?'

'In some form or other, I suppose, ever since my return to Amber.'

'I wonder,' she said, 'whether you might have been happier before you regained your memory.'

'It is one of those impossible questions,' I said. 'I might also be dead if I had not. But putting that part aside for a moment, in those times there was still a thing that drove me, that troubled me every day. I was constantly looking for ways to discover who I really was, what I was.'

'But were you happier, or less happy, than you are now?'

'Neither,' I said. 'Things balance out. It is, as you suggested, a state of mind. And even if it were not so, I could never go back to that other life, now that I know who I am, now that I have found Amber.'

'Why not?'

'Why do you ask me these things?'

'I want to understand you,' she said. 'Ever since I first heard of you back in Rebma, even before Random told me stories, I wondered what it was that drove you. Now I've the opportunity – no right, of course, just the opportunity – I felt it worth speaking out of turn and order beyond my station simply to ask you.'

A half-chuckle caught me.

'Fairly taken,' I said. 'I will see whether I can be honest. Hatred drove me at first – hatred for my brother Eric – and my desire for the throne. Had you asked me on my return which was the stronger, I would have said that it was the summons of the throne. Now, though . . . now I would have to admit that it was actually the other way around. I had not realized it until this moment, but it is true. But Eric is dead and there is nothing left of what I felt then. The throne remains, but now I find that my feelings toward it are mixed. There is a possibility that none of us has a right to it under present circumstances, and even if all family objections were removed I would not take it at this time. I would have to see stability restored to the realm and a number of questions answered first.'

'Even if these things showed that you may not have the throne?'

'Even so.'

'Then I begin to understand.'

'What? What is there to understand?'

'Lord Corwin, my knowledge of the philosophical bases of these things is limited, but it is my understanding that you are able to find anything you wish within Shadow. This has troubled me for a long while, and I never fully understood Random's explanations. If you wished, could not each of you wane in Shadow and find yourself another Amber – like this one in all respects, save that you ruled there or enjoyed whatever other status you might desire?'

'Yes, we can locate such places,' I said.

'Then why is this not done, to have an end of strife?'

'It is because a place could be found which *seemed* to be the same – but that would be all. We are a part of this Amber as surely as it is a part of us. Any shadow of Amber would have to be populated with shadows of ourselves to seem worth while. We could even except the shadow of our own person should we choose to move into a ready realm. However, the shadow folk would not be exactly like the other people here. A shadow is never precisely like that which casts it. These little differences add up. They are actually worse than major ones. It would amount to entering a nation of strangers. The best mundane comparison which occurs to me is an encounter with a person who strongly resembles another person you know. You keep expecting him to act like your acquaintance; worse yet, you have a tendency to act toward him as you would toward that other. You face him with a certain mask and his responses are not appropriate. It is an uncomfortable feeling. I never enjoy meeting people who remind me of other people. Personality is the one thing we cannot control in our manipulations of Shadow. In fact, it is the means by which we can tell one another from shadows of ourselves. This is why Flora could not decide about me for so long, back on the shadow Earth: my new personality was sufficiently different.'

'I begin to understand,' she said. It is not just Amber for you. It is the place plus everything else.'

'The place plus everything else . . . *That* is Amber,' I agreed.

'You say that your hate died with Eric and your desire for the throne has been tempered by the consideration of new things you have learned.'

'That is so.'

'Then I think I do understand what it is that moves you.'

'The desire for stability moves me,' I said, 'and something of curiosity – and revenge on our enemies . . .'

'Duty,' she said. 'Of course.'

I snorted.

'It would be comforting to put such a face on it,' I said. 'As it is, however, I will not be a hypocrite. I am hardly a dutiful son of Amber or of Oberon.'

'Your voice makes it plain that you do not wish to be considered one.'

I closed my eyes, closed them to join her in darkness, to recall for a brief while the world where other messages than light waves took precedence. I knew then that she had been right about my voice. Why had I trodden so heavily on the idea of duty as soon as it was suggested? I like credit for being good and clean and noble and high-minded when I have it coming, even sometimes when I do not – the same as the next person. What bothered me about the notion of duty to Amber? Nothing. What was it then?

Dad.

I no longer owed him anything, least of all duty. Ultimately, he was responsible for the present state of affairs. He had fathered a great brood of us without providing for a proper succession, he had been less than kind to all of our mothers and he then expected our devotion and support. He played favorites and, in fact, it even seemed he played us off against one another. He then got suckered into something he could not handle and left the kingdom in a mess. Sigmund Freud had long ago anesthetized me to any normal, generalized feelings of resentment which might operate within the family unit. I have no quarrel on those grounds. Facts are another matter. I did not dislike my father simply because he had given me no reason to like him; in truth, it seemed that he had labored in the other direction. Enough. I realized what it was that bothered me about the notion of duty: its object.

'You are right,' I said, opening my eyes, regarding her, 'and I am glad that you told me of it.'

I rose.

'Give me your hand,' I said.

She extended her right hand and I raised it to my lips.

'Thank you,' I said. 'It was a good lunch.'

I turned and made my way to the door. When I looked back she had blushed and was smiling, her hand still partly raised, and I began to understand the change in Random.

'Good luck to you,' she said, the moment my footsteps ceased.

'. . . And you,' I said, and went out quickly.

I had been planning to see Brand next, but just could not bring myself to do it. For one thing, I did not want to encounter him with my wits dulled by fatigue. For another, talking with Vialle was the first pleasant thing which had happened to me in some time, and just his once I was going to quit while I was ahead.

I mounted the stairs and walked the corridor to my room, thinking, of course, of the night of the knifings as I fitted my new key to my new lock. In my bedchamber, I drew the drapes against the afternoon's light, undressed, and got into bed. As on other occasions of rest after stress with more stress pending, sleep eluded me for a time. For a long while I tossed and twisted, reliving events of the past several days and some from even farther back. When finally I slept, my dreams were an amalgam of the same material, including a spell in my old cell, scraping away at the door.

It was dark when I awoke and I actually felt rested. The tension gone out of me, my reverie was much more peaceful In fact, there was a tiny charge of pleasant excitement dancing through the back of my head. It was a tip-of-the-tongue imperative, a buried notion that—

Yes!

I sat up. I reached for my clothes, began to dress. I buckled on Grayswandir. I folded a blanket and tucked it under my arm. Of course . . .

My mind felt clear and my side had stopped throbbing. I had no idea how long I had slept, and it was hardly worth checking at this point I had something far more important to look into, something which should have occurred to me a long while ago – had occurred, as a matter of fact I had actually been staring right at it once, but the crush of time and events had ground it from my mind. Until now.

I locked my room behind me and headed for the stairs. Candles flickered, and the faded stag who had been dying for centuries on the tapestry to my right looked back on the faded dogs who had been pursuing him for approximately as long. Sometimes my sympathies are with the stag; usually though, I am all dog. Have to have the thing restored one of these days.

The stairs and down. No sounds from below. Late, then. Good, Another day and we're still alive. Maybe even a trifle wiser. Wise enough to realize there are many more things we still need to know. Hope, though. There's that. A thing I lacked when I squatted in that damned cell, hands pressed against my ruined eyes, howling. Vialle . . . I wish I could have spoken with you for a few moments in those days. But I learned what I learned in a nasty school, and even a milder curriculum would probably not have given me your grace. Still . . . hard to say. I have always felt I am more dog than stag, more hunter than victim. You might have taught me something that would have blunted the bitterness, tempered the hate. But would that have been for the best? The hate died with its object and the bitterness, too, has passed – but looking back, I wonder whether I would have made it without them to sustain me. I am not at all certain that I would have survived my internment without my ugly companions to drag me back to life and sanity time and again. Now I can afford the luxury of an occasional stag-thought, but then it might have been fatal. I do not truly know, kind lady, and I doubt that I ever will.

Stillness on the second floor. A few noises from below. Sleep well, lady. Around, and down again. I wondered whether Random had uncovered anything of great moment. Probably not, or he or Benedict should have contacted me by now. Unless there was trouble. But no. It is ridiculous to shop for worries. The real thing makes itself felt in due course, and I'd more than enough to go around.

The ground floor.

'Will,' I said, and, 'Rolf.'

'Lord Corwin.'

The two guards had assumed professional stances on hearing my footsteps. Their faces told me that all was well, but I asked for the sake of form.

'Quiet, Lord. Quiet,' replied the senior.

'Very good,' I said, and I continued on, entering and crossing the marble dining hall.

It would work, I was sure of that, if time and moisture had not totally effaced it. And then . . .

I entered the long corridor, where the dusty walls pressed close on either side. Darkness, shadows, my footsteps . . .

I came to the door at the end, opened it, stepped out onto the platform. Then down once more, that spiraling way, a light here, a light there, into the caverns of Kolvir. Random had been right, I decided then. If you had gouged out everything, down to the level of that distant floor, there would be a close correspondence between what was left and the place of that primal Pattern we had visited this morning.

. . . On down. Twisting and winding through the gloom. The torch and lantern-lit guard station was theatrically stark within it. I reached the floor and headed that way.

'Good evening, Lord Corwin,' said the lean, cadaverous figure who rested against a storage rack, smoking his pipe, grinning around it.

'Good evening, Roger. How are things in the nether world?'

'A rat, a bat, a spider. Nothing much else astir. Peaceful.'

'You enjoy this duty?'

He nodded.

'I am writing a philosophical romance shot through with elements of horror and morbidity. I work on those parts down here.'

'Fitting, fitting,' I said. 'I'll be needing a lantern.'

He took one from the rack, brought it to flame from his candle.

'Will it have a happy ending?' I inquired.

He shrugged.

'I'll be happy.'

'I mean, does good triumph and hero bed heroine? Or do you kill everybody off?'

'That's hardly fair,' he said.

'Never mind. Maybe I'll read it one day.'

'Maybe,' he said.

I took the lantern and turned away, heading in a direction I had not taken in a long while. I discovered that I could still measure the echoes in my mind.

Before too long, I neared the wall, sighted the proper corridor, entered it. It was simply a matter of counting my paces then. My feet knew the way.

The door to my old cell stood partly ajar. I set down the lantern and used both hands to open it fully. It gave way grudgingly, moaning as it moved. Then I raised the lantern, held it high, and entered.

My flesh tingled and my stomach clenched itself within me. I began to shiver. I had to fight down a strong impulse to bolt and run. I had not anticipated such a reaction. I did not want to step away from that heavy brassbound door for fear that it would be slammed and bolted behind me. It was an instant close to pure terror that the small dirty cell had aroused in me. I forced myself to dwell on particulars – the hole which had been my latrine, the blackened spot where I had built my fire on that final day. I ran my left hand over the inner surface of the door, finding and tracing there the grooves I had worn while scraping away with my spoon. I remembered what the activity had done to my hands. I stooped to examine the gouging. Not nearly so deep as it had seemed at the time, not when compared to the total thickness of the door. I realized how much I had exaggerated the effects of that feeble effort toward freedom. I stepped past it and regarded the wall.

Faint. Dust and moisture had worked to undo it. But I could still discern the outlines of me lighthouse of Cabra, bordered by four slashes of my old spoon handle. The magic was still there, that force which had finally transported me to freedom. I felt it without calling upon it.

I turned and faced the other wall.

The sketch which I now regarded had fared less well than that of the lighthouse, but then it had been executed with extreme haste by the light of my last few matches. I could not even make out all of the details, though my memory furnished a few of those which were hidden: It was a view of a den or library, bookshelves lining the walls, a desk in the foreground, a globe beside the desk. I wondered whether I should risk wiping it clean.

I set my lantern on the floor, returned to the sketch on the other wall. With a corner of my blanket, I gently wiped some dust from a point near the base of the lighthouse. The line grew clearer. I wiped it again, exerting a little more pressure. Unfortunate. I destroyed an inch or so of outline.

I stepped back and tore a wide strip from the edge of the blanket I folded what remained into a pad and seated myself on it. Slowly, carefully then, I set to work on the light-house. I had to get an exact feeling for the work before I tried cleaning the other one.

Half an hour later I stood up and stretched, bent and massaged life back into my legs. What remained of the lighthouse was clean. Unfortunately, I had destroyed about 20 per cent of the sketch before I developed a sense of the wall's texture and an appropriate stroke across it I doubted that I was going to improve any further.

The lantern sputtered as I moved it. I unfolded the blanket, shook it out, tore off a fresh strip. Making up a new pad, I knelt before the other sketch and set to work.

A while later I had uncovered what remained of it. I had forgotten the skull on the desk until a careful stroke revealed it once again – and the angle of the far wall, and a tall candlestick . . . I drew back. It would be risky to do any more rubbing. Probably unnecessary, also. It seemed about as entire as it had been.

The lantern was nickering once again. Cursing Roger for not checking the kerosene level, I stood and held the light at shoulder level off to my left. I put everything from my mind but the scene before me.

It gained something of perspective as I stared. A moment later and it was totally three-dimensional and had expanded to fill my entire field of vision. I stepped forward then and rested the lantern on the edge of the desk.

I cast my eyes about the place. There were bookshelves on all four walls. No windows. Two doors at the far end of the room, right and left, across from one another, one closed, the other partly ajar. There was a long, low table covered with books and papers beside the opened door. Bizarre curios occupied open spaces on the shelves and odd niches and recesses in the walls – bones, stones, pottery, inscribed tablets, lenses, wands, instruments of unknown function. The huge rug resembled an Ardebil. I took a step toward that end of the room and the lantern sputtered again. I turned and reached for it. At that moment, it failed.

I growled an obscenity and lowered my hand. Then I turned, slowly, to check for any possible light sources. Something resembling a branch of coral shone faintly on a shelf across the room and a pale line of illumination occurred at the base of the closed door. I abandoned the lantern and crossed the room.

I opened the door as quietly as I could. The room it let upon was deserted, a small, windowless living place faintly lit by the still smoldering embers in its single, recessed hearth. The room's walls were of stone and they arched above me. The fireplace was a possibly natural niche in the wall to my left. A large, armored door was set in the far wall, a big key partly turned in its lock.

I entered, taking a candle from a nearby table, and moved toward the fireplace to give it a light. As I knelt and sought a flame among the embers, I heard a soft footfall in the vicinity of the doorway.

Turning, I saw him just beyond the threshold. About five feet in height, hunchbacked. His hair and beard were even longer than I remembered. Dworkin wore a nightshirt which reached to his ankles. He carried an oil lamp, his dark eyes peering across its sooty chimney.

'Oberon,' he said, 'is it finally time?'

'What time is that?' I asked softly.

He chuckled.

'What other? Time to destroy the world, of course!'

5

I kept the light away from my face, kept my voice low.

'Not quite,' I said. 'Not quite.'

He sighed.

'You remain unconvinced.'

He looked forward and cocked his head, peering down at me.

'Why must you spoil things?' he said.

'I've spoiled nothing.'

He lowered the lamp. I turned my head again, but he finally got a good look at my face. He laughed.

'Funny. Funny, funny, funny,' he said. 'You come as the young Lord Corwin, thinking to sway me with family sentiment. Why did you not choose Brand or Bleys? It was Clarissa's lot served us best.'

I shrugged and stood.

'Yes and no,' I said, determined now to feed him ambiguities for so long as he'd accept them and respond. Something of value might emerge, and it seemed an easy way to keep him in a good humor. 'And yourself?' I continued. 'What face would you put on things?'

'Why, to win your good will I'll match you,' he said, and then he began to laugh.

He threw his head back, and as his laughter rang about me a change came over him. His stature seemed to increase, and his face luffed like a sail cut too close to the wind. The hump on his back was diminished as he straightened and stood taller. His features rearranged themselves and his beard darkened. By then it was obvious that he was somehow redistributing his body mass, for the nightshirt which had reached his ankles was now midway up his shins. He breathed deeply and his shoulders widened. His arms lengthened, his bulging abdomen narrowed, tapered. He reached shoulder height on me, then higher. He looked me in the eye. His garment reached only to his knees. His hump was totally resorted. His face gave a final twist, his features steadied, were reset. His laughter fell to a chuckle, faded, closed with a smirk.

I regarded a slightly slimmer version of myself.

'Sufficient?' he inquired.

'Not half bad,' I said. 'Wait till I toss a couple logs on the fire.'

'I will help you.'

'That's all right.'

I drew some wood from a rack to the right. Any stall served me somewhat, buying reactions for my study. As I was about the work, he crossed to a chair and seated himself. When I glanced at him I saw that he was not looking at me, but staring into the shadows. I drew out the fire-building, hoping that he would say something, anything. Eventually, he did.

'Whatever became of the grand design?' he asked.

I did not know whether he was speaking of the Pattern or of some master plan of Dad's to which he had been privy. So, 'You tell me,' I said.

He chuckled again.

'Why not? You changed your mind, that is what happened,' he said.

'From what to what – as you see it?'

'Don't mock me. Even you have no right to mock me,' he said. 'Least of all, you.'

I got to my feet.

'I was not mocking you,' I said.

I crossed the room to another chair and carried it over to a position near the fire, across from Dworkin. I seated myself.

'How did you recognize me?' I asked.

'My whereabouts are hardly common knowledge.'

'That is true.'

'Do many in Amber think me dead?'

'Yes, and others suppose you might be traveling off in Shadow.'

'I see.'

'How have you been – feeling?'

He gave me an evil grin.

'Do you mean am I still mad?'

'You put it more bluntly than I care to.'

'There is a fading, there is an intensifying,' he said. 'It comes to me and it departs again. For the moment I am almost myself – almost, I say. The shock of your visit, perhaps . . . Something is broken in my mind. You know that. It cannot be otherwise, though. You know that, too.'

'I suppose that I do,' I said. 'Why don't you tell me all about it, all over again? Just the business of talking might make you feel better, might give me something I've missed. Tell me a story.'

Another laugh.

'Anything you like. Have you any preferences? My flight from Chaos to this small sudden island in the sea of night? My meditations upon the abyss? The revelation of the Pattern in a jewel hung around the neck of a unicorn? My transcription of the design by lightning, blood, and lyre while our fathers raged baffled, too late come to call me back while the poem of fire ran that first route in my brain, infecting me with the will to form? Too late! Too late . . . Possessed of the abominations born of the disease, beyond their aid, their power, I planned and built, captive of my new self. Is that the tale you'd hear again? Or rather I tell you of its cure?'

My mind spun at the implications he had just scattered by the fistful I could not tell whether he spoke literally or metaphorically or was simply sharing paranoid delusions, but the things that I wanted to hear, had to hear, were things closer to the moment. So, regarding the shadowy image of myself from which that ancient voice emerged, 'Tell me of its cure,' I said.

He braced his finger tips together and spoke through them.

'I am the Pattern,' he said, 'in a very real sense. In passing through my mind to achieve the form it now holds, the foundation of Amber, it marked me as surely as I marked it. I realized one day that I am both the Pattern and myself, and it was forced to become Dworkin in the process of becoming itself. There were mutual modifications in the birthing of this place and this time, and therein lay our weakness as well as our strength. For it occurred to me that damage to the Pattern would be damage to myself, and damage to myself would be reflected within the Pattern. Yet I could not be truly harmed because the Pattern protects me, and who but I could harm the Pattern? A beautiful closed system, it seemed, its weakness totally shielded by its strength.'

He fell silent I listened to the fire. I do not know what he listened to.

Then, 'I was wrong,' he said. 'Such a simple matter, too . . . My blood, with which I drew it could deface it. But it took me ages to realize that the blood of my blood could also do this thing. You could use it you could also change it – yea, unto the third generation.'

It did not come to me as a surprise, learning that he was grandsire to us all. Somehow, it seemed that I had known all along, had known but never voiced it. Yet . . . if anything, this raised more questions than it answered. *Collect one generation of ancestry. Proceed to confusion.* I had less idea now than ever before as to what Dworkin really was. Add to this the fact which even he acknowledged: It was a tale told by a madman.

'But to repair it . . . ?' I said.

He smirked, my own face twisting before me.

'Have you lost your taste to be a lord of the living void, a king of chaos?' he asked.

'Mayhap,' I replied.

'By the Unicorn, thy mother, I knew it would come to this! The Pattern is as strong in you as is the greater realm. What then is your desire?'

'To preserve the realm.'

He shook his/my head.

' 'Twould be simpler to destroy everything and try a new start – as I have told you so often before.'

'I'm stubborn. So tell me again,' I said, attempting to simulate Dad's gruffness.

He shrugged.

'Destroy the Pattern and we destroy Amber – and all of the shadows in polar array about it. Give me leave to destroy myself in the midst of the Pattern and we will obliterate it. Give me leave by giving me your word that you will then take the Jewel which contains the essence of order and use it to create a new Pattern, bright and pure, untainted, drawing upon the stuff of your own being while the legions of chaos attempt to distract you on every side. Promise me that and let me end it, for broken as I am, I would rather die for order than live for it. What say you now?'

'Would it not be better to try mending the one we've got than to undo the work of eons?'

'Coward!' he cried, leaping to his feet. 'I knew you would say that again!'

'Well, wouldn't it?'

He began to pace.

'How many times have we been through this?' he asked.

'Nothing has changed! You are afraid to try it!'

'Perhaps,' I said. 'But do you not feel that something for which you have given so much is worth some effort – some additional sacrifice – if there is even a possibility of saving it?'

'You still do not understand,' he said. 'I cannot but think that a damaged thing should be destroyed – and hopefully replaced. The nature of my personal injury is such that I cannot envision repair. I am damaged in just this fashion. My feelings are foreordained.'

'If the Jewel can create a new Pattern, why will it not serve to repair the old one, end our troubles, heal your spirit?'

He approached and stood before me.

'Where is your memory?' he said. 'You know that it would be infinitely more difficult to repair the damage than it would be to start over again. Even the Jewel could more easily destroy it than repair it. Have your forgotten what it is like out there?' He gestured toward the wall behind him. 'Do you want to go and look at it again?'

'Yes,' I said. 'I would like that Let's go.'

I rose and looked down at him. His control over his form had begun slipping when he had grown angry. He had already lost three or four inches in height, the image of my face was melting back into his own gnomelike features, and a noticeable bulge was growing between his shoulders, had already been visible when he had gestured.

His eyes widened and he studied my face.

'You really mean it,' he said after a moment 'All right, then. Let us go.'

He turned and moved toward the big metal door. I followed him. He used both hands to turn the key. Then he threw his weight against it I moved to help him, but he brushed me aside with extraordinary strength before giving the door a final shove. It made a grating noise and moved outward into a fully opened position. I was immediately struck by a strange, somehow familiar odor.

Dworkin stepped through and paused. He located what looked to be a long staff leaning against the wall off to his right. He struck it several times against the ground and its upper end began to glow. It lit up the area fairly well, revealing a narrow tunnel into which he now advanced. I followed him and it widened before too long, so that I was able to come abreast of him. The odor grew stronger, and I could almost place it. It had been something fairly recent . . .

It was close to eighty paces before our way took a turn to the left and upward. We passed then through a little appendix like area. It was strewn with broken bones, and a large metal ring was set in the rock a couple of feet above the floor. Affixed thereto was a guttering chain, which fell to the floor and trailed on ahead like a line of molten droplets cooling in the gloom.

Our way narrowed again after that and Dworkin took the lead once more. After a brief time, he turned an abrupt corner and I heard him muttering. I nearly ran into him when I made the turn myself. He was crouched down and groping with his left hand inside a shadowy cleft. When I heard the soft cawing noise and saw that the chain vanished into the opening I realized what it was and where we were.

'Good Wixer,' I heard him say. 'I am not going far. It is all right, good Wixer. Here is something to chew on.'

From where he had fetched whatever he tossed the beast, I do not know. But the purple griffin, which I had now advanced far enough to glimpse as it stirred within its lair, accepted the offering with a toss of its head and a series of crunching noises.

Dworkin grinned up at me.

'Surprised?' he asked.

'At what?'

'You thought I was afraid of him. You thought I would never make friends with him. You set him out here to keep me in there – away from the Pattern.'

'Did I ever say that?'

'You did not have to. I am not a fool.'

'Have it your way,' I said.

He chuckled, rose, and continued on along the passageway.

I followed and it grew level underfoot once again. The ceiling rose and the way widened. At length, we came to the cave mouth. Dworkin stood for a moment silhouetted, staff raised before him. It was night outside, and a clean salt smell swept the musk from my nostrils.

Another moment, and he moved forward once more, passing into a world of sky-candles and blue velours. Continuing after him, I had gasped briefly at that amazing view. It was not simply that the stars in the moonless, cloudless sky blazed with a preternatural brilliance, nor that the distinction between sky and sea had once again been totally obliterated. It was that the Pattern glowed an almost acetylene blue by that sky-sea, and all of the stars above, beside, and below were arrayed with a geometric precision, forming a fantastic, oblique latticework which, more than anything else, gave the impression that we hung in the midst of a cosmic web where the Pattern was the true center, the rest of the radiant meshwork a precise consequence of its existence, configuration, position.

Dworkin continued on down to the Pattern, right up to the edge beside the darkened area. He waved his staff over it and turned to look at me just as I came near.

'There you are,' he announced, 'the hole in my mind. I can no longer think through it, only around it I no longer know what must be done to repair something I now lack. If you think that you can do it, you must be willing to lay yourself open to instant destruction each time you depart the Pattern to cross the break. Not destruction by the dark portion. Destruction by the Pattern itself when you break the circuit. The Jewel may or may not sustain you. I do not know. But it will not grow easier. It will become more difficult with each circuit, and your strength will be lessening all the while. The last time we discussed it you were afraid. Do you mean to say you have grown bolder since then?'

'Perhaps,' I said. 'You see no other way?'

'I know it can be done starting with a clean slate, because once I did it so. Beyond that, I see no other way. The longer you wait the more the situation worsens. Why not fetch the Jewel and lend me your blade, son? I see no better way.'

'No,' I said. 'I must know more. Tell me again how the damage was done.'

'I still do not know which of your children shed our blood on this spot, if this is what you mean. It was done. Let it go at that. Our darker natures came forth strongly in them. It must be that they are too close to the chaos from which we sprang, growing without the exercises of will we endured in defeating it. I had thought that the ritual of traveling the Pattern might suffice for them. I could think of nothing stronger. Yet it failed. They strike out against everything. They seek to destroy the Pattern itself.'

'If we succeed in making a fresh start, might not these events simply repeat themselves?'

'I do not know. But what choice have we other than failure and a return to chaos?'

'What will become of them if we try for a new beginning?'

He was silent for a long while. Then he shrugged.

'I cannot tell.'

'What would another generation have been like?'

He chuckled.

'How can such a question be answered? I have no idea.'

I withdrew the mutilated Trump and passed it to him. He regarded it near the blaze of his staff.

'I believe it is Random's son Martin,' I said, 'He whose blood was spilled here. I have no idea whether he still lives. What do you think he might have amounted to?'

He looked back out over the Pattern.

'So this is the object which decorated it,' he said. 'How did you fetch it forth?'

'It was gotten,' I said. 'It is not your work, is it?'

'Of course not. I have never set eyes on the boy. But this answers your question, does it not? If there is another generation, your children will destroy it.'

'As we would destroy them?'

He met my eyes and peered.

'Is it that you are suddenly becoming a doting father?' he asked.

'If you did not prepare that Trump, who did?'

He glanced down and nicked it with his fingernail.

'My best pupil. Your son Brand. That is his style. See what they do as soon as they gain a little power? Would any of them offer their lives to preserve the realm, to restore the Pattern?'

'Probably,' I said. 'Probably Benedict, Gérard, Random, Corwin . . .'

'Benedict has the mark of doom upon him, Gérard possesses the will but not the wit, Random lacks courage and determination. Corwin . . . Is he not out of favor and out of sight?'

My thoughts returned to our last meeting, when he had helped me to escape from my cell to Cabra. It occurred to me that he might have had second thoughts concerning that, not having been aware of the circumstances which had put me there.

'Is that why you have taken his form?' he went on. Is this some manner of rebuke? Are you testing me again?'

'He is neither out of favor nor sight,' I said, 'though he has enemies among the family and elsewhere. He would attempt anything to preserve the realm. How do you see his chances?'

'Has he not been away for a long while?'

'Yes.'

'Then he might have changed. I do not know.'

'I believe he is changed. I know that he is willing to try.'

He stared at me again, and he kept staring.

'You are not Oberon,' he said at length.

'No.'

'You are he whom I see before me.'

'No more, no less.'

'I see . . . I did not realize that you knew of this place.'

'I didn't, until recently. The first time that I came here I was led by the unicorn.'

His eyes widened.

'That is – very – interesting,' he said. 'It has been so long . . .'

'What of my question?'

'Eh? Question? What question?'

'My chances. Do you think I might be able to repair the Pattern?'

He advanced slowly, and reaching up, placed his right hand on my shoulder. The staff tilted in his other hand as he did so; its blue light flared within a foot of my face, but I felt no heat. He looked into my eyes.

'You have changed,' he said, after a time.

'Enough,' I asked, 'to do the job?'

He looked away.

'Perhaps enough to make it worth trying,' he said, 'even if we are foredoomed to failure.'

'Will you help me?'

'I do not know,' he said, 'that I will be able. This thing with my moods, my thoughts – it comes and it goes. Even now, I feel some of my control slipping away. The excitement, perhaps . . . We had best get back inside.'

I heard a clinking noise at my back. When I turned, the griffin was there, his head swinging slowly from left to right, his tail from right to left, his tongue darting. He began to circle us, halting when he came to a position between Dworkin and the Pattern.

'He knows,' Dworkin said. 'He can sense it when I begin to change. He will not let me near the Pattern then . . . Good Wixer. We are returning now. It is all right . . . Come, Corwin.'

We headed back toward the cave mouth and Wixer followed, a dink for every pace.

'The Jewel,' I said, 'the Jewel of Judgment . . . you say that it is necessary for the repair of the Pattern?'

'Yes,' he said. 'It would have to be borne the entire distance through the Pattern, reinscribing the original design in the places where it has been broken. This could only be done by one who is attuned to the Jewel, though.'

'I am attuned to the Jewel,' I said.

'How?' he asked, halting.

Wixer made a cackling noise behind us, and we resumed walking.

'I followed your written instructions – and Eric's verbal ones,' I said. 'I took it with me to the center of the Pattern and projected myself through it.'

'I see,' he said. 'How did you obtain it?'

'From Eric, on his deathbed.'

We entered the cave.

'You have it now?'

'I was forced to cache it in a place off in Shadow.'

'I would suggest you retrieve it quickly and bring it here or take it back to the palace. It is best kept near the center of things.'

'Why is that?'

'It tends to have a distorting effect on shadows if it lies too long among them.'

'Distorting? In what fashion?'

'There is no way to tell, in advance. It depends entirely upon the locale.'

We rounded a corner, continued on back through the gloom.

'What does it mean,' I said, 'when you are wearing the Jewel and everything begins to slow down about you? Fiona warned me that this was dangerous, but she was not certain why.'

'It means that you have reached the bounds of your own existence, that your energies will shortly be exhausted, that you will die unless you do something quickly.'

'What is that?'

'Begin to draw power from the Pattern itself – the primal Pattern within the Jewel.'

'How is this achieved?'

'You must surrender to it, release yourself, blot out your identity, erase the bounds which separate you from everything else.'

'It sounds easier said that done.'

'But it can be done, and it is the only way.'

I shook my head. We moved on, coming at last to the big door. Dworkin extinguished the staff and leaned it against the wall. We entered and he secured the door. Wixer had stationed himself just outside.

'You will have to leave now,' Dworkin said.

'But there are many more things that I must ask you, and some that I would like to tell you.'

'My thoughts grow meaningless, and your words would be wasted. Tomorrow night, or the next, or the next. Hurry! Go!'

'Why the rush?'

'I may harm you when the change comes over me. I am holding it back by main will now. Depart!'

'I do not know how. I know how to get here, but—'

'There are all manner of special Trumps in the desk in the next room. Take the light! Go anywhere! Get out of here!'

I was about to protest that I hardly feared any physical violence he could muster, when his features began to Sow like melting wax and he somehow seemed much larger and longer-limbed than he had been. Seizing the light, I fled the room, a sudden chill upon me.

. . . To the desk. I tore open the drawer and snatched at some Trumps which lay scattered within it I heard footsteps then, of something entering the room behind me, coming from the chamber I had just departed. They did not seem like the footsteps of a man. I did not look back. Instead, I raised the cards before me and regarded the one on top. It was an unfamiliar scene, but I opened my mind immediately and reached for it. A mountain crag, something indistinct beyond it, a strangely stippled sky, a scattering of stars to the left . . . The card was alternately hot and cold to my touch, and a heavy wind seemed to come blowing through it as I stared, somehow rearranging the prospect.

From right behind me then, the heavily altered but still recognizable voice of Dworkin spoke: 'Fool! You have chosen the land of your doom!'

A great clawlike hand – black, leathery, gnarled – reached over my shoulder, as if to snatch the card away. But the vision seemed ready, and I rushed forward into it turning the card from me as soon as I realized I had made my escape. Then I halted and stood stock-still, to let my senses adjust to the new locale.

I knew. From snatches of legend, bits of family gossip, and from a general feeling which came over me, I knew the place to which I had come. It was with full certainty as to identity that I raised my eyes to look upon the Courts of Chaos.

6

Where? The senses are such uncertain things, and now mine were strained beyond their limits. The rock on which I stood . . . If I attempted to fix my gaze upon it, it took on the aspect of a pavement on a hot afternoon. It seemed to shift and waver, though my footing was undisturbed. And it was undecided as to the portion of the spectrum it might call home. It pulsated and flashed like the skin of an iguana. Looking upward, I beheld a sky such as I had never before set eyes upon. At the moment, it was split down the middle – half of it of deepest night-black, and the stars danced within it. When I say danced, I do not mean twinkled; they cavorted and they shifted magnitudes; they darted and they circled; they flared to nova brilliance, then faded to nothing. It was a frightening spectacle to behold, and my stomach tightened within me as I experienced a profound agrophobia. Yet, shifting my gaze did little to improve the situation. The other half of the sky was like a bottle of colored sands, continuously shaken; belts of orange, yellow, red, blue, brown, and purple turned and twisted; patches of green, mauve, gray, and dead white came and went, sometimes snaking into belthood, replacing or joining the other writhing entities. And these, too, shimmered and wavered, creating impossible sensations of distance and nearness. At times, some or all seemed literally sky-high, and then again they came to fill the air before me, gauzy, transparent mists, translucent swaths or solid tentacles of color. It was not until later that I realized that the line which separated the black from the color was advancing slowly from my right while retreating to my left. It was as if the entire celestial mandala were rotating about a point directly overhead. As to the light source of the brighter half, it simply could not be determined. Standing there, I looked down upon what at first seemed a valley filled with countless explosions of color; but when the advancing darkness faced this display away the stars danced and burned within its depths as well as above, giving then the impression of a bottomless chasm. It was as if I stood at the end of the world, the end of the universe, the end of everything. But far, far out from where I stood, something hovered on a mount of sheerest black – a blackness itself, but edged and tempered with barely perceptible Sashes of light. I could not guess at its size, for distance, depth, perspective, were absent here. A single edifice? A group? A city? Or simply a place? The outline varied each time that it fell upon my retina. Now faint and misty sheets drifted slowly between us, twisting, as if long strands of gauze were buoyed by heated air. The mandala ceased its turning when it had exactly reversed itself. The colors were behind me now, and imperceptible unless I turned my head, an action I had no desire to take. It was pleasant standing there, staring at the formlessness from which all things eventually emerged . . . Before the Pattern, even, this thing was. I knew this, dimly but surely, at the very center of my consciousness. I knew this, because I was certain that I had been here before. Child of the man I had become, it seemed that I had been brought here in some distant day – whether by Dad or Dworkin, I could not now recall – and had stood or been held in this place or one very near to it, looking out upon the same scene with, I am certain, a similar lack of comprehension, a similar sense of apprehension. My pleasure was tinged with a nervous excitement, a sense of the forbidden, a feeling of dubious anticipation. Peculiarly, at that moment, there rose in me a longing for the Jewel I had had to abandon in my compost heap on the shadow Earth, the thing Dworkin had made so much of. Could it be that some part of me sought a defense or at least a symbol of resistance against whatever was out there? Probably.

As I continued to stare, fascinated, across the chasm, it was as if my eyes adjusted or the prospect shifted once again, subtly. For now I discerned tiny, ghostly forms moving within that place, like slow-motion meteors along the gauzy strands. I waited, regarding them carefully, courting some small understanding of the actions in which they were engaged. At length, one of the strands drifted very near. Shortly thereafter I had my answer.

There was a movement. One of the rushing forms grew larger, and I realized that it was following the twisting way that led toward me. In only a few moments, it took on the proportions of a horseman. As it came on, it assumed a semblance of solidity without losing that ghostly quality which seemed to cling to everything which lay before me. A moment later, I beheld a naked rider on a hairless horse, both deathly pale, rushing in my direction. The rider brandished a bone-white blade; his eyes and the eyes of the horse both flashed red. I did not really know whether he saw me, whether we existed on the same plane of reality, so unnatural was his mien. Yet I unsheathed Grayswandir and took a step backward as he approached.

His long white hair shed tiny sparkling motes, and when he turned his head I knew that he was coming for me, for then I felt his gaze tike a cold pressure across the front of my body. I turned sidewise and raised my blade to guard.

He continued, and I realized that both he and the horse were big, bigger even than I had thought. They came on. When they reached the point nearest me – some ten meters, perhaps – me horse reared as the rider drew it to a halt. They regarded me then, bobbing and swaying as if on a raft in a gently swelling sea.

'Your name!' the rider demanded. 'Give me your name, who comes to this place!'

His voice produced a crackling sensation in my ears. It was all of one sound level, loud and without inflection.

I shook my head.

'I give my name when I choose, not when I am ordered to,' I said. 'Who are you?'

He gave three short barks, which I took to be a laugh.

'I will hunt you down and about, where you will cry it out forever.'

I pointed Grayswandir at his eyes.

'Talk is cheap,' I said. Whisky costs money.'

I felt a faint cool sensation just then, as if someone were toying with my Trump, thinking of me. But it was dim, weak, and I had no attention to spare, for the rider had passed some signal to his mount and the beast reared. The distance is too great, I decided. But this thought belonged to another shadow. The beast plunged ahead toward me, departing the tenuous roadway that had been its course.

Its leap bore it to a point far short of my position. But it did not fan from there and vanish, as I had hoped. It resumed the motions of galloping, and although its progress was not fully commensurate with the action, it continued to advance across the abyss at about half-speed.

While this was occurring, I saw that in the distance from which it had come another figure appeared to be headed my way. Nothing to do but stand my ground, fight, and hope that I could dispatch this attacker before the other was upon me.

As the rider advanced, his ruddy gaze flicked over my person and halted when it fell upon Grayswandir. Whatever the nature of the mad illumination at my back, it had tricked the delicate tracery on my blade to life once more, so that that portion of the Pattern it bore swam and sparkled along its length. The horseman was very near by then, but he drew back on the reins and his eyes leaped upward, meeting my own. His nasty grin vanished.

'I know you!' he said. 'You are the one called Corwin!'

But we had him, me and my ally momentum.

His mount's front hoofs fell upon the ledge and I rushed forward. The beast's reflexes caused it to seek equal footing for its hind legs despite the drawn reins. The rider swung his blade into a guard position as I came on, but I cross-stepped and attacked from his left. As he moved his blade cross-body, I was already lunging. Grayswandir sheared through his pale hide, entering beneath the sternum and above the guts.

I wrenched my blade free and gouts of fire poured like blood from his wound. His sword arm sagged and his mount uttered a shriek that was almost a whistle as the blazing stream fell upon its neck. I danced back as the rider slumped forward and the beast, now fully footed, plunged on toward me, kicking. I cut again, reflexively, defensively. My blade nicked its left foreleg, and it, too, began to burn.

I side-stepped once again as it turned and made for me a second time. At that moment, the rider erupted into a pillar of light. The beast bellowed, wheeled, and rushed away. Without pausing, it plunged over the edge and vanished into the abyss, leaving me with the memory of the smoldering head of a cat which had addressed me long ago and the chill which always accompanied the recollection.

I was backed against rock, panting. The wispy road had drifted nearer – ten feet, perhaps, from the ledge. I had developed a cramp in my left side. The second rider was rapidly approaching. He was not pale like the first. His hair was dark and there was color in his face. His mount was a properly maned sorrel. He bore a cocked and bolted crossbow. I glanced behind me and there was no retreat, no crevice into which I might back.

I wiped my palm on my trousers and gripped Grayswandir by the forte of the blade. I turned sideways, so as to present the narrowest target possible. I raised my blade between us, hilt level with my head, point toward the ground, the only shield I possessed.

The rider came abreast of me and halted at the nearest point on the gauzy strip. He raised the crossbow slowly, knowing that if he did not drop me instantly with his single shot, I might be able to hurl my blade like a spear. Our eyes met.

He was beardless, slim. Possibly light-eyed within the squint of his aim. He managed his mount well, with just the pressure of his legs. His hands were big, steady. Capable. A peculiar feeling passed over me as I beheld him.

The moment stretched beyond the point of action. He rocked backward and lowered the weapon slightly, though none of the tenion left his stance.

'You,' he called out. 'Is that the blade Grayswandir?'

'Yes,' I answered, 'It is.'

He continued his appraisal, and something within me looked for words to wear, failed, ran naked away through the night.

'What do you want here?' he asked.

'To depart,' I said.

There was a *chish-chá*, as his bolt struck the rock far ahead and to the left of me.

'Go then,' he said. 'This is a dangerous place for you.'

He turned his mount back in the direction from which he had come.

I lowered Grayswandir.

'I won't forget you,' I said.

'No,' he answered. 'Do not.'

Then he galloped away, and moments later the gauze drifted off also.

I resheathed Grayswandir and took a step forward. The world was beginning to turn about me again, the light advancing on my right, the dark retreating to my left I looked about for some way to scale the rocky prominence at my back. It seemed to rise only thirty or forty feet higher, and I wanted the view that might be available from its summit. My ledge extended to both my right and my left. On inspection, the way to the right narrowed quickly, however, without affording a suitable ascent I turned and made my way to the left.

I came upon a rougher spot in a narrow place beyond a rocky shoulder. Running my gaze up its height, an ascent seemed possible. I checked behind me after the approach of additional threats. The ghostly roadway had drifted farther away; no new riders advanced. I commenced climbing.

The going was not difficult, though the height proved greater than it had seemed from below. Likely a symptom of the spatial distortion which seemed to have affected my sight of so much else in this place. After a time, I hauled myself up and stood erect at a point which afforded a better view in the direction opposite the abyss.

Once again, I beheld the chaotic colors. From my right, the darkness herded them. The land they danced above was rock-cropped and cratered, no sign of any life within it. Passing through its midst, however, from the far horizon to a point in the mountains somewhere to the right, inky and serpentine, ran what could only be the black road.

Another ten minutes of climbing and maneuvering, and I had positioned myself to view its terminus. It swept through a broad pass in the mountains and ran right to the very edge of the abyss. There, its blackness merged with that which filled the place, noticeable now only by virtue of the fact that no stars shone through it Using this occlusion to gauge it, I obtained the impression that it continued on to the dark eminence about which the misty strips drifted.

I stretched out on my belly, so as to disturb the outline of the low crest as little as possible to whatever unseen eyes might flick across it Lying there, I thought upon the opening of this way. The damage to the Pattern had laid Amber open to this access, and I believed that my curse had provided the precipitating element. I felt now that it would have come to pass without me, but I was certain that I had done my part. The guilt was still partly mine though no longer entirely so, as I had once believed. I thought then of Eric, as he lay dying on Kolvir. He had said that as much as he hated me, he was saving his dying curse for the enemies of Amber. In other words, this, and these.

Ironic. My efforts were now entirely directed toward making good on my least-liked brother's dying wish. His curse to cancel my curse, me as the agent. Fitting though, perhaps, in some larger sense.

I sought, and was pleased not to discover, ranks of glowing riders setting forth or assembling upon that road. Unless another raiding party was already under way Amber was still temporarily safe. A number of things immediately troubled me, however. Mainly, if time did indeed behave as peculiarly in that place as Dara's possible origin indicated, then why had there not been, another attack? They had certainly had ample time in which to recover and prepare for another assault. Had something occurred recently, by Amber's time, that is, to alter the nature of their strategy? If so, what? My weapons? Brand's recovery? Or something else? I wondered, too, how far Benedict's outposts reached. Certainly not this far, or I should have been informed. Had he ever been to this place? Had any of the others, within recent memory, stood where I had just stood, looking upon the Courts of Chaos, knowing something that I did not know? I resolved to question Brand and Benedict in this regard as soon as I returned.

All of which led me to wonder how time was behaving with me, at that moment. Better not to spend any more time here than I had to, I decided. I scanned the other Trumps I had removed from Dworkin's desk. While they were all of them interesting, I was familiar with none of the scenes depicted. I slipped my own case then and riffled through to Random's Trump. Perhaps he was the one who had tried to contact me earlier. I raised his card and regarded it.

Shortly, it swam before my eyes and I looked upon a blurred kaleidoscope of images, the impression of Random in their midst Motion, and twisting perspectives . . .

'Random,' I said. 'This is Corwin.'

I felt his mind, but there was no response from it. It struck me then that he was in the middle of a hellride, all his concentration bent on warping the stuff of Shadow about him. He could not respond without losing control. I blocked the Trump with my hand, breaking the contact.

I cut to Gérard's card. Moments later, there was contact I stood.

'Corwin, where are you?' he inquired.

'At the end of the world,' I said. 'I want to come home.'

'Come ahead.'

He extended his hand. I reached out and clasped it, stepped forward.

We were on the ground floor of the palace in Amber, in the sitting room to which we had all adjourned on the night of Brand's return. It seemed to be early morning. There was a fire going on the grate. No one else was present.

'I tried to reach you earlier,' he said. 'I think Brand did, too. But I can't be sure.'

'How long have I been away?'

'Eight days,' he said.

'Glad I hurried. What's happening?'

'Nothing untoward,' he said. 'I do not know what Brand wants. He kept asking for you, and I could not reach you. Finally, I gave him a deck and told him to see whether he could do any better. Apparently, he could not.'

'I was distracted,' I said, 'and the time-flow differential was bad.'

He nodded.

'I have been avoiding him now that he is out of danger. He is in one of his black moods again, and he insists he can take care of himself. He is right, in that, and it is just as well.'

'Where is he now?'

'Back in his own quarters, and he was still there as of perhaps an hour ago – brooding.'

'Has he been out at all?'

'A few brief walks. But not for the past several days.'

'I guess I had best go see him then. Any word on Random?'

'Yes,' he said. 'Benedict returned several days ago. He said they had found a number of leads concerning Random's son. He helped him check on a couple of them. One led further, but Benedict felt he had best not be away from Amber for too long, things being as uncertain as they are. So he left Random to continue the search on his own. He gained something in the venture, though. He came back sporting an artificial arm – a beautiful piece of work. He can do anything with it that he could before.'

'Really?' I said. 'It sounds strangely familiar.'

He smiled, nodded.

'He told me you had brought it back for him from Tir-na Nog'th. In fact he wants to speak with you about it as soon as possible.'

'I'll bet,' I said. 'Where is he now?'

'At one of the outposts he has established along the black road. You would have to reach him by Trump.'

'Thanks,' I said. 'Anything further on Julian or Fiona?'

He shook his head.

'All right,' I said, turning toward the door. 'I guess I will go see Brand first.'

'I am curious to know what it is that he wants,' he said.

'I will remember that,' I told him.

I left the room and headed for the stairs.

7

I rapped on Brand's door.

'Come in, Corwin,' he said.

I did, deciding as I crossed the threshold that I would not ask him how he had known who it was. His room was a gloomy place, candles burning despite the fact that it was daytime and he had four windows. The shutters were closed on three of them. The fourth was only part way open. Brand stood beside this one, staring out toward the sea. He was dressed all in black velvet with a silver chain about his neck. His belt was also of silver – a fine, linked affair. He played with a small dagger, and did not look at me as I entered. He was still pale, but his beard was neatly trimmed and he looked well scrubbed and a bit heavier than he had when last I had seen him.

'You are looking better,' I said. 'How are you feeling?'

He turned and regarded me, expressionless, his eyes half-closed.

'Where the hell have you been?' he said.

'Hither and yon. What did you want to see me about?'

'I asked you where you've been.'

'And I heard you,' I said, reopening the door behind me. 'Now I am going to go out and come back in. Supposing we start this conversation over again?'

He sighed.

'Wait a minute. I am sorry,' he said. 'Why are we all so thin-skinned? I do not know . . . All right. It may be better if I do start over again.'

He sheathed his dagger and crossed to sit in a heavy chair of black wood and leather.

'I got to worrying about all the things we had discussed,' he said, 'and some that we had not. I waited what seemed an appropriate time for you to have concluded your business in Tir-na Nog'th and returned. I then inquired after you and was told you had not yet come

571

back. I waited longer. First I was impatient; and then I grew concerned that you might have been ambushed by our enemies. When I inquired again later, I learned that you had been back only long enough to speak with Random's wife – it must have been a conversation of great moment – and then to take a nap. You then departed once more. I was irritated that you had not seen fit to keep me posted as to events, but I resolved to wait a bit longer. Finally, I asked Gérard to get hold of you with your Trump. When he failed, I was quite concerned. I tried it myself then, and while it seemed that I touched you on several occasions I could not get through. I feared for you, and now I see that I had nothing to fear all along. Hence, I was abrupt.'

'I see,' I said, taking a seat off to his right 'Actually, time was running faster for me than it was for you, so from where I am sitting I have hardly been away. You are probably far more recuperated from your puncture than I am from mine.'

He smiled faintly and nodded.

'That is something, anyway,' he said, 'For my pains.'

'I have had a few pains myself,' I said, 'So don't give me any more. You wanted me for something. Let's have it.'

'Something is bothering you,' he said. 'Perhaps we ought to discuss that first.'

'All right,' I said. 'Let's.'

I turned and looked at the painting on the wall beside the door. An oil, a rather somber rendering of the well at Mirata, two men standing beside their horses nearby, talking.

'You've a distinctive style,' I said.

'In all things,' he replied.

'You stole my next sentence,' I said, locating Martin's Trump and passing it to him.

He remained expressionless as be examined it, gave me one brief, sidelong look and then nodded.

'I cannot deny my hand,' he said.

'It executed more than that card, your hand. Didn't it?'

He traced his upper lip with the tip of his tongue.

'Where did you find it?' he asked.

'Right where you left it, at the heart of things – in the real Amber.'

'So . . .' he said, rising from the chair and returning to the window, holding up the card as if to study it in a better light. 'So,' he repeated, 'you are aware of more than I had guessed. How did you learn of the primal Pattern?'

I shook my head.

'You answer my question first: did you stab Martin?'

He turned toward me once again, stared a moment, then nodded sharply. His eyes continued to search my face.

'Why?' I asked.

'Someone had to,' he explained, 'to open the way for the powers we needed. We drew straws.'

'And you won.'

'Won? Lost?' He shrugged. 'What does any of this matter now? Things did not come about as we had intended, I am a different person now than I was then.'

'Did you kill him?'

'What?'

'Martin, Random's son. Did he die as a result of the wound you inflicted?'

He turned his hands palms upward.

'I do not know,' he said. 'If he did not, it was not because I did not try. You need look no farther. You have found your guilty party. Now that you have, what are you going to do?'

I shook my head.

'I? Nothing. For all I know, the lad may still be living.'

'Then let us move on to matters of greater moment. For how long have you known of the existence of the true Pattern?'

'Long enough,' I said. 'Its origin, its functions, the effect of the blood of Amber upon it – long enough. I paid more attention to Dworkin than you might have thought. I saw no gain to he had in damaging the fabric of existence, though. So I let Rover lie sleeping for a long, long while. It did not even occur to me until I spoke with you recently that the black road might have been connected with such foolishness. When I went to inspect the Pattern I found Martin's Trump and all the rest.'

'I was not aware that you were acquainted with Martin.'

'I have never set eyes on him.'

'Then how were you aware he was the subject of the Trump?'

'I was not alone in that place.'

'Who was with you?'

I smiled.

'No, Brand, It is still your turn. You told me when last we talked that the enemies of Amber hied all the way from the Courts of Chaos, that they have access to the realm via the black road because of something you and Bleys and Fiona had done back when you were of one mind as to the best way to take the throne. Now I know what it is that you did. Yet Benedict has been watching the black road and I have just looked upon the Courts of Chaos. There is no new massing of forces, no movement toward us upon that road. I know that time flows differently in that place. They should have had more than enough time to ready a new assault I want to know what is holding them back. Why have they not moved? What are they waiting for, Brand?'

'You credit me with more knowledge than I possess.'

'I don't think so. You are the resident expert on the subject. You have dealt with them. That Trump is evidence that you have been holding back on other matters. Don't weasel, just talk.'

'The Courts . . .' he said. 'You have been busy. Eric was a fool not to have killed you immediately – if he was aware you had knowledge of these things.'

'Eric was a fool,' I acknowledged. 'You are not. Now talk.'

'But I am a fool,' he said, 'a sentimental one, at that. Do you recall the day of our last argument, here in Amber, so long ago?'

'Somewhat.'

'I was sitting on the edge of my bed. You were standing by my writing desk. As you turned away and headed toward the door, I resolved to kill you. I reached beneath my bed, where I keep a cocked crossbow with a bolt in it I actually had my hand on it and was about to raise it when I realized something which stopped me.'

He paused.

'What was that?' I asked.

'Look over there by the door.'

I looked, I saw nothing special. I began to shake my head, just as he said, 'On the floor.'

Then I realized what it was – russet and olive and brown and green, with a small geometric pattern.

He nodded.

'You were standing on my favorite rug. I did not want to get blood on it. Later, my anger passed. So I, too, am a victim of emotion and circumstance.'

'Lovely story—' I began.

'—but now you want me to stop stalling. I was not stalling, however. I was attempting to make a point. We are all of us alive by one another's sufferance and an occasional fortunate accident. I am going to propose suspending that sufferance and eliminating the possibility of accident in a couple of very important cases. First though, to answer your question, while I do not know for certain what is holding them back, I can venture a very good guess. Bleys has assembled a large strike force for an attack on Amber. It will be nowhere near the scale of the one on which you accompanied him, however. You see, he will be counting on the memory of that last attack to have conditioned the response to this one. It will probably also be preceded by attempts to assassinate Benedict and yourself. The entire affair will be a feint, though. I would guess that Fiona has contacted the Courts of Chaos – may even be there right now – and has prepared them for the real attack, which might be expected any time after Bleys's diversionary foray. Therefore—'

'You say this is a very good guess,' I interrupted. 'But we do not even know for certain that Bleys is still living.'

'Bleys is alive,' he said. 'I was able to ascertain his existence via his Trump – even a brief assessment of his current activities – before he became aware of my presence and blocked me out. He is very sensitive to such surveillance. I found him in the field with troops he intends to employ against Amber.'

'And Fiona?'

'No,' he said, 'I did no experimenting with her Trump, and I would advise you not to either. She is extremely dangerous, and I did not want to lay myself open to her influence. My estimate of her current situation is based on deduction rather than direct knowledge. I would be willing to rely on it, though.'

'I see,' I said.

'I have a plan.'

'Go ahead.'

'The manner in which you retrieved me from durance was quite inspired, combining the forces of everyone's concentration as you did.

The same principle could be utilized again, to a different end. A force such as that would break through a person's defense fairly easily – even someone like Fiona, if the effort is properly directed.'

'That is to say, directed by yourself?'

'Of course. I propose that we assemble the family and force our way through to Bleys and Fiona, wherever they may be. We hold them, locked in the full, in the flesh, just for a moment or so. Just long enough for me to strike.'

'As you did Martin?'

'Better, I trust. Martin was able to break free at the last moment. That should not occur this time, with all of you helping. Even three or four would probably be sufficient.'

'You really think you can pull it off that easily?'

'I know we had better try. Time is running. You will be one of the ones executed when they take Amber. So will I. What do you say?'

'If I become convinced that it is necessary. Then I would have no choice but to go along with it.'

'It is necessary, believe me. The next thing is that I will need the Jewel of Judgment.'

'What for?'

'If Fiona is truly in the Courts of Chaos, the Trump alone will probably be insufficient to reach her and hold her – even with all of us behind it. In her case, I will require the Jewel to focus our energies.'

'I suppose that could be arranged.'

'Then the sooner we are about it the better. Can you set things up for tonight? I am sufficiently recovered to handle my end of it.'

'Hell, no,' I said, standing.

'What do you mean?' He clenched the arms of the chair, half-rising. 'Why not?'

'I said I would go along with it if I became convinced that it was necessary. You have admitted that a lot of this is conjecture. That alone is sufficient to keep me from being convinced.'

'Forget about being convinced then. Can you afford to take the chance? The next attack is going to be a lot stronger than the last, Corwin. They are aware of your new weapons. They are going to allow for this in their planning.'

'Even if I agreed with you, Brand, I am certain I could not convince the others that the executions are necessary.'

'Convince them? Just tell them! You've got them all by the throat, Corwin! You are on top right now. You want to stay there, don't you?'

I smiled and moved toward the door.

'I will, too,' I said, 'by doing things my way. I will keep your suggestion on file.'

'Your way is going to get you dead. Sooner than you think.'

'I am standing on your rug again,' I said.

He laughed.

'Very good. But I was not threatening you. You know what I meant. You are responsible for all of Amber now. You have to do the right thing.'

'And you know what I meant. I am not going to kill a couple more of us because of your suspicions. I would need more than that.'

'When you get it, it may be too late.'

I shrugged.

'We'll see.'

I reached toward the door.

'What are you going to do now?'

I shook my head.

'I don't tell anybody everything that I know, Brand. It is a kind of insurance.'

'I can appreciate that. I only hope that you know enough.'

'Or perhaps you fear that I know too much,' I said.

For a moment a wary look danced on the muscles beneath his eyes. Then be smiled.

'I am not afraid of you, brother,' he said.

'It is good to have nothing to fear,' I said.

I opened the door.

'Wait,' he said.

'You neglected to tell me who was with you when you discovered Martin's Trump, in the place where I had left it.'

'Why, it was Random,' I said.

'Oh. Is he aware of the particulars?'

'If you mean, does he know that you stabbed his son,' I said, 'the answer is no, not yet.'

'I see. And of Benedict's new arm? I understand that you somehow got it for him in Tir-na Nog'th. I would like to know more about this.'

'Not now,' I said. 'Let's save something for our next get-together. It won't be all that long.'

I went on out and closed the door, my silent regards to the rug.

8

After visiting the kitchens, compiling an enormous meal and demolishing it, I headed for the stables, where I located a handsome young sorrel which had once belonged to Eric. I made friends with him in spite of this, and a short while later we were moving toward the trail down Kolvir which would take us to the camp of my Shadow forces. As I rode and digested, I tried to sort out the events and revelations of what, to me, had been the past few hours. If Amber had indeed arisen as the result of Dworkin's act of rebellion within the Courts of Chaos, then it followed that we were all of us related to the very forces which now threatened us. It was, of course, difficult to decide how far anything Dworkin said might now be trusted. Yet, the black road did run to the Courts of Chaos, apparently as a direct result of Brand's ritual, a thing which he had based on principles learned from Dworkin. Fortunately, for now, the parts of Dworkin's narrative which required the greatest credulity were those things which were not of any great moment, from an immediate, practical standpoint. Still, I had mixed feelings about being descended from a unicorn—

'Corwin.'

I drew rein. I opened my mind to the sending and the image of Ganelon appeared.

'I am here,' I said. 'Where did you get hold of a set of Trumps? And learn how to use them?'

'I picked up a pack from the case in the library a while back. Thought it a good idea to have a way of getting in touch with you in a hurry. As for using them, I just did what you and the others seem to do – study the Trump, think about it, concentrate on getting in touch with the person.'

'I should have gotten you a pack long ago,' I said. 'It was an oversight on my part which I am glad you've remedied. Are you just testing them now, or did something come up?'

'Something,' he said. 'Where are you?'

'As chance would have it; I am on my way down to see you.'

'You are all right?'

'Yes.'

'Fine. Come ahead then. I'd rather not try bringing you through his thing, the way you people do. It is not that urgent I will see you by and by.'

'Yes.'

He broke the contact and I rustled the reins and continued on. For a moment, I had been irritated that he had not simply asked me for a deck. Then I recalled that I had been away for over a week, by Amber's time. He had probably been getting worried, didn't trust any of the others to do it for him. Perhaps rightly so.

The descent went quickly, as did the balance of the journey to the camp. The horse – whose name, by the way, was Drum – seemed happy to be going somewhere and had a tendency to pull away at the least excuse. I gave him his head at one point to tire him a bit and it was not too long afterward that I sighted the camp. I realized at about that time that I missed Star.

I was the subject of stares and salutes as I rode into camp. A silence followed me and all activity ceased as I passed. I wondered whether they believed I had come to deliver a battle order.

Ganelon emerged from his tent before I had dismounted.

'Fast,' he observed, clasping my hand as I came down. 'Pretty horse, that.'

'Yes,' I agreed, turning the reins over to his orderly. 'What news have you?'

'Well . . .' he said. 'I've been talking to Benedict . . .'

'Something stirring on the black road?'

'No, no. Nothing like that. He came to see me after he returned from those friends of his – the Tecys – to tell me that Random was all right, that he was following a lead as to Martin's whereabouts. We got to talking of other matters after that and finally he asked me to tell him everything I knew about Dara. Random had told him about her walking the Pattern, and he had decided then that too many people other than yourself were aware of her existence.'

'So what did you tell him?'

'Everything.'

'Including the guesswork, the speculation – after Tir-na Nog'th?'

'Just so.'

'I see. How did he take this?'

'He seemed excited about it. Happy, I'd even say. Come talk with him yourself.'

I nodded and he turned toward his tent. He pushed back the flap and stepped aside. I entered.

Benedict was seated on a low stool beside a foot locker atop which a map had been spread. He was tracing something on the map with the long metal finger of the glinting, skeletal hand attached to the deadly, silver-cabled, firepinned mechanical arm I had brought back from the city in the sky, the entire device now attached to the stump of his right arm a little below the point where the sleeve had been cut away from his brown shirt, a transformation which halted me with a momentary shudder, so much did he resemble the ghost I had encountered. His eyes rose to meet my own and he raised the hand in greeting, a casual, perfectly executed gesture, and he smiled the broadest smile I had ever seen crease his face.

'Corwin!' he said, and then he rose and extended that hand.

I had to force myself to clasp the device which had almost killed me. But Benedict looked more kindly disposed toward me than he had in a long while. I shook the new hand and its pressures were perfect I tried to disregard its coldness and angularity and almost succeeded, in my amazement at the control he had acquired over it in such a brief time.

'I owe you an apology,' he said. 'I have wronged you. I am very sorry.'

'It's all right,' I said. 'I understand.'

He clasped me for a moment, and my belief that things had apparently been set right between us was darkened only by the grip of those precise and deadly fingers on my shoulder.

Ganelon chuckled and brought up another stool, which he set at the other end of the locker. My irritation at his having aired the subject I had not wanted mentioned, whatever the circumstances, was submerged by the sight of its effects: I could not remember having seen Benedict in better spirits; Ganelon was obviously pleased at having effected the resolution of our differences.

I smiled myself and accepted a seat, unbuckling my sword belt and hanging Grayswandir on the tent pole. Ganelon produced three glasses and a bottle of wine. As he set the glasses before us and poured, he remarked, 'To return the hospitality of your tent, that night, back in Avalon.'

Benedict took up his glass with but the faintest of clicks.

'There is more ease in this tent,' he said. 'Is that not so, Corwin?'

I nodded and raised my glass.

'To that ease. May it always prevail.'

'I have had my first opportunity in a long while,' he said, 'to talk with Random at some length. He has changed quite a bit.'

'Yes,' I agreed.

'I am more inclined to trust him now than I was in days gone by. We had the time to talk after we left the Tecys.'

'Where were you headed?'

'Some comments Martin had made to his host seemed to indicate that he was going to a place I knew of further off in Shadow – the black city of Heerat. We journeyed there and found this to be correct. He had passed that way.'

'I am not familiar with Heerat,' I said.

'A place of adobe and stone – a commercial center at the junction of several trade routes. There, Random found news which took him eastward and probably deeper into Shadow. We parted company at Heerat, for I did not want to be away from Amber overlong. Also, there was a personal matter I was anxious to pursue. He told me how he had seen Dara walk the Pattern on the day of the battle.'

'That's right,' I said. 'She did. I was there, too.'

He nodded.

'As I said, Random had impressed me. I was inclined to believe he was telling the truth. If this were so, then it was possible that you were also. Granting this, I had to pursue the matter of the girl's allegations. You were not available, so I came to Ganelon – this was several days ago – and had him tell me everything he knew about Dara.'

I glanced at Ganelon, who inclined his head slightly.

'So you now believe you have uncovered a new relative.' I said, 'a mendacious one, to be sure, and quite possibly an enemy – but a relative, nevertheless. What is your next move?'

He took a sip of wine.

'I would like to believe in the relationship,' he said. 'The notion somehow pleases me. So I would like to establish it or negate it to a certainty. If it turns out that we are indeed related, then I would like to understand the motives behind her actions. And I would like to learn why she never made her existence known to me directly.' He put down his glass, raised his new hand and flexed the fingers. 'So I would like to begin,' he continued, 'by learning of those things you experienced in Tir-na Nog'th which apply to me and to Dara. I am also extremely curious about this hand, which behaves as if it were made for me. I have never heard of a physical object being obtained in the city in the sky.' He made a fist, unclenched it, rotated the wrist, extended the arm, raised it, lowered it gently to his knee. 'Random performed a very effective piece of surgery, don't you think?' he concluded.

'Very,' I agreed.

'So, will you tell me the story?'

I nodded and took a sip of my wine.

'It was in the palace in the sky that it occurred,' I said. 'The place was filled with inky, shifting shadows. I felt impelled to visit the throne room. I did this, and when the shadows moved aside, I saw you standing to the right of the throne, wearing that arm. When things cleared further, I saw Dara seated upon the throne. I advanced and touched her with Grayswandir, which made me visible to her. She declared me dead these several centuries and bade me return to my grave. When I demanded her lineage, she said she was descended of you of the hell maid Lintra.'

Benedict drew a deep breath but said nothing. I continued:

'Time, she said, moved at such a different rate in the place of her birth, that several generations had passed there. She was the first of them possessed of regular human attributes. She again bade me depart. During this time, you had been studying Grayswandir. You struck then to remove her from danger, and we fought. My blade could reach you and your hand could reach me. That was all. Otherwise, it was a confrontation of ghosts. As the sun began to rise and the city to fade, you had me in a grip with that hand. I struck it free of the arm with Grayswandir and escaped. It was returned with me because it was still clasping my shoulder.'

'Curious,' Benedict said. 'I have known that place to render false prophecies – the fears and hidden desires of the visitor, rather than a true picture of what is to be. But then, it often reveals unknown truths as well. And as in most other things, it is difficult to separate the valid from the spurious. How did you read it?'

'Benedict,' I said. 'I am inclined to believe the story of her origin. You have never seen her, but I have. She does resemble you in some ways. As for the rest . . . it is doubtless as you said – that which is left after the truth has been separated out.'

He nodded slowly, and I could tell that he was not convinced but did not want to push the matter. He knew as well as I did what the rest implied. If he were to pursue his claim to the throne and succeed in achieving it, it was possible that he might one day step aside in favor of his only descendant.

'What are you going to do?' I asked him.

'Do?' he said. 'What is Random now doing about Martin? I shall seek her, find her, have the story from her own lips, and then decide for myself. This will have to wait, however, until the matter of the black road is settled. That is another matter I wish to discuss with you.'

'Yes?'

'If time moves so differently in their stronghold, they have had more than they need in which to mount another attack. I do not want to keep waiting to meet them in indecisive encounters. I am contemplating following the black road back to its source and attacking them on their home ground. I would like to do it with your concurrence.'

'Benedict,' I said, 'have you ever looked upon the Courts of Chaos?'

He raised his head and stared at the blank wall of the tent.

'Ages ago, when I was young,' he said, 'I hellrode as far as I might go, to the end of everything. There, beneath a divided sky, I looked upon an awesome abyss. I do not know if the place lies there or if the road runs that far, but I am prepared to take that way again, if such is the case.'

'Such is the case,' I said.

'How can you be certain?'

'I am just returned from that land. A dark citadel hovers within it. The road goes to it.'

'How difficult was the way?'

'Here,' I said, taking out the Trump and passing it to him. 'This was Dworkin's. I found it among his things. I only just tried it. It took me there. Time is already rapid at that point. I was attacked by a rider on a drifting roadway, of a sort not shown on the card. Trump contact is difficult there, perhaps because of the time differential. Gérard brought me back.'

He studied the card.

'It seems the place I saw that time,' he said at length. 'This solves our logistics problems. With one of us on either end of a Trump connection we can transport the troops right through, as we did that day from Kolvir to Garnath.'

I nodded.

'That is one of the reasons I showed it to you, to indicate my good faith. There may be another way, involving less risk than running our forces into the unknown. I want you to hold off on this venture until I have explored my way further.'

'I will have to hold off in any event, to obtain some intelligence concerning that place. We do not even know whether your automatic weapons will function there, do we?'

'No, I did not have one along to test.'

He pursed his lips.

'You really should have thought to take one and try it.'

'The circumstances of my departure did not permit this.'

'Circumstances?'

'Another time. It is not relevant here. You spoke of following the black road to its source . . .'

'Yes?'

'That is not its true source. Its real source lies in the true Amber, in the defect in the primal Pattern.'

'Yes, I understand that. Both Random and Ganelon have described your journey to the place of the true Pattern, and the damage you discovered there. I see the analogy, the possible connection—'

'Do you recall my flight from Avalon, and your pursuit?'

In answer, he only smiled faintly.

'There was a point where we crossed the black road,' I said. 'Do you recall it?'

He narrowed his eyes.

'Yes,' he said. 'You cut a path through it. The world had returned to normal at that point I had forgotten.'

'It was an effect of the Pattern upon it,' I said, 'one which I believe can be employed upon a much larger scale.'

'How much larger?'

'To wipe out the entire thing.'

He leaned back and studied my face.

'Then why are you not about it?'

'There are a few preliminaries I must undertake.'

'How much time will they involve?'

'Not too much. Possibly as little as a few days. Perhaps a few weeks.'

'Why didn't you mention all of this sooner?'

'I only learned how to go about it recently.'

'How *do* you go about it?'

'Basically, it amounts to repairing the Pattern.'

'All right,' he said. 'Say you succeed. The enemy will still be out there.' He gestured toward Garnath and the black road. 'Someone gave them passage once.'

'The enemy has always been out there,' I said. 'And it will be up to us to see that they are not given passage again – by dealing properly with those who provided it in the first place.'

'I go along with you on that,' he said, 'but that is not what I meant. They require a lesson, Corwin. I want to teach them a proper respect for Amber, such a respect that even if the way is opened again they will fear to use it. That is what I meant. It is necessary.'

'You do not know what it would be like to carry a battle to that place, Benedict. It is – literally – indescribable.'

He smiled and stood.

'Then I guess I had best go see for myself,' he said. 'I will keep this card for a time, if you don't mind.'

'I don't mind.'

'Good. Then you be on with your business about the Pattern, Corwin, and I will be about my own. This will take me some time, too. I must go give my commanders orders concerning my absence now. Let us agree that neither of us commence anything of a final nature without checking first with the other.'

'Agreed,' I said.

We finished our wine.

'I will be under way myself, very soon now,' I said. 'So, good luck.'

'To you also.' He smiled again. 'Things are better,' he said, and he clasped my shoulder as he passed to the entrance.

We followed him outside.

'Bring Benedict's horse,' Ganelon directed the orderly who stood beneath a nearby tree; and turning, he offered Benedict his hand. 'I, too, want to wish you luck,' he said.

Benedict nodded and shook his hand. 'Thank you, Ganelon. For many things.'

Benedict withdrew his Trumps.

'I can bring Gérard up to date,' he said, 'before my horse arrives.'

He riffled through them, withdrew one, studied it.

'How do you go about repairing the Pattern?' Ganelon asked me.

'I have to get hold of the Jewel of Judgment again,' I said. 'With it, I can reinscribe the damaged area.'

'Is this dangerous?'

'Yes.'

'Where is the Jewel?'

'Back on the shadow Earth, where I left it.'

'Why did you abandon it?'

'I feared that it was killing me.'

He contorted his features into a near-impossible grimace.

'I don't like the sound of this, Corwin. There must be another way.'

'If I knew a better way, I'd take it.'

'Supposing you just followed Benedict's plan and took them all on? You said yourself that he could raise infinite legions in Shadow. You also said that he is the best man there is in the field.'

'Yet the damage would remain in the Pattern, and something else would come to fill it. Always. The enemy of the moment is not as important as our own inner weakness. If this is not mended we are already defeated, though no foreign conqueror stands within our walls.'

He turned away.

'I cannot argue with you. You know your own realm,' he said. 'But I still feel you may be making a grave mistake by risking yourself on what may prove unnecessary at a time when you are very much needed.'

I chuckled, for it was Vialle's word and I had not wanted to call it my own when she had said it.

'It is my duty,' I told him.

He did not reply.

Benedict, a dozen paces away, had apparently reached Gérard, for he would mutter something, then pause and listen. We stood there, waiting for him to conclude his conversation so that we could see him off.

'. . . Yes, he is here now,' I heard him say. 'No, I doubt that very much. But—'

Benedict glanced at me several times and shook his head.

'No, I do not think so,' he said. Then, 'All right come ahead.'

He extended his new hand, and Gérard stepped into being, clasping it. Gérard turned his head, saw me, and immediately moved in my direction.

He ran his eyes up and down and back and forth across my entire person, as if searching for something.

'What is the matter?' I said.

'Brand,' he replied. 'He is no longer in his quarters. At least, most of him isn't. He left some blood behind. The place is also broken up enough to show there had been a fight.'

I glanced down at my shirt front and trousers.

'And you are looking for bloodstains? As you can see, these are the same things I had on earlier. They may be dirty and wrinkled, but that's all.'

'That does not really prove anything,' he said.

'It was your idea to look. Not mine. What makes you think I—'

'You were the last one to see him,' he said.

'Except for the person he had a fight with – if he really did.'

'What do you mean by that?'

'You know his temper, his moods. We had a small argument. He might have started breaking things up after I left, maybe cut himself, gotten disgusted, trumped out for a change of scene – Wait! His rug! Was there any blood on that small, fancy rug before his door?'

'I am not sure – no, I don't think so. Why?'

'Circumstantial evidence that he did it himself. He was very fond of that rug. He avoided messing it.'

'I don't buy it,' Gérard said, 'and Caine's death still looks peculiar –

and Benedict's servants, who could have found out you wanted gunpowder. Now Brand—'

'This could well be another attempt to frame me,' I said, 'and Benedict and I have come to better terms.'

He turned toward Benedict, who had not moved from where he stood a dozen paces away, regarding us without expression, listening.

'Has he explained away those deaths?' Gérard asked him.

'Not directly,' Benedict answered, 'but much of the rest of the story now stands in a better light. So much so, that I am inclined to believe all of it.'

Gérard shook his head and glared down at me again.

'Still unsettled,' he said. 'What were you and Brand arguing about?'

'Gérard,' I said, 'that is our business, till Brand and I decide otherwise.'

'I dragged him back to life and watched over him, Corwin. I didn't do it just to see him killed in a squabble.'

'Use your brains,' I told him. 'Whose idea was it to search for him the way that we did? To bring him back?'

'You wanted something from him,' he said. 'You finally got it. Then he became an impediment.'

'No. But even if that were the case, do you think I would be so damned obvious about it? If he has been killed, then it is on the same order as Caine's death – an attempt to frame me.'

'You used the obviousness excuse with Caine, too. It seems to me it could be a kind of subtlety – a thing you are good at.'

'We have been through his before, Gérard . . .'

'. . . And you know what I told you then.'

'It would be difficult to have forgotten.'

He reached forward and seized my right shoulder. I immediately drove my left hand into his stomach and pulled away. It occurred to me then that perhaps I should have told him what Brand and I had been talking about. But I didn't like the way he had asked me.

He came at me again. I side-stepped and caught him with a light left near the right eye. I kept jabbing after that, mainly to keep his head back. I was in no real shape to fight him again, and Grayswandir was back in the tent I had no other weapon with me.

I kept circling him. My side hurt if I kicked with my left leg. I caught him once on the thigh with my right, but I was slow and off-balance and could not really follow through. I continued to jab.

Finally, he blocked my left and managed to drop his hand on my biceps. I should have pulled away then, but he was open. I stepped in with a heavy right to his stomach, all of my strength behind it. It bent him forward with a gasp, but his grip tightened on my arm. He blocked my attempted uppercut with his left, continuing its forward motion until the heel of his hand slammed against my chest, at the same time jerking my left arm backward and to the side with such force that I was thrown to the ground. If he came down on me, that was it.

He dropped to one knee and reached for my throat.

9

I moved to block his hand, but it halted in midreach. Turning my head, I saw that another hand had fallen upon, Gérard's arm, was now grasping it, was holding it back.

I rolled away. When I looked up again, I saw that Ganelon had caught hold of him. Gérard jerked his arm forward, but it did not come free.

'Stay out of this, Ganelon,' he said.

'Get going, Corwin!' Ganelon said. 'Get the Jewel!'

Even as he called out, Gérard was beginning to rise. Ganelon crossed with his left and connected with Gérard's jaw. Gérard sprawled at his feet. Ganelon moved in and swung a kick toward his kidney, but Gérard caught his foot and heaved him over backward. I scrambled back into a crouch, supporting myself with one hand.

Gérard came up off the ground and rushed Ganelon, who was just recovering his feet. As he was almost upon him, Ganelon came up with a double-fisted blow to Gérard's midsection, which halted him in his tracks. Instantly, Ganelon's fists were moving like pistons against Gérard's abdomen. For several moments, Gérard seemed too dazed to protect himself, and when he finally bent and brought his arms in, Ganelon caught him with a right to the jaw that staggered him backward. Ganelon immediately rushed forward, throwing his arms about Gérard as he slammed into him and hooking his right leg behind Gérard's own. Gérard toppled and Ganelon fell upon him. He straddled Gérard then and drove his right fist against his jaw. When Gérard's head rolled back, Ganelon crossed with his left.

Benedict suddenly moved to intervene, but Ganelon chose that moment to rise to his feet. Gérard lay unconscious, bleeding from his mouth and nose.

I got shakily to my own feet, dusted myself off.

Ganelon grinned at me.

'Don't stay around,' he said. 'I don't know how I would do in a rematch. Go find the trinket.'

I glanced at Benedict and he nodded. I returned to the tent for Grayswandir. When I emerged, Gérard still had not moved, but Benedict stood before me.

'Remember,' he said, 'you've my Trump and I've yours. Nothing final without a conference.'

I nodded. I was going to ask him why he had seemed willing to help Gérard, but not me. But second thoughts had me and I decided against spoiling our fresh-minted amity.

'Okay.'

I headed toward the horses. Ganelon clapped me on the shoulder as I came up to himn.

'Good luck,' he said. 'I'd go with you, but I am needed here – especially with Benedict trumping off to Chaos.'

'Good show,' I said. 'I shouldn't have any trouble. Don't worry.'

I went off to the paddock. Shortly, I was mounted and moving. Ganelon threw me a salute as I passed and I returned it. Benedict was kneeling beside Gérard.

I headed for the nearest trail into Arden. The sea lay at my back, Garnath and the black road to the left, Kolvir to my right. I had to gain some distance before I could work with the stuff of Shadow. The day lay clean once Garnath was lost to sight, several rises and dips later. I struck the trail and followed its long curve into the wood, where moist shadows and distant bird songs reminded me of the long periods of peace we had known of old and the silken, gleaming presence of the maternal unicorn.

My aches faded into the rhythm of the ride, and I thought once again of the encounter I had departed. It was not difficult to understand Gérard's attitude, since he had already told me of his suspicions and issued me a warning. Still, it was such bad timing for whatever had happened with Brand that I could not but see it as another action intended either to slow me or to stop me entirely. It was fortunate that Ganelon had been on hand, in good shape, and able to put his fists in the right places at the proper times. I wondered what Benedict would have done if there had only been the three of us present I'd a feeling he would have waited and intervened only at the very last moment, to stop Gérard from killing me. I was still not happy with our accord, though it was certainly an improvement over the previous state of affairs.

All of which made me wonder again what had become of Brand. Had Fiona or Bleys finally gotten to him? Had he attempted his proposed assassinations singlehanded and been met with a counter-thrust, then dragged through his intended victim's Trump? Had his old allies from the Courts of Chaos somehow gotten through to him? Had one of his thorny-handed guardians from the tower finally been able to reach him? Or had it been as I had suggested to Gérard – an accidental self-injury in a fit of rage, followed by an ill-tempered flight from Amber to do his brooding and plotting elsewhere?

When that many questions arise from a single event the answer is seldom obtainable by pure logic. I had to sort out the possibilities though, to have something to reach for when more facts did turn up. In the meantime, I thought carefully over everything he had told me, regarding his allegations in light of those things which I now knew. With one exception, I did not doubt most of the facts. He had built too cleverly to have the edifice simply toppled – but then, he had had a lot of time to think these things over. No, it was in his manner of presenting events that something had been hidden by misdirection. His recent proposal practically assured me of that.

The old trail twisted, widened, narrowed again, swung to the northwest and downward, into the thickening wood. The forest had changed very little. It seemed almost the same trail a young man had ridden centuries before, riding for the sheer pleasure of it, riding to explore that vast green realm which extended over most of the continent if he did not stray into Shadow. It would be good to be doing it again for no reason other than this.

After perhaps an hour, I had worked my way well back into the forest where the trees were great dark towers, what sunlight I glimpsed caught like phoenix nests in their highest branches, an always moist twilight softness smoothing the outlines of stumps and boles, logs and mossy rocks. A deer bounded across my path, not trusting to the excellent concealment of a thicket at the right of the trail. Bird notes sounded about me, never too near. Occasionally, I crossed the tracks of other horsemen. Some of these were quite fresh, but they did not stay long with the trail. Kolvir was well out of sight had been for some time.

The trail rose again, and I knew that I would shortly reach the top of a small ridge, pass among rocks, and head downward once more. The trees thinned somewhat as we climbed, until finally I was afforded a partial view of the sky. It was enlarged as I continued, and when I came to the summit I heard the distant cry of a hunting bird.

Glancing upward, I saw a great dark shape, circling and circling, high above me. I hurried past the boulders and shook the reins for a burst of speed as soon as the way was clear. We plunged downward, racing to get under cover of the larger trees once again.

The bird cried out as we did this, but we won to the shade, to the dimness, without incident I slowed gradually after that and continued to listen, but there were no untoward sounds on the air. This part of the forest was pretty much the same as that we had left beyond the ridge, save for a small stream we picked up and paralleled for a time, finally crossing it at a shallow ford. Beyond, the trail widened and a little more light leaked through and flowed with us for half a league. We had almost come a sufficient distance for me to begin those small manipulations of Shadow which would bear me to the pathway back to the shadow Earth of my former exile. Yet, it would be difficult to begin here, easier farther along. I resolved to save the strain on myself and my mount by continuing to a better beginning. Nothing of a threatening nature had really occurred. The bird could be a wild hunter, probably was.

Only one thought nagged at me as I rode.

Julian . . .

Arden was Julian's preserve, patrolled by his rangers, sheltering several encampments of his troops at all times – Amber's inland border guard, both against incursions natural and against those things which might appear at the boundaries of Shadow.

Where did Julian go when he had departed the palace so suddenly on the night of Brand's stabbing? If he wished simply to hide, there was no necessity for him to flee farther than this. Here he was strong, backed by his own men, moving in a realm he knew far better than the rest of us. It was quite possible that he was not, right now, too far away. Also, he liked to hunt. He had his hellhounds, he had his birds . . .

A half mile, a mile . . .

Just then, I heard the sound that I feared most Piercing the green and the shade, there came the notes of a hunting horn. They came from some distance behind me, and I think from the left of the trail.

I urged my mount to a gallop and the trees rushed to a blur on either side. The trail was straight and level here. We took advantage of this.

Then from behind, I heard a roar – a kind of deep-chested coughing, growling sound backed by a lot of resonant long space. I did not know what it was that had uttered it, but it was no dog. Not even a hellhound sounded like that I glanced back, but there was no pursuit in sight. So I kept low and talked to Drum a bit.

After a time, I heard a crashing noise in the woods off to my right, but the roar was not repeated just then. I looked again, several times, but I was unable to make out what it was that was causing the disturbance. Shortly thereafter, I heard the horn once more, much nearer, and this time it was answered by the barks and the baying which I could not mistake. The hellhounds were coming – swift, powerful, vicious beasts Julian had found in some shadow and trained to the hunt.

It was time, I decided, to begin the shift. Amber was still strong about me, but I laid hold of Shadow as best I could and started the movement.

The trail began to curve to the left, and as we raced along it the trees at either hand diminished in size, fell back. Another curve, and the trail led as through a clearing, perhaps two hundred meters across. I glanced up then and saw that that damned bird was still circling, much nearer now, close enough to be dragged with me through Shadow.

This was more complicated than I had intended. I wanted an open space in which to wheel my mount and swing a blade freely if it came to that. The occurrence of such a place, however, revealed my position quite clearly to the bird, whom it was proving difficult to lose.

All right. We came to a low hill, mounted it, started downward, passing a lone, lightning-blasted tree as we did. On its nearest branch sat a hawk of gray and silver and black. I whistled to it as we passed, and it leaped into the air, shrieking a savage battle cry.

Hurrying on, I heard the individual voices of the dogs clearly now, and the thud of the horses' hoofs. Mixed in with these sounds there was something else, more a vibration, a shuddering of the ground. I looked back again, but none of my pursuit had yet topped the hill. I bent my mind toward the way away and clouds occluded the sun. Strange flowers appeared along the trail – green and yellow and purple – and there came a rumble of distant thunders. The clearing widened, lengthened. It became completely level.

I heard once again the sound of the horn. I turned for another look.

It bounded into view then, and I realized at that instant that I was not the object of the hunt, that the riders, the dogs, the bird, were pursuing the thing that ran behind me. Of course, this was a rather academic distinction, in that I was in front, and quite possibly the object of *its* hunt. I leaned forward, shouting to Drum and digging in with my knees, realizing even as I did that the abomination was moving faster than we could. It was a panic reaction.

I was being pursued by a manticora.

The last time I had seen its like was on the day before the battle in which Eric died. As I had led my troops up the rearward slopes of Kolvir, it had appeared to tear a man named Rall in half. We had dispatched it with automatic weapons. The thing proved twelve feet in length, and like this one it had worn a human face on the head and shoulders of a lion; it, too, had had a pair of eaglelike wings folded against its sides and the long pointed tail of a scorpion curving in the air above it. A number of them had somehow wandered in from Shadow to devil our steps as we headed for that battle. There was no reason to believe all of them had been accounted for, save that none had been reported since that time and no evidence of their continued existence in the vicinity of Amber had come to light. Apparently, this one had wandered down into Arden and been living in the forest since that time.

A final glance showed me that I might be pulled down in moments if I did not make a stand. It also showed me a dark avalanche of dogs rushing down the hill.

I did not know the intelligence or psychology of the manticora. Most fleeing beasts will not stop to attack something which is not bothering them. Self-preservation is generally foremost in their minds. On the other hand, I was not certain that the manticora even realized that it was being pursued. It might have started out on my trail and only had its own picked up afterward. It might have only the one thing on its mind. It was hardly a time to pause and reflect on all the possibilities.

I drew Grayswandir and turned my mount to the left, pulling back on the reins immediately as he made the turn.

Drum screamed and rose high onto his hind legs. I felt myself sliding backward, so I jumped to the ground and leaped to the side.

But I had, for the moment, forgotten the speed of the storm-hounds, had also forgotten how easily they had once overtaken Random and myself in Flora's Mercedes, had also forgotten that unlike ordinary dogs chasing cars, they had begun tearing the vehicle apart.

Suddenly, they were all over the manticora, a dozen or more dogs, leaping and biting. The beast threw back its head and uttered another cry as they struck at it. It swept that vicious tail through them, sending one flying, stunning or killing two others. It reared then and turned, striking out with its forelegs as it descended.

But even as it did this, a hound attached itself to its left foreleg, two more were at its haunches and one had scrambled onto its back, biting at its shoulder and neck. The others were circling it now. As soon as it would go after one, the others would dart in and slash at it.

It finally caught the one on its back with its scorpion sting and disembowled the one gnawing at its leg. However, it was running blood from a double dozen wounds by then. Shortly, it became apparent that the leg was giving it trouble, both for striking purposes and for bearing its weight when it struck with the others. In the meantime, another dog had mounted its back and was tearing at its neck. It seemed to be having a more difficult time getting at this one. Another came in from its right and shredded its ear. Two more plied its haunches, and when it reared again one rushed in and tore at its belly. Their barks and growls also seemed to be confusing it some-what, and it began striking wildly at the ever-moving gray shapes.

I had caught hold of Drum's bridle and was trying to calm him sufficiently to remount and get the hell out of there. He kept trying to rear and pull away, and it took considerable persuasion even to hold him in place.

In the meantime, the manticora let out a bitter, wailing cry. It had struck wildly at the dog on its back and driven its sting into its own shoulder. The dogs took advantage of this distraction and rushed in wherever there was an opening, snapping and tearing.

I am certain the dogs would have finished it, but at that moment the riders topped the hill and descended. There were five of them, Julian in the lead. He had on his scaled white armor and his hunting horn hung about his neck. He rode his gigantic steed Morgenstern, a beast which has always hated me. He raised the long lance that he bore and saluted with it in my direction. Then he lowered it and shouted orders to the dogs. Grudgingly, they dropped away from the prey. Even the dog on the manticora's back loosened its grip and leaped to the ground. All of them drew back as Julian couched the lance and touched his spurs to Morgenstern's sides.

The beast turned toward him, gave a final cry of defiance, and leaped ahead, fangs bared. They came together, and for a moment my view was blocked by Morgenstern's shoulder. Another moment, however, and I knew from the horse's behavior that the blow had been a true one.

A turning, and I saw the beast stretched out, great gouts of blood upon its breast, flowering about the dark stem of the lance.

Julian dismounted. He said something to the other riders which I did not overhear. They remained mounted. He regarded the still-twitching manticora, then looked at me and smiled. He crossed and placed his foot upon the beast, seized the lance with one hand, and wrenched it from the carcass. Then he drove it into the ground and tethered Morgenstern to its shaft. He reached up and patted the horse's shoulder, looked back at me, turned, and headed in my direction.

When he came up before me he said, 'I wish you hadn't killed Bela.'

'Bela?' I repeated.

He glanced at the sky. I followed his gaze. Neither bird was now in sight.

'He was one of my favorites.'

'I am sorry,' I said. 'I misunderstood what was going on.'

He nodded.

'All right. I've done something for you. Now you can tell me what happened after I left the palace. Did Brand make it?'

'Yes,' I said, 'and you're off the hook on that. He claimed Fiona stabbed him. And she was not around to question either. She departed during the night, also. It's a wonder you didn't bump into one another.'

He smiled.

'I'd have guessed as much,' he said.

'Why did you flee under such suspicious circumstances?' I asked. 'It made it look bad for you.'

He shrugged.

'It would not be the first time I've been falsely accused, suspected. And for that matter, if intent counts for anything, I am as guilty as our little sister. I'd have done it myself if I could. In fact, I'd a blade ready the night we fetched him back. Only, I was crowded aside.'

'But why?' I asked.

He laughed.

'Why? I am afraid of the bastard, that's why. For a long while, I had thought he was dead, and certainly hoped so – finally claimed by the dark powers he dealt with. How much do you really know about him, Corwin?'

'We had a long talk.'

'And . . . ?'

'He admitted that he and Bleys and Fiona had formed a plan to claim the throne. They would see Bleys crowned, but each would share the real power. They had used the forces you referred to, to assure Dad's absence. Brand said that he had attempted to will Caine to their cause, but that Caine had instead gone to you and to Eric. The three of you then formed a similar cabal to seize power before they could, by placing Eric on the throne.'

He nodded.

'The events are in order, but the reason is not. We did not want the throne, at least not that abruptly, nor at that time. We formed our group to oppose their group, because it had to be opposed to protect the throne. At first, the most we could persuade Eric to do was to assume a Protectorship. He was afraid he would quickly turn up dead if he saw himself crowned under those conditions. Then you turned up, with your very legitimate claim. We could not afford to let you press it at that time, because Brand's crowd was threatening out-and-out war. We felt they would be less inclined to make this move if the throne were already occupied. We could not have seated you, because you would have refused to be a puppet, a role you would have had to play since the game was already in progress and you were ignorant on too many fronts. So we persuaded Eric to take the risk and be crowned. That was how it happened.'

'So when I did arrive he put out my eyes and threw me in the dungeon for laughs.'

Julian turned away and looked back at the dead manticora.

'You are a fool,' he finally said. 'You were a tool from the very beginning. They used you to force our hand and either way you lost. If that half-assed attack of Bleys's had somehow succeeded, you wouldn't have lasted long enough to draw a deep breath. If it failed, as it did, Bleys disappeared, as he did, leaving you with your life forfeit for attempted usurpation. You had served your purpose and you had to die. They left us small choice in the matter. By rights, we should have killed you – and you know it.'

I bit my lip. There were many things I might say. But if he was telling something approximating the truth, he did have a point. And I did want to hear more.

'Eric,' he said, 'figured that your eyesight might eventually be restored – knowing the way we regenerate – given time. It was a very delicate situation. If Dad were to return, Eric could step down and justify all of his actions to anyone's satisfaction – except for killing you. That would have been too patent a move to ensure his own continued reign beyond the troubles of the moment. And I will tell you frankly that he simply wanted to imprison you and forget you.'

'Then whose idea was the blinding?'

He was silent again for a long while. Then he spoke very softly, almost a whisper: 'Hear me out, please. It was mine, and it may have saved your life. Any action taken against you had to be tantamount to death, or their faction would have tried for the real thing. You were no longer of any use to them, but alive and about you possessed the potentiality of becoming a danger at some future time. They could have used your Trump to contact you and kill you, or they could have used it to free you in order to sacrifice you in yet another move against Eric. Blinded, however, there was no need to slay you and you were of no use for anything else they might have in mind. It saved you by taking you out of the picture for a time, and it saved us from a more egregious act which might one day be held against us. As we saw it, there was no choice. It was the only thing we could do. There could be no show of leniency either, or we might be suspected of having some use for you ourselves. The moment you assumed any such semblance of value you would have been a dead man. The most we could do was look the other way whenever Lord Rein contrived to comfort you. That was all that could be done.'

'I see,' I said.

'Yes,' he agreed, 'You saw too soon. No one had guessed you would recover your sight that quickly, nor that you would be able to escape once you did. How did you manage it?'

'Does Macy's tell Gimbel's?' I said.

'Beg pardon?'

'I said— never mind. What do you know of Brand's imprisonment, then?'

He regarded me once more.

'All I know is that there was some sort of falling out within his group. I lack the particulars. For some reason, Bleys and Fiona were afraid to kill him and afraid to let him run loose. When we freed him from their compromise – imprisonment – Fiona was apparently more afraid of having him free.'

'And you said you feared him enough to have made ready to kill him. Why now, after all this time, when all of this is history and the power has shifted again? He was weak, virtually helpless. What harm could he do now?'

He sighed.

'I do not understand the power that he possesses,' he said, 'but it is considerable. I know that he can travel through Shadow with his mind, that he can sit in a chair, locate what he seeks in Shadow, and then bring it to him by an act of will without moving from the chair; and he can travel through Shadow physically in a somewhat similar fashion. He lays his mind upon the place he would visit, forms a kind of mental doorway, and simply steps through. For that matter, I believe he can sometimes tell what people are thinking. It is almost as if he has himself become some sort of living Trump. I know these things because I have seen him do them. Near the end, when we had him under surveillance in the palace he had eluded us once in this fashion. This was the time he traveled to the shadow Earth and had you placed in Bedlam. After his recapture, one of us remained with him at all times. We did not yet know that he could summon things through Shadow, however. When he became aware that you had escaped your confinement, he summoned a horrid beast which attacked Caine, who was then his bodyguard. Then he went to you once again. Bleys and Fiona apparently got hold of him shortly after that, before we could, and I did not see him again until that night in the library when we brought him back. I fear him because he has deadly powers which I do not understand.'

'In such a case, I wonder how they managed to confine him at all?'

'Fiona has similar strengths, and I believe Bleys did also. Between the two of them, they could apparently annul most of Brand's power while they created a place where it would be inoperative.'

'Not totally,' I said. 'He got a message to Random. In fact, he reached me once, weakly.'

'Obviously not totally, then,' he said. 'Sufficiently, however. Until we broke through the defenses.'

'What do you know of all their byplay with me – confining me, trying to kill me, saving me.'

'That I do not understand,' he said, 'except that it was part of the power struggle within their own group. They had had a falling out amongst themselves, and one side or the other had some use for you. So, naturally, one side was trying to kill you while the other fought to preserve you. Ultimately, of course, Bleys got the most mileage out of you, in that attack he launched.'

'But he was the one who tried to kill me, back on the shadow Earth,' I said. 'He was the one who shot out my tires.'

'Oh?'

'Well, that is what Brand told me, but it jibes with all sorts of secondary evidence.'

He shrugged.

'I cannot help you on that,' he said. 'I simply do not know what was going on among them at that time.'

'Yet you countenance Fiona in Amber,' I said. 'In fact, you are more than a little cordial to her whenever she is about.'

'Of course,' he said, smiling. 'I have always been very fond of Fiona. She is certainly the loveliest, most civilized of us all. Pity Dad was always so dead-set against brother-sister marriages, as well you know. It bothered me that we had to be adversaries for so long as we were. Things returned pretty much to normal after Bleys's death, your imprisonment, and Eric's coronation, though. She accepted their defeat gracefully, and that was that. She was obviously as frightened at the prospect of Brand's return as I was.'

'Brand told things differently,' I said, 'but then, of course, he would. For one thing, he claims that Bleys is still living, that he hunted him down with his Trump and knows that he is off in Shadow, training another force for another strike at Amber.'

'I suppose this is possible,' Julian said. 'But we are more than adequately prepared, are we not?'

'He claims further that the strike will be a feint,' I continued, 'and that the real attack will then come direct from the Courts of Chaos, over the black road. He says that Fiona is off preparing the way for this right now.'

He scowled.

'I hope he was simply lying,' he said. 'I would hate to see their group resurrected and at us again, this time with help from the dark direction. And I would hate to see Fiona involved.'

'Brand claimed he was out of it himself, that he had seen the error of his ways – and suchlike penitent noises.'

'Ha! I'd sooner trust that beast I just slew than take Brand at his word. I hope you've had the sense to keep him well guarded – though this might not be of much avail if he has his old powers back.'

'But what game could he be playing now?'

'Either he has revived the old triumvirate, a thought I like not at all, or he has a new plan all his own. But mark me, he has a plan. He has never been satisfied to be a mere spectator at anything. He is always scheming. I'd take an oath he even plots in his sleep.'

'Perhaps you are right,' I said. 'You see, there has been a new development, whether for good or ill, I cannot yet tell. I just had a fight with Gérard. He thinks I have done Brand some mischief. This is not the case, but I was in no position to prove my innocence. I was the last person I know of to see Brand, earlier today. Gérard visited his quarters a short time ago. He says the place is broken up, there are blood smears here and there, and Brand is missing. I don't know what to make of it.'

'Neither do I. But I hope it means someone has done the job properly this time.'

'Lord,' I said, 'it's tangled. I wish I had known all of these things before.'

'There was never a proper time to tell you,' he said, 'until now. Certainly not when you were a prisoner and could still be reached, and after that you were gone for a long while. When you returned with your troops and your new weapons, I was uncertain as to your full intentions. Then things happened quickly and Brand was back again. It was too late. I had to get out to save my skin. I am strong here in Arden. Here, I can take anything he can throw at me. I have been maintaining the patrols at full battle force and awaiting word of Brand's death. I wanted to inquire of one of you whether he was still around. But I could not decide whom to ask, thinking myself still suspect should he have died. As soon as I did get word, though, should it prove he was still living, I was resolved to have a try at him myself. Now this . . . state of affairs . . . What are you going to do now, Corwin?'

'I am off to fetch the Jewel of Judgement from a place where I cached it in Shadow. There is a way it can be used to destroy the black road. I intend to try it.'

'How can this be done?'

'That is too long a story, for a horrible thought has just occurred to me.'

'What is that?'

'Brand wants the Jewel. He was asking about it, and now – this power of his to find things in Shadow and fetch them back. How good is it?'

Julian looked thoughtful.

'He is hardly omniscient, if that is what you mean. You can find anything you want in Shadow the normal way we go about it – by traveling to it. According to Fiona, he just cuts out the footwork. It is therefore *an* object, not a particular object that he summons. Besides, that Jewel is a very strange item from everything Eric told me about it I think Brand would have to go after it in person, once he finds out where it is.'

'Then I must get on with my hellride. I have to beat him to it.'

'I see you are riding Drum,' Julian observed. 'He is a good beast, a sturdy fellow. Been through many a hellride.'

'Glad to hear that,' I said. 'What are *you* going to do now?'

'Get in touch with someone in Amber and get up to date on everything we haven't had a chance to talk about – Benedict, probably.'

'No good,' I said. 'You will not be able to reach him. He is off to the Courts of Chaos. Try Gérard, and convince him I am an honorable man while you are about it.'

'The redheads are the only magicians in this family, but I will try . . . You *did* say the Courts of Chaos?'

'Yes, but again, the time is too valuable now.'

'Of course. Get you gone. We will have our leisure later – I trust.'

He reached out and clasped my arm. I glanced at the manticora, at the dogs seated in a circle about it.

'Thanks, Julian. I— You are a difficult man to understand.'

'Not so. I think the Corwin I hated must have died centuries ago. Ride now, man! If Brand shows up around here, I'll nail his hide to a tree!'

He shouted an order to his dogs as I mounted, and they fell upon the carcass of the manticora, lapping at its blood and tearing out huge chunks and strips of flesh. As I rode past that strange, massive, manlike face, I saw that its eyes were still open, though glazed. They were blue, and death had not robbed them of a certain preternatural innocence. Either that, or the look was death's final gift – a senseless way of passing out ironies, if it was.

I took Drum back to the trail and began my hellride.

10

Moving along the trail at a gentle pace, clouds darkening the sky and Drum's whinny of memory or anticipation . . . A turn to the left, and uphill . . . The ground is brown, yellow, back to brown again . . . The trees squat down, draw apart . . . Grasses wave between them in the cool and rising breeze . . . A quick fire in the sky . . . A rumble shakes loose raindrops . . .

Steep and rocky now . . . The wind tugs at my cloak . . . Up . . . Up to where the rocks are streaked with silver and the trees have drawn their line . . . The grasses, green fires, die down in the rain . . . Up, to the craggy, sparkling, rain-washed heights, where the clouds rush and boil like a mud-gorged river at flood crest . . . The rain stings like buckshot and the wind clears its throat to sing . . . We rise and rise and the crest comes into view, like the head of a startled bull, horns guarding the trail . . . Lightnings twist about their tips, dance between them . . . The smell of ozone as we reach that place and rush on through, the rain suddenly blocked the wind shunted away . . .

Emerging on the farther side . . . There is no rain, the air is still, the sky smoothed and darkened to a proper starfilled black . . . Meteors cut and burn, cut and burn, cauterizing to afterimage scars, fading, fading . . . Moons, cast like a handful of coins . . . Three bright dimes, a dull quarter, a pair of pennies, one of them tarnished and scarred . . . Down then, that long, winding way . . . Hoof clops clear and metallic in the night air . . . Somewhere, a cat-like cough . . . A dark shape crossing a lesser moon, ragged and swift . . .

Downward . . . The land drops away at either hand . . . Darkness below . . . Moving along the top of an infinitely high, curved wall, the way itself bright with moonlight . . . The trail buckles, folds, grows transparent . . . Soon it drifts, gauzy, filamentous, stars beneath as well as above . . . Stars below on either side . . . There is no land . . .

There is only the night, night and the thin, translucent trail I had to try to ride, to learn how it felt, against some future use . . .

It is absolutely silent now, and the illusion of slowness attaches to every movement . . . Shortly, the trail falls away, and we move as if swimming underwater at some enormous depth, the stars bright fish . . . It is freedom, it is the power of the hellride that brings an elation, like yet unlike the recklessness that sometimes comes in battle, the boldness of a risky feat well learned, the rush of rightness following the finding of the poem's proper word . . . It is these and the prospect itself, riding, riding, riding, from nowhere to nowhere perhaps, across and among the minerals and fires of the void, free of earth and air and water . . .

We race a great meteor, we touch upon its bulk . . . Speeding across its pitted surface, down, around, then up again . . . It stretches into a great plain, it lightens, it yellows . . .

It is sand, sand now beneath our movement . . . The stars fade out as the darkness is diluted to a morning of sunrise . . . Swaths of shade ahead, desert trees within them . . . Ride for the dark . . . Crashing through . . . Bright birds burst forth, complain, resettle . . .

Among the thickening trees . . . Darker the ground, narrower the way . . . Palm fronds shrink to hand size, barks darken . . . A twist to the right, a widening of the way . . . Our hoofs striking sparks from cobblestones . . . The lane enlarges, becomes a tree-lined street . . . Tiny row houses flash by . . . Bright shutters, marble steps, painted screens, set back beyond flagged walks . . . Passing, a horse-drawn cart, loaded with fresh vegetables . . . Human pedestrians turning to stare . . . A small buzz of voices . . .

On . . . Passing beneath a bridge . . . Coursing the stream till it widens to river, taking it down to the sea . . .

Thudding along the beach beneath a lemon sky, blue clouds scudding . . . The salt, the wrack, the shells, the smooth anatomy of driftwood . . . White spray off the lime-colored sea . . .

Racing, to where the place of waters ends at a terrace . . . Mounting, each step crumbling and roaring down behind, losing its identity, joined with the boom of the surf . . . Up, up to the flat-topped, tree-grown plain, a golden city shimmering, miragelike, at its end . . .

The city grows, darkens beneath a shadowy umbrella, its gray towers stretch upward, glass and metal flashing light through the murk . . . The towers begin to sway . . .

The city falls in upon itself, soundlessly, as we pass . . . Towers topple, dust boils, rises, is pinked by some lower glow . . . A gentle noise, as of a snuffed candle, drifting by . . .

A dust storm, quickly falling, giving place to fog . . . Through it, the sounds of automobile horns . . . A drift, a brief lift, a break in the gray-white, pearl-white, shifting . . . Our hoofprints on a shoulder of highway . . . To the right, endless rows of unmoving vehicles . . . Pearl-white, gray-white, drifting again . . .

Directionless shrieks and wailings . . . Random flashes of light . . .

Rising once more . . . The fogs lower and ebb . . . Grass, grass, grass . . . Clear now the sky, and delicate blue . . . A sun racing to set . . . Birds . . . A cow to the field chewing, staring and chewing . . .

Leaping a wooden fence to ride a country road . . . A sudden chill beyond the hill . . . The grasses are dry and snow's on the ground . . . Tin-roofed farmhouse atop a rise, curl of smoke above it . . .

On . . . The hills grow up, the sun rolls down, darkness dragged behind . . . A sprinkle of stars . . . Here a house, set far back . . . There another, long driveway wound among old trees . . . Headlights . . .

Off to the side of the road . . . Draw rein and let it pass . . .

I wiped my brow, dusted my shirt front and sleeves. I patted Drum's neck. The oncoming vehicle slowed as it neared me, and I could see the driver staring. I gave the reins a gentle movement and Drum began walking. The car braked to a halt and the driver called something after me, but I kept going. Moments later, I heard him drive off.

It was country road for a time after that. I traveled at an easy pace, passing familiar landmarks, recalling other times. A few miles later and I came to another road, wider and better. I turned there, staying off on the shoulder to the right. The temperature continued to drop, but the cold air had a good clean taste to it. A sliced moon shone above the hills to my left. There were a few small clouds passing overhead, touched to the moon's quarter with a soft, dusty light. There was very little wind; an occasional stirring of branches, no more. After a time, I came to a series of dips in the road, telling me I was almost there.

A curve and a couple more dips . . . I saw the boulder beside the driveway, I read my address upon it.

I drew rein then and looked up the hill. There was a station wagon in the driveway and a light on inside the house. I guided Drum off the road and across a field into a stand of trees. I tethered him behind a pair of evergreens, rubbed his neck, and told him I would not be long.

I returned to the road. No cars in sight. I crossed over and walked up the far side of the driveway, passing behind the station wagon. The only light in the house was in the living room, off to the right. I made my way around the left side of the house to the rear.

I halted when I reached the patio, looking around. Something was wrong.

The back yard was changed. A pair of decaying lawn chairs which had been leaning against a dilapidated chicken coop I had never bothered to remove were gone. So, for that matter, was the chicken coop. They had been present the last time I had passed this way. All of the dead tree limbs which had previously been strewn about, as well as a rotting mass of them I had long ago heaped to cut for firewood, were also gone.

The compost heap was missing.

I moved to the space where it had been. All that was there was an irregular patch of bare earth of the approximate shape of the heap itself.

But I had discovered in attuning myself to the Jewel that I could make myself feel its presence. I closed my eyes for a moment and tried to do so.

Nothing.

I looked again, searching carefully, but there was no tell-tale glitter anywhere in sight. Not that I had really expected to see anything, not if I could not feel it nearby.

There had been no curtains in the lighted room. Studying the house now, I saw that none of the windows had curtains, shades, shutters, or blinds. Therefore . . .

I passed around the other end of the house. Approaching the first lighted window, I glanced in quickly. Dropcloths covered much of the floor. A man in cap and coveralls was painting the far wall.

Of course.

I had asked Bill to sell the place. I had signed the necessary papers while a patient in the local clinic, when I had been projected back to my old home – probably by some action of the Jewel – on the occasion of my stabbing. That would have been several weeks ago, local time, using the Amber to shadow Earth conversion factor of approximately two and a half to one and allowing for the eight days the Courts of Chaos had cost me in Amber. Bill, of course, had gone ahead on my request. But the place had been in bad shape, abandoned as it had been for a number of years, vandalized . . . It needed some new windowpanes, some roofing work, new guttering, painting, sanding, buffing. And there had been a lot of trash to haul away, outside as well as inside . . .

I turned away and walked down the front slope to the road, recalling my last passage this way, half-delirious, on my hands and knees, blood leaking from my side. It had been much colder that night and there had been snow on the ground and in the air. I passed near the spot where I'd sat, trying to flag down a car with a pillow case. The memory was slightly blurred, but I still recalled the ones that had passed me by.

I crossed the road, made my way through the field to the trees. Unhitching Drum, I mounted.

'We've some more riding ahead,' I told him. 'Not too far this time.'

We headed back to the road and started along it, continuing on past my house. If I had not told Bill to go ahead and sell the place, the compost heap would still have been there, the Jewel would still have been there. I could be on my way back to Amber with the ruddy stone hung about my neck, ready to have a try at what had to be done. Now, now I had to go looking for it, when I'd a feeling time was beginning to press once again. At least, I had a favorable ratio here with respect to its passage in Amber. I clucked at Drum and shook the reins. No sense wasting it, even so.

A half hour, and I was into town, riding down a quiet street in a residential area, houses all about me. The lights were on at Bill's place. I turned up his driveway. I left Drum in his back yard.

Alice answered my knock, stared a moment, men said, 'My God! Carl!'

Minutes later, I was seated in the living room with Bill, a drink on the table to my right. Alice was out in the kitchen, having made the mistake of asking me whether I wanted something to eat.

Bill studied me as he lit his pipe.

'Your ways of coming and going still tend to be colorful,' he said.

I smiled.

'Expediency is all,' I said.

'That nurse at the clinic . . . scarcely anyone believed her story.'

'Scarcely anyone?'

'The minority I refer to is, of course, myself.'

'What was her story?'

'She claimed that you walked to the center of the room, became two-dimensional, and just faded away, like the old soldier that you are, with a rainbowlike accompaniment.'

'Glaucoma can cause the rainbow symptom. She ought to have her eyes checked.'

'She did,' he said. 'Nothing wrong.'

'Oh. Too bad. The next thing that comes to mind is neurological.'

'Come on, Carl. She's all right. You know that.'

I smiled and took a sip of my drink.

'And you,' he said, 'you look like a certain playing card I once commented on. Complete with sword. What's going on, Carl?'

'It's still complicated,' I said. 'Even more than the last time we talked.'

'Which means you can't give me that explanation yet?'

I shook my head.

'You have won an all-expense tour of my homeland, when this is over,' I said, 'if I still have a homeland then. Right now, time is doing terrible things.'

'What can I do to help you?'

'Information, please. My old house. Who is the guy you have fixing the place up?'

'Ed Wellen. Local contractor. You know him, I think. Didn't he put in a shower for you, or something?'

'Yes, yes he did . . . I remember.'

'He's expanded quite a bit. Bought some heavy equipment. Has a number of fellows working for him now. I handled his incorporation.'

'Do you know who he's got working at my place – now?'

'Offhand, no. But I can find out in just a minute.' He moved his hand to rest on the telephone on the side table. 'Shall I give him a ring?'

'Yes,' I said, 'but there is a little more to it than that. There is only one thing in which I am really interested. There was a compost heap in the back yard. It was there the last time I passed this way. It is gone now. I have to find out what became of it.'

He cocked his head to the right and grinned around his pipe.

'You serious?' he finally said.

'Sure as death,' I said. 'I hid something in that heap when I crawled by, decorating the snow with my precious bodily fluids. I've got to have it back now.'

'Just what is it?'

'A ruby pendant.'

'Priceless, I suppose.'

'You're right.'

He nodded, slowly.

'If it were anyone else, I would suspect a practical joke,' he said. 'A treasure in a compost heap . . . Family heirloom?'

'Yes. Forty or fifty carats. Simple setting. Heavy chain.'

He removed his pipe and whistled softly.

'Mind if I ask why you put it there?'

'I'd be dead now if I hadn't.'

'Pretty good reason.'

He reached for the phone again.

'We've had some action on the house already,' he remarked. 'Pretty good, since I haven't advertised yet. Fellow'd heard from someone who'd heard from someone else. I took him over his morning. He's thinking about it. We may move it pretty quick.'

He began to dial.

'Wait,' I said. 'Tell me about him.'

He cradled the phone, looked up.

'Thin guy,' he said. 'Redhead. Had a beard. Said he was an artist. Wants a place in the country.'

'Son of a bitch!' I said, just as Alice came into the room with a tray.

She made a *tsking* sound and smiled as she delivered it to me.

'Just a couple hamburgers and some leftover salad,' she said. 'Nothing to get excited about.'

'Thank you. I was getting ready to eat my horse. I'd have felt bad afterward.'

'I don't imagine he'd have been too happy about it himself. Enjoy,' she said, and returned to the kitchen.

'Was the compost heap still there when you took him over?' I asked.

He closed his eyes and furrowed his brow.

'No,' he said after a moment. 'The yard was already clear.'

'That's something, anyway,' I said, and I began eating.

He made the call, and he talked for several minutes. I got the drift of things from his end of the conversation, but I listened to the entire thing after he had hung up, while I finished the food and washed it down with what was left in my glass.

'He hated to see good compost go to waste,' Bill said. 'So he pitched the heap into his pickup just the other day and took it out to his farm. He dumped it next to a plot he intends to cultivate, and he has not had a chance to spread it yet. Says he did not notice any jewelry, but then he could easily have missed it.'

I nodded.

'If I can borrow a flashlight I had better get moving.'

'Sure. I will drive you out,' be said.

'I do not want to be parted from my horse at this point.'

'Well, you will probably want a rake, and a shovel or a pitchfork. I can drive them out and meet you there, if you know where the place is.'

'I know where Ed's place is. He must have tools, though.'

Bill shrugged and smiled.

'All right,' I said. 'Let me use your bathroom, and then we had better get moving.'

'You seemed as if you knew the prospective buyer.'

I put the tray aside and rose to my feet.

'You heard of him last as Brandon Corey.'

'The guy who pretended to be your brother and got you committed?'

' "Pretended" hell! He is my brother. No fault of mine, though. Excuse me.'

'He was there.'

'Where?'

'Ed's place, this afternoon. At least a bearded redhead was.'

'Doing what?'

'Said he was an artist. Said he wanted permission to set up his easel and paint in one of the fields.'

'And Ed let him?'

'Yes, of course. Thought it was a great idea. That is why he told me about it. Wanted to brag.'

'Get the stuff. I will meet you there.'

'Right.'

The second thing I took out in the bathroom was my Trumps. I had to reach someone in Amber soonest, someone strong enough to stop him. But who? Benedict was on his way to the Courts at Chaos, Random was off looking for his son, I had just parted with Gérard on somewhat less than amicable terms. I wished that I had a Trump for Ganelon.

I decided that I would have to try Gérard.

I drew forth his card, performed the proper mental maneuvers. Moments later, I had contact.

'Corwin.'

'Just listen, Gérard! Brand is alive, if that is any consolation. I'm damn sure of that. This is important. Life and death. You've got to do something – fast!'

His expressions had changed rapidly while I had spoken – anger, surprise, interest . . .

'Go ahead,' he said.

'Brand could be coming back very soon. In fact, he may already be in Amber. You haven't seen him yet, have you?'

'No.'

'He must be stopped from walking the Pattern.'

'I do not understand. But I can post a guard outside the chamber of the Pattern.'

'Put the guard inside the chamber. He has strange ways of coming and going now. Terrible things may happen if he walks the Pattern.'

'I will watch it personally then. What is happening?'

'No time now. Here is the next thing: Is Llewella back in Rebma?'

'Yes, she is.'

'Get hold of her with her Trump. She's got to warn Moire that the Pattern in Rebma has to be guarded also.'

'How serious is this, Corwin?'

'It could be the end of everything,' I said. 'I have to go now.'

I broke the contact and headed for the kitchen and the back door, stopping only long enough to thank Alice and say good night. If Brand had got hold of the Jewel and attuned himself to it, I was not certain what he would do, but I had a pretty strong hunch.

I mounted Drum and turned him toward the road. Bill was already backing, out of the driveway.

11

I cut through fields in many places where Bill had to follow the roads, so I was not all that far behind him. When I drew up, he was talking with Ed, who was gesturing toward the southwest.

As I dismounted, Ed was studying Drum.

'Nice horse, that,' he said.

'Thanks.'

'You've been away.'

'Yes.'

We shook hands.

'Good to see you again. I was just telling Bill that I don't really know how long that artist stayed around. I just figured he would go away when it got dark, and I didn't pay too much attention. Now, if he was really looking for something of yours and knew about the compost heap, he could still be out there for all I know. I'll get my shotgun, if you like, and go with you.'

'No,' I said, 'thanks. I think I know who it was. The gun will not be necessary. We'll just walk over and do a little poking around.'

'Okay,' he said. 'Let me come along and give you a hand.'

'You don't have to do that,' I said.

'How about your horse, then? What say I give him a drink and something to eat, clean him up a bit?'

'I'm sure he'd be grateful. I know I would.'

'What's his name?'

'Drum.'

He approached Drum and began making friends with him.

'Okay,' he said. 'I'll be back in the barn for a while. If you need me for anything, just holler.'

'Thanks.'

I got the tools out of Bill's car and he carried the electric lantern, leading me off to the southwest where Ed had been pointing earlier.

As we crossed the field, I followed the beam of Bill's light, searching for the heap. When I saw what might be the remains of one, I drew a deep breath, involuntarily. Someone must have been at it, the way the clods were strewn about. The mass would not have been dumped from a truck to fall in such a dispersed fashion.

Still . . . the fact that someone had looked did not mean he had located what he had been seeking.

'What do you think?' Bill siad.

'I don't know,' I told him, lowering the tools to the ground and approaching the largest aggregate in sight 'Give me some light here.'

I scanned what remained of the heap, then fetched a rake and began taking it apart I broke each clod and spread it upon the ground, running the tines through it. After a time, Bill set the lantern at a good angle and moved to help me.

'I've got a funny feeling . . .' he said.

'So do I.'

'. . . that we may be too late.'

We kept pulverizing and spreading, pulverizing and spreading . . .

I felt the tingle of a familiar presence. I straightened and waited. Contact came moments later.

'Corwin!'

'Here, Gérard.'

'What'd you say?' said Bill.

I raised my hand to silence him and gave my attention to Gérard. He stood in shadow at the bright beginning of the Pattern, leaning upon his great blade.

'You were right,' he said. 'Brand did show up here, just a moment ago. I am not sure how he got in. He stepped out of the shadows off to the left, there.' He gestured. 'He looked at me for a moment then turned around and walked back. He did not answer when I hailed him. So I turned up the lantern, but he was nowhere in sight. He just disappeared. What do you want me to do now?'

'Was he wearing the Jewel of Judgment?'

'I could not tell. I only had sight of him for a moment in this bad light.'

'Are they watching the Pattern in Rebma now?'

'Yes. Llewella's alerted them.'

'Good. Stay on guard, then. I will be in touch again.'

'All right. Corwin – about what happened earlier . . .'

'Forget it.'

'Thanks. That Ganelon is one tough fellow.'

'Indeed,' I said. 'Stay awake.'

His image faded as I released the contact, but a strange thing happened then. The sense of contact, the path, remained with me, objectless, open, like a switched-on radio not tuned to anything.

Bill was looking at me peculiarly.

'Carl, what is happening?'

'I don't know. Wait a minute.'

Suddenly, there was contact again, though not with Gérard. She must have been trying to reach me while my attention was diverted.

'Corwin, it is important . . .'

'Go ahead, Fi.'

'You will not find what you are looking for there. Brand has it.'

'I was beginning to suspect as much.'

'We have to stop him. I do not know how much you know—'

'Neither do I any more,' I said, 'but I have the Pattern in Amber and the one in Rebma under guard. Gérard just told me that Brand appeared at the one in Amber, but was scared off.'

She nodded her small, fine-featured face. Her red tresses were unusually disarrayed. She looked tired.

'I am aware of this,' she said. 'I have him under surveillance. But you have forgotten another possibility.'

'No.' I said. 'According to my calculations, Tir-na Nog'th should not be attainable yet—'

'That is not what I was referring to. He is headed for the primal Pattern itself.'

'To attune the Jewel?'

'The first time through,' she said.

'To walk it, he would have to pass through the damaged area. I gather that is more than a little difficult.'

'So you do know about it,' she said. 'Good. That saves time. The dark area would not trouble him the way it would another of us. He has come to terms with that darkness. We must stop him, now.'

'Do you know any short cuts to that place?'

'Yes. Come to me. I will take you there.'

'Just a minute. I want Drum with me.'

'What for?'

'No telling. That is why I want him.'

'Very well. Then bring me through. We can as easily depart from there as from here.'

I extended my hand. In a moment, I held hers. She stepped forward.

'Lord!' said Bill, drawing back. 'You were giving me doubts about your sanity, Carl. Now it's mine I wonder about. She – she's on one of the cards, too, isn't she?'

'Yes. Bill, this is my sister Fiona. Fiona, this is Bill Roth, a very good friend.'

Fi extended her hand and smiled, and I left them there while I went back to fetch Drum. A few minutes later, I led him forth.

'Bill,' I said, 'I am sorry to have wasted your time. My brother has the thing. We are going after him now. Thanks for helping me.'

I shook his hand. He said, 'Corwin.' I smiled.

'Yes, that is my name.'

'We have been talking, your sister and I. Not much I could learn in a few minutes, but I know it is dangerous. So good luck. I still want the whole story one day.'

'Thanks,' I said. 'I will try to see that you get it.'

I mounted, leaned down, and drew Fiona up before me.

'Good night, Mr Roth,' she said. Then, to me, 'Start riding, slowly, across the field.'

I did.

'Brand says you are the one who stabbed him,' I said, as soon as we had gone far enough to feel alone.

'That's right.'

'Why?'

'To avoid all this.'

'I talked with him for a long while. He claimed it was originally you, Bleys, and himself, together in a scheme to seize power.'

'That is correct.'

'He told me he had approached Caine, trying to will him to your side, but that Caine would have none of it, that Caine had passed the word along to Eric and Julian. And his led to their forming their own group, to block your way to the throne.'

'That is basically correct. Caine had ambitions of his own – long-term ones – but ambitions nevertheless. He was in no position to pursue them, however. So he decided that if his lot was to be a lesser one, he would rather serve it under Eric than under Bleys. I can see his point, too.'

'He also claimed that the three of you had a deal going with the powers at the end of the black road, in the Courts of Chaos.'

'Yes,' she said, 'we did.'

'You use the past tense.'

'For myself and for Bleys, yes.'

'That is not the way Brand tells it.'

'He wouldn't.'

'He said you and Bleys wanted to continue exploiting that alliance, but that he had had a change of heart. Because of this, he claims you turned on him and imprisoned him in that tower.'

'Why didn't we just kill him?'

'I give up. Tell me.'

'He was too dangerous to be allowed his freedom, but we could not kill him either because he held something, vital.'

'What?'

'With Dworkin gone, Brand was the only one who knew how to undo the damage he had done to the primal Pattern.'

'You had a long time to get that information out of him.'

'He possesses unbelievable resources.'

'Then why did you stab him?'

'I repeat, to avoid all this. If it became a question of his freedom or his death, it were better he died. We would have to take our chances on figuring the method of repairing the Pattern.'

'This being the case, why did you consent to co-operate in bringing him back?'

'First, I was not co-operating, I was trying to impede the attempt. But there were too many trying too hard. You got through to him in spite of me. Second, I had to be on hand to try to kill him in the event you succeeded. Too bad things worked out the way they did.'

'You say that you and Bleys had second thoughts about the alliance, but that Brand did not?'

'Yes.'

'How did your second thoughts affect your desire for the throne?'

'We thought we could manage it without any additional outside help.'

'I see.'

'Do you believe me?'

'I'm afraid that I am beginning to.'

'Turn here.'

I entered a cleft in a hillside. The way was narrow and very dark, with only a small band of stars above us. Fiona had been manipulating Shadow while we had talked, leading us from Ed's field downward, into a misty, moorlike place, then up again, to clear and rocky trail among mountains. Now, as we moved through the dark defile, I felt her working with Shadow again. The air was cool but not cold. The blackness to our left and our right was absolute, giving the illusion of enormous depths, rather than nearby rock cloaked in shadow. This impression was reinforced, I suddenly realized, by the fact that Drum's hoofbeats were not producing any echoes, after-sounds, over-tones.

'What can I do to gain your trust?' she said.

'That's asking quite a bit.'

She laughed.

'Let me rephrase it. What can I do to convince you I am telling the truth?'

'Just answer one question.'

'What?'

'Who shot out my tires?'

She laughed again.

'You've figured it out, haven't you?'

'Maybe. You tell me.'

'Brand,' she said. 'He had failed in his effort to destroy your memory, so he decided he had better do a more thorough job.'

'The version I had of the story was that Bleys had done the shooting and left me in the lake, that Brand had arrived in time to drag me out and save my life. In fact, the police report seemed to indicate something to that effect'

'Who called the police?' she asked.

'They had it listed as an anonymous call, but—'

'Bleys called them. He couldn't reach you in time to save you, once he realized what was happening. He hoped that they could. Fortunately, they did.'

'What do you mean?'

'Brand did not drag you out of the wreck. You did it yourself. He waited around to be certain you were dead, and you surfaced and pulled yourself ashore. He went down and was checking you over, to decide whether you would die if he just left you there or whether he should throw you back in again. The police arrived about then and he had to clear out. We caught up with him shortly afterward and were able to subdue him and imprison him in the tower. That took a lot of doing. Later, I contacted Eric and told him what had happened. He then ordered Flora to put you in the other place and see that you were held until after his coronation.'

'It fits,' I said. 'Thanks.'

'What does it fit?'

'I was only a small-town GP in simpler times than these, and I never had much to do with psychiatric cases. But I do know that you don't give a person electroshock therapy to restore memories. EST generally does just the opposite. It destroys some of the short-term ones. My suspicions began to stir when I learned that that was what Brand had had done to me. So I came up with my own hypothesis. The auto wreck did not restore my memories, and neither did the EST. I had finally begun recovering them naturally, not as the result of any particular trauma. I must have done something or said something to indicate that this was occurring. Word of it somehow got to Brand and he decided that this would not be a good thing to have happen at that time. So he journeyed to my shadow and managed to get me committed and subjected to treatment which he hoped would wipe out those things I had recently recovered. This was just partly successful, in that its only lasting effect was to fuzz me up for the few days surrounding the sessions. The accident may have contributed, too. But when I escaped from Porter and lived through his attempt to kill me, the process of recovery continued after I regained consciousness in Greenwood and left the place. I was remembering more and more when I was staying at Flora's. The recovery was accelerated by Random's taking me to Rebma, where I walked the Pattern. If this had not occurred, however, I am convinced now that it would all have come back, anyway. It might have taken somewhat longer, but I had broken through and the remembering was an ongoing process, coming faster and faster near the end. So I concluded that Brand was trying to sabotage me, and that is what fits the things you just told me.'

The band of stars had narrowed, and it finally vanished above us. We advanced through what seemed a totally black tunnel now, with perhaps the tiniest flickering of light a great distance ahead of us.

'Yes,' she said in the darkness before me, 'you guessed correctly. Brand was afraid of you. He claimed he had seen your return one night in Tir-na Nog'th, to the undoing of all our plans. I paid him no heed at the time, for I was not even aware you still lived. It must have been then that he set out to find you. Whether he divined your whereabouts by some arcane means or simply saw it in Eric's mind, I do not know. Probably the latter. He is occasionally capable of such a feat. However he located you, you now know the rest.'

'It was Flora's presence in that place and her strange liaison with Eric that first made him suspicious. Or so he said. Not that it matters, now. What do you propose doing with him if we get our hands on him?'

She chuckled.

'You are wearing your blade,' she said.

'Brand told me, not all that long ago, that Bleys is still alive. Is this true?'

'Yes.'

'Then why am I here, rather than Bleys?'

'Bleys is not attuned to the Jewel. You are. You interact with it at near distances, and it will attempt to preserve your life if you are in imminent danger of losing it. The risk, therefore, is not as great,' she said. Then, moments later, 'Don't take it for granted, though. A swift stroke can still beat its reaction. You can die in its presence.'

The light ahead grew larger, brighter, but there were no drafts, sounds, or smells from that direction. Advancing, I thought of the layers upon layers of explanations I had received since my return, each with its own complex of motivations, justifications for what had happened while I was away, for what had happened since, for what was happening now. The emotions, the plans, the feelings, the objectives I had seen swirled like floodwater through the city of facts I was slowly erecting on the grave of my other self, and though an act is an act, in the best Steinian tradition, each wave of interpretation that broke upon me shifted the position of one or more things I had thought safely anchored, and by this brought about an alteration of the whole, to the extent that all of life seemed almost a shifting interplay of Shadow about the Amber of some never to be attained truth. Still, I could not deny that I knew more now than I had several years earlier, that I was closer to the heart of matters than I had been before, that the entire action in which I had been caught up upon my return seemed not to be sweeping toward some final resolution. And what did I want? A chance to find out what was right and a chance to act on it! I laughed. Who is ever granted the first, let alone the second of these? A workable approximation of truth, men. That would be enough . . . And a chance to swing my blade a few times in the right direction: the highest compensation I could receive from a one o'clock world for the changes wrought since noon. I laughed again and made sure my blade was loose in the sheath.

'Brand said that Bleys had raised another army—' I began.

'Later,' she said, 'later. There is no more time.'

And she was right. The light had grown large, become a circular opening. It had approached at a rate out of proportion to our advance, as though the tunnel itself were contracting. It seemed to be daylight that was rushing in through what I chose to regard as the cave mouth.

'All right,' I said, and moments later we reached the opening and passed through it.

I blinked my eyes as we emerged. To my left was the sea, which seemed to merge with the same-colored sky. The golden sun which floated/hung above/within it, bounced beams of brilliance from all directions. Behind me, now, there was nothing but rock. Our passage to this place had vanished without a sign. Not too far below and before me – perhaps a hundred feet distant – lay the primal Pattern. A figure was negotiating the second of its outer arcs, his attention so confined by this activity that he had apparently not yet noted our presence. A flash of red as he took a turn: the Jewel, hanging now from his neck as it had hung from mine, from Eric's, from Dad's. The figure, of course, was Brand's.

I dismounted. I looked up at Fiona, small and distraught, and I placed Drum's reins in her hand.

'Any advice, other than to go after him?' I whispered.

She shook her head.

Turning then, I drew Grayswandir and strode forward.

'Good luck,' she said softly.

As I walked toward the Pattern, I saw the long chain leading from the cave mouth to the now still form of the griffin Wixer. Wixer's head lay on the ground several paces to the left of his body. Body and head both leaked a normal-colored blood upon the stone.

As I approached the beginning of the Pattern, I did a quick calculation. Brand had already taken several turns about the general spiral of the design. He was approximately two and a half laps into it. If we were only separated by one winding, I could reach him with my blade once I achieved a position paralleling his own. The going, however, got rougher the further one penetrated the design. Consequently, Brand was moving at a steadily decreasing pace. So it would be close. I did not have to catch him. I just had to pick up a lap and a half and obtain a position across from him.

I placed my foot upon the Pattern and moved forward, as fast as I was able. The blue sparks began about my feet as I rushed through the first curve against the rising resistance. The sparks grew quickly. My hair was beginning to rise when I hit the First Veil, and the crackling of the sparks was quite audible now. I pushed on against the pressure of the Veil, wondering whether Brand had noticed me yet, unable to afford the distraction of a glance in his direction just then. I met the resistance with increased force, and several steps later I was through the Veil and moving more easily again.

I looked up. Brand was just emerging from the terrible Second Veil, blue sparks as high as his waist. He was grinning a grin of resolve and triumph as he pulled free and took a clear step forward. Then he saw me.

The grin went away and he hesitated, a point in my favor. You never stop on the Pattern if you can help it. If you do, it costs a lot of extra energy to get moving again.

'You are too late!' he called out.

I did not answer him. I just kept going. Blue fires fell from the Pattern tracery along Grayswandir's length.

'You will not make it through the black,' he said.

I kept going. The dark area was just ahead of me now. I was glad that it had not occurred over one of the more difficult portions of the

Pattern this time around. Brand moved forward and slowly began his movement toward the Grand Curve. If I could catch him there, it would be no contest. He would not have the strength or the speed to defend himself.

As I approached the damaged portion of the Pattern, I recalled the means by which Ganelon and I had cut the black road on our flight from Avalon. I had succeeded in breaking the power of the road by holding the image of the Pattern in my mind as we had gone across. Now, of course, I had the Pattern itself all around me, and the distance was not nearly so great. While my first thought had been that Brand was simply trying to rattle me with his threat, it occurred to me that the force of the dark place might well be much stronger here at its source. As I came up to it, Grayswandir blazed with a sudden intensity which outshone its previous light. On an impulse, I touched its point to the edge of the blackness, at the place where the Pattern ended.

Grayswandir clove to the blackness and could not be raised above it I continued forward, and my blade sliced the area before me, sliding ahead in what seemed an aproximation of the original tracery. I followed. The sun seemed to darken as I trod the dark ground. I was suddenly conscious of my heartbeat, and perspiration formed on my brow. A grayish cast fell over everything. The world seemed to dim, the Pattern to fade. It seemed it would be easy to step amiss in this place, and I was not certain whether the result would be the same as a misstep within the intact portions of the Pattern. I did not want to find out.

I kept my eyes low, following the line Grayswandir was inscribing before me, the blade's blue fire now the only thing of color left to the world. Right foot, left foot . . .

Then suddenly I was out of it and Grayswandir swung free in my hand once again, the fires partly diminished, whether by contrast with the reilluminated prospect or for some other reasons I did not know.

Looking about, I saw that Brand was approaching the Grand Curve. As for me, I was working my way toward the Second Veil. We would both be involved in the strenuous efforts these entailed in a few more minutes. The Grand Curve is more difficult, more prolonged than the Second Veil, however. I should be free and moving more quickly again before he worked his way through his barrier.

Then I would have to cross the damaged area another time. He might be free by then, but he would be moving more slowly than I would, for he would be into the area where the going becomes even more difficult.

A steady static arose with each step that I took, and a tingling sensation permeated my entire body. The sparks rose to midthigh as I moved. It was like striding through a field of electric wheat. My hair was at least partly risen by then. I could feel its stirring. I glanced back once to see Fiona, still mounted, unmoving, watching.

I pressed ahead to the Second Veil.

Angles . . . short, sharp turns . . . The force rose and rose against me, so that all of my attention, all of my strength, was now occupied in striving against it. There came again that familiar sense of timelessness, as though this was all I had ever done, all that I ever would do. And will . . . a focusing of desire to such an intensity that everything else was excluded . . . Brand, Fiona, Amber, my own identity . . . The sparks rose to even greater heights as I struggled, turned, labored, each step requiring more effort than the previous one.

I pushed through. Right into the black area again.

Reflexively, I moved Grayswandir down and ahead once more. Again, the grayness, the monochrome fog, cut by the blue of my blade opening the way before me like a surgical incision.

When I emerged into normal light, I sought Brand. He was still in the western quadrant, struggling with the Grand Curve, about two thirds of the way through it. If I pushed hard, I might be able to catch him just as he was coming out of it I threw all of my strength into moving as quickly as possible.

As I made it to the north end of the Pattern and into the curve leading back, it struck me suddenly what I was about to do.

I was rushing to spill more blood upon the Pattern.

If it came to a simple choice between further damage to the Pattern and Brand's destroying it utterly, then I knew what I had to do. Yet, I felt there had to be another way. Yes . . .

I slowed my pace just a trifle. It was going to be a matter of timing. His passage was a lot rougher than mine just then, so I had an edge in that respect. My entire new strategy involved arranging our encounter at just the right point. Ironically, at that moment, I recalled Brand's concern for his rug. The problem of keeping this place clean was a lot trickier, though.

He was nearing the end of the Grand Curve, and I paced him while calculating the distance to the blackness. I had decided to let him do his bleeding over the area which had already been damaged. The only disadvantage I seemed to possess was that I would be situated to Brand's right. To minimize the benefit this would give him when we crossed blades, I would have to remain somewhat to the rear.

Brand struggled and advanced, all of his movements in slow motion. I struggled too, but not as hard. I kept the pace. I wondered as I went, about the Jewel, about the affinity we had shared since the attunement I could feel its presence, there to my left and ahead, even though I could not see it now upon Brand's breast. Would it really act to save me across that distance should Brand gain the upper hand in our coming conflict? Feeling its presence, I could almost believe that it would. It had torn me from one assailant and found, somehow, within my mind, a traditional place of safety – my own bed – and had transported me there. Feeling it now, almost seeing the way before Brand through it, I felt some assurance that it would attempt to function on my behalf once again. Recalling Fiona's words, however, I was determined not to rely on it. Still, I considered its other functions, speculated upon my ability to operate it without contact . . .

Brand had almost completed the Grand Curve. I reached out from some level of my being and made contact with the Jewel. Laying my will upon it, I called for a storm of the red tornado variety which had destroyed Iago, I did not know whether I could control that particular phenomenon in this particular place, but I called for it nevertheless and directed it toward Brand. Nothing happened immediately, though I felt the Jewel functioning to achieve something. Brand came to the end, offered a final exertion, and passed from the Grand Curve.

I was right there behind him.

He knew it, too – somehow. His blade was out the instant the pressure was off, he gained a couple feet faster than I thought he could, got his left foot ahead of him, turned his body, and met my gaze over the lines of our blades.

'Damned if you didn't make it,' he said, touching the tip of my blade with his own. 'You would never have gotten here this soon if it weren't for the bitch on the horse, though.'

'Nice way to talk about our sister,' I said, feinting and watching him move to parry.

We were hampered, in that neither of us could lunge without departing the Pattern. I was further hampered in not wanting to make him bleed, yet. I faked a stop thrust and he drew back, sliding his left foot along the design to his rear. He withdrew his right then, stamped it, and tried a head cut without preliminaries. Damn it! I parried and then riposted by pure reflex. I did not want to catch him with the chest cut I had thrown back at him, but the tip of Grayswandir traced an arc beneath his sternum. I heard a humming in the air above us. I could not afford to take my eyes off Brand, though. He glanced downward and backed some more. Good. A red line now decorated his shirt front where my cut had taken him. So far, the material seemed to be absorbing it. I stamped, feinted, thrust, parried, stop thrust, bound, and unbound – everything I could think of to keep him retreating. I had the psychological edge on him in that I had the greater reach and we both knew I could do more things with it, more quickly. Brand was nearing the dark area. Just a few more paces . . . I heard a sound like a single bell chime, followed by a great roaring. A shadow suddenly fell upon us, as though a cloud had just occluded the sun.

Brand glanced up. I think I could have gotten him just then, but he was still a couple of feet too far from the target area.

He recovered immediately and glared at me.

'Damn you, Corwin! That's yours, isn't it?' he cried, and then he attacked, discarding what caution he still possessed.

Unfortunately, I was in a bad position, as I had been edging up on him, preparing to press him the rest of the way back. I was exposed and slightly off-balance. Even as I parried, I realized it would not be sufficient, and I twisted and fell back.

I struggled to keep my feet in place as I went down. I caught myself with my right elbow and my left hand. I cursed, as the pain was too much and my elbow slid to the side, dropping me to my right shoulder.

But Brand's thrust had gone by me, and within blue halos my feet still touched the line. I was out of Brand's reach for a death thrust, though he could still hamstring me.

I raised my right arm, still clutching Grayswandir, before me. I began to sit up. As I did, I saw that the red formation, yellow about the edges, was now spinning directly above Brand, crackling with sparks and small lightnings, its roar now changed to a wailing.

Brand took hold of his blade by the forte and raised it above his shoulder like a spear, pointed in my direction. I knew that I could not parry it, that I could not dodge it.

With my mind, I reached out to the Jewel and up to the formation in the sky . . .

There came a bright flash as a small finger of lightning reached down and touched his blade . . .

The weapon fell from his hand and his hand flew to his mouth. With his left hand, he clutched at the Jewel of Judgment, as if he realized what I was doing and sought to nullify it by covering the stone. Sucking his fingers, he looked upward, all of the anger draining from his face to be replaced by a look of fear verging on terror. The cone was beginning to descend.

Turning then, he stepped onto the blackened area, faced south, raised both his arms and cried out something I could not hear above the wailing.

The cone fell toward him, but he seemed to grow two-dimensional as it approached. His outline wavered. He began to shrink – but it did not seem a function of actual size, so much as an effect of distancing. He dwindled, dwindled, was gone, a bare instant before the cone licked across the area he had occupied.

With him went the Jewel, so that I was left with no way of controlling the thing above me. I did not know whether it was better to plantain a low profile or to resume a normal stance on the Pattern. I decided on the latter, because the whirlwind seemed to go for things which broke the normal sequence. I got back into a sitting position and edged over to the line. Then I leaned forward into a crouch, by which time the cone began to rise. The wailing retreated down the scale as it withdrew. The blue fires about my boots had subsided completely. I turned and looked at Fiona. She motioned me to get up and go on.

So I rose slowly, seeing that the vortex above me continued to dissipate as I moved. Advancing upon the area where Brand had so recently stood, I once again used Grayswandir to guide me through. The twisted remains of Brand's blade lay near the far edge of the dim place.

I wished there were some easy way out of the Pattern. It seemed pointless to complete it now. But there is no turning back once you have set foot upon it, and I was extremely leery of trying the dark route out. So I headed on toward the Grand Curve. To what place, I wondered, had Brand taken himself? If I knew, I could command the Pattern to send me after him, once I reached the center. Perhaps Fiona had an idea. Still, he would probably head for a place where he had allies. It would be senseless to pursue him alone.

At least I had stopped the attunement, I consoled myself.

Then I entered the Grand Curve. The sparks shot up about me.

12

Late afternoon on a mountain: the westering sun shone full on the rocks to my left, tailored long shadows for those to the right; it filtered through the foliage about my tomb; it countered to some extent the chill winds of Kolvir. I released Random's hand and turned to regard the man who sat on the bench before the mausoleum.

It was the face of the youth on the pierced Trump, lines now drawn above the mouth, brow heavier, a general weariness in eye movement and set of jaw which had not been apparent on the card.

So I knew it before Random said, 'This is my son Martin.'

Martin rose as I approached him, clasped my hand, said, 'Uncle Corwin'. His expression changed but slightly as he said it. He scrutinized me.

He was several inches taller than Random, but of the same light build. His chin and cheekbones had the same general cut to them, his hair was of a similar texture.

I smiled.

'You have been away a long while,' I said. 'So was I.'

He nodded.

'But I have never really been in Amber proper,' he said. 'I grew up in Rebma – and other places.'

'Then let me welcome you, nephew. You come at an interesting time. Random must have told you about it.'

'Yes,' he said. 'That is why I asked to meet you here, rather than there.'

I glanced at Random.

'The last uncle he met was Brand,' Random said, 'and under very nasty circumstances. Do you blame him?'

'Hardly. I ran into him myself a bit earlier. Can't say it was the most rewarding encounter.'

'Ran into him?' said Random. 'You've lost me.'

'He has left Amber and he has the Jewel of Judgment with him. If I had known earlier what I know now, he would still be in the tower. He is our man, and he is very dangerous.'

Random nodded.

'I know,' he said. 'Martin confirmed all our suspicions on the stabbing – and it was Brand. But what is this about the Jewel?'

'He beat me to the place where I had left it on the shadow Earth. He has to walk the Pattern with it and project himself through it, though, to attune it to his use. I just stopped him from doing that on the primal Pattern in the real Amber. He escaped, however. I was just over the hill with Gérard, sending a squad of guards through to Fiona in that place, to prevent his returning and trying again. Our own Pattern and that in Rebma are also under guard because of him.'

'Why does he want so badly to attune it? So he can raise a few storms? Hell, be could take a walk in Shadow and make all the weather he wants.'

'A person attuned to the Jewel could use it to erase the Pattern.'

'Oh? What happens then?'

'The world as we know it comes to an end.'

'Oh,' Random said again. Then, 'How the hell do you know?'

'It is a long story and I haven't the time, but I had it from Dworkin and I believe that much of what he said.'

'He's still around?'

'Later,' I said.

'Okay. But Brand would have to be mad to do something like that.'

I nodded.

'I believe he thinks he could then cast a new Pattern, redesign the universe with himself as chief executive.'

'Could this be done?'

'Theoretically, perhaps. But even Dworkin has certain doubts that the feat could be repeated effectively now. The combination of factors was unique . . . Yes, I believe Brand is somewhat mad. Looking back over the years, recalling his personality changes, his cycles of moods, it seems there was something of a schizoid pattern there. I do not know whether the deal he made with the enemy pushed him over the edge or not. It does not really matter. I wish he were back in his tower. I wish Gérard were a worse physician.'

'Do you know who stabbed him?'

'Fiona. You can get the story from her, though.'

He leaned against my epitaph and shook his head.

'Brand,' he said. 'Damn him. Any one of us might have killed him on a number of occasions – in the old days. Just when he would get you mad enough, though, he would change. After a while, you would get to thinking he wasn't such a bad guy after all. Too bad he didn't push one of us just a little harder at the wrong time . . .'

'Then I take it he is now than game?' said Martin.

I looked at him. The muscles in his jaws had tightened and his eyes narrowed. For a moment, all of our faces fled across his, like a riffling of the family cards. All of our egoism, hatred, envy, pride, and abuse seemed to flow by in that instant – and he had not even set foot in Amber yet. Something snapped inside me and I reached out and seized him by the shoulders.

'You have good reason to hate him,' I said, 'and the answer to your question is "yes". The hunting season is open. I see no way to deal with him other than to destroy him. I hated him myself for so long as he remained an abstraction. But – now – it is different. Yes, he must be killed. But do not let that hatred be your baptism into our company. There has been too much of it among us. I look at your face – I don't know . . . I am sorry, Martin. Too much is going on right now. You are young. I have seen more things. Some of them bother me – differently. That's all.'

I released my grip and stepped back.

'Tell me about yourself,' I said.

'I was afraid of Amber for a long while,' he began, 'and I guess that I still am. Ever since he attacked me, I have been wondering whether Brand might catch up with me again. I have been looking over my shoulder for years. I have been afraid of all of you, I suppose. I knew most of you as pictures on cards – with bad reputations attached. I told Random – Dad – that I did not want to meet you all at once, and he suggested that I see you first. Neither of us realized at the time that you would be particularly interested in certain things that I know. After I mentioned them though, Dad said I had to see you as soon as possible. He has been telling me all about what has been going on and – you see, I know something about it.'

'I had a feeling that you might – when a certain name cropped up not too long ago.'

634

'The Tecys?' Random said.

'The same.'

'It is difficult, deciding where to start . . .' Martin said.

'I know that you grew up in Rebma, walked the Pattern, and then used your power over Shadow to visit Benedict in Avalon,' I said. 'Benedict told you more about Amber and Shadow, taught you the use of the Trumps, coached you in weaponry. Later, you departed to walk in Shadow by yourself. And I know what Brand did to you. That is the sum of my knowledge.'

He nodded, stared off into the west.

'After I left Benedict's, I traveled for years in Shadow,' he said. 'Those were the happiest times I have known. Adventure, excitement, new things to see, to do . . . In the back of my mind, I always had it that one day when I was smarter and tougher – more experienced – I would journey to Amber and meet my other relatives. Then Brand caught up with me. I was camped on a little hillside, just resting from a long ride and taking my lunch, on my way to visit my friends the Tecys. Brand contacted me then. I had reached Benedict with his Trump, when he was teaching me how to use them, and other times when I had traveled. He had even transported me through occasionally, so I knew what it felt like, knew what it was all about. This felt the same way, and for a moment I thought that somehow it was Benedict calling me. But no. It was Brand – I recognized him from his picture in the deck. He was standing in the midst of what seemed to be the Pattern. I was curious. I did not know how he had reached me. So far as I knew, there was no Trump for me. He talked for a minute – I forget what he said – and when everything was firm and clear, he – he stabbed me. I pushed him and pulled away then. He held the contact somehow. It was hard for me to break it – and when I did, he tried to reach me again. But I was able to block him Benedict had taught me that. He tried again, several times, but I kept blocking. Finally, he stopped. I was near to the Tecys. I managed to get onto my horse and make it to their place. I thought I was going to die, because I had never been hurt that badly before. But after a time, I began to recover. Then I grew afraid once again, afraid that Brand would find me and finish what he had begun.'

'Why didn't you contact Benedict,' I asked him, 'and tell him what had happened, tell him of your fears?'

'I thought of that,' he said, 'and I also thought of the possibility that Brand believed he had succeeded, that I was indeed dead. I did not know what sort of power struggle was going on in Amber, but I decided that the attempt on my life was probably part of such a thing. Benedict had told me enough about the family that this was one of the first things to come to mind. So I decided that perhaps it would be better to remain dead. I left the Tecys before I was completely recovered and rode off to lose myself in Shadow.

'I happened upon a strange thing then,' he continued, 'a thing I had never before encountered, but which now seemed virtually omnipresent: in nearly all of the shadows through which I passed, there was a peculiar black road existing in some form or other. I did not understand it, but since it was the only thing I had come across which seemed to traverse Shadow itself, my curiosity was aroused. I resolved to follow it and learn more about it. It was dangerous. I learned very quickly not to tread the thing. Strange shapes seemed to travel it at night. Natural creatures which ventured upon it sickened and died. So I was careful. I went no nearer than was necessary to keep it in sight I followed it through many places, I quickly learned that everywhere it ran there was death, desolation, or trouble nearby. I did not know what to make of it.

'I was still weak from my wound,' he went on, 'and I made the mistake of pressing myself, of riding too far, too fast, in a day's time. That evening, I fell ill and I lay shivering in my blanket through the night and much of the next day. I was into and out of delirium during his time, so I do not know exactly when she appeared. She seemed like part of my dream much of the while. A young girl. Pretty. She took care of me while I recovered. Her name was Dara. We talked interminably. It was very pleasant. Having someone to talk with like that . . . I must have told her my whole life story. Then she told me something of herself. She was not a native of the area in which I had collapsed. She said that she had traveled there through Shadow. She could not yet walk through it as we do, though she felt she could learn to do this, as she claimed descent from the House of Amber through Benedict. In fact, she wanted very badly to learn how it was done. Her means of travel then was the black road itself. She was immune to its noxious effects, she said, because she was also related to the dwellers at its farther end, in the Courts of Chaos. She wanted to learn our ways though, so I did my best to instruct her in those things that I did know. I told her of the Pattern, even sketched it for her. I showed her my Trumps – Benedict had given me a deck – to show her the appearance of her other relatives. She was particularly interested in yours.'

'I begin to understand,' I said. 'Go on.'

'She told me that Amber, in the fullness of its corruption and presumption, had upset a kind of metaphysical balance between itself and the Courts of Chaos. Her people now had the job of redressing the matter by laying waste to Amber. Their own place is not a shadow of Amber, but a solid entity in its own right. In the meantime, all of the intervening shadows are suffering because of the black road. My knowledge of Amber being what it was, I could only listen. At first, I accepted everything that she said. Brand, to me, certainly fit her description of evil in Amber. But when I mentioned him, she said no. He was some sort of hero back where she hied from. She was uncertain as to the particulars, but it did not trouble her all that much. It was then that I realized how oversure she seemed about everything – there was a ring of the fanatic when she talked. Almost unwillingly, I found myself trying to defend Amber. I thought of Llewella and of Benedict – and of Gérard, whom I had met a few times. She was eager to learn of Benedict, I discovered. That proved the soft spot in her armor. Here I could speak with some knowledge, and here she was willing to believe the good things I had to say. So, I do not know what the ultimate effect of an this talk was, except that she seemed somewhat less sure of herself near the end . . .'

'The end?' I said. 'What do you mean? How long was she with you?'

'Almost a week,' he replied. 'She had said she would take care of me until I was recovered, and she did. Actually, she remained several days longer. She said that was just to be sure, but I think it was really that she wanted to continue our conversations. Finally though, she said that she had to be moving on. I asked her to stay with me, but she said no. I offered to go with her, but she said no to that, too. She must have realized that I planned to follow her then, because she slipped away during the night. I could not ride the black road, and I had no idea what shadow she would travel to next on her way to Amber. When I awoke in the morning and realized she had gone, I thought for a time of visiting Amber myself. But I was still afraid. Perhaps some of the things she had said had reinforced my own fears. Whatever, I decided to remain in Shadow. And so I traveled on, seeing things, trying to learn things – until Random found me and told me he wanted me to come home. He brought me here first though, to meet you, because he wanted you to hear my story before any of the others. He said that you knew Dara, that you wanted to learn more about her. I hope I have helped.'

'Yes,' I said. 'Thank you.'

'I understand that she did finally walk the Pattern.'

'Yes, she succeeded in that.'

'And afterward declared herself an enemy of Amber.'

'That, too.'

'I hope,' he said, 'that she comes to no harm from all this. She was kind to me.'

'She seems quite able to take care of herself,' I said. 'But . . . yes, she is a likable girl. I cannot promise you anything concerning her safety, because I still know so little about her, so little of her part in everything that is going on. Yet, what you have told me has been helpful. It makes her someone I would still like to grant doubt's benefit, as far as I can.'

He smiled.

'I am glad to hear that.'

I shrugged.

'What are you going to do now?' I asked.

'I am taking him to see Vialle,' Random said, 'and then to meet the others, as time and opportunity permit. Unless, of course, something new has developed and you need me now.'

'There have been new developments,' I said, 'but I do not really need you now. I had better bring you up to date, though. I still have a little time.'

As I filled Random in on events since his departure, I thought about Martin. He was still an unknown quantity so far as I was concerned. His story might be perfectly true. In fact, I felt that it was. On the other hand, I had a feeling that it was not complete, that he was intentionally leaving something out. Maybe something harmless. Then again, maybe not. He had no real reason to love us. Quite the contrary. And Random could be bringing home a Trojan Horse.

Probably though, it was nothing like that. It is just that I never trust anyone if there is an alternative available.

Still, nothing that I was telling Random could really be used against us, and I strongly doubted that Martin could do us much damage if that was his intention. No, more likely he was being as cagey as the rest of us, and for pretty much the same reasons: fear and self-preservation. On a sudden inspiration, I asked him, 'Did you ever run into Dara again after that?'

He flushed.

'No,' he said, too quickly. 'Just that time. That's all.'

'I see,' I said, and Random was too good a poker player not to have noticed; so I had just bought us a piece of instant insurance at the small price of putting a father on guard against his long-lost son.

I quickly shifted our talk back to Brand. It was while we were comparing notes on psychopathology that I felt the tiny tingle and the sense of presence which heralds a Trump contact I raised my hand and turned aside.

In a moment the contact was clear and Ganelon and I regarded one another.

'Corwin,' he said, 'I decided it was time to check. By now, you have the Jewel, Brand has the Jewel, or you are both still looking. Which one is it?'

'Brand has the Jewel,' I said.

'More's the pity,' he said. 'Tell me about it.'

So I did.

'Then Gérard had the story right,' he said.

'He's already told you all this?'

'Not in such detail,' Ganelon replied, 'and I wanted to be sure I was getting it straight. I just finished speaking with him.' He glanced upward. 'It would seem you had best be moving then, if my memories of moonrise serve me right.'

I nodded.

'Yes, I will be heading for the stairway shortly. It is not all that far from here.'

'Good. Now here is what you must be ready to do—'

'I know what I have to do,' I said. 'I have to get up to Tir-na Nog'th before Brand does and block his way to the Pattern. Failing that, I have to chase him through it again.'

'That is not the way to go about it,' he said.

'You have a better idea?'

'Yes, I do. You have your Trumps with you?'

'Yes.'

'Good. First, you would not be able to get up there in time to block his way to the Pattern—'

'Why not?'

'You have to make the ascension, then you have to walk to the palace and make your way down to the Pattern. That takes time, even in Tir-na Nog'th – especially in Tir-na Nog'th, where time tends to play tricks anyway. For all you know, you may have a hidden death wish slowing you down. I don't know. Whatever the case, he would have commenced walking the Pattern by the time you arrived. It may well be that he would be too far into it for you to reach him this time.'

'He will probably be tired. That should slow him some.'

'No. Put yourself in his place. If you were Brand, wouldn't you have headed for some shadow where the time flow was different? Instead of an afternoon, he could well have taken several days to rest up for this evening's ordeal. It is safest to assume that he will be in good shape.'

'You are right,' I said. 'I can't count on it. Okay. An alternative I had entertained but would rather not try if it could be avoided, would be to kill him at a distance. Take along a crossbow or one of our rifles and simply shoot him in the midst of the Pattern. The thing that bothers me about it is the effect of our blood on the Pattern. It may be that it is only the primal Pattern that suffers from it, but I don't know.'

'That's right. You do not know,' he said. 'Also, I would not want you to rely on normal weapons up there. That is a peculiar place. You said yourself it is like a strange piece of Shadow drifting in the sky. While you figured how to make a rifle fire in Amber, the same rules may not apply up there.'

'It is a risk,' I acknowledged.

'As for the crossbow – supposing a sudden gust of wind deflected the bolt each time you shot one?'

'I am afraid I do not follow you.'

'The Jewel. He walked it part way through the primal Pattern, and he has had some time to experiment with it since then. Do you think it possible that he is partly attuned to it now?'

'I do not know. I am not at all that sure how the process works.'

'I just wanted to point out that if it does work that way, he may be able to use it to defend himself. The Jewel may even have other properties you are not aware of. So what I am saying is that I would not want you to count on being able to kill him at a distance. And I would not even want you to rely on being able to pull the trick you did with the Jewel again – not if he may have gained some measure of control over it.'

'You do make things look a little bleaker than I had them.'

'But possibly more realistic,' he said.

'Conceded. Go on. You said you had a plan.'

'That is correct. My thinking is that Brand must not be allowed to reach the Pattern at all, that once he sets foot upon it the probability of disaster goes way up.'

'And you do not think I can get there in time to block him?'

'Not if he can really transport himself around almost instantaneously while you have to take a long walk. My bet is that he is just waiting for moonrise, and as soon as the city takes form he will be inside, right next to the Pattern.'

'I see the point, but not the answer.'

'The answer is that you are not going to set foot in Tir-na Nog'th tonight.'

'Hold on a minute!'

'Hold on, hell! You imported a master strategist, you'd better listen to what he has to say.'

'Okay, I am listening.'

'You have agreed that you probably cannot reach the place in time. But someone else can.'

'Who and how?'

'All right. I have been in touch with Benedict. He has returned. At this moment he is in Amber, down in the chamber of the Pattern. By now, he should have finished walking it and be standing there at its center, waning. You proceed to the foot of the stairs to the sky-city. There you await the rising of the moon. As soon as Tir-na Nog'th takes form, you will contact Benedict via his Trump. You tell him that all is ready, and he will use the power of the Pattern in Amber to transport himself to the place of the Pattern in Tir-na Nog'th. No matter how fast Brand travels, he cannot gain much on that.'

641

'I see the advantages,' I said. 'That is the fastest way to get a man up there and Benedict is certainly a good man. He should have no trouble dealing with Brand.'

'Do you really think Brand will make no other preparations?' Ganelon said. 'From everything I've heard about the man, he's smart even if he is daft. He just may anticipate something like this.'

'Possibly. Any idea what he might do?'

He made a sweeping gesture with one hand, slapped his neck and smiled.

'A bug,' he said. 'Pardon me. Pesky little things.'

'You still think—'

'I think you had better remain in contact with Benedict the entire time he is up there, that is what I think. If Brand gets the upper hand, you may need to pull Benedict back immediately to save his life.'

'Of course. But then—'

'But then we would have lost a round. Admitted. But not the game. Even with the Jewel fully attuned, he would have to get to the primal Pattern to do his real damage with it – and you have that under guard.'

'Yes,' I said. 'You seem to have everything figured. You surprised me, moving so fast.'

'I've had a lot of time on my hands recently, which can be a bad thing unless you use it for thinking. So I did. What I think now is that you had best move fast. The day isn't getting any longer.'

'Agreed,' I said. 'Thanks for the good counsel.'

'Save your thanks till we see what comes of it,' he said, and then he broke the contact.

'That one sounded important,' Random said. 'What's up?'

'Appropriate question,' I answered, 'but I am all out of time now. You will have to wait till morning for the story.'

'Is there anything I can do to help?'

'As a matter of fact,' I said, 'yes, if you'll either ride double or go back to Amber on a Trump. I need Star.'

'Sure,' Random said. 'No trouble. Is that all?'

'Yes. Haste is all.'

We moved toward the horses.

I patted Star a few times and then mounted.

'We'll see you in Amber,' Random said. 'Good luck.'

'In Amber,' I said. 'Thanks.'

I turned and headed toward the place of the stairway, treading my tomb's lengthening shadow eastward.

13

On the highest ridge of Kolvir there is a formation which resembles three steps. I sat on the lowest of these and waited for more to occur above me. It takes night and moonlight to do this, so half of the requirements had been met.

There were clouds to the west and northeast. I was leery of those clouds. If they massed sufficiently to block all moonlight, Tir-na Nog'th faded back to nothingness. This was one reason why it was always advisable to have a backup man on the ground, to Trump you to safety should the city vanish about you.

The sky overhead was clear, however, and fitted with familiar stars. When the moon came up and its light fell upon the stone at which, I rested, the stairway in the sky would come into being, sweeping upward to a great height, taking its way to Tir-na Nog'th, the image of Amber that rode the night's middle air.

I was weary. Too much had occurred in too brief a time. Suddenly to be at rest, to remove my boots and rub my feet, to lean back and rest my head, even against stone, was a luxury, a pure animal pleasure. I drew my cloak together before me against the growing chill. A hot bath, a full meal, a bed would be very good things. But these assumed an almost mythic quality from that vantage. It was more than sufficient simply to rest as I was, to let my thoughts move more slowly, drifting, spectatorlike, back over the day's happenings.

So much . . . but now, at least, I had some answers to some of my questions. Not all of them, certainly. But enough to slake my mind's thirst for the moment . . . I now had some idea as to what had been going on during my absence, a better understanding of what was happening now, a knowledge of some of the things that had to be done, of what I had to do . . . And I felt, somehow, that I knew more than I realized, consciously, that I already possessed pieces that would fit the growing picture before me, if I were only to jiggle them, flip them, rotate them properly. The pace of recent events, particularly today's, had not allowed me a moment's reflection. Now, though, some of the pieces seemed to be turning at odd angles . . .

I was distracted by a stirring above my shoulder, a tiny effect of brightening in the higher air. Turning, then standing, I regarded the horizon. A preliminary glow had occurred out over the sea at the point where the moon would ascend. As I watched, a minute arc of light came into view. The clouds had shifted slightly also, though not enough to cause concern. I glanced up then, but the overhead phenomenon had not yet begun. I withdrew my Trumps, however, riffled them, and cut out Benedict's.

Lethargy forgotten, I stared, watching the moon expand above the water, casting a trail of light over the waves. A faint form was suddenly hovering on the threshold of visibility high overhead. As the light grew, a spark limned it here and there. The first lines, faint as spider webbing, appeared above the rock. I studied Benedict's card, I reached for contact . . .

His cold image came alive. I saw him in the chamber of the Pattern, standing at the design's center. A lighted lantern glowed beside his left foot. He became aware of my presence.

'Corwin,' he said, 'is it time?'

'Not quite,' I told him. 'The moon is rising. The city is just beginning to take form. So it will only be a little longer. I wanted to be certain you were ready.'

'I am ready,' he said.

'It is good that you came back when you did. Did you learn anything of interest?'

'Ganelon called me back,' he said, 'as soon as he learned what had happened. His plan seemed a good one, which is why I am here. As for the Courts of Chaos, yes. I believe I have learned a few things—'

'A moment,' I said.

The moonbeam strands had assumed a more tangible appearance. The city overhead was now clear in outline. The stairway was visible in its entirety, though fainter in some places than in others. I stretched forth my hand, above the second stair, the third . . .

Cool, soft, I encountered the fourth stair. It seemed to give somewhat beneath my push, however.

'Almost,' I said to Benedict. 'I am going to try the stairs. Be ready.'

He nodded.

I mounted the stone stairs, one, two, three. I raised my foot then and lowered it upon the fourth, ghostly one. It yielded gently to my weight I was afraid to raise my other foot, so I waited, watching the moon. I breathed the cool air as the brightness increased, as the path in the waters widened. Glancing upward, I saw Tir-na Nog'th lose something of its transparency. The stars behind it grew dimmer. As his occurred, the stair became firmer beneath my foot. All resiliency went out of it I felt that it might bear my full weight. Casting my eyes along its length, I now saw it in its entirety, here translucent, there transparent, sparkling, but continuous all the way up to the silent city that drifted above the sea. I raised my other foot and stood on the fourth stair. If I'd the mind, a few more steps would send me along that celestial escalator into the place of dreams made real, walking neuroses and dubious prophecy, into a moonlit city of ambiguous wish fulfillment, twisted time, and pallid beauty. I stepped back down and glanced at the moon, now balanced on the world's wet rim. I regarded Benedict's Trump in its silvery glow.

'The stair is solid, the moon is up,' I said.

'All right. I am going.'

I watched him there at the center of the Pattern. He raised the lantern in his left hand and for a moment stood unmoving. An instant later he was gone, and so was the Pattern. Another instant, and he stood within a similar chamber, this time outside the Pattern, next to the point where it begins. He raised the lantern high and looked all around the room. He was alone.

He turned, walked to the wall, set the lantern beside it. His shadow stretched toward the Pattern, changed shape as he turned on his heel, moved back to his first position.

This Pattern, I noted, glowed with a paler light than the one in Amber – silvery white, without the hint of blue with which I was familiar. Its configuration was the same, but the ghost city played strange tricks with perspective. There were distortions – narrowings, widenings – which seemed to shift for no particular reason across its surface, as though I viewed the entire tableau through an irregular lens rather than Benedict's Trump.

I retreated down the stairs, settled once again on the lowest step. I continued to observe.

Benedict loosened his blade in its scabbard.

'You know about the possible effect of blood on the Pattern?' I asked.

'Yes. Ganelon told me.'

'Did you ever suspect – any of this?'

'I never trusted Brand,' he told me.

'What of your journey to the Courts of Chaos? What did you learn?'

'Later, Corwin. He could come any time now.'

'I hope no distracting visions show up,' I said, recalling my own journey to Tir-na Nog'th and his own part in my final adventure there.

He shrugged.

'One gives them power by paying them heed. My attention is reserved for one matter tonight.'

He turned through a full circle, regarding every part of the chamber, halted when he had finished.

'I wonder if he knows you are there?' I said.

'Perhaps. It does not matter.'

I nodded. If Brand did not show up, we had gained a day. The guards would ward the other Patterns, Fiona would have a chance to demonstrate her own skill in matters arcane by locating Brand for us. We would then pursue him. She and Bleys had been able to stop him once before. Could she do it alone now? Or would we have to find Bleys and try to convince him to help? Had Brand found Bleys? What the hell did Brand want that kind of power for anyhow? A desire for the throne I could understand. Yet . . . The man was mad, leave it at that. Too bad, but that's the way it was. Heredity or environment? I wondered wryly. We were all of us, to some degree, mad after his fashion. To be honest, it had to be a form of madness, to have so much and to strive so bitterly for just a little more, for a bit of an edge over the others. He carried this tendency to its extreme, that is all. He was a caricature of this mania in all of us. In this sense, did it really matter which of us was the traitor?

Yes, it did. He was the one who had acted. Mad or not, he had gone too far. He had done things Eric, Julian, and I would not have done. Bleys and Fiona had finally backed away from his thickening plot. Gérard and Benedict were a notch above the rest of us – moral, mature, whatever – for they had exempted themselves from the zero-sum power game. Random had changed, quite a bit, in recent years. Could it be that the children of the unicorn took ages in which to mature, that it was slowly happening to the rest of us but had somehow passed Brand by? Or could it be that by his actions Brand was causing it in the rest of us? Like most such questions, the benefit of these was in the asking, not the answering. We were enough like Brand that I knew a particular species of fear nothing else could so provoke. But yes, it did matter. Whatever the reason, he was the one who had acted.

The moon was higher now, its vision superimposed upon my inward viewing of the chamber of the Pattern. The clouds continued to shift, to boil nearer the moon. I thought of advising Benedict, but it would serve no other end than distraction. Above me, Tir-na Nog'th rode like some supernatural ark upon the seas of night.

. . . And suddenly Brand was there.

Reflexively, my hand went to Grayswandir's hilt, despite the fact that a part of me realized from the very first that he stood across the Pattern from Benedict in a dark chamber high in the sky.

My hand fell again. Benedict had become aware of the intruding presence immediately, and he turned to face him. He made no move toward his weapon, but simply stared across the Pattern at our brother.

My earliest fear had been that Brand would contrive to arrive directly behind Benedict and stab him in the back. I would not have tried that though, because even in death Benedict's reflexes might have been sufficient to dispatch his assailant. Apparently, Brand wasn't that crazy either.

Brand smiled.

'Benedict,' he said. 'Fancy . . . You . . . Here.'

The Jewel of Judgment hung fiery upon his breast.

'Brand,' Benedict said, 'don't try it.'

Still smiling, Brand unclasped his sword belt and let his weapon fall to the floor. When the echoes died, he said, 'I am not a fool, Benedict. The man hasn't been born who can go up against you with a blade.'

'I don't need the blade, Brand.'

Brand began walking, slowly, about the edge of the Pattern.

'Yet you wear it as a servant of the throne, when you could have been king.'

'That has never been high on my list of ambitions.'

'That is right.' He paused, only part way about the Pattern. 'Loyal, self-effacing. You have not changed at all. Pity Dad conditioned you so well. You could have gone so much further.'

'I have everything that I want,' Benedict said.

'. . . To have been stifled, cut off, so early.'

'You cannot talk your way past me either, Brand. Do not make me hurt you.'

The smile still on his face, Brand began moving again, slowly. What was it he was trying to do? I could not figure his strategy.

'You know I can do certain things the others cannot,' Brand said. 'If there is anything at all that you want and think that you cannot have, now is your chance to name it and learn how wrong you were. I have learned things you would scarcely believe.'

Benedict smiled one of his rare smiles.

'You have chosen the wrong line,' he said. 'I can walk to anything that I want.'

'Shadows!' Brand snorted, halting again. 'Any of the others can clutch a phantom! I am talking of reality! Amber! Power! Chaos! Not daydreams made solid! Not second best!'

'If I had wanted more than I have, I knew what to do. I did not do it.'

Brand laughed, began walking again. He had come a quarter of the way about the Pattern's periphery. The Jewel burned more brightly. His voice rang.

'You are a fool, to wear your chains willingly! But if things do not call out to you to possess them and if power holds no attraction, what of knowledge? I learned the last of Dworkin's lore. I have gone on since then and paid dark prices for greater insight into the workings of the universe. This you could have without that price tag.'

'There would be a price,' Benedict said, 'one that I will not pay.'

Brand shook his head and tossed his hair. The image of the Pattern wavered for a moment then, as a wisp of cloud crossed the moon. Tir-na Nog'th faded slightly, returned to normal focus.

'You mean it you really mean it,' Brand said, apparently not aware of the moment of fading. 'I shan't test you further then. I had to try.' He halted again, staring. 'You are too good a man to waste yourself on that mess in Amber, defending something that is obviously falling apart. I am going to win, Benedict. I am going to erase Amber and build it anew. I am going to rub out the old Pattern and draw my own. You can be with me. I want you on my side. I am going to raise up a perfect world, one with more direct access to and from Shadow. I am going to merge Amber with the Courts of Chaos. I am going to extend this realm directly through all of Shadow. You will command our legions, the mightiest military ibices ever assembled. You—'

'If your new world would be as perfect as you say, Brand, there would be no need for legions. If, on the other hand, it is to reflect the mind of its creator, then I see it as something less than an improvement over the present state of affairs. Thank you for your offer, but I hold with the Amber which already exists.'

'You are a fool, Benedict. A well-meaning one, but a fool nevertheless.'

He began to move again, casually. He was within forty feet of Benedict. Thirty . . . He kept moving. He finally paused about twenty feet away, hooked his thumbs behind his belt, and simply stared. Benedict met his gaze. I checked the clouds again. A long mass of them continued a moonward slide. I could pull Benedict out at any time, though. It was hardly worth disturbing him at the moment.

'Why don't you come and cut me down then?' Brand finally said. 'Unarmed as I am, it should not be difficult. The fact that the same blood flows in both our veins makes no difference, does it? What are you waiting for?'

'I already told you that I do not wish to hurt you,' Benedict said.

'Yet you stand ready to, if I attempt to pass your way.'

Benedict simply nodded.

'Admit that you fear me, Benedict. All of you are afraid of me. Even when I approach you weaponless like this, something must be twisting your guts. You see my confidence and you do not understand it. You must be afraid.'

Benedict did not reply.

'. . . And you fear my blood on your hands,' Brand went on, 'you fear my death curse.'

'Did you fear Martin's blood on your own?' Benedict asked.

'That bastard puppy!' Brand said. 'He was not truly one of us. He was only a tool.'

'Brand, I have no desire to kill a brother. Give me that trinket you wear about your neck and come back with me now to Amber. It is not too late to set matters right.'

Brand threw back his head and laughed.

'Oh, nobly spoken! Nobly spoken, Benedict! Like a true lord of the realm! You would shame me with your excessive virtue! And what is the sticking point of this all?' He reached down and stroked the Jewel of Judgment. 'This?' He laughed again and strode forward. 'This bauble? Would its surrender buy us peace, amity, order? Would it ransom my life?'

He halted once more, ten feet from Benedict now. He raised the Jewel between his fingers and looked down at it.

'Do you realize the full powers of this thing?' he asked.

'Enough of th—' Benedict began, and his voice cracked in his throat.

Brand hurriedly took another step forward. The Jewel was bright before him. Benedict's hand had begun to move toward his blade, but it did not reach it. He stood stiffly now, as if suddenly transformed into a statue. Then I began to understand, but by then it was too late.

Nothing that Brand had been saying had really mattered. It had simply been a running line of patter, a distraction thrown up before him while he sought cautiously after the proper range. He was indeed partly attuned to the Jewel, and the limited control this gave him was still sufficient to enable him to produce effects with it effects which I was unaware it could produce, but of which he had known all along. Brand had carefully contrived his arrival a good distance from Benedict, tried the Jewel, moved a little nearer, tried again, kept up this movement this testing, until he found the point where it could affect Benedict's nervous system.

'Benedict,' I said, 'you had better come to me now,' and I exerted my will, but he did not budge nor did he reply. His Trump was still functioning, I felt his presence, I observed events because of it, but I could not reach him. The Jewel was obviously affecting more than his motor system.

I looked to the clouds again. They were still growing, they were reaching for the moon. It seemed they might come across it soon. If I could not pull Benedict out when it happened, he would fall to the sea as soon as the light was fully blocked, the city disrupted. Brand! If he became aware of it he might be able to use the Jewel to dissipate the clouds. But to do that he would probably have to release Benedict. I did not think he would do it. Still . . . The clouds seemed to be slowing now. This entire line of reasoning could become unnecessary. I thumbed out Brand's Trump though, and set it aside.

'Benedict, Benedict' said Brand, smiling, 'of what use is the finest swordsman alive if he cannot move to take up his blade? I told you that you were a fool. Did you think I would walk willingly to my slaughter? You should have trusted the fear you must have felt. You should have known that I would not enter this place helpless. I meant it when I said that I was going to win. You were a good choice though, because you are the best. I really wish that you had accepted my offer. But it is not that important now. I cannot be stopped. None of the others has a chance, and with you gone things are going to be much easier.'

He reached beneath his cloak and produced a dagger.

'Bring me through, Benedict!' I cried, but it was no use. There was no response, no strength to trump me up there.

I seized Brand's Trump. I recalled my Trump battle with Eric. If I could hit Brand through his Trump, I might be able to break his concentration sufficiently for Benedict to come free. I turned all of my faculties upon the card, preparing for a massive mental assault.

But nothing. The way was frozen and dark.

It had to be that his concentration on the task at hand, his mental involvement with the Jewel, was so complete that I simply could not reach him. I was blocked at every turn.

Suddenly, the stairway grew paler above me and I cast a quick glance at the moon. A limb of cumulus now covered a portion of its face. Damn!

I returned my attention to Benedict's Trump. It seemed slow, but I did recover the contact, indicating that somewhere, inside it all, Benedict was still conscious. Brand had moved a pace nearer and was still taunting him. The Jewel on its heavy chain burned with the light of its use. They stood perhaps three paces apart now. Brand toyed with the dagger.

'. . . Yes, Benedict,' he was saying, 'you probably would have preferred to die in battle. On the other hand, you might look upon this as a kind of honor – a signal honor. In a way, your death will allow the birth of a new order . . .'

For a moment, the Pattern faded behind them. I could not tear my eyes from the scene to examine the moon, however. There, within the shadows and the flickering light, his back to the Pattern, Brand did not seem to notice. He took another step forward.

'But enough of this,' he said. 'There are things to be done, and the night grows no younger.'

He stepped nearer and lowered the blade.

'Good night, sweet Prince,' he said, and he moved to close with him.

At that instant, Benedict's strange mechanical right arm, torn from this place of shadow and silver and moonlight, moved with the speed of a striking snake. Thing of glinting, metallic planes like the facets of a gem, wrist a wondrous weave of silver cable, pinned with flecks of fire, stylized, skeletal, a Swiss toy, a mechanical insect, functional, deadly, beautiful in its way, it shot forward with a speed that I could not follow, while the rest of his body remained steady, a statue.

The mechanical fingers caught the Jewel's chain about Brand's neck. Immediately, the arm moved upward, raising Brand high above the floor. Brand dropped the dagger and clutched at his throat with both hands.

Behind him, the Pattern faded once again. It returned with a much paler glow. Brand's face in the lantern light was a ghastly, twisted apparition. Benedict remained frozen, holding him on high, unmoving, a human gallows.

The Pattern grew dimmer. Above me, the steps began to recede. The moon was half-occluded.

Writhing, Brand raised his arms above his head, catching at the chain on either side of the metal hand that held it. He was strong, as all of us are. I saw his muscles bunch and harden. By then, his face was dark and his neck a mass of straining cables. He bit his lip; the blood ran into his beard as he drew upon the chain.

With a sharp snap followed by a rattling, the chain parted and Brand fell to the floor gasping. He rolled over once, clutching at his throat with both hands.

Slowly, very slowly, Benedict lowered his strange arm. He still held the chain and the Jewel. He flexed his other arm. He sighed deeply.

The Pattern grew even dimmer. Above me, Tir-na Nog'th became transparent. The moon was almost gone.

'Benedict!' I cried. 'Can you hear me?'

'Yes,' he said, very softly, and he began to sink through the floor.

'The city is fading! You've got to come to me right away!'

I extended my hand.

'Brand . . .' he said, turning.

But Brand was sinking also, and I saw that Benedict could not reach him. I clasped Benedict's left hand and jerked. Both of us fell to the ground beside the high outcrop.

I helped him to his feet. Then we both seated ourselves on the stone. For a long while, we did not say anything. I looked again and Tir-na Nog'th was gone.

I thought back over everything that had happened, so fast, so sudden, that day. A great weight of weariness lay upon me now, and I felt that my energies must be at their end, that shortly I must sleep. I could scarcely think straight Life had simply been too crowded recently. I leaned my head back against the stone once more, regarding cloud and star. The pieces . . . the pieces which it seemed should fit, if only the proper jiggle, twist or flip were applied . . . They were jiggling, twisting, and flipping now, almost of their own accord . . .

'Is he dead, do you think?' Benedict asked, pulling me back from a half-dream of emerging forms.

'Probably,' I said. 'He was in bad shape when things fell apart.'

'It was a long way down. He might have had time to work some escape along the lines of his arrival.'

'Right now it does not really matter,' I said. 'You've drawn his fangs.'

Benedict granted. He was still holding the Jewel, a much dimmer red than it had been so recently.

'True,' he finally said. 'The Pattern is safe now. I wish . . . I wish that some time, long ago, something had not been said that was said, or something done that was not done. Something, had we known, which might have let him grow differently, something which would have seen him become another man than the bitter, bent thing I saw up there. It is best now if he is dead. But it is a waste of something that might have been.'

I did not answer him. What he had said might or might not be right. It did not matter. Brand might have been borderline psychotic, whatever that means, and then again maybe not. There is always a reason. Whenever anything has been mucked up, whenever anything outrageous happens, there is a reason for it. You still have a mucked-up, outrageous situation on your hands, however, and explaining it does not alleviate it one bit. If someone does something really rotten, there is a reason for it. Learn it, if you care, and you learn why he is a son of a bitch. The fact is the thing that remains, though. Brand had acted. It changed nothing to run a posthumous psychoanalysis. Acts and their consequences are the things by which our fellows judge us. Anything else, and all that you get is a cheap feeling of moral superiority by thinking how you would have done something nicer if it had been you. So as for the rest, leave it to heaven. I'm not qualified.

'We had best get back to Amber,' Benedict said. 'There are a great number of things that must be done.'

'Wait,' I said.

'Why?'

'I've been thinking.'

When I did not elaborate, he finally said, 'And . . . ?'

I riffled slowly through my Trumps, replacing his, replacing Brand's.

'Haven't you wondered yet about the new arm you wear?' I asked him.

'Of course. You brought it from Tir-na Nog'th, under unusual circumstances. It fits. It works. It proved itself tonight.'

'Exactly. Isn't the last a lot of weight to dump on poor coincidence? The one weapon that gave you a chance up there, against the Jewel. And it just happened to be a part of you – and you just happened to be the person who was up there, to use it? Trace things back and trace them forward again. Isn't there an extraordinary – no, preposterous – chain of coincidences involved?'

'When you put it that way . . .' he said.

'I do. And you must realize as well as I do that there has to be more to it than that.'

'All right. Say that. But how? How was it done?'

'I have no idea,' I said, withdrawing the card I had not looked upon in a long, long while, feeling its coldness beneath my finger tips, 'but the method is not important. You asked the wrong question.'

'What should I have asked?'

'Not "How?" but "Who?"'

'You think that a human agency arranged that entire chain of events, up through the recovery of the Jewel?'

'I don't know about that. What's human? But I do think that someone we both know has returned and is behind it all.'

'All right. Who?'

I showed him the Trump that I held.

'Dad? That *is* ridiculous! He must be dead. It's been so long.'

'You know he could have engineered it. He's that devious. We never understood all of his powers.'

Benedict rose to his feet. He stretched. He shook his head.

'I think you have been out in the cold too long, Corwin. Let's go home now.'

'Without testing my guess? Come on! That is hardly sporting. Sit down and give me a minute. Let's try his Trump.'

'He would have contacted someone by now.'

'I don't think so. In fact – come on. Humor me. What have we got to lose?'

'All right. Why not?'

He sat down beside me. I held the Trump where both of us could make it out. We stared at it. I relaxed my mind, I reached for contact. It came almost immediately.

He was smiling as he regarded us.

'Good evening. That was a fine piece of work,' Ganelon said. 'I am pleased that you brought back my trinket. I'll be needing it soon.'

THE COURTS OF CHAOS

To Carl Yoke, First Reader —

From Lucetania to Euclid Park,
Sarcobatus Flats to Cygnus X-1 —
May you live another ten thousand years,
May your liar be safe from trendeltiles.
May the diminutive deities
break their collective leg.

1

Amber: high and bright atop Kolvir in the middle of the day. A black road: low and sinister through Garnath from Chaos to the south. Me: cursing, pacing and occasionally reading in the library of the palace in Amber. The door to that library: closed and barred.

The mad prince of Amber seated himself at the desk, returned his attention to the opened volume. There was a knock on the door.

'Go away!' I said.

'Corwin. It's me – Random. Open up, huh? I even brought lunch.'

'Just a minute.'

I got to my feet again, rounded the desk, crossed the room. Random nodded when I opened the door. He carried a tray, which he took to a small table near the desk.

'Plenty of food there,' I said.

'I'm hungry, too.'

'So do something about it.

He did. He carved. He passed me some meat on a slab of bread. He poured wine. We seated ourselves and ate.

'I know you are still mad . . .' he said, after a time.

'Aren't you?'

'Well, maybe I am more used to it. I don't know. Still . . . Yes. It was sort of abrupt, wasn't it?'

'Abrupt?' I took a large swallow of wine. 'It is just like the old days. Worse even. I had actually come to like him when he was playing at being Ganelon. Now that he is back in control he is just as peremptory as ever, he has given us a set of orders he has not bothered to explain and he has disappeared again.'

'He said he would be in touch soon.'

'I imagine he intended that last time, too.'

'I'm not so sure.'

'And he explained nothing about his other absence. In fact, he has not really explained anything.'

'He must have his reasons.'

'I am beginning to wonder, Random. Do you think his mind might finally be going?'

'He was still sharp enough to fool you.'

'That was a combination of low animal cunning and shapeshifting ability.'

'It worked, didn't it?'

'Yes. It worked.'

'Corwin, could it be that you do not want him to have a plan that might be effective, that you do not want him to be right?'

'That is ridiculous. I want this mess cleared up as much as any of us.'

'Yes, but wouldn't you rather the answer came from another quarter?'

'What are you getting at?'

'You do not want to trust him.'

'I will admit that I have not seen him – as himself – in a hell of a long time, and . . .'

He shook his head.

'That is not what I mean. You are angry that he is back, aren't you? You hoped that we had seen the last of him.'

I looked away.

'There is that,' I finally said. 'But not for a vacant throne, or not *just* for it. It is him, Random. Him. That's all.'

'I know,' he said. 'But you have to admit he suckered Brand, which is not an easy thing to do. He pulled a stunt I still do not understand, getting you to bring that arm back from Tir-na Nog'th, somehow getting me to pass it along to Benedict, seeing to it that Benedict was in the right place at the proper moment, so that everything worked and he got the Jewel back. He is also still better than we are at Shadow play. He managed it right on Kolvir when he took us to the primal Pattern. I cannot do that. Neither can you. And he was able to whip Gérard. I do not believe that he is slowing down. I think he knows exactly what he is doing, and whether we like it or not, I think be is the only one who can deal with the present situation.'

'You are trying to say that I should trust him?'

'I am trying to say that you have no choice.'

I sighed.

'I guess you've put your finger on it,' I said. 'No sense in my being bitter. Still . . .'

'The attack order bothers you, doesn't it?'

'Yes, among other things. If we would wait longer, Benedict could field a greater force. Three days is not much time to get ready for something like this. Not when we are so uncertain about the enemy.'

'But we may not be. He spoke in private with Benedict for a long while.'

'And that is the other thing. These separate orders. This secrecy . . . He is not trusting us any more than he has to.'

Random chuckled. So did I.

'All right,' I said. 'Maybe I would not either. But three days to launch a war.' I shook my head. 'He had better know something we don't.'

'I get the impression that it is more a peremptory strike than a war.'

'Only he did not bother to tell us what we are preempting.'

Random shrugged, poured more wine.

'Perhaps he will say when he gets back. You did not get any special orders, did you?'

'Just to stand and wait. What about you?'

He shook his head.

'He said that when the time comes, I will know. At least with Julian, he told him to have his troops ready to move on a moment's notice.'

'Oh? Aren't they staying in Arden?'

He nodded.

'When did he say this?'

'After you left. He trumped Julian up here to give him the message, and they rode off together. I heard Dad say that he would ride partway back with him.'

'Did they take the eastern trail over Kolvir?'

'Yes. I saw them off.'

'Interesting. What else did I miss?'

He shifted in his seat.

'The part that bothers me,' he said. 'After Dad had mounted and waved a good-bye, he looked back at me and said, "And keep an eye on Martin".'

'That is all?'

'That is all. But he was laughing as he said it.'

'Just natural suspicion at a newcomer, I guess.'

'Then why the laugh?'

'I give up.'

I cut a piece of cheese and ate it.

'Might not be a bad idea, though. It might not be suspicion. Maybe he feels Martin needs to be protected from something. Or both. Or neither. You know how he sometimes is.'

Random stood.

'I had not thought through to the alternative. Come with me now, huh?' he said. 'You have been up here all morning.'

'All right.' I got to my feet, buckled on Grayswandir. 'Where is Martin, anyway?'

'I left him down on the first floor. He was talking with Gérard.'

'He is in good hands, then. Is Gérard going to be staying here, or will he be returning to the fleet?'

'I do not know. He would not discuss his orders.'

We left the room. We headed for the stairway.

On the way down, I heard some small commotion from below and I quickened my pace.

I looked over the railing and saw a throng of guards at the entrance to the throne room, along with the massive figure of Gérard. All of them had their backs to us. I leaped down the final stairs. Random was not far behind me.

I pushed my way through.

'Gérard, what is happening?' I asked.

'Damned if I know,' he said. 'Look for yourself. But there is no getting in.'

He moved aside and I took a step forward. Then another. And that was it. It was as if I were pushing against a slightly resilient, totally invisible wall. Beyond was a sight that tied my memory and feelings into a knot I stiffened, as fear took hold of me by the neck, clasped my hands. No mean trick, that.

Martin, smiling, still held a Trump in his left hand, and Benedict – apparently recently summoned – stood before him. A girl was nearby, on the dais, beside the throne, facing away. Both, men appeared to be speaking, but I could not hear the words.

Finally, Benedict turned and seemed to address the girl. After a time, she appeared to be answering him. Martin moved off to her left. Benedict mounted the dais as she spoke. I could see her face then. The exchange continued.

'That girl looks somewhat familiar,' said Gérard, who had moved forward and now stood at my side.

'You might have gotten a glimpse of her as she rode past us,' I told him, 'the day Eric died. It's Dara.'

I heard his sudden intake of breath.

'Dara!' he said. 'Then you . . .' His voice faded.

'I was not lying,' I said. 'She is real.'

'Martin!' cried Random, who had moved up on my right 'Martin! What's going on!'

There was no response.

'I don't think he can hear you,' Gérard said. 'This barrier seems to have cut us off completely.'

Random strained forward, his hands pushing against something unseen.

'Let's all of us give it a shove,' he said.

So I tried again. Gérard also threw his weight against the invisible wall.

After half a minute without success, I eased back.

'No good,' I said. 'We can't move it.'

'What is the damned thing?' Random asked. 'What is holding—'

I'd had a hunch – only that, though – as to what might be going on. And only because of the *déjà vu* character of the entire piece. Now, though . . . Now I clasped my hand to my scabbard, to assure myself that Grayswandir still hung at my side.

It did.

Then how could I explain the presence of my distinctive blade, its elaborate tracery gleaming for all to see, hanging where it had suddenly appeared, without support, in the air before the throne, its point barely touching Dara's throat?

I could not.

But it was too similar to what had happened that night in the dream city in the sky, Tir-na Nog'th, to be a coincidence. Here were none of the trappings – the darkness, the confusion, the heavy shadows, the tumultuous emotions I had known – and yet the piece was set much as it had been that night. It was very similar. But not precisely so. Benedict's stance seemed somewhat off – farther back, his body angled differently. While I could not read her lips, I wondered whether Dara was asking the same strange questions. I doubted it. The tableau – like, yet unlike, that which I had experienced – had probably been colored at the other end – that is, if there were any connection at all – by the effects of Tir-na Nog'th's powers upon my mind at that time.

'Corwin,' Random said, 'that looks like Grayswandir hanging in front of her.'

'It does, doesn't it?' I said. 'But as you can see, I am wearing my blade.'

'There can't be another just like it . . . can there? Do you know what is happening?'

'I am beginning to feel as if I may,' I said. 'Whatever, I am powerless to stop it.'

Benedict's blade suddenly came free and engaged the other, so like my own. In a moment, he was fighting an invisible opponent.

'Give him hell, Benedict!' Random shouted.

'It is no use,' I said. 'He is about to be disarmed.'

'How can you know?' Gérard asked.

'Somehow, that is me in there, fighting with him,' I said. 'This is the other end of my dream in Tir-na Nog'th. I do not know how he managed it, but this is the price for Dad's recovering the Jewel.'

'I do not follow you,' he said.

I shook my head.

'I do not pretend to understand how it is being done,' I told him. 'But we will not be able to enter until two things have vanished from that room.'

'What two things?'

'Just watch.'

Benedict's blade had changed hands, and his gleaming prosthesis shot forward and fixed itself upon some unseen target. The two blades parried one another, locked, pressed, their points moving toward the ceiling. Benedict's right hand continued to tighten.

Suddenly, the Grayswandir blade was free, and moving past the other. It struck a terrific blow to Benedict's right arm at the place where the metal portion joined it. Then Benedict turned and the action was blocked to our view for several moments.

Then the sight was clear again, as Benedict dropped to one knee, turning. He clutched at the stump of his arm. The mechanical hand/arm hung in the air near Grayswandir. It was moving away from Benedict and descending, as was the blade. When both reached the floor, they did not strike it but passed on through, vanishing from sight.

I lurched forward, recovered my balance, moved ahead. The barrier was gone.

Martin and Dara reached Benedict before we did. Dara had already torn a strip from her cloak and was binding Benedict's stump when Gérard, Random and I got there.

Random seized Martin by the shoulder and I turned him.

'What happened?' he asked.

'Dara . . . Dara told me she wanted to see Amber,' he said. 'Since I live here now, I agreed to bring her through and show her around. Then—'

'Bring her through? You mean on a Trump?'

'Well, yes.'

'Yours or hers?'

Martin raked his lower lip with his teeth.

'Well, you see . . .'

'Give me those cards,' said Random, and he snatched the case from Martin's belt. He opened it and began going through them.

'Then I thought to tell Benedict, since he was interested in her,' Martin went on, 'Then Benedict wanted to come and see—'

'What the hell!' Random said. 'There is one of you, one of her, and one of a guy I've never even seen before! Where did you get these?'

'Let me see them,' I said.

He passed me the three cards.

'Well?' he said. 'Was it Brand? He is the only one I know who can make Trumps now.'

'I would not have anything to do with Brand,' Martin replied, 'except to kill him.'

But I already knew they were not from Brand. They were simply not in his style. Nor were they in the style of anyone whose work I knew. Style was not foremost in my mind at that moment, however. Rather, it was the features of the third person, the one whom Random had said he had never seen before. I had. I was looking at the face of the youth who had confronted me with a crossbow before the Courts of Chaos, recognized me and then declined to shoot.

I extended the card.

'Martin, who is this?' I asked.

'The man who made these extra Trumps,' he said. 'He drew one of himself while he was about it. I do not know his name. He is a friend of Dara's.'

'You are lying,' Random said.

'Then let Dara tell us,' I said, and I turned to her.

She still knelt beside Benedict, though she had finished bandaging him and he was now sitting up.

'How about it?' I said, waving the card at her. 'Who is this man?'

She glanced at the card, then up at me. She smiled.

'You really do not know?' she said.

'Would I be asking if I did?'

'Then look at it again and go look in a mirror. He is your son as much as mine. His name is Merlin.'

I am not easily shocked, but this had nothing of ease about it. I felt dizzy. But my mind moved quickly. With the proper time differential the thing was possible.

'Dara,' I said, 'what is it that you want?'

'I told you when I walked the Pattern,' she said, 'that Amber must be destroyed. What I want is to have my rightful part in it.'

'You will have my old cell,' I said. 'No, the one next to it. Guards!'

'Corwin, it is all right,' Benedict said, getting to his feet. 'It is not as bad as it sounds. She can explain everything.'

'Then let her start now.'

'No. In private. Just family.'

I motioned back the guards who had come at my call.

'Very well. Let us adjourn to one of the rooms up the hall.'

He nodded, and Dara took hold of his left arm. Random, Gérard, Martin and I followed them out I looked back once to the empty place where my dream had come true. Such is the stuff.

2

I rode up over the crest of Kolvir and dismounted when I came to my tomb. I went inside and opened the casket. It was empty. Good. I was beginning to wonder. I had half-expected to see myself laid out before me, evidence that despite signs and intuitions I had somehow wandered into the wrong shadow.

I went back outside and rubbed Star's nose. The sun was shining and the breeze was chill. I had a sudden desire to go to sea. I seated myself on the bench instead and fumbled with my pipe.

We had talked. Seated with her legs beneath her on the brown sofa, Dara had smiled and repeated the story of her descent from Benedict and Lintra, the hellmaid, growing up in and about the Courts of Chaos, a grossly non-Euclidean realm where time itself presented strange distribution problems.

'The things you told me when we met were lies,' I said. 'Why should I believe you now?'

She had smiled and regarded her fingernails.

'I had to lie to you then,' she explained, 'to get what I wanted from you.'

'That being . . . ?'

'Knowledge, of the family, the Pattern, the Trumps, of Amber. To gain your trust. To have your child.'

'The truth would not have served as well?'

'Hardly. I come from the enemy. My reasons for wanting these things were not the sort of which you would approve.'

'Your swordplay . . . ? You told me then that Benedict had trained you.'

'I learned from the great Duke Borel himself, a High Lord of Chaos.'

'. . . and your appearance,' I said. 'It was altered on a number of occasions when I saw you walk the Pattern. How? Also, why?'

'All whose origins involve Chaos are shapeshifters,' she replied.

I thought of Dworkin's performance the night he had impersonated me.

Benedict nodded.

'Dad fooled us with his Ganelon disguise.'

'Oberon is a son of Chaos,' Dara said, 'a rebel son of a rebel father. But the power is still there.'

'Then why is it we cannot do it?' Random asked.

She shrugged.

'Have you ever tried? Perhaps you can. On the other hand, it may have died out with your generation. I do not know. As to myself, however, I have certain favored shapes to which I revert in times of stress. I grew up where this was the rule, where the other shape was actually sometimes dominant. It is still a reflex with me. This is what you witnessed – that day.'

'Dara,' I said, 'why did you want the things that you said you wanted – knowledge of the family, the Pattern, the Trumps, Amber? And a son?'

'All right' She sighed. 'All right. You are by now aware of Brand's plans – the destruction and rebuilding of Amber . . . ?'

'Yes.'

'This involved our consent and co-operation.'

'Including the murder of Martin?' Random asked.

'No,' she said. 'We did not know who he intended to use as the – agent.'

'Would it have stopped you had you known?'

'You are asking a hypothetical question,' she said. 'Answer it yourself. I am glad that Martin is still alive. That is all that I can say about it.'

'All right,' Random said. 'What about Brand?'

'He was able to contact our leaders by methods he had learned from Dworkin. He had ambitions. He needed knowledge, power. He offered a deal.'

'What sort of knowledge?'

'For one thing, he did not know how to destroy the Pattern—'

'Then you *were* responsible for what he did,' Random said.

'If you choose to look at it that way.'

'I do.'

668

She shrugged, looked at me.

'Do you want to hear this story?'

'Go ahead.' I glanced at Random and he nodded.

'Brand was given what he wanted,' she said, 'but he was not trusted. It was feared that once he possessed the power to shape the world as he would, he would not stop with ruling over a revised Amber. He would attempt to extend his dominion over Chaos as well. A weakened Amber was what was desired, so that Chaos would be stronger than it now is – the striking of a new balance, giving to us more of the shadowlands that lie between our realms. It was realized long ago that the two kingdoms can never be merged, or one destroyed, without also disrupting all the processes that lie in flux between us. Total stasis or complete chaos would be the result. Yet, though it was seen what Brand had in mind, our leaders came to terms with him. It was the best opportunity to present itself in ages. It had to be seized. It was felt that Brand could be dealt with, and finally replaced, when the time came.'

'So you were also planning a double-cross,' Random said.

'Not if he kept his word. But then, we knew that he would not. So we provided for the move against him.'

'How?'

'He would be allowed to accomplish his end and then be destroyed. He would be succeeded by a member of the royal family of Amber who was also of the first family of the Courts, one who had been raised among us and trained for the position. Merlin even traces his connection with Amber on both sides, through my forebear Benedict and directly from yourself – the two most favored claimants to your throne.'

'You are of the royal house of Chaos?'

She smiled.

I rose. Strode away. Stared at the ashes on the grate.

'I find it somewhat distressing to have been involved in a calculated breeding project,' I said, at length. 'But be that as it may, and accepting everything you have said as true – for the moment – why are you telling us all of these things now?'

'Because,' she said, 'I fear that the lords of my realm would go as far for their vision as Brand would for his. Farther, perhaps. That balance I spoke of. Few seem to appreciate what a delicate thing it is. I have traveled in the shadowlands near to Amber, and I have walked in Amber herself. I also have known the shadows that lie by Chaos' side. I have met many people and seen many things. Then, when I encountered Martin and spoke with him, I began to feel that the changes I had been told would be for the better would not simply result in a revision of Amber more along the lines of my elders' liking. They would, instead, turn Amber into a mere extension of the Courts, most of the shadows would boil away to join with Chaos. Amber would become an island. Some of my seniors who still smart at Dworkm's having created Amber in the first place are really seeking a return to the days before this happened. Total Chaos, from which all things arose. I see the present condition as superior and I wish to preserve it. My desire is that neither side emerge victorious in any conflict.'

I turned in time to see Benedict shaking his head.

'Then you are on neither side,' he stated.

'I like to think that I am on both.'

'Martin,' I said, 'are you in this with her?'

He nodded.

Random laughed.

'The two of you? Against both Amber and the Courts of Chaos? What do you hope to achieve? How do you plan to further this notion of balance?'

'We are not alone,' she said, 'and the plan is not ours.'

Her fingers dipped into her pocket. Something glittered when she withdrew them. She turned it in the light. It was our father's signet ring that she held.

'Where did you get that?' Random asked.

'Where else?'

Benedict stepped toward her and held out his hand. She gave it to him. He scrutinized it.

'It *is* his,' he said. 'It has the little markings on the back that I've seen before. Why do you have it?'

'First, to convince you that I am acting properly when I convey his orders,' she said.

'How is it that you even know him?' I asked.

'I met him during his – difficulties – some time back,' she told us. 'In fact, you might say that I helped to deliver him from them. This was after I had met Martin, and I was inclined to be more sympathetic toward Amber. But then, your father is also a charming and persuasive man. I decided that I could not simply stand by and see him remain prisoner to my kin.'

'Do you know how he was captured in the first place?'

She shook her head.

'I only know that Brand effected his presence in a shadow far enough from Amber that he could be taken there. I believe it involved a fake quest for a nonexistent magical tool which might heal the Pattern. He realizes now that only the Jewel can do it.'

'Your helping him to get away . . . How did this affect your relations with your own people?'

'Not too damned well,' she said. 'I am temporarily without a home.'

'And you want one here?'

She smiled again.

'It depends on how things turn out. If my people have their way, I would as soon go back – or stay with what shadows remain.'

I withdrew a Trump, glanced at it.

'What of Merlin? Where is he now?'

'They have him,' she said. 'I fear he may be their man now. He knows his parentage, but they have had charge of his education for a long while. I do not know whether he could be gotten away.'

I raised the Trump, stared at it.

'No good,' she said. 'It will not function between here and there.'

I recalled how difficult Trump communication had been when I had been to the fringes of that place. I tried anyway.

The card grew cold in my hand and I reached out. There was the faintest flicker of a responding presence. I tried harder.

'Merlin, this is Corwin,' I said. 'Do you hear me?'

I seemed to hear a reply. It seemed to be, 'I cannot—' And then there was nothing. The card lost its coldness.

'Did you reach him?' she asked.

'I am not sure,' I said. 'But I think so. Just for a moment.'

'Better than I thought,' she said. 'Either conditions are good or your minds are very similar.'

'When you began waving Dad's signet around you spoke of

orders,' Random said. 'What orders?' And why is he sending them through you?'

'It is a matter of timing.'

'Timing? Hell! He just left here this morning!'

'He had to finish one thing before he was ready for another. He had no idea how long it would take. But I was just in touch with him before I came here – though I was hardly prepared for the reception I walked into – and he is now ready to begin the next phase.'

'Where did you speak with him?' I asked. 'Where is he?'

'I have no idea where he is. He contacted me.'

'And . . . ?'

'He wants Benedict to attack immediately.'

Gérard finally stirred from the huge armchair in which he had sat listening. He rose to his feet, hooked his thumbs in his belt and looked down at her.

'An order like that would have to come directly from Dad.'

'It did,' she said.

He shook his head.

'It makes no sense. Why contact you – someone we have small reason to trust – rather than one of us?'

'I do not believe that he can reach you at the moment. On the other hand, he was able to reach me.'

'Why?'

'He did not use a Trump. He does not have one for me. He used a reverberation effect of the black road, similar to the means by which Brand once escaped Corwin.'

'You know a lot of what has been going on.'

'I do. I still have sources in the Courts, and Brand transported himself there after your struggle. I hear things.'

'Do you know where our father is right now?' Random asked.

'No, I do not know. But I believe that he has journeyed to the real Amber, to take counsel with Dworkin and to re-examine the damage to the primal Pattern.'

'To what end?'

'I do not know. Probably to decide on the course of action he will take. The fact that he reached me and ordered the attack most likely means that he has decided.'

'How long ago was this communication?'

'Just a few hours – my time. But I was far from here in Shadow. I do not know what the time differential is. I am too new at this.'

'So it could be something extremely recent. Possibly only moments ago,' Gérard mused. 'Why did he talk with you rather than one of us? I do not believe that he could not reach us if he wished to.'

'Perhaps to show that he looks upon me with favor,' she said.

'All of this may be entirely true,' Benedict stated. 'But I am not moving without a confirmation of that order.'

'Is Fiona still at the primal Pattern?' Random asked.

'Last I heard,' I told him, 'she had set up camp there. I see what you mean . . .'

I shuffled out Fi's card.

'It took more than one of us to get through from there,' he observed.

'True. So give me a hand.'

He rose, came to my side. Benedict and Gérard also approached.

'This is not really necessary,' Dara protested.

I ignored her and concentrated on the delicate features of my red-haired sister. Moments later, we had contact.

'Fiona,' I asked, seeing from the background, that she was still in residence at the heart of things, 'is Dad there?'

'Yes,' she said, smiling tightly. 'He is inside with Dworkin.'

'Listen, urgency prevails. I do not know whether or not you know Dara, but she is here—'

'I know who she is, but I have never met her.'

'Well, she claims she has an attack order for Benedict, from Dad. She has his signet to back it up, but he did not speak of this earlier. Do you know anything about it?'

'No,' she said. 'All we did was exchange greetings when he and Dworkin were out here earlier to look at the Pattern. I had some suspicions then, though, and this confirms them.'

'Suspicions? What do you mean?'

'I think Dad is going to try to repair the Pattern. He has the Jewel with him, and I overheard some of the things he said to Dworkin. If he makes the attempt, they will be aware of it in the Courts of Chaos the moment that he begins. They will try to stop him. He would want to strike first to keep them occupied. Only . . .'

'What?'

'It is going to kill him, Corwin. I know that much about it. Whether he succeeds or fails, he will be destroyed in the process.'

'I find it hard to believe.'

'That a king would give up his life for the realm?'

'That Dad would.'

'Then either he has changed or you never really knew him. But I do believe he is going to try it.'

'Then why send his latest order by someone he knows we do not really trust?'

'To show that he wants you to trust her, I would guess, once he has confirmed it.'

'It seems a roundabout way of doing things, but I agree that we should not act without that confirmation. Can you get it for us?'

'I will try. I will get back to you as soon as I have spoken with him.'

She broke the contact.

I turned toward Dara, who had heard only our side of the conversation.

'Do you know what Dad is going to do right now?' I asked her.

'Something involving the black road,' she said. 'He had indicated that much. What, though, or how, he did not say.'

I turned away. I squared my cards and encased them. I did not like this turning of events. This entire day had started badly, and things had been going downhill ever since. It was only a little past lunchtime, too. I shook my head. When I had spoken with him, Dworkin had described the results of any attempt to repair the Pattern, and they had sounded pretty horrendous to me. Supposing Dad tried it, failed, and got himself killed in the attempt? Where would we be then? Right where we were now, only without a leader, on the eve of battle – and with the succession problem stirring again. That whole ghastly business would be in the back of our minds as we rode to the wars, and we would all begin our private arrangements to fight one another once more as soon as the current enemy was dealt with. There had to be another way of handling things. Better Dad alive and on the throne than a revival of the succession intrigues.

'What are we waiting for?' Dara asked. 'Confirmation?'

'Yes,' I replied.

Random began to pace. Benedict seated himself and tested the dressing on his arm. Gérard leaned against the mantelpiece. I stood and thought. An idea came to me just then. I pushed it away immediately, but it returned. I did not like it, but had nothing to do with practicalities. I would have to move quickly, though, before I had a chance to talk myself around to another viewpoint. No. I would stick with this one. Damn it!

There came a stirring of contact. I waited. Moments later, I regarded Fiona again. She stood in a familiar place that it took me several seconds to recognize: Dworkin's sitting room, on the other side of the heavy door at the back of the cave. Dad and Dworkin were both with her. Dad had dropped his Ganelon disguise and was his old self once again. I saw that he wore the Jewel.

'Corwin,' Fiona said, 'it is true. Dad did send the attack order with Dara, and he expected this call for confirmation. I—'

'Fiona, bring me through.'

'What?'

'You heard me. Now!'

I extended my right hand. She reached forward and we touched.

'Corwin!' Random shouted. 'What's happening!'

Benedict was on his feet, Gérard already moving toward me.

'You will hear about it shortly,' I said, and I stepped forward.

I squeezed her hand before I released it and I smiled.

'Thanks, Fi. Hello, Dad. Hi, Dworkin. How's everything?'

I glanced once at the heavy door, saw that it stood open. Then I passed around Fiona and moved toward them. Dad's head was lowered, his eyes narrowed. I knew that look.

'What is this, Corwin? You are here without leave,' he said. 'I have confirmed that damned order, now I expect it to be carried out.'

'It will be,' I said, nodding. 'I did not come here to argue about that.'

'What, then?'

I moved nearer, calculating my words as well as the distance. I was glad that he had remained seated.

'For a time we rode as comrades,' I said. 'Damned if I did not come to like you then. I never had before, you know. Never had guts enough to say that before either, but you know it is true. I like to think that that is how things could have been, if we had not been what we are to each other.' For the barest moment, his gaze seemed to soften as I positioned myself. Then, 'At any rate,' I went on, 'I am going to believe in you that way rather than this way, because there is something I would never have done for you otherwise.'

'What?' he asked.

'This.'

I seized the Jewel with an upward sweeping motion and snapped the chain up over his head. I pivoted on my heel then and raced across the room and through the door. I drew it shut behind me and snapped it to. I could see no way to bar it from the outside, so I ran on, re-tracing the route through the cave from that night I had followed Dworkin along it. Behind me, I heard the expected bellow.

I followed the twistings. I stumbled only once. Wixer's smell still hung heavy in his lair. I pounded on and a final turning brought me a view of daylight ahead.

I raced toward it, slipping the Jewel's chain over my head as I went I felt it fall to my breast, I reached down into it with my mind. There were echoes in the cave behind me.

Outside!

I sprinted toward the Pattern, feeling through the Jewel, turning it into an extra sense. I was the only person other than Dad or Dworkin fully attuned to it. Dworkin had told me that the Pattern's repair might be effected by a person's walking the Grand Pattern in such a state of attunement, burning out the smear at each crossing, replacing it with stock from the image of the Pattern that he bore within him, wiping out the black road in the process. Better me than Dad, then. I still felt that the black road owed something of its final form to the strength my curse against. Amber had given it I wanted to wipe that out, too. Dad would do a better job of putting things together after the war than I ever could, anyway. I realized, at that moment, that I no longer wanted the throne. Even if it were available, the prospect of administering to the kingdom down all the dull centuries that might lie before me was overwhelming. Maybe I would be taking the easy way out if I died in this effort Eric was dead, and I no longer hated him. The other thing that had driven me – the throne – seemed now to have been desirable only because I'd thought he had wanted it so. I renounced both. What was left? I had laughed at Vialle, then wondered. But she had been right. The old soldier in me was strong-est. It was a matter of duty. But not duty alone. There was more . . .

I reached the edge of the Pattern, quickly made my way toward its

beginning. I glanced back at the cavemouth. Dad, Dworkin, Fiona –
none of them had yet emerged. Good. They could never make it in
time to stop me. Once I set foot on the Pattern, it would be too late
for them to do anything but wait and watch. I thought for a fleeting
instant of Iago's dissolution, pushed that thought away, strove to calm
my mind to the level necessary for the undertaking, recalled my battle
with Brand in this place and his strange departure, pushed that away,
too, slowed my breathing, prepared myself.

A certain lethargy came upon me. It was time to begin, but I held
back for a moment, trying to fix my mind properly on the grand task
that lay before me. The Pattern swam for a moment in my vision.
Now! Damn it! Now! No more preliminaries! Begin, I told myself.
Walk!

Still, I stood, contemplating the Pattern as in a dream. I forgot
about myself for long moments as I regarded it. The Pattern, with its
long black smear to be removed . . .

It no longer seemed important that it might kill me. My mind
drifted, considering the beauty of the thing . . .

I heard a sound. It would be Dad, Dworkin, Fiona, coming. I had
to do something before they reached me. I had to walk it, in a
moment . . .

I pulled my gaze away from the Pattern and glanced back toward
the cavemouth. They had emerged, come partway down the slope
and halted. Why? Why had they stopped?

What did it matter? I had the time I needed in which to begin. I
began to raise my foot, to step forward.

I could barely move. I inched my foot ahead with a great effort of
will. Taking this first step was proving worse than walking the Pattern
itself, near to the end. But it did not seem so much an external
resistance I fought against as it did the sluggishness of my own body.
It was almost as if—

Then I had me an image of Benedict beside the Pattern in Tir-na
Nog'th, Brand approaching, mocking, the Jewel burning upon his
breast.

Before I looked down, I knew what I would see.

The red stone was pulsing in time with my heartbeat.

Damn them!

Either Dad or Dworkin – or both of them – reached through it at this instant, paralyzing me. I did not doubt that either of them could manage it alone. Still, at this distance, it was not worth surrendering without a fight.

I continued to push forward with my foot, sliding it slowly ahead toward the edge of the Pattern. Once I made it, I did not see how they . . .

Drowsing . . . I felt myself beginning to fall. I had been asleep for a moment. It happened again.

When I opened my eyes, I could see a portion of the Pattern. When I turned my head, I saw feet. When I looked up, I saw Dad holding the Jewel.

'Go away,' he said to Dworkin and Fiona, without turning his head toward them.

They withdrew as he placed the Jewel about his own neck. He leaned forward then and extended his hand. I took it and he drew me to my feet.

'That was a damfool thing to do,' he said.

'I almost made it.

He nodded.

'Of course, you would have killed yourself and not accomplished anything,' he said. 'But it was well done nevertheless. Come on, let's walk.'

He took my aim, and we began to move about the periphery of the Pattern.

I watched that strange sky-sea, horizonless about us, as we went. I wondered what would have happened had I been able to begin the Pattern, what would be happening at that moment.

'You have changed,' he finally said, 'or else I never really knew you.'

I shrugged.

'Something of both perhaps. I was about to say the same of you. Tell me something?'

'What?'

'How difficult was it for you, being Ganelon?'

He chuckled.

'Not hard at all,' he said. 'You may have had a glimpse of the real me.'

'I liked him. Or rather, you being him. I wonder whatever became of the real Ganelon?'

'Long dead, Corwin. I met him after you had exiled him from Avalon, long ago. He wasn't a bad chap. Wouldn't have trusted him worth a damn, but then I never trust anyone I don't have to.'

'It runs in the family.'

'I regretted having to kill him. Not that he gave me much choice. All this was very long ago, but I remembered him clearly, so he must have impressed me.'

'And Lorraine?'

'The country? A good job, I thought. I worked the proper shadow. It grew in strength by my very presence, as any will if one of us stays around for long – as with you in Avalon, and later that other place. And I saw that I had a long while there by exercising my will upon its time-stream.'

'I did not know that could be done.'

'You grow in strength slowly, beginning with your initiation into the Pattern. There are many things you have yet to learn. Yes, I strengthened Lorraine, and made it especially vulnerable to the growing force of the black road. I saw that it would lie in your path, no matter where you went. After your escape, all roads led to Lorraine.'

'Why?'

'It was a trap I had set for you, and maybe a test. I wanted to be with you when you met the forces of Chaos. I also wanted to travel with you for a time.'

'A test? What were you testing me for? And why travel with me?'

'Can you not guess? I have watched all of you over the years. I never named a successor. I purposely left the matter muddled. You are all enough like me for me to know that the moment I declared for one of you I would be signing his or her death warrant No. I intentionally left things as they were until the very end. Now, though, I have decided. It is to be you.'

'You communicated with me, as yourself, briefly, back in Lorraine. You told me then to take the throne. If you had made up your mind at that point why did you continue the masquerade?'

'But I had not decided then. That was merely a means to assure your continuing. I feared you might come to like that girl too much, and that land. When you emerged a hero from the Black Circle you might have decided to settle and stay there. I wanted to plant the notions that would cause you to continue your journey.'

I was silent for a long while. We had moved a good distance about the Pattern.

Then, 'There is something that I have to know,' I said. 'Before I came here I was speaking with Dara, who is in the process of trying to clear her name with us—'

'It *is* clear,' he said. 'I have cleared it.'

I shook my head.

'I refrained from accusing her of something I have been thinking about for some time. There is a very good reason why I feel she cannot be trusted, despite her protests and your endorsement Two reasons, in fact.'

'I know, Corwin. But she did not kill Benedict's servants to manage her position at his house. I did it myself, to assure her getting to you as she did, at just the appropriate time.'

'You? You were party to her whole plot? Why?'

'She will make you a good queen, son. I trust the blood of Chaos for strength. It was time for a fresh infusion. You will take the throne already provided with an heir. By the time he is ready for it, Merlin will long have been weaned from his upbringing.'

We had come all the way around to the place of the black smear. I stopped. I squatted and studied it.

'You think this thing is going to kill you?' I finally asked.

'I know that it is.'

'You are not above murdering innocent people to manipulate me. Yet you would sacrifice your life for the kingdom.'

I looked up at him.

'My own hands are not clean,' I said, 'and I certainly do not presume to judge you. A while back, though, when I made ready to try the Pattern, I thought how my feelings had changed – toward Eric, toward the throne. You do what you do, I believe, as a duty. I, too, feel a duty now, toward Amber, toward the throne. More than that, actually. Much more, I realized, just then. But I realized something else, also, something that duty does not require of me. I do not know when or how it stopped and I changed, but I do not want the throne, Dad. I am sorry it messes up your plans, but I do not want to be king of Amber. I am sorry.'

I looked away then, back down at the smear. I heard him sigh.

Then, 'I am going to send you home now,' he said. 'Saddle your horse and take provisions. Ride to a place outside Amber – any place, fairly isolated.'

'My tomb?'

He snorted and chuckled faintly.

'That will do. Go there and wait my pleasure. I have some thinking to do.'

I stood. He reached out and placed his right hand on my shoulder. The Jewel was pulsing. He looked into my eyes.

'No man can have everything he wants the way that he wants it,' he said.

And there was a distancing effect, as of the power of a Trump, only working in reverse. I heard voices, then about me I saw me room I had earlier departed. Benedict, Gérard, Random and Dara were still there. I felt Dad release my shoulder. Then he was gone and I was among them once again.

'What is the story?' Random said. 'We saw Dad sending you back. By the way, how did he do that?'

'I do not know,' I said. 'But he confirms what Dara has told us. He gave her the signet and the message.'

'Why?' Gérard asked.

'He wanted us to learn to trust her,' I said.

Benedict rose to his feet 'Then I will go and do as I have been bid.'

'He wants you to attack, then fall back,' Dara said. 'After that, it will only be necessary to contain them.'

'For how long?'

'He said only that this will become apparent.'

Benedict gave one of his rare smiles and nodded. He managed his card case with his one hand, removed the deck, thumbed out the special Trump I had given him for the Courts.

'Good luck,' Random said.

'Yes,' Gérard agreed.

I added my wishes and watched him fade. When his rainbow afterimage had vanished I looked away and noticed that Dara was crying silently. I did not remark on it.

'I, too, have orders now – of a sort,' I said. 'I had best be moving.'

'And I will get back to the sea,' said Gérard.

'No,' I heard Dara say as I was moving toward the door.

I halted.

'You are to remain here, Gérard, and see to the safety of Amber herself. No attack will come by sea.'

'But I thought Random was in charge of the local defense.'

She shook her head.

'Random is to join Julian in Arden.'

'Are you sure?' Random asked.

'I am certain.'

'Good,' he said. 'It is nice to know he at least thought of me. Sorry, Gérard. That's the breaks.'

Gérard simply looked puzzled. 'I hope he knows what he is doing,' he said.

'We have been through that already,' I told him. 'Good-bye.'

I heard a footfall as I left the room. Dara was beside me.

'What now?' I asked her.

'I thought I would walk with you, wherever you are going.'

'I am just going up the hill to get some supplies. Then I am heading for the stables.'

'I will go with you.'

'I am riding alone.'

'I could not accompany you, anyway. I still have to speak with your sisters.'

'They're included, huh?'

'Yes.'

We walked in silence for a time, then she said, 'The whole business was not so cold-blooded as it seemed, Corwin.'

We entered the supply room.

'What business?'

'You know what I mean.'

'Oh. That. Well, good.'

'I like you. It could be more than that one day, if you feel anything.'

My pride handed me a snappy reply, but I bit it back. One learns a few things over the centuries. She had used me, true, but then it seemed she had not been entirely a free agent at the time. The worst that might be said, I suppose, was that Dad wanted me to want her. But I did not let my resentment on this interfere with what my own feelings really were, or could become.

So, 'I like you, too,' I said, and I looked at her. She seemed as if she needed to be kissed just then, so I did. 'I had better get ready now.'

She smiled and squeezed my arm. Then she was gone. I decided not to examine my feelings just then. I got some things together.

I saddled Star and rode back up over the crest of Kolvir until I came to my tomb. Seated outside it, I smoked my pipe and watched the clouds. I felt I had had a very full day, and it was still early afternoon. Premonitions played tag in the grottoes of my mind, none of which I would have cared to take to lunch.

3

Contact came suddenly as I sat drowsing. I was on my feet in an instant. It was Dad.

'Corwin, I have made my decisions and the time has come,' he said. 'Bare your left arm.'

I did this, as his form continued to grow in substantiality, looking more and more regal the while, a strange sadness on his face, of a sort I had never seen there before.

He took hold of my arm with his left hand and drew his dagger with his right.

I watched as he cut my arm, then resheathed his blade. The blood came forth, and he cupped his left hand and caught it. He released my arm, covered his left hand with his right and drew away from me. Raising his hands to his face, he blew his breath into them and drew them quickly apart.

A crested red bird the size of a raven, its feathers all the color of my blood, stood on his hand, moved to his wrist, looked at me. Even its eyes were red, and there was a look of familiarity as it cocked its head and regarded me.

'He is Corwin, the one you must follow,' he told the bird. 'Remember him.'

Then he transferred it to his left shoulder, from whence it continued to stare at me, making no effort to depart.

'You must go now, Corwin,' he said, 'quickly. Mount your horse and ride south, passing into Shadow as soon as you can. Hellride. Get as far away from here as possible.'

'Where am I going, Father?' I asked him.

'To the Courts of Chaos. You know the way?'

'In theory. I have never ridden the distance.'

He nodded slowly.

'Then get moving,' he said. 'I want you to create as great a time differential as you can between this place and yourself.'

'All right,' I said, 'but I do not understand.'

'You will, when the time comes.'

'But there is an easier way,' I protested. 'I can get there faster and with a lot less bother simply by getting in touch with Benedict with his Trump and having him take me through.'

'No good,' Dad said. 'It will be necessary for you to take the longer route because you will be carrying something which will be conveyed to you along the way.'

'Conveyed? How?'

He reached up and stroked the red bird's feathers.

'By your friend here. He could not fly all the way to the Courts – not in time, that is.'

'What will he bring me?'

'The Jewel. I doubt that I will be able to effect the transfer myself when I have finished what I have to do with it. Its powers may be of some benefit to us in that place.'

'I see,' I said. 'But I still need not ride the entire distance. I can Trump through after I receive it.'

'I fear not. Once I have done what must be done here, the Trumps will all become inoperative for a period of time.'

'Why?'

'Because the entire fabric of existence will be undergoing an alteration. Move now, damn it! Get on your horse and ride!'

I stood and stared a moment longer.

'Father, is there no other way?'

He simply shook his head and raised his hand. He began to fade.

'Good-bye.'

I turned and mounted. There was more to say, but it was too late. I turned Star toward the trail that would take me southward.

While Dad was able to play with the stuff of Shadow atop Kolvir, I had never been able to. I required a greater distance from Amber in order to work the shifts.

Still, knowing that it could be done, I felt that I ought to try. So, working my way southward across bare stone and down rocky passes where the wind howled, I sought to warp the fabric or being about me as I headed toward the trail that led to Garnath.

. . . A small clump of blue Sowers as I rounded a stony shoulder.

I grew excited at this, for they were a modest part of my working. I continued to lay my will upon the world to come beyond each twisting of my way.

A shadow from a triangular stone, across my path . . . A shifting of the wind . . .

Some of the smaller ones were indeed working. A backward twist to the trail . . . A crevice . . . An ancient bird's nest, high on a rocky shelf . . . More of the blue flowers . . .

Why not? A tree . . . Another . . .

I felt the power moving within me I worked more changes.

A thought came to me then, concerning my newfound strength. It seemed possible that it might have been purely psychological reasons which had barred me from performing such manipulations earlier. Until very recently I had considered Amber herself the single, immutable reality from which all shadows took their form. Now I realized she was but first among shadows, and that the place where my father stood represented the higher reality. Therefore, while the proximity made it difficult it did not make it impossible to effect changes in this place. Yet, under other circumstances I would have saved my strength until I had reached a point where it was easier to shift things about.

Now, now though, the need for haste lay upon me. I would have to exert myself, to rush, to do my father's bidding.

By the time I reached the trail leading down the southern face of Kolvir, the character of the land had already changed. I looked upon a series of gentle slopes, rather than the steep descent which normally marked the way. I was already entering the shadowlands.

The black road still lay like a dark scar to my left as I headed downward, but this Garnath through which it had been cut was in slightly better shape than that which I knew so well. Its lines were softer, from flocks of greenery which lay somewhat nearer the dead swath. It was as though my curse upon the land were slightly mitigated. Illusion of feeling, of course, for this was no longer exactly my Amber. But, *I am sorry for my part in this*, I addressed everything mentally, half-prayerlike. *I ride now to try to undo it. Forgive me, oh spirit of this place.* My eyes moved in the direction of the Grove of the Unicorn, but it was too far to the west masked by too many trees, for me even to glimpse that sacred glade.

The slope grew more level as I descended, becoming a series of gentle foothills. I let Star move faster as we crossed them, bearing to the southwest, then finally the south. Lower, lower. At a great distance to my left the sea sparkled and shone. Soon the black road would come between us, for I was descending into Garnath in its direction. No matter what I did with Shadow, I would not be able to erase that ominous presence. In fact, the fastest course I could follow would be one that paralleled it.

We came at last to the floor of the valley. The Forest of Arden towered far to my right, sweeping westward, immense and venerable. I rode on, working what changes I could to bear me even farther from my home.

While keeping the black road on hand, I stayed a good distance from it I had to, since it was the one thing I could not change. I kept shrubs, trees and low hills between us.

I reached out then, and the texture of the land changed.

Veins of agate . . . Heaps of schist . . . A darkening of the greenery . . .

Clouds swimming across the sky . . . The sun shimmering and dancing . . .

We increased our pace. The land sank lower still. Shadows lengthened, merged. The forest retreated. A rocky wall grew to my right, another to my left . . . A cold wind pursued me down a rough canyon. Strata streaks – red, gold, yellow and brown – flashed by. The floor of the canyon grew sandy. Dust devils spun about us. I leaned farther forward as the way began to rise once again. The walls slanted inward, grew closer together.

The way narrowed, narrowed. I could almost touch either wall . . .

Their tops came together. I rode through a shadowy runnel, slowing as it darkened . . . Phosphorescent designs burst into being. The wind made a moaning noise.

Out then!

The light from the walls was blinding, and giant crystals rose all about us. We plunged past, following an upward trail that led away from this region and through a series of mossy dells where small, perfectly circular pools lay still as green glass.

Tall ferns appeared before us and we made our way among them. I heard a distant trumpeting noise.

Turning, pacing . . . Red now the ferns, wider and lower . . . Beyond, a great plain, pinking into evening . . .

Forward, over pale grasses . . . The smell of fresh earth . . . Mountains or dark clouds far ahead . . . A rush of stars from my left . . . A quick spray of moisture . . . A blue moon leaps into the sky . . . Flickerings among the dark masses . . . Memories and a rumbling noise . . . Stormsmell and rushing air . . .

A strong wind . . . Clouds across the stars . . . A bright fork spearing a shattered tree to my right, turning it to flame . . . A tingling sensation . . . The small of ozone . . . Sheets of water upon me . . . A row of lights to my left . . .

Clattering down a cobbled street . . . A strange vehicle approaching . . . Cylindrical, chugging . . . We avoid one another . . . A shout pursues me . . . Through a lighted window the face of a child . . .

Clattering . . . Splashing . . . Storefronts and homes . . . The rain lets up, dies down, is gone . . . A fog blows by, lingers, deepens, is pearled by a growing light to my left . . .

The terrain softens, grows red . . . The light within the mist brightens . . . A new wind, from behind, a growing warmth . . . The air breaks apart . . .

Sky of pale lemon . . . Orange sun rushing toward noon . . .

A shudder! A thing not of my doing, totally unanticipated . . . The ground moves beneath us, but there is more to it than that. The new sky, the new sun, the rusty desert I have just now entered – all of them expand and contract, fade and return. There comes a cracking sound, and with each fading I find Star and myself alone, amid a white nothingness – characters without a setting. We tread upon nothing. The light comes from everywhere and illuminates only ourselves. A steady cracking noise, as of the spring thaw come upon a Russian river I had once ridden beside, fills my ears. Star, who has paced many shadows, emits a frightened sound.

I look all about me. Blurred outlines appear, sharpen, grow clear. My environment is restored, though with a somewhat washed-out look to it. A bit of the pigment has been drained from the world.

We wheel to the left, racing for a low hill, mounting it, halting finally at its summit.

The black road. It too seems denatured – but even more so than the rest. It ripples beneath my gaze, almost seems to undulate as I watch. The cracking noise continues, grows louder . . .

A wind comes out of the north, gentle at first but increasing in force. Looking in that direction, I see a mass of dark clouds building.

I know that I must move as I have never moved before. Ultimates of destruction and creation are occurring at the place I visited – when? No matter. The waves mow outward from Amber and this, too, may pass away – and me along with it. If Dad cannot put it all back together again.

I shake the reins. We race southward.

A plain . . . Trees . . . Some broken buildings . . . Faster . . .

The smoke of a forest afire . . . A wall of flame . . . Gone . . .

Yellow sky, blue clouds . . . An armada of dirigibles crossing . . .

Faster . . .

The sun drops like a piece of hot iron into a bucket of water, stars become streaks . . . A pale light upon a straight trail . . . Sounds dopplered from dark smears, the wailing . . . Brighter the light, fainter the prospect . . . Gray, to my right, my left . . . Brighter now . . . Nothing but the trail my eyes to ride . . . The wailing heightens to a shriek . . . Forms run together . . . We race through a tunnel of Shadow . . . It begins to revolve . . .

Turning, turning . . . Only the road is real . . . The worlds go by . . . I have released my control of the sets and ride now the thrust of the power itself, aimed only to remove me from Amber and hurl me toward Chaos . . . There is wind upon me and the cry in my ears . . . Never before have I pushed my power over Shadow to its limit . . . The tunnel grows as slick and seamless as glass . . . I feel I am riding down a vortex, a maelstrom, the heart of a tornado . . . Star and I are drenched with sweat . . . There is a wild feeling of flight upon me, as though I am pursued . . . The road is become an abstraction . . . My eyes sting as I try to blink away the perspiration . . . I cannot hold this ride much longer . . . There comes a throbbing at the base of my skull . . .

I draw back gently upon the reins and Star begins to slow . . .

The walls of my tunnel of light grow grainy . . . Blotches of gray,

black, white, rather than a uniformity of shading . . . Brown . . . A
hint of blue . . . Green . . . The wailing descends to a hum, a rumble,
fading . . . Gentler the wind . . . Shapes come and go . . .

Slowing, slowing . . .

There is no path. I ride on mossy earth. The sky is blue, the clouds
are white. I am very light-headed. I draw rein. I—

Tiny.

I was shocked as I lowered my eyes. I stood at the outskirts of a toy
village. Houses I could hold in the palm of my hand, miniscule loads,
tiny vehicles crawling along them . . .

I looked back. We had crushed a number of these diminutive
residences. I looked all around. There were fewer to the left I guided
Star carefully in that direction, kept moving until we had left that
place. I felt bad about it – whatever it was – whoever dwelled there.
But there was not a thing that I could do.

I moved again, passing through Shadow, until I came to what
seemed a deserted quarry beneath a greenish sky. I felt heavier here. I
dismounted, took a drink of water, walked around a bit.

I breathed deeply of the damp air that engulfed me. I was far from
Amber now, about as far as one ever need go, and well on my way
to Chaos. I had seldom come this far before. While I had chosen
this place for a rest stop because it represented the nearest thing to
normalcy I could catch hold of, the changes would soon be getting
more and more radical.

I was stretching my cramped muscles when I heard the shriek, high
in the air above me.

I looked up and saw the dark form descending, Grayswandir
coming by reflex into my hand. But the light caught it at a proper
angle as it came down, and the winged form took fire on its way.

My familiar bird circled, circled, descended to my outstretched
arm. Those frightening eyes regarded me with a peculiar intelligence,
but I did not spare them the attention I might have on another
occasion. Instead, I sheathed Grayswandir and reached for the thing
the bird bore.

The Jewel of Judgment.

I knew by this that Dad's effort, whatever it had amounted to, was
finished. The Pattern had either been repaired or botched. He was
either alive or dead. Choose a couple from either column. The effects

of his act would be spreading outward from Amber through Shadow now, like the ripples in the proverbial pond. I would learn more of them soon enough. In the meantime, I had my orders.

I drew the chain over my head and let the Jewel fall upon my breast I remounted Star. My bloodbird emitted a short cry and rose into the air.

We moved again.

. . . Over a landscape where the sky whitened as the ground darkened. Then the land flared and the sky grew black. Then the reverse. And again . . . With each stride the effect shifted, and as we moved faster it built to a stroboscopic series of still-shots about us, gradually growing to a jerky animation, then the hyperactive quality of a silent film. Finally, all was a blur.

Points of light flashed past, like meteors or comets. I began to feel a throbbing sensation, as of a cosmic heartbeat. Everything began to turn about me, as though I had been caught up in a whirlwind.

Something was going wrong. I seemed to be losing control. Could it be that the effects of Dad's doings had already reached the area of Shadow through which I passed? It seemed hardly likely. Still . . .

Star stumbled. I clung tightly as we went down, not wishing to be separated in Shadow. I struck my shoulder on a hard surface and lay there for a moment, stunned.

When the world came together about me again, I sat up and looked around.

A uniform twilight prevailed, but there were no stars. Instead, large rocks of various shapes and sizes drifted and hovered in the air. I got to my feet and looked all about.

It was possible, from what I could see of it, that the irregular stony surface on which I stood was itself but a mountain-sized boulder drifting with the others. Star rose and stood shivering at my side. An absolute silence contained us. The still air was cool. There was not another living thing in sight I did not like his place. I would not have halted here of my own volition. I knelt to inspect Star's legs. I wanted to leave as soon as possible, preferably mounted.

As I was about this, I heard a soft chuckle which might have come from a human throat.

I paused, resting my hand upon Grayswandir's hilt and seeking the source of the sound.

Nothing. Nowhere.

Yet I had heard it. I turned slowly, looking in every direction. No . . .

Then it came again. Only his time, I realized that it had its source overhead.

I scanned the floating rocks. Shadow-draped, it was difficult to distinguish—

There!

Ten meters above the ground and thirty or so to my left, what appeared to be a human form stood atop a small island in the sky, regarding me. I considered it. Whatever it was, it seemed too far off to pose a threat I was certain that I could be gone before it could reach me. I moved to mount Star.

'No good, Corwin,' called the voice I least wanted to hear just then. 'You are locked here. There is no way you can depart without my leave.'

I smiled as I mounted, then drew Grayswandir.

'Let's find out,' I said. 'Come bar my way.'

'Very well,' he replied, and flames sprang from the bare rock, towering full circle about me, licking, sprawling, soundless.

Star went wild. I slammed Grayswandir back into the scabbard, whipped a corner of my cloak across Star's eyes, spoke soothing words. As I did this, the circle enlarged, the fires receding toward the edges of the great rock on which we stood.

'Convinced?' came the voice. 'This place is too small. Ride in any direction. Your mount will panic again before you can shift into Shadow.'

'Good-bye, Brand,' I said, and I began to ride.

I rode in a large counterclockwise circle about the rocky surface, shielding Star's right eye from the flames about the periphery of things. I heard Brand chuckle again, not realizing what I was doing.

A pair of large rocks . . . Good. I rode on by, continuing the course. Now a jagged hedge of stone to my left, a rise, a dip . . . A mess of shadow the fires cast, across my path . . . There. Down . . . Up. A touch of green to that patch of light . . . I could feel the shifting begin.

The fact that it is easier for us to take a straight course does not make it the only way. We all pursue it so much of the time, though, that we tend to forget that one can also make progress by going around in circles . . .

I could feel the shift more strongly as I neared the two large rocks again. Brand caught on about then, also.

'Hold it, Corwin!'

I threw him a finger and cut between the rocks, heading down into a narrow canyon speckled with points of yellow light. According to specifications.

I drew my cloak away from Star's head and shook the reins. The canyon cut abruptly to the right. We followed it into a better-lighted avenue which widened and brightened as we went.

. . . Beneath a jutting overhang, sky of milk shading to pearl on its other side.

Riding deeper, faster, farther . . . A jagged cliff crowned the upper talus to my left, greening in twisted sign of shrubbery beneath a pink-touched sky.

I rode until the greenery was bluery beneath a yellow sky, till the canyon rose to meet a lavender plain where orange rocks rolled as the ground was shaken beneath us in time with our hoofbeats. I crossed there under wheeling comets, coming to the shore of a blood-red sea in a place of heavy perfumes. I rode a large green sun and a small bronze one out of the sky as I paced that shore, while skeletal navies clashed and serpents of the deep circled their orange and blue-sailed vessels. The Jewel pulsed upon me and I drew strength from it. A wild wind came up and lofted us through a copper-clouded sky above a wailing chasm which seemed to extend forever, black-bottomed, spark-shot, fuming with heady scents . . .

At my back, the sound of thunder, ceaseless . . . Fine lines, like the craqueleur of an old painting, abreast of us, advancing, every-where . . . Cold, a fragrance-killing wind pursues . . .

Lines . . . The cracks widen, blackness flows to fill . . . Dark streaks race by, up, down, back upon themselves . . . The settling of a net, the labors of a giant, invisible spider, world-trapping . . .

Down, down and down . . . The ground again, wrinkled and leathery as a mummy's neck . . . Soundless, our throbbing passage . . . Softer the thunder, falling the wind . . . Dad's last gasp? Speed now and away . . .

A narrowing of lines, to the fineness of an etching, fading then in the three suns' heat . . . And faster yet . . .

A rider, approaching . . . Hand to hilt in time to my own . . . Me. Myself coming back? Simultaneous, our salutes . . . Through one another, somehow, the air like a sheet of water that one dry instant. What Carroll mirror, what Remba, Tir-na Nog'th effect . . . Yet far, far to my left, a black thing writhing . . . We pace the road . . . It leads me on . . .

White sky, white ground and no horizon . . . Sunless and cloudless the prospect . . . Only that thread of black, far off, and gleaming pyramids everywhere, massive, disconcerting . . .

We tire. I do not like this place . . . But we have outrun whatever process pursues. Draw rein.

I was tired, but I felt a strange vitality within me. It seemed as though it arose from within my breast . . . The Jewel. Of course. I made an effort to draw upon this power again. I felt it flow outward through my limbs, barely halting at my extremities. It was almost as if—

Yes. I reached out and lay my will upon my blank and geometrical surroundings. They began to alter.

It was a movement. The pyramids shuffled by, darkening as they passed. The world turned upside down and I stood as on the underside of a cloud, watching landscapes flash by beneath/above.

Light streamed upward past me, from a golden sun beneath my feet. This, too, passed, and the fleecy ground darkened, firing waters upward to erode the passing land. Lightnings jumped up to strike the world overhead, to break it apart. In places it shattered and its pieces fell about me.

They began to swirl as a wave of darkness passed.

When the light came again, bluish this time, it held no point source and described no land.

. . . Golden bridges cross the void in great streamers, one of them flashing beneath us even now. We wind along its course, standing the while still as a statue . . . For an age, perhaps, this goes on. A phenomenon not unrelated to highway hypnosis enters through my eyes, lulls me dangerously.

I do what I can to accelerate our passage. Another age goes by.

Finally, far ahead, a dusky, misty blotch, our terminus, growing very slowly despite our velocity.

By the time we reach it, it is gigantic – an island in the void, forested over with golden, metallic trees . . .

I stop the motion which has borne us thus far and we move forward under our own power, entering that wood. Grass like aluminum foil crunches beneath us as we pass among those trees. Strange fruit, pale and shiny, hangs about me. There are no animal sounds immediately apparent. Working our way inward, we come to a small clearing through which a quicksilver stream flows. There, I dismount.

'Brother Corwin,' comes that voice again. 'I have been waiting for you.'

4

I faced the wood, watched him emerge from it. I did not draw my weapon, as he had not drawn his. I reached down into the Jewel with my mind, though. After the excercise I had just completed, I realized that I could do a lot more than control weather with it. Whatever Brand's power, I felt I'd a weapon now with which to confront it directly. The Jewel pulsed more deeply as I did this.

'Truce,' Brand said. 'Okay? May we talk?'

'I do not see that we have anything more to say to one another,' I told him.

'If you do not give me a chance you will never know for certain, will you?'

He came to a halt about seven meters away, flung his green cloak back over his left shoulder and smiled.

'All right. Say it, whatever it is,' I said.

'I tried to stop you,' he said, 'back there, for the Jewel. It is obvious that you know what it is now, that you realize how important it is.'

I said nothing.

'Dad has already used it,' he continued, 'and I am sorry to report that he has failed in what he set out to do with it.'

'What? How could you know?'

'I can see through Shadow, Corwin. I would have thought our sister had filled you in more thoroughly on these matters. With a little mental effort, I can perceive whatever I choose now. Naturally, I was concerned with the outcome of this affair. So I watched. He is dead, Corwin. The effort was too much for him. He lost control of the forces he was manipulating and was blasted by them a little over halfway through the Pattern.'

'You lie!' I said, touching the Jewel.

He shook his head.

'I admit that I am not above lying to gain my ends, but this time I am telling the truth. Dad is dead. I saw him fall. The bird brought you the Jewel then, as he had willed it. We are left in a universe without a Pattern.'

I did not want to believe him. But it was possible that Dad had failed. I had the assurance of the only expert in the business, Dworkin, as to the difficulty of the task.

'Granting for the moment what you have said, what happens next?' I asked.

'Things fall apart,' he replied. 'Even now, Chaos wells up to fill the vacuum back at Amber. A great vortex has come into being, and it grows. It spreads ever outward, destroying the shadow worlds, and it will not stop until it meets with the Courts of Chaos, bringing all of creation full circle, with Chaos once more to reign over all.'

I felt dazed. Had I struggled from Greenwood, through everything, to here, to have it end this way? Would I see everything stripped of meaning, form, content, life, when things had been pushed to a kind of completion?

'No!' I said. 'It cannot be so.'

'Unless . . .' Brand said softly.

'Unless what?'

'Unless a new Pattern is inscribed, a new order created to preserve form.'

'You mean ride back into that mess and try to complete the job? You just said that the place no longer exists.'

'No. Of course not. The location is unimportant. Wherever there is a Pattern there is a center. I can do it right here.'

'You think that you can succeed where Dad failed?'

'I have to try. I am the only one who knows enough about it and has sufficient time before the waves of Chaos arrive. Listen, I admit to everything Fiona has doubtless told you about me, I have schemed and I have acted. I have dealt with the enemies of Amber. I have shed our blood. I tried to burn out your memory. But the world as we know it is being destroyed now, and I live here too. All of my plans – everything! – will come to nothing if some measure of order is not preserved. Perhaps I have been duped by the Lords of Chaos. It is difficult for me to admit that, but I see the possibility now. It is not too late to foil them, though. We can build the new bastion of order right here.'

'How?'

'I need the Jewel – and your assistance. This will be the site of the new Amber.'

'Supposing – *arguendo* – I give it to you. Would the new Pattern be exactly like the old one?'

He shook his head.

'It could not be, any more than the one Dad was attempting to create would have been like Dworkin's. No two authors can render the same story in the same fashion. Individual stylistic differences cannot be avoided. No matter how hard I might try to duplicate it, my version would be slightly different.'

'How could you do this,' I asked, 'when you are not fully attuned to the Jewel? You would need a Pattern to complete the process of attunement – and, as you say, the Pattern has been destroyed. What gives?'

Then, 'I said that I would need your help,' he stated. 'There is another way to attune a person to the Jewel. It requires the assistance of someone who is already attuned. You would have to project yourself through the Jewel once more, and take me with you – into and through the primary Pattern that lies beyond.'

'And then?'

'Why, when the ordeal is past I will be attuned, you give me the Jewel, I inscribe a new Pattern and we are back in business. Things hold together. Life goes on.'

'What of Chaos?'

'The new Pattern will be unmarred. They will no longer have the road giving them access to Amber.'

'With Dad dead, how would the new Amber be run?'

He smiled crookedly.

'I ought to have something for my pains, oughtn't I? I will be risking my life with this, and the odds are not all that good.'

I smiled back at him.

'Considering the payoff, what is to prevent me from taking the gamble myself?' I said.

'The same thing that prevented Dad from succeeding – all the forces of Chaos. They are summoned by a kind of cosmic reflex when such an act is begun. I have had more experience with them than you. You would not have a chance. I might.'

'Now let us say that you are lying to me, Brand. Or let us be kind and say that you did not see clearly through all the turmoil. Supposing Dad did succeed? Supposing there is a new Pattern in existence right now? What would happen if you were to do another, here, now?'

'I . . . It has never been done before. How should I know?'

'I wonder?' I said. 'Might you still get your own version of reality that way? Might it represent the splitting off of a new universe – Amber and Shadow – just for you? Might it negate ours? Or would it simply stand apart? Or would there be some overlapping? What do you think, given that situation?' He shrugged his shoulders.

'I have already answered that. It has never been done before. How should I know?'

'But I think that you do know, or can make a very good guess at it. I think that that is what you are planning, that that is what you want to try – because that is all you have left now. I take this action on your part as an indication that Dad has succeeded and that you are down to your last card. But you need me and you need the Jewel for it. You cannot have either.'

He sighed.

'I had expected more of you. But all right. You are wrong, but leave it at that. Listen, though. Rather than see everything lost, I will split the realm with you.'

'Brand,' I said, 'get lost. You cannot have the Jewel, or my help. I have heard you out, and I think that you are lying.'

'You are afraid,' he said, 'afraid of me. I do not blame you for not wanting to trust me. But you are making a mistake. You need me now.'

'Nevertheless, I have made my choice.'

He took a step toward me. Another . . .

'Anything you want, Corwin. I can give you anything you care to name.'

'I was with Benedict in Tir-na Nog'th,' I said, 'looking through his eyes, listening with his ears, when you made him the same offer. Shove it, Brand. I am going on with my mission. If you think that you can stop me, now is as good a time as any.'

I began walking toward him. I knew that I would kill him if I reached him. I also felt that I would not reach him.

He halted. He took a step backward.

'You are making a big mistake,' he said.

'I do not think so. I think that I am doing exactly the right thing.'

'I will not fight with you,' he said hastily. 'Not here, not above the abyss. You have had your chance, though. The next time that we meet, I will have to take the Jewel from you.'

'What good will it be to you, unattuned?'

'There might still be a way for me to manage it – more difficult, but possible. You have had your chance. Goodbye.'

He retreated into the wood. I followed after, but he had vanished.

I left that place and rode on, along a road over nothing. I did not like to consider the possibility that Brand might have been telling the truth, or at least a part of it. But the things he had said kept returning to plague me. Supposing Dad had failed? Then I was on a fool's errand. Everything was already over, and it was just a matter of time. I did not like looking back, just in case something was gaining on me. I passed into a moderately paced hellride. I wanted to get to the others before the waves of Chaos reached that far, just to let them know that I had kept faith, to let them see that in the end I had tried my best I wondered then how the actual battle was going. Or had it even begun yet, within that time frame?

I swept along the bridge, which widened now beneath a brightening sky. As it assumed the aspect of a golden plain, I considered Brand's threat. Had he said what he had said simply to raise doubts, increase my discomfort and impair my efficiency? Possibly. Yet, if he required the Jewel he would have to ambush me. And I had a respect for that strange power he had acquired over Shadow. It seemed almost impossible to prepare for an attack by someone who could watch my every move and transport himself instantaneously to the most advantageous spot. How soon might it come? Not too soon, I guessed. First, he would want to frazzle my nerves – and I was already tired and more than a little punchy. I would have to rest, to sleep, sooner or later. It was impossible for me to go that great distance in a single stretch, no matter how accelerated the hellride.

Fogs of pink and orange and green fled past swirled about me, filling up the world. The ground rang beneath us like metal. Occasional musical tones, as of rung crystal occurred overhead. My thoughts danced. Memories of many worlds came and went in random fashion. Ganelon, my friend-enemy, and my father, enemy-friend, merged and parted, parted and merged. Somewhere one of them asked me who had a right to the throne. I had thought it was Ganelon, wanting to know our several justifications. Now I knew that it had been Dad, wanting to know my feelings. He had judged. He had made his decision. And I was backing out. Whether it was arrested development, the desire to be free of such an encumbrance, or a matter of sudden enlightenment based on all that I had experienced in recent years, growing slowly within me, granting me a more mature view of the onerous role of monarch apart from its moments of glory, I do not know. I remembered my life on the shadow Earth, following orders, giving them. Faces swam before me – people I had known over the centuries – friends, enemies, wives, lovers, relatives. Lorraine seemed to be beckoning me on, Moire laughing, Deirdre weeping. I fought again with Eric. I recalled my first passage through the Pattern, as a boy, and the later one when, step by step, my memory was given back to me. Murders, thieveries, knaveries, seductions returned because, as Mallory said, they were there. I was unable, even, to place them all correctly in terms of time. There was no great anxiety because there was no great guilt. Time, time, and more time had softened the edges of harsher things, had worked its changes on me. I saw my earlier selves as different people, acquaintances I had outgrown. I wondered how I could ever have been some of them. As I rushed onward, scenes from my past seemed to solidify in the mists about me. No poetic license here. Battles in which I had taken part assumed tangible form, save for a total absence of sound – the flare of weapons, the colors of uniforms, banners and blood. And people – most of them now long dead – moved from my memory into silent animation about me. None of these were members of my family, but all of them were people who had once meant something to me. Yet there was no special pattern to it. There were noble deeds as well as shameful; enemies as well as friends – and none of the persons involved took note of my passage; all were caught up in some long-past sequence of actions. I wondered then at the nature of the place through which I rode. Was it some watered-down version of Tir-na Nog'th, with some mind-sensitive substance in the vicinity that drew from me and projected about me this 'This Is Your life' panorama? Or was I simply beginning to hallucinate? I was tired, anxious, troubled, distressed, and I passed along a way which provided a monotonous, gentle stimulation of the senses of the sort leading to reverie . . . In fact, I realized that I had lost control over Shadow sometime back and was now simply proceeding in a linear fashion across this landscape, trapped in a kind of externalized narcissism by the spectacle . . . I realized then that I had to stop and rest – probably even sleep a little – though I feared doing so in this place. I would have to break free and make my way to a more sedate, deserted spot . . .

I wrenched at my surroundings. I twisted things about. I broke free.

Soon I was riding in a rough, mountainous area, and shortly thereafter I came to the cave that I desired.

We passed within, and I tended to Star. I ate and drank just enough to take the edge off my hunger. I built no fire. I wrapped myself in my cloak and in a blanket I had brought. I held Grayswandir in my right hand. I lay facing the darkness beyond the cavemouth.

I felt a little sick. I knew that Brand was a liar, but his words bothered me anyway.

But I had always been good at going to sleep. I closed my eyes and was gone.

5

I was awakened by a sense of presence. Or maybe it was a noise and a sense of presence. Whatever, I was awake and I was certain that I was not alone. I tightened my grip on Grayswandir and opened my eyes. Beyond that, I did not move.

A soft light, like moonlight, came in through the cave mouth. There was a figure, possibly human, standing just inside. The lighting was such that I could not tell whether it faced me or faced outward. But then it took a step toward me.

I was on my feet, the point of my blade toward its breast. It halted.

'Peace,' said a man's voice, in Thari. 'I have but taken refuge from the storm. May I share your cave?'

'What storm?' I asked.

As if in answer, there came a roll of thunder followed by a gust of wind with the smell of rain within it.

'Okay, that much is true,' I said. 'Make yourself comfortable.'

He sat down, well inside, his back against the right-hand wall of the cave. I folded my blanket for a pad and seated myself across from him. About four meters separated us. I located my pipe and filled it, then tried a match which had been with me from the shadow Earth. It lit, saving me a lot of trouble. The tobacco had a good smell, mixed with the damp breeze. I listened to the sounds of the rain and regarded the dark outline of my nameless companion. I thought over some possible dangers, but it had not been Brand's voice which had addressed me.

'This is no natural storm,' the other said.

'Oh? How so?'

'For one thing, it is coming out of the north. They never come out of the north, here, this time of year.'

'That's how records are made.'

'For another, I have never seen a storm behave this way. I have been watching it advance all day – just a steady line, moving slowly, front like a sheet of glass. So much lightning, it looks like a monstrous insect with hundreds of shiny legs. Most unnatural. And behind it, things have grown very distorted.'

'That happens in the rain.'

'Not that way. Everything seems to be changing its shape. Flowing. As if it is melting the world – or stamping away its forms.'

I shuddered. I had thought that I was far enough ahead of the dark waves that I could take a little rest. Still, he might be wrong, and it could just be an unusual storm. But I did not want to take the chance. I rose and turned to the rear of the cave. I whistled.

No response. I went back and groped around.

'Something the matter?'

'My horse is gone.'

'Could it have wandered off?'

'Must have. I'd have thought Star'd have better sense, though.'

I went to the cave mouth but could see nothing. I was half-drenched in the instant I was there. I returned to my position beside the left wall.

'It seems like an ordinary enough storm to me,' I said. 'They sometimes get pretty bad in the mountains.'

'Perhaps you know this country better than I do?'

'No, I am just traveling through – a thing I had better be continuing soon, too.'

I touched the Jewel. I reached into it, then through it, out and up, with my mind. I felt the storm about me and ordered it away, with red pulses of energy corresponding to my heartbeats. Then I leaned back, found another match and relit my pipe. It would still take a while for the forces I had manipulated to do their work, against a stormfront of this size.

'It will not last too long,' I said.

'How can you tell?'

'Privileged information.'

He chuckled.

'According to some versions, this is the way that the world ends – beginning with a strange storm from out of the north.'

'That's right,' I said, 'and this is it. Nothing to worry about, though. It will be all over, one way or the other, before too long.'

'That stone you are wearing . . . It is giving off light.'

'Yes.'

'You were joking about this being the end, though – were you not?'

'No.'

'You make me think of that line from the Holy Book – *The Archangel Corwin shall pass before the storm, lightning upon his breast* . . . You would not be named Corwin, would you?'

'How does the rest of it go?'

'. . . *When asked where he travels, he shall say, "To the ends of the Earth", where he goes not knowing what enemy will aid him against another enemy, nor whom the Horn will touch.*'

'That's all?'

'All there is about the Archangel Corwin.'

'I have run into this difficulty with Scripture in the past. It tells you enough to get interested, but never enough to be of any immediate use. It is as though the author gets his kicks by tantalizing. One enemy against another? The Horn? Beats me.'

'Where *do* you travel?'

'Not too far, unless I can find my horse.'

I returned to the cave mouth. It was letting up now, with a glow like a moon behind some clouds to the west, another to the east I looked both ways along the trail and down the slope to the valley. No horses anywhere in sight. I turned back to the cave. Just as I did, however, I heard Star's whinny far below me.

I called back to the stranger in the cave. 'I have to go. You can have the blanket.'

I do not know whether he replied, for I moved off into the drizzle then, picking my way down the slope. Again, I exerted myself through the Jewel, and the drizzle halted, to be replaced by a mist.

The rocks were slippery, but I made it halfway down without stumbling. I paused then, both to catch my breath and to get my bearings. From that point, I was not certain as to the exact direction from which Star's whinny had come. The moon's light was a little stronger, visibility a bit better, but I saw nothing as I studied the prospect before me. I listened for several minutes.

Then I heard the whinny once more – from below, to my left, near a dark boulder, cairn or rocky outcrop. There did seem to be some

705

sort of turmoil in the shadows at its base. Moving as quickly as I dared, I laid my course in that direction.

As I reached level ground and hurried toward the place of the action, I passed pockets of ground mist, stirred slightly by a breeze from out of the west, snaking silvery, about my ankles. I heard a grating, crunching sound, as of something heavy being pushed or rolled over a rocky surface. Then I caught sight of a gleam of light, low on the dark mass I was approaching.

Drawing nearer, I saw small, manlike forms outlined in a rectangle of light, struggling to move a great rocky slab. Faint echoes of a clattering sound and another whinny came from their direction. Then the stone began to move, swinging like the door that it probably was. The lighted area diminished, narrowed to a sliver, vanished with a boming sound, all of the struggling figures having first passed within.

When I finally reached that rocky mass all was silent once again. I pressed my ear to the stone, but heard nothing. But, whoever they were, they had taken my horse. I had never liked horse thieves, and I had killed my share in the past. And right now, I needed Star as I had seldom needed a horse. So I groped about, seeking the edges of that stony gate.

It was not too difficult to describe its outlines with my fingertips. I probably located it sooner than I would have by daylight, when everything would have blended and merged more readily to baffle the eye. Knowing its situation, I sought further then after some handhold by which I might draw it. They had seemed to be little guys, so I looked low.

I finally discovered what might have been the proper place and seized hold of it I pulled then, but it was stubborn. Either they were disproportionately strong or there was a trick to it that I was missing.

No matter. There is a time for subtlety and a time for brute force. I was both angry and in a hurry, so the decision was made.

I began to draw upon the slab once again, tightening the muscles in my arms, my shoulders, my back, wishing Gérard were nearby. The door creaked. I kept pulling. It moved slightly – an inch, perhaps – and stuck. I did not slacken, but increased my effort. It creaked again.

I leaned backward, shifted my weight and braced my left foot against the rocky wall at the side of the portal. I pushed with it as I drew back. There was more creaking and some grinding as it moved again – another inch or so. Then it stopped and I could not budge it.

I released my grip and stood, flexing my arms. Then I put my shoulder to it and pushed the door back to its fully closed position. I took a deep breath and seized it again.

I put my left foot back where it had been. No gradual pressure his time. I yanked and shoved simultaneously.

There was a snapping sound and a clattering from within, and the door came forward about half a foot, grinding as it moved. It seemed freer now, though, so I got to my feet, reversed my position – back to wall – and found sufficient purchase to push it outward.

It moved more easily this time, but I could not resist placing my foot against it as it began to swing and thrusting forward as hard as I could. It shot through a full hundred and eighty degrees, slammed back against the rock on the other side with a great booming noise, fractured in several places, swayed, fell and struck the ground with a crash that made it shudder, breaking off more fragments when it hit.

Grayswandir was back in my hand before it struck, and I had dropped into a crouch and stolen a quick look about the corner.

Light . . . There was illumination beyond . . . From little lamps depending from hooks along the wall . . . Beside the stairway . . . Going down . . . To a place of greater light and some sounds . . . Like music . . .

There was no one in sight. I would have thought that the godawful din I had raised would have caught someone's attention, but the music continued. Either the sound – somehow – had not carried, or they did not give a damn. Either way . . .

I rose and stepped over the threshold. My foot struck against a metal object I picked it up and examined it. A twisted bolt. They had barred the door after themselves. I tossed it back over my shoulder and started down the stair.

The music – fiddles and pipes – grew louder as I advanced. From the breaking of the light, I could see that there was some sort of hall off to my right, from the foot of the stair. They were small steps and there were a lot of them. I did not bother with stealth, but hurried down to the landing.

When I turned and looked into the hall, I beheld a scene out of some drunken Irishman's dream. In a smoky, torchlit hall, hordes of meter-high people, red-faced and green clad, were dancing to the music or quaffing what appeared to be mugs of ale while stamping their feet, slapping tabletops and each other, grinning, laughing and shouting. Huge kegs fined one wall, and a number of the revelers were queued up before the one which had been tapped. An enormous fire blazed in a pit at the far end of the room, its smoke being sucked back through a crevice in the rook wall, above a pair of cavemouths running anywhere. Star was tethered to a ring in the wall beside that pit, and a husky little man in a leather apron was grinding and honing some suspicions-looking instruments.

Several faces turned in my direction, there were shoots and suddenly the music stopped. The silence was almost complete.

I raised my blade to an overhand, épée en garde position, pointed across the room toward Star. All faces were turned in my direction by then.

'I have come for my horse,' I said. 'Either you bring him to me or I come and get him. There will be a lot more blood the second way.'

From off to my right, one of the men, larger and grayer than most of the others, cleared his throat.

'Begging your pardon,' he began, 'but how did you get in here?'

'You will be needing a new door,' I said. 'Go and look if you care to, if it makes any difference – and it may. I will wait.'

I stepped aside and put the wall to my back.

He nodded.

'I will do that.'

And he darted by.

I could feel my anger-born strength flowing into and back out of the Jewel. One part of me wanted to cut and slash and stab my way across the room, another wanted a more humane settlement with people so much smaller than myself; and a third and perhaps wiser part suggested that the little guys might not be such pushovers. So I waited to see how my door-opening feat impressed their spokesman.

Moments later, he returned, giving me wide berth.

'Bring the man his horse,' he said.

A sudden flurry of conversation occurred within the hall. I lowered my blade.

'My apologies,' said the one who had given the order. 'We desire no trouble with the like of you. We will be foraging elsewhere. No hard feelings, I hope?'

The man in the leather apron had untethered Star and started in my direction. The revelers drew back to make way as he led my mount through the hall.

I sighed.

'I will just call it a day and forgive and forget,' I said.

The little man seized a flagon from a nearby table and passed it to me. Seeing my expression, he sipped from it himself.

'Join us in a drink, then?'

'Why not?' I said, and I took it and quaffed it as he did the same with the second one.

He gave a gentle belch and grinned.

' 'Tis a mighty small draught for a man of your size,' he said then. 'Let me fetch you another, for the trail.'

It was a pleasant ale, and I was thirsty after my efforts.

'All right,' I said.

He called for more as Star was delivered to me.

'You can wrap the reins around this hook here,' he said, indicating a low projection near the doorway, 'and he will be safe out of the way.'

I nodded and did that as the butcher withdrew. No one was staring at me any longer. A pitcher of the brew arrived and the little man refilled our flagons from it. One of the fiddlers struck up a fresh tune. Moments later, another joined him.

'Sit a spell,' said my host, pushing a bench in my direction with his foot. 'Keep your back to the wall as you would. There will be no funny business.'

I did, and he rounded the table and seated himself across from me, the pitcher between us. It was good to sit for a few moments, to take my mind from my journey for just a little while, to drink the dark ale and listen to a lively tune.

'I will not be apologizing again,' said my companion, 'nor explaining either. We both know it was no misunderstanding. But you have got the right on your side, it is plain to see.' He grinned and winked. 'So I am for calling it a day, too. We will not starve. We will just not feast tonight. 'Tis a lovely jewel you are wearing. Tell me about it?'

'Just a stone,' I said.

The dancing resumed. The voices grew louder. I finished my drink and he refilled the flagon. The fire undulated. The night's cold went out of my bones.

'Cozy place you've got here,' I said.

'Oh, that it is. Served us for time out of mind, it has. Would you be liking the grand tour?'

'Thank you, no.'

'I did not think so, but 'twas my hostly duty to offer. You are welcome to join in the dancing, too, if you wish.'

I shook my head and laughed. The thought of my cavorting in this place brought me images out of Swift.

'Thanks anyway.'

He produced a clay pipe and proceeded to fill it. I cleaned my own and did the same. Somehow all danger seemed past. He was a genial enough little fellow, and the others seemed harmless now with their music and their stepping.

Yet . . . I knew the stories from another place, far, so far from here . . . To awaken in the morning, naked, in some field, all traces of this spot vanished . . . I knew, yet . . .

A few drinks seemed small peril. They were warming me now, and the keening of the pipes and the wailings of the fiddles were pleasant after the brain-numbing twistings of the hellride. I leaned back and puffed smoke. I watched the dancers.

The little man was talking, talking. Everyone else was ignoring me. Good. I was hearing some fantastic yarn of knights and wars and treasures. Though I gave it less than half an ear, it lulled me, even drew a few chuckles.

Inside, though, my nastier, wiser self was warning me: All right, Corwin, you have had enough. Time to take your leave . . .

But, magically it seemed, my glass had been refilled, and I took it and sipped from it. One more, one more is all right.

No, said my other self, he is laying a spell on you. Can't you feel it?

I did not feel that any dwarf could drink me under the table. But I was tired, and I had not eaten much. Perhaps it would be prudent . . .

I felt myself nodding. I placed my pipe on the table. Each time that I blinked it seemed to take longer to reopen my eyes, I was pleasantly warm now, with just the least bit of delicious numbness in my tired muscles.

I caught myself nodding, twice. I tried to think of my mission, of my personal safety, of Star . . . I mumbled something, still vaguely awake behind closed eyelids. It would be so good, just to remain this way for half a minute more . . .

The little man's voice, musical, grew monotonous, dropped to a drone. It did not really matter what he was say—

Star whinnied.

I sat bolt upright, eyes wide, and the tableau before me swept all sleep from my mind.

The musicians continued their performance, but now no one was dancing. All of the revelers were advancing quietly upon me. Each held something in his hand – a flask, a cudgel, a blade. The one in the leather apron brandished his cleaver. My companion had just fetched a stout stick from where it had leaned against the wall. Several of them lofted small pieces of furniture. More of them had emerged from the caves near the fire pit, and they bore stones and clubs. All traces of gaiety had vanished, and their faces were now either expressionless, twisted into grimaces of hate or smiling very nasty smiles.

My anger returned, but it was not the white-heat filing I had left earlier. Looking at the horde before me, I had no wish to tackle it. Prudence had come to temper my feelings. I had a mission. I should not risk my neck here if I could think of another way of handling things. But I was certain that I could not talk my way out of this one.

I took a deep breath. I saw that they were getting ready to rush me, and I thought suddenly of Brand and Benedict in Tir-na Nog'th, Brand not even fully attuned to the Jewel. I drew strength from that fiery stone once again, growing alert and ready to lay about me if it came to that. But first, I would have a go at their nervous systems.

I was not certain how Brand had managed it, so I simply reached out through the Jewel as I did when influencing the weather. Strangely, the music was still playing, as though this action of the little people was but some grisly continuation of their dance.

'Stand still.' I said it aloud and I wined it, rising to my feet 'Freeze. Turn to statues. All of you.'

I felt a heavy throbbing within/upon my breast I felt the red forces move outward, exactly as on those other occasions when I had employed the Jewel.

My diminutive assailants were poised. The nearest ones stood stock-still, but there were still some movements among those to the rear. Then the pipes let out a crazy squeal and the fiddles fell silent. Still, I did not know whether I had reached them or whether they had halted of their own accord on seeing me stand.

Then I felt the great waves of force which flowed out from me, embedding the entire assembly in a tightening matrix. I felt them all trapped within this expression of my will, and I reached out and un-tethered Star.

Holding them with a concentration as pure as anything I used when passing through Shadow, I led Star to the doorway. I turned then for a final look at the frozen assembly and pushed Star on ahead of me up the stair. As I followed, I listened, but there were no sounds of renewed activity from below.

When we emerged, dawn was already paling the east. Strangely, as I mounted, I heard the distant sounds of fiddles. Moments later, the pipes came in on the tune. It seemed as though it mattered not at all whether they succeeded or failed in their designs against me; the party was going to go on.

As I headed us south, a small figure hailed me from the doorway I had so recently quitted. It was their leader with whom I had been drinking. I drew rein, to better catch his words.

'And where do you travel?' he called after me.

Why not?

'To the ends of the Earth!' I shouted back.

He broke into a jig atop his shattered door.

'Fare thee well, Corwin!' he cried.

I waved to him. Why not, indeed? Sometimes it's damned hard to tell the dancer from the dance.

6

I rode fewer than a thousand meters to what had been the south, and everything stopped – ground, sky, mountains. I faced a sheet of white light. I thought then of the stranger in the cave and his words. He had felt that the world was being blotted by that storm, that it corresponded to something out of a local apocalyptic legend. Perhaps it had. Perhaps it had been the wave of Chaos of which Brand had spoken, moving this way, passing over, destroying, disrupting. But this end of the valley was untouched. Why should it remain?

Then I recalled my actions on rushing out into the storm. I had used the Jewel, the power of the Pattern within it, to halt the storm over this area. And if it had been more than an ordinary storm? The Pattern had prevailed over Chaos before. Could this valley where I had stopped the rainfall be but a small island in a sea of Chaos now? If so, how was I to continue?

I looked to the east, from whence the day brightened. No sun stood new-risen in the heavens, but rather a great, blindingly burnished crown, a gleaming sword hanging through it From somewhere I heard a bird singing, notes almost like laughter. I leaned forward and covered my face with my hands. Madness . . .

No! I had been in weird shadows before. The farther one traveled, the stranger they sometimes grew. Until . . . What was it I'd thought that night in Tir-na Nog'th?

Two lines from a story of Isak Dinesen's returned to me, lines which had troubled me sufficiently to cause me to memorize them, despite the fact that I had been Carl Corey at the time: '. . . Few people can say of themselves that they are free of the belief that this world which they see around them is in reality the work of their own imagination. Are we pleased with it, proud of it, then?'. A summation of the family's favorite philosophical pastime. Do we make the Shadow worlds? Or are they there, independent of us, awaiting our footfalls? Or is there an unfairly excluded middle? Is it a matter of more or less, rather than either-or? A dry chuckle arose suddenly as I realized that I might never know the answer for certain. Yet, as I had thought that night, there is a place, a place where there comes an end to Self, a place where solipsism is no longer the plausible answer to the locales we visit, the things that we find. The existence of this place, these things, says that here, at least, there is a difference, and if here, perhaps it runs back through our shadows, too, informing them with the not-self, moving our egos back to a smaller stage. For this, I felt, was such a place, a place where the 'Are we pleased with it, proud of it, then?' need not apply, as the rent vale of Garnath and my curse might have nearer home. Whatever I ultimately believed, I felt that I was about to enter the land of the completely not-I. My powers over Shadow might well be canceled beyond this point.

I sat up straight and squinted against the glare. I spoke a word to Star and shook the reins. We moved ahead.

For a moment, it was like riding into a fog. Only it was enormously brighter, and there was absolutely no sound. Then we were falling.

Falling, or drifting. After the initial shock, it was difficult to say. At first, there was a feeling of descent – perhaps intensified by the fact that Star panicked when it began. But there was nothing to kick against, and after a time Star ceased all movement save for shivering and heavy breathing.

I held the reins with my right hand and clutched the Jewel with my left I do not know what I willed or how I reached with it, exactly, but that I wanted passage through this place of bright nothingness, to find my way once more and move on to the journey's end.

I lost track of time. The feeling of descent had vanished. Was I moving, or merely hovering? No way to say. Was the brightness really brightness, still? And that deadly silence . . . I shuddered. Here was even greater sensory deprivation than in the days of my blindness, in my old cell. Here was nothing – not the sound of a scuttling rat nor the grinding of my spoon against the door; no dampness, no chill, no textures. I continued to reach . . .

Flicker.

It seemed there had been some momentary breaking of the visual field to my right, near subliminal in its brevity. I reached out and felt nothing.

It had been so brief a thing that I was uncertain whether it had really occurred. It could easily have been an hallucination.

But it seemed to happen again, this time to my left. How long the interval between, I could not say.

Then I heard something like a groan, directionless. This, too, was very brief.

Next – and for the first time, I was certain – there came a gray and white landscape like the surface of the moon. There and gone, perhaps a second's worth, in a small area of my visual field, off to my left Star snorted.

To my right appeared a forest – gray and white – tumbling, as though we passed one another at some impossible angle. A small-screen fragment, less than two seconds' worth.

Then pieces of a burning building beneath me . . . Colorless . . .

Snatches of wailing, from overhead . . .

A ghostly mountain, a torchlit procession ascending a switchback trail up its nearest face . . .

A woman hanging from a tree limb, taut rope about her neck, head twisted to the side, hands tied behind her back . . .

Mountains, upside down, white; black clouds beneath . . .

Click. A tiny thrill of vibration, as if we had momentarily touched something solid – Star's hoof on stone, perhaps. Then gone . . .

Flicker.

Heads, rolling, dripping black gore . . . A chuckle from nowhere . . . A man nailed to a wall, upside down . . .

The white light again, rolling and heaving, wavelike . . .

Click. Flicker.

For one pulsebeat, we trod a trail beneath a stippled sky. The moment it was gone, I reached for it again, through the Jewel.

Click. Flicker. Click. Rumble.

A rocky trail, approaching a high mountain pass . . . Still monochrome, the world . . . At my back, a crashing like thunder . . .

I twisted the Jewel like a focus knob as the world began to fade. It came back again . . . Two, three, four . . . I counted hoofbeats, heartbeats against the growling background . . . Seven, eight, nine . . . The world grew brighter. I took a deep breath and sighed heavily. The air was cold.

Between the thunder and its echoes, I heard the sound of rain. None fell upon me, though.

I glanced back.

A great wall of rain stood perhaps a hundred meters to the rear. I could distinguish only the dimmest of mountain outlines through it. I clucked to Star and we moved a little faster, climbing to an almost level stretch that led between a pair of peaks like turrets. The world ahead was still a study in black and white and gray, the sky before me divided by alternate bands of darkness and light. We entered the pass.

I began to tremble. I wanted to draw rein, to rest, eat, smoke, dismount and walk around. Yet, I was still too close to that storm-screen to so indulge myself.

Star's hoofbeats echoed within the pass, where rock walls rose sheer on either hand beneath that zebra sky. I hoped these mountains would break this stormfront, though I felt that they could not. This was no ordinary storm, and I had a sick feeling that it stretched all the way back to Amber, and that I would have been trapped and lost forever within it but for the Jewel.

As I watched that strange sky, a blizzard of pale flowers began to fall about me, brightening my way. A pleasant odor filled the air. The thunder at my back softened. The rocks at my sides were shot with silver streaks. The world was possessed of a twilight feeling to match the illumination, and as I emerged from the pass, I saw down into a valley of quirked perspective, distances impossible to gauge, filled with natural-seeming spires and minarets reflecting the moon-like light of the sky-streaks, reminiscent of a night in Tir-na Nog'th, interspersed with silvery trees, spotted with mirror-like pools, traversed by drifting wraiths, almost terraced-seeming in places, natural and rolling in others, cut by what appeared to be an extension of the line of trail I followed, rising and falling, hung over by an elegiac quality, sparked with inexplicable points of glitter and shine, devoid of any signs of habitation.

I did not hesitate, but began my descent. The ground about me here was chalky and pale as bone – and was that the faintest line of a black road far off to my left? I could just about make it out.

I did not hurry now, as I could see that Star was tiring. If the storm did not come on too quickly, I felt that we might take a rest beside one of the pools in the valley below. I was tired and hungry myself.

I kept a lookout on the way down, but saw no people, no animals. The wind made a soft, sighing noise. White flowers stirred on vines beside the trail when I reached the lower levels where regular foliage began. Looking back, I saw that the stormfront still had not passed the mountain crest, though the clouds continued to pile behind it.

I made my way on down into that strange place. The flowers had long before ceased to fall about me, but a delicate perfume hung in the air. There were no sounds other than our own and that of the constant breeze from my right. Oddly shaped rock formations stood all about me, seeming almost sculpted in their purity of line. The mists still drifted. The pale grasses sparkled damply.

As I followed the trail toward the valley's wooded center, the perspectives continued to shift about me, skewing distances, bending prospects. In fact, I turned off the trail to the left to approach what appeared to be a nearby lake and it seemed to recede as I advanced. When I finally came upon it, however, dismounted and dipped a finger to taste, the water was icy but sweet.

Tired, I sprawled after drinking my fill, to watch Star graze while I began a cold meal from my bag. The storm was still fighting to cross the mountains. I looked for a long while, wondering about it. If Dad had failed, then those were the growls of Armageddon and this whole trip was meaningless. It did me no good to think that way, for I knew that I had to go on, whatever. But I could not help it I might arrive at my destination, I might see the battle won, and then see it all swept away. Pointless . . . No. Not pointless. I would have tried, and I would keep on trying to the end. That was enough, even if everything was lost. Damn Brand, anyway! For starting—

A footfall.

I was into a crouch and I was turned in that direction with my hand on my blade in an instant.

It was a woman that I faced, small, clad in white. She had long, dark hair and wild, dark eyes, and she was smiling. She carried a wicker basket, which she placed on the ground between us.

'You must be hungry, Knight at arms,' she said in strangely accented Thari. 'I saw you come. I brought you this.'

I smiled and assumed a more normal stance.

'Thank you,' I said. 'I am. I am called Corwin. Yourself?'

'Lady,' she said.

I quirked an eybrow. 'Thank you – Lady. You make your home in this place?'

She nodded and knelt to uncover the basket.

'Yes, my pavilion is farther back, along the lake.' She gestured with her head, eastward – in the direction of the black road.

'I see,' I said.

The food and the wine in the basket looked real, fresh, appetizing, better than my traveler's fare. Suspicion was with me, of course. 'You will share it with me?' I asked.

'If you wish.'

'I wish.'

'Very well.'

She spread a cloth, seated herself across from me, removed the food from the basket and arranged it between us. She served it then, and quickly sampled each item herself. I felt a trifle ignoble at this, but only a trifle. It was a peculiar location for a woman to be residing, apparently alone, just waiting around to succor the first stranger who happened along. Dara had fed me on our first meeting, also; and as I might be nearing the end of my journey, I was closer to the enemy's places of power. The black road was too near at hand, and I caught Lady eying the Jewel on several occasions.

But it was an enjoyable time, and we grew more familiar as we dined. She was an ideal audience, laughing at all my jokes, making me talk about myself. She maintained eye contact much of the time, and somehow our fingers met whenever anything was passed. If I were being taken in in some way, she was being very pleasant about it.

As we had dined and talked, I had also kept an eye on the progress of that inexorable-seeming stormfront. It had finally breasted the mountain crest and crossed over. It had begun its slow descent of the high slope. As she cleared the cloth, Lady saw the direction of my gaze and nodded.

'Yes, it is coming,' she said, placing the last of the utensils in the basket and seating herself beside me, bringing the bottle and our cups. 'Shall we drink to it?'

'I will drink with you, but not to that.'

She poured.

'It does not matter,' she said. 'Not now,' and she placed her hand on my arm and passed me my cup.

I held it and looked down at her. She smiled. She touched the rim of my cup with her own. We drank.

'Come to my pavilion now,' she said, taking my hand, 'where we will wile pleasurably the hours that remain.'

'Thanks,' I said. 'Another time and that wiling would have been a fine dessert to a grand meal. Unfortunately, I must be on my way. Duty nags, time rushes, I've a mission.'

'All right,' she said. 'It is not that important. And I know all about your mission. It is not all that important either, now.'

'Oh? I must confess that I fully expected you to invite me to a private party which would result in me alone and palely loitering on the cold side of some hill sometime hence if I were to accept.'

She laughed.

'And I must confess that it was my intention to so use you, Corwin. No longer, though.'

'Why not?'

She gestured toward the advancing line of disruption.

'There is no need to delay you now. I see by this that the Courts have won. There is nothing anyone can do to halt the advance of the Chaos.'

I shuddered briefly and she refilled our cups.

'But I would rather you did not leave me at this time,' she went on. 'It will reach us here in a matter of hours. What better way to spend this final time than in one another's company? There is no need even to go as far as my pavilion.'

I bowed my head, and she drew up close against me. What the hell. A woman and a bottle – that was how I had always said I wanted to end my days. I took a sip of the wine. She was probably right. Yet, I thought of the woman-thing which had trapped me on the black road as I was leaving Avalon, I had gone at first to aid her, succumbed quickly to her unnatural charms – then, when her mask was removed, saw that there was nothing at all behind it. Damned frightening, at the time. But, not to get too philosophical, everybody has a whole rack of masks for different occasions. I have heard pop psychologists inveigh against them for years. Still, I have met people who impressed me favorably at first, people whom I came to hate when I learned what they were like underneath. And sometimes they were like that woman-thing – with nothing much really there. I have found that the mask is often far more acceptable than its alternative. So . . . This girl I held to me might really be a monster inside. Probably was. Aren't most of us? I could think of worse ways to go if I wanted to give up at this point. I liked her.

I finished my wine. She moved to pour me more and I stayed her hand.

She looked up at me. I smiled.

'You almost persuaded me,' I said.

Then I closed her eyes with kisses four, so as not to break the charm, and I went and mounted Star. The sedge was not withered, but he was right about the no birds. Hell of a way to run a railroad, though.

'Good-bye, Lady.'

I headed south as the storm boiled its way down into the valley. There were more mountains before me, and the trail led toward them. The sky was still streaked, black and white, and these lines seemed to move about a bit; the overall effect was still that of twilight, though no stars shone within the black areas. Still the breeze, still the perfume about me – and the silence, and the twisted monoliths and the silvery foliage, still dew-damp and glistening. Rag ends of mist blew before me. I tried to work with the stuff of Shadow, but it was difficult and I was tired. Nothing happened. I drew strength from the Jewel, trying to transmit some of it to Star, also. We moved at a steady pace until finally the land tilted upward before us, and we were climbing toward another pass, a more jagged thing than the one by which we had entered. I halted to look back, and perhaps a third of the valley now lay behind the shimmering screen of that advancing storm-thing. I wondered about Lady and her lake, her pavilion. I shook my head and continued.

The way steepened as we neared the pass, and we were slowed. Overhead, the white rivers in the sky took on a reddish cast which deepened as we rode. By the time I reached the entrance, the whole world seemed tinged with blood. Passing within that wide, rocky avenue, I was struck by a heavy wind. Pushing on against it, the ground grew more level beneath us, though we continued to climb and I still could not see beyond the pass.

As I rode, something raided in the rocks to my left. I glanced that way, but saw nothing. I dismissed it as a falling stone. Half a minute later, Star jerked beneath me, let out a terrible neigh, turned sharply to the right, then began to topple, leftward.

I leaped clear, and as we both fell I saw that an arrow protruded from behind Star's right shoulder, low. I hit the ground rolling, and when I halted I looked up in the direction from which it must have come.

A figure with a crossbow stood atop the ridge to my right, about ten meters above me. He was already cranking the weapon back to prepare for another shot.

I knew that I could not reach him in time to stop him. So I cast about for a stone the size of a baseball, found one at the foot of the escarpment to my rear, hefted it and tried not to let my rage interfere with the accuracy of my throw. It did not, but it may have contributed some extra force.

The blow caught him on the left arm, and he let out a cry, dropping the crossbow. The weapon clattered down the rocks and landed on the other side of the trail, almost directly across from me.

'You son of a bitch!' I cried. 'You killed my horse! I'm going to have your head for it!'

As I crossed the trail, I looked for the fastest way up to him and saw it off to my left. I hurried to it and commenced climbing. An instant later, the light and the angle were proper and I had a better view of the man, bent nearly double, massaging his arm. It was Brand, his hair even redder in the sanguine light.

'This is it, Brand,' I said. 'I only wish someone had done it a long time ago.'

He straightened and watched me climb for a moment. He did not reach for his blade. Just as I got to the top, perhaps seven meters away from him, he crossed his arms on his breast and lowered his head.

I drew Grayswandir and advanced. I admit that I was prepared to kill him in that or any other position. The red light had deepened until we seemed bathed in blood. The wind howled about us, and from the valley below came a rumble of thunder.

He simply faded before me. His outline grew less distinct, and by the time I reached the place where he had been standing he had vanished entirely.

I stood for a moment, cursing, remembering the story that he had somehow been transformed into a living Trump, capable of transporting himself anywhere in a very brief time.

I heard a noise from below . . .

I rushed to the edge and looked down. Star was still kicking and blowing blood, and it tore my heart to see it. But that was not the only distressing sight.

Brand was below. He had picked up the crossbow and begun preparing it once more.

I looked about for another stone, but there was nothing at hand. Then I spotted one farther back, in the direction from which I had come. I hurried to it, resheathed my blade and raised the thing. It was about the size of a watermelon. I returned with it to the edge and sought Brand.

He was nowhere in sight.

Suddenly, I felt very exposed. He could have transported himself to any vantage and be sighting in on me at that instant I dropped to the ground, falling across my rock. A moment later, I heard the bolt strike to my right. The sound was followed by Brand's chuckle.

I stood again, knowing it would take him at least a little while to recock his weapon. Looking in the direction of the laughter, I saw him, atop the ledge across the pass from me – about five meters higher than I was, and about twenty meters distant.

'Sorry about the horse,' he said. 'I was aiming for you. But those damned winds . . .'

By then I had spotted a niche and I made for it, taking the rock with me for a shield. From that wedge-shaped fissure, I watched him fit the bolt.

'A difficult shot,' he called out, raising the weapon, 'a challenge to my markmanship. But certainly worth the effort I've plenty more quarrels.'

He chuckled, sighted and fired.

I bent low, holding the rock before my middle, but the bolt struck about two feet to my right.

'I had sort of guessed that might happen,' he said, beginning to prepare his weapon once again. 'Had to learn the windage, though.'

I looked about for smaller stones to use for ammunition as I had earlier. There were none nearby. I wondered about the Jewel then. It was supposed to act to save me in the presence of immediate peril.

But I had a funny feeling that this involved close proximity, and that Brand was aware of this and was taking advantage of the phenomenon. Still, mightn't there be something else I could do with the Jewel to thwart him? He seemed too far away for the paralysis trick, but I had beaten him once before by controlling the weather. I wondered how far off the storm was. I reached for it I saw that it would take minutes I did not possess in order to set up the conditions necessary to draw lightning upon him. But the winds were another matter. I reached out for them, felt them . . .

Brand was almost ready to shoot again. The wind began to scream through the pass.

I do not know where his next shot landed. Nowhere near me, though. He fell to readying his weapon again. I began setting up the factors for a lightningstroke . . .

When he was ready, when he raised the weapon this time, I raised the winds once more. I saw him sight, I saw him draw a breath and hold it. Then he lowered the bow and stared at me.

'It just occurred to me,' he called out, 'you've got that wind in your pocket, haven't you? That is cheating, Corwin.' He looked all about. 'I should be able to find a footing where it will not matter, though. Aha!'

I kept working to set things up to blast him, but conditions were not ready yet. I looked up at that red- and black-streaked sky, something cloud-like forming above us. Soon, but not yet . . .

Brand faded and vanished again. Wildly, I sought him everywhere.

Then he faced me. He had come over to my side of the pass. He stood about ten meters to the south of me, with the wind at his back. I knew that I could not shift it in time. I wondered about throwing my rock. He would probably duck and I would be throwing away my shield. On the other hand . . .

He raised the weapon to his shoulder.

Stall! cried my own voice within my mind, while I continued to tamper with the heavens.

'Before you shoot, Brand, tell me one thing. All right?'

He hesitated, then lowered the weapon a few inches.

'What?'

'Were you telling me the truth about what happened – with Dad, the Pattern, the coming of Chaos?'

He threw back his head and laughed, a series of short barks.

'Corwin,' he stated then, 'it pleases me more than I can say to see you die not knowing something that means that much to you.'

He laughed again and began to raise the weapon. I had just moved to hurl my rock and rush him. But neither of us completed either action.

There came a great shriek from overhead, and a piece of the sky seemed to detach itself and fall upon Brand's head. He screamed and dropped the crossbow. He raised his hands to tear at the thing that assailed him. The red bird, the Jewel bearer, born of my blood from my father's hand, had returned, to defend me.

I get go the rock and advanced upon him, drawing my blade as I went. Brand struck the bird and it flapped away, gaining altitude, circling for another dive. He raised both arms to cover his face and head, but not before I saw the blood that flowed from his left eye socket.

He began to fade again even as I rushed toward him. But the bird descended like a bomb and its talons struck Brand about the head once again. Then the bird, too, began to fade. Brand was reaching for his ruddy assailant and being slashed by it as they both disappeared.

When I reached the place of the action the only thing that remained was the fallen crossbow, and I smashed it with my boot.

Not yet, not yet the end, damn it! How long will you plague me, brother? How far must I go to bring it to an end between us?

I climbed back down to the trail. Star was not yet dead and I had to finish the job. Sometimes I think I'm in the wrong business.

7

A bowl of cotton candy.

Having traversed the pass, I regarded the valley that lay before me. At least, I assumed that it was a valley. I could see nothing below its cover of cloud/mist/fog.

In the sky, one of the red streaks was turning yellow; another, green. I was slightly heartened by this, as the sky had behaved in a somewhat similar fashion when I had visited the edge of things, across from the Courts of Chaos.

I hitched up my pack and began down the trail. The winds diminished as I went. Distantly, I heard some thunder from the storm I was fleeing. I wondered where Brand had gone. I had a feeling that I would not be seeing him again for a time.

Partway down, with the fog just beginning to creep and curl about me, I spotted an ancient tree and cut myself a staff. The tree seemed to shriek as I severed its limb.

'Damn you!' came something like a voice from within it.

'You're sentient?' 'I'm sorry . . .'

'I spent a long time growing that branch. I suppose you are going to burn it now?'

'No,' I said. 'I needed a staff. I've a long walk before me.'

'Through this valley?'

'That's right.'

'Come closer, that I may better sense your presence. There is something about you that glows.'

I took a step forward.

'Oberon!' it said. 'I know thy Jewel.'

'Not Oberon,' I said. 'I am his son. I wear it on his mission, though.'

'Then take my limb, and have my blessing with it. I've sheltered your father on many a strange day. He planted me, you see.'

'Really? Planting a tree is one of the few things I never saw Dad do.'

'I am no ordinary tree. He placed me here to mark a boundary.'

'Of what sort?'

'I am the end of Chaos and of Order, depending upon how you view me. I mark a division. Beyond me other rules apply.'

'What rules?'

'Who can say? Not I. I am only a growing tower of sentient lumber. My staff may comfort you, however. Planted, it may blossom in strange climes. Then again, it may not. Who can say? Bear it with you, however, son of Oberon, into the place where you journey now. I feel a storm approaching. Good-bye.'

'Good-bye,' I said. 'Thank you.'

I turned and walked on down the trail into the deepening fog. The pinkness was drained from it as I went I shook my head as I thought about the tree, but its staff proved useful for the next several hundred meters, where the going was particularly rough.

Then things cleared a bit. Rocks, a stagnant pool, some small, dreary trees festooned with ropes of moss, a smell of decay . . . I hurried by. A dark bird was watching me from one of the trees.

It took wing as I regarded it, flapping in a leisurely fashion in my direction. Recent events having left me a little bird-shy, I drew back as it circled my head. But then it fluttered to rest on the trail before me, cocked its head and viewed me with its left eye.

'Yes,' it announced then, 'You are the one.'

'The one what?' I said.

'The one I will accompany. You've no objection to a bird of ill omen following you, have you, Corwin?'

It chuckled then, and executed a little dance.

'Offhand, I do not see how I can stop you. How is it that you know my name?'

'I've been waiting for you since the beginning of Time, Corwin.'

'Must have been a bit tiresome.'

'It has not been all that long, in this place. Time is what you make of it.'

I resumed walking. I passed the bird and kept going. Moments later, it flashed by me and landed atop a rock off to my right.

'My name is Hugi,' he stated. 'You are carrying a piece of old Ygg, I see.'

'Ygg?'

'The stuffy old tree who waits at the entrance to this place and won't let anyone rest on his branches. I'll bet he yelled when you whacked it off.' He emitted peals of laughter then.

'He was quite decent about it.'

'I'll bet. But then, he hadn't much choice once you'd done it. Fat lot of good it will do you.'

'It's doing me fine,' I said, swinging it lightly in his direction.

He fluttered away from it.

'Hey! That was not funny!'

I laughed.

'I thought it was.'

I walked on by.

For a long while, I made my way through a marshy area. An occasional gust of wind would clear the way nearby. Then I would pass it, or the fogs would shift over it once again. Occasionally, I seemed to hear a snatch of music – from what direction, I could not tell – slow, and somewhat stately, produced by a steel-stringed instrument.

As I slogged along, I was hailed from somewhere to my left:

'Stranger! Halt and regard me!'

Wary, I halted. Couldn't see a damned thing through that fog, though.

'Hello,' I said. 'Where are you?'

Just then, the fogs broke for a moment and I beheld a huge head, eyes on a level with my own. They belonged to what seemed a giant body, sunk up to the shoulders in a quag. The head was bald, the skin pale as milk, with a stony texture to it. The dark eyes probably seemed even darker than they really were by way of contrast.

'I see,' I said then. 'You are in a bit of a fix. Can you free your arms?'

'If I strain mightily,' came the reply.

'Well, let me check about for something stable you can grab onto. You ought to have a pretty good reach there.'

'No. That is not necessary.'

'Don't you want to get out? I thought that was why you hollered.'

'Oh, no. I simply wanted you to regard me.'

I moved nearer and stared, for the fog was beginning to shift again.

'All right,' I said. 'I have seen you.'

'Do you feel my plight?'

'Not particularly, if you will not help yourself or accept help.'

'What good would it do me to free myself?'

'It is your question. You answer it.'

I turned to go.

'Wait! Where do you travel?'

'South, to appear in a morality play.'

Just then, Hugi flew out of the fog and landed atop the head. He pecked at it and laughed.

'Don't waste your time, Corwin. There is much less here than meets the eye,' he said.

The giant lips shaped my name. Then: 'He is indeed the one?'

'That's him, all right,' Hugi replied.

'Listen, Corwin,' said the sunken giant. 'You are going to try to stop the Chaos, aren't you?'

'Yes.'

'Do not do it. It is not worth it. I want things to end. I desire a release from this condition.'

'I already offered to help you out. You turned me down.'

'Not that sort of release. An end to the whole works.'

'That is easily done,' I said. 'Just duck your head and take a deep breath.'

'It is not only personal termination that I desire, but an end to the whole foolish game.'

'I believe there are a few other folks around who would rather make their own decisions on the matter.'

'Let it end for them, too. There will come a time when they are in my position and will feel the same way.'

'Then they will possess the same option. Good day.'

I turned and walked on.

'You will, too!' he called after me.

As I hiked along, Hugi caught up with me and perched on the end of my staff.

'It's neat to sit on old Ygg's limb now he can't— Yikes!'

Hugi sprang into the air and circled.

'Burned my foot! How'd he do that?' he cried.

I laughed.

'Beats me.'

He fluttered for a few moments, then made for my right shoulder.

'Okay if I rest here?'

'Go ahead.'

'Thanks.' He settled. 'The Head is really a mental basket case, you know.'

I shrugged my shoulders and he spread hit wings for balance.

'He is groping after something,' he went on, 'but proceeding incorrectly by holding the world responsible for his own failings.'

'No. He would not even grope to get out of the mud,' I said.

'I meant philosophically.'

'Oh, that sort of mud. Too bad.'

'The whole problem lies with the self, the ego, and its involvement with the world on the one hand and the Absolute on the other.'

'Oh, is that so?'

'Yes. You see, we are hatched and we drift on the surface of events. Sometimes, we feel that we actually influence things, and this gives rise to striving. This is a big mistake, because it creates desires and builds up a false ego when just being should be enough. That leads to more desires and more striving and there you are, trapped.'

'In the mud?'

'So to speak. One needs to fix one's vision firmly on the Absolute and learn to ignore the mirages, the illusions, the fake sense of identity which sets one apart as a false island of consciousness.'

'I had a fake identity once. It helped me a lot in becoming the absolute that I am now – me.'

'No, that's fake, too.'

'Then the me that may exist tomorrow will thank me for it, as I do that other.'

'You are missing the point. That you will be fake, too.'

'Why?'

'Because it will still be full of those desires and strivings that set you apart from the Absolute.'

'What is wrong with that?'

'You remain alone in a world of strangers, the world of phenomena.'

'I like being alone. I am quite fond of myself. I like phenomena, too.'

'Yet the Absolute will always be there, calling to you, causing unrest.'

'Good, then there is no need to hurry. But yes, I see what you mean. It takes the form of ideals. Everyone has a few. If you are saying that I should pursue them, I agree with you.'

'No, they are distortions of the Absolute, and what you are talking about is more striving.'

'That is correct.'

'I can see that you have a lot to unlearn.'

'If you are talking about my vulgar instinct for survival, forget it.'

The trail had been leading upward, and we came now to a smooth, level place, almost paved-seeming, though strewn lightly with sand. The music had grown louder and continued to do so as I advanced. Then, through the fog, I saw dim shapes moving, slowly, rhythmically. It took several moments for me to realize that they were dancing to the music.

I kept moving until I could view the figures – human-seeming, handsome folk, garbed in courtly attire – treading to the slow measures of invisible musicians. It was an intricate and lovely dance that they executed, and I halted to watch some of it.

'What is the occasion,' I asked Hugi, 'for a party out here in the middle of nowhere?'

'They dance,' he said, 'to celebrate your passage. They are not mortals, but the spirits of Time. They began this foolish show when you entered the valley.'

'Spirits?'

'Yes. Observe.'

He left my shoulder, flew above them and defecated. The dropping passed through several dancers as if they were holograms, without staining a brocaded sleeve or a silken shirt, without causing any of the smiling figures to miss a measure. Hugi cawed several times then and flew back to me.

'That was hardly necessary,' I said. 'It is a fine performance.'

'Decadent,' he said, 'and you should hardly take it as a compliment, for they anticipate your failure. They but wish to get in a final celebration before the show is closed.'

I watched for a time anyway, leaning upon my staff, resting. The figure described by the dancers slowly shifted, until one of the women – an auburn-haired beauty – was quite near to me. Now, none of the dancers' eyes at any time met my own. It was as if I were not present.

But that woman, in a perfectly timed gesture, cast with her right hand something which landed at my feet.

I stooped and found it substantial. It was a silver rose – my own emblem – that I held. I straightened and fixed it at the collar of my cloak. Hugi looked the other way and said nothing. I had no hat to doff, but I did bow to the lady. There might have been a slight twitch at her right eye as I turned to go.

The ground lost its smoothness as I walked, and finally the music faded. The trail grew rougher, and whenever the fogs cleared the only views were of rocks or barren plains. I drew strength from the Jewel when I would otherwise have collapsed, and I noted that each such fix was of shorter duration now.

After a time, I grew hungry and I halted to eat what rations I had left.

Hugi stood on the ground nearby and watched me eat.

'I will admit to a certain small admiration for your persistence,' he said, 'and even for what you implied when you spoke of ideals. But that is about it. Earlier, we were talking about the futility of desire and of striving—'

'You were. It is not a major concern in my life.'

'It should be.'

'I have had a long life, Hugi. You insult me by assuming I have never considered these footnotes to sophomore philosophy. The fact that you find consensus reality barren tells me more about you than it does about that state of affairs. To wit, if you believe what you say I feel sorry for you, in that you must for some inexplicable reason be here desiring and striving to influence this false ego of mine rather than free of such nonsense and on your way to your Absolute. If you do not believe it, then it tells me that you have been sent to hinder and discourage me, in which case you are wasting your time.'

Hugi made a gargling noise. Then: 'You are not so blind that you deny the Absolute, the beginning and end of everything?'

'It is not indispensable to a liberal education.'

'You admit the possibility?'

'Perhaps I know it better than you, bird. The ego, as I see it, exists at an intermediate stage between rationality and reflex existence. Blotting it out is a retreat, though. If you come from that Absolute – of a self-canceling All – why do you wish to go back home? Do you so despise yourself that you fear mirrors? Why not make the trip worthwhile? Develop. Learn. Live. If you have been sent on a journey why do you wish to cop out and run back to your point of departure? Or did your Absolute make a mistake in sending something of your caliber? Admit that possibility and that is the end of the news.'

Hugi glared at me, then sprang into the air and flew off. Going to consult his manual, perhaps . . .

I heard a peal of thunder as I rose to my feet. I began walking. I had to try to keep ahead of things.

The trail narrowed and widened a number of times before it vanished completely, leaving me to wander across a gravelly plain. I felt more and more depressed as I traveled, trying to keep my mental compass set in the proper direction. I almost came to welcome the sounds of the storm, for they at least gave me a rough idea as to which way was north. Of course, things were a bit confusing in the fog, so that I could not be absolutely certain. And they were growing louder . . . Damn.

. . . And I had been grieved by the loss of Star, troubled by Hugi's futilitarianism. This was definitely not a good day. I began to doubt that I was going to complete my journey. If some nameless denizen of this dark place did not ambush me before too long, there was a strong possibility that I would wander here until my strength failed or the storm caught me. I did not know whether I would be able to beat back that canceling storm another time. I began to doubt it.

I tried using the Jewel to disperse the fog, but its effects seemed blunted. By my own sluggishness, perhaps. I could clear a small area, but my rate of travel quickly bore me through it. My sense of Shadow was dulled in this place which seemed in some way the essence of Shadow.

Sad. It would have been nice to go out with opera – in a big Wagnerian finale beneath strange skies, against worthy opponents – not scrabbling about in a foggy wasteland.

I passed a familiar-seeming outcrop of stone. Could I have been moving in a circle? There is a tendency to do that when completely lost. I listened for the thunder, to take my bearings again. Perversely, all was silent I moved to the outcrop and seated myself on the ground, resting my back against it. No sense to merely wandering. I would wait a time for the thunder's signal I withdrew my Trumps as I sat there. Dad had said that they would be out of commission for a time, but I had nothing better to do.

One by one, I went through them all, trying to reach everyone, save for Brand and Caine. Nothing. Dad had been right. The cards lacked the familiar coldness. I shuffled the entire deck then and cast my fortune, there on the sand. I got an impossible reading and put them all away again. I leaned back and wished I had some water left. For a long while, I listened for the storm. There were a few growls, but they were directionless. The Trumps made me think of my family. They were up ahead – wherever that might be – waiting for me. Waiting for what? I was transporting the Jewel. To what end? At first, I had assumed that its powers might be necessary in the conflict. If so, and if I were indeed the only one who could employ them, then we were in bad shape. I thought of Amber then, and I was shaken with remorse and a kind of dread. Things must not end for Amber, ever. There had to be a way to roll back the Chaos . . .

I threw away a small stone I had been toying with. Once I released it, it moved very slowly.

The Jewel. Its slowdown effect again . . .

I drew more energy and the stone shot away. It seemed that I had just taken strength from the Jewel a little while ago. While this treatment energized my body, my mind still felt fogged up. I needed sleep – with lots of rapid eye movements. This place might seem a lot less unusual if I were rested.

How close was I to my destination? Was it just beyond the next mountain range, or an enormous distance farther? And what chance had I of staying ahead of that storm, no matter what the distance? And the others? Supposing the battle was already concluded and we had lost? I had visions of arriving too late, to serve only as grave-digger . . . Bones and soliloquies, Chaos . . .

And where was that damned black road now that I finally had a use for it? If I could locate it, I could follow it I had a feeling that it was somewhere off to my left . . .

I reached out once again, parting the fogs, rolling them back . . . Nothing . . .

A shape? Something moving?

It was an animal, a large dog perhaps, moving to remain within the fog. Was it stalking me?

The Jewel began to pulse as I moved the fog even farther back. Exposed, the animal seemed to shrug itself. Then it moved straight toward me.

8

I stood as it came near. I could see then that it was a jackal, a big one, its eyes fixed on my own.

'You are a little early,' I said. 'I was only resting.'

It chuckled.

'I have come merely to regard a Prince of Amber,' the beast said. 'Anything else would be a bonus.'

It chuckled again. So did I.

'Then feast your eyes. Anything else, and you will find that I have rested sufficiently.'

'Nay, nay,' said the jackal. 'I am a fan of the House of Amber. And that of Chaos. Royal blood appeals to me, Prince of Chaos. And conflict.'

'You have awarded me an unfamiliar title. My connection with the Courts of Chaos is mainly a matter of genealogy.'

'I think of the images of Amber passing through the shadows of Chaos. I think of the waves of Chaos washing over the images of Amber. Yet at the heart of the order Amber represents moves a family most chaotic, just as the House of Chaos is serene and placid. Yet you have your ties, as well as your conflicts.'

'At the moment,' I said, 'I am not interested in paradox hunting and terminology games. I am trying to get to the Courts of Chaos. Do you know the way?'

'Yes,' said the jackal. 'It is not far, as the carrion bird flies. Come, I will set you in the proper direction.'

It turned and began walking away. I followed.

'Do I move too fast? You seem tired.'

'No. Keep going. It is beyond this valley certainly, is it not?'

'Yes. There is a tunnel.'

I followed it, out across sand and gravel and dry, hard ground. There was nothing growing at either hand. As we walked, the fogs thinned and took on a greenish cast – another trick of that stippled sky, I assumed.

After a time, I called out, 'How much farther is it?'

'Not too far now,' it said. 'Do you grow tired? Do you wish to rest?'

It looked back as it spoke. The greenish light gave to its ugly features an even more ghastly cast. Still, I needed a guide; and we were heading uphill, which seemed to be proper.

'Is there water anywhere near about?' I asked.

'No. We would have to backtrack a considerable distance.'

'Forget it. I haven't the time.'

It shrugged and chuckled and walked on. The fog cleared a little more as we went, and I could see that we were entering a low range of hills. I leaned on my staff and kept up the pace.

We climbed steadily for perhaps half an hour, the ground growing stonier, the angle of ascent steeper. I found myself beginning to breathe heavily.

'Wait,' I called to him. 'I do want to rest now. I thought you said that it was not far.'

'Forgive me,' it said, halting, 'for jackalocentrism. I was judging in terms of my own natural pace. I erred in this, but we *are* almost there now. It lies among the rocks just ahead. Why not rest there?'

'All right,' I replied, and I resumed walking.

Soon we reached a stony wall which I realized was the foot of a mountain. We picked our way among the rocky debris which lined it and came at last to an opening which led back into darkness.

'There you have it,' said the jackal. 'The way is straight, and there are no troublesome side branches. Take your passage through, and good speed to you.'

'Thank you,' I said, giving up thoughts of rest for the moment and stepping inside. 'I appreciate this.'

'My pleasure,' he said from behind me.

I took several more steps and something crunched beneath my feet and rattled when kicked aside. It was a sound one does not readily forget. The floor was strewn with bones.

There came a soft, quick sound from behind me, and I knew that I did not have time to draw Grayswandir. So I spun, raising my staff before me and thrusting with it.

This maneuver blocked the beast's leap, striking it on the shoulder.

But it also knocked me over backward, to roll among the bones. The staff was torn from my hands by the impact, and in the split second of decision allowed me by my opponent's own fall I chose to draw Grayswandir rather than grope after it.

I managed to get my blade unsheathed, but that was all. I was still on my back with the point of my weapon to my left when the jackal recovered and leaped again. I swung the pommel with all of my strength into its face.

The shock ran down my arm and up into my shoulder. The jackal's head snapped back and its body twisted to my left I brought the point into line immediately, gripping the hilt with both hands, and I was able to rise to my right knee before it snarled and lunged once more.

As soon as I saw that I had it on target, I threw my weight behind it, driving the blade deep into the jackal's body. I released it quickly and rolled away from those snapping jaws.

The jackal shrieked, struggled to rise, dropped back. I lay panting where I had fallen. I felt the staff beneath me and seized it I brought it around to guard and drew myself back against the cave wall. The beast did not rise again, however, but lay there thrashing. In the dim light, I could see that it was vomiting. The smell was overpowering.

Then it turned its eyes in my direction and lay still.

'It would have been so fine,' it said softly, 'to eat a Prince of Amber. I always wondered – about royal blood.'

Then the eyes closed and the breathing stopped and I was left with the stink.

I rose, back still against the wall, staff still before me, and regarded it. It was a long while before I could bring myself to retrieve my blade.

A quick exploration showed me that I was in no tunnel, but only a cave. When I made my way out, the fog had grown yellow, and it was stirred now by a breeze from the lower reaches of the valley.

I leaned against the rock and tried to decide which way to take. There was no real trail here.

Finally, I struck off to my left. That way seemed somewhat steeper, and I wanted to get above the fog and into the mountains as soon as I could. The staff continued to serve me well. I kept listening for the sound of running water, but there was none about.

I struggled along, always continuing upward, and the fogs thinned and changed color. Finally, I could see that I was climbing toward a wide plateau. Above it, I began to catch glimpses of the sky, many-colored and churning.

There were several sharp claps of thunder at my back, but I still could not see the disposition of the storm. I increased my pace then, but began to grow dizzy after a few minutes. I stopped and seated myself on the ground, panting. I was overwhelmed with a sense of failure. Even if I made it up to the plateau, I had a feeling that the storm would roar right across it. I rubbed my eyes with the heels of my hands. What was the use of going on if there was no way I could make it?

A shadow moved through the pistachio mists, dropped toward me. I raised my staff, then saw that it was only Hugi. He braked himself and landed at my feet.

'Corwin,' he said, 'you have come a good distance.'

'But maybe not good enough,' I said. 'The storm seems to be getting nearer.'

'I believe that it is. I have been meditating and would like to give you the benefit of—'

'If you want to benefit me at all,' I said, 'I could tell you what to do.'

'What is that?'

'Fly back and see how far off the storm really is, and how fast it seems to be moving. Then come and tell me.'

Hugi hopped from one foot to the other. Then, 'All right,' he said, and leaped into the air and batted his way toward what I felt to be the northwest.

I leaned on the staff and rose. I might as well keep climbing at the best pace I could manage. I drew upon the Jewel again, and strength came into me like a red lightning flash.

As I mounted the slope, a damp breeze sprang up from the direction in which Hugi had departed. There came another thunder-clap. No more growls and rumbles.

I made the most of the influx of energy, climbing quickly and efficiently for several hundred meters. If I were going to lose, I might as well make it to the top first I might as well see where I was and learn whether there was anything at all left for me to try.

My view of the sky grew more and more clear as I climbed. It had changed considerably since last I had regarded it. Half of it was of uninterrupted blackness and the other half those masses of swimming colors. And the entire heavenly bowl seemed to be rotating about a point directly overhead. I began to grow excited. This was the sky I was seeking, the sky which had covered me that time I had journeyed to Chaos. I struggled higher. I wanted to utter something heartening, but my throat was too dry.

As I neared the run of the plateau, I heard a napping sound and Hugi was suddenly on my shoulder.

'The storm is about ready to crawl up your arse,' he said. 'Be here any minute.'

I continued climbing, reached level ground and hauled myself up to it. I stood for a moment then, breathing heavily. The wind must have kept the area clear of fog, for it was a high, smooth plain, and I could see the sky for a great distance ahead. I advanced, to find a point from which I could see beyond the farther edge. As I moved, the sounds of the storm came to me more clearly.

'I do not believe you will make it across,' Hugi said, 'without getting wet.'

'You know that is no ordinary storm,' I croaked. 'If it were, I'd be thankful for the chance of getting a drink.'

'I know. I was speaking figuratively.'

I growled something vulgar and kept going.

Gradually, the vista before me enlarged. The sky still did its crazy veil dance, but the illumination was more than sufficient. When I reached a position where I was positive what lay before me, I halted and sagged against my staff.

'What is the matter?' Hugi asked.

But I could not speak. I simply gestured at the great wasteland which commerced somewhere below the farther lip of the plateau to sweep on for at least forty miles before butting up against another range of mountains. And far off to the left and still running strong went the black road.

'The waste?' he said. 'I could have told you it was there. Why didn't you ask me?'

I made a noise halfway between a groan and a sob and sank slowly to the ground.

How long I remained so, I am not certain. I felt more than a little delirious. In the midst of it I seemed to see a possible answer, though

739

something within me rebelled against it. I was finally roused by the noises of the storm and Hugi's chattering.

'I can't beat it across that place,' I whispered. 'There is no way.'

'You say you have failed,' Hugi said. 'But this is not so. There is neither failure nor victory in striving. It is all but an illusion of the ego.'

I rose slowly to my knees.

'I did not say that I had failed.'

'You said that you cannot go on to your destination.'

I looked back, to where lightnings now flashed as the storm climbed toward me.

'That's right, I cannot do it that way. But if Dad failed, I have got to attempt something that Brand tried to convince me only he could do. I have to create a new Pattern, and I have to do it right here.'

'You? Create a new Pattern? If Oberon failed, how could a man who can barely stay on his feet do it? No, Corwin. Resignation is the greatest virtue you might cultivate.'

I raised my head and lowered the staff to the ground. Hugi fluttered down to stand beside it and I regarded him.

'You do not want to believe any of the things that I said, do you?' I told him. 'It does not matter, though. The conflict between our views is irreducible. I see desire as hidden identity and striving as its growth. You do not.' I moved my hands forward and rested them on my knees. 'If for you the greatest good is union with the Absolute, then why do you not fly to join it now, in the form of the all-pervading Chaos which approaches? If I fail here, it will become Absolute. As for me, I must try, for so long as there is breath within me, to raise up a Pattern against it. I do this because I am what I am, and I am the man who could have been king in Amber.'

Hugi lowered his head.

'I'll see you eat crow first,' he said, and he chuckled.

I reached out quickly and twisted his head off, wishing that I had time to build a fire. Though he made it look like a sacrifice, it is difficult to say to whom the moral victory belonged, since I was planning on doing it anyway.

9

. . . Cassis, and the smell of the chestnut blossoms. All along the Champs-Elysées the chestnuts were foaming white . . .

I remembered the play of the fountains in the Place de la Concorde . . . And down the Rue de la Seine and along the quais, the smell of the old books, the smell of the river . . . The smell of chestnut blossoms . . .

Why should I suddenly remember 1905 and Paris on the shadow Earth, save that I was very happy that year and I might, reflexively, have sought an antidote for the present? Yes . . .

White absinthe, Amer Picon, grenadine . . . Wild strawberries, with Crème d'Isigny . . . Chess at the Café de la Régence with actors from the Comédie Française, just across the way . . . The races at Chantilly . . . Evenings at the Boîte à Fursy on the Rue Pigalle . . .

I placed my left foot firmly before my right, my right before my left. In my left hand, I held the chain from which the Jewel depended – and I carried it high, so that I could stare into the stone's depths, seeing and feeling there the emergence of the new Pattern which I described with each step. I had screwed my staff into the ground and left it to stand near the Pattern's beginning. Left . . .

The wind sang about me and there was thunder near at hand. I did not meet with the physical resistance that I did on the old Pattern. There was no resistance at all. Instead – and in many ways worse – a peculiar deliberation had come over all my movements, slowing them, ritualizing them. I seemed to expend more energy in preparing for each step – perceiving it, realizing it and ordering my mind for its execution – than I did in the physical performance of the act. Yet the slowness seemed to require itself, was exacted of me by some unknown agency which determined precision and an adagio tempo for all my movements. Right . . .

. . . And, as the Pattern in Rebma had helped to restore my faded memories, so this one I was now striving to create stirred and elicited the smell of the chestnut trees, of the wagonloads of vegetables moving through the dawn toward the Halles . . . I was not in love with anyone in particular at the time, though there were many girls – Yvettes and Mimis and Simones, their faces merge – and it was spring in Paris, with Gipsy bands and cocktails at Louis' . . . I remembered, and my heart leaped with a kind of Proustian joy while Time tolled about me like a bell . . . And perhaps this was the reason for the recollection, for this joy seemed transmitted to my movements, informed my perceptions, empowered my will . . .

I saw the next step and I took it . . . I had been around once now, creating the perimeter of my Pattern. At my back, I could feel the storm. It must have mounted to the plateau's rim. The sky was darkening, the storm blotting the swinging, swimming, colored lights. Flashes of lightning splayed about, and I could not spare the energy and the attention to try to control things.

Having gone completely around, I could see that as much of the new Pattern as I had walked was now inscribed in the rock and glowing palely, bluely. Yet, there were no sparks, no tingles in my feet, no hair-raising currents – only the steady law of deliberation, upon me like a great weight . . . Left . . .

. . . Poppies, poppies and cornflowers and tall poplars along country roads, the taste of Normandy cider . . . And in town again, the smell of the chestnut blossoms . . . The Seine full of stars . . . The smell of the old brick houses in the Place des Vosges after a morning's rain . . . The bar under the Olympia Music Hall . . . A fight there . . . Bloodied knuckles, bandaged by a girl who took me home . . . What was her name? Chestnut blossoms . . . A white rose . . .

I sniffed then. The odor was all but gone from the remains of the rose at my collar. Surprising that any of it had survived this far. It heartened me. I pushed ahead, curving gently to my right. From the corner of my eye, I saw the advancing wall of the storm, slick as glass, obliterating everything it passed. The roar of its thunder was deafening now.

Right, left . . .

The advance of the armies of the night . . . Would my Pattern hold against it? I wished that I might hurry, but if anything I was moving with increasing slowness as I went on. I felt a curious sense of bilocation, almost as if I were within the Jewel tracing the Pattern there myself while I moved out here, regarding it and mimicking its progress. Left . . . Turn . . . Right . . . The storm was indeed advancing. Soon it would reach old Hugi's bones. I smelled the moisture and the ozone and wondered about the strange dark bird who had said he'd been waiting for me since the beginning of Time. Waiting to argue with me or be eaten by me in this place without history? Whatever, considering the exaggeration usual in moralists, it was fitting that, having failed to leave me with my heart all laden with rue over my spiritual condition, he be consumed to the accompaniment of theatrical thunder . . . There was distant thunder, near thunder and more thunder now. As I turned in that direction once more, the lightning flashes were nearly blinding. I clutched my chain and took another step . . .

The storm pushed right up to the edge of my Pattern, and then it parted. It began to creep around me. Not a drop fell upon me or the Pattern. But slowly, gradually, we came to be totally engulfed within it.

It seemed as if I were in a bubble at the bottom of a stormy sea. Walls of water encircled me and dark shapes darted by. It seemed as if the entire universe were pressing in to crush me. I concentrated on the red world of the Jewel. Left . . .

The chestnut blossoms . . . A cup of hot chocolate at a sidewalk café . . . A band concert in the Tuileries Gardens, the sounds climbing through the sunbright air . . . Berlin in the twenties, the Pacific in the thirties – there had been pleasures there, but of a different order. It may not be the true past, but images of the past that rush to comfort or torment us later, man or nation. No matter. Across the Pont Neuf and down the Rue Rivoli, buses and fiacres . . . Painters at their easels in the Luxembourg Gardens . . . If all were to fall well, I might seek a shadow like this again one day . . . It ranked with my Avalon. I had forgotten . . . The details . . . The touches that make for life . . . The smell of the chestnuts . . .

Walking . . . I completed another circuit. The wind screamed and the storm roared on, but I was untouched. So long as I did not permit it to distract me, so long as I kept moving and maintained my focus on the Jewel . . . I had to hold up, had to keep taking these slow, careful steps, never to stop, slower and slower but constantly moving . . .

Faces . . . It seemed that rows of faces regarded me from beyond the Pattern's edge . . . Large, like the Head, but twisted – grinning, jeering, mocking me, waiting for me to stop or step wrongly . . . Waiting for the whole thing to come apart around me . . . There was lightning behind their eyes and in their mouths, their laughter was the thunder . . . Shadows crawled among them . . . Now they spoke to me, with words like a gale from off a dark ocean . . . I would fail, they told me, fail and be swept away, this fragment of a Pattern dashed to pieces behind me and consumed . . . They cursed me, they spat and vomited toward me, though none of it reached . . . Perhaps they were not really there . . . Perhaps my mind had been broken by the strain . . . Then what good were my efforts? A new Pattern to be shaped by a madman? I wavered, and they took up the chorus, 'Mad! Mad! Mad!' in the voices of the elements.

I drew a deep breath and smelled what was left of the rose and thought of chestnuts once again, and days filled with the joys of life and organic order. The voices seemed to soften as my mind raced back through the events of that happy year . . . And I took another step . . . And another . . . They had been playing on my weaknesses, they could feel my doubts, my anxiety, my fatigue . . . Whatever they were, they seized what they saw and tried to use it against me . . . Left . . . Right . . . Now let them feel my confidence and wither, I told myself. I have come this far. I will continue. Left . . .

They swirled and swelled about me, still mouthing discouragements. But some of the force seemed gone out of them. I made my way through another section of arc, seeing it grow before me in my mind's red eye.

I thought back to my escape from Greenwood, to my tricking Flora out of information, to my encounter with Random, our fight with his pursuers, our journey back to Amber . . . I thought of our flight to Rebma and my walking of the reversed Pattern there for a restoration of much of my memory . . . Of Random's shotgun wedding and my sojourn to Amber, where I fought with Eric and fled to Bleys . . . Of the battles that followed, my blinding, my recovery, my escape, my journey to Lorraine and then to Avalon . . .

Moving into even higher gear, my mind skimmed the surface of subsequent events . . . Ganelon and Lorraine . . . The creatures of the Black Circle . . . Benedict's arm . . . Dara . . . The return of

Brand and his stabbing . . . My stabbing . . . Bill Roth . . . hospital records . . . My accident . . .

. . . Now, from the very beginning at Greenwood, through it all, to this moment of my struggle to assure each perfect maneuver as it appeared to me, I felt the growing sense of anticipation I had known – whether my actions were directed toward the throne, vengeance, or my conception of duty – felt it, was aware of its continuous existence across those years up until this moment, when it was finally accompanied by something else . . . I felt that the waiting was just about over, that whatever I had been anticipating and struggling toward was soon to occur.

Left . . . Very, very slowly . . . Nothing else was important. I threw all of my will into the movements now. My concentration became total. Whatever lay beyond the Pattern, I was now oblivious to it. Lightnings, faces, winds . . . It did not matter. There was only the Jewel, the growing Pattern and myself – and I was barely aware of myself. Perhaps this was the closest I would ever come to Hugi's ideal of merging with the Absolute. Turn . . . Right foot . . . Turn again . . .

Time ceased to have meaning. Space was restricted to the design I was creating. I drew strength from the Jewel without summoning it now, as part of the process in which I was engaged. In a sense, I suppose, I was obliterated. I became a moving point, programmed by the Jewel, performing an operation which absorbed me so totally that I had no attention available for self-consciousness. Yet, at some level, I realized that I was a part of the process, also. For I knew, somehow, that if anyone else were doing it, it would be a different Pattern emerging.

I was vaguely aware that I had passed the halfway point. The way had become trickier, my movements even slower. Despite the matter of velocity, I was somehow reminded of my experiences on originally becoming attuned to the Jewel, in that strange, many-dimensional matrix which seemed to be the source of the Pattern itself.

Right . . . Left . . .

There was no drag. I felt very light, despite the deliberation. A boundless energy seemed to wash constantly through me. All of the sounds about me had merged into a white noise and vanished.

Suddenly then, I no longer seemed to be moving slowly. It did not seem as if I had passed a Veil or barrier, but rather that I had undergone some internal adjustment.

It felt as if I were moving at a more normal pace now, winding my way through tighter and tighter coils, approaching what would soon be the design's terminus. Mainly, I was still emotionless, though I knew intellectually that at some level a sense of elation was growing and would soon burst through. Another step . . . Another . . . Perhaps half a dozen more paces . . .

Suddenly, the world went dark. It seemed that I stood within a great void, with only the faint light of the Jewel before me and the glow of the Pattern like a spiral nebula through which I was striding. I wavered, but only for an instant. This must be the last trial, the final assault. I would have to be sufficient to the distraction.

The Jewel showed me what to do and the Pattern showed me where to do it. The only thing missing was a view of myself. Left . . .

I continued, executing each move with all of my attention. An opposing force began to rise against me finally, as on the old Pattern. But for this, I was prepared by years of experience. I struggled for two more steps against the mounting barrier.

Then, within the Jewel, I saw the ending of the Pattern. I would have gasped at the sudden realization of its beauty, but at this point even my breath was regulated by my efforts. I threw all of my strength into the next step, and the void seemed to shake about me, I completed it, and the next was even more difficult I felt as if I were at the center of the universe, treading on stars, struggling to impart some essential motion by what was basically an act of will.

My foot slowly advanced, though I could not see it. The Pattern began to brighten. Soon its blaze was almost blinding.

Just a little farther . . . I strove harder than I ever had on the old Pattern, for now the resistance seemed absolute. I had to oppose it with a firmness and constancy of will that excluded everything else, though I seemed not to be moving at all now, though all of my energies seemed diverted into the brightening of the design. At least, I would go out with a splendid backdrop . . .

Minutes, days, years . . . I do not know how long this went on. It felt like forever, as if I had been engaged in this single act for all of eternity . . .

Then I moved, and how long that took I do not know. But I completed the step and began another. Then another . . .

The universe seemed to reel about me. I was through.

The pressure was gone. The blackness was gone . . .

For an instant, I stood at the center of my Pattern. Without even regarding it, I fell forward onto my knees and bent double, my blood pounding in my ears. Head swimming, I panted. I began to shake, all over. I had done it, I realized dimly. Come whatever may, there was a Pattern. And it would endure . . .

I heard a sound where there should have been none, but my jaded muscles refused to respond, even reflexively, until it was too late. Not until the Jewel was jerked from my limp fingers did I raise my head and roll back onto my haunches. No one had been following me through the Pattern – I was certain that I would have been aware of it. Therefore . . .

The light was almost normal, and blinking against it, I looked up into Brand's smiling face. He wore a black eyepatch now, and he held the Jewel in his hand. He must have teleported himself in.

He struck me just as I raised my head, and I fell onto my left side. He kicked me in the stomach then, hard.

'Well, you've done it,' he said. 'I did not think you could. Now I have another Pattern to destroy before I set things right I need this to turn the battle at the Courts first, though.' He waved the Jewel. 'Good-bye for now.'

And he vanished.

I lay there gasping and clutching at my stomach. Waves of blackness rose and fell, like a surf, within me, though I did not completely succumb to unconsciousness. A feeling of enormous despair washed over me, and I closed my eyes and moaned. There was no Jewel for me to draw upon now, either.

The chestnut trees . . .

10

As I lay there hurting, I had visions of Brand appearing on the battlefield where the forces of Amber and Chaos fought, the Jewel pulsing about his neck. Apparently his control over it was sufficient, as he saw it, to enable him to turn things against us. I saw him lashing out with lightning bolts among our troops. I saw him summoning great winds and hailstorms to strike at us. I almost wept. All of this, when he could still redeem himself by coming in on our side. Just winning was not enough for him now, though. He had to win for himself, and on his own terms. And I? I had failed. I had thrown up a Pattern against the Chaos, a thing I had never thought I could do. Yet, this would be as nothing if the battle was lost and Brand returned and wiped out my work. To have come this close, passing through everything that I had, and then to fail here . . . It made me want to cry 'Injustice!' though I knew the universe did not run in accordance with my notions of equity. I gnashed my teeth and spat some dirt I had mouthed. I had been charged by our father to take the Jewel to the place of battle. I had almost made it.

A sense of strangeness came over me then. Something was calling for my attention. What?

The silence.

The raging winds and the thunder had ceased. The air was still. In fact, the air felt cool and fresh. And on the other side of my eyelids, I knew that there was light.

I opened my eyes. I saw a sky of a bright, uniform white. I blinked, I turned my head. There was something off to my right . . .

A tree. A tree stood where I had planted the staff I had cut from old Ygg. It was already far taller than the staff itself had been. I could almost see it growing. And it was green with leaves and white with a sprinkling of buds; a few blossoms had opened. From that direction, the breeze brought me a faint and delicate scent which offered me some comfort.

I felt along my sides. I did not seem to have any broken ribs, though my guts still felt knotted from the kick I had taken. I rubbed my eyes with my knuckles and ran my hands through my hair. I sighed heavily then and rose to one knee.

Turning my head, I regarded the prospect. The plateau was the same, yet somehow not the same. It was still bare but was no longer harsh. Likely an effect of the new illumination. No, there was more to it than that . . .

I had continued to turn, completing my scanning of the horizon. It was not the same place where I had commenced my walk. There were differences both subtle and gross: altered rock formations, a dip where there had been a rise, a new texture to the stone beneath and near me, in the distance what appeared to be soil. I stood and it seemed that now, from somewhere, I caught the scent of the sea. This place had an entirely different feeling to it than the one to which I had mounted – so long ago, it seemed. It was too much of a change for that storm to have wrought. It reminded me of something.

I sighed again, there at the Pattern's center, and continued to consider my surroundings. Somehow, in spite of myself, my despair was slipping away and a feeling of – 'refreshment', seems somehow the best word – was rising within me. The air was so clean and sweet, and the place had a new, unused feeling about it I—

Of course. It was like the place of the primal Pattern. I turned back to the tree and regarded it again, higher already. Like, yet unlike . . . There was something new in the air, the ground, the sky. This was a new place. A new primal Pattern. Everything about me then was a result of the Pattern in which I stood.

I suddenly realized that I was feeling more than refreshment. It was now a sense of elation, a kind of joy that was moving through me. This was a clean, fresh place and I was somehow responsible for it.

Time passed. I just stood there watching the trees, looking around me, enjoying the euphoria that had come over me. Here was some kind of victory, anyway – until Brand came back to wipe it out.

Suddenly, I was sober again. I had to stop Brand, I had to protect this place. I was at the center of a Pattern. If this one behaved like the other, I could use its power to project me anywhere I desired. I could use it to go and join the others now.

I dusted myself off. I loosened my blade in the scabbard. Things might not be as hopeless as they had seemed earlier. I had been told to convey the Jewel to the place of battle. So Brand had done it for me; it would still be there. I would simply have to go and take it back from him, somehow, to make things turn the way they were supposed to have fallen.

I looked all around me. I would have to return here, to investigate this new situation at another time, if I survived what was to come. There was mystery here. It hung in the air and drifted on the breeze. It could take ages to unravel what had occurred when I had drawn the new Pattern.

I saluted the tree. It seemed to stir as I did so. I adjusted my rose and pushed it back into shape. It was time to move again. There was a thing I had yet to do.

I lowered my head and closed my eyes. I tried to recall the lay of the land before the final abyss at the Courts of Chaos. I saw it then, beneath that wild sky, and I peopled it with my relatives, with troops. I seemed to hear the sounds of a distant battle as I did this. The scene adjusted itself, came clearer. I held the vision an instant longer, then charged the Pattern to take me there.

. . . A moment later, it seemed, I stood upon a hilltop beside a plain, a cold wind whipping my cloak about me. The sky was that crazy, turning, stippled thing I remembered from last time – half-black, half-psychedelic rainbows. There were unpleasant fumes in the air. The black road was off to the right now, crossing that plain and passing beyond it over the abyss toward that nighted citadel, firefly gleams flickering about it Gauzy bridges drifted in the air, extending from far in that darkness, and strange forms traveled upon them as well as upon the black road. Below me on the field was what seemed to be the main concentration of troops. At my back, I heard something other than Time's winged chariot.

Turning toward what must have been north by a succession of previous reckonings regarding its course, I beheld the advance of that devil-storm through distant mountains, flashing and growling, coming on like a sky-high glacier.

So I had not stopped it with the creation of a new Pattern. It seemed that it had simply passed by my protected area and would continue until it got to wherever it was going. Hopefully then, the thing would be succeeded by whatever constructive impulses were now spreading outward from the new Pattern, with the reimposition of order throughout the places of Shadow. I wondered how long it would take for the storm to get here.

I heard the sound of hoofs and turned, drawing my blade . . .

A horned rider on a great black horse was bearing down upon me, something like firelight glowing in his eyes.

I adjusted my position and waited. He seemed to have descended from one of the gauzy roadways which had drifted in this direction. We were both fairly far removed from the main scene of action. I watched as he mounted the hill. Odd horse, that. Nice chest. Where the hell was Brand? I wasn't looking for just any fight.

I watched the rider as he came on, and the crooked blade in his right hand. I repositioned myself as he moved in to cut me down. When he swung, I was ready with a parry that pulled his arm within reach. I caught hold of it and dragged him from his mount.

'That rose . . .' he said as he fell to the ground. I do not know what else he might have said, because I cut his throat, and his words and everything else about him were lost with the fiery slash.

I whirled then, drawing Grayswandir away, sprinted several paces and had hold of the black charger's bridle. I spoke with the horse to calm him and led him away from the flames. After a couple of minutes we were on better terms, and I mounted.

He was skittish at first, but I just had him pace the hill top lightly while I continued to observe. The forces of Amber appeared to be on the offense. Smoldering corpses were all over the field. The main force of our enemies was drawn back onto a height near the lip of the abyss. Lines of them, not yet broken but hard pressed, were falling, backing slowly toward it. On the other hand, more troops were crossing that abyss and joining the others who held the heights. Estimating their growing numbers and their position quickly, I judged that these might be readying an offense of their own. Brand was nowhere in sight.

Even if I had been rested and wearing armor I would have had second thoughts about riding down and joining in the fray. My job right now was to locate Brand. I doubted that he would be directly involved in the fighting. I looked off to the sides of the battle proper, seeking a lone figure. No . . . Perhaps the far side of the field. I would have to circle to the north. There was too much that I could not see to the west.

I turned my mount and made my way down the hill. It would be so pleasant to collapse, I decided. Just to fall down in a heap and sleep. I sighed. Where the hell was Brand?

I reached the bottom of the hill and turned to cut through a culvert. I needed a better view—

'Lord Corwin of Amber!'

He was waiting for me as I rounded a bend in the depression, a big, corpse-colored guy with red hair and a horse to match. He wore coppery armor with greenish tracings, and he sat facing me, still as a statue.

'I saw you on the hilltop,' he said. 'You are not mailed, are you?'

I slapped my chest.

He nodded sharply. Then he reached up, first to his left shoulder, then to his right, then to his sides, opening fastenings upon his breastplate. When he had them undone, he removed it, lowered it toward the ground on his left side and let it fall. He did the same with his greaves.

'I have long wanted to meet you,' he said. 'I am Borel. I do not want it said that I took unfair advantage of you when I killed you.'

Borel . . . The name was familiar. Then I remembered. He had Dara's respect and affection. He had been her fencing teacher, a master of the blade. Stupid, though, I saw. He had forfeited my respect by removing his armor. Battle is not a game, and I had no desire to make myself available to any presumptuous ass who thought otherwise. Especially a skilled ass, when I was feeling beat. If nothing else, he could probably wear me down.

'Now we shall resolve a matter which has long troubled me,' he said.

I replied with a quaint vulgarism, wheeled my black and raced back the way I had come. He gave chase immediately.

As I passed back along the culvert, I realized that I did not have a sufficient lead. He would be upon me in a matter of moments with my back all exposed, to cut me down or force me to fight. However, while limited, my choices included a little more than that.

'Coward!' he cried. 'You flee combat! Is this the great warrior of whom I have heard so much?'

I reached up and unfastened my cloak. At either hand, the culvert's lip was level with my shoulders, then my waist.

I rolled out of the saddle to my left, stumbled once and found my footing. The black went on. I moved to my right, facing the draw.

Catching my cloak in both hands, I swung it in a reverse-veronica maneuver a second or two before Borel's head and shoulders came abreast of me. It swept over him, drawn blade and all, muffling his head and slowing his arms.

I kicked then, hard. I was aiming for his head, but I caught him on the left shoulder. He was spilled from his saddle, and his horse, too, went by.

Drawing Grayswandir, I leaped after him. I caught him just as he had brushed my cloak aside and was struggling to rise. I skewered him where he sat and saw the startled expression on his face as the wound began to flame.

'Oh, basely done!' he cried. 'I had hoped for better of thee!'

'This isn't exactly the Olympic Games,' I said, brushing some sparks from my cloak.

I chased down my horse then and mounted. This took me several minutes. As I continued northward, I achieved higher ground. From there, I spotted Benedict directing the battle, and in a draw far to the rear, I caught a glimpse of Julian at the head of his troops from Arden. Benedict was apparently holding them in reserve.

I kept going, toward the advancing storm, beneath the half-dark, half-painted, revolving sky. I soon reached my goal, the highest hill in sight, and began to mount it. I halted several times on the way up, to look back.

I saw Deirdre in black armor, swinging an ax; Llewella and Flora were among the archers, Fiona was nowhere in sight Gérard was not there either. Then I saw Random on horseback, swinging a heavy blade, leading an assault toward the enemy's high ground. Near him was a knight clad in green whom I did not recognize. The man swung a mace with deadly efficiency. He wore a bow upon his back, and he'd a quiver of gleaming arrows at his hip.

The sounds of the storm came louder as I reached the summit of my hill. The lightning flickered with the regularity of a neon tube and the rain sizzled down, a fiberglass curtain that had now passed over the mountains.

Below me, both beasts and men – and more that a few beast-men – were woven in knots and strands of battle. A cloud of dust hung over the field. Assessing the distribution of forces, however, it did not appear to me that the growing forces of me enemy could be pushed much farther. In fact, it seemed that it was just about time for the counterattack. They appeared to be ready up in their craggy places, and just waiting for the order.

I was about a minute and a half off. They advanced, sweeping down the slope, reinforcing their lines, pushing our troops back, driving ahead. And more were arriving from beyond the dark abyss. Our own troops began a reasonably orderly retreat. The enemy pressed harder, and when things seemed about ready to be turned into a rout an order must have been given.

I heard the sound of Julian's horn, and shortly thereafter I saw him astride Morgenstern leading the men of Arden onto the field. This balanced the opposing forces almost exactly and the noise level rose and rose while the sky turned above us.

I watched the conflict for perhaps a quarter of an hour, as our own forces slowly withdrew across the field. Then I saw a one-armed figure on a fiery striped horse suddenly appear atop a distant hill. He bore a raised blade in his hand and he was faced away from me, toward the west. He stood unmoving for several long moments. Then he lowered the blade.

I heard trumpets in the west, and at first I saw nothing. Then a line of cavalry came into view. I started. For a moment, I thought Brand was there. Then I realized it was Bleys leading his troops to strike at the enemy's exposed flank.

And suddenly, our troops in the field were no longer retreating. They were holding their line. Then, they were pressing forward.

Bleys and his riders came on, and I realized that Benedict had the day again. The enemy was about to be ground to pieces.

Then a cold wind swept over me from out of the storm, and I looked that way again.

The storm had advanced considerably. It must have started moving faster just recently. And it was darker now than it had been, with brighter flashes and louder roars. And this cold, wet wind was increasing in intensity.

I wondered then . . . would it simply sweep over the field like an annihilating wave and that be that? What of the effects of the new Pattern? Would these follow, to restore everything? Somehow, I doubted this. If this storm smashed us, I'd a feeling we would stay smashed. It would require the force of the Jewel to permit us to ride it out until order was restored. And what would be left if we survived it? I simply could not guess.

So what was Brand's plan? What was he waiting for? What was he going to do?

I looked out over the battlefield once more . . .

Something.

In a shadowy place on the heights where the enemy had regrouped, been reinforced, and down which it had stormed . . . something.

A tiny flash of red . . . I was sure I had seen it.

I kept watching, waiting. I had to see it again, to pinpoint it . . .

A minute passed. Two, perhaps . . .

There! And again.

I wheeled the black charger. It looked possible to make it around the enemy's near flank and up to that supposedly vacant height I raced down the bin and began that course.

It had to be Brand with the Jewel. He had chosen a good, safe spot, from which he commanded a view of the entire battlefield as well as the approaching storm. From there, he could direct its lightning into our troops as the front advanced. He would signal a retreat at the proper moment, hit us with the storm's strange furies, then sidetrack the thing to bypass the side he was backing. It seemed the simplest and most effective use of the Jewel under the circumstances.

I would have to get close fast. My control of the stone was greater than his, but it diminished with distance, and he would have the Jewel on his person. My best bet would be to charge right into him, to get within control range at all costs, take over command of the stone and use it against him. But he might have a bodyguard up there with him. That troubled me, because dealing with it could slow me disastrously. And if he did not, what was to prevent him from teleporting himself away if the going got too rough? Then what could I do? I would have to start all over, hunting him again. I wondered whether I could use the Jewel to keep him from transporting himself. I did not know. I resolved to try.

It might not have been the best of plans, but it was the only one I had. There was no longer time to plot.

As I rode, I saw that there were others headed for that height, also. Random, Deirdre and Fiona, mounted and accompanied by eight horsemen, had made their way through the enemy lines, with a few other troops – friends or foes, I could not tell, maybe both – riding hard behind them. The knight clad in green seemed to be moving the fastest, gaining on them. I did not recognize him – or her, as the case might be. I did not doubt the objective of the vanguard, however – not with Fiona there. She must have detected Brand's presence and be leading the others to him. A few drops of hope fell upon my heart. She might be able to neutralize Brand's powers, or minimize them. I leaned forward, still bearing to my left, hurrying my horse along. The sky kept turning. The wind whistled about me. A terrific clap of thunder rolled by. I did not look back.

I was racing them. I did not want them to get there before me, but I feared that they would. The distance was just too great.

If only they would turn and see me coming, they would probably wait. I wished there had been some way of giving them a sign of my presence earlier. I cursed the fact that the Trumps no longer worked.

I began shouting. I screamed after them, but the wind blew my words away and the thunder rolled over them.

'Wait for me! Damn it! It's Corwin!'

Not even a glance in my direction.

I passed the nearest engagements and rode along the enemy's flank out of range of missiles and arrows. They seemed to be retreating faster now and our troops were spreading out over a larger area. Brand must be getting ready to strike. Part of the rotating sky was covered by a dark cloud which had not been above the field minutes before.

I turned toward my right, behind the retreating forces, racing on toward those hills the others were already mounting.

The sky continued to darken as I neared the foot of the hills, and I feared for my kinsmen. They were getting too close to him. He would have to do something. Unless Fiona was strong enough to stop him . . .

The horse reared and I was thrown to the ground at the blinding flash which had occurred before me. The thunder cracked before I hit the earth.

I lay there for several moments, dazed. The horse had run off, was perhaps fifty meters away, before he halted and began to move about uncertainly. I rolled onto my stomach and looked up the long slope. The other riders were also down. Their group had apparently been struck by the discharge. Several were moving, more were not. None had yet risen. Above them, I saw the red glow of the Jewel, back beneath an underhang, brighter and steadier now, and the shadowy outline of the figure who wore it.

I began crawling forward, upward and to my left I wanted to get out of line of sight with that figure before I risked rising. It would take too long to reach him crawling, and I was going to have to skirt the others now, because his attention would be with them.

I made my way carefully, slowly, using every bit of cover in sight, wondering whether the lightning would be striking in the same place again soon – and if not, when he would begin pulling disaster down upon our troops. Any minute now, I judged. A glance back showed me our forces spread over the far end of the field, with the enemy pulled back and coming this way. Before too long, in fact, it seemed I might have them to worry about, too.

I made it into a narrow ditch and wormed my way south for perhaps ten meters. Out again then on the far side, to take advantage of a rise, then some rocks.

When I raised my head to take stock of the situation, I could no longer see the glow of the Jewel. The cleft from which it had shone was blocked by its own eastern shoulder of stone.

I kept crawling, though, near to the lip of the great abyss itself, before I bore to my right once more. I reached a point where it seemed safe to rise, and I did so. I kept expecting another flash, another thunderclap – nearby or on the field – but none came. I began to wonder . . . why not? I reached out, trying to sense the presence of the Jewel, but I could not. I hurried toward the place where I had seen the glow.

I glanced back over the abyss to be sure that no new menaces were approaching from that direction. I drew my blade. When I reached my goal, I stayed close to the escarpment and worked my way northward. I dropped low when I came to its edge and peered around.

There was no red glow. No shadowy figure either. The stony

recess appeared to be empty. There was nothing suspicious anywhere in the vicinity. Could he have teleported again? And if so, why?

I rose and passed about the rocky rise. I continued moving in that direction. I tried once more to feel the Jewel, and this time I made a faint contact with it – somewhere off to my right and above, it seemed.

Silent, wary, I moved that way. Why had he left his shelter? He had been perfectly situated for what he had been about. Unless . . .

I heard a scream and a curse. Two different voices. I began to run.

11

I passed the niche and kept going. Beyond it, there was a natural trail winding upward. I mounted this.

I could see no one as yet, but my sense of the Jewel's presence grew stronger as I moved. I thought that I heard a single footfall from off to my right and I whirled in that direction, but there was no one in sight. The Jewel did not feel that near either, so I continued.

As I neared the top of the rise, the black drop of Chaos hanging behind, I heard voices. I could not distinguish what was being said, but the words were agitated.

I slowed as I neared the crest, lowered myself and peered around the side of a rock.

Random was a small distance ahead of me and Fiona was with him, as were Lords Chantris and Feldane. All, save Fiona, held weapons as if ready to use them, but they stood perfectly still. They were staring toward the edge of things – a shelf of rock slightly above their level and perhaps fifteen meters distant – the place where the abyss began.

Brand stood in that place, and he was holding Deirdre before him. She was unhelmed, her hair blowing wild, and he had a dagger at her throat. It appeared that he had already cut her slightly. I dropped back.

I heard Random say softly, 'Is there nothing more you can do, Fi?'

'I can hold him here,' she said, 'and at this range, I can slow his efforts at weather control. But that is all. He's got some attunement with it and I do not. He also has proximity going for him. Anything else I might try, he can counter.'

Random gnawed his lower lip.

'Put down your weapons,' Brand called out. 'Do it now, or Deirdre's dead.'

'Kill her,' Random said, 'and you lose the only thing that's keeping you alive. Do it, and I'll show you where I'll put my weapon.'

Brand muttered something under his breath. Then: 'Okay. I will start by mutilating her.'

Random spat.

'Come on!' he said. 'She can regenerate as well as the rest of us. Find a threat that means something, or shut up and fight it out!'

Brand was still. I thought it better not to reveal my presence. There must be something I could do. I ventured another look, mentally photographing the terrain before I dropped back. There were some rocks way off to the left, but they did not extend far enough. I saw no way that I might sneak up on him.

'I think we are going to have to rush him and chance it,' I heard Random say. 'I don't see anything else. Do you?'

Before anyone answered him, a strange thing occurred. The day began to grow brighter.

I looked all about me for the source of the illumination, then sought it overhead.

The clouds were still there, the crazy sky doing its tricks beyond them. The brightness was in the clouds, however. They had paled and were now glowing, as if they masked a sun. Even as I watched, there was a perceptible brightening.

'What is he up to now?' Chantris asked.

'Nothing that I can tell,' Fiona said. 'I do not believe it is his doing.'

'Whose then?'

There was no answer that I could overhear.

I watched the clouds grow brighter. The largest and brightest of them seemed to swirl then, as if stirred. Forms tossed within it, settled. An outline began to take shape.

Below me, on the field, the sounds of battle lessened. The storm itself was muted as the vision grew. Something was definitely forming in the bright place above our heads – the lines of an enormous face.

'I do not know, I tell you,' I heard Fiona say in response to something mumbled.

Before it finished taking form, I realized that it was my father's face in the sky. Neat trick, that. And I had no idea what it represented either.

The face moved, as if he were regarding us all. There were lines of strain there, and something of concern to his expression. The brightness grew a little further. His lips moved.

When his voice came down to me it was somehow at an ordinary conversational level, rather than the vast booming I had expected:

'I send you this message,' he said, 'before undertaking the repair of the Pattern. By the time you receive it, I will already have succeeded or failed. It will precede the wave of Chaos which must accompany my endeavor. I have reason to believe the effort will prove fatal to me.'

His eyes seemed to sweep across the field.

'Rejoice or mourn, as you would,' he went on, 'for this is either the beginning or the end. I will send the Jewel of Judgment to Corwin as soon as I have finished with it I have charged him to bear it to the place of conflict. All of your efforts there will be as nothing if the wave of Chaos cannot be averted. But with the Jewel, in that place, Corwin should be able to preserve you until it passes.'

I heard Brand's laugh. He sounded quite mad now.

'With my passing,' the voice continued, 'The problem of the succession will be upon you. I had wishes in this regard, but I see now that these were futile. Therefore, I have no choice but to leave this on the horn of the Unicorn.

'My children, I cannot say that I am entirely pleased with you, but I suppose this works both ways. Let it be. I leave you with my blessing, which is more than a formality. I go now to walk the Pattern. Goodbye.'

Then his face began to fade and the brightness drained out of the cloudbank. A little while, and it was gone. A stillness lay upon the field.

'. . . and, as you can see,' I heard Brand saying, 'Corwin does not have the Jewel. Throw down your weapons and get the hell out of here. Or keep them and get out I do not care. Leave me alone. I have things to do.'

'Brand,' Fiona said, 'can you do what he wanted of Corwin? Can you use it to make that thing miss us?'

'I could if I would,' he said. 'Yes, I could turn it aside.'

'You will be a hero if you do,' she said gently. 'You will earn our gratitude. All past wrongs will be forgiven. Forgiven and forgotten. We—'

He began to laugh wildly.

'*You* forgive *me*?' he said. You, who left me in that tower, who put

761

the knife into my side? Thank you, sister. It is very kind of you to offer to forgive me, but excuse me if I decline.'

'All right,' Random said, 'what *do* you want? An apology? Riches and treasure? An important appointment? All of these? They are yours. But this is a stupid game you are playing. Let us end it and go home, pretend it was all a bad dream.'

'Yes, let us end it,' Brand replied. 'You do that by throwing down your weapons first. Then Fiona releases me from her spell, you all do an about-face and march north. You do it or I kill Deirdre.'

'Then I think you had better go ahead and kill her and be ready to fight it out with me,' he said, 'because she will be dead in a little while anyway, if we let you have your way. All of us will.'

I heard Brand's chuckle.

'Do you honestly think I am going to let you die? I need you – as many of you as I can save. Hopefully Deirdre, too. You are the only ones who can appreciate my triumph. I will preserve you through the holocaust that is about to begin.'

'I do not believe you,' Random said.

'Then take a moment and think about it. You know me well enough to know that I will want to rub your noses in it. I want you as witnesses to what I do. In this sense, I require your presence in my new world. Now, get out of here.'

'You will have everything you want plus our gratitude,' Fiona began, 'if you will just—'

'Go!'

I knew that I could delay no longer. I had to make my move. I also knew that I could not reach him in time. I had no choice but to try using the Jewel as a weapon against him.

I reached out and felt its presence. I closed my eyes and summoned my powers.

Hot. Hot, I thought. It is burning you, Brand. It is causing every molecule in your body to vibrate faster and faster. You are about to become a human torch—

I heard him scream.

'Corwin,' he bellowed. 'Stop it! Wherever you are! I'll kill her. Look!'

Still willing the Jewel to burn him, I rose to my feet I glared at him across the distance that separated us. His clothing was beginning to smolder.

'Stop it!' he cried, and he raised the knife and slashed Deirdre's face. I screamed and my eyes swam. I lost control of the Jewel. But Deirdre, her left cheek bloody, sank her teeth into his hand as he moved to cut her again. Then her arm was free, and she jabbed her elbow into his ribs and tried to pull away.

As soon as she moved, as soon as her head dropped, there was a silver flash. Brand gasped and let go the dagger. An arrow had pierced his throat. Another followed an instant later and stood out from his breast, a little to the right of the Jewel.

He stepped backward and made a gurgling noise. Only there was no place to which he might step, from the edge of the abyss.

His eye went wide as he began to topple. Then his right hand shot forward and caught hold of Deirdre's hair. I was running by then, shouting, but I knew that I could not reach them in time.

Deirdre howled, a look of terror on her bloodstreaked face, and she reached out to me . . .

Then Brand, Deirdre and the Jewel were over the edge and falling, vanished from sight, gone . . .

I believe that I tried to throw myself after them, but Random caught hold of me. Finally, he had to hit me, and it all went away.

When I came around, I lay upon the stony earth farther back from the edge of that place where I had fallen. Someone had folded my cloak into a pillow for me. My first vision was of the turning sky, reminding me somehow of my dream of the wheel the day I had met Dara. I could feel the others about me, hear their voices, but I did not at first turn my head. I just lay there and regarded the mandala in the heavens and thought upon my loss. Deirdre . . . she had meant more to me than all the rest of the family put together. I cannot help it. That is how it was. How many times had I wished she were not my sister. Yet, I had reconciled myself to the realities of our situation. My feelings would never change, but . . . now she was gone, and this thought meant more to me than the impending destruction of the world.

Yet, I had to see what was happening now. With the Jewel gone, everything was over. Yet . . . I reached out, trying to feel its presence, wherever it might be, but there was nothing. I began to rise then, to see how far the wave had advanced, but a sudden arm pushed me back.

'Rest, Corwin.' It was Random's voice. 'You're beat. You look as if you have crawled through hell. There is nothing you can do now. Take it easy.'

'What difference does the state of my health make?' I replied. 'In a little while, it will not matter.'

I made to rise again, and this time the arm moved to support me.

'All right, then,' he said. 'Not that much worth seeing, though.'

I suppose that he was right. The fighting appeared to be over except for a few isolated pockets of resistance by the enemy, and these were rapidly being enveloped, their combatants slain or captured, everyone moving in this direction, withdrawing before the advancing wave which had reached the far end of the field. Soon our height would be crowded with all of the survivors from both sides. I looked behind us. No new forces were approaching from the dark citadel. Could we retreat to that place when the wave finally reached us here? Then what? The abyss seemed the ultimate answer. 'Soon,' I muttered, thinking of Deirdre. 'Soon . . .' Why not?

I watched the stormfront, flashing, masking, transforming. Yes, soon. With the Jewel gone along with Brand—

'Brand . . .' I said. 'Who was it finally got him?'

'I claim that distinction,' said a familiar voice which I could not place.

I turned my head and stared. The man in green was seated on a rock. His bow and quiver lay beside him on the ground. He flashed an evil smile in my direction.

It was Caine.

'I'll be damned,' I said, rubbing my jaw. 'A funny thing happened to me on the way to your funeral.'

'Yes. I heard about it.' He laughed. 'You ever kill yourself, Corwin?'

'Not recently. How'd you manage it?'

'Walked to the proper shadow,' he said, 'waylaid the shadow of myself there. He provided the corpse.' He shuddered. 'An eerie feeling, that. Not one I'd care to repeat.'

'But why?' I said. 'Why fake your death and try to frame me for it?'

'I wanted to get to the root of the trouble in Amber,' he said, 'and destroy it. I thought it best to go underground for that. What better way than by convincing everyone that I was dead? I finally succeeded, too, as you saw.' He paused. 'I'm sorry about Deirdre, though. But I had no choice. It was our last chance. I did not really think he would take her with him.'

I looked away.

'I had no choice,' he repeated. 'I hope you can see that.'

I nodded.

'But why did you try to make it look as if I had killed you?' I asked.

Just then Fiona approached with Bleys. I greeted them both and turned back to Caine for my answer. There were things I wanted to ask Bleys, too, but they could wait.

'Well?' I said.

'I wanted you out of the way,' he said. 'I still thought you might be behind the whole thing. You or Brand. I had it narrowed down that far. I thought it might even be the two of you in it together – especially with him struggling to bring you back.'

'You have that wrong,' said Bleys. 'Brand was trying to keep him away. He had learned that his memory was returning and—'

'I gather,' Caine replied, 'but at the time it looked that way. So I wanted Corwin back in a dungeon while I searched for Brand. I lay low then and listened in on the Trumps to everything everyone said, hoping for a due as to Brand's whereabouts.'

'That's what Dad meant,' I said.

'What?' Caine asked.

'He implied there was an eavesdropper on the Trumps.'

'I do not see how he could have known. I had learned to be completely passive about it I had taught myself to deal them all out and touch all of them, lightly at the same time, waiting for a stirring. When it came, I would shift my attention to the speakers. Taking you one at a time, I even found I could sometimes get into your minds when you were not using the Trumps yourselves – if you were sufficiently distracted and I allowed myself no reaction.'

'Yet he knew,' I said.

'It is entirely possible. Likely, even,' said Fiona, and Bleys nodded.

Random drew nearer.

'What did you mean when you asked about Corwin's side?' he inquired. 'How could you even know about it unless—'

Caine merely nodded. I saw Benedict and Julian together in the distance, addressing their troops. At Caine's silent movement, I forgot them.

'You?' I croaked. 'You stabbed me?'

'Have a drink, Corwin,' Random said, passing me his flask. It was a dilute wine. I gulped it. My thirst was immense, but I stopped after several good swigs.

'Tell me about it,' I said.

'All right I owe you that,' he said. 'When I learned from Julian's mind that you had brought Brand back to Amber, I decided that an earlier guess had been correct – that you and Brand were in it together. That meant you both had to be destroyed. I used the Pattern to project myself into your chambers that night. There, I tried to kill you, but you moved too fast and you somehow managed to Trump out before I got a second chance.'

'Well, damn your eyes,' I said. 'If you could touch our minds couldn't you have seen that I was not the man you were looking for?'

He shook his head.

'I could pick up only surface thoughts and reactions to your immediate environment. Not always that, even. And I had heard your curse, Corwin. And it was coming true. I could see it all around us. I felt that we would all be a lot safer with you and Brand both out of the way. I knew what he could do, from his actions back before your return. I could not get at him just then, though, because of Gérard. Then he began to grow stronger. I made one effort later, but it failed.'

'When was that?' Random asked.

'That was the one Corwin got blamed for. I masked myself. In case he managed to get away as Corwin had, I did not want him knowing I was still around. I used the Pattern to project myself into his chambers and tried to finish him off. We were both hurt – there was a lot of blood around – but he managed to Trump away, too. Then I got in touch with Julian a while back and joined him for this battle, because Brand just had to show up here. I had some silver-tipped arrows made because I was more than half convinced that he was no longer like the rest of us. I wanted to kill him fast and do it from a distance. I practiced my archery and came looking for him. I finally found him.

Now everyone tells me I was wrong about you, so I guess your arrow will go unused.'

'Thanks a lot.'

'I might even owe you an apology.'

'That would be nice.'

'On the other hand, I thought that I was right. I was doing it to save the rest—'

I never did get Caine's apology, because just then a trumpet blast seemed to shake the entire world – directionless, loud, prolonged. We cast about, seeking its source.

Caine stood and pointed.

'There!' he said.

My eyes followed his gesture. The curtain of the stormfront was broken off to the northwest, at the point where the black road emerged from it. There, a ghostly rider on a black horse had appeared and was winding his horn. It was a while before more of its notes reached us. Moments later, two more trumpeters – also pale, and mounted on black steeds – joined him. They raised their horns and added to the sound.

'What can it be?' Random asked.

'I think I know,' Bleys said, and Fiona nodded.

'What, then?' I asked.

But they did not answer me. The horsemen were beginning to move again, passing along the black road, and more were emerging behind them.

12

I watched. There was a great silence on the heights about me. All of the troops had halted and were regarding the procession. Even the prisoners from the Courts, hemmed by steel, turned their attention that way.

Led by the pale trumpeters came a mass of horsemen mounted on white steeds, bearing banners, some of which I did not recognize, behind a man-thing who bore the Unicorn standard of Amber. These were followed by more musicians, some of them playing upon instruments of a sort I had never seen before.

Behind the musicians marched horned man-shaped things in light armor, long columns of them, and every twentieth or so bore a great torch before him, reaching high above his head. A deep noise came to us then – slow, rhythmic, rolling beneath the notes of the trumpets and the sounds of the musicians – and I realized that the foot soldiers were singing. A great deal of time seemed to pass as this body advanced along that black way across the distant track below us, yet none of us stirred and none of us spoke. They passed, with the torches and the banners and the music and the singing, and they finally came to the edge of the abyss and continued over the near-invisible extension of that dark highway, their torches flaring against the blackness now, lighting their way. The music grew stronger, despite the distance, with more and more voices added to that chorus, as the guard continued to emerge from that flashing storm curtain. An occasional roll of thunder passed by, but this could not drown it; nor did the winds which assailed the torches extinguish any so far as I could see. The movement had a hypnotic effect. It seemed that I had been watching the procession for countless days, years perhaps, listening to the tune I now recognized.

Suddenly, a dragon sailed through the storm front, and another, and another. Green and golden and black as old iron, I watched them soar on the winds, turning their heads to trail pennons of fire. The lightning flashed behind them and they were awesome and magnificent and of incalculable size. Beneath them came a small herd of white cattle, tossing their heads and blowing, beating the ground with their hoofs. Riders passed beside and among these, cracking long black whips.

Then came a procession of truly bestial troops from a shadow with which Amber sometimes has commerce – heavy, scaled, taloned – playing upon instruments like bagpipes, whose skirling notes came to us with vibrance and pathos.

These marched on, and there were more torch bearers and more troops with their colors – from shadows both distant and near. We watched them pass and wind their way into the far sky, like a migration of fireflies, their destination that black citadel called the Courts of Chaos.

There seemed no end to it. I had lost all track of time. But the storm front, strangely, was not advancing as all this went on. I had even lost something of my sense of person, to be caught up in the procession which passed us. This, I knew, was an event which could never be repeated. Bright flying things darted above the columns and dark ones floated, higher.

There were ghostly drummers, beings of pure light and a flock of floating machines; I saw horsemen, clad all in black, mounted on a variety of beasts; a wyvern seemed to hang in the sky for a moment, like part of a fireworks display. And the sounds – of hoofbeats and footfalls, of singing and skirling, of drumming and trumpeting – mounted to a mighty wave that washed over us. And on, on, on out over the bridge of darkness, wound the procession, its lights lining the great span for a vast distance now.

Then, as my eyes drifted back along those lines, another shape emerged from the glistening curtain. It was a cart draped all in black and drawn by a team of black horses. At each corner rose a staff which glowed with blue fire, and atop it rested what could only be a casket, draped with our Unicorn flag. The driver was a hunchback clad in purple and orange garments, and I knew even at that distance that it was Dworkin.

It is thus, then, I thought. *I do not know why, but somehow it is fitting, fitting that it be the Old Country to which you travel now. There were many things that I might have said while you lived. Some of them I did say, but few of the right words were ever spoken. Now it is over, for you are dead. As dead as all of those who have gone before you into that place where the rest of us soon may follow. I am sorry. It was only after all these years, on your assuming another face and form, that I finally knew you, respected you, even came to like you – though you were a crochety old bastard in that form, too. Was the Ganelon self the real you all along, or was it only another form adopted for convenience's sake, Old Shape-shifter? I will never know, but I like to think that I finally saw you as you were, that I met someone I liked, someone I could trust, and that it was you. I wish that I might have known you even better, but I am grateful for this much . . .*

'Dad . . . ?' Julian said softly.

'He wanted to be taken beyond the Courts of Chaos and into the final darkness when his time came at last,' Bleys said. 'So Dworkin once told me. Beyond Chaos and Amber, to a place where none reigned.'

'And so it is,' Fiona said. 'But is there order somewhere beyond that wall they come through? Or does the storm go on forever? If he succeeded, it is but a passing matter and we are in no danger. But if he did not . . .'

'It does not matter,' I said, 'whether or not he succeeded, because I did.'

'What do you mean?' she asked.

'I believe that he failed,' I said, 'that he was destroyed before he could repair the old Pattern. When I saw this storm coming – actually, I experienced a part of it – I realized that I could not possibly make it here in time with the Jewel, which he had sent to me after his efforts. Brand had been trying to get it from me all along the way – to create a new Pattern, he said. Later, that gave me the idea. When I saw that all else was failing, I used the Jewel to create a new Pattern. It was the most difficult thing I ever did, but I succeeded. Things should hold together after this wave passes, whether we survive it or not. Brand stole the Jewel from me just as I completed it. When I recovered from his attack I was able to use the new Pattern to project me here. So there is still a Pattern, no matter what else happens.'

'But Corwin,' she said, 'what if Dad succeeded?'

'I do not know.'

'It is my understanding,' Bleys said, 'from things that Dworkin told me, that two distinct Patterns could not exist in the same universe. Those in Rebma and Tir-na Nog'th do not count, being but reflections of our own . . .'

'What would happen?' I said.

'I think there would be a splitting off, the founding of a new existence – somewhere.'

'Then what would its effect be upon our own?'

'Either total catastrophe or no effect whatsoever,' Fiona said. 'I can make a case for its going either way.'

'Then we are right back where we started,' I said. 'Either things are going to fall apart shortly or they are going to hold.'

'So it would seem,' Bleys said.

'It does not matter, if we are not going to be around after that wave gets to us,' I said. 'And it will.'

I turned my attention back to the funeral cortege. More horsemen had emerged behind the wagon, followed by marching drummers. Then pennons and torches and a long line of foot soldiers. The singing still came to us, and far, far out over the abyss it seemed the procession might finally have reached that dark citadel.

. . . *I hated you for so long, blamed you for so many things. Now it is over, and none of these feelings remain. Instead, you had even wanted me to be king, a job for which – I see now – I am not fated. I see that I must have meant something to you after all. I will never tell the others. It is enough to know it myself. But I can never think of you in the same fashion again. Already your image blurs. I see Ganelon's face where yours should be. He was my companion. He risked his neck for me. He was you, but a different you – a you that I had not known. How many wives and enemies had you outlived? Were there many friends? I think not. But there were so many things about you of which we knew nothing. I never thought that I would see your passing. Ganelon – Father – old friend and enemy, I bid you farewell. You join Deirdre, whom I have loved. You have preserved your mystery. Rest in peace, if that be your will. I give you this withered rose I have borne through hell, casting it into the abyss. I leave you the rose and the twisted colors in the sky. I will miss you . . .*

Finally, the long line came to an end. The last marchers emerged from the curtain and moved away. The lightning still flared, the rain still poured and the thunder rumbled. No member of the procession that I could recall had seemed wet, however. I had been standing at the edge of the abyss, watching them pass. There was a hand on my arm.. How long it had been there, I could not tell. Now that the passage was complete, I realized that the stormfront was advancing again.

The rotation of the sky seemed to be bringing more darkness upon us. There were voices off to my left. It seemed they had been talking for a long while, but I had not been hearing their words. I realized that I was shaking, that I ached all over, that I could barely stand.

'Come and lie down,' Fiona said. 'The family has shrunken enough for one day.'

I let her lead me away from the edge.

'Would it really make any difference?' I asked. 'How much longer do you think we have?'

'We do not have to stay here and wait for it,' she said. 'We will cross the dark bridge into the Courts. We have already broken their defense. The storm may not reach that far. It may be stopped here by the abyss. We ought to see Dad off, anyway.'

I nodded.

'It would seem we have small choice but to be dutiful unto the end.'

I eased myself down and sighed. If anything, I felt even weaker now.

'Your boots . . .' she said.

'Yes.'

She pulled them off. My feet throbbed.

'Thanks.'

'I'll get you some rations.'

I closed my eyes. I dozed. Too many images played within my head to make for a coherent dream. How long this lasted, I do not know, but an old reflex drew me to wakefulness at the sound of an approaching horse. Then a shadow passed over my eyelids.

I looked up and beheld a muffled rider, silent, still. I was regarded.

I looked back. No threatening gesture had been made, but there was a feeling of antipathy in that cold gaze.

'There lies the hero,' said a soft voice.

I said nothing.

'I could slay you easily now.'

I recognized the voice then, though I had no idea as to the reason behind the sentiment.

'I came upon Borel before he died,' she said. 'He told me how ignobly you had bested him.'

I could not help it, I could not control it. A dry chuckle rose in my throat. Of all the stupid things to get upset about. I might have told her that Borel had been far better equipped and far fresher than I, and that he had come to me looking for a fight. I might have told her that I do not recognize rules when my life is at stake, or that I do not consider war a game. I could have said a great number of things, but if she did not know them already or did not choose to understand them, they would not have made a bit of difference. Besides, her feelings were already plain.

So I simply said one of the great trite truths: 'There is generally more than one side to a story.'

'I will settle for the one I have,' she told me.

I thought about shrugging, but my shoulders were too sore.

'You have cost me two of the most important persons in my life,' she said then.

'Oh?' I said. 'I'm sorry for you.'

'You are not what I was led to believe. I had seen you as a truly noble figure – strong, yet understanding and sometimes gentle. Honorable . . .'

The storm, much closer now, was flaring at her back. I thought of something vulgar and said it. She let it pass as if she had not heard me.

'I am going now,' she said, 'back to my own people. You have won the day thus far – but that way lay Amber.' She gestured toward the storm. I could only stare. Not at the raging elements. At her. 'I doubt there is anything of my new allegiance left for me to renounce,' she continued.

'What about Benedict?' I asked softly.

'Don't . . .' she said, and she turned away. There was a silence. Then, 'I do not believe that we will ever meet again,' she said, and her horse carried her off to my left, in the direction of the black road.

A cynic might have decided that she had simply chosen to toss in her lot with what she now saw as the winning side, as the Courts of Chaos would likely survive. I simply did not know. I could think only of what I had seen when she had gestured. The cowling had slipped away and I had gotten a glimpse of what she had become. It had not been a human face, there within the shadows. But I turned my head and watched until she was gone. With Deirdre, Brand and Dad gone, and now a parting with Dara on these terms, the world was much emptier – whatever was left of it.

I lay back and sighed. Why not just remain here when the others departed, wait for the storm to wash over me, and sleep . . . dissolve? I thought of Hugi. Had I digested his flight from life as well as his flesh? I was so tired that it seemed the easiest course . . .

'Here, Corwin.'

I had been dozing again, though only for a moment. Fiona was beside me once more, with rations and a flask. Someone was with her.

'I did not wish to interrupt your audience,' she said. 'So I waited.'

'You heard?' I asked.

'No, but I can guess,' she said, 'since she is gone. Here.'

I swallowed some wine, turned my attention to the meat, the bread. Despite my state of mind, they tasted good to me.

'We will be moving soon,' Fiona said, casting a glance at the raging stormfront. 'Can you ride?'

'I think so,' I said.

I took another drink of the wine.

'But too much has happened, Fi,' I told her. 'I have gone numb emotionally. I broke out of a sanitarium on a shadow world. I have tricked people and I've killed people. I have calculated and I have fought. I won back my memory and I have been trying to straighten out my life, I have found my family, and found that I love it. I have been reconciled with Dad. I have fought for the kingdom. I have tried everything I know to hold things together. Now it appears that it has all come to nothing, and I have not enough spirit left to mourn farther. I have gone numb. Forgive me.'

She kissed me.

'We are not yet beaten. You will be yourself again,' she said.

I shook my head.

'It is like the last chapter of *Alice*,' I said. 'If I shout, "You are only a pack of cards!" I feel we will all fly into the air, a hand of painted pasteboards. I am not going with you. Leave me here. I am only the Joker, anyway.'

'Right now, I am stronger than you are,' she said. 'You are coming.'

'It is not fair,' I said softly.

'Finish eating,' she said. 'There is still some time.'

As I did, she went on, 'Your son Merlin is waiting to see you. I would like to call him up here now.'

'Prisoner?'

'Not exactly. He was not a combatant. He just arrived a little while ago, asking to see you.'

I nodded and she went away. I abandoned my rations and took another swig of wine. I had just become nervous. What do you say to a grown son you only recently learned existed? I wondered about his feelings toward me. I wondered whether he knew of Dara's decision. How should I act with him?

I watched him approach from a place where my relatives were clustered, far off to my left. I had wondered why they had left me by myself this way. The more visitors I received the more apparent it became. I wondered whether they were holding up the withdrawal because of me. The storm's moist winds were growing stronger. He was staring at me as he advanced, no special expression on that face so much like my own. I wondered how Dara felt now that her prophecy of the destruction seemed to have been fulfilled. I wondered how her relationship with the boy actually stood. I wondered . . . many things.

He leaned forward to clasp my hand.

'Father . . .' he said.

'Merlin.' I looked into his eyes. I rose to my feet, still holding his hand.

'Do not get up.'

'It is all right.' I clasped him to me, then released him. 'I am glad,' I said. Then: 'Drink with me.' I offered him the wine, partly to cover my lack of words.

'Thank you.'

He took it, drank some and passed it back.

'Your health,' I said and took a sip myself. 'Sorry I cannot offer you a chair.'

I lowered myself to the ground. He did the same.

'None of the others seemed to know exactly what you have been doing,' he said, 'except for Fiona, who said only that it had been very difficult.'

'No matter,' I said. 'I am glad to have made it this far, if for no other reason than this. Tell me of yourself, son. What are you like? How has life treated you?'

He looked away.

'I have not lived long enough to have done too much,' he said.

I was curious whether he possessed the shapeshifting ability, but restrained myself from asking at this point. No sense in looking for our differences when I had just met him.

'I have no idea what it was like,' I said, 'growing up in the Courts.'

He smiled for the first time.

'And I have no idea what it would have been like anywhere else,' he responded. 'I was different enough to be left to myself a lot. I was taught the usual things a gentleman should know – magic, weapons, poisons, riding, dancing. I was told that I would one day rule in Amber. This is not true anymore, is it?'

'It does not seem too likely in the foreseeable future,' I said.

'Good,' he replied. 'This is the one thing I did not want to do.'

'What do you want to do?'

'I want to walk the Pattern in Amber as Mother did and gain power over Shadow, so that I might walk there and see strange sights and do different things. Do you think I might?'

I took another sip and I passed him the wine.

'It is quite possible,' I said, 'that Amber no longer exists. It all depends on whether your grandfather succeeded in something he attempted – and he is no longer around to tell us what happened. However, one way or the other, there is a Pattern. If we live through this demon storm, I promise you that I will find you a Pattern, instruct you and see you walking it.'

'Thanks,' he said. 'Now will you tell me of your journey here?'

'Later,' I told him. 'What did they tell you of me?'

He looked away.

'I was taught to dislike many of the things about Amber,' he finally said. Then, after a pause: 'You, I was taught to respect, as my father. But I was reminded that you were of the party of the enemy.' Another pause. 'I remember that time on patrol, when you had come to this place and I found you, after your fight with Kwan. My feelings were mixed. You had just slain someone I had known, yet – I had to admire the stance you took. I saw my face in your own. It was strange. I wanted to know you better.'

The sky had rotated completely and the darkness was now above us, the colors passing over the Courts. The steady advance of the flashing stormfront was emphasized by this. I leaned forward and reached for my boots, began pulling them on. Soon it would be time to begin our retreat.

'We will have to continue our conversation on your home ground,' I said. 'It is about time to fly the storm.'

He turned and considered the elements, then looked back out over the abyss.

'I can summon a filmy if you wish.'

'One of those drifting bridges such as you rode on the day we met?'

'Yes,' he answered. 'They are most convenient I—'

There had been a shout from the direction of my assembled relatives. Nothing threatening seemed to be about when I regarded them. So I got to my feet and took a few steps toward them, Merlin rising to follow me.

Then I saw her. A white form, pawing air it seemed, and rising out of the abyss. Her front hoofs finally struck its brink, and she came forward and then stood still, regarding us all: our Unicorn.

13

For a moment, my aches and my fatigue fell away. I felt a tiny twinge of something like hope as I considered the dainty white form which stood before us. A part of me wanted to rush forward, but something much stronger kept me motionless, waiting.

How long we stood thus, I could not tell. Below, on the slopes, the troops had been readying themselves for travel. The prisoners had been bound, horses loaded, equipment secured. But this vast army in the process of march ordering its gear had suddenly halted. It was not natural that they should have become aware so quickly, but every head that I could see was turned in this direction, toward the Unicorn on the brink, limned against that wild sky.

I was suddenly aware that the wind at my back had grown still, though the thunder continued to rumble and explode and the lightning flares threw dancing shadows before me.

I thought of the other time I had seen the Unicorn – at the recovery of the Shadow-Caine's body, the day I had lost a fight with Gérard. I thought of the stories I had heard . . . Could she really help us?

The Unicorn took a step forward and halted.

She was such a lovely thing that somehow I was heartened just by looking upon her. It was a kind of aching feeling that she aroused, though; hers was a beauty of the sort to be taken in small doses. And I could somehow sense the unnatural intelligence within that snowy head. I wanted very badly to touch her, but knew that I could not.

She cast her gaze all about. Her eyes lighted upon me, and I would have looked away if I had been able. This was not possible, however, and I returned that gaze in which I read an understanding beyond my own. It was as if she knew everything about me, and in this instant had comprehended all of my recent trials – seeing, understanding, possibly sympathizing. For a moment, I felt that I saw something of pity and a strong love reflected there – and perhaps a touch of humor.

Then her head turned and the gaze was broken. I sighed involuntarily. At that moment, in the lightning's glare, I thought I caught a glimpse of something shining at the side of her neck.

She advanced another step, and now she was looking upon the crowd of my kinsmen toward which I had been moving. She lowered her head and made a small whickering noise. She tapped at the earth with her right front hoof.

I felt Merlin at my side. I thought upon things I would be losing if it all ended here.

She took several dancing steps forward. She tossed her head and lowered it. It seemed that she did not like the notion of approaching so large a group of people.

At her next step, I saw the glitter again, and more. A tiny spark of red shone through her fur farther down on her neck. She was wearing the Jewel of Judgment. How she had retrieved it, I had no idea. And it did not matter. If she would just deliver it, I felt that I could break the storm – or at least shield us from this section of it until it had passed.

But that one glance had been enough. She paid me no more heed. Slowly, carefully, as if ready to bolt at the slightest disturbance, she advanced upon the spot where Julian, Random, Bleys, Fiona, Llewella, Benedict and several nobles stood.

I should have realized then what was occurring, but I did not. I simply watched the sleek beast's movements as she picked her way forward, passing about the periphery of the group.

She halted once again and lowered her head. Then she shook her mane and dropped to her front knees. The Jewel of Judgment hung suspended from her twisted, golden horn. The tip of her horn was almost touching the person before whom she knelt.

Suddenly, in my mind's eye, I saw our father's face in the heavens, and his words came back to me: 'With my passing, the problem of the succession will be upon you . . . I have no choice but to leave this on the horn of the Unicorn.'

A murmur moved through the group, as I realized this same thought must be occurring to the others. The Unicorn did not stir at this disturbance, however, but remained a soft white statue, not even seeming to breathe.

Slowly, Random reached forward and removed the Jewel from her horn. His whisper carried to me.

'Thank you,' he said.

Julian unsheathed his blade and placed it at Random's feet as he knelt. Then Bleys and Benedict and Caine, Fiona and Llewella. I went and joined them. So did my son.

Random stood silent for a long while. Then, 'I accept your allegiance,' he said. 'Now get up, all of you.'

As we did, the Unicorn turned and bolted. She raced down the slope and was out of sight in a matter of moments.

'I had never expected anything like this to happen,' Random said, still holding the Jewel at eye level. 'Corwin, can you take this thing and stop that storm?'

'It is yours now,' I said, 'and I do not know how extensive the disturbance is. It occurs to me that in my present condition I might not be able to hold up long enough to keep us all safe. I think it is going to have to be your first regal act.'

'Then you are going to have to show me how to work it. I thought we needed a Pattern to perform the attunement.'

'I think not. Brand indicated that a person who was already attuned could attune another. I have given it some thought since then, and I believe I know how to go about it. Let's get off to one side somewhere.'

'Okay. Come on.'

Already, something new had come into his voice and posture. The sudden role had begun working its change immediately, it seemed. I wondered what sort of king and queen he and Vialle would become. Too much. My mind felt disassociated. Too much had happened too recently. I could not contain all of the latest events in one big piece of thinking. I just wanted to crawl off somewhere and sleep around the clock. Instead, I followed him to a place where a small cooking fire still smoldered.

He poked at the fire and tossed a handful of sticks onto it. Then he seated himself close to it and nodded to me. I went over and sat down beside him.

'About this king business,' he said. 'What am I going to do, Corwin? It caught me totally unprepared.'

'Do? Probably a very good job,' I replied.

'Do you think there were many hard feelings?'

'If there were, they did not show,' I said. 'You were a good choice,

Random. So much has happened recently . . . Dad sheltered us actually, maybe more than was good for us. The throne is obviously no plum. You have a lot of hard work ahead of you. I think the others have come to realize this.'

'And yourself?'

'I wanted it only because Eric did. I did not realize it at the time, but it is true. It was the winning counter in a game we had been playing across the years. The end of a vendetta, really. And I would have killed him for it. I am glad now that he found another way to die. We were more alike than we were different, he and I. I did not realize that until much later either. But after his death, I kept finding reasons for not taking the throne. Finally, it dawned on me that it was not really what I wanted. No. You are welcome to it. Rule well, brother. I am sure that you will.'

'If Amber still exists,' he said after a time, 'I will try. Come, let us be about this business with the Jewel. That storm is getting uncomfortably near.'

I nodded and took the stone from his fingers. I held it by its chain with the fire behind it. The light came through; its insides seemed clear.

'Lean closer and stare into the Jewel with me,' I directed.

He did this, and while we both regarded the stone, I told him, 'Think of the Pattern,' and I commenced thinking of it myself, trying to summon to mind its loops and swirls, its palely glowing lines.

I seemed to detect a slight flaw near to the stone's center. I considered it as I thought upon the twistings, the turns, the Veils . . . I imagined the current which swept through me every time I essayed that complex way.

The imperfection in the stone grew more distinct.

I lay my will upon it summoning it into fullness, clarity. A familiar feeling came over me as this occurred. It was that which had taken me on the day I had attuned myself to the Jewel. I only hoped that I was strong enough now to go through the experience once again.

I reached out and clasped Random by the shoulder.

'What do you see?' I asked him.

'Something like the Pattern,' he said, 'only it seems to be three dimensional. It lies at the bottom of a red sea . . .'

'Come with me then,' I said. 'We must go to it.'

Again, that feeling of movement, drifting at first, then falling with increasing velocity toward the never fully seen sinuosities of the Pattern within the Jewel. I willed us ahead, feeling my brother's presence beside me, and the ruby glow which surrounded us darkened, becoming the blackness of a clean night sky. This special Pattern grew with each thudding heartbeat. Somehow, the process seemed easier than it had before – perhaps because I was already attuned.

Feeling Random beside me, I drew him along as that familiar shape grew and its starting point became apparent. As we were moved in that direction, I once again tried to encompass the totality of this Pattern and was lost once more in what seemed its extra-dimensional convolutions. Great curves and spirals and knotted-seeming traceries wound before us. The sense of awe I had felt earlier swept over me, and from somewhere nearby I was aware of this in Random, also.

We progressed to the section of the beginning and were swept into it. There was a shimmering brightness all about us flashed through with sparks as we were woven into the matrix of light. This time, my mind was entirely absorbed by the process and Paris seemed far away . . .

A subconscious memory reminded me of the more difficult sections, and here I employed my desire – my will, if you like – to hurry us along the dazzling route, recklessly drawing strength from Random to accelerate the process.

It was as if we negotiated the luminous interior of an enormous and elaborately convoluted seashell. Only our passage was soundless, and we ourselves disembodied points of sentience.

Our velocity seemed to increase constantly, as did a mental aching I did not recall from the previous traversal of the design. Perhaps it was related to my fatigue, or to my efforts to hurry things so. We crashed through the barriers; we were surrounded by steady, flowing walls of brightness. I felt myself growing faint, dizzy, now. But I could not afford the luxury of unconsciousness, nor could I permit us to move more slowly with the storm as near as I remembered it. Again, regretfully, I drew strength from Random – this time just to keep us in the game. We sped ahead.

This time, I did not experience the tingling, fiery sensation of somehow being shaped. It must have been an effect of my attunement. My previous passage through it might have rendered me some small immunity in this regard.

After a timeless interval, it seemed that I felt Random falter. Perhaps I represented too great a drain upon his energies. I began to wonder whether I would leave him with sufficient strength to manipulate the storm if I leaned upon him any further. I resolved not to draw upon his resources any more than I already had. We were well along the way. He should be able to continue without me, if it came to that. I would simply have to hang on as best I could now. Better for me to be lost here than both of us.

We swept on, my senses rebelling, the dizziness recurring. I set my will to our progress and forced everything else from my mind. It seemed we were nearing the terminus when a darkening began which I knew was not a part of the experience. I fought down panic.

It was no good. I felt myself slipping away. So close! I was certain we were almost finished. It would be so easy to—

Everything swam away from me. My last sensation was a knowledge of Random's concern.

It was flickering orange and red between my feet. Was I trapped in some astral hell? I continued to stare as my mind slowly cleared. The light was surrounded by darkness and . . .

There were voices, familiar . . .

Things cleared. I was lying on my back, feet toward a campfire.

'It is all right, Corwin. It is all right.'

It was Fiona who had spoken. I turned my head. She was seated on the ground above me.

'Random . . . ?' I said.

'He is all right, also – Father.'

Merlin was seated off to the right.

'What happened?'

'Random bore you back,' Fiona said.

'Did the attunement work?'

'He thinks so.'

I struggled to sit up. She tried to push me back, but I sat up anyway.

'Where is he?'

She gestured with her eyes.

I looked and I saw Random. He was standing with his back to us

783

about thirty meters away, on a shelf of rock, facing the storm. It was very close now, and a wind whipped his garments. lightning trails crissed and crossed before him. The thunder boomed almost constantly.

'How long – has he been there?' I asked.

'Only a few minutes,' Fiona replied.

'That is how long it has been – since our return?'

'No,' she said. 'You have been out for a fairly long while. Random talked with the others first, then ordered a troop withdrawal. Benedict has taken them all to the black road. They are crossing over.'

I turned my head.

There was movement along the black road, a dark column heading out toward the citadel. Gossamer strands drifted between us; there were a few sparks at the far end, about the nighted hulk. Overhead, the sky had completely reversed itself, with us beneath the darkened half. Again, I felt the strange feeling of having been here long, long ago, to see that this, rather than Amber, was the true center of creation. I grasped after the ghost of a memory. It vanished.

I searched the lightning-shot gloom about me.

'All of them – gone?' I said to her. 'You, me, Merlin, Random – we're the only ones left here?'

'Yes,' Fiona said. 'Do you wish to follow them now?'

I shook my head.

'I am staying here with Random.'

'I knew you would say that.'

I got to my feet as she did. So did Merlin. She clapped her hands and a white horse came ambling up to her.

'You have no further need for my ministrations,' she said. 'So I will go and join the others in the Courts of Chaos. There are horses for you tethered by those rocks.' She gestured. 'Are you coming, Merlin.

'I will stay with my father, and the king.'

'So be it. I hope to see you there soon.'

'Thanks, Fi,' I said.

I helped her to mount and watched her ride off.

I went over and sat down by the fire again. I watched Random, who stood unmoving, facing the storm.

'There are plenty of rations and wine,' Merlin said. 'May I fetch you some?'

784

'Good idea.'

The storm was so close that I could have walked down to it in a couple of minutes. I could not tell yet whether Random's efforts were having any effect. I sighed heavily and let my mind drift.

Over. One way or another, all of my efforts since Greenwood were over. No need for revenge any longer. No. We had an intact Pattern, maybe even two. The cause of all our troubles, Brand, was dead. Any residuum of my curse was bound to be wiped out by the massive convulsions sweeping through Shadow. And I had done my best to make up for it. I had found a friend in my father and come to terms with him as himself before his death. We had a new king, with the apparent blessing of the Unicorn, and we had pledged him our loyalty. It seemed sincere to me. I was reconciled with my entire family. I felt that I had done my duty. Nothing drove me now. I had run out of causes and was as close as I might ever be to peace. With all this behind me, I felt that if I had to die now, it was all right. I would not protest quite so loudly as I would have at any other time.

'You are far from here, Father.'

I nodded, then smiled. I accepted some food and began eating. As I did, I watched the storm. Still too early to be certain, but it seemed that it was no longer advancing.

I was too tired to sleep. Or something like that. My aches had all subsided and a wondrous numbness had come over me. I felt as if I were embedded in warm cotton. Events and reminiscences kept the mental clockwork turning within me. It was, in many ways, a delicious feeling.

I finished eating and built up the fire. I sipped the wine and watched the storm, like a frosted window set before a fireworks display. Life felt good. If Random succeeded in pulling this one off, I would be riding into the Courts of Chaos tomorrow. What might await me there, I could not tell. Perhaps it might be a gigantic trap. An ambush. A trick. I dismissed the thought. Somehow, right now, it did not matter.

'You had begun telling me of yourself, Father.'

'Had I? I do not recall what I said.'

'I would like to get to know you better. Tell me more.'

I made a popping noise with my lips and shrugged.

'Then this.' He gestured. 'This whole conflict. How did it get started? What was your part in it? Fiona told me that you had dwelled in Shadow for many years without your memory. How did you get it back and locate the others, and return to Amber?'

I chuckled. I regarded Random and the storm once more. I took a drink of wine and drew up my cloak against the wind.

'Why not?' I said then. 'If you've a stomach for long stories, that is . . . I suppose that the best place to begin is at Greenwood Private Hospital, on the shadow Earth of my exile. Yes . . .'

14

The sky turned, and turned again as I spoke. Standing against the storm, Random prevailed. It broke before us, parting as if cloven by a giant's axblade. It rolled back at either hand, finally sweeping off to the north and the south, fading, diminishing, gone. The landscape it had masked endured, and with it went the black road. Merlin tells me that this is no problem, though, for he will summon a strand of gossamer when the time comes for us to cross over.

Random is gone now. The strain upon him was immense. In repose, he no longer looked as once he did – the brash younger brother we delighted in tormenting – for there were lines upon his face which I had never noticed before, signs of some depth to which I had paid no heed. Perhaps my vision has been colored by recent events, but he seemed somehow nobler and stronger. Does a new role work some alchemy? Appointed by the Unicorn, anointed by the storm, it seems that he had indeed assumed a kingly mien, even in slumber.

I have slept – even as Merlin now dozes – and it pleased me to be, for this brief while before his awakening, the only spot of sentience on this crag at the rim of Chaos, looking back upon a surviving world, a world that has been scoured, a world which endures . . .

We may have missed Dad's funeral, his drifting into some nameless place beyond the Courts. Sad, but I lacked the strength to move. And yet, I have seen the pageant of his passing, and I bear much of his life within me. I have said my good-byes. He would understand. And good-bye, Eric. After all this time I say it, in this way. Had you lived so long, it would have been over between us. We might even one day have become friends, all our causes for strife passed. Of them all, you and I were more alike than any other pair within the family. Save, in some ways, Deirdre and myself . . . But tears on this count were shed long ago. Good-bye again, though, dearest sister, you will always live somewhere in my heart.

And you Brand . . . With bitterness do I regard your memory, mad brother. You almost destroyed us. You nearly toppled Amber from her lofty perch on the breast of Kolvir. You would have shattered all of Shadow. You almost broke the Pattern and redesigned the universe in your own image. You were mad and evil, and you came so close to realizing your desires that I tremble even now. I am glad that you are gone, that the arrow and the abyss have claimed you, that you sully no more the places of men with your presence nor walk in the sweet airs of Amber. I wish that you had never been born and, failing that, that you had died sooner. Enough! It diminishes me to reflect so. Be dead and trouble my thinking no more.

I deal you out like a hand of cards, my brothers and sisters. It is painful as well as self-indulgent to generalize like this, but you – I – we – seem to have changed, and before I move into the traffic again I require a final look.

Caine, I never liked you and I still do not trust you. You have insulted me, betrayed me and even stabbed me. Forget that. I do not like your methods, though I cannot fault your loyalty this time around. Peace, then. Let the new reign begin with a clean slate between us.

Llewella, you possess reserves of character the recent situation did not call upon you to exercise. For this, I am grateful. It is sometimes pleasant to emerge from a conflict untested.

Bleys, you are still a figure clad in light to me – valiant, exuberant and rash. For the first, my respect, for the second, my smile. And the last seems to have at least been tempered in recent times. Good. Stay away from conspiracies in the future. They do not suit you well.

Fiona, you have changed the most. I must substitute a new feeling for an old one, princess, as we have become for the first time friends. Take my fondness, sorceress. I owe you.

Gérard, slow, faithful brother, perhaps we have not all changed. You stood rock-like and held to what you believed. May you be less easily gulled. May I never wrestle you again. Go down to your sea in your ships and breathe the clean salt air.

Julian, Julian, Julian . . . Is it that I never really knew you? No. Arden's green magic must have softened that old vanity during my long absence, leaving a juster pride and something I would fain call fairness – a thing apart from mercy, to be sure, but an addition to your armory of traits I'll not disparage.

And Benedict, the gods know you grow wiser as time burns its way to entropy, yet you still neglect single examples of the species in your knowledge of people. Perhaps I'll see you smile now this battle's done. Rest, warrior.

Flora . . . Charity, they say, begins at home. You seem no worse now than when I knew you long ago. It is but a sentimental dream to regard you and the others as I do, totting up by balance sheets, looking for credits. We are not enemies, any of us, now, and that should be sufficient.

And the man clad in black and silver with a silver rose upon him? He would like to think that he has learned something of trust, that he has washed his eyes in some clear spring, that he has polished an ideal or two. Never mind. He may still be only a smart-mouthed meddler, skilled mainly in the minor art of survival, blind as ever the dungeons knew him to the finer shades of irony. Never mind, let it go, let it be. I may never be pleased with him.

Carmen, *voulez-vous venir avec moi?* No? Then good-bye to you too, Princess of Chaos. It might have been fun.

The sky is turning once more, and who can say what deeds its stained-glass light might shine upon? The solitaire has been dealt and played. Where there had been nine of us now there are seven and one a king. Yet Merlin and Martin are with us, new players in the ongoing game.

My strength returns as I stare into the ashes and consider the path I have taken. The way ahead intrigues me, from hell to hallelujah. I have back my eyes, my memories, my family. And Corwin will always be Corwin, even on Judgment Day.

Merlin is stirring now, and this is good. It is time to be about. There are things to do.

Random's last act after defeating the storm was to join with me drawing power from the Jewel, to reach Gérard through his Trump. They are cold once more, the cards, and the shadows are themselves again. Amber stands. Years have passed since we departed it, and more may elapse before I return. The others may already have Trumped home, as Random has done, to take up his duties. But I must visit the Courts of Chaos now, because I said that I would, because I may even be needed there.

We ready our gear now, Merlin and I, and soon he will summon a wispy roadway.

When all is done in that place, and when Merlin has walked his Pattern and gone to claim his worlds, there is a journey that I must make. I must ride to the place where I planted the limb of old Ygg, visit the tree it has grown to, I must see what has become of the Pattern I drew to the sound of pigeons on the Champs-Elysées. If it leads me to another universe, as I now believe it will, I must go there, to see how I have wrought.

The roadway drifts before us, rising to the Courts in the distance. The time has come. We mount and move forward.

We are riding now across the blackness on a road that looks like cheesecloth. Enemy citadel, conquered nation, trap, ancestral home . . . We shall see. There is a faint flickering from battlement and balcony. We may even be in time for a funeral. I straighten my back and I loosen my blade. We will be there before much longer.

Good-bye and hello, as always.

NOVELS

This Immortal (1966)

The Dream Master (1966)

Lord of Light (1967)

Isle of the Dead (1969)

Creatures of Light and Darkness (1969)

Damnation Alley (1969)

Jack of Shadows (1971)

Today We Choose Faces (1973)

To Die in Italbar (1973)

Bridge of Ashes (1976)

Deus Irae (1976) with Philip K. Dick

Doorways in the Sand (1976)

My Name is Legion (1976)

Roadmarks (1979)

The Bells of Shoredan (1979)

Changeling (1980)

Madwand (1981)

The Changing Land (1981)

Coils (1982) with Fred Saberhagen

Dilvish, The Damned (1982)

Eye of the Cat (1982)

The Black Throne (1990) with Fred Saberhagen

The Mask of Loki (1990) with Thomas T. Thomas

Bring Me the Head of Prince Charming (1991) with Robert Sheckley

Flare (1992) with Thomas T. Thomas

If at Faust You Don't Succeed (1993) with Robert Sheckley

A Night in the Lonesome October (1993)

Wilderness (1994)

A Farce to be Reckoned With (1995) with Robert Sheckley

Home is the Hangman (1996)

Donnerjack (1997) with Jane M. Lindskold

AMBER NOVELS

Trumps of Doom (1985)

Blood of Amber (1986)

Sign of Chaos (1987)

Knight of Shadows (1989)

Prince of Chaos (1991)

SHORT STORY COLLECTIONS

Four for Tomorrow (1967)

The Doors of His Face, The Lamps of His Mouth, and Other Stories (1971)

The Last Defender of Camelot (1980)

Unicorn Variations (1983)

Frost and Fire (1989)

ROGER ZELAZNY was born in 1937. His first published story was 'Passion Play' which appeared in *Amazing Stories* in 1962, the same year he graduated from Columbia University with an MA. For the next five years, Zelazny was a prolific writer, sometimes resorting to the pseudonym of Harrison Denmark. He rose quickly to prominence, winning Nebula awards in 1965 for 'He Who Shapes' (published in 1966 as *The Dream Master*) and 'The Doors of His Face, the Lamps of His Mouth'. He followed this with a Hugo award in 1966 for the novel *This Immortal* (originally titled '. . . And Call Me Conrad'). In 1967 he started writing full time. That year he published *Lord of Light*, which went on to win a Hugo in 1968. His 1969 novel *Damnation Alley* was adapted as a film of the same name in 1977. During the '70s he started to focus more on his fantasy sequence, the Amber series, although he never stopped writing SF. His short fiction continued to receive acclaim; he received a Hugo and a Nebula for 'Home is the Hangman' in 1976, and further Hugos for 'Twenty-Four Views of Mount Fuji, by Hokusai' in 1986, 'Unicorn Variation' in 1982 and 'Permafrost' in 1987. He died in 1995.